# THE DARK

A DIVISION 53 NOVEL
BOOK ONE

E.M. JOHNSON

# DIVISION 53 SERIES

In a bleak future where blades are the dominant weapon, the economy is down, the U.S. is fragmented due to minor secessions, and dangerous criminals call for a stronger arm of law enforcement; a system of skilled, handcrafted agents exists to protect the innocent and defenseless. Their methods are effective but harsh, so Division 53 of Homeland Security is a hidden sector, and the members of the American Security Association are separated from civilians.

This series is about people who belong to and are affected by Division 53 in their daily lives. Some thrive in this system, some reject it, and others have been harmed by it. One fact is always the same though: they cannot escape it.

## Books in the series:

**The Dark**

**The Haven**

**The Hunt**

**The Shield**

**The Streets**

**The System**

**The Ripper**

**The Conspiracy**

**THE DARK**
Division 53 Series, Book One
By E.M. Johnson

Published by
DEMIPRISM
PO BOX 706
Ankeny, Iowa. 50023
USA



Support the author here at www.division53.com

Learn more about Demiprism at www.demiprism.com

This is a work of fiction. All of the characters, events, and locations are either products of the author's imagination or are used fictitiously.



Cover Illustration: Ahmet Nergiz
Cover Design & Interior Layout: Demiprism

ISBN:
978-1-967526-00-0 (pbk)
978-1-967526-01-7 (epub)

Second Edition, First Print May 2025

**To Audra, Shawn, Farah, Kate, Kaity, Tom, and Carol in 2015**


Thank you for reading back when this was passed around on floppy disks and printed in the school computer labs (which caused printing limits to be put in place). Thank you for all of your early edits – your love for the story and the characters are why they made it this far. You're the reason why these guys aren't just the people in my head anymore, and now they can be in other peoples' too. Stay amazing!


**To Shawn, Jill, and Callie in 2025**


Thank you for helping me with this whirlwind rewrite of a story that all three of you love. If it wasn't for your enthusiasm, encouragement, and attention, there's no way this insanity I embarked upon would've been finished. I'll try not to do this again – but no promises. ♥

# THE DARK

A DIVISION 53 NOVEL
BOOK ONE

E.M. JOHNSON

# PROLOGUE



September 20, 2025 (11 years ago)
Cavington, Minnesota

It was hot and the air was dry – stifling when the sparse and inconsistent wind wasn't blowing. Cavington was a moderately-sized town with clean, narrow streets. The highway arced around the town, bypassing it after nearly touching the modestly industrial west end with its few warehouses, factories, and corporate chain stores. Downtown was full of mostly family or locally-owned storefronts, homes, and offices. The east side was purely residential.

At the moment, downtown was unusually crowded – full of agitated, chattering people who seemed to be flowing inconsistently in one direction.

Two boys – one ten, the other nearly twelve – made their way through the thick crowd, trying to see what was making the street so congested. A blonde-haired, blue-eyed, eleven-year-old girl followed them, keeping rather quiet but surveying the crowd with interest. All three wore backpacks and sweatshirts, even despite the heat.

The oldest and tallest was a solid boy with brown hair, Caucasian skin, and calculating green eyes. He walked with a purpose, only glancing about slightly, to make certain of their location. "Jeez, what the hell's going on? They never said it'd be this crowded here."

The younger boy, a very shifty, slender child with tan skin and wild, short black hair that refused to stay flat, shrugged. He had unique, darting eyes – completely black, even where the white would be on a typical person. The only distinction between the iris, pupil, and the rest of his eye was that his irises had gray highlights in them, and occasionally the pupil flashed white as the light hit it. He tried to keep his hold on his friend's coat while they cut through the crowd, knowing that he was the most likely to get left behind. He heard someone call out.

"Would you hurry up! We're gonna miss the hanging!"

He looked around to see who had said it, repeating to his friends in his normal hushed tone what he had heard. "They're going to hang someone."

"People still do that?" the girl said in bewildered disbelief.

"That's what they said," the smaller boy said sheepishly.

"I know, I'm not saying you're wrong, Malk. I mean, what cretins still hold public hangings?"

The older boy yawned and grabbed his collar, fluffing it to try and get cooler air in his shirt. "Backwoods towns like this, I guess. There's a reason we're here. You wanna see it? We don't have anything else to do until it gets dark. Might help get you two ready for later."

The young one shrugged and continued following his friend. "Whatever."

The girl didn't respond.

Before long, they could see a pair of crude gallows in a small, open park. Being smaller than many of the people around them, they were able to slip through the majority of the milling rabble and get close to the front of the crowd. The area around the gallows was blocked off with sawhorses, a few uniformed officers standing by them to keep people away. The crowd was mostly grumbling and aggravated, but there were definitely some who seemed pleased and even excited about the impending event.

When they got closer to the barriers, they were able to see the blocked-off area better. There were a few officers around the platform and three on the platform. Two officers next to the platform were holding two teens in place. The teens were resisting them somewhat, leaning over and conversing desperately with several other kids that were beyond the barrier, also being corralled by officers.

"Do you see the criminals?" the girl asked, craning her neck.

"Uh, that fat guy is the sheriff," the older boy said, peering. "The kids are the criminals."

"The *kids*?!" the younger boy said in disbelief.

"Yeah. The two of them in the barrier are handcuffed. The other three must be their friends."

"I can see them." She narrowed her eyes. "I don't like this place. What person would sentence *kids* to death? Kids are supposed to be innocent and protected."

"We're not," the taller boy responded insolently.

"Speak for yourself, but you know normal kids are supposed to be," she retorted sharply.

"There's a reason we're here," the smaller boy said, watching the police and children, a disgusted expression on his face.

The officers holding the two handcuffed kids pulled them away from the others, moving them toward the platform. The two were crying quietly, their expressions full of misery and terror. One was a girl and one was a boy, and they both had dark brown hair and Caucasian skin. They were dressed in matching plain red outfits – probably law enforcement-issued clothing.

The other kids beyond the barrier were more audibly miserable – one of the girls, the brown-haired one, was crying, her face in her hands as she alternated between watching and hiding her eyes. The other girl, a blonde, looked furious, and one of the officers had a hand firmly on her shoulder. The boy had tears on his face, but his arms were around the crying girl. All three looked younger than their friends, but not by much.

After a few minutes, the officers tugged the handcuffed young teens toward the gallows.

The younger boy's eyes grew wide and he drew a ragged breath as he watched them ascend the stairs. The others noticed.

"What?"

"Traphian, Arista, they're darks."

Traphian tried to see. "Both of them?"

"How can you tell that from all the way over here?" the girl asked quietly.

"I can see their eyes."

"Wow… you have really good eyesight."

"You're sure?" Traphian asked, a little mystified.

"Yeah. I think they're twins; they look almost exactly alike. Oh, God, maybe they were right; maybe people in these parts do kill darks off before they can get to be adults."

The other boy, Traphian, put his arm around his friend's shoulders. "Don't worry, I won't let them get anywhere near you, Malkarai. If anyone tries anything, they'll pay for it."

Malkarai shrugged his friend's arm off his shoulders, bit his lip, and watched mutely as one of the officers put a hood on each of the young darks and then slipped nooses over their heads.

The crowd's volume rose, sounding like an angry beehive.

"That's awful," Arista whispered. "Isn't anyone gonna stop them?"

Neither of her companions answered.

Then, on the obese man's beckon, the planks were pulled out from below the two teens.

They dropped a few feet, jerked suddenly, and went limp as they hung there.

Malkarai had flinched visibly at the snapping noise.

They could hear the tear-stained girl gasp – a crying, strangled gasp – even over the yells of the crowd. Some of the yells were decidedly triumphant, but just as loud were the ones of anger and protest.

Arista looked at Malkarai, her eyebrows knitted up and a frown on her lips, but he didn't look horrified, as she'd expected.

Malkarai hissed angrily, and his friends could hear the speed of his breathing increase in shuddering rage. "No wonder we were sent here. Listen to all the vile people here. Twisted evil bastards…"

"Yeah, well, at least it was easy to find *our* evil bastard," Traphian muttered, an incredibly dark expression on his face as he glared at the officers on the gallows.

"What the hell could two kids have possibly done that would warrant *this*?" Arista asked.

Traphian exhaled and then inhaled deeply before glancing around and then going up to a woman a short distance away – one who looked rather smug. He tapped her on the shoulder. When she looked at him, he asked, "Why were the two kids hanged? What did they do?"

"They're thieves and darks. Nipping the bud before it gets worse."

Traphian frowned. "Thieves? Hanging isn't a fair punishment for stealing."

"It is here. They've been stealing as long as they could walk and they wouldn't stop. They've been warned and punished. Damn kids don't obey the law anymore."

"Are they siblings?"

"Yeah, twins. Mutant brats without any discipline or regard for others at all." She noticed Malkarai, standing behind Traphian. She gave him a cold look before saying, "We don't trust dark people."

Malkarai's black eyes narrowed.

Traphian scowled, taking a half step so he was more between Malkarai and the woman. "Those two had friends; they were standing up by the gallows. Are you saying that they're up there, crying for them, and they don't trust them?"

"No, but one of those three isn't much better, and the other two fell in with the wrong crowd; they don't understand what's going on in the undersides of this town. You don't either. I'm warning you, stay clean. We don't take any chances anymore. Kid or not, if you're disobeying the law, you'll get busted. 'Specially darks."

The woman turned away from them, and Traphian went back by his friends, grabbing Malkarai by the arm. "Let's get out of here. I can't believe these people."

Malkarai held back, pulling his arm out of Traphian's grasp. "No, wait… can we try asking those other kids?"

Traphian glanced at the other kids, irritated. "Why bother? Look at this crowd – I believe that dumb bitch that they just needed an excuse to kill some darks. Do you really want to get more attention and end up on the gallows next to them?"

"I want to know if they were actually committing crimes or just getting blamed for them," Malkarai said, seriously and firmly. "I'd trust them to tell the truth."

"Malk, it doesn't matter if they're innocent or not; they killed them."

"It matters to me," Malkarai said quietly, staring intently at Traphian.

Traphian sighed and threw his hands up.

Arista took Malkarai's hand and gave him a look of solidarity, nodding slightly.

They went over to the side as the crowd started to disperse, mostly aided by the police officers who were telling people to calm down and go about their business.

The bodies of the twins were taken down and laid on the platform, a sheet spread over them as several people stood by them, waiting for the crowd to leave.

Arista frowned as they watched the other kids, waiting for them to no longer be engaged. The officers that had been holding them back were telling them to go home.

The long-haired girl had stopped sobbing, and the boy had an arm around her shoulders.

The girl with short blonde hair snarled and said something to the officers, throwing their hands off and turning, stalking away from the gallows. When she saw Malkarai, she stopped and stared. Her eyes were a cold and icy gray, and the skin was red around them.

"Who the hell are you?" she hissed.

Malkarai didn't answer immediately; being both startled and naturally very shy. Arista squeezed his hand, frowning at the girl. That gave him a bit of courage. "We-we're visitors."

She glared and put her hands on her hips, her voice harsh and sarcastic. "Really? I couldn't tell. What do you want? Want to stare at them like the rest? It's not a sideshow, you know."

Traphian stepped in front of Malkarai. He was taller than the girl, so when he narrowed his eyes he was glaring down at her. "Hey, he didn't insult you. Don't treat him like that."

The girl glared at him and curled her lip, her hands tightening into fists. "I'll treat him how I want to, what are you gonna say about it? You don't own the place."

Malkarai saw Traphian unzip his sweatshirt and pull the side of it back. He grabbed his friend's arm before he could slip his knife out, presumably, to scare her. "Traphian, don't."

"You don't deserve that," Traphian muttered mutinously.

"Don't make a terrible day worse. It's okay," Malkarai insisted.

The other two were aware of the altercation now. They came up behind the first girl.

The long-haired girl's eyes widened as she saw Malkarai, and she came around in front of her friend, putting her hands on her upper arms. "Cypha, don't be mean. He didn't say anything about them."

"I wasn't gonna beat up the little one, just the big one." She glared at Traphian. "He's the one who's picking a fight with me."

"Cypha, stop it!" she said insistently.

Cypha shrugged her friend's firm hands off her and crossed her arms, still glaring at Traphian, who Malkarai had pushed to the side. Arista put a hand on his arm and stared at him pleadingly until he sighed and his muscles relaxed.

"Do you want something?" the boy asked. His tone was impatient.

Malkarai had regained his steady, though quiet, voice. "I'm really sorry about your friends. This is horrible."

"Thanks," he replied, fairly automatically. "You aren't staying here, right?"

"No, I'm not. We're just passing through."

"Do it sooner rather than later," Cypha said grumpily.

Malkarai eyed her briefly before looking at the other two. The other girl had turned back around, standing between her friends. He nodded. "We won't be here long. I wanted to ask you about your friends. Were they really guilty, or were they killed because they were darks?"

Arista added to her friend's question. "Were they framed, or did they really steal?"

The boy swallowed, taking a moment before he replied. "Yes and no. Yeah, they stole, but they didn't want to. Their mother forced them to do what they did, but no one believed them but us, because they are darks and she isn't. That's the way things always go around here. If a dark is blamed for anything, then they're as good as dead." He gestured agitatedly toward the gallows. "As you can see…"

Cypha spoke again, but her tone was insistent, not combative. "Watch your back. If you see one sign of trouble, stay away from it. These people are idiots. They don't care if you did anything; if you were there, you'd get in trouble."

Malkarai nodded. "Thanks." He glanced at his friends and moved to go. "We won't bother you anymore. I'm sorry."

"W-wait," the long-haired girl said, causing the three to hesitate. "Um, wh-what are you in town for? Is there anything we can help with?"

"Where are your parents?" the boy asked.

Arista glanced at Traphian, but Malkarai replied with a fairly trained smile. "We're fine. We have something to do, then we'll be gone. Thanks for the offer. Take care."

Traphian nodded to them and Arista said, "I'm sorry," before following Malkarai and Traphian back toward the dispersing crowd.

The girl with the long hair wiped her eyes with the back of her hand, realizing that they were still wet. "I wonder where they came from."

"They aren't from around here, that's obvious." The boy paused for a moment, watching them.

Cypha looked at her friend. "You gotta stop offering help to every random kid you meet, Saty."

She looked back, indignant. "Why?"

"One of these days you're gonna find one more dangerous than me."

"Like who?" she scoffed.

The boy nodded toward the retreating kids. "Like them."

Saty looked at them and frowned. "Just cuz Cypha was mean and the one stood up to her?"

"No, they looked like trouble. They had healing bruises and band-aids on their hands. And why were they wearing coats and backpacks when it's this hot?"

"The tall kid had a knife," Cypha said, watching the crowd until they couldn't see the other three anymore, and then looking at her friends.

"He did?" Saty asked, surprised.

"Yeah, that's why I dropped it. His friend stopped him from grabbing it, but I saw it in his sweatshirt."

"They gave me the same vibes as like… Josh's mom and her friends," the boy said. "Nicer than knights though."

"Everyone's nicer than knights," Cypha grumbled.

"What do you mean, Dyspro?" Saty asked, looking at him.

"I dunno… it's like… they felt like they're able to hurt you, even if they aren't acting threatening. Although the bigger guy was. Their clothes were nice and clean too, so they probably aren't street kids."

Saty shook her head, "They *are* kids though…"

"Yeah, they're our age, but they're not normal. I'd be surprised if we saw them again. Maybe they *will* get picked up by the police," Dyspro said.

"Even the girl?"

"Yeah. She didn't look any more innocent than the other two did. She was just real quiet."

"How could kids do things like that and not have gotten in trouble for it?" Saty protested.

"That doesn't mean anything; they could've escaped getting caught," Cypha said. "Hell, if Fayta and Martra could be killed when they're only thirteen years old, why can't three kids the same age be threats?"

Saty didn't respond, inhaling as she fought to not start crying again.

Dyspro cast a furtive glance at the gallows and then turned to his friends. "We should go," he said seriously.

"Yeah," Cypha agreed shortly, wiping her arm quickly over her eyes before turning and heading to the street.

He put a hand on Saty's shoulder as she inhaled deeply, both following Cypha.

# 1



Malkarai, now twenty-one years old, walked down a dry, dirty city street alone. He was just under six feet tall and muscular but lean in build – a strong but unimposing figure. His jet-black hair was long but not past his jawline, heavy enough to make it lay flat, and loosely covered most of his unshaven face. There was a long scar that reached from his left ear to his chin, a pale contrast to his sallow tan complexion.

He wore a dark-colored, heavy traveling cloak over a long black coat that clinked slightly as he walked, despite his smooth gait. There was a bag hanging from one shoulder, hidden under the cloak. He had on worn, dark blue jeans and black leather boots, and his hands were buried in the pockets of the coat. His black eyes searched the street, taking the area in.

The streets here were pretty wide and there was substantial space between buildings. The sidewalks were mostly devoid of walking people, although the vehicle traffic was pretty steady.

The section of town he was walking through was a mixture of small, local shop fronts with the occasional restaurant and ill-repaired parking lots north of downtown, near the river. The area was clean but had a lot of empty or abandoned buildings littered with graffiti and half-hearted boards and chains.

At a fairly busy intersection, he stopped, exhaling, his warm breath visible in the air. After a few moments, he reached over and pushed the 'Walk' button on the signal post. He waited, patiently at first, but increasingly impatiently as he noticed people in the cars waiting for the lights at the corner staring at him.

He reached over and pushed the button a few more times before putting his hands in his coat pockets, staring at the signal across the street stubbornly until it changed, his brow tight. He crossed halfway, stopped to let someone who wasn't paying attention to him turn right, and then continued to the other sidewalk and down the street.

A few blocks later, he reached his destination and entered a small, unassuming hotel. It was fairly clean inside but poorly kept up – like the rest of the neighborhood. Some of the trim around the walls in the lobby was missing, there were a few patches in the drywall that hadn't been painted, and the front of the desk needed repair. However, he could see no dust or dirt on any of the surfaces, not even on the half-full bookshelf to his right. After taking stock of the room and the man sitting in an easy chair near the doors, reading a paper, he stepped up to the desk, and the attentive worker addressed him.

"Good morning," she said, her eyes locking right onto his after she'd looked up at him. There was the briefest of pauses before she asked, "How can I help you?"

His voice was low and quiet, but easy enough to hear. He didn't want to make this person suspicious, so he kept his tone friendly. "I'm interested in several rooms. I'm in charge of finding housing for my extended family for the next two days, and my bag with my laptop and my phone got stolen and I'm waiting for insurance to decide if they want to grace me with replacements, so I thought it might be easier to just come and ask in person."

The girl smiled faintly. She was looking him over and didn't seem sold. "That's unfortunate."

"Yeah. How many rooms do you have free right now?"

She stared at him – at his eyes – for a moment longer before looking at the computer, which seemed almost as old as the building itself. He could hear it whirring somewhere under the desk.

"Er… well, we have four rooms with queen-size beds free at the moment. How many do you need?"

"Are they close to each other at all?"

She picked up a laminated map of the hotel and circled the rooms with a dry-erase marker. "Well… four and six are in the same hall, and ten and eleven are on the next floor, next to each other."

"Hmmm… four's all you have?"

"At the moment, yes. We had one recently vacated, but it hasn't been cleaned yet. How soon do you need the rooms?"

"Later today. Not right now."

"Oh, well, then another one will open up after it's cleaned."

"Where's that in relation to the others?"

"It's in the same hall as four and six. Seven, so it's across from six."

He nodded, examining the map and considering what she'd told him. "How much do rooms run a night?"

"$85.00."

"Do you have any group rates?"

"Sorry, we do not."

"All right. I'll have to see if that's enough rooms to hold us. I think she was saying eight, but maybe they can get cozy. Is it possible for you to hold them for just an hour at the most? I need to go call her."

The girl hesitated but then nodded. "I can probably hold them for an hour, but no longer, all right? My manager wouldn't be happy if I locked them out completely."

"That's fine, I'll try to be quick. Thank you. Uh, can you break a dollar so I can get change for the pay phone?"

She nodded and opened a drawer as he reached into his coat and dug out his wallet.

He exchanged a dollar for the coins and put them in his pocket. "Thank you."

Malkarai left and went to the right, heading up the street until he reached an alleyway. He turned down it and circled back around to the hotel. After examining and counting the windows at the back of the building and making sure the alley was deserted, he stopped at one and pulled a crate over to reach the window. He pulled a six-inch wire out of his pocket, put a crook in it near one end, and then bent the other end with a smaller crook. Holding the end with the larger crook, he fed it in between the sliding panels of the window, working with the tool to flip the lock for the window up and unlock the panels.

After a few minutes, the lock flipped and he withdrew the tool before dropping it back in his pocket. He pushed the window aside, looked around to make sure the room was empty, and hoisted himself up and inside, pulling his coat and cloak in after him carefully to keep the items inside from clattering together loudly.

Inside the room, he went to the door, opened it enough to double-check the number on it, and then closed it and fastened the deadbolt before moving into the bathroom. He took a small spray bottle out of his coat and sprayed the sink. While glancing about at the rest of the bathroom, he put the bottle away and took out a flashlight, which he pushed the button on three times and pointed at the sink. The light was a black light that illuminated several spots on the ceramic. It seemed like the interior of the sink had been cleaned with chemicals, but the drops on the outer countertop had been neglected.

"Hmmm… still bleeding from her attempt, huh?" He turned off the flashlight, put it back in his pocket, and looked at the garbage can next to the vanity to see a moderate amount of ash inside the metal can.

"Now, who burns their bathroom garbage if they have nothing to hide…?" He looked around again and then moved out to the main room.

Malkarai walked over to the bed and threw back the covers. He took out the same flashlight and pushed the button once, turning on a normal light bulb, and examined the sheets and pillow. After a few minutes, he found a straight brown hair several inches long. He held it up to the light for a few moments and then dropped it. Then he moved around the room, searching through drawers. The Bible was still there, but the occupant hadn't left anything.

He crouched by the garbage can near the door and found an envelope underneath some used tissues. He shook the trash to the side and fished out the envelope. It was ripped in four, but easily enough put back together. It held the logo of a train company.

"Mmmm… jackpot." He stuffed the envelope pieces inside his coat and put away his flashlight before undoing the deadbolt and heading for the window.

After exiting and closing the panel, but leaving it unlocked, he headed around the block again and entered the hotel from the front.

The woman at the desk looked up as he entered and approached. "Welcome back."

He gave her a small, tired smile, acting annoyed. "Thanks. I'm sorry, but it seems that the five rooms won't be enough. I'll have to see if I can find something else, or at least another place close by to put the rest. You don't need to hold the rooms for me anymore though."

"I'm sorry they won't work for you."

"I wish she'd given me more than six hours to find everyone rooms. My apologies for wasting your time," he said, already taking a step away from the desk.

"It's all right. Have a nice day."

"You too," he said before leaving.

Malkarai headed back where he'd come from after he left the hotel, walking back down the street and glaring at the obnoxiously laggy crosswalk before he'd even gotten to it. After dealing with that again, he went to a café that he'd seen on his first trip down the street and entered.

He went up to the counter, ordered a drink and a sandwich, and then found a secluded table and opened his bag, digging out a small, thin laptop. He opened the screen and powered it on. Immediately he entered a passcode and then looked around idly, waiting for the operating system to load, taking in the people around him and scanning for threats; although he couldn't see how there could be any here. There was a smattering of people in the restaurant, but the lunch hour hadn't really started yet. He aimed to vacate before it got busy anyway.

Once the OS had loaded, he entered several authentication codes and passwords into the computer and then connected to a wireless broadband network instead of the café's public wi-fi. When he had connectivity, he started some scripts to give him the necessary digital privacy he needed. After a few different approaches, he was able to get access to the train company's internal network to review their passenger lists, departure times, and surveillance videos.

He searched the passenger lists for a few names, fairly quickly finding one he recognized. He copied down the platform number, destination name, and schedule. Then he moved to the surveillance to visually confirm his man had actually gotten on the train he had a ticket for.

After watching the platform for a short time while he ate his lunch, he found his target. The man had short brown hair, a brown leather jacket, worn blue jeans, a dark blue backpack over one shoulder, and a sword sheath on his back, the leather restraint strap snapped in place over its hilt. He paused the playback after he watched him board a train and pulled a notebook from his bag so he could write down the information about the train, the time of his boarding, the departure, and what time it was scheduled to arrive at its first, second, third, and fourth destinations. The man had only paid for a ticket to the second destination, but that didn't mean that he wouldn't do something forensically disorienting like purchasing another ticket later.

After watching some more videos to make sure he didn't leave the train, Malkarai navigated out of the surveillance footage. Forty-five minutes later, he logged out of, turned off, and put away his computer. Then he stood up, gathered his garbage, threw it out, and went back up to the counter.

He waited in line for a few minutes and then bought a cookie for the road. After paying, he dropped the quarters from the hotel in the tip jar and then headed for the door.

Malkarai went outside, put the cookie in his pocket, and pulled out his phone, pressing a button on the main screen before holding it up to his ear. After a few rings his call was answered.

"Hello, this is Stika."

"It's Malkarai. He moved again," he said as he took a right and walked down the street.

Stika sighed. "Awesome," she said sarcastically.

"I know where he went. I'm following."

"Where to now?"

"Cavington, Minnesota, to begin with."

She hesitated before responding. "That's the middle of dark-hater territory, Malk."

"Yeah. He's getting smarter."

"Perhaps, but unless you intend to just hide the whole time, you're going to have a hell of a time tracking him. No one's gonna give you any favors there."

"No one gives me any favors anywhere, Stika. I'll be fine."

"You're going to follow?"

"Of course, I'm going to follow."

"Do you want me to take this up higher?"

"No," he said firmly.

"I can send Teffifa to scare him out. She's mostly healed."

"She'd scare everyone out, and she's not that healed; don't let her lie to you."

"Look up the town before you get there. It's ringing bells for some reason."

"Yeah, I'll check it out. I'll talk to you later."

"Be careful."

Malkarai ended the call and then opened up a GPS program, getting directions to Cavington, Minnesota.

He stared at the destination on the map for a few moments, his eyebrows knitting up. It was ringing bells for him too, but he wasn't sure why. He'd been to so many towns around the Northwest and Northern Midwest, that he wouldn't be surprised if he had been there before, but it was bugging him beyond that.

Malkarai shook his head and pulled keys out of a pocket in his coat as he approached a dark blue car with Iowa plates parked two blocks away from the café. After unlocking it, he took his cloak and bag off, tossed them in the back seat, and then got in the front. He put his phone in the dash mount, plugging the power cord in it, before buckling himself in.

He turned the car on and locked the doors, staring at his phone while the electronics in the car kicked in. After a few moments of deliberation, he picked it up, opened up a browser, and searched for the town.

"Why are you running to *that* place…? Is it *because* it's dangerous for darks? If that's the case, that won't matter, because I haven't given a fuck about that for years…" he muttered, glaring at his phone as he browsed. "What's your plan here?"

# 2

The brown-haired man shifted his backpack on his shoulder as he stepped off the train, looking around through the iron fence along the platform. There were buildings around, but they were mostly industrial. There was a lot of concrete and gravel outside of the station, and it looked pretty barren. Only a few other people deboarded as he did, and he followed them into the station.

Inside, he looked around for the familiar tourist rack full of brochures, coupons, and other local propaganda. After perusing it for a few minutes, he collected a map, several inn advertisements, and a local coupon packet. He looked around for rideshare or taxi information but didn't find anything, which meant this area probably relied on the app ones. "Okay, hoofing it again, I guess," he grumbled, since using an app was not an option. He went over to a chair in the room, took his bag off, and opened it up, pulling a bunch of rumpled brochures and similar literature for Omaha out of the bag. He tossed them in a garbage can nearby and then put the bag back on, tucking some of his new information in his coat pocket.

He opened up the map and examined it. Downtown seemed congested enough for his purposes, and there were several inns, restaurants, and stores there too. If he wasn't going to have access to vehicles, then downtown was the best choice.

He put the map away and headed outside. He did a quick scope to see if there were any taxis or rideshare cars were sitting outside of the station, looking for easy fares, but the lot only held parked cars.

It took him a while, but eventually, he made his way to the center of town.

Cavington looked like fairly typical small-town America; old, but properly lit and well-repaired. The storefronts he was passing had a traditional, antiquated feel with brick fronts, wooden and stone molding, and classic artistic metal accents. The streetlamps matched like there had been a historical revival of the place. Still, it said a lot that the place still looked nice, albeit a little dirty. Everything seemed to look dirty this time of year though. In the cold months, until the snow showed up, the world was just dead, and it felt as such.

It was cold and windy, and his skin stung. Blinking green eyes to get the tears from the wind out of them, he put a hand up to block it, looking around for one of the inns on the list.

He was looking for a motel or inn or something similar because the last place he should be was out on the streets at night while being followed, and for the same reason he wanted a place with thin walls, where someone else would hear if something happened to him. He knew that it would be a deterrent to his pursuer. The problem with most chain hotels was that you could set a bomb off in your toilet and your neighbor would never know.

Eventually, he found one of the inns and scoped the front of it. It seemed nice, but not too fancy. His budget couldn't handle fancy. He went inside and up to the desk, glancing around the room, which looked like a comfortable sitting room with a few non-homey elements, like a tile aisle going through the middle of the carpet, and the metal spinning rack full of cards, postcards, and paperback books.

He checked the price and reserved a room for the night, letting the clerk know it may be more than one night, but he wasn't sure yet.

"If you guys have to reserve the room, that's okay, I'll find another one. I can't really commit to more than a night at a time though."

"That's fine, it shouldn't be a problem – unless you're still around at Christmas time," she said as she handed him a key, eyeing him.

He laughed and took the key. "Wouldn't that be nice?"

"You're upstairs and on the right-hand side as you reach the top of the stairs."

"Okay, thank you."

He headed for the stairs, went up to the room, opened the door, and went inside. He did a quick walk-through, checking out the amenities. There was a microwave and mini-fridge in addition to the television.

"Score, I'm not restricted to take-out," he said to himself before going back to the door, giving the room another glance, and then leaving and locking up behind himself.

Downstairs, he went back up to the desk. "Hey, sorry to bug you again."

The woman looked up from the computer. "Is there something wrong with the room?"

"No, not at all. Where's the nearest grocery store? I wanna get a few things to eat in."

"Oh, uh, Henny's is a few minutes away." She pointed to her right. "Go that way out of here, down to 9th street, and it's just two blocks south. It's on the corner so it's pretty easy to see."

"Great, thank you," he said, tapping the desk briefly before heading for the door.

It took him more than a few minutes to get there since he was not driving, but he found the store easily enough. It was definitely a locally run place. There were signs both on the side of the building and above the door that said, 'Henny's' in large font over a smaller, 'Food Market.'

A bell on the door jingled as he entered, and he was almost immediately greeted by the young woman leaning on the counter to the right of the door. She had long brown hair up in a ponytail and was wearing a pale green sweater and jeans. Her figure suggested she was in her late teens or early twenties. "Welcome," she said in a friendly tone.

He did a double take but then smiled at her. "Thanks."

The inside was clean, brightly lit, and had fairly well-stocked, old metal shelves. He noticed the complete lack of gaudy advertisements and racks for special goods. There were some display boxes situated on the counter at the front of the store, but that was the extent of the advertisements. Most of the products were brand-name or of a single off-brand, but there was no extra marketing wasted on them. At the moment it looked like he was the only customer in the store, which he honestly thought was pretty surprising.

He moved over by the cooler on the far left-hand wall to see what they had for lunch meat and other fresh ingredients. He aimed to make good use of that mini-fridge.

"Hey, Dad?" the girl called to the back of the store.

"What, Saty?" a man replied from the back room.

"Do you need me to stick around to help close tonight?"

"Nah, I've got it. You can take off at 6:30 again."

"I'll stick around for a little bit longer. I think Patricia's having Brendan over tonight. They kinda make me sick these days."

Her father laughed as he came out of the back room and then up front with a box of items. "One day you'll find some guy that makes her sick, don't worry."

"All the guys I find make her sick, but not the same way hers sicken me."

"She's just got different tastes. You two require very different boys. Hand me that box cutter."

The girl reached over, took a utility knife off the end of the counter, and handed it to her father, who opened the box. She also greeted another customer by name as she came in.

After gathering bread, lunch meat, cheese, a few cans of food, two drinks, and condiments, the man came up to the counter.

The girl flashed him a smile. "Hi there. This all today?"

He couldn't help but smile back as he set his food on the counter. "Yeah, this is it."

As she checked the prices on each of the items, she glanced at him, checking him out. "Are you visiting or just passing through?"

He gave her a calculating look. "Is it that obvious?"

She smirked and typed the prices into the register with her right hand. "Well, you're not a knight or police officer, and no one else around here really carries a sword but them."

"Oh." He'd honestly forgotten he still had it on. "It's my emotional support sword."

She laughed.

"Is it that problematic to have one here?"

"No, it's just not common. I doubt you'll need it in Cavington. We're not that exciting of a town."

He smiled. "I sincerely hope so."

"Really, don't worry about it. No one else will even say anything unless you take it out. It's just that I people-watch, so it's something I noticed. Your total's $26.35, by the way."

He opened his wallet and then handed her two twenties. "People-watch, huh?"

She smiled, counting out his change. "Yeah. Gotta pass the time somehow, and getting a rare visitor like yourself makes for interesting conversation."

He laughed and took the change and then the bag of food from her. "Wow, I didn't think I qualified as rare, but I guess you probably have your regulars."

She smiled, glancing at the other lady that was in the store. "Sure do."

"I guess this is what it feels like to be a dark, huh?" he said, deciding to try and scope the current climate.

Her expression turned serious as she looked back at him.

"They don't deserve that kind of attention. It's pretty aggravating."

"Incredibly," she said, her tone betraying that she had feelings on this matter, despite her customer service face being on.

He settled, holding his groceries at his side, and gave her an inquisitive look. "Is this place still pretty bad for them?"

"It's better than it was. No darks live here, but most people don't like them. There's still an embarrassing number of people that believe the bad stereotypes and the rest are just awkward about them because we almost never see any."

"I see. That's unfortunate," he said, trying to sound sympathetic. "Thanks for entertaining my weird questions. Have a good night."

"You too," she said, friendly, but still eyeing him curiously.

He made his exit. Outside, he headed toward the inn again, shaking his head. *Christ, if I stand out here, then you're going to be a goddamn sideshow. I really hope this place works to my advantage.*

# 3



Satyrna Hennessin blew her bangs out of her eyes as she watched the street through the windows of the small grocery and convenience store her parents owned, distracted from the stocking she'd been asked to do.

She had long, straight brown hair that reached the middle of her back, emerald green eyes under swept bangs, and a magnetic, casual beauty about her. She was wearing comfortable-fit jeans that hung over her black canvas tennis shoes and a dark-red, long-sleeved shirt that hugged her fit form flatteringly.

"Earth to Satyrna. Those crackers aren't going to stock themselves," her elder sister, Patricia, called from behind the counter, where she was stocking mints while waiting for the handful of customers in the store to finish their shopping.

Satyrna sighed and glanced at her before resuming her task. "Oh, stuff it. When can I take a supper break?"

"You leave in an hour."

"So…? I'm hungry."

Patricia sighed at her and turned around to put the overstock of mints on a high shelf behind her. "Oh, stop whining. Eat a snack or something. It's not like we sell auto parts, you know."

Satyrna finished stocking the crackers and came around the counter to grab a box of cookies while her sister greeted and checked out a customer who was holding the hand of a toddler. Satyrna waved at the little kid and gave him a smile before heading back to the other side of the store.

"Have a good day," Patricia said to the customer as he led the toddler out the door, his groceries in his other hand. She glanced at the other customers and then resumed putting candy in the display next to the counter, and putting the overstock boxes back up behind her.

Patricia had dirty blonde, shoulder-length hair, and hazel eyes. She was wearing a knee-length jean skirt, white knit tights, brown heeled boots, and a white sweater. She was attractive too, but her looks were less natural than her younger sister's. She actually had make-up on, whereas Satyrna had completely neglected it that morning.

"Why are you so dressed up, anyway?" Satyrna asked, giving her a look. "You're stocking candy and tampons."

Patricia gave her a look over her shoulder. "Excuse me for acting like I *like* my job."

Satyrna rolled her eyes and put away a few more boxes of cookies before she stopped, distracted by something outside of the window again.

Patricia turned around and leaned against the counter, noticing that her sister was staring again. "Hey, slacker, stop gaping."

She glanced at Patricia and then pointed subtly out the window at a man who was standing near the corner, a phone up to his ear. "Hey, look at him."

"Who? I can see at least four guys out there, Satyrna."

"The one with the black hair and the long dark coat." She narrowed her eyes as she looked at him, trying to see his eyes better. "I think… I think he's a dark."

"I can't see."

"I can. I'm pretty sure, anyway. I haven't seen a dark around here in a long time."

Patricia leaned over the counter a little more, trying to better see him. "There're a lot of strange characters around here these days."

Satyrna gave her a look. "I never said he was strange. Darks aren't strange."

"Yeah, they are. I haven't seen any since the Harakins."

"Okay, you mean *rare*. And yes, they're rare here." She frowned and counted on her fingers. "But there was that one last year, and one a few years before that, and Cypha, Dyspro, and I saw that one after my friends died."

"Yeah, fine, I guess. That's really not that many, Satyrna. Also, those were all kids, and the one last year was a toddler. He's an adult. And I meant strange weird too."

Satyrna frowned. "That's not fair."

"He's dressed weird."

"He's dressed for *the cold*," Satyrna insisted.

"That's a heck of a lot of black."

Satyrna rolled her eyes. "Oh, this again."

"Shady types *love* black," Patricia said. "And darks can be dangerous too. Just cuz someone is dark doesn't mean you can automatically say they're a saint. I know you sanctify them."

"Name one example of a dangerous dark," Satyrna pressed, annoyed.

"That woman two years ago who went crazy and killed her boyfriend and son."

"How about one that the media hasn't completely hyped to hell?" Satyrna said with a scowl.

"Fine, even if you accept that that's an outlier-"

"Which it is," Satyrna interjected insistently.

Patricia shook her head. "They still have a reputation – and there's usually a reason for that."

"Yeah, people need someone 'other' to hate on," Satyrna grumbled. She settled back on her heels and crossed her arms, a bitter look on her face. "They're no different from the rest of us; I don't see why people are so against them."

Patricia sighed. "Like you said, people always need someone to blame stuff on. Why are you getting so worked up? It's not like you know that guy."

Satyrna looked back at the man, who pulled the phone down from his head and tapped the screen a few times before glancing around and starting to walk. She turned and went back over to the counter with her empty box as the bell above the door jingled for an adolescent boy coming in. He made a beeline for the candy, not waiting for a greeting.

"You *know* darks are a sensitive topic for me," Satyrna said as she got close to her sister.

Patricia shook her head as Satyrna broke down her box and set it behind the counter. "Yeah, but you know nothing about that one – I wouldn't say he was radiating goodness. He looked shifty as hell."

Satyrna sat down on one of the stools behind the counter and strained a bit to examine the stranger, who was nearly out of sight to their left now. "He doesn't look bad, he looks kinda… I don't know; cautious, troubled… alert. Actually, I think he's rather handsome."

Her sister pushed her shoulder, exasperated. "You would. Why is it that you always go for the weirdos?"

Satyrna caught herself and stuck her tongue out at her. "*I'm* a weirdo, according to you. Weirdos are more fun."

Patricia sighed. "I can't argue that first point."

"Just because I don't fawn over the stupid knights, like you do, doesn't mean that my interests are flawed."

"I thought you liked Brendan."

"Yeah, sure. And I obviously like Josh – but would I ever date either of them? Hell no."

"Josh doesn't count; he wouldn't date you either."

"Regardless, I'm not asking either of them to hook me up with any of their coworkers. They're a bunch of egotistical jerks."

"You went out with the head knight, Satyrna."

She bristled at the mention of that disliked part of her dating life. "Yeah, and if even the top of the ladder pissed me off, what makes you think I'd like being with any of the others? They're a bunch of assholes – *especially* him."

"Hypocrite." Patricia nodded her head slightly toward the kid, who had made his way around to the batteries. She'd been watching him the whole time they were chatting at the counter.

"Is that the same one?" Satyrna murmured.

"Yep."

"What the hell…" she muttered before sighing and sliding slowly off her stool.

The kid had apparently realized his time was up and he'd been noticed, because he glanced at them briefly, snatched a pack of batteries, and bolted for the door.

"Hey! Stop!" Patricia called.

"I got him," Satyrna said as she went around the counter and chased after him.

Outside, the kid had darted around people and headed down the street, but Satyrna almost immediately ran into several people.

"Ugh! Stop! Thief! Someone grab that kid!" she yelled as she went around, trying to keep the kid in sight.

Down the street, people were stopping as they heard her calls but weren't doing anything; startled or unsure what was happening.

Except for one, who heard her calls for help, altered their course to be closer to the path the kid was taking, and snatched him as he went past.

"Agh! Let go of me!"

Satyrna ran up, breathing a little heavy. "Thank you so much!" She blushed, realizing that the man who had grabbed him was the one they'd just been discussing.

"What'd he do?" Malkarai asked, looking at the adolescent, who was struggling and trying to dislodge his grip from his coat.

A man came up, looking indignant. "Hey, buddy, let go of that kid!"

Satyrna immediately stepped up to the other man, a fierce expression on her face. "Back off! The kid's a thief. He just stole from our store."

"Oh- uh, all right." He took a step away, shaking his head at her.

Satyrna shook her head, deciding he wasn't worth wasting any more breath on, and turned to the one who had actually helped. She was going to say something to him but lost her train of thought. *I was right… absolutely a dark – and even better looking up close. Jeez.* She took a deep breath, pretending she was still catching her breath.

Malkarai looked at the kid and lifted him off the ground slightly because he was trying to get leverage to pull away from him.

Satyrna was impressed; the kid wasn't small. She saw the batteries sticking out of the kid's coat pocket and grabbed them. "There!"

Malkarai looked at the batteries, confused. "That's what he stole?"

"Yeah – this time."

"What do you want to do with him?" he asked, looking up at her face. His brow knitted up slightly when Satyrna just stared levelly at him, not flinching or looking wary of him. If anything, she looked excited, and it confused him.

"Uhhh…" she looked around briefly. "Um, how good of a hold on him do you have?"

"He's not going anywhere if I don't want him to."

The kid scowled and kicked at him, but he just stepped away calmly, dodging it.

"Normally I'd just let him go since I have the stuff… but he's actually gotten away with a lot of *other* stuff and not gotten caught, so… could you bring him back to the store for me?"

"Where's your store?"

"Not even a block that way," she said, pointing west. "Once we get him back there my sister can call the police."

"Will this take long?"

"Probably not – the police station is only a few blocks away."

He nodded to her and set the kid back on the ground, taking hold of both of his upper arms. "Lead on."

"Oh, fuck you! C'mon! Let me go!" the kid yelled, struggling.

Satyrna frowned at the kid. "Maybe if you hadn't stolen five hundred dollars worth of stuff from us. Our charity has a limit."

She turned and headed back to the store, glancing back to make sure that Malkarai was following.

He pushed the kid along in front of him, still holding him by the upper arms. The kid was trying to drag his feet but failed to even slightly hinder Malkarai's pace.

Back at the store, Satyrna opened the door and held it as Malkarai brought the kid inside.

Patricia perked up and then her eyes widened when she saw Malkarai. "Oh," she said simply, shocked. "You got him! Nice job!" she added lamely.

Satyrna looked at her, both annoyed with this response, but also proud of her sister for not saying something stupid or unintentionally insulting. "Yeah, he caught the kid for me. Can you call the cops so they can pick this little shit up?"

"Yeah," Patricia said before grabbing the phone off the wall and dialing one of the numbers they had written on notepapers stuck to the wall next to it. "Uh, get Dad up here."

Satyrna glanced at Malkarai. "Sorry, could you keep hold of him for just a few more minutes?"

He nodded patiently and Satyrna headed into the back of the store.

A short while later, after two officers had come around, handcuffed the thief, and taken Malkarai, Satyrna, Patricia, and their father's statements, Malkarai declined to be identified and excused himself.

Satyrna watched him go and bit her lower lip contemplatively, crossing her arms as he passed the front window.

"Good work, Saty," her father said.

"Eh, Patricia should've told me it was the kid as soon as he came in. I didn't know what he looked like. I would've been more alert."

"I forgot you weren't here for the other times," Patricia said defensively. "It worked out okay. We got him."

"Yeah, thanks to that guy." Satyrna exhaled shortly like she'd decided something. She looked up at her dad. "Can I go?"

Her father smirked at her. "For any good reason?"

"Maybe."

He waved a hand dismissively. "Make sure you've got your phone on you."

"Thanks!" She gave him a quick hug, ran behind the counter, snatched her purse from behind it, and then hurried out the door.

"Where's she going?" Patricia asked, startled by Satyrna's sudden exit.

He chuckled as he came around the counter, next to her. "Chasing down her dark knight, probably."

Patricia sighed, frowning. "She left her coat."

Her father laughed.

Outside, Satyrna looked to her left, trying to find the dark man. After a few moments, she spotted him almost where he'd caught the thief for her earlier.

She hurried down the street, holding her purse at her side, before catching up to him. "Hey!"

He glanced at her as she fell into step at his side. "Did they still need me?"

"Nope, and I got the okay to leave too!"

"Oh. Then what is it?"

"Thank you for catching him."

"It was nothing," he said dismissively, looking away.

Satyrna chewed on her lower lip briefly before turning and holding out her hand to him in greeting. "I can't believe I didn't introduce myself throughout all of that. My name is Satyrna."

He glanced at her but didn't stop walking, turning his eyes ahead again. "Not sure if you're reckless or naïve, but darks are trouble. You shouldn't be talking to one."

"Well, I guess we have something in common."

"You're not a dark," he said coldly.

"I never said I was. I meant I was trouble too."

He scoffed humorlessly and looked away. "I doubt that."

She sighed, deciding her next angle. "What's your name?"

"You're better off not knowing it."

"Oh, come on, how is knowing your name problematic?"

He paused before answering, and even then, his response was hesitant. "Malkarai."

"Wow, that's a cool name." Satyrna suddenly remembered the guy from last night. "Oh! Are you here to meet up with someone?"

He looked at her sharply. "What?"

She was a little startled at the sudden interest. "Well, see, there was a guy yesterday afternoon who was asking about how darks are treated here; it sounded like he was trying to scope the environment."

Malkarai stopped, looking directly at her, his expression serious. "Where'd he go?"

"I don't know," she said with a shrug. "I only sold him food. I don't know where he went after that."

He sighed and looked around, seeming uncertain about something.

"Are you friends?"

"Not exactly. Yes, I'm looking for him."

She paused, not sure how to pursue that. "Where are you from?"

"West."

"Just west?"

"Yeah."

"West of here? The West Coast? Western Minnesota?" she urged.

"West of here."

"Is this your first time in the area?"

"No."

She perked up. "That's surprising. When were you here?"

His expression hardened. "A while ago, I think. I don't know. I travel a lot, and there's no shortage of places that treat darks like shit, so it all blurs together."

"Ugh! That pisses me off! There's nothing wrong with darks, and there's no reason to fear them like people do."

"Yeah, well, people suck."

"Not all people. You seem like a good person."

"Why?"

Satyrna's brow lifted as she looked at him. He was actually looking back at her, looking both guarded and curious. "What do you mean, 'why?'" she asked. "You just caught a thief for me."

"That's not a big deal."

She waved a hand, still making eye contact with him. "Nobody else on this street even tried."

He grunted softly, apparently unable to counter that.

"This guy you're looking for…shouldn't you call him or something?"

Malkarai looked away, glancing down the street. "He won't answer my calls if he even has a phone."

"Oh."

"I need to find him."

"It sounded like he was expecting you."

"Yeah, but he doesn't necessarily want me to find him."

"How come?" she pressed, intrigued.

"I'm here on business. He doesn't want me to catch up to do business with him."

"Really? That sounds…"

"Obnoxious."

Satyrna snickered. "Not what I was thinking."

"It's obnoxious and I'm annoyed. The officers at the store reminded me of something. This place has a different policing system, right?"

"Than most of the US? Yes."

"What's different? Those were police officers that came to the store, right?"

"Yeah. We still have cops and they basically handle all the civic issues, but we also have this other law enforcement squad called the knights. They're like a combination of SWAT and detectives and just more competent police. They focus on things like gangs, drugs, the bad stuff. Anything that would likely involve fighting. They work with the police on some things, or the police will give them information on things that the knights should handle."

"Does that work?"

"Yeah, for the most part, I guess. I think they fuck things up sometimes too though," Satyrna muttered.

"How so?" he asked.

"When Cavington seceded from the US like so many other towns and stuff did at that time, the people who set up our government wanted more security. They saw what happened in other places and didn't want criminals to see the town as a good place to set up a base or anything like that. So, the knights and police strictly enforce our laws and drive those elements out." She scowled, getting more incensed. "However, they've also used their positions to act like ignorant tyrants that thought it was perfectly fine to publicly execute children for petty theft."

Malkarai frowned, still watching her. "That's fucked up. Wait, what's going to happen to the kid you just called the police on?"

She waved her hands defensively. "He won't get treated like that. My friends were the last victims of that bullshit. I'm positive they only did it because they were dark too. If they'd been little kids with normal eyes, they would've just sent them to a juvenile facility. No, they had to make an *example* of them. Sometimes I really hate this place. I know exactly why we have a terrible reputation."

Malkarai was quiet for a few moments. "What was the legal justification for that?"

"I was young, so I can't say I know exactly what they said or did. I know that they were caught stealing really expensive stuff – multiple times. But, they were my friends… I knew that they weren't doing it because they wanted to. Their mother made them do it – she's the one who wanted the jewelry and things they stole. The sheriff proposed death by hanging to make an example of them, and the head knight signed off on it, and people were pissed, but not enough to actually prevent it before it happened. They were trying to send a strong message against crime, but it really just made them look like monsters. There are laws against public executions, hanging, and capital punishment against children now. The fact that there weren't laws before was just a fucking loophole that *no one* should've taken advantage of. They didn't think they needed to say it, you know?"

He looked bothered, his eyebrows knitted up as he stared at the ground just beyond her. "What happened to their mother?"

"She just left town. I never heard of her again. Dyspro, Cypha, Josh, and I told people that it was her, but either they didn't believe us, or they didn't care. It still makes me *so mad*."

"How old were they?"

"Thirteen – they were older than the rest of us. Still nowhere near old enough to have an adult punishment given to them though."

"What were their names?"

"Fayta and Martra."

He was quiet for a moment. "Were they twins? Dark brown hair?"

Satyrna stared at him. "Yeah, how did you know that?"

"I was here the day that they were hanged." He shook his head, shutting his eyes for a moment. "I'd almost forgotten about that. I think I tried to block it out."

Her eyes widened. "You were *here*? By yourself?"

"No, I was with two other kids."

"How old were you?"

"Ten, I think."

She stepped closer to him, putting her hands on his arms as she spoke quickly, excited. "That was *you*?! You came up and asked us about them afterward – you and your friends, right? I was the one that was bawling the whole time, and I think Cypha tried to fight your friend."

He'd tensed when she touched him, but nodded, looking up at her again. "Yeah, that was me. I'm surprised *you* remember me…I have a feeling that was not an easy day for you."

"It wasn't – it was awful. But I always remember the darks I meet, and one after such a traumatic event? Yeah, I never forgot you. Why were you here then? Were you with your parents?"

"We were here alone, no chaperones. Not like I ever had parents anyway," he said with a shrug. "Where were *your* parents that day? You guys were alone there too, weren't you?"

"Oh. Yeah – we all snuck out," she said quietly, taking her hands off his arms, just realizing how up in his space she'd gotten in her excitement. "We weren't supposed to be there. Our parents were pissed about the execution, but they didn't want us to see it. We weren't going to let our friends be alone though."

He frowned, taking her in. "They wanted to keep you safe."

"Yeah, I know. They didn't want us to know about or deal with that bull while we were kids, so they tried to protect us. But karma caught up to the sheriff at least, because he died shortly after it." She made a contemplative face, her brow knitted up. "I honestly should go back and look at newspaper articles from then now that I'm not as young and stupid."

"I'm kind of surprised that you turned that thief in, knowing what happened to your friends," he said, looking at her appraisingly. "Are you sure he'll be treated fairly?"

Satyrna sighed. "Yes. He's stolen quite a bit of stuff from us, and it's never been food. Yeah, we're more sympathetic to thieves than most people, but my parents still have a business to run, and that kid's either doing it for the thrills or for a gang. Either way, we couldn't just let it continue. We *have* helped out people who tried to lift food. Quite a few times, actually. He's different. Also, the hangings and capital punishment for petty crimes are gone. Like I said, that sheriff is gone, and the new one that was elected is a lot more moderate. I'm not afraid to call the police anymore.

"The current head knight has issues, but he's not a bad person, and is a hell of a lot better than the old head knight, who used those things as control and power tactics. There are laws in place now, but even if a law doesn't cover it, the new head knight doesn't allow that crap. He thought it was barbaric."

Malkarai frowned and started walking again. "It is."

She kept pace with him, glancing at him as they went. "He does still encourage and embrace the idea of having a strong fighting force though. Earlier this year they had to face off against some drug dealers that turned violent fast. They even found some evidence that they were trying to find people to smuggle in a gun for them."

"How do *you* know about that?" Malkarai asked, eyeing her curiously.

She didn't look at him, watching the sidewalk in front of them. "I have friends on the squad. I think I mentioned Josh; he's one of my best friends, and he's a knight. My sister's boyfriend is too. Also, there's one high school here – so I went to school with some of the others."

"I see. Did they have to deal with a gun?"

"I don't think so. I think they stopped it before it happened."

"That's good. Guns are outlawed, but shootings still happen, and it's really annoying and dangerous for law-abiding people to fight against them when you only have a melee weapon. Is it good that fewer people have them? Absolutely. Following the law makes it more challenging though."

"Melee? Like a sword?"

"Yeah."

"Why did they outlaw them for everyone then?" Satyrna asked, looking at him again.

"They were getting out of control. There were too many mass shootings, and not even all of law enforcement could be trusted with them. They treated it like prohibition and removed it for everything besides military issue."

"Did that work?

"Yes, somewhat. There are a lot fewer mass shootings, but the number is unfortunately not zero, because the sociopaths who commit the shootings still can dig guns up from black markets. There are almost no kids taking out their classmates at least."

"That's good… but what does law enforcement do to protect themselves against guns?" Satyrna asked, her eyebrows knitted up.

"Depends on the squad. There are still bullet-proof vests and body armor, and most systems have training on how to counter shooters. For ranged situations, some people specialize in bows and arrows or crossbows. They have ways around it."

"You know a lot about law enforcement…"

Malkarai shrugged, looking around evasively as they reached a busy street. "I know a lot about a lot of random shit."

Satyrna smiled and followed him as he crossed with the light. "What else do you know about?"

"You do not have the time, and I do not have the social stamina to get into that," he said as they reached the other curb.

Satyrna laughed.

A young man and woman walking from the north noticed them and walked up.

"Hey, Satyrna," the man greeted.

She looked toward them and smiled, waving.

He was dressed in tan carpenter-style pants, a sleeveless white shirt, and a blue flannel button-up shirt – all of it worn-in. He was clean-shaven, had deep blue eyes, mid-length and styled brown hair, and a strong, muscular build. "I thought you had work tonight."

"Yeah, but I just finished."

The woman was eyeing Malkarai, who had stopped when Satyrna did. He didn't look comfortable and was looking for a chance to go around them and continue walking.

"Who's your friend?" she asked Satyrna, looking straight at Malkarai as she did so. She was wearing a long, light brown coat with a low collar that hid her clothing except for light blue jeans and work boots. She had straight, blonde hair that followed her jawline and piercing cold gray eyes.

"This is Malkarai," Satyrna said brightly. "He just caught that thief that's been taking stuff from the store."

Cypha took her eyes off him, glancing at Satyrna. "Huh."

"This is Dyspro and Cypha," Satyrna said to Malkarai, gesturing to each of them in turn.

He just nodded slightly, seeming uncomfortable. They had no problems looking at him either, and the steady eye contact was starting to tire him out – he was used to dealing with evasiveness.

"Nice to meet you," Dyspro said. "I see you made the mistake of getting too close to Satyrna and activating her friend trap."

Cypha snickered.

Malkarai sighed. "Yeah."

Satyrna narrowed her eyes at them, putting a hand on her hip. "Well, at least *one* of us is capable of making friends."

"I make plenty of friends," Dyspro said, lifting his chin.

"No, you hit on cute chicks and tick off their guys or their brothers," Cypha retorted. "That's not making friends, dumbass."

"That's how I met Sam and Joey."

"And you talk to them *so* often," Cypha said sarcastically.

"Yeah, I should talk to them again," Dyspro mused, scratching his chin. "They're better company than you are."

Cypha rolled her eyes. "Anyway, what's your story, Malkarai?"

He frowned. "Uh…"

"He's looking for someone that I saw yesterday, so we were talking about that a little bit," Satyrna put in defensively.

"Who?"

"This tall, brown-haired guy with a sword and a backpack. He bought food from us last night and was asking me about the situation for darks here, so when I ran into Malkarai *today*, I told him about him."

"Oh, well, that's lucky for you," Cypha said, looking from Satyrna to Malkarai.

"Yeah," he said simply.

"So, are you still looking for him?"

"Yes. Well, trying." He eyed Satyrna.

Dyspro snickered. "Why don't you just call the guy?"

"I have a phone, but he does not, and I don't know where he's holed himself up." He looked at Satyrna again. "How much food did he buy?"

"Um, at least four meals worth. Bread, lunch meat, drinks, some single-serving stuff."

Malkarai sighed. "Yeah, he's holing up."

"Is he expecting you?" Cypha asked.

"Yeah, but he doesn't want me to find him. Which is why he's burrowed into a town that's deep in dark-hater territory."

Dyspro frowned. "But you followed anyway?"

"I can't say it scares me. I've seen too much shit."

Satyrna perked up again. "Oh! Cypha, do you recognize him?"

"Who? Malkarai? No."

"Dyspro?"

"No. We've met before?"

"Well, sorta. Do you remember when those three kids approached us after Fayta and Martra died? Cypha nearly got in a fight then; she snapped at the younger boy and the older one was ready to beat her up for being rude to him. The younger boy was a dark and he wanted to know why they were killed."

Dyspro laughed. "Cypha snaps at everyone, and she was always getting into fights then."

Satyrna gave him an unamused look.

Cypha looked at Malkarai, her eyes narrowing again. "Hmm… I remember that. Tiny, dark kid with a bodyguard who got pissy with me and a girl who didn't really talk. Were *you* that dark?"

Malkarai shifted from foot to foot, uncomfortable. However, he nodded.

"Jeez, you sure have grown," Dyspro said. "You're a hell of a lot taller than I would've thought you'd be. You were a small kid."

"Mm, no, I can see it," Cypha said. "You used to be a cute little munchkin too, Dyspro."

"Nuh-uh," he protested vehemently, but Cypha ignored him.

Malkarai shrugged. "I've done a lot of training."

"What happened to your bodyguard and the girl?" Cypha asked.

He sighed, looking around and avoiding eye contact. "Long story. We don't see much of each other anymore."

"Is that why you aren't as jumpy?"

"Part of it, I guess. He was like my big brother; I didn't have to stand up for myself then." He quickly averted his words, like he was avoiding getting too personal. "It's a good thing these two stopped you when they did; if you had started a fight with Traphian you probably would've ended up seriously hurt."

Cypha narrowed her eyes again. "Why do you say that?"

"He had a blade and no reason to spare you, and he only half listened to me. I have a feeling you weren't armed."

She snapped her fingers. "Right, I remember that. I saw it in his sweatshirt. I realized that continuing to pick a fight was a bad idea, no matter how bad of a mood I was in. What the hell would a kid that age need a blade for? What was he? Twelve?"

"Yeah, eleven or twelve, but I was ten and I had one, possibly two. I'm pretty sure he was only going to take it out to scare you... but it's just better if the knives don't come out at all. It's too easy to escalate if there are blades involved."

Cypha looked at Dyspro meaningfully. "I'll be damned."

"Huh?"

"You were right. Well, *we* were right. I agreed with you."

Dyspro perked up and he elbowed Satyrna. "Did you hear that, Saty? She said I was right!"

Satyrna smirked. "Uh-oh, it's already gone to his head."

Cypha rolled her eyes.

"Right about what?" Malkarai asked, confused.

She looked back at him. "Dyspro guessed that you guys were fighters."

"Oh, right," Satyrna said, remembering.

Malkarai glanced between Cypha and Dyspro. "Why'd you think that?"

"Our friend Josh's mom was a knight," Dyspro explained, "and you gave me the vibe that she and her friends from the squad always gave me. Like, don't fuck around, cuz they know how to hurt you, they just aren't because you're not a problem. So, don't *become* a problem, you know?"

"Oh," Malkarai said quietly. "I guess."

"What about the girl you were with then? Is she still around?" Cypha asked.

Malkarai closed his eyes and turned his head away, shaking it slightly. "No."

He didn't say anything else, and the three glanced at each other, none of them comfortable pressing it.

Cypha shifted and pulled a pocket knife out of the inside of her coat, offering it to him. "Look, you guys had the right idea when you were little. If you're gonna hang around here, you're going to need a weapon on you. People around here don't trust darks, and you're better off being able to defend yourself. Lots of law enforcement doesn't care for people like you, and the rest of the people are such small-town hicks that they won't give you the time of day. We don't have any darks here, and so they just see all the shit in the news and have no reason to change their minds. Avoid the authorities, don't give them a reason to notice you, and keep your hands visible with everyone else."

Malkarai sighed. "I've run into situations like this often enough; I know how to handle myself. I don't need your blade. I have my own."

"You do? Let me see."

Malkarai hesitated, staring at her.

Cypha crossed her arms, raising a brow. "Well?"

"Why?"

"Morbid curiosity."

The other two were staring at him too, so Malkarai hesitantly opened his cloak up, taking the inner trench coat edge with it and holding it back enough to let them see the sheathed sword hanging from a black leather belt at his hip.

"Oh…" Satyrna said quietly. "I had no idea you were armed."

Dyspro laughed and walked a few feet away and then back, shaking his head bemusedly.

Satyrna gave him a look. "What is it?"

"All three of us are standing here staring at what the guy's got in his trench coat. It looks like he's flashing us."

Cypha laughed and Malkarai dropped his coat and started to walk away.

Satyrna's jaw dropped and she glared at Dyspro before running after Malkarai. "Wait, Malkarai, please! He was just joking around."

"I don't have time for jokes. I'm busy."

"Please, don't run away…" Satyrna said as Cypha and Dyspro exchanged a look and then started following them. "We just want to help. You're not gonna find it easy to walk around here. The only reason no one's bugged you so far is I've been with you."

He looked at her but didn't stop. "What the hell are they gonna do to me? Glares don't do anything to a dark that's spent more than a few months outside their home."

Satyrna shook her head. "No… they're usually worse than that. People will accuse you of stuff that you haven't done, say rude things, bump you, push you… It's awful. They'll want you out, so they'll try and get you in trouble."

"Which is why I was making sure you were armed," Cypha put in as she put her knife back in her pocket. "The gangs will look for any reason to screw someone up, and law enforcement won't always step in to help out. And you definitely look like an out-of-towner."

Malkarai sighed. "Yeah, well, don't worry about it. I can take care of myself."

Cypha nodded toward his hip. "Can you use that?"

"I wouldn't carry it on me if I couldn't use it, and I've got far more than just that on me."

"Why?"

"In my profession, you need them all, and usually more."

Cypha laughed humorlessly. "What are you? A weapon salesman?"

"No."

"Then what are you?"

"It doesn't matter, just don't meet up with me in a dark alley."

Cypha gave him a frightened look and Dyspro shook his head.

"Sorry, that was terrible phrasing. I'm not a criminal," he assured them with a sigh. "My job is perfectly legal. It's just not… lacking danger."

"Because you're a dark, or just because of your job?" Dyspro asked appraisingly.

"Both, unfortunately."

"Have you guys eaten?" Satyrna asked, changing the subject again.

"No," Dyspro replied.

Cypha nodded down the street. "We were heading to Barry's."

"Great! Let's all go there. I'm starving and freezing. Patricia wouldn't let me take a dinner break."

"Well, you got off at six, so…" Cypha replied.

"Six-thirty, but still! I worked all day."

"Also, where is your coat?" Cypha added, scoldingly.

"I forgot it," Satyrna said dismissively and started urging the others to walk faster. "So, c'mon. Let's go."

"When are you moving out?" Dyspro asked. "You keep talking about it. You need less Patricia in your life."

"I need more of a job than just working at the store. I can't afford it right now. Anyway, even if I move out, I'll still keep working at the store – they're paying for school as long as I work there, you know that."

"You can still work there and not live at home though."

"Patricia still lives at home."

"She's just waiting for things to happen with Brendan and she'll move in with him," Dyspro said. "At the speed she's going, you'll be graduated before that happens. Spare yourself the stress and move out first."

Satyrna sighed. "I know. I'll see if I can afford anything, but I'll probably need another job."

Dyspro nudged her with his elbow. "Stay at our place. It's not like we're swarmed with people – and it's free."

"I'll think about it. I'll need internet when school starts again."

Satyrna noticed that Malkarai wasn't with them, turned around, and called to him. "Malkarai, come with us."

He didn't turn, even though he had to have heard her. He wasn't far away, apparently having taken advantage of their distraction to slip away recently.

Satyrna ran up and put a hand on his arm. "Malkarai."

He pulled his arm closer to himself and looked at her out of the corner of his eye. "What?"

"Come with us."

"Where?"

She motioned toward a bar near the end of the street with a sign that said, 'Grant's Pub 'n Grill.' It was two stories high, and reasonably large, with a parking lot to the east of it. "Our friend's restaurant."

"Why?"

She frowned slightly. "I don't know. For the social interaction?"

"Yeah, because I just scream social," he said, his voice dripping with sarcasm.

"Oh, come on. It's supper time. Eat with us. Who's it gonna kill?"

He sighed, but didn't respond to that question. "You sure you want to be caught with a dark in a bar of all places?"

She looked at Dyspro, asking for help. He sighed, but obliged, "If you want to talk about safe places in this town, this is prime real estate. The owner's my best friend, and he's a great guy that doesn't stand for bullshit."

"He's a better guy than Dyspro is," Cypha said with a smirk.

Dyspro flipped her off, but didn't argue with her. "And anyway, what's a bar brawl to kick off the week?"

Satyrna smirked at Dyspro and looked at Malkarai. "I can't say that it's going to help you look for your guy… but it's cold out here, I highly doubt he's going to be just walking around."

Malkarai sighed, staring down the street, but not protesting that.

"Come hang out with us a little longer?" Satyrna asked again, tentatively but insistently.

"Yeah, sure," he said, slightly begrudgingly. He eventually turned and followed them.

# 4

In the restaurant, it was dark and busy. The whole dining area was one large room with a big bar on the left-hand side, directly in front of the door. There were occupied stools all around the three sides and gaps at both ends of the bar for employees to exit. On the end nearest the door, there was another door to the kitchen, space for people to stand and sit to wait for a table, and a hostess stand, although it was currently empty and a sign that said, 'Please seat yourself,' was sitting on top of it. The room extended pretty far to the right and was filled with tables. They could see through the windows along two of the walls, but from the outside, they hadn't been able to see in. There was also a hallway leading back farther into the building on the opposite side of the bar from the door, and a few other doors along that same wall that were closed.

Dyspro waved to the bartender, who waved back and then returned to washing a glass. Cypha cast a long, deadly glare at someone sitting at the bar, but no one there acknowledged her, so it was unclear who it was aimed at.

Satyrna led them to an empty table near the right-hand wall of the room. Malkarai was right behind her due to Dyspro and Cypha lingering at the entrance, so when she hesitated to sit, he took the seat closest to the wall. She promptly sat down next to him, shifting it slightly to her left as she pulled it in to the table.

Cypha smirked at Satyrna and pulled out the seat next to her, slumping comfortably in it.

Dyspro tipped his head toward the back wall of the restaurant as he sat between Malkarai and Cypha. "Did you spot the knights over there, Saty?"

She looked where he'd gestured as Malkarai's eyes narrowed. "Oh, no, I did not."

"Thought maybe you had, since you sat way over here."

Cypha glanced behind herself but then relaxed back in her seat again. "They're way too far away to see, don't worry about it," she said, looking at Malkarai.

He sighed softly but didn't say anything. He was looking around the bar, his head tilted forward so his hair was mostly covering his eyes.

"Oh, I get the emo look now," Dyspro said, snickering as he watched Malkarai do this.

Malkarai eyed him.

A waitress with short brown hair came over to their table, holding menus, although she didn't set them down. "I thought it was you guys. How are you doing today, Cypha, Satyrna?" She bluntly ignored Dyspro's presence, going so far as to stand mostly with her back facing him.

A smirk formed on Satyrna's face as she looked at Dyspro, who looked amused. "I'm doing well, Leah."

"Fine," Cypha replied flatly, seeming less entertained by this behavior.

"How's the store?"

"Good. We caught a chronic shoplifter today."

"That's good. Kid or adult?"

"Kid."

"What a punk. Well, I know you guys don't need menus, but does your friend?"

Malkarai shook his head and Leah tucked the menu she'd started to pull out back in the stack. "No, thanks."

"All right, then. What can I get for you all?"

Satyrna eyed Malkarai for a few moments, looking a little pouty, but then looked at Leah.

Cypha and Satyrna ordered, and Leah wrote down their orders on a notepad. She didn't look at Dyspro, but when he held a hand up to his mouth, acting like he was yelling even though he spoke in a normal voice, and told her what he wanted, she marked something on the paper and then looked at Malkarai.

"Whiskey. Middle shelf, but I don't care what kind."

"No food?"

He shook his head.

"Got an I.D.?"

Malkarai hesitated briefly before he dug out his wallet from his coat, opened it underneath the table, and then handed her his driver's license.

Leah looked at it, looked at him, and then put his I.D. on the table in front of him. "'K, I'll be back shortly."

Malkarai put his I.D. away under the table and then put his wallet away as Cypha shook her head at Dyspro.

"What'd I do?" Dyspro asked with a laugh.

"What *did* you do?" she retorted.

"I'm as innocent as the day I was born. I dunno what her problem is."

"Bull shit," Cypha replied, putting stress on each word.

Satyrna smirked. "Dyspro, stop dating and dumping the waitresses here. It makes eating here really awkward."

"Awkward? Maybe from *my* end. You guys get to watch a fun show!"

Malkarai was mostly ignoring them, watching Leah. She'd stopped at one table to check on the patrons, but then gone behind the bar and stuck their order up in the kitchen window. Afterward, she said something to the bartender, and they both looked in his direction and the bartender shrugged, looking minutely annoyed.

"This isn't fun, it's just sad," Cypha said.

Satyrna shook her head and looked at Malkarai, noticing he was watching something across the restaurant intently, looking perturbed. "What's wrong?"

"She figured it out; she told the bartender."

Dyspro sighed, looking at the bar. "That twit. Barry won't care. I mean, he's our friend."

"Isn't she dating a knight now though?" Cypha asked, her eyes narrowed as she looked at Leah.

"Yeah, she was boasting about it like it'd make me jealous, but I just laughed at her and told her to enjoy her downgrade." Dyspro snapped his fingers. "Ah, that's why she's giving me the cold shoulder."

"She gives you the cold shoulder cuz she's a petty bitch," Cypha scoffed.

"This is pointless," Malkarai muttered. "I should leave. This is going to cause problems for me."

"What? No. You're here with us, right?" Satyrna insisted, putting a hand on his upper arm. "Just stay for a bit, okay?"

"I'd rather avoid the trouble."

Satyrna sighed, frowning at him. "Leaving after you've ordered and not paid will probably cause more trouble."

Malkarai immediately went to pull his wallet out again, but Satyrna dropped her hand to his lower arm. "No, no, that's not what I meant. Just drink your drink and leave like a normal person. That'll be way less suspicious, okay?"

Cypha leaned on a hand, propping her chin up with her palm. "Yeah, just lurk with us until we go. It's not that big of a deal, and you can't undo her knowing."

"The longer you're around locals the less antsy people will be," Dyspro added.

He sighed, sounding disgruntled. However, he folded his arms on the table and leaned over them, keeping his head low as he continued to look around the room, not at them.

Cypha gave Satyrna a long look, an eyebrow raised. Satyrna just frowned indignantly at her.

Malkarai noticed the bartender coming to their table before the rest of them. He was pretty tall and stocky and had mid-length dark brown hair that he had drawn back and styled so it wasn't loose. He'd apparently decided to deliver their drinks himself because he came up with a tray full of glasses.

"Hey!" Dyspro greeted cheerfully. "To what do we owe the pleasure? Did Leah complain about me? I swear, I'm behaving."

Barry gave Dyspro an amused look as he put his soda in front of him. "Now, that I don't believe. No, although she's being a chatty old lady about your new friend. I wanted to say hi and it's busy, so this might be the only way we're gonna get to talk tonight if you're not at the bar. They can spare a few minutes for me to deliver things and say hi, especially if they don't want to get weak drinks for being impatient."

"Okay, you being too busy to socialize is normal though," Cypha said before taking a sip of the water he'd put in front of her.

"Unfortunately," Barry agreed, holding the tray at his side after putting Malkarai's drink in front of him. "Anyway, hi, I'm Barry."

Malkarai nodded slightly. "Hi," he said, putting a hand around the glass.

Satyrna eyed Malkarai for a moment before smirking and looking at Barry. "He's not very talkative. This is Malkarai – he caught a thief for me earlier tonight, and I've been trying to give him a little social barrier so Cavington doesn't do what it does best."

"Yeah, I get it. Well, welcome, and I hope no one gives you a hard time while you're here. Well, aside from Saty. Unfortunately, you're not going to avoid that."

"Hey!" Satyrna said with a laugh.

Cypha snorted, amused.

Malkarai eyed Satyrna, a smirk tugging at his mouth. "Yeah, believe me, I picked up on that," he said before taking a sip of his drink.

"Satyrna's got a lot of gall, accusing *me* of being obnoxious," Dyspro scoffed.

"She's cute, people are okay with her being obnoxious," Cypha said.

Dyspro looked offended, but Barry laughed and said, "Yeah, she has a point."

Satyrna snickered and grinned at Dyspro.

After setting his glass down on the table, Dyspro looked up at Barry. "Have you seen Josh lately?"

"A day or two ago, yeah. He stopped in for a late lunch after patrol, so we got to talk a while."

"Christ, really? Good to know the asshole isn't dead."

Barry smirked. "You seem to have a lot of big feelings on that, Dyspro."

"Well, yeah! I don't think I've seen the dickhead in like two *months*!"

"Maybe stop bashing his job."

"I cannot. You all know this. He's fine. The *rest* of them, however…"

Barry shrugged. "He's wanted to be a knight since he was little; he is not going to separate the two."

"Yeah, grow up, Dyspro," Cypha said with a smirk.

Dyspro narrowed his eyes at her. "You bitch about them even more than I do!"

Cypha laughed. "No, I don't – Satyrna does."

Satyrna shrugged.

"Okay, fine. That's true."

Barry rolled his eyes. "Anyway, he works like six days a week, so good luck meeting up with him to try and pretend you've changed your tune."

"That's gross."

"I work seven."

"That's even grosser!" Dyspro protested. "But we can at least find *you*."

"Josh is absolutely avoiding everyone," Barry said. "He's not scheduled for six days; he picks shifts up. Actually, he was complaining that Kalyfa told him to stop taking two shifts in a day."

"Why is he picking so many shifts up?" Cypha asked bluntly.

Barry shrugged. "He wants to work. Like I said, being a knight was his dream – maybe stop bitching about them."

Satyrna sighed, leaning on a fist, her elbow on the table next to her soda. She seemed disgruntled about that request.

"And they are *not* all bad. Yeah, there are some pricks, but there are quite a few of them that are decent guys." Barry glanced over at the table of knights that Dyspro had identified earlier. "Donald, Mark, and Ben are good people."

"Ugh, you and your stupid good points. You're such a buzzkill," Dyspro said.

Barry shook his head with a smile. "I'm sorry that I have to be the adult. Anyway, I'm the adult here too, so I gotta get back up to the bar so Leah can get back to her other tables. Say bye before you leave. Welcome again, Malkarai. Good luck."

Malkarai just nodded to him.

"See ya," Cypha said.

After Barry was gone, Malkarai broke the silence. "You're sure he won't tell anyone?"

"Yes," Dyspro said immediately.

"Barry's a mediator," Cypha said. "That's why he's standing in the middle. If he was gonna tell anyone we're hanging out with a new dark, it'd only be Josh – and Josh would keep it absolutely quiet."

"How do you know that for sure?" Malkarai asked.

"Josh would've been there with us that day, except he's the one of us who always followed the rules," Satyrna said.

Dyspro nodded soberly.

"Yeah," Cypha agreed. "You ran into Cavington's resident dark fan club – and there's four of us, with Barry as an honorary fifth."

Malkarai looked at her.

"Barry's only honorary cuz we didn't meet him until high school," Dyspro added. "So, he didn't know Fayta and Martra."

"I see."

A few moments later, Leah came up to the table with a tray of food. She continued to pretend Dyspro wasn't there, set everyone's food and some utensils down, and then glanced around the table. "Did you guys need anything else?"

Cypha reached forward, grabbing the ketchup from the condiment caddy in the middle of the table. "Nah, I'm good."

Satyrna shook her head.

"All right, enjoy. I'll be back later."

"She's so mature and adult," Dyspro said in a sarcastically admiring tone as he pulled his food across the table from where Leah had put it between Cypha and Satyrna.

Cypha snorted and Satyrna snickered.

Satyrna noticed Malkarai smirk, but he immediately took a drink of his whiskey, covering his mouth.

She pushed her plate of chicken and fries over toward him slightly. "Would you like some?"

He shook his head.

"I don't mind sharing, honest."

"I'm not hungry."

"Okay," she said tentatively, pulling her plate back by her.

"I ate before I caught your thief."

"Oh." Satyrna picked up a piece of chicken and took a bite, giving him an appraising look, realizing he could've used that as a reason to avoid coming in, but didn't.

"What are you trying to find this guy for, Malkarai?" Dyspro asked.

"Work."

"What kind of work?"

"Private investment."

Cypha gave him a confused look. "What does that mean, exactly?"

"I'm here to meet with a client – he's the client."

Satyrna looked at him, curious. "A client that doesn't want to meet with you?"

"Yeah. They're usually… sensitive dealings. Sometimes they're combative."

"That's why you've got a sword, then?" Cypha said.

"Yeah."

"What, are you like a debt collector?"

Malkarai glanced at Dyspro. "Yeah, kind of."

"Huh," Dyspro said, his eyebrows furrowed.

"Who do you work for?" Satyrna asked.

Malkarai hesitated. "I can't say. They prefer to remain anonymous."

"That's kinda suspicious," Dyspro said, his brow still furrowed.

Malkarai sighed over his glass, which he was holding a few centimeters from his chin. "My job has a lot of rules, and one is that I have to maintain secrecy."

"Even from friends?" Satyrna asked innocently.

He snorted quietly. "We would have to have friends to keep it from. Everyone I know is my coworkers."

"What about us?"

"Well, since you're not my coworkers, no, I can't tell you."

Dyspro sighed and shook his head, looking down to work on his meal, apparently giving up on the questioning.

Cypha just chewed on the inside of her lip, staring at Malkarai passively.

Satyrna continued to press though. "Well, what brought you here eleven years ago? Why were you and your friends in town?"

"Pretty much the same reason; work."

"At *ten?*" she said, surprised.

"Yeah."

"Aren't there child labor laws against that?" Cypha said.

"Probably. I didn't have any parents – none of us did – so we'd been training to do this job for a few years at that point. Well, not Arista. She was new. Besides, there was an adult that we were working with too, they just weren't with us at that particular time."

"What was the other guy's name again?" Cypha asked after taking a drink of her water.

"Traphian."

"Are they still working?"

Malkarai shook his head.

"How come?"

His eyes narrowed at some point across the room. "Can't say."

Cypha made a nonplussed face before shaking her head and going back to her burger.

"What do you do for fun?" Satyrna asked.

"Eh… when I'm not working, I teach, train, study, and read."

"Train? What does that entail?"

"Practicing, sparring, weight training, speed training."

"All that for business work?" Dyspro asked, his jaw dropping.

"That's so I'm not scrawny and so no one will mess me up. Genetics are against me in terms of build."

"Sheesh…" he muttered.

Cypha eyed Malkarai. "What do you use besides the sword?"

"Knives and some other things. Pretty much anything can be a weapon."

"What do you prefer?"

"Dual-wielding knives."

Satyrna's brow wrinkled. "What kind of knives?"

"I have fighting knives."

"On you?" Dyspro asked.

Malkarai glanced at him. "Yes."

"Can I see one?"

He hesitated. "Well, they're kind of hidden."

"It's dark in here," Dyspro urged.

Malkarai sighed, but eventually reached down, below the table, and produced a nine-inch knife with a sharp, matte black blade and a serrated top edge. It had a black leather handle with a small hilt. He kept it under the height of the table and handed it to Dyspro.

Dyspro held it at table level as well, so he could examine it. "Nice… but don't you lose reach with these?"

"Yeah, but it doesn't matter. I out-skill almost everyone I go up against."

Dyspro handed it to Cypha under the table. Her brow raised as she looked it over.

Satyrna leaned over to look at it in Cypha's lap. She looked up at Malkarai, her eyebrows lifted. "What's easier to fight with?"

"Sword. Knives are pretty tough, especially since most people prefer to use swords. You can get hit a lot easier when you use knives."

"Then why fight with them?"

"For the speed and the challenge. They're also easier to hide."

Cypha handed the knife to Satyrna, who just passed it right back to Malkarai. "Where do you keep them?"

Malkarai reached under the table again to put it away. "On my lower legs."

"Oh, you have leg sheaths?"

"Yeah. I prefer my primary weapons to always be on my person. Most places will ask you to remove your sword or take off your coat. Also, it's a pain in the ass to fight in a trench coat, so I usually take this off," he said, shrugging his shoulders.

"What's in the coat?"

He took a sip of his drink. "Field medicine and pointy things. You two seem to have fighting experience. What kind?"

Dyspro shrugged, stabbing at some fries with his fork. "Mostly just brawling for me. I'm more the fist-to-jaw sort – I can't say I get into that many fights though."

"I've brawled a lot too, but I find myself in knife fights quite a bit," Cypha said.

"You usually piss people off worse than me," Dyspro put in.

"I piss off the *wrong* people more often than you."

Malkarai smirked, his eyes narrowed. "The wrong people?"

"He's gotten in fights because of stupid shit, like girls hitting on him and him returning it where their boyfriend sees it, or dumb shit that teenagers fight about. I piss off people in gangs. I don't look for fights, but they don't like me because I'm a street kid, but I don't declare loyalty to any gang."

Satyrna shook her head. "She spent half of high school in the assistant principal's office."

Cypha smirked. "That's a *slight* exaggeration."

"What do you mean, 'street kid?'" Malkarai asked.

"I spent most of my time outside, even when I had a home. I didn't have one for a while though. My asshole father dumped me when I was little, and I ran away from the children's home. I had a home as an older kid and teenager, but I spent a lot of time avoiding it with my friends."

"I see. What is your definition of 'gang' here? Because I'm very surprised to hear that multiple organized gangs have a presence in this small of a city…"

"They aren't gangs like what you'd find in major cities, no," Cypha agreed. "Mostly young shits that wanted to fight authority with their own kind of organization. They're not like the groups you'd find elsewhere, and the knights are generally okay with that – because if they keep picking at their seams, then they'll stay small, stupid, unorganized, and lower in threat. They call themselves gangs, so that's what the knights call them too. I think Olivia called them clubs who find it fun to pick fights with each other, and honestly, that's a pretty accurate description."

"Oh." Malkarai motioned between Dyspro and Satyrna with his glass. "And you two…? What are your stories?"

"Our parents are friends, so we've been buddies since we were born. Our older brothers and sisters and us all lined up pretty even, but his parents had two more kids. My parents decided I was enough," Satyrna explained.

"We all agree, you're enough," Dyspro put in.

Satyrna pouted. "You're so mean to me."

Cypha snorted. "He's a lot more of a problem than you, Saty. His parents probably went nuts after taking care of him, so what was two more gonna hurt?"

Dyspro shrugged, not protesting this. "And I am not mean to you, Satyrna. Who else would clean up all the problems you cause?"

She dropped her jaw. "All the problems *I* cause?! What are you talking about? You cause everything and then leave it up to me to talk your way out of it!"

"I'd say it's more 50/50. I've decked plenty of guys for messing with or hitting on you when you didn't appreciate it, and then had to deal with him and his buddies afterward."

"Okay, but that's totally not 50/50. More like 70/30. They don't hit on me that much."

"Yeah, they do," Cypha put in between bites of her burger.

"But I don't ask for all of them to be flattened! Some of them are kinda cute."

Dyspro shook his head with a sigh. "Then date one of them and appease your parents."

"I just said they were cute, not that I'd date them. Bah, last time I dated a guy cuz he was infatuated with me it ended poorly."

"Yeah, we know. You're still bitching about it." Cypha reached forward and grabbed a napkin from the middle of the table to clean her hands. "I've told you – you require somebody you can work on. He was not somebody you could work on. He wanted you to worship him and be a good little girlfriend and just let him do everything for you. I could tell it was doomed to fail from the start."

Satyrna sighed. "Thanks for the warning on that one."

"Who am I to tell you who to date? Next time, just ask my opinion and I'll give it."

"Fine." Satyrna turned to Malkarai, hoping to get the conversation off her dating life. "How about you? Got any exes to bitch about?"

He shook his head slowly, not gracing her with a look or a vocal response. He was looking somewhere in the distance, not exactly at one of the televisions hanging around the bar, but it could've been.

"Really? Nothing?"

"Nothing I am going to talk about."

She sighed. "Well, thanks for saving my butt on that. So, new topic? Weather?"

"It sucks," Cypha said simply before sticking fries in her mouth.

"You just hate winter."

"I hate the cold, yeah."

Dyspro shook his head, cleaning ketchup off of his plate with one of his remaining fries. "Get a thicker coat."

"I like my coat just fine. Coats are expensive."

"So are doctor bills. Get more layers."

"Yeah, I'll work on that. Wanna go shopping, Saty?"

Satyrna smirked. "Sure. Thriftmark again?"

"Of course. Best shit this town's got."

"Agreed," Dyspro said as he rattled his empty glass on the table so the ice clinked. He looked around to see where Leah was. "Think there's any chance she'll give me a refill?"

"Not a chance."

Satyrna looked at Malkarai again, trying to get him involved. "You said before that you teach. What do you teach?"

"Kids."

"What kids? What do you teach them?"

"Kids that are in my profession. I teach weapon play and science."

Cypha cocked an eyebrow. "That's an interesting combo."

He shrugged.

"You teach them science?" Satyrna pursued.

"Yeah."

"Why don't they go to school for that?"

"Their schedules revolve around what we do, so they don't have the time to go to regular school. We teach them. Usually, they learn far more and far faster than what kids do in normal schools."

"How much faster? Do they finish high school and stuff really early?"

"Yeah. They're usually finished with that and moving on to specialized classes by sixteen or seventeen, depending on their maturity. I have two degrees right now. Those come from legit colleges though, not us. I might start another one in a year or so. I've got nothing else to worry about but work."

Dyspro and Satyrna looked impressed.

"Jeez, and I'm finding one program to be a pain…" Satyrna mused.

"You have other things to worry about, like friends and family."

"Oh, yeah… you said you never knew your parents. None of you do?"

He shook his head. "That's one of the nice things about the job. They find kids they feel have potential in orphanages and then raise them in the system. At about twelve, if they feel that they're not fit for the job, they'll release them back – but they'll be educated and fed and clothed. The others continue with their training."

"They were letting you and your friends work at ten though."

"It wasn't really an option to let any of us go. Traphian was good at the job and well… they made sure I was good at mine. Arista was actually shadowing us. They didn't let all the kids go and do the sort of training we were… but it made a difference. We were all farther ahead of the others."

"But the others aren't working anymore?"

Malkarai shook his head. "It's just me now."

Cypha made a face. "Well, that worked well, didn't it?"

Malkarai looked bothered. "They were… abnormal cases. They got what they wanted out of me though, so I'm sure that our employers are happy with the results anyway. Whatever. I can work hard enough for the three of us."

"Don't kill yourself," Satyrna said gently. Regardless, it caused his expression to flicker between being bothered and distaste. "You gotta have some fun. What's the point of working so much if you don't get to have a little bit of recreation? I mean, that's why we work – so that we can be comfortable and afford to relax."

"So down that whiskey and have another," Dyspro said, raising his empty glass to Malkarai.

"I've gotta work tonight," Malkarai responded soberly.

"Is taking one night off gonna hurt?"

"Probably."

Cypha shook her head at him with a sigh. "Oh, lighten up. Being that serious isn't good for anyone."

"You're gonna have ulcers in your twenties," Dyspro said with a shake of his head.

"I'll be fine."

Satyrna eyed him. "If you gotta work, why are you drinking?"

"To warm up. And it makes talking to people easier."

Satyrna raised her brow. "Contrary to popular belief, alcohol doesn't make you warmer, it constricts your blood vessels."

"I know that. But there's heat in here. Also, I wanted the alcohol to calm my anxiety. That much of the stereotype is true; we're not social. It's not fun to talk to people when they just stare at you like you're a freak."

Satyrna frowned. "I'm sorry. Am I giving you anxiety?"

Malkarai nodded slightly and looked at her. "A different kind though, because you three obviously aren't afraid of me. You didn't force me in here though. I chose to come."

"How come?" Cypha asked bluntly. "Seems masochistic."

Dyspro gave her a look, his eyebrows lifted. "Wow, that's such a big word, Cypha. And you even said all the silly-bulbs!"

She looked at him and then reached up and flicked him in the ear.

"Ow!" he exclaimed, rubbing his ear. "Okay, I deserved that, but not nice!"

Malkarai smirked briefly, but stopped, finishing his drink.

Satyrna gave her friends a tired look.

"Anyway," Cypha said, looking back at Malkarai.

"The cover *is* nice. Yeah, I'm not welcome here. I'm not stupid; you don't care that I'm dark, and I know that's rare. So… yeah, I'll be social for now. It helps me, and it appeases her," he motioned to Satyrna.

"Oh, thanks for appeasing me," she mumbled begrudgingly.

"You're welcome. If you feel like you need to pay me back for catching that kid, forget it. Any good person would've done the same thing."

"You're not imposing on us, Malkarai," Satyrna urged. "Yeah, you catching the thief was what started this… but if hanging around us keeps you from getting messed with, by all means, hang around us. I would like to help you out. Any good person would, right?"

He shook his head. "Any smart person wouldn't."

"That's not what we're discussing, is it?"

"No, I suppose it isn't."

"So, it's settled then. If you need some sort of cover, let us know. I work at the store tomorrow during the day, but I'll be working with my dad. He's a big softy; he lets me go whenever I want. Dyspro should be working, and Cypha's gonna be busy job-hunting-" Cypha scoffed quietly, "but I can spare the time. I've got all December to work full-time."

"I can't tell you no, can I?"

"No," Dyspro said. "She won't listen."

Cypha nodded.

Malkarai sighed. "I'll see how tomorrow goes. I'll be fine at night. No one will even see me, but yeah, daylight will probably be a problem."

"You know where to find me."

# 5



About an hour later, the four left the tavern. Dyspro, Cypha, and Satyrna invited Malkarai to stay with them for a while, and to their surprise, he agreed. They had waited until the knights had left before they attempted to vacate.

Outdoors it was dark and breezy. Satyrna shivered when they left the tavern. "I wish I hadn't forgotten my coat."

Malkarai unclasped his cloak and slipped it off his shoulders. He held it out to her, revealing the bag that he had over his shoulder. At first, she just looked at him, but he shook it a little bit to show that he meant for her to take it.

"Take it, I don't bite."

She took it, but kept on looking at him in surprise.

"Put it on, you said you were cold."

"Won't you be?"

"No, I have a coat. Actually, I was roasting…"

She put his cloak over her shoulders and continued walking with the others. After a few moments, she spun twice, causing the cloak to billow up and twirl around her, and then looked back at Malkarai brightly.

He gave her an incredulous look. "What?"

"This thing is so cool. I've never seen a real one before."

Cypha gave her an amused look. "Satyrna, you're a dork."

She laughed. "Oh, shut up! I mean, how many people wear capes around?"

Malkarai sighed and put a hand on his brow. "It's not a cape… It's a traveling cloak."

"Oh."

Cypha laughed.

Malkarai shifted the bag on his shoulder and stuck his hands in the pockets of his trench coat. Every few moments he'd look around, examining buildings, signs, and people, not focusing on his companions' conversation.

After walking for forty-five minutes or so, they went into the woods just southeast of the town. It wasn't long before they came to a small but rather well kept-up stone house. The grass in the area had grown long with weeds and brush, but directly around the house was trimmed short, and there was a well-worn path up to the door. It wasn't much to look at, but it looked sturdy and in good maintenance. Cypha went up to the door, unlocked it, and went in. Dyspro and Satyrna followed, but Malkarai was reluctant and came in last.

The primitive little house had one main room which had a table with three chairs; a gas stove; a small fireplace; a wooden box with food in it, and some dishes stacked on another wooden box, all on the left side of the room. The other side had a long bench with a back and flat cushions that were rather worn, but still looked plushy enough to be comfortable. A chair with a similar cushion sat across from it. Next to the chair was a small table and there were candles placed around the room. A short hallway with four doors extended off the middle of the room. There were several long pieces of wood leaning against the corner in the hallway, and a toolbox on the floor below them. The walls and floor were knotty stained wood, giving it a cabin feel. In all, it was very rough but seemed hospitable enough.

When Malkarai came inside, Cypha was lighting one of the candles with a lighter. She started lighting the others placed around the room with the first candle.

Dyspro flopped down on the wooden chair with the cushion and Satyrna sat down on the bench across from him, still wearing Malkarai's cloak. Cypha finished lighting the candles and put the original candle back in its holder. She looked at Dyspro, who had leaned the chair back so it was resting against the stone wall, on two legs. He had his eyes closed.

"Work too hard today, muscle man?"

"Isn't that always the case?"

"Do us a favor and go to bed so we don't hafta look at your ugly mug. I'll hit you in the head with a frying pan if you wanna go to sleep fast."

He acted like he was thinking about it and then shook his head. "Nah, I'll go the natural way, thank you."

Malkarai looked between the two and asked, "You two aren't together, are you?"

Cypha looked at Malkarai and laughed. "Hell no! We just live together cuz I couldn't afford a place in town, and it's easier to live with someone than alone. Renting around here sucks. He's trying to turn this place into something livable, and he said I could live here while he does."

Dyspro made a face, keeping his eyes shut.

Cypha dropped down by the fireplace and started building a fire. "I like it a hell of a lot better out here than in town. No nosy-ass neighbors."

Malkarai hesitated, then asked, "Are you squatters?"

"Nah, we're not that underhanded."

"This is a hunting cabin that belongs to a friend of my family's," Dyspro said, opening his eyes. "In exchange for keeping it up and making sure no one is doing anything illegal on his land, we get to stay here for free."

"Oh…I didn't see an address or mailbox."

"We have post office boxes."

"I see. What do you do?"

"I'm a general contractor. 'Mr. Fix-it.' I've yet to succeed at fixing Saty though."

Satyrna stuck her tongue out at him.

When Malkarai looked at her, Cypha gave him a cold look and then turned away. "I'm between jobs at the moment."

Satyrna shook her head and changed the subject. "Are you going to leave right after you've finished with your business?"

Malkarai looked at her, "Yeah."

"Will it take a while?"

"It could. Depends."

"On what?"

"On whether or not I want it to, and how well he's holed himself up."

"How long does it usually take?"

"A few days to a week. Shorter if he moves again."

"I see."

Dyspro yawned suddenly and then shook his head. "Sheesh, sorry. I'm goin' to bed. See you in the morning."

"All right. Good night."

"Good night." He went into the short hallway across from the door and into a room, closing the door behind him.

Cypha took off her long coat and hung it off of one of the chairs at the table. Underneath she was dressed much like Dyspro, with pale blue jeans and a white beater tank top. She was very slim – almost bony in places – but obviously strong and tough. There were quite a few scars on her arms.

She asked Satyrna, "Are you staying here or going home?"

"I don't know. I'll probably go home. I didn't even grab a coat, so it's not like I have anything I need for sleeping."

Cypha looked at Malkarai. "Malkarai, where're you staying? At an inn?"

He shook his head.

"The hotel?"

"No."

"Then where're you planning on sleeping?" Satyrna asked.

"Wherever I can find a place to. I'll probably end up outside of town."

Satyrna perked up, looking displeased. "Outside of town? You're going to leave?"

He eyed her. "That's where I parked my car."

"Oh. I didn't realize you drove – but no, that makes sense."

"I tried looking from the car yesterday, but didn't find anything, so I walked the town today. That's why I had a coat *and* cloak on."

"I see. So, you're going to sleep in your car?" Satyrna asked tentatively.

"That was my plan."

Cypha frowned. "Why in the hell would you want to stay there?"

"I'd do a lot to avoid people."

"Okay, granted, but hotels have heat."

"Heat's overrated."

"I disagree with that." Cypha shrugged. "We have an extra bed; Satyrna stays here quite a bit. You can sleep there if you want."

"I'm not staying here."

"You're gonna get hypothermia sleeping outside."

"Satyrna can stay here; I'm leaving. I have a lot of stuff to do before I go to sleep."

"No, I should go home. I have work in the morning anyway," Satyrna said with a yawn.

"You want me to walk you home?" Cypha asked as she stood.

"I'll be fine, Cypha."

Cypha narrowed her eyes and then shoved Malkarai toward Satyrna. He didn't look like he appreciated that. "You, escort her home."

"What?" he said, rather affronted.

"You're going into town, right?"

"Well, yeah–"

"So is she. Walk her home." Cypha tried to grab his bag off his shoulder and he snatched it back roughly. She gave him a look. "Leave your shit here and when you're done working, come back."

"No."

"You want to get messed with, fine, be a dick. We want you to leave this town how you came in."

"I'll walk her home. I'm not coming back here," Malkarai retorted.

Cypha sighed. "Look, we're going out on a limb and trusting you here. Would you just roll with it?"

Satyrna put a hand gently on Malkarai's arm. He looked back at her. "Malkarai… we're only trying to help you out. Is there something in your bag you need for work?"

"No, it's just clothes and shit," he replied begrudgingly.

"Then leave it here," said Satyrna. "They're not gonna go through it. Dyspro's unconscious and she will be in five minutes."

"I'm not worried about that. There's a lock on my bag…"

"Then what's your hang-up?"

"You don't have a room anywhere, just leave the thing here." Cypha shook her head at him in exasperation.

He sighed but begrudgingly slipped his bag off his shoulder and dropped it on the floor next to the bench.

Cypha eyed him for a moment, but then nodded and handed him a key. "All right, lock the door behind you when you come back. I'm going to bed. Too much walking today."

"Go to bed. Good night, Cypha. Come on, Malkarai, I'd better get home."

Satyrna went outside and Malkarai followed, shutting the door and locking it.

He wordlessly walked by her side, looking around as though he was watching for something.

Satyrna eyed him as they walked, twisting her fingers around in the hem of his cloak. "Malkarai?"

"Hmm?"

"Was I annoying you earlier? Asking questions and everything?"

"No."

"You didn't really seem to want to answer anything."

"Because I can't."

"All because of your job?"

"Yeah."

"Well, can you answer questions about yourself?"

"It mostly depends on the question, but I don't particularly like talking about myself."

"I understand. I'm sorry, I'm just curious. It's rare to see a dark around here… People are so prejudiced and mean to them… most darks just avoid the place. You would if you didn't have to work, right?"

"Yeah."

She nodded. After a few more moments of silence, she spoke up. "You know, if you don't like answering questions, you could ask them. Or even talk about the weather or something."

"Don't like awkward silence, huh?"

"No… awkward silences always seem to equal bad things."

He sighed. "All right… uh, how old are you?"

"Twenty."

"Are you going to school?"

"Yeah. I'm on break right now though."

"Already?"

"Yeah, our semesters are kinda weirdly set up."

"Is Dyspro in school? He seems pretty young to be contracting solo."

"No. He's considering going to a technical school, but he doesn't have the money for it right now. He works for a bunch of people, doing odd jobs."

"I see. Cypha's apparently not on the same level as you two."

Satyrna shook her head. "Because she was abandoned when she was little, she prefers to be on her own and resists help. She manages herself remarkably well, but she doesn't have any of the advantages we do… We do what we can to help her out, but she doesn't take charity well."

"Independent people like to stay independent."

"Mm-hmm. But, we got her to go to quite a bit of grade school and through high school, so I'm fine with holding off on any charity. She'll be okay on her own. She's just got a lot of issues she wants to sort out herself."

Malkarai nodded as he took in the street they had just stepped onto.

Satyrna looked at him curiously. "Are you still looking for that guy?"

"Yeah, and no. He's probably not out right now."

"Then why do you keep on looking around like you think you're being followed?"

"Because I might be."

She frowned. "You always walk around like you're being hunted? Why bother going outside?"

"No, I'm not afraid when I'm by myself. I couldn't care less if someone tried to mess with me; I could take care of them before they did any damage. But when I'm with you, I'll look out for you. I don't care much for other people, but you and the others were doing what you could to keep people and the knights from seeing me tonight, you let me stay with you, and you warned me about the locals and about the way my kind's treated around here."

Satyrna's eyebrows lifted in surprise. "Oh, thank you."

He paused. "I like you three."

Satyrna smiled. "Does that mean you'll stick around for a bit?"

"I'll see." He quickly changed the subject. "So, that guy that was asking about a dark…"

"Yeah?"

"Could you describe him to me?"

"Er, well… he had short brown hair, green eyes, a leather jacket… oh! And he had a sword on his back. I think I mentioned that, but I can't remember now. That's how I could tell he wasn't local. Not many people walk around armed in this town. Not unless they're knights or police, and I unfortunately know most of them, at least by sight. He was a nice guy; smiled at me and laughed a few times too. He seemed kinda nervous though. That's who you're looking for, right?"

"Yeah, that sounds like him. Did he say his name?"

"Nope."

"How did he pay?"

"Um, cash, I think. Yeah, cash."

"Do you think he's staying at an inn? Did he mention anything?"

"No, I don't think he said anything. There are a few inns and things downtown by us, otherwise, there's a hotel on the west side."

"Thanks."

"So, since you're collecting a debt, I assume he doesn't want to do business with you?"

"Not especially. He won't let me get close enough to talk to him, so I need to corner him."

They walked in silence for a few moments. Satyrna was using the light from the streetlights to subtly study Malkarai, who was looking around again. They had reached the main part of the town and there weren't many other people outdoors. The streets weren't barren, but the life on it was scattered and few.

They walked down one of the main streets, Malkarai just following Satyrna.

"Where'd you get that scar?" she asked, finally breaking the silence.

He chuckled humorlessly. "Which one?"

"The one on your face. It looks like it was deep."

"I got it when I was younger."

"From what?"

"Switchblade."

"When you were young? How old?"

"Thirteen, I think."

"Who would do that to a thirteen-year-old?"

"Traphian; he was fourteen or fifteen then."

Satyrna looked surprised but concerned. "Why? Wasn't he your friend?"

"Yeah. We were fighting."

"While training?"

"No, it was an argument." His tone suddenly turned bitter. "That we both lost. I just got a half an inch-deep slice in my face to show my half of the loss. Where's your place?"

Satyrna tore her gaze from him. "Oh, it's right over here. Down this street."

She walked down the street and went up to a house built with brick. It had a homey appearance, with electric light burning in a few of the windows. There was a gentle flickering of a TV in one of the upper-floor windows.

"Well, this is it. I guess I'll see you tomorrow."

"Yeah, if you can find me."

"Oh, come on, you're not going to disappear on us, are you? I want to help."

"I might. It depends."

"On what?"

"On whether or not I want to."

She gave him a mildly amused look and went up to the door, tried the doorknob, and then knocked on it.

The door opened and Patricia stood in the doorway with her hand on her hip. "Jeez, about time. Where have you been all night?"

"Out," Satyrna said simply. "I met up with Cypha and Dyspro."

"Did you walk all the way home from their house? It's so late, Saty. That's dangerous."

Satyrna rolled her eyes and motioned over her shoulder. "I didn't walk home alone, *he* walked me."

Patricia looked to where Satyrna had nodded. She curled her lip and slowly looked at Satyrna. "An invisible man walked you home?"

"What?" Satyrna turned around. Malkarai was gone. She looked up and down the street, but there was no sign of him anywhere. "Oh, jeez, he actually succeeded this time."

"Have you been drinking? You know what Mom'll do if she found out you were. You still have six months until it's legal."

"No! There was someone here. He walked with me from Dyspro and Cypha's place."

"Who was it? Was it that guy from the store?"

"Yeah, it was the guy that caught our thief. His name's Malkarai. He spent the evening with us."

Patricia sighed. "I knew you'd go chasing him down... Satyrna, that was so stupid."

"It was *not* that stupid. He's a good guy, Patricia. And he's a guy I've met before."

"Say what?"

"The dark that I met after Fayta and Martra were hanged – that was him."

"Huh," she said, surprised. "What a small world. Come in already, it's cold out here."

Patricia let Satyrna in and closed the door, looking around outside once more before she did so. Satyrna was just about to go up the stairs to her room when Patricia asked her, "Where'd you get that coat... thing?"

She remembered that she still had Malkarai's cloak on and turned around. "Shoot."

"What? Whose is it? Did you steal it?"

"No, it's Malkarai's. And stop treating me like a delinquent, Patricia."

"Hey, I'm not the one running off to hang out with darks all night."

Satyrna shook her head and ignored her, opened the door, and went outside, looking around to see if he was anywhere in the area. She looked down toward the end of the street and could see a middle-aged man under a streetlight. It looked like he was talking to seemingly nothing. She looked harder and could make out the form of a person dressed completely in black next to him.

"He didn't disappear, he just blended into the darkness," she said and started down the street toward them as the other man went back by his door, taking a drag on a cigarette. She caught the person in black a short distance down the street. It was Malkarai.

She tapped him on the shoulder and he looked at her.

"What's wrong?" he asked.

"I still have your cloak. Here." She took the long cloak off and gave it to him.

"Oh, thanks," he said, blushing. "I figured I'd just get it back tomorrow."

Satyrna smiled. "You can still come and say hi tomorrow, but I'll get my own coat."

He flung the cloak over his shoulders and said, "You'd better get inside before you catch something. I'll see you tomorrow, I have things to do."

Malkarai headed off down the street, sticking to the shadows. Satyrna stood, watching him for a few moments before walking back to her house.

# 6



Cypha woke paranoid, feeling like she was being watched. As soon as she opened her eyes, she cried out and punched upward, catching hair but nothing else.

Satyrna shook her head at her. "You're lucky I'm quick, Cypha."

"What the hell are you doing with your face in my face?!"

Satyrna stepped lightly over to the door. "Making sure you get up. Come on."

Cypha sat up scowling. "You are such a pain in the ass."

"You like it. I'm better than an alarm clock."

"More obnoxious than one too," Cypha muttered as she climbed out of bed and went to look at her phone, which was plugged into a solar-powered charging device on the window sill.

"Get dressed," said Satyrna. "I'll be waiting out here." She left and shut Cypha's door behind her. "Want some breakfast?"

"No. I'll eat later."

"You sure? I brought donuts."

"Well… if that's the case… Got one of those crème-filled ones?"

"Yeah. You know, it's not really crème though. It's more like pudding."

"Whatever the hell it is, it's good. I call dibs on one."

"'Kay."

"Oh, would you two shut the hell up?" Dyspro groaned from behind his closed door.

Satyrna grinned, standing by the open door to the extra room. "Morning, sunshine. You have work to do today too."

"Yeah, but not for like four hours!"

"You're wasting the day away. We only have so many hours of light in the winter. Get your ass up, lazybones."

Cypha opened her door and stumbled into the main room, scowling and rubbing her eyes. She had on light blue jeans and a washed-out red v-neck shirt. "Seriously, Saty, it's seven-thirty."

"Employers are impressed by early risers."

"I don't want to give anyone false hopes. I'm not a morning person."

"You're not an anything person. Have a donut." Satyrna stepped out to the main room but called back to Dyspro. "The donuts leave with me, Dyspro!"

"Good. I hope you have a happy life together. I'm going back to sleep."

Satyrna shook her head at him and opened up the storage container with the donuts in it. She took one and motioned toward one with white frosting. "Pretty sure that's got crème-pudding in it."

Cypha took it and stuck it in her mouth before getting a cup and filling it with drinking water from a beaten-up cooler in the corner near the stove. "Do ah need t' showah?"

"Your mouth could be cleaned out, yeah."

Cypha gave her a half-hearted dirty look and took the donut out of her mouth. "Seriously. Do I look grungy?"

"A little. Just wash your face. Your hair should be fine for today. Comb it."

"K."

"You can stop by my house and shower, you know," Satyrna offered.

Cypha sat down at the table with her donut and water and started eating her breakfast. "Yeah, and I can also stop by your house and borrow some household chemicals to make an explosive; doesn't mean I will."

Satyrna sighed and sat down. "Hey, I can keep trying, can't I? You're gonna get hypothermia from that pump."

"They're not hip to me at the Y yet. I'll just go there again." Cypha glanced over at Satyrna and furrowed her brow after taking her in. "What the hell do you have makeup on for?"

She shrugged. "Felt like it."

"You don't need it."

"I didn't put that much on. Eyeliner and mascara. Whoop-de-doo. Wanna borrow some? I've got it in my purse."

"No thanks. That shit bothers my eyes." Cypha took a few more bites out of the donut before looking at Satyrna in disbelief, realization crossing her features. "I know what's up! Is he here?"

"Who?"

"Malkarai."

"No. His bag's still over there though." Satyrna motioned toward the other end of the room.

"You've got the hots for him."

Satyrna made a face. "What the hell makes you think that?"

"Well, you had me and Dyspro help you reel him in last night."

"So what? He never hit on me. He caught a thief."

"No, he did his damnedest to avoid all of us. Seriously, you do – you're crushing on the anti-social little bastard."

"Cypha, don't be stupid. He's here on some business thing for a few days and then he'll be gone again."

"I said it already – you need a guy you have to work on, not someone who worships you. That dude was fighting just being around people. You see him as a challenge."

"Yeah, the aversion was intriguing, I'll admit that. I want to know about him. Also, I'm interested in the fact that he's dark. Someone in this town needs to stand up for them."

Cypha nodded slowly. "Sure, sugarcoat it all you want."

Satyrna sighed. "Why do you think it's always about whether I'm attracted to the guys or not? What's wrong with just being friendly?"

"Nothing, but seriously, Satyrna... yeah, you're stubborn, but I haven't seen you try that hard in years."

"I've never run into a dark my age before, Cypha... Well, not since we met Malkarai the first time anyway. I mean, I know you're still pissed about what they did to Fayta and Martra."

"Of course, I am. What the hell can we do about that now though?"

"Well, we can't really do anything about them – but we can help out any other darks that show up here. The intolerance here makes me sick."

"Yeah, me too." Cypha sighed, her donut gone, water cup hovering in front of her mouth. She smirked. "You can't tell me that you didn't find him attractive though."

"I never said that," Satyrna said with a wry smile. "He's very cute. Could use a shave, but..."

"Personally, the armory trips my trigger. Wonder how good he is with them. If he trains as much as he says he does, he's gotta be pretty good."

Satyrna shook her head as she stood up. "The sharp things *would* appeal to you."

"A guy can betray you. A knife won't. A knife does exactly what it's supposed to every time you stick it somewhere."

Satyrna laughed.

"They appeal to you too, whether you want to admit it or not. You've always thought people who can stand up for themselves were attractive."

"Well, yeah..."

"But then you get upset when they actually do it," Cypha said with a laugh.

"I just don't like conflict for the sake of conflict. There's so much of it."

"Try and explain that to your guy radar."

Satyrna sighed in exasperation. She tossed Cypha her coat. "Let's get going. I have work and you have employers to hound."

"Yeah, can't wait," Cypha sighed and put her coat on before going into her room to comb her hair. "You and me are hitting the thrift store tonight. I need new gloves and a hat before the sky craps on us."

"Sure. Stop by the store when you're tired of badgering people."

"Will do."

**1:30 p.m.**

Malkarai opened his eyes to bright sunlight as it finally reached his face through an opening in the tree cover above his car. He groaned softly and rubbed his face with the back of his hand, pushing the ski cap on his head up, onto his forehead.

"Shit, it's cold…" he mumbled as he sat up, rubbing his shoulders under his cloak.

He looked at his watch and sighed before looking around, blinking in the light. He yawned and put his seat upright before rubbing his chin and scowling.

*I think it's about time I shaved… Looking like a hobo isn't going to help me here if I've gotta look for the bastard during daylight…*

He pushed the cloak onto the passenger seat, unlocked and opened the car door, and then climbed out and stood up straight, stretching his arms above his head. He took a small bottle out of the inside of his coat, checked the label, and then poured some into his mouth. He rinsed it around for a few minutes before spitting it out. Then he took off his hat, ran his fingers through his hair while looking at himself in the backseat car window to make sure it wasn't doing anything weird, put the hat and mouthwash away, and reached into the car to pull his cloak out.

After putting the cloak over his shoulders, closing the car door, locking it, and putting his keys away, he headed into town to find a bathroom and mirror.

**6:00 p.m.**

Satyrna looked up as the bell on the door rang, and waved to Cypha as she headed over to the counter.

"Any luck?"

"Eh, there were three that didn't outright tell me no. I guess I'll see if they call me. Hopefully one of them does before the stupid phone company turns my phone off."

Satyrna smiled a little. "Pretty self-defeating cycle, huh?"

Cypha leaned against the counter. "Yeah, no kidding. Anyway, how long do you have left?"

"Dad said I could go whenever I wanted. He and Mom are in the back, eating supper."

"All right. Wait for them to finish and then head out?"

"Sure."

Cypha picked up a pen and started taking it apart. "So, did your pet project come around?"

"No. Didn't really expect him to, though."

"Yeah, he was pretty anti-social."

"To say the least." Satyrna sighed, staring through the front windows. "Hope he isn't having any problems."

"Yeah, well, he hasn't been in town long enough for the knights to know about him."

"He has been if Leah squealed," Satyrna muttered.

"Oh. I forgot about her."

"And it really doesn't take anything for a gang to mess with a lone dark." Satyrna shook her head with a sigh. "I still wish he'd been more receptive to help."

"He seems pretty tough. I don't think he'll have any problems taking care of himself."

"Yeah, but that's just another reason I wish he'd been friendlier."

Cypha looked up at her. "Huh? How do you figure?"

"It's rare to see a dark that is perfectly aware of all the shit they get, and yet seems to be coming out on top despite it all. He's lasted this long, has a job, apparently has enough money – his clothes seemed fairly nice – clean and hole-less, at least – and he seemed clean. I think we'd have noticed if he was high or anything, right?"

"Yeah, he didn't strike me as a user. He wasn't jumpy or twitchy." Cypha shook her head, looking at the pen again. "I'm pretty sure he was noticing a lot more things than we were last night. He never stopped looking around. A little suspicious, yes, but not crooked and not dirty."

"He's aware. I hope nothing happens to him while he's here."

"Oh, hey, Cypha," Satyrna's father said as he came up to the front.

"Hey, Mr. Hennessin."

"How are you?"

"Cold. Is it okay if I steal Satyrna?"

"Yeah, go ahead. Got something planned?"

Satyrna scooped up her purse and coat. "Yeah, shopping."

He made a face. "Shopping? That's a response I expect out of your sister, not you, Saty."

Satyrna pointed at Cypha. "She's cold. We're getting cheap layers."

He laughed. "All right. I'll see you at home later."

"Bye!" Satyrna called into the back as she pulled her coat on, "Bye, Mom!"

The two heard her mother respond as they were heading out the door, "Don't stay out too late again, Satyrna!"

Cypha looked at Satyrna as they headed down the street. "Seriously, nine was too late for her?"

Satyrna shrugged. "One day they'll figure out I'm older than twelve."

"It'll help when your sister stops bitching about you."

"Yeah, probably. I feel like I have two mothers sometimes. Want one?"

"No, thanks."

Malkarai leaned against a wall just inside of an alley, dug his phone out of his pocket, and turned it on. He waited, then tapped a hotkey icon and put it up to his ear.

After about half a minute his call was answered.

"Hello, Stika here."

"It's Malkarai."

"Oh, there you are. Are you keeping your phone off?"

"Yeah, I haven't had power for a bit, and I don't want to run the car out of gas if I'm not going anywhere."

"Does it also have to do with Carlisle calling you yesterday?"

"More than a little, yes."

Stika sighed. "How's the search going?"

"Slowly. I think I may have found him, but I'm not positive. He's been holed up all day. He might be until tomorrow."

"You know he's where you are?"

"Yeah, he never left Cavington unless it was by foot. I checked the train station again, the two car rental and taxi places. The bus station hasn't had any arrivals since before he got here, and won't have anything leaving for the next three days. I have an eyewitness who saw he was here, so it's just a matter of waiting it out."

"All right. Hey, did you look up that place before you got there?"

"Yeah."

"I did too. Be careful, Malk. Their law enforcement isn't real cooperative with us."

"I know. They're vigilantes."

"Well, not quite, but yeah, they're not gonna work with you. Don't do anything rash."

"I'll try not to."

"They know you're there. I had to let them know."

He sighed. "All right. Thanks for the heads up."

"Are you going to try and get your phone charged today?"

"Maybe. I've been sleeping in my car."

Stika sighed. "Don't get yourself sick. It's cold out."

"I'll be fine. I only sleep when the sun's out anyway."

"The sun doesn't help much in December."

"When it snows I'll worry about finding a bed. I don't feel like dealing with people here more than I have to."

"All right."

Malkarai looked up as he heard voices he recognized and saw Satyrna and Cypha. Satyrna saw him at the same time. "Shit. Hey, I'll talk to you later."

"Did something happen?"

"No. Someone saw me. It's fine. Bye."

He ended the call and dropped his phone into his pocket as Satyrna stepped over by him, hesitantly.

"Hey, sorry… you didn't have to hang up."

"I was done."

"Talking to a friend?" she ventured.

"No, my boss. Do you want something?"

Satyrna sighed. "You always assume that people only approach people for a reason?"

"Why else would someone walk up to me?"

"To say hi. Lighten up."

Malkarai sighed and stuck his hands in his pockets.

"How's work going?"

"Slowly. He's still avoiding me."

"Sorry. Anything we can do to help?"

He shook his head slowly. "There's no point for me to get you involved in what I'm doing."

"He's not avoiding us though."

"No," he said firmly. "You shouldn't be hanging around me either, you know."

"Everyone here already knows we support darks, so to hell with them."

Cypha coughed as she leaned against the corner of the opposite building. Satyrna looked back at her.

"I didn't forget, chill."

Cypha shrugged. "I was just coughing."

Satyrna looked back at him. "Your stuff's still at their place. Why didn't you stay there?"

"I didn't go to sleep until dawn. I slept in my car."

Satyrna gave him a judging look. "Dawn?"

"I worked all night. It's far easier to work at night when you're a dark."

"Well, sure, I guess… but what a screwed-up sleep schedule…"

He shrugged. "I don't need a guardian. I can sleep whenever the hell I want."

Satyrna shook her head. "I think you need to sleep more. You're cranky."

Malkarai sighed and turned to go.

Satyrna exchanged an exasperated look with Cypha, who just smirked. Satyrna reached out and grabbed Malkarai by the arm. "Oh, stop it. You really need to relax."

"No, I really need to work. Leave me alone."

"You said yourself he's avoiding you."

"Yeah, but if he takes off, I'll lose him again. I need to keep alert."

"Do you think he'll try and run at the time you're most active?"

Malkarai scowled.

"Have you eaten yet today?"

"No."

"Well, that explains a lot!"

Cypha snickered.

Malkarai cast an unamused glare over his shoulder at Satyrna.

She just grinned. "You're very grouchy right now."

"Trying to find someone who keeps doing everything he can to avoid you can get really aggravating."

"Yeah, I know," she said pointedly.

Malkarai shook his head. "The last thing you should be doing is trying to find me."

"I wasn't; honest. Cypha and I were headed to the thrift store. I'll admit, I was hoping you'd stop by the store, but since you were asleep most of the day, I'd imagine that was silly of me."

"Look, you hanging around me isn't a good idea."

"Keeping you from getting screwed up is. No one's gonna do anything to us, okay?"

He muttered something under his breath.

"What?"

“Nothing.”

“I won’t make you be social, but would you join us for supper?” She looked over at Cypha. “That deli on Third sound okay to you?”

She shrugged. “Whatever.”

Satyrna looked back at Malkarai. “Meet us there in like an hour and a half, okay? Third and Main.”

“I’ll see.”

“I’m pretty sure that was the most positive thing you’ve said to me this whole conversation, so I’ll take that.”

He grunted and headed down the alley. “See ya.”

Satyrna shook her head and turned toward Cypha. “Crimony,” she said, exasperated.

Cypha smirked. “Not giving up on him yet, huh?”

“You were harder. Anyway, let’s go get you clothes.”

# 7



When Satyrna and Cypha arrived at the deli, Dyspro was already there, waiting. Satyrna had called him a half hour earlier to inform him of their dinner plans. He looked at his phone as they walked up.

"Sheesh. Typical girls; you're late."

"Oh, bite me, Tanen."

Satyrna smirked. "Last minute discovery. She's got plenty of layers now."

"Good, now she'll just be a bitch instead of a cold bitch."

Cypha slugged him in the shoulder and he flinched and rubbed it.

"Have you seen Malkarai?"

"No; should I have?"

Satyrna shrugged. "I invited him to join us."

Dyspro shrugged and opened the door. "Not surprised. Anyway, are we getting this to go or are we eating here?"

"I'd prefer to go."

Satyrna spun around, her face delighted. Cypha and Dyspro looked over their shoulders at the man who'd appeared near the corner of the building.

"You came!"

"I got stared down trying to get a burger somewhere else," Malkarai muttered, eyeing the handful of people inside the restaurant balefully.

Cypha shook her head and stepped inside. "Toldja so. We can get it to go."

Malkarai followed them in, but Dyspro waited until he'd passed to come in and let go of the door.

Dyspro stepped up by Cypha as she ordered, and Satyrna looked over to Malkarai. "So, are we still a convenience for you?"

"I can't say you're not convenience, no."

"You coulda just sucked it up and eaten at the other place though."

"Yeah, and eaten whatever they'd spit on my food…? No, thank you."

"Get any farther with your guy in the leather jacket?"

He wasn't looking at her, examining the menu on the wall. "Not really."

Satyrna chewed on her lip, finally turning away to glance at the menu. "Is this a normal thing?"

"Them hiding? When they're aware we're here, yes."

"Shouldn't you be used to it then?"

"Most of the time they don't know I'm here. And I've been dealing with this for nearly two weeks, so it's getting irritating."

Satyrna stepped up and ordered her meal. Instead of watching Malkarai though, as he ordered, she watched the cashier exchange a distasteful glance with the person making the sandwiches. It angered her.

Malkarai looked rather surprised when she suddenly grabbed his hand with both of hers. "So, where should we go to eat?"

He gave her a bewildered look at first but noticed the defiance in her face and went with it. "Er, I don't know. You pick."

"Watch them," she whispered before looking over at Dyspro, who was sipping his drink as he watched them. "What do you think?"

"I dunno. Home?"

Satyrna made a face. "That's too far out."

He shrugged.

"Your place is close," Cypha suggested as she put a lid on her own drink.

"Works for me." Satyrna picked up her sandwich with one hand, still holding onto Malkarai's hand.

He watched the sandwich maker carefully as he finished and wrapped up his order, then he slipped his sandwich into a pocket and picked up a cup. He tried to dislodge his hand, but Satyrna held it tight. He gave her a look and then pulled it away. She let it go this time.

Satyrna glowered at the people behind the counter as he filled his cup and then headed straight for the door.

Dyspro elbowed Satyrna as they followed Malkarai outside. "Relax, Saty."

"It pisses me off."

"I know, but there's no reason to ignite it."

When Cypha came outside and let the door shut, Malkarai faced them. "Thank you. I'm going to go back to work. Have a nice night."

Satyrna narrowed her eyes. "Why are you so anti-people?"

He shrugged.

"You're really gonna leave us, huh?" she said with a sigh.

"Yup. See ya later."

Cypha looked over at Satyrna as Malkarai crossed the street. "Wow, you're just gonna let him go?"

"Yeah, I have to admit I had you pegged for more stubborn than that."

Satyrna shook her head and just started walking toward her house.

Cypha and Dyspro exchanged looks. Cypha shrugged as she followed Satyrna.

After they'd walked a few blocks, Dyspro spoke up. "So, what's up your butt?"

"Nothing."

"Why'd you give up on him so suddenly?"

She shrugged. "He's got this all figured out. Why should I try and hide him?"

"That's not your motivation."

"Yeah, it is."

"She's totally into him," Cypha said, her straw between her teeth.

"Oh, yeah."

Satyrna sighed and shook her head. "You guys need to drop that."

"Whatever, it's the truth."

"I haven't chased a guy since I dumped the last one, and I'm not starting now."

"It's been five months, Saty. That's pretty long for you."

"He's a passerby, guys! He'll be gone in a few days! Just cuz I'm trying to help him out doesn't mean I want him. I'm more realistic than that. Besides, you keep telling me to pay attention to red flags… why are you giving me shit for trying to listen this time?"

Cypha snorted. "I dunno, I think there are fewer red flags with this one than the last one."

Satyrna sighed, giving her an exasperated look.

"You're still trying awfully hard with this guy though," Dyspro said.

"I tried harder to win over Cypha."

Cypha shrugged. "That's true. She didn't give up on me."

Dyspro stretched his arms out to his sides. "Well, all right. Stop pouting then."

"I don't like being shot down," Satyrna said simply.

"We know."

December 3, 2036
1:50 a.m.

A young dark woman crept along the side of a building, following the dark man in front of her. He either didn't know she was there or he just wasn't acknowledging her presence – but he also seemed rather concerned by the gang of people that were behind her, following him. She was nervous and on edge, not only because she didn't know why these people were following him, but also because she didn't want them to notice her too.

She had been following Malkarai since he had left Marion, but that was two weeks ago. She didn't understand what he was doing exactly, for this was very different from the other missions she had followed him on; it had taken a much longer time, involved way more locations – and he'd associated himself with people.

The two were headed toward the east end, where Dyspro and Cypha's home was. He was still in the heart of the town though, and dark buildings surrounded them. This particular street was worn concrete, almost smooth from constant traffic, and the streetlights lining it glared in the darkness, reflecting dully off of the oily road. The streets were deserted. It was almost two in the morning, so nearly all the lights were out in the windows of the homes and buildings. Malkarai wasn't looking around like before. She knew that he could sense the small gang behind him. She assumed he'd first known they were watching and tailing him at least two hours ago, but figured he didn't want them to follow him while he was working. The group had grown to seven now, so he couldn't pretend not to notice them any longer.

Malkarai moved down a narrow alley and then stopped and turned, facing the knights boldly. He didn't draw a weapon, but she could see that he had a hand resting on the bump at his hip where the hilt of his sword sat.

As the people began to move to take up his challenge, the dark girl pulled herself swiftly onto a fire escape to see the skirmish better and be out of the way.

Malkarai didn't do anything as they approached. The alley was so narrow, however, that most were forced to wait at the end of the alley, either just inside the mouth or on the sidewalk by the street.

One of them held a long double-edged sword that glinted in the streetlight as he approached Malkarai. He was tall and lean, but under shoulder-length, shaggy blonde hair he had a strong jaw and intense, gray-blue eyes. Malkarai had done his research, so he knew exactly who this was: the head knight, Kalyfa Desfete.

His tone was harsh and piercing, almost taunting. "Hey, stranger, we'd like to know just what you're doing wandering all over our town."

"I wasn't wandering."

"Oh, then what were you doing?"

"Trying to get you off my tail."

"Well, it didn't work; it just pissed us off. You shouldn't do that."

Malkarai spread his arms, his voice dripping with sarcasm. "I'm sorry, and here I thought we were all having a wonderful time. Would you like me to try that over for *another* two hours?"

"Shut up, smart ass. What were you doing with Satyrna Hennessin last night?"

"Who?"

"Satyrna Hennessin. The naïve little brunette you were with all last night."

"I don't know what you're talking about."

The knight looked at him sharply. "Don't mess with me, Faerstathe."

Malkarai sneered slightly, not expecting this attack to be focused on that girl. "How do you know I was with her?"

"I have my connections. I want you to stay away from her, dark. She's too good – too innocent – to be hanging with the likes of you."

"Desfete, why the hell would you care?"

The knights whispered to themselves, surprised at the stranger's familiar use of the head knight's last name.

Kalyfa, however, was not surprised. He turned and hissed in Malkarai's face, leaning over slightly to be at Malkarai's height. "She's my girl, asshole. You keep the hell away from her."

If Malkarai was surprised or confused, he didn't show it. "Interesting. She and her friends dislike the knights as a whole; are you the cause for that?"

"You don't get what's going on around here, and they have old prejudices. We have to do a lot of shit to keep this town safe."

"So, you're the judge and the jury, are you?"

"Says the pot to the tea kettle, dark. I know what you are."

Malkarai's brow tightened. "Then you know you shouldn't mess with me."

"Your government doesn't rule here, Faerstathe."

"Well, since you're smart enough to realize that, you should've deduced that there's a threatening target here. Thus, I follow. You and the government have always agreed on that."

"Yes, within boundaries. But, you're in our jurisdiction now. You're not a big shot here. You and your kind are not to associate with civilians here."

Malkarai's lip curled up. "I performed a simple law enforcing act, and she followed me. The girl wouldn't go away. If you really knew her, you'd know she's got some sort of weird fascination with my darkness. It's pretty obvious."

Kalyfa narrowed his eyes. "I don't need you telling me what she's like, dirtbag."

Three people rushed Malkarai from behind Kalyfa. Ready for this, he met them with his sword unsheathed. He blocked the fastest one, swiftly disarmed him, and then worked on the other two.

While he was engaged, Kalyfa struck him on the side. Malkarai noticed this at the last moment and rolled with it, but, even though the thick layers of cloth had helped cushion the blow, skin had definitely been cut. This threw him off-balance, but he caught himself on the wall and kicked away one of the knights before getting his sword back up in front of him to fight.

Malkarai blocked as Kalyfa took the displaced knights' positions and tried again to cut him with his long blade. Malkarai focused on him and flung the sword from Kalyfa's hands before he jumped to the middle of the alley, away from the wall.

It was all very chaotic and poorly orchestrated. It was for this reason that Malkarai hated gang fights. There was no organization, no reason. He scowled as he felt warm blood drip down his side, stopping where his belt held his jeans up.

He worked hard to keep a space open so that only two knights at the most could get at him in the narrow alley. Despite the advantage of skill and location, he still had trouble keeping them away. What they lacked in experience, they made up for in numbers and fervor. However, he managed to avoid getting hit deeply again.

Kalyfa took his time rearming himself, but after he had retrieved his sword, he stood, watching Malkarai battling the other knights.

"Hiding behind your cronies, are you, Kalyfa? How very brave of you," Malkarai hissed, irritated that the deciding person in the fight was just watching.

When he didn't respond, Malkarai decided to spur things along. Instead of disarming or shoving one of the knights fighting him away, he let his blade taste flesh, cutting a deep wound in one's arm and gouging the other shallowly in the stomach.

Then he threw the less injured one into his fellows, letting the other fall to the concrete. The knights shouted, unnerved.

Malkarai stood up straight, holding his sword out to the side, at the ready, but plainly showing the knights' blood on the sharp blade, daring any others to challenge him.

Kalyfa came forward, eyes narrowed.

Malkarai glared at him and gripped his sword handle.

At first, the challenger just stood there with his sword hanging at his side, at the ready but not brandished. "That's how you want to play, huh?"

"I don't want to play with children, period," Malkarai sneered as he slipped a hand into his coat, resting it over his cut.

The knight lunged at Malkarai. He swung his blade around and the sword flew from Malkarai's hand when he blocked it. The knights cheered their leader as they saw the sword fly through the air, hit a wall, and then clatter against the concrete.

"Yeah, Desfete!"

"Get him!"

"Make him pay for messing with us!"

Kalyfa knew that he hadn't truly won that. Malkarai had let go of the sword, and he wasn't sure why.

Malkarai didn't leave him much time to be confused though, because as the sword flew from his grip, the hand that seemed to be holding his injured side emerged with a knife in it, and then both his hands were around the knight's neck, the one bearing the blade in front of his throat. His body was close to the knight's, completely inside of his striking range. "Drop the sword," he hissed.

The alley went silent as Kalyfa's sword clattered to the cement.

The knights paused for a beat and then started to move to help their leader.

Malkarai's black eyes flicked toward them. "If any of you move, I'll kill him."

"Stop, all of you!" one of the knights near the street yelled.

The knights nearest them stopped and watched impatiently, gripping the handles of their weapons nervously, but not making any moves.

Kalyfa gritted his teeth, realizing that forcing Malkarai to dispose of his sword only gave him a chance to get closer to him. He thought he knew what he was dealing with, but reality certainly was not what he had expected.

"Sheath your blades," Malkarai ordered.

They didn't.

Clearly uncomfortable, Kalyfa choked out, "Do it!"

The others' expressions grew indignant, but they slipped their weapons into their sheaths.

Malkarai forced Kalyfa to move, keeping the knife to his throat until he found his sword. Then he addressed the other knights.

Malkarai's voice was a low and venomous hiss. "If any of you follow me, I'll fight harder and people will die. I'm not playing around anymore; I will kill. You're not dealing with some punk here. Let me do my job, and no other knights will get hurt. Do you understand?"

The knights' hatred-filled faces bobbed slightly in agreement – except for the vocal one. He hung to the back of the others, his arms crossed. Malkarai shoved Kalyfa toward them. The closest few caught him and when they looked back at Malkarai, he and his sword had disappeared.

"Should we find him?"

"Just tell us, we'll go!"

"No, let him go," Kalyfa said darkly, rubbing his throat as he bent over to retrieve his sword. "We don't need more injuries. Help Jason and Kel up; we'll take them to the ER."

"This shit wouldn't happen if you didn't try and teach every potentially threatening stranger a lesson," the vocal knight near the street muttered loud enough for Kalyfa to easily hear.

"I appreciate that you have a head on your shoulders, Brendan, but you cross the line far too much." Kalyfa turned and gave him a withering look. "Watch your mouth or you'll regret it."

The woman slipped silently off of the fire escape and darted across the alley to the safety of the shadows along that wall, and then followed them out of the alley, after the male dark.

Close to an hour later, Malkarai dropped heavily into a sheltered gully on the eastern end of town. He was very close to Dyspro and Cypha's, but he had no intention of going there.

He got comfortable in the matted, dead long grass and weeds and then unbuttoned his trench coat and dug inside of it for a few moments. After finding what he was looking for, he pulled three small bottles out of his coat.

He pulled the right side of his coat aside and lifted the sliced T-shirt underneath. The cut was fairly shallow, but it hurt. He opened up one of the bottles and poured the clear liquid over the wound. It fizzed and bubbled up. He blew on it to get rid of the foam and then closed up the plastic bottle and opened one of the two small ones. He dropped only a few drops on the wound with this bottle and then closed it. The second was a powder that he applied a little more liberally but still didn't use very much of.

After doing this, he pulled his shirt back down, put the jacket back over and buttoned it up, pulled his hat out of his pocket and put it on, and then pulled the cloak close around him, laying his head back.

With a sigh, Malkarai stared up at the bright stars overhead.

*You're lucky for tonight. Tomorrow will be different. Well, if I make it to tomorrow.*

He frowned.

*No... I'll make it. This isn't bad enough to do any damage. Besides, if I got hung up because of an infection I'm pretty sure Stika would just kill me anyway. Too bad it wouldn't be literally.*

Malkarai shut his eyes, turning off the starlight. *I hate it when it's nice out like this. I miss you even more.*

# 8



Cypha woke to someone knocking on the door. She sighed angrily and climbed out of bed, wrapping her blanket around her. As she went out to the main room, she banged her fist on Dyspro's door. The sunlight was bright when she opened the door, causing her to blink and cover her eyes with a hand.

"I thought we gave you a key," she muttered bitterly.

Satyrna smirked. "You did, I just wanted to be a pain in the ass and get someone up. Did I wake you up?"

She sighed. "Yeah, you pain in the ass. The door was unlocked," she added in irritation.

Satyrna stepped inside and shut the door. She noticed Malkarai's bag was still on the floor next to the bench, untouched, and made a pensive face. "Dyspro up yet?"

"Nah, I think he's still asleep. He was zonked when I went to bed last night."

"He's been working a ton lately."

"I know. It's kinda odd for December. Hopefully, the payoff's good. Oh well, he has to get up and work again sometime today. Might as well get our heads bitten off now and get it over with. You can have the honors this time."

"Oh, thank you."

"You're welcome." Cypha lay down on the bench and curled up in her blanket.

Satyrna shook her head at her as she took off her coat, and then walked to Dyspro's door and knocked on it. He didn't answer, so she slowly opened it and looked in. He was still asleep. She sighed. "Oh great."

She walked in and shook him until he opened his eyes. He squinted at her and said, "Hello? Damn, it's just you."

"Dork. Get up."

He sat up and stretched. "Why can't it ever be someone new? It's always one of you two."

"If it was someone new you would *not* be this relaxed about it. Come on."

He threw the covers off and looked around the room. "You see my shirt?"

"No. I don't feel like being helpful this morning, so I'll be out here."

"Thanks for your assistance."

"You're welcome."

Satyrna went out to the main room and saw that Cypha was beginning to doze off. She rolled her eyes and went to see what they had for food, hoping to be able to scrape something together for breakfast.

She started when she heard the doorknob turn on the still-unlocked front door. Not knowing who it could be, she looked around and grabbed a pan to defend herself.

Dyspro came into the room, pulling his shirt over his head. "Shit, it's cold out here. Cypha, would it kill ya to start a fire?"

"Shut up," she mumbled.

"Dyspro!"

He looked at Satyrna as his shirt slipped over his torso. She pointed to the door.

Dyspro moved quickly, grabbing the door and blocking entry. Doing so, the person collided with him.

"Ugh!" Malkarai said quietly, startled. He dropped several pieces of chopped wood on the floor.

"Oh, shit. Sorry, Malkarai. Are you all right?"

Malkarai grimaced and rubbed his chest where the wood had been shoved into it. "Yeah, I'm fine," he groaned. "What the hell was that for?"

Dyspro moved and picked up the dropped pieces of wood. "Sorry, I thought someone was breaking into our shack."

Satyrna set the pan down on the table. "Malkarai! When did you get here?"

He stepped inside, still rubbing his chest. "I came back here about half an hour or so ago to change clothes, and I thought it was cold, so I got some wood because you're out. I didn't think I'd get beaten for it; you guys gave me a key."

"Sorry," Dyspro said again. "My reflexes are faster than my brain this morning."

"Did you sleep here last night?" Satyrna asked.

"No."

"Why not? Did you sleep in your car again?" she asked scoldingly.

"No, I slept outside for a change of scenery," he retorted. "Do you sleep here too? What the hell are you doing here so early?"

Satyrna smirked. "I'm their obnoxious alarm clock."

"Obnoxious and unnecessary alarm clock."

Cypha pulled the blanket over her head. "Close the door and shut up, I'm trying to sleep!"

Dyspro walked over and pulled her off the bench, onto the floor. "If I gotta get up, so do you."

She kicked him and pulled her blanket back over her. "Leave me alone, you got more sleep than me."

"Yeah, fifteen minutes more."

"I don't care; I want those fifteen minutes back." She curled up again. "I'm not getting out until somebody starts a fire."

Satyrna rolled her eyes and shut the door. Dyspro put some of the wood in the fireplace and searched for matches. Malkarai set down the rest of the wood and the axe on the hearth and found the matches before Dyspro did. He crouched down and worked on lighting the wood.

Satyrna sat down at the table and watched him, waiting for the warmth. She noticed something conspicuous on his neck as he leaned forward.

"Malkarai, there's something on your neck."

He put his hand on it and then looked at his hand. "Shit, I thought I got all of it."

"What is it? I don't think that was there last night, I would have noticed something that obvious."

"It wasn't. Well, I hope it wasn't. That would say a lot for my hygiene."

"What is it?"

Malkarai rubbed the dried substance between his fingers and then reached up to get the rest off his neck. "Blood. How the hell did I get it back there?"

Satyrna's eyes widened. "Blood! What happened?"

He held a match under the wood, dropping it when the flame got too close to his fingers. It went out after a few seconds. Dyspro handed him a can of lighter fluid. "I met up with some of those knights you told me about."

Her brow raised. "You did? What did they do to you?"

Malkarai squirted some of the lighter fluid on the wood and then lit another match. The small flame caused a rather good-sized fire to start up. "Not much, I did more to them."

Dyspro sat down at the table. "What'd you do to them?"

"Taught them a lesson. Nothing life-threatening, but definitely not something they could ignore. I only hurt two of them."

"How many were there?"

He stood up as the flames spread to some of the other logs in the fireplace. "About seven."

"Damn it," said Satyrna with a scowl. "What did they do to you?"

"I'm fine, Satyrna, don't worry."

"You've got blood on you, so you apparently got hurt, so it *is* something to worry about. You can't just ignore a blade wound, especially not from a sword," Satyrna insisted. "Where are you hurt?"

Malkarai sighed and pulled his cloak back. A long patch of coat along his side was darker than the rest and looked rather damp still.

Satyrna started cussing worriedly. "Damn it, Malkarai, that's bad. Damn it! I hate the knights! I hope it isn't serious. Let me take a look at it."

"Satyrna, I'm fine."

"Malkarai, it won't do any good to leave it be. Take off your cloak and coat and let me see it."

He sighed and took off his cloak. His coat, when he got it off, clattered as it hit the floor because of all the items he had stowed in it.

"What the hell is in that?" Dyspro asked, his eyebrows raised.

"A lot of shit."

Dyspro gave him a look, but he didn't elaborate.

Satyrna took one look at the wound through the slash in his shirt and told him to sit down. He obeyed reluctantly. She asked Dyspro where they had their rags stashed.

"In a cardboard box in the closet."

"Are they clean?"

"Yeah, if Cypha cleaned them when she was supposed to," he said intentionally loudly.

They heard a muffled response from Cypha's blanket. "They're clean."

Satyrna went to the hallway closet, pulled them out, and brought them over by Malkarai. Then she took a pot from the pile of dishes. "I'm going to get some water. Take your shirt off, or I won't be able to clean it."

"You said you were just going to look at it."

"You want it to get worse? That thing's really bad. Doesn't it hurt?"

"Don't know."

"Why not?"

"My side's numb."

She sighed and slammed the door behind her as she went to get some water.

Malkarai raised his eyebrows to the closed door. "Did I mention that I made it numb?"

Dyspro chuckled. "Satyrna's amusing when she's mad."

Malkarai sighed and leaned back in the chair, arms crossed. "Oh yeah, very entertaining."

"She mostly only swears when she's worried or really angry. That's a good thing though; it means she cares about you."

Malkarai gave him a look. "I'm not interested."

Dyspro stretched his arms above his head. "Well, if anything, she's definitely got a keen and kind interest in darks. Humor her. You won't find many people like her."

"Yeah, I know."

When Satyrna came back she put the pot on the rack over the fire and then went to Malkarai's right side.

"Take off your shirt."

He hesitated and pulled it up partially.

Satyrna looked at his face when he only went far enough to uncover the wound. "All the way?"

"Why?"

"Because I don't want it to fall in your wound while I'm cleaning and treating it."

He sighed, avoiding her eyes as he pulled the shirt up and off, revealing a well-defined muscular torso littered with dozens of small pale scars and a mostly scabbed slice along his right side.

Satyrna blinked, distracted by all of the scars. "Huh… I guess you're used to this," she said quietly.

"I told you it wasn't a problem."

"Well, regardless, I'm going to clean it." She went over to the pot, moved it to the table, and then took out a clean cloth and dipped it in the water. Then she knelt at his side and started cleaning the blood away from his wound.

"Satyrna, you don't have to take care of it."

"If you don't get it taken care of, it'll get infected."

"I can take care of it myself."

She ignored his protests and continued cleaning his wound.

He sighed and then contented himself with closely watching her work.

"What did they hit you with? This is really big."

"Broadsword. Most of them just had standard swords, but one had a ridiculously large one."

"Did they follow you?"

"No, I easily got away."

"Where did you sleep?"

"Some ditch."

"Why didn't you come back here? We told you you're welcome to."

He didn't respond to that.

"Are you sure you're all right?"

"Yeah, I'm fine." He was quiet for a few moments before saying, "Satyrna, the one who had the broadsword said that you were his girlfriend."

She looked up, her expression furious. "That *asshole*."

Malkarai regarded her contemplatively. "I take it he was blowing smoke?"

"Yes," she said firmly. "I broke up with him *six months ago*. I am *not* his girlfriend."

Dyspro pushed his chair out a few feet and propped his feet up on the corner of the table. "Kalyfa's persistent, huh?"

"He didn't want to break up, and so now he's telling people half a freaking year later that we're still together? Ugh!"

Dyspro shrugged. "You know, you really should return his calls once, Saty. He's not gonna stop until you talk with him."

She scowled. "I do *not* owe him any more of an explanation than I've already given him."

"What happened?" Malkarai asked.

"We went out for a while this past year, but he started talking about the future and marriage and crap, and I said 'nuh-uh,' and dumped him. His vision of the future and marriage do *not* align with mine, not to mention the timeline. I mean, I'm twenty! I'm not done with nursing school! I'm not even thinking about marriage – not to him anyway. He can't get it through his thick head that I didn't like him that much. He may have been head over heels, but I was just entertaining it so people would get off my back and stop telling me I wouldn't know until I gave him a try. Well, I gave him a try, and I don't want him."

Malkarai felt a little better about her messing around with his wound knowing that she was going to nursing school, but he was still watching her like a hawk. However, he was more than a little irritated that he'd gotten himself wrapped up in this tiff between Desfete and his ex. "He was protecting you."

"Protecting me from what? You? Just cuz you're a dark doesn't mean that you're gonna disembowel me and murder my family and friends."

Satyrna rinsed the blood-covered rag, turning the water in the pot a watery red. She wrung it out and put it on Malkarai's cut. While she sat there, applying pressure, she spotted an odd-shaped scar on his right arm in the shape of a dragon, its coils twisted in an intricate pattern with two bat-like wings on its back.

"Whoa, where'd you get this thing?"

Malkarai looked at his arm and quickly covered it with his hand.

Satyrna looked up at his face. "What is it?"

"Nothing."

"That isn't nothing. It looks cool. How'd you get it like that?"

He hesitated. "It's a brand. You take a red-hot metal shape, like they do with cows, and press it on yourself for a few moments so that it stays indented in your skin. Doesn't feel too nice."

Her eyes widened. "Then why'd you do it?"

"It's hard to explain why."

"Can I see it again?"

"No."

"Oh, come on. It's just a dragon."

Malkarai sighed and took his hand off the scar. Satyrna stared at it for a few moments.

"That's badass, but *ow*," Dyspro said as he leaned forward to see it.

"It was cool when we first thought of it. It stayed cool until we were separated. Now it's just a bad reminder. It's like it's just there to remind me how it didn't work out – just like everything else in my life." He put his hand over the scar again and looked at the fire.

"What do you mean? Does someone else have the same one? Who was the other person?"

Malkarai shook his head. "I don't want to talk about it."

"Was it a girl?"

His lip curled. "No."

"When did you get in the fight?" Dyspro asked as he got up and started to dig through their food.

"About two. They had been following me since midnight."

Satyrna grumbled as she ripped a long, wide strip from a rag. She was about to put it over his wound but stopped and grabbed the first rag to soak up blood from it. "Shit, it's bleeding again."

Cypha sat down by the fire, still curled up in her blanket, and yawned. "Uh-oh, Satyrna's swearing again. What's wrong?" She obviously hadn't been listening to the conversation.

"Malkarai got sliced by some of the knights. Where have you been?" Dyspro said and opened up the jar of peanut butter so he could make a sandwich.

"Sleeping. You all right?" Cypha took the blanket off her head.

"Yeah."

"No, he isn't."

Malkarai sighed and leaned back in his chair further. Cypha raised her eyebrows when she saw him and gave his toned body a careful once-over. "Whoa."

He looked at her. "What?"

"Why the hell do you cover yourself up with all that black? Most guys'd kill to look like you. You should be showing that bod off, not hiding it."

He blushed and looked away evasively. "I told you once, camouflage. I work at night."

Satyrna sat back, wiping the blood on her hands on one of the rags. As she came to a realization her expression became one of fear. "Oh no! At night they always have knights on patrol, and Patricia's boyfriend, Brendan, was saying how he was going on it last night, and how he wasn't looking forward to it. He was one of the ones there."

Malkarai stood up and went over to his bag.

"Where are you going?" Satyrna asked Malkarai, watching him.

"Relax, I'm not going anywhere," he said, turning the combination on the small lock holding the zipper shut on his bag. "I heard Brendan. Kalyfa said something to him at some point and called him by name. He was trying to stop Kalyfa from messing with me."

"Yeah, Brendan doesn't like the fact that they stalk any new people in town," Cypha said before yawning and covering her mouth up.

"Who did you hurt, Malkarai?" said Dyspro.

He sat back down and shrugged. "How the hell would I know?"

"What did they look like?"

He pulled out a new T-shirt and a small tube of something. "Like knights. Well, when I was done with them, they were bloody knights. I don't know; it was dark and I didn't care much what they looked like, I was trying to keep myself from being stabbed. Brendan wasn't one of the ones that I hurt though, I'm sure of that. He stood back and didn't engage."

Dyspro leaned forward. "What about Josh? You know who he is?"

Malkarai shook his head and took the cap off the tube. "I can't tell you if he was one of the ones or not, sorry."

"Shit."

"What's that?" Satyrna asked curiously, watching Malkarai.

"Super glue."

"For what?"

He contorted a little, leaning so he could reach his side with the tube. "Ghetto stitches."

Satyrna's jaw dropped. "Don't! Are you crazy?"

"No, I'm not crazy." He glanced at her, but when she didn't move toward him, he proceeded to hold the wound together and close it with dabs of super glue.

"That's so unsanitary!"

"Not really. It's more unsanitary to leave it open."

"You could get real stitches, you know," she insisted.

"It's not that serious. Super glue's fine. It'll keep it shut at the very least."

Satyrna shook her head in disbelief.

Dyspro smirked and exchanged a look with Cypha. "That's your favorite method of fixing, isn't it?"

She shrugged. "It's the cheapest."

"So yeah."

"Yeah," she agreed.

Satyrna sighed, obviously not okay with this method. "Can I put a bandage on it at least?"

"Yeah, after it's dried." He closed up the cap and tossed it in his bag.

"Why the hell did they attack you?" Dyspro asked. "Did you do something to upset them?"

"I've done a whole lot of nothing since I got here. Apparently, they just didn't like the fact that I was wandering around at night. Do you guys have a curfew here?"

"No…"

"Do other places?" Cypha asked, brow furrowed.

"Some cities do, yes. Usually, it's just for kids though. Trying to keep kids safe since they can't keep the streets themselves safe."

"They just attacked you cuz you were walking around? That's so stupid!" Satyrna exclaimed.

Malkarai shrugged. "I'm used to dealing with stupid."

"Does this kind of crap happen to you often?"

"Idiotic authority figures trying to teach me unnecessary lessons? No. Usually, they're cooperative."

"Do you deal with them a lot?"

"Eh, occasionally. I usually try and avoid them."

"Why?"

"Because people in uniforms tend to be egotistical. And I'm anti-social."

Satyrna gave him a bemused look.

Malkarai leaned over and touched the wound slightly to see if the super glue had dried.

"Dry?"

"Yeah. Go ahead."

Satyrna leaned forward again and ran the long fabric strip around his torso, tying it off on the side opposite the cut.

"Still, that's pretty strange, for them to go on a manhunt like that…" Dyspro said.

"One guy saw me and just kept following me. He called friends. I got sick of it when I realized they'd grown to seven."

Satyrna's shoulders slumped and she looked at her lap with a disappointed sigh.

"What?" Malkarai asked, eyeing her.

"It's just… it didn't help. I probably just made it worse, because Kalyfa's such a misguidedly overprotective dick. All I wanted to do was help – and now you did what you should, and stood up for yourself, and they'll just go and use it as further justification for their stupid prejudice, and- and…"

"Don't blame yourself for what happened last night."

"It's my fault though."

"It's Desfete's fault," Malkarai immediately retorted. "We don't have history, but he is in charge of those Neanderthals. He could've easily just approached me himself and had a civil chat, but he decided to hold a witch hunt instead."

"He probably did the witch hunt instead of the civil chat *because* of me…"

Malkarai shrugged. "I let you drag me along. You didn't force me to do anything against my will the other night."

Dyspro snorted. "Could've fooled us," he said with a smirk.

"Yeah, I was a grouchy, resistant little shit, but if I wanted to go, I would've just left. Regardless, you are not at fault."

Satyrna sighed. "No matter what, this is gonna be a pain in the ass when I get home. I'm sure Brendan will tell Patricia about it, and then she'll probably tell Mom and Dad, and they'll tell me to stay at home until this blows over. The knights will blame everything on you; that's what they always do. They never see the dark's side of it, they always blame them, and that's that. They never look into it."

Dyspro frowned. "I agree they're a bunch of dickbags, Satyrna, but they don't usually flat-out lie like that. Kalyfa doesn't work like that."

"They'll do something like that. He absolutely knows how to spin a story. He's a politician, you can't forget that," she retorted fiercely.

Malkarai shook his head and pulled his shirt on. "It's better if they don't look into my side of things. Don't tell them to. Look, I'm not going to stick around. Thank you, all of you, for helping me out, but it's pretty obvious that I shouldn't be hanging around you." He stood up and grabbed his coat.

Satyrna frowned. "Because Kalyfa acted like an overprotective dick?"

He put his coat on, checking something inside of it. "No, because I shouldn't be hanging around the people who live here, period."

She stood up. "Malkarai, that's the kind of sentiment we want to change around here!"

He looked at her, his stare cold. "You don't understand what's going on, Satyrna. Yeah, because I'm a dark I'm going to piss people off. But, I went against the rules by associating with you three. Now I've gone and injured two knights and pissed off the head knight. I need to finish what I was sent here to do and get the hell out of town." He shifted the coat on his shoulders and then picked up his cloak and grabbed his bag from the floor.

"What rules?" Satyrna asked quietly.

"The rules of my profession." He reached into his jeans pocket and pulled out the key Cypha gave him. He tossed it on the table. Then he put the bag over his shoulder, put the cloak on, and opened the door. "Thanks for everything, and goodbye."

There was a sour look on Satyrna's face as the door shut behind him. "Dick," she muttered.

Cypha gave her a look. "Satyrna, why are you upset? He's trying to keep himself and us out of trouble."

"I figured he'd have enough spine to try and change things. No, he's just as weak as everyone wants him to be."

Dyspro shook his head. "I'd call that guy a few things, but spineless is not one of them."

She gave him a questioning look, still perturbed.

He pointed at where Malkarai had been sitting. "The guy fought off a gang of knights last night – Kalyfa included – and emerged the better! Yeah, he had a slice from it, but you'll notice he didn't flinch once the entire time you were messing around with it. I mean, he had like fifty scars on him. He's probably used to crap like that. He didn't once whine about how darks are treated. It's not like he was ignorant of it – he saw Fayta and Martra die. He's a fighter… but he knows where to pick his fights and where to just let it go."

Satyrna frowned. "I don't like letting it go."

"Yeah, me neither," Cypha put in. "But you can't just force one of them to take the abuse for you."

"I know…"

Dyspro scratched his chin. "What are you gonna do about your family?"

Satyrna stared at the fire for a few moments. "I think I'm gonna hang out here for a little while. It just sounds less stressful to not be in town."

"School's all over, right?"

"Yeah. Finals were over three days ago."

"Then go back home and get your things. Midday has got to be the best time for you to sneak out. You can stay here until it blows over or gets sorted out. It's time you moved out anyway. Leave them a note or call them after you're back here."

She sighed and picked up her coat. "Will one of you come with me?"

Dyspro stood. "I will. Let me get a coat."

Satyrna and Dyspro walked through town slowly. Satyrna kept looking around, hoping she'd spot Malkarai, even though she knew there was no making him come back. Dyspro watched her, his hands in the pockets of his coat.

"Let him go, Satyrna."

She frowned. "He's the first dark I've run into in a long time, Dyspro–"

"It's more than that, I know. But you should drop it. You gave it a try, let him go."

She sighed. "I don't want what happened to Fayta and Martra to ever happen again."

"He's not like them. He can protect himself. He has. He was a tiny kid, but look at him now. I wouldn't pick a fight with him."

"That's why he could do a lot of good for other darks that aren't tough like him."

Dyspro shook his head.

"You don't want it to continue, do you?"

"Of course not, but I'm realistic. We're all solid supporters of the underdog, but we're a minority here. I don't want to look for more trouble. You drag me into enough of it."

Satyrna smiled and grabbed hold of his hand with both of hers. "Oh, come on, you like it."

Dyspro smiled a little. "No, I'm used to it. That doesn't mean I like it." Dyspro stared forward, his carefree expression going a little darker. He nodded in that direction. "Satyrna, look."

She looked up and frowned in both annoyance and confusion, letting go of Dyspro's hand.

Kalyfa sauntered up to them, two knights flanking him. "Good morning. Thanks for sparing us the walk."

"What do you want, Kalyfa?" Satyrna hissed at him.

He gave Satyrna a sober look. "Satyrna, stop it."

"I'll stop it when you get a clue! Stop telling people I'm your girlfriend!"

He scowled. "This isn't about your inability to focus on things – this is about your safety." He looked at Dyspro meaningfully. "All of yours."

Dyspro frowned. "What are you talking about?"

"The outsider you're harboring."

Satyrna bristled. "Kalyfa, leave him alone! You jerks attacked him when he was trying to do his job!"

Kalyfa laughed once; a loud, humorless laugh. He threw his arms out. "Exactly! Satyrna, you're so naïve. If you knew just what he was trying to do, you wouldn't be so judgmental."

"You're just being dicks because he's a dark."

Kalyfa cocked his head to the side. "Well, it did make him a more obvious target. Darks don't come here without a reason, but that's not why I sought him out. He knows he's not supposed to associate with people here, but he did it anyway. That's why we approached him last night."

"So, it was your fault."

"He was rather argumentative when we approached him. In the end, he injured two of my knights. That's inexcusable, no matter what he is."

"He only stood his ground. If you didn't go and target every minority that you think poses a threat upon your insecure little seat of power, you'd see that some of them are actually good!"

Kalyfa sighed. "Yeah, some of them are – but not him."

Satyrna sneered at him. Dyspro grabbed her arm firmly, telling her to stay put.

"Well, I can see *you're* not going to be cooperative." He looked at Dyspro. "Dyspro Tanen, I have a proposition for you."

"What?"

"Bring me that dark. I know you're perfectly capable of dealing with one man. It'll be even easier if he's a friend of yours. I can make it worth your while."

"I'd sooner die than help the knights put another dark in their grave," Dyspro hissed.

Kalyfa sighed. "Well, that's dramatic, but if that's how you feel about it." He motioned to a few knights who had come up behind them without them knowing it.

They stepped forward and grabbed Dyspro by the arms, causing him to let go of Satyrna.

"No, Dyspro!" Satyrna cried.

Kalyfa grabbed Satyrna as the others wrestled the struggling Dyspro away from her. She immediately reacted by facing him more directly and kneeing upward.

He reacted quickly, turning and getting the bulk of the force in his thigh, but he cringed and held onto her tighter, although farther away. "Ah, fuck…" he hissed. "Satyrna, stop it. This is for your own good."

"Assault is for our own good?!"

"No, I'm taking you two into protective custody until he's gone. We'll pick up Vatale later. Please try and cooperate. We really don't want to have to force you."

Satyrna scowled, fighting against Kalyfa's grip. "You are such an ignorant asshole, Kalyfa… Let me go!"

He sighed. "I'm not the ignorant one, Satyrna. Stop fighting us."

"Get your hands off me," Dyspro hissed.

"You don't have an option, Tanen, stop fighting."

The knights holding Dyspro started taking him north and Kalyfa followed, another knight flanking Satyrna.

# 9



It had been nearly four hours since Satyrna and Dyspro had left. Cypha, having finished cleaning the whole place and eaten lunch, banged her fist down on the table impatiently.

"Damn it, where are they?"

She looked at the clock on her phone with a scowl on her face.

*This isn't good. Something's happened. Even if they'd run into people on the way, they'd be back by now. It isn't like she's packing up her entire house; just some clothes and a few other things. It should've taken ten minutes.*

She chewed on her lip for a few moments, debating a course of action.

"Ah hell… I'm just gonna find out where the hell they are."

She snatched up the key from the table, stood, threw on her coat, and then grabbed her pocketknife off the stove and stuffed it in a pocket inside the coat. She locked the door behind her before making her way quickly through the woods and into town.

She made it all the way through town and to Satyrna's house without spotting them. She had noticed that Satyrna's parents were at their store, but decided to keep clear of them for now. There was no point worrying them needlessly.

At the Hennessin residence, Cypha knocked. No one answered so she twisted the doorknob.

"Locked. Hmm."

She looked around, and, figuring the street was fairly clear, she took a hidden key from a crack in the brick wall as inconspicuously as possible. She unlocked the door and shoved the key back in its hiding place.

The house was a clean, homey place and was well-furnished. The furniture was cushioned and there was carpet on the floors where it wasn't hardwood. There were stairs directly in front of her and rooms to either side. Cypha started up the stairs.

She made it to the second floor and looked around, but couldn't see anything. The door to Patricia's room was ajar, but the lights were out. She could see the TV in Satyrna's parents' room was off, the bathroom was empty, and Satyrna's bedroom and the other room's doors were closed.

Slowly, because she felt a little like she was breaking and entering, she made her way down the hall and opened Satyrna's door.

The brightly decorated room was empty. Her bed was unmade, and there were a few pairs of clothing lying on the chair in the corner. One of the drawers on her dresser was slightly open, and things were lying scattered about the room. It wasn't messy, but Satyrna obviously hadn't been there to pack things up.

Cypha walked over to the bed and turned around, giving the room a good look, mostly because she wasn't sure where to go from there.

After a few minutes, she left, shut the door, and made her way downstairs.

At the bottom of the stairs, she looked at the room to her left, which was the living room. Beyond the dining room was the kitchen. She headed for that. When she reached it, she sighed. Someone was sitting at the table, and they nearly dropped their coffee on themselves when they heard her.

Patricia quickly looked and saw her. "Oh my God, you scared me! Don't you even bother to knock anymore?"

"I did. You didn't answer. I'm looking for Satyrna and Dyspro. Have they been here?"

She set her mug down. "No."

"Shit."

"Did you call her?"

"Yeah. She never answers her phone even if she has it on her, and Dyspro isn't answering his."

Patricia shrugged. "Don't know why our parents even bothered getting her one… I haven't seen her since about eight this morning. She said she was going to your place."

"Yeah, she was there. Then she went into town with Dyspro, and I haven't seen them since."

"I wish she'd stop running off like that. What do you think they're doing?"

"Don't know. I'll find them. If they come here, tell them I'm looking for them."

Patricia nodded.

"All right, I'll catch you later." Cypha turned to go.

"Wait," Patricia said.

She looked around.

"You were with Satyrna the other night, right?"

"Yeah, we've hung out the past few nights."

"Was she drinking?"

Cypha sighed. "Patricia, you know she doesn't. She doesn't lie to you."

"That's what I want to believe, but I'm still afraid. The people that you, she, and Dyspro are around most aren't the best kind of people. I mean, she had some random dark walk her home… She may be twenty, but she's still my little sister."

"Yeah, I know. Don't worry; they wouldn't mess with any of us. Even if they did, we can handle ourselves. And as for that dark, I think he's an okay guy. I wouldn't have let him take her home if I had thought otherwise. Dyspro and I look out for her, you know that. I'll see you later."

Patricia watched as she left and then she sat back down and took a long drink of her coffee. "Oh, leave the door unlocked," she called. "I'm waiting for Brendan."

"Hot date?"

She laughed. "Yeah, right. A hot date at two on a Wednesday."

Cypha smirked.

As soon as the door closed behind her, Cypha swore out loud. *Not good.*

As she made her way down the street and toward the center of town, Cypha thought hard about what to do.

"They've been taken… that's all I can figure. But by who?"

She frowned.

*Well, that's the easy part. It was one of two people. The knights or the dark. So, which do I search for?*

That was answered for her. As she came around a corner, she spotted Malkarai across the street, watching something intently. It was hard to tell exactly what he was looking at from a distance.

She glanced upward to see what he was looking at, but couldn't see anything in the windows of the building behind her. After making sure the street was clear, she crossed and went right up to him.

"Malkarai."

He jumped slightly and looked at her.

"Where are they?"

"What?" He looked confused.

"Do you have them?"

"What? Look, I gave you your key back, and I never took anything else."

She frowned. "No, I'm not talking about objects."

Now he looked upset. "Then what are you missing that I could've taken?"

"Satyrna and Dyspro."

"What?"

"I can't find them, and neither are answering their phones, which leads me to conclude that either you or the knights snatched them. And, if you didn't, well, then, I guess that leaves only one other option, doesn't it?"

Malkarai sighed in aggravation. "Shit. How long have they been gone?"

"Well, they left just after you did. They went to get some of Satyrna's things. She was gonna wait for things to blow over and stay at our place for a little bit. I haven't seen or heard from them since, and Satyrna's sister says she hasn't seen her either."

He looked up at the building he'd been staring at, but then tore his gaze away in reluctance.

"So, since I'm sure you're the reason they were picked up, you're going to come and help me get them back."

"Where from?"

"The knights use this old castle, the Garevn castle. I don't know all that they do in there, but there's a lot of space for keeping people."

Malkarai gave her a bewildered look. "A castle in southern Minnesota?"

She sighed. "Yes. You know, gonna have knights, gotta have a castle? Anyway, it was imported like a century ago. It's not real fancy. I'd compare it more to a prison than a castle, but that's what it was when they imported all the rock. All the fancy crap's been sold off or put away under lock and key by old man Garevn. It's just a stronghold for the pissant good old hometown-boy knights now."

"Wow… they never told me about that," he muttered, mildly impressed, but mostly bitter.

"Anyway, I'd wager they have them there. Kalyfa would want to keep Satyrna close to him."

"Not at the police station?" Malkarai asked, wagging a thumb over his shoulder.

"I doubt it. The cops and the knights don't really work together without good reason – and I'm sure the knights see you as a personal problem."

He sighed, his jaw tight as he considered this. "Wouldn't it be wiser to not immediately attempt a jailbreak?"

"Probably – but either way, if we're going to find a knight to ask about this, the castle would be the best place to look. I think Kalyfa has an office in city hall, but I have no idea where it is. Knights don't wear uniforms either."

He sighed. "All right. Lead on."

"This way."

Malkarai glanced back at the building once, but then followed her until she turned down a different street, and then went north for a while until they went through what appeared to be a dead-end alley. In a dark corner, there was a narrow gap between buildings and this led to a path leading away from the town. The path went into the woods, where the stark, leafless trees reached over the dead-plant-ridden path. Boot marks could be seen among the dead foliage, and several times they could see a stick broken on a tree, or a bush squashed on one side. They were fresh, they could tell, because they would have gone back to their original shape if left for a while.

Cypha licked her lips grimly. "Looks like a struggle."

"Mm-hmm," he replied, examining other things along the path. He pointed out to Cypha how firm the path was and how deep the prints went. They saw at least one set that looked more like dragging than steps.

Farther on the path became harder to see, and they had to take care to not wander off into the forest. Cypha was sure of the way, though, so they kept on going.

Malkarai spotted something up ahead, on the side of the path, but he didn't say anything at first, thinking that it could just be a log or brush – or a trap. Either way, it was wiser to take it slow. When they grew closer Cypha saw it too. She ran to it and came to a skid-stop at its side, stooped down.

"Satyrna! Malkarai, come here, it's Satyrna!"

Malkarai ran to her and crouched down at Satyrna's side. The young woman was curled up next to a tree, hugging her arms against herself, and she was missing her coat. Her eyes were shut, and she hadn't reacted to Cypha's voice. She was fairly visible from the direction they'd approached from, but blocked from view from the castle. There was a cut on her forehead, the drip of blood already dried to her skin. He put his fingers on her neck to check her pulse. "She's alive, she's just unconscious."

He took his cloak off and picked her up in his arms, gently wrapping her limp form in the long cloak and then holding her close to him to warm her. "You see Dyspro?"

Cypha stood and walked around, searching the area thoroughly, including going as close to the castle as she dared, but she couldn't find anything. When she came back to where Malkarai stood, examining the area, she shook her head, a worried expression on her face. "Not a trace."

"Then we'd better get Satyrna someplace warm. They probably have him in the castle, and there isn't much we can do for him at the moment if he's in there; they outnumber us. She probably escaped – we should get out of the area quickly."

Cypha followed, still looking around, as Malkarai walked back quickly. With Cypha leading, they took a shorter way back to the house, cutting through the woods instead of going through town. Malkarai could feel that Satyrna was warming up with the heat of his body and the warmth of the thick, insulating cloak around her. However, he was surprised when she stirred. She slowly opened her eyes and looked up at him.

"Malkarai?" she said softly, confused.

"Yeah," he replied, looking down at her.

"Where are we?"

"Cypha and I found you outside the castle. We're heading back to Dyspro and Cypha's."

She opened her eyes wide. "Did you find Dyspro?"

"No, was he near you?"

She slumped back in his arms, laying her head and hand upon his chest. "I dunno where he is."

Cypha gave Malkarai a worried look and continued walking silently.

"What happened to you?"

"I…" she trailed off, frowning as she stared at his chest.

"Satyrna?" he prompted after a few moments.

She shut her eyes, her head resting more heavily against him. "Sleepy… talk later…"

Cypha looked from Satyrna to Malkarai, still looking very worried. "What's wrong with her?"

"If I'd had to guess, I'd think she'd been drugged," he said quietly, watching Satyrna for a few moments before focusing on his footing.

"What the fuck? They *drugged* her?!" Cypha whispered fiercely.

"Either that or she hit her head. She has a cut on it. Maybe it's both."

"Should we take her to the hospital instead?"

"We're almost to your place, let's start there and we can take her to the hospital if she doesn't improve."

Cypha sighed heavily, increasing her pace.

It was only about twenty minutes before they reached the house. Satyrna had dozed the rest of the trek and didn't say much more that they could comprehend. Cypha opened the door and Malkarai set Satyrna next to the fire. She curled up in Malkarai's cloak and sat there with her face practically hidden by the cloth.

Cypha crouched down near her. "Saty, are you okay?"

Satyrna nodded slightly, her face still buried.

"What happened to Dyspro?"

Satyrna shook her head, but didn't respond otherwise.

"Does your head feel okay?"

She shrugged. "Foggy."

"Do you want me to get something cold to put on it?"

Satyrna shook her head slightly.

"Er, all right… We can take you to the hospital."

"I'm fine," she insisted, blearily.

"You don't sound fine."

"I think this jackass messed me up somehow," she mumbled.

"Did you fall or hurt your head? You have a cut."

Satyrna touched her forehead gently. "No, that's from a branch."

"Oh. Okay. Do you wanna just rest then?"

She nodded slightly and pulled the cloak up higher, covering her eyes.

Cypha stood up and glanced at Malkarai. She motioned to Satyrna. "Is that okay? Just sleeping that off?"

He nodded. "If she doesn't have a head wound, she should be okay."

Cypha sighed in relief, picked up a log, and threw it on the dying fire before going over to their pantry box and moving things around so she could find something to make.

Malkarai shifted, eyeing the door longingly. Feeling bad about leaving while Dyspro was missing though, he eventually dropped his bag on the floor and took a seat on the bench.

He started playing with things in his coat idly until Cypha went to get water from outside. He realized that the side of his coat was fairly hard with dried blood and made a face. "Damn it…"

When Cypha came back in she saw that Satyrna was asleep again. She nodded toward her and said to Malkarai. "Could you put her in the extra bed? It can't be too comfortable there."

He stood, crossed to the hearth, picked her up, and silently took her to the extra room. When he came out, he said, "I'm going to wash my clothes out. There isn't much we can do until we find out what happened to her and Dyspro, and I obviously can't just walk away from this anymore. You have a tub or something I could use?"

"Yeah, in the closet across from the room you just put her in."

He got a medium-sized metal tub and took it outside. It only took a few minutes to find the pump on the north side of the cottage and fill the basin. He was both surprised and impressed to see that the pump was quite modern, and had a filter attached to it. There was an outhouse near it, which answered another one of his questions about how they survived out here. He imagined that this place was probably a small paradise in the summer. When he came back inside, he set the tub by the fire so it would warm up.

"Mind if I steal some of your heat?"

"Nah, I got the stove going."

"Uh, if you guys have filtered water, why isn't it connected to the house?"

Cypha glanced at him. "Dyspro hasn't gotten around to it yet."

"Oh."

"He installed the filter, but because the owner didn't explicitly want the place modernized, stuff like that comes out of his pocket. Maybe next spring he'll put a sink in, he just hasn't yet."

"I see. So, he does know what he's doing."

"Yeah, he's obnoxious, but he's good at what he does. He put the drywall up in here and insulated it too, which is why it's pretty comfortable in here most of the time. We've got an LP tank out back, but so far it only supplies the stove. He has plans to hook up a water heater and maybe even a furnace, but that's pretty far in the future."

Malkarai sniffed the air. "What are you making?"

She stirred the contents of the pot on the stove. "I think it's soup. That's what it said on the package. It doesn't look like the picture much anymore though, so you tell me when you eat it."

He furrowed his brow and sat down at the table.

"Dyspro does most of the cooking. I never was that great at making anything over a stove, with or without the directions. I'm getting better out of necessity. Satyrna's the best of the three of us, but," Cypha waved a hand vaguely toward the other half of the house.

"So, you're going to feed the rest of us?"

"Yep. Hey, I said I'm getting better." Cypha knocked the spoon against the rim of the pot, shaking soup off of it, and then set it to the side. She sat down and looked at him. "What about you? Can you cook? Wanna take over?"

Malkarai shook his head. "That's not in my skill repertoire."

"Hm, really? What do you do at home? Survive on take-out?"

"We have a cafeteria."

"Oh. Man, you live in a facility?"

"Something like that."

She stared at the wall for a few moments, her expression contemplative. "Wonder if that would be nicer or worse than going it on your own, as long as you were free to go whenever you wanted." She eyed him. "You're free to go whenever you want, right?"

"For the most part. I mostly only leave for work though."

"I suppose that's not that bad, if working means you get to travel."

Malkarai shrugged. "Travel can be interesting, yeah. Home is nice because I don't get stared at and I can hide in my room."

"Do you often hide in your room?"

"Yeah."

She looked at him, thoughtfully. "Why do you hide? It's not like you seem to get social interaction out here."

He sighed. "I have no family, all the people I live with either hate me or don't give a shit that I'm there, and my friends are gone. I'm just going through the motions. It's easier to hide."

"That sucks," she said, frowning.

"Eh, it's normal now."

"Well, I think it's safe to say you found some new friends."

He glanced at her. "You shouldn't be offering that."

"Why?"

“Look at this bullshit I’ve caused.”

Cypha scoffed and stood up, checking the soup again. “Yeah, if you think that kind of crap is going to drive us, especially Saty, away, you need to wise up.”

He sighed, frowning.

“What should we do to get Dyspro out of there?” Cypha asked as she stirred the soup. “You have any ideas?”

“I’m thinking about it. I need to talk to Satyrna about what exactly happened. Hopefully, it’s just some kind of precaution, and we don’t have to do anything. We’ll figure something out. We’ll talk to Satyrna and then I’ll think about it.”

# 10



Satyrna woke slowly and stretched. At first, she was disoriented, wondering what time it was, and why it was so bright for the morning. She relaxed, staring at the ceiling. Then she remembered what had happened and sat up straight in bed. She winced and rubbed the cut on her forehead as Malkarai came to the doorway, rousted by the sound of the bed frame creaking.

"Malkarai?" she said in surprise. "When did you-?" she cut herself off, remembering being carried. She blushed and put her hands on the bed at her sides as it made her lightheaded.

He took a step into the room, his brow furrowed. "Uh, are you okay?"

"Y-yeah. I'm just lightheaded." She frowned, touching her forehead again. "This stings."

"You said you cut yourself on a branch."

"Right," she murmured.

Malkarai came closer, reaching to pull her hand away but then hesitating, seeming uncomfortable. "You should stop rubbing it before it bleeds."

Satyrna dropped her hand and looked up at him for a few moments before looking at her fingers. She rubbed the dried blood on her finger with her thumb. "Wh-where's Cypha?"

"She's right out here, cooking," he replied, gesturing toward the main room.

"What about Dyspro?" she insisted.

"No, we're pretty sure he's in the castle. We're still sorting that out."

"Is she up?" Cypha called.

"Yes," Malkarai replied, raising his voice.

"Good!"

He took a step back toward the door. "Uh, stay in bed if you're still lightheaded, but if you're hungry, Cypha's got something out here that resembles soup," he said in his normal, soft voice.

Cypha called from the other room. "I heard that! Surprisingly."

Malkarai rolled his eyes at the joke aimed at the volume of his voice. "Funny."

"What?"

"Shut up."

"What?"

Satyrna smiled brightly and slowly got up from the bed, still wrapped in Malkarai's cloak.

"You can stay in here if you want. We can bring it to you," Malkarai said, looking concerned.

Satyrna shook her head. "It's okay. I'm not dizzy."

"All right…" he said, watching her for a moment before leaving the room.

She walked out into the main room and Cypha looked over.

"Hey, sleeping beauty. How are you feeling?"

"Better. My head was just foggy as hell earlier."

"But it's clear now?"

"Yeah, clearing."

Cypha looked at Malkarai. "Fine, you're off the hook."

He gave her a bemused look.

Cypha motioned to the pot of soup. "Dare to try some of this? I think the dark one's afraid to."

"I never said that I was afraid to."

Satyrna walked over to the stove and looked in the pot. "I don't blame him."

Cypha gave her a look and Satyrna smiled, being snarky.

"Sit down or I'll stuff it down both of your throats."

Satyrna sat down and said, "I'm sure it's fine. No need to choke us with it."

Cypha dished out the soup and took her place at the table.

Satyrna looked cautiously at Malkarai. "Malkarai…?" she asked tentatively. "How did you know something had happened to us?"

He eyed her, stirring his soup slowly. He looked back down at his bowl before responding. "Cypha was worried about you, and ran into me while she was searching."

"You agreed to help?" She looked hopeful and pleased.

"Since it's my fault, yes."

Satyrna frowned.

Cypha looked at her friend. "Satyrna, what happened?"

She sighed, looking at her spoon intently. "Well… they confronted the two of us and took us into custody. I escaped. I don't know where Dyspro is. They separated us in the castle."

Cypha's brow knitted up. "What for?"

"They were afraid we were in danger," she said meekly.

Malkarai glanced at her but returned his attention to his bowl after a few moments.

Cypha looked between the two of them. "Well, that's lame. You're not in any danger. Is she?" The last phrase was rather pointed.

Malkarai shook his head. "I have no intention of hurting any of you. You've done nothing but be kind to me."

Satyrna watched him. "But if we weren't kind to you...?"

"Well, then I probably wouldn't pay you any mind. That's the norm for me. I'm not a harbinger of doom. I'm just a guy who has a job to do. I only fight if someone else fights me first."

Satyrna nodded, accepting this.

After a few minutes, Cypha dropped her spoon in her empty bowl and dumped both in a basin next to the stove. "I'm going to get some more food. We were short even before I made lunch, and if we have to hole up out here to avoid knights, we'll need sustenance."

"Do you want me to go?" Satyrna asked.

Cypha gave her an incredulous look. "Your brain is chloroform soup. Stay here and recover."

"I could go-" Malkarai started to offer, but Cypha put up a finger.

"That's an even worse idea than her going."

He frowned. "I am really good at staying hidden when I need to."

"Are you gonna swoop from the rafters at the grocery store? Just stay put and make sure she takes it easy."

"What if the knights bother you?" Satyrna pressed.

"I have my phone. If I don't show up or I don't call, well, just add me to the rescue list."

Satyrna sat back, pulled her legs close to her, and hugged the cloak tight around her, looking disgruntled. "Got some money?"

She hesitated but responded reluctantly as she put her coat on. "Some."

"Wait," Malkarai said.

Cypha looked at him as he dug into his pocket and pulled out his wallet. He pulled a few bills from it and held them out to her. "Use this."

She looked from his outstretched hand to his face. "I can't take your money."

"Take it. You guys have done enough for me, the least I can do for now is throw a few bucks in."

Cypha sighed and begrudgingly took the money from Malkarai. Then she slammed the door behind her and started for town.

Satyrna leaned forward as Malkarai closed his wallet to put it away. "Wait, what was that silver thing?"

He hesitated.

She looked up at his face. "What is it?"

He sighed softly, flipped the wallet open, and lifted the leather flap to show her a silver badge, which he then shut and put back in his pocket.

She blinked. "You're a cop?"

"No."

"Then why do you have a badge?"

"It's my clearance for carrying arms in public places."

"Oh…I've never heard of that. Is that what a weapon license looks like?"

"No, it's not a license, although I technically have one to back it. It doesn't expire, unlike licenses."

"Oh." She watched him, not completely accepting his explanation, but not wanting to dig too deep either.

Malkarai stood up, put his dishes in the basin with Cypha's, and checked to see if the water in the tub was warmed up at least a little. It was, so he tossed his cut shirt that he'd removed earlier and some more dirty clothing from his bag into the water. He was about to take his shirt off when he remembered that Satyrna was still there.

"Do you mind if I wash my shirt and coat out?"

"Huh? No. I saw you without it already; what's there new to be seen, besides less blood?"

"That's kind of what I figured," he said with a shrug. He took his shirt off and put it in the tub. Then he took all of his weapons and other items out of his coat, set them on the table, and put the coat in as well. After swirling them around a little bit, he sat back.

"Why don't you just put another one on?"

"This is all I've got."

"Oh. How long have you been away from home?"

"A few weeks."

"Sheesh… your job is involved."

"It isn't usually, but this guy is good at evading."

"Hm." Satyrna leaned forward, looking at the surprising number of items on the table. "Is that your blood on those, or is it someone else's?"

"Huh?" He looked at the battle instruments on the table. "Oh, probably mine. I always keep them clean. Didn't think any got on them though." He picked a bottle up and rubbed it with his fingers. The dark red rubbed off easily but left a residue, showing it was still wet. "Yeah, it's mine. Where are those rags?"

She pointed to the closet in the hall. After getting a small rag he wet it with water from the tub and cleaned off the bottles and weapons with blood on them. He soon finished and threw the rag in the tub with his clothes. Then he dug around near the dishes before finding dish soap, which he also squirted into the tub of clothes and water.

While he was washing the clothing, Satyrna was taking inventory of the weapons. There was one sword, which he'd had on his belt previously, three daggers, two switchblades, a pocket knife, and two leather pouches of different sizes which seemed to hold something metal. There were also about half a dozen small bottles, and two of them had a skull and crossbones on them. A few of the others seemed to be medicine. "What the hell do you need all that stuff for?"

He shrugged. "You never know what you're gonna need. Self-defense is often necessary in my line of work."

"You can't defend yourself with just a sword and those knives?"

"I can, but if I get disarmed, it's nice to have backups. Plus, a little bit of variety makes things less tedious."

"What's in the pouches?"

He put a finger on one, "Throwing darts," and then on the other. "Lock picking set."

Satyrna raised her brow. "Why would you need to pick locks?"

He shrugged. "Better than breaking locks. I'm not often welcomed in at the front door of places. Some people who do my job rely completely on wooing our targets or presenting a social façade that gets them where they need to be. I don't really get to work like that. No one will grant me special treatment because I'm charming or attractive. I don't like to work with fear, but sometimes that's the only way to get what my boss wants. Mostly I just sneak in to where I need to be and address the person I need to talk to."

"Sounds underhanded," Satyrna muttered, her chin on her knees.

"Yeah, well, that's about the only way a dark can survive around here – being underhanded."

Satyrna frowned.

They sat there for a few minutes, silent, until Malkarai shifted in his seat, and the rag bandage caught on the chair back, cutting into his wound. He grimaced, moaned softly, and loosed the bandage completely. He looked at his wound and tossed the rag in the tub.

"How is that doing?"

"It stopped bleeding, but it hurts like hell still. Those bandages always annoyed me."

"They keep the wound clean."

He shrugged. "I prefer it when they aren't wrapped all the way around."

"Why did you carry me all the way here if you were in pain?"

He shrugged again.

"Why? It could have opened it up again."

"You were basically asleep. Don't worry about it; you weren't heavy, and I'm used to still functioning with injuries."

"You *are* misleadingly strong," she said quietly.

"What happened to you and Dyspro? Did they jump you?"

"Not really. Kalyfa and some others came up to us, spouting some garbage about how you were dangerous. He gave Dyspro a proposition – to catch you and bring you to them. Dyspro refused, and they grabbed him and dragged him away, saying some shit about how we were going into protective custody. I tried to get to Dyspro, but Kalyfa grabbed me so I kneed him. He asked me to cooperate, and, when I kept struggling, he dragged me to the castle too – but they separated us as soon as we got inside. They put me in one of the interior rooms – at least, there wasn't a window and it wasn't in the basement. There was a cot and a chair and a table, but it wasn't one of the rooms with electricity, just a lantern. I tried to get out and the last time he dragged me back in, his… his gloves smelled really strong – like an… acrid smell. It was gross. I started getting panicked after that, and it got harder and harder to concentrate."

Malkarai frowned, his brow furrowed deeply. "I thought so… That sleaze must've put a drug on his gloves or in his sleeve or something to make you docile."

She frowned at him. "I… I wasn't sure, I thought I was having a panic attack or something, but…"

"No, this seems entirely unnatural. Panic and fear are logical here, but your adrenaline should've been going. You shouldn't have been sleepy."

She sighed heavily, frowning still as she looked at the floor.

"And they were still saying it was protective custody?"

Satyrna nodded, looking at him.

"That's not okay. What the fuck is Kalyfa playing at?"

"Kalyfa didn't do it. It was another knight – this older guy. He got mad because I tried to leave twice and he dragged me back in each time, and I smelled that stuff the last time, and afterward it was harder to walk."

Malkarai's eyes were narrowed. "Do you know what knight it was?"

"I don't know his name."

"All right."

"Uh, it was only a little bit before Kalyfa came in. I demanded to know where Dyspro was, but he told me not to worry about it, that we were separated because he wanted to talk to me."

"What about?"

She scowled. "He wanted a heart-to-heart, but I was not in the mood. He was always doing this before-"

"Kidnapping you?" Malkarai interrupted.

"No, butting in and protecting me when he didn't need to. This was extreme. You scare him."

Malkarai shrugged. "I kicked their asses last night."

"Well, he pissed me off, and me being pissed upset him. We got to yelling… and…"

"What?"

She looked like she was concentrating. "He called me a naïve little child. I told him that he was a bigot for pulling all this bullshit because you're a dark, and he just got… furious. But he didn't say anything. Like he was angry and stuttering, but didn't get anything out and looked frustrated. He told me to stay put and left in a huff. He didn't lock the door behind him, so after like thirty seconds, I ran. I didn't see the other guy, and I didn't want to go slow so he could catch up. I made it out of the castle without anyone stopping me and made it to where you guys found me. I was so foggy and scared, I just hid and sat there." She put her fingers over the cut on her forehead that had long since scabbed over. "The stuff he made me inhale messed my head up." She curled up more in the cloak, looking very pale.

"Are you all right?"

She closed her eyes for a moment and nodded. "I'll be fine; I'm just kinda shaken up. He's not going to be happy…" She put her face in her hands. "And God… what happened to Dyspro? What he said before they grabbed him scares me…"

"What?"

"He said he'd rather die than help them. Kalyfa said, 'Well if that's how you feel about it,' and then they all took him down. What if they kill him, Malkarai!?"

Malkarai looked disconcerted. "That really seems unlikely. At the very least, what you've told me about Kalyfa tells me he wouldn't do that."

"I mean, yes, probably… I hope," Satyrna mumbled.

"And you have friends that are knights, right? They wouldn't allow that – even for standing up for a dark."

"No, they wouldn't… You're right, Josh wouldn't allow that." She shook her head. "There are other good knights too, like Brendan. This stupid shit is making me emotional and irrational."

"Yeah, this situation is fucked up," he muttered.

"No, I meant the stuff he made me inhale."

He glanced at her. "Oh. I doubt the situation is helping it though."

"Well, no," she begrudgingly agreed.

"I can't believe that Dyspro just said no like that. I could have easily dealt with the knights."

She shook her head. "The fact that it was you wasn't the only reason. He'd never help the knights do anything to a dark, no matter what it came to."

"What's the castle like?" Malkarai asked.

"Dark rock walls, metal fixtures, and repo and surplus army furniture and supplies. That's pretty much all they've got in there. There's one big main hall where they do training and things, and some meeting rooms in the center back, but the rooms on the left and right sides are smaller and used for storage, equipment, bunking, and apparently imprisonment thinly veiled as protective custody now too," she said with bitterness. "Some of the rooms have lights, but not all of them. Mostly they use battery-operated and rechargeable stuff. They don't use all of it regularly, and laying wire through the whole thing would be expensive and involve drilling. I've been there before – with Josh when we were all little, and with Kalyfa later. It was cool and kinda spooky when I was a kid, now it's just kind of an eyesore. Josh owns the place since his grandpa handed it over after he retired, but he basically just lets Kalyfa decide what he wants to do with it and signs off on it. The knights pay for any changes or upgrades, so it doesn't have a lot."

Malkarai nodded, looking thoughtful. After a few minutes, he said, "I'll get him out."

She perked up. "What?"

"I'll get Dyspro out of the castle."

"Why?"

"They shouldn't be holding someone just for talking to me. These guys are irrational and too emotion-driven. If that one didn't see why drugging you was a terrible, illegal move, I'm not sure how much I can trust the rest of them. I don't feel like he's safe in there, so I'll get him out."

She smiled, a little surprised. "Thank you. You don't have to do anything for us."

He frowned. "Yeah, I do. I'm the reason Kalyfa's pissed. I'm the one who started all of this. You and your friends have helped me out ever since you met me. No one's ever done that for me. Most people avoid me, with good reason. And when I got in trouble, you guys paid for it. So, yes, I do have to do this."

She shrugged. "We just want people to stop thinking so poorly of darks. We don't want what happened to Fayta and Martra to ever happen again. We didn't think anything would happen because we talked to you, but Kalyfa was mad at you because you were with me."

"I figured, but that's not really why they attacked me. I should have warned you. It would have saved a whole hell of a lot of trouble."

"Warned me about what?" she asked tentatively.

He shook his head. "I can't tell you. I can't make you go away yet. I gotta get him out. Kalyfa apparently wants to keep this under the table, and that's fine by me. I'll play this stupid game by his stupid rules." Before Satyrna could respond, he looked up. "Satyrna, once I get Dyspro out of there, I'm going to have to leave. I can't stay here. I have to get back."

Satyrna slumped back in her chair, an unhappy expression on her face. "I was kinda hoping you'd stay with us, at least for a little while."

"This went sideways. I have to clear outta here."

"Why?"

"Because Kalyfa's pissed at me, mainly."

"What about if he wasn't?"

"It'd be the same, just a few days later."

"Why?"

"Because I need to go back."

"Back where?"

"Home."

"Where is home for you?"

"I can't say."

"Why not?"

"It's part of the contract. We can't tell anyone."

Satyrna frowned. "Your job, is it something bad?"

"Based on your perspective, yes, I guess it could be."

Satyrna stared at him. "Malkarai?"

"What?"

"Why are you doing this job, if it's bad?"

"I said it could be bad according to one's perspective. I never said I thought it was bad."

"I don't think you're an evil person, Malkarai."

"You don't know me."

"I'd like to."

He looked at her. "Why?"

Satyrna put her shoulders back slightly, still frowning. His stare was demanding an answer bigger than his question. "I like you. You've been telling me to stay away from you from the beginning, but I've yet to see why, aside from some misguided lesson you've had drilled into your head that you're a toxic person. I think the complete opposite. I think you've had to deal with a lot of bullshit in your life, but I don't think *you're* the cause for it."

"It doesn't matter if I've caused it or not if it just follows me around."

"I want to get to know you better, and maybe help you swat away some of this stupidity."

Malkarai shook his head, looking down at the fire. "You need help."

"No, you do," she retorted. "You're the one who thinks associating with people is a crime."

Malkarai ground his teeth, still staring at the fire. "It's against the rules; not a crime, like Kalyfa seems to think."

"You follow the rules pretty closely."

"It's easy to follow the rules when you don't want to be around people."

"I don't believe that you really don't want to be around people."

"People are exhausting and stress me out."

"Sure, people who fear or dislike you. You've had friends before – friends that didn't see your darkness as a downside, just like us. You need friends again."

"If you want me to magically revert back to how I was when I was ten, Satyrna, that is *not* what I want."

"No, that's impossible, and I don't think that would be good for you anyway. You're strong and independent now, and very world-wise. But that doesn't mean you can't have friends anymore. I honestly think you *need* those two things. Having people that you feel comfortable with… that's just as good for your mind and body as training, studying, and working hard. You can't do everything alone, we're social creatures."

"Darks aren't."

Satyrna huffed. "Don't *you* buy into that stereotype too. That's lazy and wrong."

"Fine, *I'm* not," he protested. "I've been tested, and I sure as hell did not land in the social track. I'm an introvert who prefers to spend his rare time off alone."

"Introverts still need people – they need *their* people. Your people are gone."

"I still have some people," he muttered.

"Besides us?"

He eyed her. "Satyrna, you've known me a total of two and a half days."

"How long do you think it takes to make friends?"

"More than two and a half days."

She scoffed. "Fine – how about eleven years?"

"That doesn't count."

"Friends are people you think about and want the best for – and I've actually thought about you frequently for the past eleven years, and I've hoped the best for you and wondered if you were still doing okay."

He sighed, his shoulders slumping slightly as he looked at her, regarding her thoughtfully. "Seriously?"

"Yes," she insisted. "Did I ever think I'd get to see you again? No. I didn't even know your name until the other day. I certainly hoped I would see you again though. I wanted to believe that you were doing well, and maybe I could see you somewhere, and see that you were doing okay."

"Does this count as okay?"

"You're alive, you're strong, you're smart, and you're healthy. Yes, I think it does."

He shook his head, looking at the fire with a small snort.

"Oh, believe me, I can tell that you aren't perfectly fine. You need help, but still, I think you're doing okay, and it made me happy to know that you were."

"I'm sure I can't live up to the made-up me you concocted over the past eleven years."

"You've surpassed it because that was a shallow construct. Look, my point is, it doesn't matter to me if you have this job that has you traveling all over the place. Your friends don't need to be in the same place as you to still be there for you. You just keep telling me that your job says you can't have friends though, and I think that's *wrong*."

"We can have friends. We can't talk about the job."

She chewed on the inside of her lip momentarily. "Okay, then why are you resisting us?"

"Because me being your friend has caused the knights to take two of you into protective custody," he said, waving a hand toward the front of the house, looking at her. "I get it, you want to be my friend – but being my friend isn't good for you, Satyrna."

She frowned. "If my ex wasn't a raging douchebag, would it be okay?"

Malkarai rolled his eyes and shrugged, looking back at the fire. "I don't know. Maybe."

"How far away do you live?"

He didn't respond immediately, hesitating.

"A distance or a time, that's okay, right?"

He looked at the ceiling for a few moments, calculating. "Probably about an hour, maybe an hour and a half driving."

Satyrna leaned forward slightly, her eyebrows lifting. "Really?"

"Pretty sure. I didn't drive here from home. I've been following this guy for two weeks."

"Honestly, that's closer than I expected."

"It doesn't change anything – I can't be here, and you can't go there. You're better off giving me a phone number or an online handle because once I leave here, we can't see each other again."

Satyrna sighed, frowning.

"Or just dropping it entirely."

"Is your job that great that it's worth dealing with this bull?" she asked quietly. "Not being able to spend time with people, not being able to talk about it, not being able to associate with anyone but your coworkers?"

Malkarai made a small noise of amusement. "What, do you think I should just quit?"

"I mean, not necessarily… but it really sounds like this job has taken over your life."

"My life *is* this job. Without this job, I wouldn't exist."

"Because they raised you?"

"More than just that. The job is the reason I have the knowledge, strength, skills, and life I have. Without it, I might've been just as doomed as your friends."

Satyrna frowned and looked at the fire, putting her feet on her chair seat and pulling his cloak up and around her, covering her mouth with the edge.

"You seem to think I can just quit and it'll fix my problems – but without this job, I'd have entirely different problems. Also, I'm under contract. I can't just quit."

She sighed. After a few minutes of silence, she asked, "This resistance… it's not cuz you don't like us, right?"

"No, it's not."

"I'll take that as a minor win."

# 11

Cypha hurried through town, trying to get done as soon as possible. She decided to go to Satyrna's family's store, where she knew she'd be a bit safer. Satyrna's father, who was stocking some shelves near the front of the store, greeted her when she came in. He was fairly tall, had short brown hair, brown eyes, and a trimmed mustache and beard with traces of gray in them.

"Hey, Cypha, what are you looking for?"

"Not much, just getting food. We ran out."

He looked concerned. "Oh, you need to ask for some?"

She shook her head quickly. "No, I have money."

"Oh, good, then go ahead and look around."

She quickly picked out the basics and took them to the counter, where she paid for them. Satyrna's mother, a woman of average height, mid-length dirty-blonde hair, with smile- and worry-wrinkles next to her hazel eyes, took the money from her and counted it. She put it in a drawer and gave her change for it, looking up at Cypha as she did so.

"Is Satyrna at your house?"

"Yeah."

"Good. Patricia told us she had run off. You found her?"

"Yeah."

"Is she all right?"

"Yeah, she's fine."

"What about Dyspro, was he with her?"

"No, but we know where he is." Cypha stuck the change in her pocket. "Thanks. See ya later." She picked up her food and hurried out the door and toward the edge of town before they could ask any more questions.

Satyrna's mother exchanged worried glances with her husband, who crossed his arms, watching Cypha hurry down the street. "Dregan…"

"Those three get into so much trouble… I would've thought it'd stop after high school."

"What should we do about it?"

He shook his head and sighed. "Wait and see what happens. Half the time all we can do is scold her and pick up the pieces, Anna."

"I'm not happy with just doing that. She's our baby, Dregan."

"Cypha said she's fine."

"And what about Dyspro?"

He put a few more items on the shelf. "Like I said, just wait until she comes to us. Interfering before has just made her mad at us. It's not like it ever helped any."

His wife sighed and crossed her arms. "You're too lenient."

"She's not Patricia, dear. Satyrna gets too much joy out of doing whatever the hell she wants. She's always gotten herself out of scrapes in the past, why should this time be any different?"

"What if something's seriously wrong?"

"You always wonder that. Cypha wouldn't go grocery shopping if Dyspro was really in danger, hon."

Anna sighed and looked back at the inventory sheet on the clipboard in front of her. "I suppose. I'll never stop worrying about her though."

"Which is why you'll always get gray faster than me. She has a phone; she knows how to use it."

"She doesn't."

"She does for emergencies. I figure, as long as she's not calling, things are okay."

Anna shook her head. "I don't like that policy."

He smiled. "Which is why Satyrna stresses you out more than the other two ever did. Relax."

"She is so your daughter, Dregan. I really feel like you just cloned her and said, 'Here, have fun.'"

He shrugged. "You are a very forgiving woman, Anna."

She sighed and headed for the back of the store to check a few things on the list. "You'd better hope it stays that way."

When Cypha reached the path to her house, she started to run – all the way to the house and inside the door. When she went in, she dropped the food on the table. The bag tipped over and its contents spilled out. She quickly locked the door.

Satyrna jumped when Cypha slammed the door. Both she and Malkarai stared at her in surprise.

"What's wrong?"

She caught her breath and looked out the window briefly before taking a step back. "Some of the chuckleheads were following me."

"Were they trying to catch you?" Satyrna asked, panicked.

Cypha shook her head, peering out the window. "No, they were just following me. They weren't chasing me, but they were far too close for my liking."

Malkarai got up and looked out the other window, standing to the side of the glass so he was out of sight. "Are they out there now?"

"I think so. It was like… they didn't want to confront me. They kept talking to each other like they were trying to make a plan or something."

Malkarai nodded toward the woods. "I see them. Two or three of them."

Satyrna drew in her breath sharply and huddled farther down in Malkarai's cloak. "Oh God, don't let them come in here."

Cypha glanced at her and then gave Malkarai a look that said, *What's wrong with her?*

He shook his head and grabbed his sword off the table, moving again so he was still not in sight. "I won't let them get in here. If they come up to the house, both of you stay inside."

"That's a stupid move," Cypha said dryly. "Honestly, you should get your ass back in one of the bedrooms, both of you, before they see you and know I'm not alone."

Satyrna looked at Malkarai, who exhaled, staring into the woods at the knights. When they started moving toward the house, he nodded and went past Satyrna, touching her shoulder as he went. "She's right. Let's go in back."

Satyrna followed him into the back and Cypha went around the table, crossing her arms as she stood by the fireplace, peering at the knights as they approached the house.

They seemed hesitant, and eventually one of them pushed another one toward the house, apparently encouraging him – or jeering at him. A combination of both.

He kept glancing at his fellows, but eventually made his way up to the door and reached up, doing something to the door she couldn't see. She heard a soft shifting sound, but then he turned and retreated quickly, going right past his comrades and heading down the path. The other two followed him, saying something to him as they went.

"What the fuck…?" she muttered.

"What is it?" Malkarai asked quietly.

"Uh, they're leaving, I think."

"What'd they do?" he asked, peeking out from the extra bedroom door.

"I don't know. One of the idiots came up to the door and did something, and then they all just bolted."

"Did you see which ones they were?" Satyrna asked from just behind Malkarai.

"Uh, yeah, but I can't think of their names. Well, one of them was Matt Hoffman."

Satyrna came out when Malkarai did, giving Cypha a contemplative look. "Didn't you beat him up once…?"

Cypha grinned. "Yeah, in ninth grade."

Malkarai snorted in amusement and Satyrna gave Cypha a fond look.

He went up to the window, checking to make sure that they were gone.

"I'm gonna see what he did to the door," Cypha said, shooing Malkarai away from it and unlocking the door.

As she opened it, a piece of folded paper fluttered to the threshold. She picked the paper up, shut and locked the door, and made an increasingly annoyed face as she read it.

"What does it say?" Satyrna asked, trying to peek over her shoulder to read.

"Uh… the handwriting sucks ass… It says, 'For your safety, report to the castle immediately. We understand that any actions you've taken were limited to not provoke additional risk to you or your friends' safety. We are taking additional measures regarding this. If the threat to the public is still in Cavington after 24 hours a warrant for neutralization will be issued and become effective immediately. Do not attempt further engagement with the dark, they are extremely dangerous and have attacked and injured two knights without just cause.' What the fuck – neutralization?! They're gonna fucking put a kill order on you?!"

Malkarai shrugged, lifting a hand, making a gesture of, 'I guess.' He held out a hand for the note and Cypha handed it over so he could read it himself.

"Why mention it to the sheriff?" Satyrna asked.

"You need that for that kind of warrant. They can't operate unchecked," Cypha said. "It really feels like they're trying to though."

Malkarai sighed. "Yeah, they might want some kind of paper trail for this, but this doesn't really align with what Kalyfa seemed to want. I think this is more likely to be a brilliant idea concocted by those particular knights than something Kalyfa ordered."

"Hm, you think?" Cypha asked.

"Yeah, that shit wouldn't fly. Definitely not for my employers. I'm going to act like it is from Kalyfa though. It's safer to consider all information and just keep an eye out for developments and revealed truth than dismiss it."

Cypha nodded thoughtfully.

"This is so stupid, that fight was self-defense!" Satyrna protested.

"Yeah, but no one's gonna vouch for me on that. It's my word against theirs, Satyrna," he responded, more than a little bitterness in his voice. "I embarrassed them and hurt two of them."

Satyrna shut her mouth, staring at him indignantly for a few moments before saying, "B-Brendan! He was there! He could speak for you."

"Kalyfa wouldn't want this to get there if what you say about him is true," Malkarai retorted. "He'd probably turn this back on those knights' heads before he ever let it get to the point where Brendan would have to commit career suicide standing up for me."

She exhaled heavily, disgruntled.

"What are you going to do?" Cypha asked.

"Nothing."

"What? Why not?" Satyrna protested.

Malkarai scoffed. "Maybe if I broke both of my legs and one of my hands, they'd have a chance of catching me, but I still don't think they could defeat me unless I let them."

Cypha snorted in amusement. Satyrna was staring at him, her eyebrows furrowed.

"I don't have to do anything. By the time they try and get me, I'll be gone. Besides, I'm not under their power. Whatever they do to me, no matter what they can get the sheriff to sign, will be illegal according to the U.S. government, and will probably piss the government off greatly too."

"Do you work for the federal government?"

"Let's just say that they like me."

"I'm still trying to figure out why those morons didn't just knock on the door and ask me to go with them." Cypha asked, still annoyed. "They followed me from town – they know I'm here."

Satyrna eyed Cypha. "It was a spectacle when they picked up me and Dyspro. They wouldn't do that to you."

Cypha snorted. "Why the fuck not?"

"The Garevns. Yeah, there's no one to see out here, but they're chickens. It's not like you'll just keep your mouth shut after the fact if they did something stupid."

Cypha sighed and rolled her eyes, but dropped it. She took the paper from Malkarai and reread the note. "Does it mention Dyspro on this thing…? No. What the hell is their play here?"

Satyrna shook her head slowly. "Do you think they're just doing this because I escaped and they don't know where I am?"

"It's possible," Malkarai said.

"Chiseling bastards," Cypha hissed. "This is a win-win situation for them."

"Yeah, of course, it is," Malkarai said. "This is their town; I'm an intruder. Either they get me out, or they remove me. I'm sure they're hoping I just leave."

Cypha gave Malkarai a calculating look. "What's your reason for not just leaving?"

He inhaled and exhaled silently, looking out the window with a frown on his face. "I mean, that's the option with the least amount of conflict, but… I have two reasons I don't want to do that."

"What are those?" Satyrna asked insistently.

"They're both ego. First, just leaving would be like telling him, 'Fine, I'll listen to whatever you say. It doesn't matter what these other people think of me, just what the knights demand.' It's stupid, but I'm not going to just ignore that you guys have stuck your necks out for me and want to be my friend."

Cypha looked at Satyrna but didn't say anything.

"Second, professionally, this is *not* what he's agreed to. He's crossing lines, and if he wants it to be this way, then I have a professional obligation to ignore his threats."

"You guys have an… agreement?" Satyrna asked, perplexed.

"Not him and I specifically, but the knights and the government. My superior followed protocol and told him I was here, and his response was to hunt me out. Was that because he dislikes people like me, or was it because I was around you guys? I don't know. Probably an equal amount of both. They attacked me, I responded, and I came out the victor. He wants me to concede."

"Jeez, this is fucked," Cypha muttered.

"Yes," Malkarai agreed.

Satyrna swallowed. "What are you going to do, then?"

"I… need to think on it. Regardless of what I do, I'm going to have to go home eventually. It's just a matter of what I can take care of before I do. No matter what, I'm sure I won't be allowed back here."

Satyrna swallowed, looking down at the floor when she felt tears well up in her eyes.

Cypha looked from Malkarai to Satyrna, watching her. After a few moments, she asked gently, "You gonna be okay, Saty?"

"I want to kick Kalyfa's ass!" she sobbed. She got up and walked into the extra room. They heard her slam the door and flop down on the bed. The door hadn't shut though, and it creaked open.

Cypha picked up the bag of food and looked at Malkarai, who looked uncomfortable. "What's wrong with her?"

He spoke more quietly than usual, aware that Satyrna's door was open, and explained to Cypha what Satyrna had told him had happened at the castle earlier.

"God… I can't believe that asshole drugged her."

Malkarai shrugged. "She pissed him off. If he's okay crossing that line, he could have done worse. I'm glad she got out of there when she did."

"Yeah, same," Cypha said as she started unpacking the grocery bag.

He paused. "She and Kalyfa didn't break up amiably, right?"

"She broke up with him, and he was blindsided. She explained why, but I guess he didn't get it, and she's just been avoiding him since."

Malkarai sighed and crossed his arms.

"I think she ignores at least a text a week from him. She ignores most texts though, to be honest. She doesn't like her phone much."

Malkarai rolled his eyes and looked out the front window. "That explains why she wasn't as keen on just being friends digitally."

Cypha smirked. "Yeah, that's not Saty's style."

"It's my style."

"She might make an exception for you," Cypha said with a shrug as she finished putting the food away.

He eyed her, his eyebrows knitted up.

"She likes you, *and* she thinks you're cute."

Malkarai blushed, frowning at her. "I *extra* don't need that shoved into this mess…"

Cypha smirked and shrugged as she shoved the empty grocery bag into a bag with a bunch of others. "Just letting you know."

"Yeah, I'm not completely oblivious," he muttered. "That's why I've been insisting this is a bad idea, and I need to go back. No matter how this turns out, I can't come back to Cavington."

"She never takes no for an answer. That's just how Satyrna is. If she sees an inch of hope, she'll attack it and stretch it to a mile. Do you *want* to stay?"

"I honestly don't know. I mean, this is all I've ever known, so not doing it anymore… is a little terrifying. I can't say I'm terribly happy where I am though. But, even if I *did* manage to remove myself from my job, I don't think Cavington is a good place for me to be."

"Mm, because of our knight infestation?"

"And despite whatever the knights are or aren't doing these days, this region really is unfriendly to darks."

Cypha sighed. "Unfortunately, yes. Yeah, it really doesn't sound like her idealism will win out this time."

He shrugged.

"Aren't you cold?" she asked.

"Not really."

"You want to borrow a shirt or something? You're making me feel cold. Well, not that I mind you standing there half-naked…" She smirked, raising an eyebrow.

He rolled his eyes and shook his head and gestured to the drying rack he'd set up out of the way in the corner of the sitting area of the main room. "Nah. I have enough shirts, and they'll be dry in a little bit. Besides, I don't think I'd fit in one of your shirts. I'd probably stain it with blood too, knowing my luck."

She laughed. "No, not mine. One of Dyspro's. He wouldn't miss it. Half his shit looks the same anyway."

"I'll pass,'" he said.

She leaned against the table. "What happened to your friend? Why were you two separated? Is he still working for the same people, just not with you?"

"Oh, Traphian?"

"Yeah."

"Traphian ran away from our home. I helped him plan it. He was going to take me with him, but I chickened out at the last minute and didn't follow. He had to leave without me because we were almost discovered. I haven't really been able to talk with him since. He altered his name and changed his hair and what he could of his appearance, but I knew it was him every time I saw him. He's changed his hair back recently, I think. I mean, he's grown up since then. Plus, he's got one of these, and that's a dead giveaway." He moved his right arm slightly, referring to the dragon scar he had on it.

"Why didn't you get away too?"

"At the time, I had too much keeping me there. Now… it's too risky. They'd hunt me down. He was a teenager, I'm not."

"Can't you just quit?"

He shook his head. "I signed a contract. I chose to stay, and when I did it was for life."

"I say risk it."

"Not with these people. They've grown up on swordplay and disguise; they don't think twice about hurting anyone."

"What do you mean?"

"We're all well-trained combatants. Each of us alone is a hard fight… I don't want to imagine everyone together. I'm not afraid of the knights; I *am* afraid of my coworkers coming after me."

She nodded slowly. "So, they'd be pissed that you left."

"Yeah."

"How come they didn't gang up on your friend then?"

"He stayed low, evaded, and grew up quickly. He was a functioning agent when he left, but his training wasn't even done yet, so they saw him as less of an asset than say, what I'd be now."

"I see. Well, that sucks."

Malkarai nodded vaguely.

"Did you have a chance to start figuring out a plan?"

Malkarai paced back and forth a few times in the middle of the room, his arms still crossed across his chest. "I have a few ideas… but I need to work through which one is the best one. I know I need to talk to the guy I'm following first though."

"Really? Why?"

He hesitated, chewing over how to respond. "It just has to happen before shit goes down with the knights."

"Why haven't you talked to him yet? That's why you're here in the first place, right?"

"Yeah. I haven't been trying as hard as I should've."

"Oh," Cypha said, an eyebrow lifting. "How come?"

Malkarai shook his head. "Many reasons. This is pushing me to commit though."

"What's his name?"

"Trebo."

"Is he just passing through Cavington?"

"Yeah; he's running from me."

Cypha's eyebrows furrowed as she gave him a look. "Well, I suppose it makes sense why he came here then."

Malkarai looked at her.

"Because this place is a pretty shitty place to go if you're a dark."

Malkarai made a soft noise of amusement, shaking his head in agreement.

# 12



A woman yawned as she walked down the cold, dry, and dirty street. She wore a black trench coat, a skirt, calf-high tactical boots, and a vest that was split and tied in the front, all of tough black leather. She had a white T-shirt and gray leggings underneath. A double sword sheath lay across her back, one hilt over each shoulder. Her shoulder-length hair was black with bright red highlights, her skin was a healthy peach color, her cheeks reddish from the cold, and her irises were a vibrant crimson due to the contacts she wore. She was pretty short, incredibly muscular, and there were scars of varying lengths scattered across all of her visible skin, including a few on her face. She looked about her as she slipped her hands in her pockets, running her tongue along her teeth idly.

*Where the hell did you go, you dumbass? You're not supposed to hide from me, just your target. You must really wanna die if you'd follow the shithead here.*

She sighed and tossed some of her hair behind her shoulder.

*If Stika hadn't forbidden me from trying again, I'd hunt down the bastard myself. But no, gotta let Malkarai do it. He'll take fucking forever. He's already letting it take fucking forever. The system's got some idiots up there. 'Oh, Teffifa couldn't handle it? Send the dark, he'll do it. He always does it.' Yeah right. What do you think he is? He'll never finish it. I couldn't finish it; he most certainly won't.*

Teffifa sighed. "I really hope he doesn't try any stupid shit again… I don't feel like hauling his ass to the ER in the middle of a Podunk town like this. We both look like hoodlums here."

Her eyes darted to the side as she spotted something move in an alley. The cat hissed at the garbage can it fell off of and ran down the alley. She smiled at the feline and turned into the alley, following the cat for the hell of it. She kicked a can out of her way as she walked, seeming perfectly relaxed.

A man with short, shaggy brown hair and a mustache and shallow beard, wearing a brown leather jacket and blue jeans, came into view in the alley she was walking down, and she looked toward him sharply. He was holding a grocery bag in one hand. He stared at her; his bright, green eyes grew wide as a sinister smile spread over her lips. He turned and took off the way he had come, but she was already on his tail.

"Oh, don't run, Trebo, you'll be tired!"

"Get away from me, you psychotic bitch!"

Teffifa laughed. "But this is so much fun!"

"Why the hell are you after me again, Ripper?! I already beat you!"

"If you call that beating! I never go away, you know that!"

"I beat you! Shit, half your arm was ripped open!"

"Oh, that was just a little scratch. Didn't hurt a bit!"

"Of course, it didn't, your frigging imbalance cut it all off!"

"That isn't all my imbalance is gonna cut off!"

He skidded to a stop, his heart sinking in his chest as he reached a dead end.

She laughed as she saw his predicament. "Ah! Caught like a rat, eh, Trebo? That's what you're going by today, right? Or have you made up another lame-ass name?"

He turned around, silent.

She grinned and drew both her swords. "Oh, where to start? I could always cut off an arm and watch you try and fight with only one, but that'd be unsportswomanlike. Unless… I could just cut off your left, so you could still fight with your right. Or I could just make it quick and do it the traditional Ripper way, and slice your throat. Nah, that's too quick. The system doesn't want you dead that fast, not after you were a pain in their ass for this long."

He unstrapped and drew his sword from over his left shoulder, watching her. She licked her lips with a smile but didn't attack him.

"Teffifa, do you ever get tired of being a mental case?"

"Nope, I enjoy it."

Trebo shook his head. "If the system knew you were like this on the hunt, they would've had you institutionalized years ago."

"Well, you won't be the first to tell them, I can guarantee you that!"

She jumped forward, taking a hard slash at him with both of her blades. He blocked her attack, pushing her away. With this first strike, the two of them went at it, slashing and stabbing. Teffifa moved in a manner that alternated her blades and made one always available for striking. This kept Trebo on the defensive, for immediately after he had blocked one attack, another was upon him.

"Why the hell are you here, anyway? Malkarai's here!"

"Exactly."

"Malkarai's your superior, Ripper!"

"Eh, that's debatable. But, Stika doesn't think he'll finish the mission. So, I'm following his tail. Believe me, if he doesn't finish it, I will."

"Then what the hell are you doing now?!"

"Oh, I'm just toying with you. This is Malk's mission now; he has to make the first attempt. I just don't want you to go and relax on us."

"You sick bitch!" he hissed.

She grinned and brought both her blades together again. This gave Trebo a brief moment's rest, but not much. "Honestly, meathead, you need to think up more creative insults than that." She hacked at him, neatly clipping his right arm through the leather jacket.

"Shit!"

She smiled and drew back, sheathing both of her blades. Trebo slapped a hand to the twin slices that now graced his upper arm. She winked, tipped her head to him, then turned on her heel and headed down the alley. "I'll see you around, Trebo!" The name sounded more like an insult than anything.

"Ah, hell."

Cypha jolted out of sleep, at first annoyed, and then a little panicked, hearing someone knocking on the front door of the cottage.

"Fuck," she whispered, tossing her covers back and climbing out of bed and going to her door. She opened it and peered out at the main room. It was dark except for the low flickering firelight, but she could see that the bench where Malkarai had bedded down was empty. The blanket he'd used was folded at the end of it, the pillow sitting on top.

There was another knock, so she stuffed her feet in her boots, put her phone in her pocket, and grabbed a sweatshirt from her dresser, pulling it on as she went to the door.

Mid-knock, she opened the door, glaring at the guy outside of it.

He jumped but then dropped his hand.

She recognized him and the girl behind him as knights. He was one of the captains.

"What do you want, Isaac?" she demanded. "It's fucking dark out."

He cleared his throat. "Kalyfa wants you to come to the castle."

"Yeah, the note said that. I'm not keen on answering this party invite."

He looked perplexed. "Note? What note?"

"The note your fellow dinguses left on my door last night."

He was starting to look more worried. "Can I see it?"

Cypha sighed and turned, looking to see where it went. It was still on the table, so she grabbed it, opened it, and pulled her phone out. "One moment." After snapping a picture of it, she handed him the note.

He looked disappointed she did so, especially after he read the note. He sighed and folded it up, putting it in his pocket. "Uh, I need to take this. My message is different. Kalyfa wants you to come to the castle for your safety. I haven't heard anything about this warrant business."

"Hm, then what was that little stunt last night?"

"We sent a group to locate you and pass along the request for you to come to the castle, but they reported that they could not find you."

"Yeah, they followed me at a distance and then tried to shove a note through my door like it was a fucking locker before running away like scared little school girls. Real professional."

Isaac shook his head, annoyed. "I'll let Kalyfa know. Please come with us to the castle."

"Yeah, you keep saying that. Why?"

"You and your friends are in danger, and he thinks it's safer for you there."

"That's nice. I think I'm plenty safe right here."

"He wants you to be in protective custody…"

"Protective custody is just imprisonment if I don't want to be there. I thought you guys all cleaned your shit up after old man Garevn left. What the fuck is with this dark prejudice? Not a good color for the squad."

"It's not because he's a dark."

"Then what is it, huh? Cuz I have yet to hear why any of us are in fucking danger."

"Faerstathe is here because there's a dangerous criminal on the run, and he associated with you three publicly, so if you're not safe, that criminal could easily get to any of you to get leverage over him."

"Faerstathe…?"

"Malkarai. The dark."

"Can't say I'm on a full-name basis with the guy, but seriously? Cuz there's a criminal involved in this, we're in danger? Jesus, Olivia and Josh were and are always dealing with criminals, I can't say I've ever lost a minute of sleep over it."

"This guy is different…"

Cypha glanced at the girl and then back to Isaac before rolling her eyes and sighing. "I suppose I don't really have a choice in the matter, do I?"

"I mean… you do, but we'll just keep bothering you and standing watch out here if you refuse."

The girl glanced at Isaac, frowning.

Cypha groaned. "What does Josh have to say about all of this bullshit, anyway?"

"I don't know. Kalyfa didn't include him."

She scoffed. "How long am I going to be there? Should I bring clothing? Something to do?"

"Er, yeah, probably. It's the castle, so you'll want your coat. I don't know how long it's for. Until the danger has passed."

"The *least* you guys could do is get us a nice, heated place to be trapped in."

"It's not *that* cold."

"It's just made out of fucking rock. Fine. Aubrey looks like she doesn't want to freeze to death, and I can't sleep with guilt. Hold on, let me get my shit," she said, sighing as she shut her door.

After grabbing her keys from the hook by the door, she checked that the screen was in front of the fire and went back to her room. Immediately after passing the doorway, she pulled her phone from her pocket, unlocked it, and hit the button for Josh's contact info. She held the phone up to her ear as she pulled out a bag and put a book and clothing in it as she talked.

Her call was answered after a few rings.

"Hello…? Cypha?" Josh answered, perplexed.

"Hey, doofus. Let me guess, you're working."

"Uh, yeah, I'm on patrol. Why are you awake?"

"Because I have some of your coworkers standing outside my door, dragging my ass to your homey little castle on the hill for 'my safety.'"

"You… *what?*"

"Yeah, I guess you apparently aren't important enough to be included in this little extra credit project. But I really think you should be, because Dyspro's ass is already in the castle and has been since yesterday morning. So was Satyrna, but she got drugged by one of your coworkers and then escaped. So, maybe, you know, you should get involved and ask your boss what the fuck is happening."

"I-I didn't know about *any* of this, Cypha," he protested, sounding distressed.

"Yeah, I'm sure they all knew you'd have issues with it. Which you should. So, maybe stop being a good little lemming and do something about it."

"Cypha, I- I didn't know-"

"If you don't, I'm gonna call your mom."

She heard him make a noise, apparently flabbergasted, but didn't give him time to reply.

"Anyway, I need to leave. They're gonna get impatient. See you later. At least, I better."

She hung up and threw her bag over her shoulder before going to the door, grabbing her coat, and going outside. She pulled the door shut and pretended to lock it, although she just unlocked it again. "Let's go. There'd better be a fucking bed up there I can use, because it is asininely early."

"Thank you," Isaac said gratefully, turning and walking with Cypha. Aubrey followed.

Josh huffed softly, pulling his phone down from his ear and looking at the screen, confirming his suspicion that she'd hung up on him. He looked at the time and looked around him at the dark street he was standing on, distressed. He still had ten hours before he was off-duty and even able to check into what the hell she was talking about.

He was half-considering calling his mother himself.

# 13



Satyrna awoke when it was still dark. She blinked a few times, staring at the table to the side of the bed she was in, trying to figure out where she was. It took her a few moments, but eventually, she remembered she was in the extra room at Cypha and Dyspro's, and she'd gone in there earlier – last night? She wasn't sure. She just remembered being upset that Kalyfa was messing with her relationships, because he was actively trying to drive Malkarai out of town at least partially because she'd dared to befriend him.

She sighed, feeling bad again. Dyspro was still in knight custody, Malkarai was going to leave, and she and Cypha were afraid of going out because the knights wanted them in custody too.

Her thoughts felt a lot clearer now than they did even before she last fell asleep. She'd been better yesterday evening, but obviously, that inhalant had been affecting her more than she thought. She was still miserable though.

Eventually, she became aware of someone standing in the doorway. She turned her eyes toward the person and gasped, sitting up and scooting toward the headboard.

They took a step toward her. "What's wrong? Are you okay?"

Satyrna sighed, her shoulders dropping as she relaxed. Her heart was racing. "Oh, Malkarai… I thought…"

"I didn't mean to startle you," he said, coming a little closer, but stopping at about the foot of the bed.

"It's okay, I'm just frayed. How long were you there?"

"Only a few moments, I thought I heard you moving."

"What time is it?"

"After six."

She hesitated. "In the morning?"

"Yeah."

"Jeez," she mumbled, rubbing her eyes.

"Who did you think I was?"

"Kalyfa," she muttered. "Or maybe another knight. I don't know."

"You are really shaken up," he said gently.

"I'm angry. Why are you already up?"

"I've been up since 3:30. I didn't get a chance to go out last night, so I got up early this morning. I'm used to running on five hours of sleep, tops."

"Were you outside?"

"Yeah, I was in town."

"That's dangerous… they're hunting for you."

Malkarai shook his head. "If I don't want anyone to find me, they won't be able to."

Satyrna pushed the covers aside, frowning as she looked down. She still had the cloak around her, mostly, but it had been unclasped. "How… I don't remember getting under the covers."

"Cypha and I undid the cloak, took off your shoes, and put you under the covers."

"Oh. When was that?"

"Around eight, when it was obvious you were out for the night."

"I see." She was quiet for a few moments before looking up at him. "What's the guy you're following's name?"

He hesitated. "You could hear us, huh?"

"Yeah, I didn't fall asleep immediately."

"His current alias is Trebo. He's gone by a few names."

"Oh. Why are you going to talk to him?"

"To wrap up this job so I can focus on dealing with these knights."

"You know where he is?"

"Yeah, I'm pretty sure I found him."

Satyrna slid her legs over the side of the bed and stood up. "That's good, I guess." She grabbed the cloak, pulled it out of the covers, and wrapped herself back up in it. "Do you have your shirt on? I can't tell; it's too dark in here."

"Yeah. My stuff was dry last night."

"How's your wound feel?"

"Eh, it's itchy."

She sighed and went out into the main room. "Maybe you should've used real stitches."

"The super glue works just fine, thank you very much."

She sat down on the bench and looked out the window at the slowly lightening woods nearby before looking at Malkarai, who had leaned against the wall near the hall. "Where did you sleep last night?"

"Where you're sitting."

"Why didn't you use Dyspro's bed?"

"I'm not using anything unless the owner tells me it's all right to." He poked a straying log into the fire with his boot toe.

"I suppose it's an improvement over your car."

"And the ground."

Satyrna gave him an exasperated look. "You were serious about that?"

"Yes."

"Malkarai…"

He just shrugged dismissively. "It was only a few hours."

"So last night was probably the best sleep you've had all week, huh?"

"Yeah."

Satyrna shook her head, sighing. "Where is your car parked, anyway?"

"Outside of town, on the west side."

"Why outside of town?"

"So it doesn't get ticketed or towed. Being on foot has been more useful for me this time."

"You could probably move it over here."

He shook his head. "I don't want anyone to know I'm here."

"Do you think the knights know your car?"

"I mean, they might put together the pieces – but the car has a tracking chip in it. It's not *my* car. It's a work car."

"Oh," she said softly.

"So, yeah, it's better to leave it where it is."

She inhaled deeply and exhaled, pulling the cloak closer around her. "You don't want this thing back anytime soon, do you?"

"Why?"

"Cuz I like it, and my coat disappeared in the castle."

"It's just a stupid cloak. You could buy one downtown for forty bucks."

"Yeah, I guess, but it's warm – and it's yours."

He gave her an appraising look, but she didn't acknowledge it. "Just keep it," he said, turning away.

Satyrna looked up at him, perplexed. "Keep it?"

"Yeah."

"What are you gonna use instead?"

"It doesn't matter."

She stared at him, but he wasn't making eye contact. "How's the plan?" she asked pointedly.

"It's coming along pretty well. I have a feeling it'll be mostly improvisation though. I don't know the layout of the building."

"What's your plan?"

"I need to go and talk to my guy today, in the daylight, and then I was going to walk up to the front doors of the castle and call Kalyfa out."

Satyrna leaned forward slightly. "Call him out how?"

"On how illegal this shit is he's pulling."

"How…how do you expect that to go?"

Malkarai shrugged. "He'll probably try and fight me again."

"But… you'll beat him again, and it'll make it worse, won't it?" Satyrna said, frowning.

"I'm hoping to cause a reaction."

Satyrna stared at him, her eyes narrowing as she worked through what he wasn't saying. "Why?"

"Because my employers need to remind him of their agreement. What we do is necessary, and this treatment is dangerous – for us and for everyone else."

"If… if you take care of your work, why don't you just leave town after that?" Satyrna pressed, tentatively. "You don't need to put yourself in danger like this. You can just report to them what happened, and have someone else handle it. Can't you?"

"I don't want to go back."

Satyrna's eyes widened. She stood up and went over to him, pulling his shoulder so he faced her again.

"What?" he muttered. "Isn't that what you want?"

"You're not talking about quitting," she hissed. "You're talking about letting them kill you."

"You want everyone to end up happy, right?"

Satyrna slapped him across the face.

Malkarai winced, but then slowly opened his eyes, glaring at her.

She was furious. "Malkarai!" she yelled. "That is *not* a solution!"

"Do you want the knights to knock this off? Do you want you and your friends to be left alone? Well, this will end it. If I'm dead, my bosses will punish the knights for this, I'll be free of my job, I won't be unhappy anymore, and I'm sure it'll please a few people from where I'm from too. If you want the best possible outcome; here it is."

"I sure as hell won't be happy with that outcome!"

"Just drop it – I'm not worth saving."

"Yes, you are!"

"I know you want us to have some kind of friendship or something, but Satyrna, that isn't going to happen. If I just dropped it and went back home, we'd never interact again. What I have waiting for me back there – death is better."

"It's been fine for you so far!"

He shook his head, looking at the floor and walking away a few steps. "It has not. And it'll be even worse after all this."

"Why?"

"Because of what I'll lose."

"What are you going to lose?" she demanded, both confused and upset.

"I don't have any friends left. I… I let myself get idiotically optimistic that maybe I could, maybe I had made friends here, but that fucking note was a wake-up call that I can't have that. I lost my family years ago and I'm not allowed friends. So… I don't want to go back. I want it to end. I can't auto-pilot forever. This might actually do some good for other people though."

"Damn it, Malkarai… I can't see how this would do enough good for *anyone* to be worth you *dying*. Don't do this to me… We can't handle another dark losing their life because of this town. Because of us…" She angrily wiped tears out of her eyes. "You don't have to die," she said forcefully.

He stared at her, his expression unsettled. He didn't like seeing her cry. "What do you propose instead?"

"*Anything!*"

"Doing nothing still means I have to go home with even less than I came here with, and I was already on the precipice."

"Can't you *talk* to Kalyfa and get him to knock this shit off? This whole thing is just *asinine*."

"We tried talking last time, and he still ended up fighting me. I don't see how it would go any better this time."

"What about if we went together? Or if we got Dyspro's family to come with us and convince him to let him go with them? I-I really think there has to be a peaceful resolution to this."

"I'm pretty sure seeing you standing next to me will just enrage him."

"I don't fucking care! I-I'd rather stand next to you than him."

He shook his head. "I don't want to be used as ammo against your ex."

"*That's not* why I would rather stand next to you," Satyrna insisted, desperation in her voice.

"Then why-"

He cut off as she stepped up to him, grabbing him and then wrapping her arms around his torso. She hugged him tightly, gripping his shirt at his back as she pressed her cheek against his shoulder.

Satyrna felt him flinch and both heard and felt his sudden intake of breath. His whole body had stiffened, but she didn't let go.

"I don't want you to die… I want to get to know you better. I want you to live, for everyone to stop being ridiculous, and for us to just act like normal human beings!"

"Satyrna…" He lifted a hand and almost put it on the back of her shoulder, but didn't. "You're making this worse on me."

"How?" she demanded.

"I can't have this."

"What? Friends? Affection? *Anyone* on your side?"

"Yes," he replied quietly.

She let go, standing up and looking him in the eyes, fiercely. He shrank back a few inches, obviously uncomfortable with sustained and deliberate eye contact. She was still holding onto his shirt, although her grip had moved to the front. "You need it more than *anyone*. Do you want it?"

"Of course I do," he muttered.

"Then fight for *that*! You'll fight for your job; this is *way* more worth it."

"How?" he said, a trace of desperation in his voice. "They aren't leaving me any options."

"Go and actually *talk*. Don't just dismiss the long shot without even trying it. If we bring other people, they would probably be less likely to attack you."

He sighed. "That's true."

She pushed gently on his chest. "See, we have options."

"Can you talk to Dyspro's family? Would they agree to go with us?"

"I'm sure his siblings would. My sister probably would too. She'll probably complain about it, but she's technically on my side with most things."

His eyes narrowed briefly.

"Don't worry about that. Yes, I can talk to them."

"Okay. I need to talk to Trebo."

"Why does that have to be done before this?"

"It just has to be."

She sighed and shrugged. "Okay." She looked toward the hallway, her eyes narrowing slightly. "Hm."

"What is it?"

Satyrna let go of him and went back toward Cypha's room, pushing the slightly ajar door open farther. "We've been way too loud to not wake up Cypha." She peered at the bed in the low light. "Cypha, are you awake?"

Malkarai inhaled deeply, trying to swallow the frog in his throat.

"Malkarai, could you hand me a candle?"

He glanced back at her and then took one off of the fireplace. "Lit, yes?"

"Yes."

He lit it in the fire and then brought it back to her, peering into the room.

Satyrna took the candle and went into Cypha's room, scanning her unmade bed and then looking around the room. "Damn it."

"She's gone?"

"Yes." Satyrna lit up the bed table with the candle and then checked the windowsill. "Her phone is gone."

"Where's yours? Could she have messaged you?"

“It was in my coat.”

“Oh. Well, that sucks.”

“Yeah,” Satyrna said, disgruntled.

Malkarai gestured to Cypha’s bed. “Does it look like there was a struggle?”

“No, not really. I mean, she usually makes her bed after she gets up. Well, straightens the covers out. But it just kinda looks like she got up unexpectedly, not like she was forced out of bed.”

He looked at Satyrna. “The door was unlocked when I got back here.”

Satyrna pursed her lips together, thinking. “Why would they take her but not me? I mean, if you had been asleep out there, they most likely would’ve seen you. She’d have woken you up at least.”

“Yeah, I’m not a heavy sleeper.”

“So, she left while you were gone… Maybe she went willingly – or she answered the door and just didn’t let them see I was here.”

“No matter how she went, I think it’s pretty clear the knights got her too.”

Satyrna nodded, looking at him. “She wouldn’t have left me here alone otherwise.”

Malkarai shook his head. “It doesn’t change much. Does she have anyone you’d want to get to petition on her behalf?”

“I mean… she’s pretty much just got us and Josh.”

“Okay. He’s not going to help, is he?”

Satyrna shrugged. “I doubt it. If you thought Brendan had a conflict of interest, Josh’s would be worse. Well, he’d have more of a crisis over it.”

Malkarai smirked slightly. “Maybe we need some of that.”

Satyrna snorted, amused. “Maybe we do. Regardless, I don’t have a phone, and finding him is way harder than finding the rest of us, especially when he doesn’t want to be found, so just forget about him for now.” She blew the candle out and went out to the main room again. “Where was this from?”

“The mantle,” he replied, following her.

She put it back and then went over to the food box, shifting things. “Let’s eat and then we should go and do our things in town.”

A few hours later, after the sun had come up and they’d talked over timing and a list of people and things they needed to address, Malkarai and Satyrna locked up the cottage and headed into town. The entire way, Malkarai kept an eye out for knights, but he never saw any to his knowledge. When they made it to Third Street, he and Satyrna stopped.

"Before you go…" Malkarai took a switchblade from his coat and handed it to her. "Hide it. You know, just in case."

She smiled an evil little smile and turned the knife in her hand slowly, opening and closing the spring-loaded blade a few times. It was solid and well-made and opened smoothly. "Thanks. Maybe he'll stop treating me like a child if I can point a knife at his stupid face."

Satyrna thought she caught Malkarai smirking, but if there was one, then it was gone as fast as it came. She slipped the knife into her jeans and then adjusted the cloak on her shoulders.

"Maybe. Don't take it out for threats though – I was thinking more it might be functionally useful somehow."

"I suppose," she said with a sigh.

"Tell Dyspro's siblings, if they agree to help, that they should meet me and you at the inn at Central and Sixth at three."

Satyrna nodded. "Good luck with… Trebo, was it?"

"Yeah. Thanks," he said and started down the street. "See you in a few hours."

# 14



Malkarai walked into the inn and up to the desk where a woman was reading a book. He cleared his throat, and she looked up.

"Can I help you?"

"Yeah, is there a man by the name of Trebo here?"

She got a better look at him and saw he was a dark, and her congenial tone turned icy. "What's it of your business?"

"He's a friend of mine."

"We don't have that name registered. Is that his last name?"

Malkarai thought for a moment, honestly not sure what alias he might be using this time. He took a shot. "No. D'vane?"

The receptionist nodded, begrudgingly.

"What room is he in?"

"12."

"Is he in?"

"I don't know. You can see. It's upstairs."

"Thanks." Malkarai started down a hallway and then went up the stairs, shaking his head and muttering under his breath, "Well, *that* name is a hell of a choice, man…" He soon found room 12 and knocked on it.

There was no response.

Malkarai hesitated, listening. After a few moments, he knocked again, leaning close to the door to listen better. He heard slight movement inside, but still no response.

"Open up. I need to talk to you."

There was the faintest of sounds, like a foot on the carpet, but still nothing happened to the door.

"Please. There has to be a good reason for me to break protocol, so hear me out."

The door opened. A man not much older than himself stood there. He had shaggy brown hair that just went past his ears, green eyes, and a tall, strong build. He was wearing a nondescript brown T-shirt and blue jeans and was clean-shaven.

"You should shave more often. The hobo look just isn't you," Malkarai said casually.

Trebo's tone was suspicious and his eyes narrow. "Is this a social call or a work one?"

"Relax; I'm not here to work."

Trebo eyed Malkarai distrustfully.

"I need to talk to you."

"Well, here I am."

"Can I come in?"

"Why?"

"Because I'm already in deep enough shit, don't make me in danger of exposing confidential information too."

Trebo stared unfalteringly at him, eyes still narrowed for a few moments before opening the door farther. He had his sword in his hand. "All right, but take all your weapons and put them on the bed. I'm not taking chances."

Malkarai took his coat off and dropped it on the bed next to a mostly packed duffel bag. Then he drew his sword and set it on top of his coat. "Going somewhere?"

"Yeah. I intended to move since you had already found out where I was and I'm still not sure where your loyalty lies." He looked Malkarai up and down. "Do you have any others?"

"If I did, do you honestly think I would tell you?" Malkarai said smugly.

Trebo ignored him, closed the door, and said, "All right, what do you want?"

"What exactly are you thinking? 'D'vane'? Really?"

Trebo crossed his arms as he leaned against the chest of drawers. "Oh, so you didn't sneak in here."

"No, I walked in the front door."

He relaxed slightly and sighed, still gazing at Malkarai with an unenthused expression. "What do you want?"

"I need to tell you something… and request something of you, I suppose."

"What makes you think I'm going to do anything for you?"

"It's to your advantage that you do."

Trebo furrowed his brow, interested and concerned at the same time. "What is it…?"

"I'm dropping the mission."

He sighed. "They won't let you do that, you know."

"No, they won't. Especially since you've been such a pain in their ass lately."

"Then how do you propose you 'drop' it?"

Malkarai looked his target in the eye, evading the question. "Run. Leave the country. You're already mobile, just get out of here."

Trebo raised an eyebrow, searching Malkarai's face for a few moments before responding. "Why?"

"I'm not going to finish it."

"Well, great, I'm glad to hear that, but you know I'm still here for a reason."

"Yeah, but you need to drop it. Give it up."

He frowned, shifting against the dresser. "I don't think you get to decide that for me. I've waited this long."

"I'm trying to tell you that there's nothing to wait for anymore," Malkarai insisted.

"You're standing right in front of me, you dumbass."

"Not for long."

Trebo tipped his head, giving Malkarai a perplexed look. "What are you talking about?"

"Look, things here in Cavington have gotten bad."

"What do you mean?"

"Their law enforcers are after me."

"What the hell for? They're supposed to work *with* you."

"I stopped a thief when I first arrived in town. The girl the kid stole from pursued me after the thief was handled. Well, she turned out to be the head knight's ex – one he is most definitely not ready to let go of."

"Why'd she pursue *you*?" Trebo asked, confused.

Malkarai gave him a look, his eyebrows knitted up. "Thanks," he said sarcastically.

Trebo sighed and looked at the ceiling for a moment. "Oh, shut up. I meant you're a dark. A very suspicious-looking dark at that."

"That's exactly why she pursued me. Because I'm dark. I can't explain the girl. Anyway, she eventually got me talking – mostly cuz she wouldn't shut up and she eventually hit a topic of interest."

"What was that?" Trebo asked, humoring him.

"We'd met before. Eleven years ago."

Trebo stared at him. "What? Seriously?"

"Yes."

Trebo scoffed. "Well, that's an unexpected turn of events. That was *not* my plan, by the way."

"If it was, I'd have applauded how magnificently you were able to set things up."

"I'm a goddamn wizard, but this time wasn't my doing."

Malkarai rolled his eyes. "Don't make yourself feel good. Anyway, it didn't exactly work out in my favor, because she convinced me to go to a tavern with her and her two friends, and it pissed off Kalyfa Desfete, the head knight."

"Oh, great," Trebo muttered.

"Yeah. Stika announced my presence, so when one of his knights spotted me, he joined the patrol and they followed me around until I got sick of it and faced them." Malkarai told him about what had happened the past few days, since his fight with the knight patrol.

Trebo shook his head thoughtfully, his eyes on the floor as he listened to Malkarai.

"I'm here now because I'm going to go and confront Kalyfa, and I'm not so sure it's going to end well for me, so I want you to go. Go before the system figures out what happened. It'll give you a head start."

"Why did they rough you up?" Trebo asked.

Malkarai shrugged. "Kalyfa probably knows exactly what I am and what I do, but the other knights are just following his orders. His men attacked me first, so I don't know if that was orchestrated or just bad communication – but the fact of the matter is that *they* attacked first and Kalyfa didn't tell them to stand down."

"What did you tell them you're here for?"

"I told Satyrna and the others I deal in private investment and I'm meeting with a client – which is kind of true – but I don't blame them for being a little suspicious. I haven't had to make up shit to cover my ass in a long time. No one ever sees me, so I've gotten kind of out of practice explaining myself. No one ever asks me, 'So, what do you do for a living?'"

Trebo scoffed. "Yeah, that's a nice conversation starter."

"Yeah, there's nowhere to go from there. The conversation's pretty much over by that point. Last night, some knights dropped a note off threatening to put a kill order out on me. By this point, I was only still there because Dyspro's state was in question. Satyrna's afraid they hurt him."

"What did the note say?"

"That, unless I got out of town, they'd tell the sheriff I attacked them without a reason and get a warrant to eliminate me. He wants me gone, dead, or, at the very least, in deep shit. I broke a rule by being around those three."

"Dear God, the associating with civilians rule is just so you're not having social time when you leave on missions," Trebo groaned.

"Yeah, I know. Kalyfa is pissed that I associated with Satyrna, of all people. Whatever. My guess is he has a vendetta against the system, but I don't know for sure. He doesn't want us in Cavington, but there's an agreement in place."

"Oh, yeah, why the hell are you telling me this, instead of calling your superiors?"

"Well…I have my reasons."

"Enlighten me," Trebo said pointedly, his head tipped as he stared at Malkarai.

Malkarai sighed. "I want out."

"Finally. Why now? You could have done it ages ago, you know."

"No, I couldn't… Look, I can't… I can't do it your way."

"Why not?"

"You didn't sign the contract. You didn't have the record I do. You didn't have the rank I do. Stika was able to get capture listed as an option on your record, but that won't happen for me. My desertion will definitely cause more problems than yours. If the knights don't kill me, I'm sure the ASA will."

"Do you expect me to just hop the border and let you walk into a trap?"

"If you were the brilliant mastermind you claim to be, you would."

Trebo shook his head, frowning at him. "Malkarai, why do you want to die?"

Malkarai just stared at him for a few moments before changing the subject. "You're off the hook for now. Get good and lost. Leave the country. Just stop hanging around here. Oh." Malkarai reached into his back pocket, causing Trebo to tense up. He pulled out his wallet, slipped the badge and its attached leather piece out, and held it out to him. "This is better with you than with me. Use it if you need to."

Trebo hesitantly took the silver badge. "Malk… you're serious about this, huh?"

"Yes, I am. I tried to do this before, a different way – a cowardly way. At least this way I'll get to save somebody else."

"Are you dumping the ASA because of those three?"

"No, I'm dumping the ASA because of Arista. This is just a convenient situation for it. But, Satyrna doesn't want me to just sacrifice myself. She and her friends have been trying to protect darks ever since their two friends were executed as children. I'm going to let her think I have a fighting chance – she's out gathering reinforcements for me."

"But you're hoping they kill you, huh?"

"It would make everything easier for everyone, yes. I'm not going to tell Satyrna that though."

Trebo shook his head and handed the badge back to Malkarai, making him take it. "There's a flaw in your plan."

"What's that?"

"Teffifa's here."

He blinked, his eyes widening. "What?"

"She followed you."

"She's not healed."

"No, she's not, but Stika apparently wanted insurance. She's not me, but she can follow you better than most."

"Are you *positive* she's here?"

"Yeah, the bitch cut my coat and gave me these," he moved his left arm, motioning to the twin slashes on his bicep that looked like they'd been recently treated with disinfectant and butterfly closures.

Malkarai groaned, tipping his head back and looking at the ceiling briefly. "Was it just her?"

"Yeah, pretty sure. Who else would be with her?"

"She has two partners."

"Oh, right. No, I didn't see the other two. You should talk to her. She could tell them you're dead. Give *her* your badge. Not me."

"I can't talk to her. Then she'll know I'm not."

"She'll be better evidence than you just going missing. And why the hell would I dig for your badge? So it looks like I killed an agent? I don't think so. Anyway, killing you would just legitimatize this asinine manhunt. I'm innocent so far."

Malkarai frowned and sat down on the edge of the bed, rubbing his forehead. "Shit. Well, whatever; if I'm dead, it won't matter who tells them."

Trebo sighed, rubbing an old scar under his shirt sleeve on his right bicep, the uninjured one, with his thumb. "Why do you want to die?"

"Why not?"

"That's not an answer."

"Why would I want to keep going? I'm alone there, Traphian. I'm sick of it."

Trebo stared at him for a few moments, complacently. "I don't go by that name anymore."

Malkarai looked up at him, at first not realizing what he'd said. "What? Oh. Shut the fuck up; you're using your real last name – you can claim your first name too. You've never been anything else to me, no matter how many lame aliases you made up."

Trebo sighed, set his sword down on the dresser, and walked over to Malkarai, grabbing his arm and turning it over to stare at his forearm, then letting go and looking at the right. He didn't see what he was looking for though.

Malkarai took his right arm away from him, making a face. "I'm not that pathetic. Give me more credit than that."

He raised an eyebrow, looking at Malkarai judgingly. "What'd you do then?"

Malkarai shook his head. "It doesn't matter. Stika put an end to it."

"They'll care if you disappear, Malkarai. And I don't just mean for contract or administrative reasons. You had other people there. More than just Arista."

"I don't care."

"What if you don't die doing this? Sounds like you're getting help with it while we speak."

"I don't know, but it's time for a change, no matter what. I'm going crazy."

"Arista wouldn't want you to get yourself killed."

"Don't tell me what she would or wouldn't have wanted," he responded sharply.

Trebo narrowed his eyes. "I know that well enough. She would not have wanted you to kill yourself over her."

"Tell me what else I have going for me now then."

"Life."

"One like yours? Where you can't even go by your name or settle in a place for more than a few days? Yeah, that sounds great."

"It's a whole lot better than having my soul owned by the ASA."

Malkarai snorted. "It was bearable when we were all in it together. But you left and then Arista disappeared. With you both gone, what makes you think I'm happy there? I don't want them hunting me down either. What other option do I have?"

"I still think you should ask Teffifa to tell them you're dead. She'll do it."

"Why do you think she'll do it?"

"You're competition for her."

"You act like it's some kind of game."

"No, it's a job. With you gone, she'd get more work. You know she'd love getting more work."

Malkarai sighed.

"Hell, if Stika knows you're suicidal, it'll only help the lie."

"I don't know where to find her," he said, defeatedly.

"Call her."

"My phone's dead. I haven't been in a place with outlets long enough to let it charge."

"Do you have it on you?"

"The phone, yes. The charger is in my bag at Dyspro and Cypha's place."

Trebo sighed. "She's not that hard to find, Malkarai. She's the Ripper, for crying out loud. You act like she hides like you."

"She should. She's too flipping obvious," he muttered bitterly.

Trebo shook his head and went to the window. "Teffifa wants to stand out. It's in her nature. Anyway, you're wasting time. What do you intend to do to free them?"

Malkarai eyed him. "Why?"

"Well, if that girl wants to keep you alive, she needs all the help she can get. She doesn't know what she's up against in you."

Malkarai blinked and sat upright. "You want to help?"

Trebo turned around with a smile. "Well, if we're going to break rules, why not break them all? I always loved doing that."

Malkarai stared at him blankly for a few moments, surprised.

"Unless you're still sore about that thing I left in your face..." Trebo's smile disappeared.

Malkarai shook his head. "No, no... I just... didn't think you'd want to help..."

"I've been waiting for you to say 'up yours' to the system for seven years, Malkarai. Yeah, I wanna help. I don't want you to die even more than that girl doesn't." He paused. "And I really am sorry about that."

"About what?"

"The gash. I mean, the scar's pretty obvious..." he frowned. "Is that why you wear your hair long now?"

Malkarai scoffed quietly. "No, but it helps hide it, yes."

"Oh... still, I'm sorry."

Malkarai waved a hand at him dismissively. "I forgave you for that years ago. Chill out." He ran his thumb over the scar along his jaw. "The scar's kinda cool. My jaw aches sometimes though."

"Sorry."

"You say sorry again I'm gonna give you one to match."

Trebo smirked. "Noted."

Malkarai looked up at him, a sincere expression on his face. "Thank you. If I'm going to succeed at this, I'm going to need a miracle. Can I call you Traphian though? Trebo is so damn lame."

He frowned. "Hey, I liked it. But, yeah, you can call me Traphian. Just, not where people can hear you. I'd prefer to not be followed anymore."

"You're still gonna be followed."

Traphian grinned. "Not if we have Teffifa tell them you killed me before you cacked it."

Malkarai's eyebrows raised. "We're putting an awful lot on Teffifa."

"Yeah, well, I'm sure she doesn't want to go up against either of us again, so she'll do it. But let's refine this plan of yours, shall we?"

"All right."

# 15

Satyrna and Patricia stepped out of their house, Patricia buttoning up her coat. "All right, I'll go talk to Brendan. Satyrna, don't do anything stupid, okay?"

Satyrna sighed. "Patricia, I'm going to do what I have to."

"We all will – but I mean it. Don't throw away everything you have for this dark. He's a stranger, no matter how nice you may think he is. If things turn out to be different than you thought, then stop. I'll let you know what I find out, okay?"

Satyrna nodded. "Thanks. See you later."

At the corner, the two sisters parted ways. Patricia headed for the castle, Satyrna for the inn Malkarai had designated.

Satyrna had barely left her street when she was aware of the two knights across the street, walking along the buildings. She licked her suddenly dry lips and felt the lump that the knife made, just for reassurance. They didn't waste any time; they crossed and walked straight over to her.

She broke into a run, but one quickly caught up to her and shoved her into an alley and up against a wall. "Just-!" she cried when she saw the one approaching pulling something out of his pocket. They both stopped briefly. "Just don't *drug* me, *please.*"

The one that had caught her looked at his partner, bewildered. "Drug you?"

The other one pulled his phone from his pocket, frowning. "Why would you think we would drug you?"

"I don't know! The last guy that was guarding me did."

The knights exchanged a concerned look.

"We don't do that," one insisted.

"Yeah, well that guy certainly fucking did," Satyrna protested.

"We won't. Will you come with us peacefully?"

"If you aren't going to do anything illegal, I guess," she said, still displeased.

"Thank you."

"Uh, I'll call Kalyfa…" the one with the phone said before unlocking his screen.

Teffifa hummed to herself as she wandered down a street, searching as idly as she had the night before. She perked up as she heard a low voice from the shadows.

"Teffifa…"

She smiled, not even looking in his direction. "Ah, there you are. Where the hell have you been? I've been looking for you. Why don't you answer your stupid phone?"

"It's dead. Why are you here?" Malkarai asked.

"Stika wanted me to shadow you."

His voice turned venomous. "I told her I wanted to do this alone!"

"Yeah, well, she's afraid you'll try and kill the wrong person."

"What?"

She turned her head and gave the shadows where he was hiding a steady look.

"You know too?" he exclaimed angrily.

She looked away. "I found your sorry ass."

"Who else knows?!"

"Just us two. That's why she sent me. I'm just backup. I won't do a thing unless you need me to, but I'm not going back until it's over."

"You coulda helped the other night instead of letting that gang beat the shit out of me."

She cocked her head, looking back at the shadows. "What are you talking about? What gang?"

"You weren't following me two nights ago?"

"No. I didn't get here until yesterday morning, and I hadn't found you until now. You're a bitch to track, Malk."

He was quiet for a few moments. "Who the hell was following me then? I figured it was an ASA spy… They weren't bad."

Teffifa shrugged. "You should be worried about Trebo, not who the ASA sent to watch your ass."

"And you should be less concerned with him and more with what your real objective here is. You attacked him again," he replied with a scowl.

"How do you know that?"

"That's irrelevant."

"I mean, not really. So, you *do* know where he is? I thought maybe he'd just been hiding too well, but I guess I was wrong. Why didn't *you* help me?"

"You weren't supposed to be attacking him."

"I played around with him a little. The guy practically walked into me. He knew I was here."

"You fought him."

"And you expect me not to? Relax, Malk, he's already kicked my ass once."

"Yeah, and I had to sew you up. You know you're not healed yet. I really don't want to have to re-stitch that arm, and I'm sure it wouldn't feel very good for you either."

"Yeah, yeah," Teffifa said. "Stika told me not to try it again. I just wanted to scare the shithead a little. The result would've been the same if I had fought him or not – it's not like I could wave my hands and tell him he never saw me."

Malkarai sighed and moved on. "You're here to help me. I need your help now."

"You haven't even confronted him yet."

"I don't need help with him."

She turned completely toward the shadows where Malkarai's voice was coming from. "What?"

"Come here."

When Teffifa reached where she surmised her peer was, she jumped and whipped out one of her swords, pointing it at Traphian. His eyes widened and he took a step back.

"Faerstathe, what the hell is going on here?!"

Malkarai stood up and knocked her sword away from Traphian. "Teffifa, cool it. Things have changed. I need you to listen to me."

She looked at him, her red eyes wild. "Malkarai, he's standing right there! Why haven't you finished it yet? I thought you were having problems getting him alone, that's why you hadn't done it yet. Did you even intend to finish it?!"

"Originally, yeah. I did. But then I woke up."

Traphian eyed him.

She shook her head, reaching for her other sword, her eyes still wide. "Aw, fuck. Me being here just fucked up your elopement plans, didn't it? Look, I don't care that much," she said rapidly. "I'm not here to fight. This probably wouldn't even be a fair fight; he fucked my arm up-"

Malkarai stood between her and Traphian, his arms wide. Traphian just gave her a jaded look from over Malkarai's shoulder. "Teffifa, stand down," Malkarai said firmly. "We aren't going to fight you. That's not why I was looking for you."

"Why the fuck wouldn't you? I'm a loose end! I know you two are standing here, not slitting each other's throats!"

"Man, is that really what you guys think of me?" Traphian scoffed.

"It's certainly what the system thinks you'll do!" She was starting to look slightly less panicked though, like she was working through what she was seeing.

"Until I ran into you, I don't think I'd drawn enough blood on one of the agents to even warrant a Band-Aid," Traphian said, his eyes narrowed.

"And do you think I could live with myself if I ever hurt one of you guys?" Malkarai pressed.

She frowned, glancing between them for a few moments before resting on Malkarai. "I dunno. I thought you'd turned that off the past few years."

"Yeah, I had. I woke up. Just stop, okay?" Malkarai said. "Something far more pertinent than hunting down my brother is going on. We're in danger here."

Her lip curled. "Well, yeah, *you* are – you just dropped some serious bombs *and* you're in dark-hater territory."

"I know that, but that's not what I meant. We're all in trouble because we're agents."

She narrowed her eyes. "No one knows we exist, Malkarai."

"The police do. And, the police in this town do not support us. You know about the knights, don't you?"

After explaining the situation to Teffifa, Malkarai moved on to the current problem. "Now, what I need you to do is–"

She put up her hands. "Wait, wait, wait. So, let me get this straight."

He paused unwillingly but nodded slightly.

"This girl pissed off her ex-boyfriend by talking to you, and all hell broke loose because of it."

"Mostly because of what I am, but yes. He doesn't give a shit that it was her that pursued me, not the opposite."

"And so, you intend to go in there and… what? Get that guy and girl out?"

"Yes."

"Why the hell do you even care? I mean, you can leave, and they'll just let them go."

"Maybe."

"Maybe? Why maybe?"

"Dyspro apparently told them he'd rather die than help them get me. I've already seen how personally charged these knights are – I can see a tempered reaction happening, whether I leave or not. And also, they have an agreement with the government – treating agents like this is wrong. We're supposed to be on the same side. If Traphian was actually a threatening criminal, then this bullshit that Kalyfa is pulling would've truly put innocent people in harm's way."

"Eh, that's giving a little too much credit to these local yokels. What makes you think they've thought any of this through with anything bigger than their small heads?"

Traphian snorted in amusement, but Malkarai ignored her.

"The police seem to be on a par with the other police forces we've dealt with, but these knights are something else. They're trained to fight and damage, not just subdue; they deal with the big issues in town; and they aren't uniformed. All of these are dangerous elements."

Teffifa sighed, looking pensively out at the street. "You do realize that you're just walking into his waiting arms, Malkarai, right?"

"Yes, but Satyrna is doing her best to make sure I don't get killed."

She shook her head. "That girl's best won't do it. Look, I don't see why you have Trebo here working with you. You should be running, you moron," she added to Traphian. "Cuz when he's done, we're just gonna have to go after you anyway. Well, someone is. You don't get to just send a card to Chicago saying, 'Just kidding!' You're damn near a level six now."

Traphian sneered.

Malkarai sighed. "Teffifa, that's where you come in, okay?"

She looked at him, but stayed quiet, listening.

"I want you to cover for me, tell Stika I'm dead. Tell her I took care of Trebo, but that I was injured too badly to survive. I mean, you can embellish all you want. Tell her I tried to take care of the wound or whatever. If you want to give her something of proof, Traphian and I can both give you something. You can't call the police here to clean up, so you won't need a body immediately. We can both leave and it's not on you, it can just look like we tricked you."

Teffifa stared at him. "Why?"

"Because it's either this or I really kill myself. The anger shit's wearing thin. I can't handle it anymore."

"No, why should I tell Stika this? That's treason and a lot of other shit I don't want on my record, Malkarai. I know how to check a pulse. I'm very familiar with mortal wounds."

"Because then you won't get sent after either me or Traphian again. Because they won't send your partners after us. Because I won't be at the agency anymore – you'll get more work. Because I've never asked you to do anything like this before, Teffifa, and I've covered for you dozens of times. Please."

She looked at Malkarai for a few more moments before glancing at Traphian. "So, you're gonna run off together. Aw, that's so sweet."

Traphian sighed and made a face. "You're such a freak."

"Will you do it?" Malkarai pressed, looking anxious.

She frowned at him contemplatively. "The last thing I want to do is lie. I hate lying. You know how hard lies are to keep straight when your head is as chaotic as mine is?"

"Your brain being chaotic should honestly be helpful in this situation," Malkarai insisted. "If you mess up any details, anxiety and stress can easily be blamed for that."

She sighed. "That's why I don't lie, dumbass."

"Good. Your good record will help."

She looked sidelong at Traphian for a few moments, still frowning, before looking back to Malkarai. "Yeah. Fine."

Malkarai looked relieved. "You'll do it then?"

"Yeah. But if they ever find your ass, you are covering for me in every way possible, Faerstathe."

He smiled. "I promise I will. Thank you."

"But, one other question…"

"Yeah?"

"Why am I in danger too?"

"Did Stika announce you?"

"To the authorities? Nah, you were already here."

"Well, if they find out that there's another agent here, you can bet they'll be pissed. They've probably already noticed you're here. You stand out more than me."

She frowned. "I suppose I should get going then, huh?"

"Yeah, probably."

Teffifa hesitated for a few moments, silently staring at the ground. "I think I should do something first."

"What?"

"Make sure you actually live through this crazy shit you plan on doing tonight."

Malkarai's brow knitted up. "Why does everyone think I won't make it?"

Traphian scoffed. "Because you didn't want to."

"Because you tried to kill yourself before," Teffifa responded in the like.

Malkarai sighed. "Things have changed."

"Yeah, you haven't tried to do it since. But I have to wonder just how hard you'll try to avoid injury anyway."

"I'm not going to try and die, Teffifa. I've been scolded enough for one day about my death apparently being a terrible thing."

"He's helping, right?" Teffifa pointed at Traphian.

"Yes."

"Then let me. Besides, you should keep yourself in plain view, so he doesn't think you're trying to liberate those kids." She nodded at Traphian. "He and I are as good as you. Better, together. We can do it for you."

Malkarai stared at her, thinking that over. It made sense. "Why? Why do you want to help me?"

"Cuz yeah, you're a pain in my ass, Faerstathe, but we're friends. If I'm gonna lie to the ASA about your fate, I'm gonna at least make sure it's for a good reason and that my stories line up. I'll make sure you're actually gonna live, and then I'll go back to the agency."

Malkarai sighed, smiling. "Thanks."

Teffifa kicked him in the shin lightly. "Just cuz she's gone, don't think you've got no friends left."

Malkarai avoided her eyes, but a smile lingered on his lips.

"So, what's the plan?"

Malkarai looked around and shook his head. "I'd rather not discuss it out here." He looked at Traphian. "Can we go back to your room?"

Traphian sighed and nodded. "I must be crazy… inviting two agents back to my room."

"I think your record is against you if you're trying to plead sane to anything, buddy," Teffifa scoffed.

Malkarai smirked. "Relax. I'll keep her under control."

Teffifa gave him a look. "What's that supposed to mean?"

"That you're… excitable."

Traphian laughed. "Yeah, that's one way to put it."

Teffifa crossed her arms. "You're both jealous."

Traphian shook his head and Malkarai just smiled.

In the room at the inn, Traphian and Malkarai sat on the bed and Teffifa leaned against the wall near the window.

"So… who else is supposed to be there to save your ass?"

"Satyrna, Dyspro's siblings, and you guys."

Teffifa frowned. "That's it?"

Malkarai shrugged. "Yeah. Satyrna's sister is going to talk to her boyfriend, who's a knight, to keep him out of things."

"How many siblings does Dyspro have?"

"Three sisters, one brother. Honestly, I'm hoping that the whole thing stays peaceful because I'm there with their family. It was asinine that they fought me in the first place – we're not supposed to be enemies."

"Where are these two being held?"

"We're about ninety percent sure it's the castle. It's possible that they put them somewhere besides where Satyrna was, but doubtful. This is a knight affair, not a police one."

Traphian made a face. "Castle?"

"It's a stronghold. Looks like a prison minus the bars."

"How freaking random."

"Yeah," Malkarai agreed.

"Where in the castle?"

"I don't know. See, that's something that Patricia was going to try and find out. Satyrna was fairly certain Brendan would be sympathetic to our problem."

"Okay, so we find out from her where to go and sneak in."

Malkarai nodded. "It's important to not be seen. When you find them, let me know. That's when I'll draw their attention."

"How should we let you know?" Traphian asked.

Malkarai nodded to Teffifa. "You call me."

"You gonna charge your phone?"

"Yeah. You have your charger?"

She dug in a pocket on the inside of her coat and then tossed him a black cord. Malkarai dug his phone out from his coat and plugged it into an outlet. He stared at the screen on the phone as it turned back on. "Wow, I missed a lot of calls."

"Yeah. I called you nearly fifty times. Stika was trying to get a hold of you too."

He made a face. "I only missed thirteen calls, not fifty. I told her my phone was dying. I forgot to turn it off the last time I called her, so the battery ran dry."

"What if we get separated?" Traphian asked, looking at Teffifa.

"Well, that'd be a shame, wouldn't it?"

He raised an eyebrow. "Not at all."

"You can't call me even if you still have your phone," Malkarai said with a shake of his head. "They keep track of our phones. After this ends, I intend to let this die again."

"I'll take it back with me along with your badge. Be sure to get some blood on them."

Malkarai smirked. "All right."

"What if we get separated?" Traphian reiterated, impatiently.

Malkarai looked at Teffifa and then back at him. "Don't. I don't know what this place is like inside."

"We'll be able to cover more ground separately," Teffifa pointed out.

"Hopefully we won't need to cover much ground if Satyrna's sister comes through."

"Good point."

"I know you two can think on your feet. Just, do what you do best."

Teffifa grinned.

Malkarai gave her a reprimanding look. "On second thought, Traphian, you do what you do best, Teffifa, you do what you do third best."

She laughed and cocked her head. "What would be one and two?"

"Going berserk and getting injured. Don't get caught, okay?"

She waved a hand at him. "Puh, ye of little faith."

"And, don't – don't – kill anyone, okay?"

Teffifa sighed and Traphian gave Malkarai a look. "Wow, you're going all out, aren't you?"

"If my new goal is to survive, I don't care to make these people any more pissed off with me."

"Can I at least hurt them a little?" Teffifa begged.

Malkarai shrugged, conceding. "Nothing crippling or potentially fatal, okay? Don't forget they're law enforcers."

"All right… Okay, after we get the kids free, what do we do? Join you?"

"Well, ideally, no. You should get them out of the building and stay there. Keep those two out of it. We don't want them to know they're gone until I've left. I suppose you two could come back and linger outside in case I do need help with combat."

"What do you intend to do?" Traphian asked, watching Malkarai pace the floor between the bed and the dresser.

"Well, talk to Kalyfa, I suppose. I don't know what will happen. He may get aggressive, he may not. Maybe I'll be able to convince him that I intend to leave town. Maybe he'll just try to stab my heart out as soon as he sees me. I don't know."

"You seem to hold a lot of stock in the knights' fighting ability."

"I know Kalyfa's good. The knights are mediocre, at best. But, there're more of them than us. Besides, I don't particularly care if I get hurt, but none of the kids are like us. I don't want them hurt at all."

"All right."

3:10 p.m.

A few hours later, Malkarai, standing in the shadows, watched the front of the inn for people to show up and wait. There were two teenage girls and a guy his age loitering there, looking around. He assumed these were at least some of Dyspro's siblings, but didn't feel like appearing until necessary.

The boy was of average height and seemed fairly athletic. He was pretty calm though, and, if he was indeed Dyspro's brother, was a lot less talkative than his brother. The older girl had the same sort of temperament as him, but she seemed more reprimanding. She had brown eyes and dirty blonde hair that seemed to want to be naturally wavy but had been dried to straightness.

The other girl acted like a female Dyspro, which made Malkarai believe he had guessed their identities correctly. She had shoulder-length, straight, brown hair, blue eyes and was constantly poking at her sister, both verbally and physically. She seemed a fair bit more energetic than her sister and, due to her younger age, seemed a little skinnier. Her older sister seemed to be constantly, automatically, telling her to be quiet or stop being obnoxious. Her brother offered her no help, visibly smirking most of the time.

After a while, two blonde girls walked up together, one with long wavy hair and brown eyes, the other with short, straight hair and hazel eyes. The boy turned and greeted them as they approached.

"Hey, Patricia. Hey, Lauren."

Patricia smiled. "Hi, Seth. Long time no see."

The youngest girl waved happily at the two and the other just smiled, her irritation dismissed.

"Lauren! I haven't seen you in at least a week! Why haven't you been around?" The youngest threw herself on the long-haired girl, hugging her tight.

Lauren laughed. "Sorry, Kirena, I've been working a lot."

Patricia looked around. "Has Satyrna shown up yet?"

"Nope, just us," Kirena replied, rather perkily.

"Is she supposed to be here by now?" the youngest blonde asked warily.

Patricia made a face. "Well, I'd assume so, but I don't see the dark she was hanging around either."

Malkarai frowned and slipped back, around the corner, paused, and then came back around, not hiding this time. He figured coming out of hiding right next to them would be a bad plan if he wanted them to trust him.

"I'm here. Satyrna's not though."

Kirena and Patricia jumped, but the other young one just looked at him steadily. "You've been over there a while, haven't you?" she asked.

Malkarai's face broke into an amused smile. He'd thought she'd seen him a few times. He was pretty impressed. "Yeah. You've got very good eyes."

She smiled slightly. "Thanks."

"What's your name? I caught the rest of yours. Kirena, Seth, Lauren, and Patricia," he said to each to prove he had.

"Akena."

"I'm Malkarai Faerstathe."

Seth was eyeing him warily. "Why were you hiding over there?"

"Standing out in the open is not a good plan for me right now. I'm sure you're all aware of the situation."

They nodded.

"Well, I hate to the bearer of worse news, but if Satyrna hasn't come back here by now, she's probably been taken too."

Patricia looked quite distressed and Seth sighed audibly.

"So, I propose we go inside instead of standing on the sidewalk."

Lauren looked at Seth, who looked at the building suspiciously. "What's in there?"

"Two more allies and a private room. We have a plan, but I don't feel comfortable explaining it out here in the open."

Seth still looked doubtful, but Lauren sighed and slugged him in the arm. "Oh, stop worrying, Seth. He's trying to help. Let's just go inside. It's cold out here anyway."

Malkarai waited until it looked like Seth had conceded and then headed for the door. Inside the lobby, he glanced back at them. "Okay, one of the allies is perfectly normal-looking. The other's... well, kinda scary. She scares me sometimes. But, it's mostly for show. So, don't get too freaked out, okay? They're going to help us out."

The others nodded guardedly.

Malkarai smirked slightly. There wasn't much he could say that could prepare them for Teffifa, but a little warning was better than nothing.

Traphian was pacing near the door when Malkarai knocked and came in. "The door's unlocked," Malkarai said warningly to him.

He made a face. "Teffifa's been watching you. Chill."

Teffifa looked over to examine the group as they came into the room, smirked slightly at the stares Kirena and Patricia gave her, and looked back out the window. "What's she look like, Malk?"

"Satyrna?"

"Yeah."

"Long brown hair, green eyes. Almost half a foot shorter than me. She's wearing my cloak. Oh, and her hair is braided today."

"'K."

"She out there?" Lauren asked.

"Nope. Just wanted a good description in case she did show up."

Malkarai turned to the others as Traphian locked the door and leaned against it. "Uh, make yourself comfortable, I guess. Patricia, were you able to talk to Brendan?"

Patricia nodded.

Kirena sat down on the edge of the bed and was joined by Lauren a few moments later. The others continued to stand, Seth warily, Akena calmly, looking around.

"He said he doesn't know much, but he did talk to Josh this morning. Josh is their friend." Malkarai nodded. "He's not happy," Patricia said with a sigh.

"I'd imagine he's not," Lauren put in.

Patricia shook her head in agreement and continued. "Kalyfa's told them it's for their protection, but, while the other knights accept what he said without much question, Josh is aggravated because it's Dyspro in there. Apparently, he's hurt. He asked about it, but Kalyfa didn't respond except for saying it wasn't serious. He didn't know how it happened, but the other knights said that the dark, you, probably did it."

Malkarai shook his head, but he looked displeased. "I'd never hurt a civilian. They don't know the truth because Kalyfa's not telling them the truth. Satyrna was afraid they'd hurt him…"

"Josh is upset because he wants to get Dyspro help, but Kalyfa's refusing to let anyone in by him. Brendan knows where he is though – and Cypha."

"Good, they have her too," said Malkarai.

"Yeah. You thought someone else was involved?" Patricia cocked her head questioningly.

"No, but she just went missing this morning, so we didn't know what happened to her."

"Where are they?" Traphian asked.

"Third floor on the west side of the building. They're under lock and key though."

Teffifa shook her head. "Not a problem for me. Traphian?"

"Me neither."

The kids glanced between the two, and Malkarai spoke up.

"All right, I'm gonna ask you to map this place out as best you can, Patricia, but the plan is for these two," he motioned at Traphian and Teffifa, "to go in and search for the three of them, free them, and get them out some way other than the front door. Meanwhile, the rest of you will be with me, in plain sight. I intend to go to Kalyfa and ask for him to release them. I don't know how he'll react to seeing me, since the last time he approached me he attacked me; but I'm hoping he'll be civil with you guys asking for the same thing as me. If anything happens though, get out of danger, immediately. Do not fight them. I'm already on the knights' bad side, you don't need to be."

Akena frowned. "Do you think they'll fight you?"

"Me, yes. You, hopefully not. I wanted to do this alone, but I think Satyrna's right, that the more people who are protesting what they're doing, the more likely they'll listen. It's important that we don't allude to the fact that we'll be freeing them at the very moment we're distracting them though. If they know, things will change completely. Then, yeah, they probably will use force."

"What if they agree to let them go? They'll be pissed if they're in the process of being freed, not to mention it'll just reaffirm their fears."

"Desfete won't let them go," Malkarai said. "He has refused to listen to anything I've had to say so far, so my guess is whatever his issue is, it's with something higher than me, and I'm just a target. If Dyspro is hurt, we need to get him out of there – not to mention this has to be bad for his work."

"What do you intend to say to Desfete?" Seth asked.

"Well, that I had never meant any harm to them, that he's in the wrong, there is an agreement between him and my bosses and this interferes with that, and that I will not leave town until they have been set free. Whatever else may be needed will have to be thought up on the spot, but that's not a big issue for me. It's not like he'll listen anyway."

"Why are they so upset with you?" Akena asked meekly.

Malkarai sighed, pausing. He figured his usual explanation for curious civilians would work. "I'm a law enforcer, like them, but I'm employed by the federal instead of local government. I'm more of an undercover type than a police officer. The knights do not like people like me. So, when we're here, we have special rules. One is that we're not supposed to associate with civilians. Normally, we don't, except for asking questions that could lead us to our targets. However, this case was a little different. The rules are there so we don't just have social time when we're on cases, but Kalyfa took it a little too literally. He hates our kind because he feels this is not our jurisdiction."

"They are imprisoning Dyspro, Cypha, and Satyrna because they were hanging out with you?" Lauren said in disbelief.

"Yeah, basically. Because I spent an hour and a half in a bar with them, he's holding them in protective custody. He was afraid because I was friendly with them. It's asinine, yes, but, I abided by his wishes; I left them alone after I'd told them what had happened."

"We shouldn't have to bust them out of there," Seth said, a little bitterly. "They should just release them if you're gone."

Lauren looked at Seth. "That's not what Satyrna wants."

Patricia nodded begrudgingly. "She wants to make a statement."

"Well, she's making a great statement, being held up there in that castle!" Seth exclaimed, motioning north with an arm.

Malkarai inched back toward where Traphian was standing.

Kirena shook her head. "She doesn't want them to treat her friend like crap."

"Kirena," Akena said, scolding her language.

Kirena stuck her tongue out at her. "I'd stand up for him too if he was my friend."

"We can't really wait around for the knights to decide it's safe to let them go – Dyspro's hurt," Patricia reminded him.

"Yeah," Lauren insisted. "Come on, Seth, if Dyspro thinks he's worth standing up to Desfete for, he can't be bad. Dyspro's impetuous, but he's not stupid."

Seth sighed in resignation, obviously outnumbered. "I'm in it to get Dyspro and the others out."

Lauren shook her head at him and Patricia looked at Teffifa, who was still watching the street outside. "Any sign of my sister?"

Teffifa shook her head. "Nope, none. When do you wanna act, Faerstathe?"

"At dark."

# 16

Satyrna paced back and forth in the room in the castle she'd been stuck in all day. The room was mostly wood, but two of the walls were made from stone, and there was no window. In the room with her, there was a chair, a cot, and a table with a lantern, a walkie-talkie, and the remains of what they'd brought her for lunch on it. She was long past wanting to rest, so the blanket and pillow on the cot were undisturbed, and she'd set Malkarai's cloak in the middle of it instead.

This was frustratingly nerve-wracking. She had already tried asking to use the restroom as a means of maybe making a break for it, but they'd apparently actually had plumbing and a proper bathroom put in the building at some point, so that only got her to the other end of the hall and then right back in this room. She'd also asked if she could at least be stuck with Cypha or Dyspro if they were going to just imprison her, but the knight she'd asked that hadn't returned.

She looked up as she heard footsteps in the hall outside the door, but was surprised when the lock clicked and her door opened.

Her excitement almost immediately dissipated and she rolled her eyes with a sigh, turning away as Kalyfa came into the room. "Ugh. What do you want?"

He sighed, hesitating briefly before shutting the door behind him. He was holding a teal piece of clothing in his hand. "You've been badgering people all day, I figured you'd be happy to see someone who can actually do something."

"Yeah, maybe if that someone wasn't an asshat," Satyrna muttered, turning around and facing him, her arms crossed. "You took your sweet time today. What, are you still at a loss for words?"

He shook his head, looking away momentarily before his eyes returned to her. "I was busy all day. I only got back to the castle a little bit ago."

"Doing what? Harassing an innocent dark?"

"I get it, you're pissed, but are you really that naive that you still don't understand why we're doing this?"

"I don't think it's naivete that's causing me to think you're a misguided jerk. What the hell do you think you're protecting us from, anyway?"

"Faerstathe put you three in danger."

Satyrna tipped her head. "Faerstathe? Do you mean Malkarai?"

"Yes," Kalyfa said impatiently. "The dark you're protecting is Malkarai Faerstathe. He didn't even tell you his name?"

"I never asked his last name. He didn't ask ours either. Until you snatched me and Dyspro, he wasn't even around us anymore. Cypha looked for him and made him help her find us."

"He's been around you long enough for people to see."

Satyrna rolled her eyes again. "Big deal. It's not a secret that we were friends with darks."

"I told you, he put you in danger. You evidently can't see that, but he did."

"How the hell do you figure that? He's not going to hurt me. I met Malkarai because he caught a thief for me! He took care of me yesterday after one of your jackass knights drugged me and I nearly got hypothermia. Something I'm still pissed about, by the way. Drugging someone to subdue them *has* to be breaking some law."

He stared at her. "Drugged you? Who drugged you?"

"The asshole you had watching me yesterday. He put some shit on his glove or something, and after he dragged me back in here, I was all fuzzy in the head and my heart was racing. I thought I was having a panic attack, but it made me tired as hell. I ended up sleeping most of yesterday because it messed me up so bad."

Kalyfa looked serious and perturbed, looking off to the side for a few moments, his jaw locked. "That was *not* sanctioned, requested, or permitted. I'll deal with him."

"Get control of your men, Kalyfa," Satyrna said, her eyes narrowed.

He looked at her, hesitating. His expression was bothered. "I'm trying. He was a leftover. You know I'm trying to weed out the problems left over from the previous squad. I tried to use people I trust on this, but obviously I misjudged him."

"Yeah, a bit," she replied bluntly.

Kalyfa sighed heavily, changing the subject. "Anyway. Just because Faerstathe has been nice to you doesn't make him a saint, Satyrna. He's put you all in danger."

"Oh, but, because his eyes are different, that makes him a bad person? I'm so sick of people not trusting darks just because they're darks!"

"That is *not* the issue."

Satyrna frowned. "Don't you even start in on how darks are supposed to be genetically predisposed to evil deeds. That's absolute crap."

He turned to her abruptly. "Satyrna! That's not why he's dangerous!"

She shut her mouth, glaring at him.

"I'll admit, his mutation makes my job a lot more difficult politically, but, beyond that, it makes no difference. I'm rather offended that you thought I was prejudiced like that. Did you get to know me at all before you dumped me?"

Satyrna just glared at him. "I'm not going to grace that with a response."

He eyed her but didn't say whatever was going through his head. He turned his head away. "Did he tell you why he's here?"

"Why?" she asked, suspicious.

"I'm trying to make you understand. I already know why he's here. Do you?"

Satyrna hesitated, but replied. "He was looking for someone as part of his job. He has some business to discuss with him for a private investor."

"Private investment? That's what Faerstathe told you he does?"

"He told us that he can't talk about it, but yeah, he was trying to track down a client."

"What if that guy he's after saw you with him? Yeah, he's not heartless. He's ruthless, yes, but not inhuman. I know that. More importantly, his target knows this."

"Why would it matter if that guy knows we helped him out?"

"He's trying to avoid Faerstathe. Wouldn't it make sense, if he was threatened and backed into a corner, that he'd try and take hostages and appeal to the dark's humane side? Faerstathe isn't a businessman, Satyrna."

Satyrna blinked and dropped her gaze, her mind racing, eyes on the floor. *Malkarai wouldn't hurt me... but would that smiling guy really do it either? I suppose... if Malkarai were to pull one of those weapons on me, I'd get freaked too... but...* She looked up at Kalyfa abruptly. "Why'd you attack Malkarai?"

"I approached him. Things didn't go well."

"You *attacked* him!"

"I spoke to him. There was poor communication, and some of my men attacked before I finished. It might have ended peacefully, but when you attack someone like Faerstathe, they don't just take it quietly."

"You cut his side – they didn't do that."

"No, but he fought us and was winning. I was not about to lose any of my men, so I fought."

"Oh, and what is with this line of bull you're telling people – that I'm still your girlfriend?! You are *not* allowed to just say that," she hissed.

"I wanted to *scare* him, Satyrna. I wanted him to leave you alone. Yes, I'm perfectly aware you are not my girlfriend anymore."

"He listened to you; he left us alone."

"The damage had been done. I wanted to make sure you three were safe. The dark's kind is bad, but the people they chase are much worse. If he'd finished his job that night, I wouldn't have had to take the steps I did, but he didn't. He's been putzing around in town for *days*, and that puts all of you in danger. His job isn't supposed to take days."

She made a disapproving face. "It's just a job, Kalyfa. What makes you think that he can't be separated from his job?"

He sighed. "Because their job is their life, Satyrna. They are orphans when the system takes them in, and from the moment they're adopted, they're trained to do one job – a job that they do until old age or injury prevents them from performing. Even then, most take on administrative positions in the system. These are not normal people. They know one world and only one world."

She looked disconcerted but still confident. "He's just a person, Kalyfa. Yeah, he's got a job that is in charge of his life – but he's not a mindless drone. If he had the chance, he'd leave it. His best friend did that, years ago."

"Where's his best friend now?"

"Why would I know that?"

"He's probably dead, Satyrna. They don't just let their agents go rogue. They're handcrafted."

"Malkarai could. They'd never find him – especially not here."

"If you're implying that I protect Faerstathe, you have another thing coming."

She frowned. "You protect all the less than stellar people in this town just like you protect the good ones. You protect me without question."

"You're very different from Faerstathe, Satyrna. I actually care about you."

"And I care what happens to him."

Kalyfa stared at her, his eyes narrowing slightly.

"What?"

"You…"

"Care about people being executed, yes! That was a fucking barbaric proposal, and I'm not forgiving you for it."

"No, there's something else to it."

"Stop trying to dig for things, Kalyfa," she said with a sigh.

"I don't have to dig very hard, Satyrna. You're easier to read than a billboard. I knew it was coming before you broke up with me. It made it easier to try and fix it before it happened."

"Yeah, that worked for you."

"It lasted longer than I thought it would," he shrugged. "Satyrna, associating yourself with this guy is dangerous."

"You don't understand everything, Kalyfa. If his life was that dangerous, why is he still alive? He's already older than most darks get."

"He's alive because he's cunning, strong, and vicious. Satyrna, don't do this to yourself."

Satyrna made a face, but Kalyfa's phone rang before she could speak.

He took it out and answered it before it could ring again. "Yeah? … All right. Be there in a minute. Don't do anything."

He put the phone away and looked at Satyrna. "If you value your life… you'll cooperate with us."

She frowned disapprovingly but didn't move.

He tossed the clothing item in his hand to her. "There's your coat."

She caught it and held it up to check that it was what he said it was. "Wait."

He hesitated while she rummaged in the pockets.

"Okay, it's here." She made a shooing gesture and Kalyfa shook his head before opening the door and leaving, locking the door behind him.

Satyrna sighed but pulled her phone out of her coat pocket and tossed the garment on top of the cloak. She flipped it open and pushed the power button, but it didn't turn on.

"Damn."

Closing the phone with a snap, she tossed it gently on top of her coat and ran her hands over her face and into her hair, pacing the floor in front of the cot.

**5:40 p.m.**

Cypha awoke to the sound of metal scraping metal. She could hear someone messing around with the lock on the door. With nothing else to do and terrible reception, she'd spent most of the day just dozing, waiting for anything to happen. Her room was currently dark because she'd turned her lantern off.

She sat up on the cot, rubbing her eyes, and said to the person at the door. "Who's there?"

When a response wasn't immediately given, she reached over to the table next to the cot and picked up the walkie-talkie. The red light saying it was on and idle was still illuminated, so she apparently hadn't missed a message due to a dead battery. That meant that whoever was at the door was probably not a knight.

There was a heavy click. "I'm here to get you out," the man replied as he opened the door and stepped inside, illuminating the room somewhat.

"I won't argue with that. Is Satyrna with you?"

"No, she got picked up by the knights earlier."

Cypha stood up and grabbed her phone and her bag from the table before stretching and coming over to him. "Are you a knight?"

"Nope."

"Are you with Malkarai?"

"Yes."

"Huh. Where'd he find you?" she asked, peering at him. She didn't recognize him. He had brown hair and bright green eyes and was tall, built, and pretty handsome, but unfamiliar to her.

"We're old friends."

"Malkarai has friends?"

He laughed. "Yeah. Feel honored, you've met one of the few friends Malk has left. You don't have to come with me, but if you do, we should get going."

Cypha shrugged and gestured for him to lead.

He went to the left out of the door. "You're Cypha, I'm guessing."

"Yeah."

"I'm supposed to get Dyspro too, he's nearby."

"Huh, I had no idea. They were keeping us all separated."

At the other end of the hallway, there was a door open. The light from inside it was spilling into the less-bright hallway. Her rescuer put up a hand to motion for her to stop as he did, listening.

She could barely pick up quick, angry voices.

"I can't, I just can't… I'm sorry."

A hoarse, hushed voice spoke. "Josh, I thought-"

The first speaker was upset. "I can't do it! I've taken an oath… I can't take you out of here. You have no idea how much I want to, but I can't… Kalyfa says that it's best for you if you stay."

"Bastard."

"Dyspro, don't make me the bad guy here. If it were up to me none of this would have happened. Kalyfa's ordered me to stay out of it completely."

"Would it kill you to do something decent for a friend?" Dyspro said angrily.

Josh sighed, upset. "Goddammit, Dyspro… It's not like that. I've been trying! There's no swaying him this time. He knows more than the rest of us about this, and he's refusing to tell us."

Cypha grabbed her rescuer by the sleeve of his leather jacket and took off down the hallway. When they grew closer to where the voices were coming from, they saw a man step out of a room.

He had mid-length dark brown hair that was usually pretty tamed but was messed up at the moment. His concerned expression reached his blue eyes. "Who's there?"

"Josh, what the hell are you doing?" Cypha demanded, exasperated.

"Cypha! Thank God, you're free! Get him out of here."

She glared at him. "Why couldn't you?"

"I'm loyal, Cypha… I can't go against Kalyfa… Just get him to a doctor and I'll forget I ever saw you. Please."

"To a doctor?! What happened to him?!"

The man who was with her went inside the room.

Josh swallowed and glanced at Dyspro before looking back to Cypha. "It was Carter and… Just get him out of here. I have to go. I'm not supposed to be here."

Cypha shook her head at him in disbelief as he went down the hallway, but then she went into the room. Dyspro was on the cot. She ran over to his side.

Dyspro was heavily bruised, and in a few places, she could make out some spots of dull, dark blood that looked like they'd dripped from a split lip. They showed up ominously on his white shirt.

"Dyspro! What the hell happened?!"

He looked away from the new man and over to Cypha. One eye was black and blue. He swallowed in pain as he shifted on the cot. "I broke my leg – or, well, they broke it. It was Leah's bastard of a boyfriend that did it. I shouldn't have fought, but the dickhead egged me on. Pretty sure I've messed it up bad though. They couldn't set it."

"Damn it… So Kalyfa didn't hurt you?"

"No, it was my ex's new meat. Kalyfa's pissed off and told everyone else – including Josh – to stay away from me since then. He said he was going to work on getting me to the hospital, but he only came around this afternoon, so I think he laid into some subordinates for not telling him about how bad it was earlier."

She sighed and looked at her rescuer. "Josh's right, we have to get him out of here."

"Yeah," he agreed. He put Dyspro's left arm over his shoulders and eased him off the bed before motioning for Cypha to do the same with his right. Together they lifted him to his feet.

"Can you walk at all?" he asked Dyspro.

Dyspro winced and shook his head. "Hell, I don't think I can stand."

"We'll carry you the whole way then. Come on."

A floor below, Josh left the stairs and headed for the room where the current knight on duty was stationed. He stopped abruptly when he reached that hallway, seeing a woman clad in black leather who most certainly was not on the squad leaving the room. He stared at her, bewildered.

When she spotted him, Teffifa swiftly pulled a sword out, pointing it at him with her right hand. "Heyo, buddy. If you don't want trouble, just turn right around and keep going."

Josh glanced at the door, putting a hand on the sword at his left hip, but not drawing it. "Who's in there? Are they okay still?"

"What makes you think anyone in there *wouldn't* be okay?"

He looked back at her. "Are you with that guy upstairs that was with Cypha?"

She pulled the door shut so their conversation was more private. "Hm, depends. I'm here to liberate some victims of a kidnapping ring," she said with a smirk.

He sighed and shut his eyes briefly before pointing to the second door down on the left. "Saty is in there," he said quietly. "Just… you didn't see me, and I didn't see you."

She tipped her head, still smirking as she regarded him. "You're their knight friend, huh?"

Josh swallowed and turned around, shaking his head as he waved a hand, walking back to the stairs. "I wasn't here."

Kalyfa came down the stairs into the main hall, looking around for the source of his summons. His eyes soon rested on the man in the trench coat, near the doors. One of his captains, Meredith, was standing near them, and there were five people between Malkarai and the doors. Kalyfa scowled slightly and strode over to him.

The main hall was a large room that shared a ceiling with the third floor of the building. Two double doors were in the center front, where everyone else was standing. To either side of the room, stone staircases led up to the second floor, and directly across from the front doors was a long balcony hallway that extended from one wing to the other, hanging over an open, shadowed area that had folded-up tables, chairs, and training equipment. There were also doors below the balcony that led to meeting rooms and storage on the first floor. All of the staircases to the third floor were internal to the wings.

Workout equipment, weights, cabinets of supplies, training pads, and blunted weapons were hanging and stored around the room. In the center were three training dummies, one of which was tipped over, and a padded workout mat.

Kalyfa glanced around the room to see if there was anyone else in there, or if Meredith was alone. He spotted a forgotten training sword near one of the training dummies, but otherwise, the room was empty and in its usual state.

Kalyfa stopped by his captain, within fifteen feet of Malkarai, his eyes narrowed at him. "What do you want, Faerstathe?"

"To talk about this."

Kalyfa looked at the Tanens and Patricia and then looked back at him. "There's nothing to talk about." Kalyfa crossed his arms. "Get out of town. You're endangering *even more* people."

"I can't do that. But, you can't do what you've been doing either."

"And why can't I?"

"You're imprisoning people not because of what they did, but because you're afraid of someone else they know. Desfete, no matter what law system you abide by, that's not legal."

"They're not imprisoned."

"You're holding them hostage!" Seth blurted out. Malkarai glanced at him and lifted a hand calmly, motioning for him to stand down.

Kalyfa looked at Seth. "No, I'm protecting them." He gestured to Malkarai. "This is the person that's put your brother and his friends in danger. The best thing for you all to do is to leave here now, and stop associating with him."

"He isn't threatening us," Patricia spoke up. "My sister didn't want to be here, but she apparently is again."

"I can give you a means by which to communicate with them, but they need to stay here so we can make sure they stay safe." Kalyfa looked back to Malkarai, scowling. "Faerstathe, you've put all of their lives in danger. Now you're putting their family in danger too!"

"I have not, Desfete. You act like I'm a wanted criminal. I'm not. I'm part of the government's law enforcement."

"So, you're okay with dragging innocent people in front of your government's enemies?" Kalyfa retorted. "You're not a very responsible law enforcer."

"I didn't approach them for some sort of plot! We met once, long ago. After I snatched some thief for Satyrna, the three of them insisted I stick around. They wanted to make sure you guys didn't hassle me, so they tried to help me blend in."

"Yeah, you blend in… that's not gonna happen."

"Not when you have every person of authority in this town looking for me, no. If you'd just let things be, I'd already be out of town. But, no, you felt the need to be a self-righteous prick. They weren't in danger."

Kalyfa narrowed his eyes. "Self-righteous? Faerstathe, you have a very warped idea of justice and safety."

"I do not. My view of justice is just a lot more black and white than yours."

"You need less black and more white."

Malkarai laughed dryly. "I don't need *you* telling me that."

Satyrna stared at the door as she heard metallic scratching at the doorknob. She expected the door to unlock and open, but it took a few minutes before anything happened. By that point, she was holding the walkie-talkie like a weapon, ready to react.

She was *not* expecting a short, goth-looking woman with two swords and red eyes to open the door.

A thin smile spread across her lips. "Ah, he was right. Satyrna, I presume?"

Satyrna stared at her, opening her mouth to speak, but not sure where to start. "Uh… yes…"

"Perfect. Come with me."

"*Who are you?*"

"I'm Teffifa. Malkarai is my partner."

"Malkarai never said *anything* about having a partner."

"He didn't know I was here until this morning. Not that he'd talk about me anyway – he never talks."

Satyrna couldn't contest that. "Uh, did the plan change…?"

"Yeah, a bit. He got more info and some new bodies to use. You still want out of this place, right?"

"Yes," Satyrna immediately replied, setting down the walkie-talkie, picking up her phone, putting on her coat, and sliding the phone into her pocket. Then she grabbed Malkarai's cloak and put it on over her coat before going to the door.

"Okay, the name of the game is stealth and speed. Let's go find your friends and get out of here."

Satyrna followed her from the room and down the hallway to the right. She looked at the doors as they passed them, heading to the opposite end of the hallway as the bathroom. "I don't know where they are; they wouldn't tell me."

"That's okay, your sister gave us a pretty good idea. You were the unknown, and the knight friend I'm supposed to pretend I didn't see pointed you out."

Satyrna narrowed her eyes slightly, looking at Teffifa – well, her black and red hair, since she was facing away from her. "…Josh?"

"He said he wasn't here," she replied amicably. "But, yeah, probably. Ah," she said, stopping.

Satyrna peered past her and up the stairs, seeing Dyspro and Cypha coming down with an unfamiliar man. She stepped into the stairwell with Teffifa, her eyes widening as the trio got closer. She realized he wasn't unfamiliar – she recognized him. "Trebo!"

His head snapped up at that.

Cypha's eyes widened and she looked from Satyrna to him. "What?! Seriously?"

Satyrna shook her head and took a step back toward the door, but Teffifa grabbed her arm, holding her in place. "N-no, this is what Kalyfa warned me about- *this* is what he was afraid of!"

"How in the fu-…" Traphian muttered. "Don't- chill out, okay?"

Teffifa gave Satyrna a perplexed look. "What'd Kalyfa tell you?"

"He- he said that we were in danger because Malkarai spent time with us in public – so the guy he was after could come after us as leverage!"

"That actually makes sense," Dyspro muttered as they got to the solid landing in front of Teffifa and Satyrna.

Traphian groaned.

Teffifa nodded. "Yeah, actually. He's overreacting a bit, but that's legit."

"Teffifa, could you please *help* the situation for once?" Traphian hissed.

She smirked and snorted softly, gesturing with a hand. "Every other mission, yeah, Kalyfa would be right. He's not this time."

"*This* time?" Satyrna pressed.

Traphian sighed. "Hi, I've never hurt anyone innocent before, and I'm not going to start now. Also, please don't call me Trebo in here. The knights obviously have some kind of dime on me."

"What are we supposed to call you instead?" Dyspro said between clenched teeth, shifting on his good leg.

"Traphian, I guess. Or nothing. Nothing is probably safer."

Satyrna's eyes widened. "Oh," she said quietly.

Cypha stared at Traphian before looking back at Satyrna. "He was after his friend?"

"Yeah, that's why he's been dragging his ass for two weeks," Teffifa said nonchalantly. "Anyway, can we have all these massive revelations outside before we lose our between-shift buffer and knights start getting up in our business?"

Satyrna peered at Teffifa. "You aren't Arista, are you?"

Teffifa snorted, amused. "Sheesh, you guys know a lot of shit for some randos he just met. No, I'm not Arista. She's Gandhi. Seriously though, we need to move it."

Satyrna sighed and looked at Cypha and Dyspro, trying to gauge their thoughts on the matter.

"I want to get the fuck out of here, so yes, let's just move," Dyspro insisted. "Like she said, figure out who is a friend and who is an enemy outside, please."

Teffifa turned and tugged the cloak so Satyrna followed, but as they moved, Satyrna looked back at Dyspro. "What happened to you?"

"Leah's boy toy picked a fight," he said, his voice tight.

She groaned. "Dyspro…"

"Hey, a little bit of pity would be nice!"

"When I'm done being annoyed at you, maybe. What did you hurt?"

"He broke my leg. Not sure how bad, but it hurts like hell."

"When?"

"Last night, but I guess the chickenshit and his buddies never told his boss, because Kalyfa only found out a little while ago. Hopefully, he gets demoted or fired," Dyspro grumbled. "Let's see Leah boast about that."

Cypha rolled her eyes. "Priorities, Dyspro."

"Let me be petty, it distracts me."

"Mood," Teffifa said flatly.

As Teffifa led them past the bathrooms, Traphian asked, quietly, "How'd you know who I was?"

Satyrna glanced back at him. "I sold you food."

His eyebrows lifted. "Oh. Right. Fuck, the *one* person on the outside of that inn I talked to, and he found you? His skills are better than I fucking thought."

Teffifa snickered. "It wasn't your expert-level skills that kept us off your ass, D'vane."

He sighed darkly. "Glad you both have some sort of affection left for me."

"Oh, I wouldn't say that."

Traphian shook his head moodily. "Did you call him?" he asked Teffifa.

She nodded. "Didn't answer, of course."

"Who are you, anyway?" Cypha asked. "We established the guy with two names' deal. What the heck are you doing in here?"

Teffifa glanced back at her. "Me? I'm technically not supposed to be in here."

Cypha's eyes narrowed.

"I'm Malk's partner. Babysitter. Backup. Take your pick."

"I thought Malkarai was going to come and get us," Satyrna said.

"Traphian said he was gonna help him, so I volunteered too. Of course, now I have to go back and tell the goons on the upper level that their pet's dead. I'm not looking forward to that, but if I'm involved, I can at least get my story straight."

"Dead?" Cypha asked, flatly.

"Yep."

Satyrna frowned, quickening her steps so she caught up to Teffifa, looking at her. "He isn't planning on making that reality, is he?"

Teffifa glanced at her, but then looked back when she saw how serious Satyrna's expression was. "Uh, pretty sure I'm just spinning a tale, yes."

"Okay…"

Teffifa nodded to a large window they were approaching. "There we go. Haste, ladies."

# 17

"Faerstathe, I don't appreciate you hiding behind innocent bystanders," Kalyfa said, glaring at him.

Malkarai glanced back at the others. "Who's hiding? They're pissed you have their siblings and friends, and I'm not happy at this attack on my profession. We came here together. Desfete, I am not the enemy."

He scowled. "Then why haven't you just finished this and removed the danger?"

Malkarai sighed in annoyance. However, before he could refute Kalyfa, a knight came running across the hall from the back left corner. He went up to Kalyfa and muttered a few things. *Shit. Please be out by now...*

Kalyfa responded quietly, looking at the knight in concern, and after the knight shook his head Kalyfa responded audibly. "Go find out. Jamal and Hendrick are back there too."

Meredith watched Kalyfa. "Orders?"

"Stay here for now," he replied. He turned back to Malkarai as the knight left. "Faerstathe, who did you call?"

Malkarai cocked his head, feigning ignorance. "What?"

"You called for backup, didn't you?"

"No," he replied honestly. "My phone's been dead for two days now."

Kalyfa glared at him. "Bullshit."

Malkarai just shrugged. "Looks to me like you should be focused less on me and more on your internal issues, Desfete."

"Don't tell me what I should be focused on, Faerstathe! *You* caused this!"

"How about we talk about what you shouldn't be focused on, then? Like Satyrna, Cypha, and Dyspro."

"Watch your tongue, Faerstathe. I've lost patience with you. I want you to get out of town now," Kalyfa hissed. "I'll let them go when I feel they are safe."

"Making me leave town will not cause my target to leave. Even if I'm gone, someone else will be sent to acquire him. Now, either you let me finish my job, or you'll be stuck with this same situation for much longer."

"If this person you're after harms a single civilian while you're here wasting my fucking time, I will personally deliver your head to your superiors," Kalyfa hissed.

The Tanens and Patricia glanced at each other, getting uncomfortable and alarmed. They glanced at the knights and each other before looking to see how Malkarai would respond.

Malkarai laughed. "I don't think you'd make the impression you're aiming to make."

"I think they'd get the hint."

Satyrna hesitated at the window after they'd forced it open. She looked out at the roof, not feeling great about this plan. There was another window about ten yards away, and the ground was about twelve feet from the edge of the roof. She glanced back at Dyspro.

"How's it look?" Cypha asked, judging Satyrna's expression.

"It'd be no problem if he weren't hurt," Satyrna said. "In fact, I think he'd enjoy it immensely."

Dyspro smirked.

Traphian spoke up. "We can take it easy and lower him down. There's something on the ground below that should give us a few extra feet so we can reach him."

Cypha gave the two a suspicious look. "Thought ahead, have we?"

Teffifa shrugged. "Yes. Always plan your course of exit before entering. Patricia said that Brendan suspected he was injured, so we made accommodations."

Satyrna and Cypha exchanged a long look before turning to Dyspro. "Well, your call, bud," Cypha said with a sigh.

Dyspro glanced backward and nodded. "Yeah, whatever. It won't kill me. Probably. Most likely."

"All right," said Satyrna. "I'll go out first."

Cypha nodded and shifted most of Dyspro's weight onto herself so Traphian could let go.

He and Satyrna easily got onto the roof outside the window.

"Shit. Don't move," Teffifa hissed, drawing both swords slowly.

Cypha stared at her, listening. Footsteps and voices were approaching. Her grip tightened around Dyspro's chest.

A lot of things happened at once.

Teffifa jumped to a ready stance, swords brandished, facing the hallway where three knights had appeared.

The knights shouted in surprise and drew their weapons.

Traphian grabbed Satyrna and rolled to the side, away from the window. He held her back to his chest, a hand over her mouth, listening to Teffifa engage the knights.

Satyrna, still not trusting him, was terrified at first. However, she didn't fight. She quickly realized what he was doing though and calmed down, listening as well.

Dyspro, seeing that Traphian and Satyrna intended to hide, reached out and yanked the window down, so it was mostly shut, with the arm that wasn't around Cypha's shoulders.

Cypha looked at him in confusion, but he just put a finger to his lips.

Teffifa, teeth bared in a focused grin, locked blades with the front two knights. The other one could not approach due to the size of the hallway. "Hello, boys. What brings you to this charming hallway on this delightful evening?"

They seemed disarmed by her conversational tone. "H-hand over the kids!"

"Well, I see we have a conflict of interest then. These two are coming with me. I'm breaking up a suspected kidnapping ring."

"W-what the hell are you talking about?!"

"Interesting. That sounds like just the thing a flunkie in a kidnapping ring would say." She twirled both swords; twisting their blades in their hands awkwardly and forcing them to take a step back to regain their grip.

A glance was exchanged between them, and they both attacked at the same time.

However, what was meant to break her down was exactly what she enjoyed most. She easily met both swords and parried them, metal striking metal wherever they tried to hit.

Cypha blinked, watching Teffifa's whirling blades. "God, I really hope she is on our side," she muttered low enough for just Dyspro to hear.

He nodded, watching her raptly.

Teffifa was ambidextrous, and neither arm usually presented a weak point, but her left arm was pulling a bit. She narrowed her eyes, a strong smirk remaining on her face, as she pushed the two knights, pressuring them to move backward into their companion. She slacked off with her right arm, trying to keep the two side by side.

Teffifa's teeth gritted when she felt several stitches break on her left bicep, and then she decided she needed to finish this. She went into motion, pulling a furious, fast circuit, slapping their swords several times to make them vibrate, and then knocking them out of their hands and to the ground. Then she swung her swords backward over her shoulders, holding the hilts to either side of her face to protect it, and put her head down, running into both of them and knocking them into the third knight and down on the ground.

While they were down, she knocked one out with one of the hilts, but her left arm didn't do what she wanted it to, and she missed the other one. The third one scrambled out from under his fellows and then sprinted off down the hallway.

"Shit," she said through gritted teeth, seeing his retreat, but focused on the knight who was fighting his way to his sword.

She stepped on his forearm and reminded herself, disappointedly, that she couldn't stab him in any way, shape, or form, and instead, whapped him in the head with the flat of her right sword.

"Stop that."

He gave her an angry, frantic look, still reaching with his fingertips, even though his arm wasn't moving anywhere.

"Look, all we have here is a conflict of interest," Teffifa said. "Honestly, though, are you that attached to these two? I'm sure they're far more important to me than you. Just let us go. I'll even give you a cut or something so you can show your boss you fought hard."

"What are you?!"

She grinned. "I'm one of the good guys! Silly boy, can't you see that?"

He just stared at her, bewildered. "They'll catch you."

Teffifa sighed. "Irrelevant to this conversation, bud. Now, I can give you a nice headache, or you can run back to your boss and say all's well. What's your choice?"

He blinked.

Teffifa waited but then repeated, "What's your choice?"

"Er, I'll let you go…"

"Good answer."

She moved her foot and kicked his sword away. Then she picked up his friend's sword and motioned with it for him to leave.

He sat up; staring at her in confusion, but then got up and ran when he realized she wasn't going to attack.

Cypha gaped at Teffifa, who dropped the sword in a corner. "What the hell did you do that for?"

She turned around. "Because I couldn't have beaten him if I fought him."

Dyspro and Cypha gave her incredulous looks. The fight they'd just witnessed was contradictory to that statement.

Teffifa held up her left hand to show them the blood that had run from inside her sleeve, down the back of her hand, staining most of the flesh red.

"Oh my God! Where'd they hit you?" said Cypha.

"Your coat's not even cut," Dyspro said in confusion.

"I have stitches. They ripped open. These guys, I'm sorry to say, are not worth furthering that injury. Also, it kind of hampers my fighting. It unbalances it. So, time for the three of us to move it! Switch sides with me, so I don't have to use that arm."

Cypha blinked, but then she shifted to Dyspro's other side using his help.

"Traphian, you get the girl out of here. I'll take care of these two."

"All right," he responded from outside. "Watch the blood; they'll be able to track you like that."

"Noted." Teffifa sheathed her swords and then grabbed Dyspro, and the three took off as fast as they could down the hallway the knights hadn't fled down.

Satyrna turned and looked at Traphian, confused and fearful.

He sighed and looked around. "Come on."

She hesitated but then followed him toward the edge of the roof.

When he had reached the edge, he walked along it for a short way, examining the dark ground below. After he'd gone about twenty paces he stopped and crouched down. He glanced at her and then dropped off the roof.

Satyrna slowly walked over, trying to see where he had gone. She spotted him standing below.

He held up his arms. "Jump. I'll catch you."

She hesitated, twisting her fingers around in the hems of Malkarai's cloak. She wasn't afraid of the drop; she was still unsure about whether or not Teffifa and Traphian were truly 'the good guys.'

Traphian shook his hands impatiently. "Come on, we need to get out of here. Malkarai may need my help."

She glanced back at the castle, uncomfortable now that she was separated from Dyspro and Cypha. She could just go back and go in through the window. She doubted she could take Teffifa on her own, but she could at least fight alongside Cypha if need be.

"Satyrna?"

She looked down at him. "How do I know that you're actually here because Malkarai asked you to be?"

His eyes narrowed slightly. "He's my friend."

"He was. He refuses to talk about you now. He said you hadn't talked for years."

"It's kinda hard to talk when one of us is on the run from the organization he works for. He told me to run and hide because he probably wasn't going to live through this, but I insisted on helping him. Teffifa's gonna tell them that we're both dead."

She stared at him levelly. "I only have your word. I don't even know if she's his ally or yours."

"We're all allies right now."

Satyrna sighed, still debating. Eventually, she figured she might as well get the hell off the roof and decide the truth later. "Are we going to get Cypha and Dyspro out?"

"As soon as we regroup, yes. We're not leaving them in there."

"Fine." She grabbed the cloak and wrapped it around her neck to keep from getting caught on the gutter, and was about to crouch down and swing over the edge when someone grabbed her from behind.

Satyrna cried out in surprise, but she was dragged backward on the roof, toward the window she'd just come from.

She saw another knight hurry down to the edge of the roof and look over, to see where the person she'd been talking with was, but he apparently didn't see anything. He walked back over. "Nothing. Let's get her downstairs, where we can watch her."

She felt the man holding her nod, and then he forced her toward the window and inside. They took her down the hall, heading for the stairs that would lead to the first floor and the main hall.

"Let them go home with their families. Then I'll finish my mission and leave. I'm a little preoccupied with this glaringly illegal hostage situation until then."

Kalyfa's eyes widened with rage, but he calmed himself before speaking. "They're not leaving until you are well out of this town. Seeing how delusional and negligent you are, now I'm afraid we're going to have to protect their siblings too!"

Everyone in the hall was distracted by a woman's yell coming from the hallway at the top of the lefthand stairwell. "Let go of me!"

"Saty," Patricia whispered, looking alarmed.

Two knights entered with a struggling Satyrna after a few moments. One hurried down the stairs and over to Kalyfa and Meredith as the other had her kneel at the top of the stairs, keeping her restrained.

"We caught her trying to jump off the first-floor roof," the knight said to Kalyfa. "There was an unknown man with her, but he got away. The other two are with an unknown woman somewhere in the castle, we believe."

Satyrna spotted Malkarai and the two locked eyes. He looked somber, disappointed.

Kalyfa was frowning. "Satyrna, I figured you'd have enough sense to listen to me."

She tore her eyes off Malkarai and looked at Kalyfa. "I respect him more than you right now, Kalyfa. Let us go. Dyspro's hurt."

Dyspro's siblings cried out at that, but Kalyfa talked over them. "A doctor was coming tonight to take care of that."

She gave him an annoyed look. "Yeah, what makes you think that's a home visit sort of injury? He needs to go to the hospital."

Kalyfa narrowed his eyes at her slowly as Seth said, "You need to let him go with us!"

Malkarai looked away, back at Kalyfa. "I told you I wasn't trying to free them. Now, please, release them to their friends and family. They'll be safer with them than here."

Kalyfa glared at Malkarai, drawing his sword. "You have endangered these people, Faerstathe; not us. I'm tired of this. You're just wasting my time." He looked at Meredith and the knight that had just come up to him. "Meredith, Jamal, subdue him by force if he won't comply."

Malkarai rolled his eyes and waved a hand back at the siblings behind him before taking off his coat, discarding it on the floor, and drawing the sword at his hip. "Okay, we're at this point now?"

"We don't have to be. Surrender and I'll just hand you over to your government and we'll handle your target for you since you apparently cannot."

Malkarai laughed. "Fat chance, Desfete."

Kalyfa sighed, giving Malkarai a jaded look. "Fine, this is your doing." He motioned for Meredith to go left as Jamal ran forward to engage Malkarai, eagerly.

"Kalyfa!" another knight called as he ran into the hall. "There's some psycho bitch with two swords loose in the castle!"

Kalyfa stopped and looked up to the top of the stairs. "I *know*, Tony," he said irritably. "Get the civilians out of here."

The knight holding Satyrna glanced at the civilians and then stopped Tony from going down the stairs. "No, you watch her. I'll handle the civilians."

Tony scowled but stopped and went over to Satyrna so the other knight could go down the stairs. He went up to the Tanens and Patricia, who for the most part were trying to stay clear of the fight, except for Seth, who looked angry about how the situation had gone and was clearly providing a barrier between his sisters and Patricia, and the knights.

Malkarai, seeing that Kalyfa was delayed in engaging, moved forward to Jamal. Putting one of the training dummies to his right between him and Meredith, he deflected Jamal's chopping slash, spinning with the maneuver to elbow him hard in the chest and knock the wind out of him. Malkarai quickly grabbed Jamal's shirt and pulled him back hard before letting go, sending him crashing over the tipped-over training dummy behind him and leaving him severely dazed.

Before Malkarai could move to rush Kalyfa, Meredith ran forcefully into the training dummy that was between them, pushing it over to obstruct his path to Kalyfa. The obstacle hit the discarded training sword over to where it stopped, stuck in the padded training mat. Malkarai stopped short and took a step back to avoid hitting the dummy.

Kalyfa hadn't expected Malkarai to take Jamal out already, but he quickly reoriented himself and jumped over the dummy, attacking Malkarai so that he had to move toward Meredith, who had picked up on the plan and was trying to keep Malkarai between them.

Satyrna resisted Tony taking over from his peer and quickly climbed to her feet, fighting him.

Aggravated, he smacked her in the head and grabbed her arm. "Stop resisting!"

The knight at the bottom of the stairs turned, hearing Tony striking her. He was alarmed and angry.

Traphian came in the front door, sword already drawn. He saw Seth inching toward the knight at the bottom of the stairs, grabbed his shoulder, and pushed him back by his siblings. "Don't," he said warningly before immediately going to the knight, switching his sword to his left hand, and delivering a right hook to the knight's solar plexus, causing him to gasp, crumple, and fight for air on his knees.

No one else noticed the altercation at the top of the stairs until Satyrna bent forward suddenly and then threw her head backward as hard as she could. Tony turned his head in time to avoid getting hit directly in the face but still was struck hard on the side of his head. He let go of her, cursing loudly at her, and she immediately took off down the stairs.

Kalyfa and Meredith, who had pressured Malkarai into staying between them near the training mats, both stopped attacking.

Malkarai heard the noise but did not stall. He used the distraction and took a minor hit on his upper arm from Meredith when she reacted to him chancing a shoulder charge on Kalyfa, knocking the head knight onto his side.

After taking Kalyfa down, however, Malkarai stepped on the loose practice sword and twisted his ankle as it slid. He also fell to the ground and lost his sword as it went flying out of his hand.

Traphian ran past Malkarai and intercepted Meredith who had been pursuing Malkarai, and pushed her back a few steps.

Kalyfa got to his feet, glanced at the top of the stairs, yelling, "What the fuck are you trying to pull?" before taking a step toward Malkarai, his sword pointing at him.

Malkarai recovered and rolled over, reaching for his left knife on his leg as he watched Kalyfa, preparing to get back up and re-engage.

Because he was watching Kalyfa, Malkarai saw Satyrna swing her arm down at Kalyfa's shoulder, embedding his switchblade in his back.

Kalyfa lurched and dropped to his knee from both surprise and pain.

Satyrna took a step back, putting her hands up to her mouth as she apparently registered what she'd done.

Behind her, Tony was almost down the stairs, sword drawn and one nostril bleeding freely, murderous intent on his face as he glared directly at her.

Kalyfa turned to see who stabbed him, dropped his sword, and reached for the knife, but Malkarai jumped to his feet and shoved Kalyfa over with his right hand while his left hand ripped the more convenient knife out of his back to use against Tony.

Kalyfa, unprepared for this, let out an agonized gasp before hitting his forehead on the stone floor and crumpling limply.

Satyrna's eyes widened and she took another step away, terrified to see Malkarai rushing her after tearing the knife out of Kalyfa.

Malkarai switched the knife to his right hand and reached out for her, pulling her close to him and twisting to take the sword slash from Tony himself, falling away from the strike to lessen some of the momentum and force of the blade.

Meredith was startled by Traphian's sudden appearance and hadn't fully engaged with him, only focused on resisting getting pushed away from Kalyfa. Both she and Traphian had stopped briefly when Kalyfa went down, and she didn't pursue when Traphian abandoned her and sprinted to try to help Malkarai.

Traphian was still a moment or two behind Malkarai, so although he led with his sword extended, he was only able to stab Tony's dominant arm and slice shallowly into his armpit after he'd already started the swing. Tony howled in pain, recoiled, and let go of his sword, not finishing the strike. He dropped his sword and fell against the wall, clutching his wound.

Satyrna struggled as Malkarai's weight fell on her. She grabbed him, but went to the ground anyway, not sure what had just happened. She looked up and her eyes widened when she saw Traphian and the knight.

Malkarai shuddered in pain but tried to get up to fight. He only relaxed when he saw Traphian standing next to him and Satyrna.

Satyrna gripped Malkarai tight, not letting him move. She looked at him, pushing his hair out of his face, but he didn't look at her. His jaw was tight, rigid; his teeth clenched.

Traphian checked the two knights by the stairs, then looked back at Kalyfa, who was still out on the floor, and then to Meredith, who was also taking in the situation. She went to Kalyfa, shifting him and trying to wake him.

Akena and Patricia ran over to Malkarai and Satyrna, calling out.

"Oh my God!" said Patricia, her hands over her mouth.

"Are you two okay?"

Malkarai sat up once Satyrna had loosened her grip, holding an arm to his side. He looked at her, his expression pained. The knight's swing hadn't finished, but it had definitely connected.

"Malkarai…"

He grimaced and his chest heaved, keeping his arm tight against his torso.

"Get out, all of you," he said loud enough for Patricia and Akena to hear, his voice noticeably strained. "Don't follow me when I leave. Don't try to find me."

Satyrna grabbed his arm as he stood up, but he only used it to help her to her feet, resisting her pull.

Traphian stepped close to Malkarai and whispered something. Malkarai responded in kind.

Traphian nodded. "Okay, girls, let's get out of here."

"What about my brother and Cypha?" Akena demanded.

Traphian pointed over her head, toward the door.

She turned and looked. Teffifa and Cypha were supporting Dyspro as they approached Seth and Lauren, apparently having come down the other set of stairs.

Akena ran over to them, and Patricia turned back to Satyrna.

"Are you okay, Saty? Are you hurt?"

Satyrna nodded vaguely, watching Malkarai.

He was looking at his side under his arm. With a sigh, he raised his head, put his arm back, and then caught her eye.

"Thank you," she whispered, not sure how to react to what had just happened.

He seemed disconcerted. "Take this," he pressed the switchblade into her hands. "And don't follow me," he reiterated and turned around to retrieve his coat. Then he strode quickly for the door, throwing his coat on as he went.

"Malkarai–" Satyrna tried to follow, but Traphian grabbed her wrist. She looked back at him.

"Don't," he said.

She frowned, staring him in the eye, but when she turned back, Malkarai was gone. She stopped resisting Traphian's pull and turned around moodily.

Traphian sighed at her. "Come on, we have to get out of here before they reorganize."

Satyrna ignored him and walked over to where Malkarai's sword had ended up. She bent over and picked it up. Then she looked at the switchblade in her other hand. She closed it, staring at the handle that was wet with blood. The sparing blood on the blade was probably Kalyfa's, but the more plentiful blood she was sure was Malkarai's. Her throat knotted up. *Why are you doing this…?*

"Satyrna?" came her sister's voice. "Come on, they really want us to get out of here."

She nodded and walked with Patricia, who put her hand on Satyrna's back.

Traphian looked around anxiously when they joined him and urged them outside. "The Tanens and Cypha already went out. Hurry. I don't know how unconscious Kalyfa is."

Neither of the two knights near the stairs were even trying to get up to pursue them, and Meredith just watched them leave, making no move to leave Kalyfa, who was starting to stir.

The cold air hit Satyrna hard outside. She took a deep breath of it, cooling her lungs and trying to fix her throat. "Where'd he go?" she asked, her voice fairly forced.

"I don't know," Traphian answered.

"He didn't tell you?"

"No. He told me to get everyone out; that he was disappearing."

"Jerk," she muttered bitterly.

Traphian looked at her, but she didn't make eye contact. He looked at Patricia, but she just shrugged.

"How's Dyspro?" Patricia asked.

"Well, his leg's broken. Not sure how bad yet. Seems all right other than that. A little bruised."

"Is Cypha okay?"

"She's fine."

They caught up to the others near the end of the path. Seth and Teffifa met them first. Teffifa had her sword drawn in her right hand. They relaxed when they recognized them, however. Cypha and Lauren were supporting Dyspro.

"Satyrna, you okay?" Seth asked.

She nodded.

Traphian eyed Teffifa's left hand, which was red and empty, her second sword still sheathed. "How're the stitches?"

"A bunch of them are ripped out. Thanks for that, by the way."

"I'll have to return the gratitude." Traphian lifted his left arm, referring to his bicep and the sliced coat.

Satyrna eyed him. "Why is she thanking you for her stitches?"

Teffifa put her single sword over her shoulder and turned to continue walking with the rest. "He gave me the cut in the first place."

Satyrna narrowed her eyes at Traphian.

He sighed. "Thanks, Teffifa. She paid me back, okay? And, I told you, Malkarai wanted us to be here. Do you really not trust me yet?"

"Well, he talked to you without doing anything to you, so I suppose I can trust you a little," Satyrna said.

Patricia looked at Satyrna. "These two are with him, Satyrna. They went in to find you because the knights don't know them."

She glanced at her sister. "Malkarai was hunting him when I met him."

Traphian sighed. "Yeah, and so was Teffifa."

"I still want to," she muttered.

"Please don't."

"Well, all three of them made the plans to get you guys out," Patricia insisted.

Satyrna accepted this, albeit begrudgingly. "So, why did he just run off?"

"He doesn't want to get you guys involved anymore."

"Get us involved – he just took a sword in the ribs for me!" Satyrna said. "I'd say I'm pretty involved now!"

The others glanced at each other furtively.

Akena asked the question that was on everyone's mind. "…Is he gonna die?"

Traphian shrugged. "I wouldn't be surprised if he did. That's not a good place to take a hit."

Kirena cried out, not accepting that answer. "No! We can get him to the hospital! Come on, we can't just let him go like that!"

Lauren put her hand on Kirena's arm and shook her head slowly. "Kirena, calm down."

"We can't take him to the hospital anyway," Traphian muttered. "The knights will want vengeance."

"But…" Kirena closed her eyes, not content with just leaving Malkarai alone, but knowing well that her cries were upon deaf, albeit reluctantly deaf, ears. "He shouldn't die… Not after saving the others…"

"Moron," Satyrna muttered bitterly.

Teffifa shook her head. "Don't short-sell him too quickly. If he wants to live, he'll live."

"That's a big if right now, Teffifa."

Satyrna looked meaningfully at Traphian as the group entered the town through the alley path. "He is, isn't he?"

Traphian looked at her, playing dumb. "Huh?"

"You know what I'm asking," Satyrna replied quite pointedly.

He shrugged. "He was. Don't know if he still is."

Kirena looked at the two of them in exasperation. "Oh, come on, why the secrecy? Is he what?"

Teffifa shook her head. "He's gotten better. I mean, he had some drive this time. I haven't seen him actually interested in anything in damn near four years now. That's part of the reason I went along with it – he *wanted* to do this."

Traphian sighed heavily but didn't speak.

Satyrna looked between the two but decided to ask her questions when the others weren't around.

It was quite dark, and thus, the streets were fairly deserted. This was fortunate because the group did not scream innocence. Seth was in the front, followed by Cypha and Lauren supporting Dyspro, Akena, Kirena, and Teffifa – both of her swords sheathed now, but still quite obvious – and then Satyrna, Patricia, and Traphian bringing up the rear. Satyrna and Teffifa were bloody, and Satyrna was clutching two weapons, one of them bloody. If Satyrna hadn't been so preoccupied and worried, she thought she might've enjoyed the fact that they looked like a pretty formidable gang at the moment.

"Where are we headed?" Patricia asked, looking down a familiar street as they passed it.

"Hospital for Dyspro and Teffifa," Lauren responded.

"I'm not letting them look at me," Teffifa corrected.

Cypha looked at her. "Your arm's torn open."

"Yeah, well, I'll wait and get it taken care of at home or something."

Akena looked at her curiously. "Why won't you go to the hospital?"

"They can put your stitches back in, you know," Cypha said, a trace of incredulity in her voice.

"Yeah, but they usually ask for identity at hospitals. Can't give that out. Not here, anyway. It'd be different if I was supposed to be here, but I'm not."

Satyrna shook her head. "You guys are all the same."

She eyed Satyrna with a smirk. "Yeah, kinda."

Satyrna sighed at her. "I'll help you with your arm. I haven't given stitches before, but I can at least clean it up and bandage it for you."

Teffifa looked at her curiously. "Are you a medic or something?"

"I'm in school for nursing."

"Ah, okay. Yeah, I'll let you look at it. I can coach you if you feel ambitious enough to stitch."

Satyrna stared at her. "What? Coach me?"

"Yeah. Sewing people up isn't that graceful of an art. I could probably do it myself if it wasn't on my arm."

Traphian shook his head at Teffifa. The others cast her surprised glances.

"What are you guys?" Cypha asked, her voice hushed.

Teffifa laughed. "Oh, come on, don't be so paranoid. Like I told those knights in there, I'm one of the good guys!"

"You're chasing him," Cypha replied, pointing at Traphian.

"Yeah, and he's not one of the good guys at the moment."

"Thanks for the modifier," Traphian muttered, staring at buildings as they passed.

Satyrna looked at him. "Yeah, why was Malkarai after you?"

"Because their bosses told him to go after me. It's a long story."

Teffifa wagged a thumb at Traphian. "He deserted. They're not terribly fond of people who do that."

"Teffifa, you really shouldn't be saying this."

She shrugged. "All right, I'll stop trying to save your face."

He shook his head with a sigh, a dark expression hovering over his face.

Satyrna eyed him. "Were they trying to capture you?"

"Well, kind of. Capturing would've been an appropriate alternative, yes. People like her and Malk don't usually capture though. Not when there's just one of them. They have the option of doling out punishment – they have the authority. Kind of like the knights back there, except their employers trust their judgment. They don't make the decisions though." He stopped, seemingly perplexed. "I can't say anything else. It's gotten me in enough trouble as it is."

"That it has, meathead," Teffifa said.

"Shut up, lunatic," Traphian snapped back.

Satyrna smirked. The two of them were irritated with each other, but she had this feeling that they weren't really enemies, more like rival siblings. "Want me to fix your arm after we get Dyspro to the hospital then?"

"Yeah, sure."

"Dyspro, you're awfully quiet up there."

He grunted. "Yeah; in pain."

"What happened, exactly?"

"They took me up to that room that Cypha and – uh, Traphian, was it?"

"Yeah."

"I've been in that room they found me in the whole time. Last night, I think, Leah's boyfriend and some other guys came in, talking shit and shoving me around. I fought back. Broke his nose. Well, they outnumbered me, so when they were holding me down, I think her boy toy jumped on my leg – definitely intending to mess it up. I passed out from the pain when something in it snapped. Kalyfa was not pleased with them, I gathered that much."

"Was he really intending to get you a doctor?" Lauren asked.

"I think so. He and someone else looked at my leg this afternoon, but they didn't feel confident enough to do anything to it themselves. Gave me ice and stuff though."

Cypha shook her head. "Can't believe that bitch would sic her boyfriend on you."

"I can. She's a spineless little twit," Seth said bitterly.

Dyspro sighed. "He wouldn't do it one on one. Had to have his buddies and an enclosed area before he did anything. I've been giving her shit for a long time."

"Shows a lot for his character," Satyrna snorted.

"He's dating Leah – he doesn't have much character," Dyspro responded.

Kirena and Akena exchanged looks but didn't comment.

"Hey, she's gone pretty far downhill since I dumped her, okay?"

"'K, Dyspro."

Cypha snickered.

He sighed and changed the topic. "Josh came in just about fifteen minutes before you guys showed up, and he says he tried to convince Kalyfa to let me go, but the wuss shoulda just gotten me out; screw asking."

"You know it's more complicated than that," Satyrna said with a sigh.

"It shouldn't be."

"But it is."

"Here we are!" Lauren said brightly as they approached the hospital, hoping to divert the conversation.

Teffifa hung back, and Traphian followed suit.

Cypha and Lauren proceeded toward the doors until the others realized they'd dropped back.

"Is this where we part ways then?" Patricia asked.

"Yeah," said Teffifa. "I can't go in there, and he shouldn't. We should remain faceless – for our and Malk's sake."

Satyrna glanced at Dyspro and then looked back at Teffifa. "Well, should I help you?"

"Only if you want to."

She glanced at her friends again.

Dyspro shook his head. "Go on, Saty, help her out. She got our asses out of there."

She nodded, a sincere look on her face. "I'll come and see how you're doing as soon as I'm done, okay?"

"Sounds good. I got a big enough posse as it is."

"Are we gonna see you two again, or are you gonna disappear like Malkarai did?" Kirena asked meekly.

Traphian exchanged a glance with Teffifa.

She shrugged. "I dunno. I'll probably split after I gather up some things."

"I'll probably be lurking around somewhere. I need to not exist for a while, and this seems to be a halfway decent place to do it."

"If you're hiding from the federal government, yeah, it's halfway decent for it."

"Satyrna, are you going to come home tonight?" Patricia asked gently.

Satyrna shrugged, avoiding eye contact. "Doubt it. I'll go home with Cypha. I've got blood to wash off."

Patricia nodded slowly. "All right. Let me know what you want to tell Mom and Dad. I'm going to meet with Brendan before I go home."

Cypha was getting impatient. Dyspro was heavy. "All right, enough. We're not dying. Move on. Inside if you're going inside, adios if you're not."

Lauren giggled, and the three of them headed inside. Akena, Kirena, and Patricia followed. Seth hesitated and looked at Traphian and Teffifa. "Thank you."

Teffifa waved a hand at him. "Don't mention it. You should teach that he-bitch dating his ex-girlfriend a lesson though."

Seth smirked and nodded. "Oh, believe me; Dyspro won't let this one go."

"Good. See ya later."

He went inside and Satyrna turned to Teffifa. "Well, shall we fix your arm?"

"Yeah, after we make a trip to the closest drugstore. We'll need a few things." Teffifa turned to Traphian. "We'll be using your place. Take Malk's stuff from her. We'll meet you there after we shop."

Teffifa took Malkarai's sword from Satyrna and shoved it into Traphian's hands. Satyrna gave Traphian a bemused look as she started to lead her down the street.

"Er, see you later, I guess."

"Yeah, I guess." He sighed and shook his head before turning toward the inn.

10:30 p.m.

After getting some first aid supplies, Teffifa and Satyrna headed back to the inn. A few minutes into the walk, Satyrna chanced conversation.

"Hey, Teffifa?"

"Hmm?"

"Are you really Malkarai's partner?"

"Sometimes. He doesn't often need a partner when he works and I already have two other partners, but they pair us up occasionally."

"Why?"

"We kinda complement each other. He's calm and cool. I'm more tempered. He's stealthy, I prefer scare tactics. Neither of us are social workers – we rely on fear and subterfuge to get to the people we need to. Plus, I know he's suicidal. No one else really did. Stika wanted to keep an eye on him."

"Doesn't he have any friends where you're from?"

"He used to. Traphian left, and Arista's gone. He's been pretty… apathetic since she left."

"Apathetic?"

"No emotion, no concern. He did what they told him to, and that was it." She didn't seem pleased about this but didn't elaborate.

Satyrna thought back to what she'd said earlier, that he actually cared about what had happened tonight. "But he didn't care about what he was doing?"

"No. He wasn't invested in any of it. I mean, he knew what he was doing, and why he was doing it, but there was no heart in the matter – well, not the right kind anyway. It was like a reflex. I do what I do because I want to – because I feel that it's right. I think Malkarai did it that way once, but he hasn't for years. He's really good – one of the best… but he doesn't really care if he's working or not. He seems just as happy working as he does when he's just putzing around the lab – he's not. He hasn't been happy doing anything since Arista left."

Satyrna frowned, her brow knitted in concern. After a few moments, she asked, "Lab? What did he do in a lab?"

"He's pretty gifted in chemistry and biology – especially anatomy and physiology. He always mixed poisons and some pharmaceuticals for us at the agency. He tests the crap on himself first before offering them to other people – the medicine, I mean. They're mostly stronger variations of existing medicines with the unnecessary things taken out. They're meant to be taken in small doses and get quick results."

Satyrna blinked, impressed. "Wow… That's what all those bottles were in his coat?"

"Yeah. Well, that and poisons. I don't like that he carries those around on his person, but he says they're for darts and stuff. Still makes me nervous though."

Satyrna looked at Teffifa. "Why?"

"That's how he tried to kill himself. He swallowed poison."

Satyrna gasped softly. "He didn't use a blade?"

"Nah. He didn't want it to look like suicide. He wanted it to look like an accident. But, I found him, and Stika guessed correctly and had his stomach pumped. He recovered, but he was a lot different afterward."

"Because of the poison?"

"No. I don't think so, anyway. It was like, we succeeded in saving him, but he died anyway. He was completely different after that. That was about two or three months after Arista disappeared."

Satyrna nodded slowly as they walked into the inn. "But he's changed since he got here?"

"Yeah. That's why I'm okay with pretending this. You guys woke him up. He's not back to normal, but he's showing interest again. Maybe Traphian will be able to fix what Arista broke."

"Your employers aren't gonna be happy about it though, are they?"

"Probably not. Which is why, if he's still out there kicking, he'd better hide his ass pretty good for a few months."

Satyrna was quiet until they reached Traphian's room. Teffifa knocked.

"Open up, meathead."

Traphian opened the door with an unamused expression on his face. "Watch the names. I could kick you out, you know."

"And I could still drag your ass back to Marion with me. So, shut up and let us in."

Traphian sighed and stood back to let Teffifa and Satyrna in. Inside, Teffifa unstrapped her sword sheath from her back and dropped it on the floor. Then she shed her coat and tossed it on one of the chairs before sitting down. Her top was sleeveless leather over a cotton undershirt, so it was pretty easy to see the half-stitched slice in her left arm. Satyrna sat in the other chair and scooted it over by her, looking at the wound carefully.

Traphian flopped on the bed and turned the TV on.

"Yikes…this is a really big cut."

"Yeah, he got me good."

Satyrna glanced at Traphian, but he had his eyes on the television. "Yeah, well, it didn't slow you down any," he muttered.

"I didn't feel it until later, that's why."

Satyrna eyed Teffifa, an eyebrow cocked.

She shrugged. "I have a nifty little chemical imbalance. Anyway, we should probably clean this first."

"Yeah." Satyrna stood and took the disinfectant out of the bag of medical supplies before following Teffifa into the bathroom.

Teffifa looked back and forth between the tub and the sink a few times before moving to the sink. Then she turned it on and put her arm under, moving it up and down to get the full length of the slice.

Satyrna watched. The cut went from just under her deltoid to the middle of her lower arm, but the stitches had only popped from the skin over her bicep. The ones at the top and most of the ones at the lower end were still intact.

After Teffifa had cleaned the cut, picked out the broken stitches, and rinsed the whole thing with disinfectant, Satyrna handed her a fistful of paper towels to dry her arm with.

"All righty then, let's do this!"

Satyrna shook her head at Teffifa as she walked out to the main room, dabbing at the water and blood.

# 18

December 5, 2036
12:00 midnight

After Teffifa coached her through stitching her arm, Satyrna sat back and asked, "How's that feel?"

"Feels fine. Thanks."

"No problem. Thanks for teaching me."

"Yup." Teffifa ran a finger over the medical tape, securing it as Satyrna started to gather up the supplies and put them back in the bag.

"Headed off to the hospital now?"

Satyrna nodded and then stood to go wash her hands. "Yeah, I'm worried about Dyspro."

"All right, don't linger around here then."

After Satyrna returned, Teffifa handed her the bag of medical supplies. Satyrna gave her a look. "What's this for?"

"Never know who might need it."

"Looks to me like you do."

Teffifa shook her head. "We have plenty of supplies back home. Don't worry about it. Put 'em to good use."

Satyrna sighed and nodded.

"Now get out of here. Tell the kid I hope his leg heals quickly."

Satyrna picked up Malkarai's sword and switchblade, which Traphian had cleaned while Satyrna and Teffifa were busy, and headed for the door. "Thanks, I will. See you later, I guess."

Teffifa grinned. "Hopefully, you won't."

She smiled faintly and waved before leaving.

When the door had shut, Teffifa went and washed her hands and the few drips of blood on her upper arm. Then she put her coat and sword sheath back on and went to the door, holding the roll of paper towels, which she'd pilfered from the supply bag before Satyrna left.

She paused and looked at Traphian, her hand on the doorknob. "Hey."

He looked over at her.

"I'm going to go find him and then clear outta town. What are you two planning?"

"I'm not sure. He said to move and he'd find me if it was safe."

"Yeah, probably not a good idea to come crawling right back here. When are you moving?"

"I'm going to move in the morning. It'll take me too long to find a place at night."

"Okay, well, you two do what you will, but don't make this story I'm telling look wrong. Details can be hazy, but I'm not that fucking stupid that I'd get the location and manner wrong. Stick to the plan or I'll come clean."

"Yeah, yeah, we'll stick to it."

"And stay out of sight. It'll be bad for all of us if you go raising hell again."

"I'm not a moron, Ripper. I only did this to get him out in the first place."

"No one who'd fight the ASA is real gifted in the common sense area, D'vane."

He sighed. "Thank you for this."

"Yeah, whatever. Thanks for the help and the bathroom. See ya."

"Bye."

Teffifa shut the door behind her. When she was at the end of the hall, she heard his door lock click. She nodded to the desk attendant in the lobby as she headed outside. On the street, she took out her phone and called Malkarai.

It rang several times before it was picked up.

"Yeah?" He sounded strained.

"Where are you?"

"Eastern edge of downtown."

"Get yourself where I can see you. I don't feel like searching for your bony ass all night. I'm on Central."

"Yeah, sure."

Teffifa closed her phone and put it in her pocket before turning east and heading for the outskirts of town.

Satyrna watched the sky as she headed to the hospital, praying for clear skies and no wind. There were a few thin clouds, but most of the sky was filled with bright, clear stars.

*Ugh... how the hell did all of this happen? Everything just went so... wrong.*

She looked down at the weapons in her hands and swallowed as she shoved the knife in her pocket, looking back up and away from the sword, which she gripped tightly, making her knuckles go white.

*Fucking Kalyfa... he can just never give up, can he? He gets it in his head that he's right, and he won't stop for anything. I shouldn't have had to stick a knife in your back to get you to stop!*

She wiped her eyes with her sleeve, upset and angry.

"You jackass…"

When she'd left downtown and reached residences, Teffifa stopped, sniffing the air, smelling old blood.

"Yeah… he's here…" she muttered.

She looked around, scanning the area until she saw a shadowed figure approaching her slowly.

Teffifa rested a hand on one of her hilts until he was close enough for her to be sure that it was indeed her colleague.

He nodded to her as he stopped. He seemed tired and was swaying a little. He looked pale. "Did anything else happen after I left?"

"No. We booked it just after you did. Most of them are at the hospital."

Malkarai's face knitted up. "Why?"

"They took the boy there. He has a broken leg. The brunette girl headed there after she was done with Traphian and me."

"Satyrna?"

"Yeah."

"What was she doing with you two?"

"Helping fix your stitch job."

He glanced at her arm. "What'd you do to it?"

She shrugged. "Fighting didn't agree with it."

He sighed. "You don't agree with it."

She nodded. "Yeah, whatever. Anyway, I need your phone and badge. Based on how you smell, I'd say you have more than enough blood to make them look messed up."

He dug through his pockets for a few moments and then handed over the thin leather wallet insert with his badge and the phone. Then he dug through another pocket and handed her car keys.

"Where's your car? Wait, no, don't tell me that. We'll have to find it anyway."

"I'm sure Swip will enjoy searching for it."

"Probably." Teffifa hesitated. "So… what's your next course of action?"

"Crawl out to the woods and die."

She raised an eyebrow at him. "Literally or figuratively?"

He shrugged, looking around evasively. "Don't know yet. I'll see how things go."

Teffifa shook her head. "Well, don't take too long to figure out which one you wanna do. You've lost a lot of blood."

"Yeah." He eyed her. "Your sense of smell creeps me out, Teffifa."

She smirked. "Hey, come on, you can't tell me that you can't smell blood from like fifty yards by now."

"I can smell it, yeah, but not like you."

She handed him the roll of paper towels. "A schoolgirl with a cold could smell you right now. Clean yourself up and get something to eat."

Malkarai took the roll and laughed. "Get out of here."

"Seriously, take care of that properly. Satyrna has the supplies from fixing my arm, and now she knows how to stitch too. You're welcome."

He smirked. "What's that supposed to mean?"

"It means, don't go fucking up and dying anyway. I'm putting my ass on the line here. Make it worth it. Keep your head down, you know they'll look into this."

"All right, I will. Thank you."

"Yeah, whatever. I'm gonna go. Good luck, Malk."

He nodded to her. "Thanks – for everything. See ya."

She shook her head and turned. "No, you won't."

Malkarai watched her for a few moments before walking in the opposite direction, to the east.

When Satyrna got to the hospital, she found Cypha waiting for her in the hall outside of Dyspro's room.

"Hey," Cypha said as she stood up from her leaning position.

"Hey. How is he?"

"Unconscious. They knocked him out when they did surgery to set his leg. They've got it in a cast now, but he'll sleep through 'til tomorrow. It was a nasty break."

Satyrna glanced in the room, which affirmed Cypha's words. She could see Dyspro sleeping, but the room was dim and vacant otherwise. "Did everyone else go home?"

"Yeah, they left like fifteen minutes ago. Lauren had to get Kirena and Akena home before their parents had a fit."

Satyrna nodded and then turned to her. "Well, should we get home then?"

"Yeah."

They got the weapons Satyrna had just checked in to security and headed out of the hospital. Cypha gave her a look. "You're covered in blood."

"Yeah, I know."

"And you're toting a sword."

"Yeah."

"Didn't they give you problems in there?"

"Nah. I checked them in and explained who I was seeing, and they didn't question it. I'm sure they figured they weren't mine."

Cypha snickered. "I'm kinda surprised they don't know the two of you by face. You've dragged him in there at least half a dozen times by now."

Satyrna smiled. "You think our, 'He fell down,' excuse will work anymore?"

"I don't think it worked the first time."

# 19



Cypha stumbled into the main room, rubbing her eyes.

Satyrna, who was sitting on the bench, staring out the window, looked over at her.

The fire was lit and there was wood stacked next to it. Cypha scratched her head, trying to wake up. "Jeez, did you cut all that?"

"Yeah."

"How long have you been up?"

"I don't know. It's snowing."

"Oh, great." Cypha walked over to the window and looked out at the flurrying flakes of white.

"It's been going pretty steadily too. I don't know if it will accumulate though. It might."

"I hope not," Cypha scowled. "I hate snow more than I hate cold."

Satyrna didn't respond, staring out the window again.

Cypha walked over to dig out something to eat.

"Are you going to job hunt today?"

"I don't know. Probably not. I'm running out of places to go. Dyspro said he's probably going to get discharged today."

"Did he call you?"

"Texted, yeah. He probably texted you too."

"Probably."

"Is your phone still dead?" Cypha asked as she located the box of granola bars she was looking for, pulled one out, and stood up.

"Yeah."

"You can use my charger to charge it."

"Eh, maybe."

"Are you purposely avoiding people?"

Satyrna sighed. "The only one I *want* to call me can't, so, sure, I guess."

"Is that why you're staring out the window?"

"Yeah. And I'm thinking, I guess."

"About yesterday?"

"Not just yesterday. There's so much going on here… I was there for all of it, I mean, it was about us, but I still don't understand what happened, or why."

Cypha tore open her granola bar. "What do you mean?"

"I just don't understand this guy… There's so much he won't tell me. I'm picking up on a lot of things, but I don't know why they are the way they are."

"Like what?"

"Like, why was he suicidal?"

She sat down at the table, facing Satyrna. "He was suicidal?" she asked before taking a bite.

"Yeah. I started catching onto it before all hell broke loose, but Teffifa told me he tried to poison himself four years ago."

"He failed?" Cypha cocked an eyebrow, the granola bar hovering in front of her mouth. "How do you fail at poisoning yourself?"

"She found him and some other lady – Stika, I think she called her – had his stomach pumped. So, he succeeded, but they interfered."

Cypha shook her head and took another bite. "Saty's found a mystery."

Satyrna sighed. "Stop acting like this is some project I've discovered. This guy needs serious help."

"Why do you feel you need to help him?"

"I feel obligated…I screwed things up."

"Satyrna, you tried to help him out. Yeah, shit got bad… but that's no one's fault but Kalyfa's."

Satyrna's eyes were locked on something outside, but they were wet and irritated. She sounded distressed. "It's mine, Cypha. I made him come with us into that bar, Kalyfa got pissed because he thought I was in danger, and he took that sword for *me*."

"He made choices there too, Satyrna. It's not all you."

"He wouldn't have been in trouble if it hadn't been for me interfering."

Cypha sighed but didn't speak for a few minutes. "Want to go see Dyspro with me?"

Satyrna nodded.

"We can figure out when they're setting him loose."

"Yeah." She rubbed her eyes with her sleeve.

"He's going to his parents' for a little while though."

"Why?"

"Heat and running water. His mom is concerned. He's gonna leave me here all alone," Cypha sniffed.

"I'll be here. I don't feel like going home and dealing with my family more than necessary right now."

"Think they'll be hard on you?"

"They don't like the trouble that follows darks and you know it. They wouldn't want me to be around him. They didn't like us hanging around Fayta and Martra very much."

"They're just worried about you. And Fayta and Martra *did* get in trouble a lot."

"I know, but Malkarai isn't the same, no matter how Kalyfa is reacting to him. You guys are right; I need to move out. I need distance. I'll see what this break brings… maybe I'll get a place before school starts again."

"You're not gonna stay out here with us?"

Satyrna shook her head. "I need to be in town and have some form of electricity and internet. Half my homework is done on the computer."

"All right. Relax though, okay? This is no way to spend a holiday break; moping in front of a cold window. Let's go visit Dyspro."

"Yeah, okay." Satyrna heaved herself off the bench and put on her coat.

When Cypha had changed, she and Satyrna went into town. They went to the hospital first but were turned away because Dyspro had to see a doctor and have some scans done before he left.

Back on the street, they headed toward downtown.

"I want something warm to eat."

"You have an oven and stove-" Satyrna started.

"That has *meat* in it."

"Dyspro needs to get some kind of fridge out there. But right now, it's so cold, you could probably store meat outside."

"That does not help my desire for protein right now. Anyway, Dyspro's going to be laid up for at least a month. I either need a cooler or a wooden box to keep stuff safe from animals – and have to pay close attention to the temperature. Those are future problems. Current Cypha is hungry and wants someone else to cook for her."

Satyrna smirked. "All right, fine." She pointed to a man by the front of a store a few yards in front of them. "Oh, isn't that Traphian? By the window?"

Cypha strained her neck to see and nodded. He was looking at what appeared to be a physical paper map. "I think so."

"You wanna see what he's doing? Maybe he's hungry too."

"Yeah, sure. Is that what it's gonna take to make you actually willing to eat in town with me?"

Satyrna shrugged as she made her way over to him. "Maybe."

Cypha followed her. "He still has a key to our house, all right? If he shows up while we're gone, he can get in."

"If he shows up while we're gone, he can escape again," Satyrna insisted.

Cypha shrugged.

When they got near Traphian, Satyrna called out to him to catch his attention. "Traphian?"

He turned his head quickly and looked at her sharply, startled. When he saw who it was, he sighed in relief, relaxed, and looked around to see if anyone else had heard her.

"What's wrong?" Satyrna asked.

"Uh, don't say my name out loud. Teffifa's back at the agency, yes, but right now's a very risky time to be out and about. They have people spying for them that even Malkarai didn't know about."

She nodded. "I understand; I'm sorry. What should we call you?"

"Nothing; don't say my real name or my fake one. Either one will give me away."

Cypha raised an eyebrow. "So, they know you pretty well?"

"Yeah; they raised me. I'm sure they have a nice thick file on me."

"Malkarai is a law enforcer, right?" Satyrna asked, her voice quiet but insistent.

Traphian looked at her and nodded slowly. "Well, he was until yesterday, anyway."

"I saw his badge. He tried to say he had it so he could carry weapons around, but I could tell he was being evasive."

"Well, yeah. He isn't supposed to tell people what he is."

"Why not?" Cypha asked bluntly.

"It's confidential. *That's* why they were hunting for me. I was talking about it."

"Why were you talking about it?" Satyrna pressed.

"I wanted them to give agents the option to quit. Their contracts basically say they can't. Malk needed out."

"How come?" Satyrna asked.

Traphian looked around. "We really shouldn't be discussing this out here."

"Did you hurt anyone?" Cypha asked.

He looked at her, his brow knitting up slightly. "Only minor injuries, so I could escape – until Teffifa came after me. Hers was the worst because she's too hard to fight. I didn't give her a life-threatening injury though."

"But it was just agents?"

"Yeah. I've never had anything against anyone outside of the system. Well, not anything that I'd hurt people for."

"All right," Cypha said with finality. "Come have lunch with us. I'm getting hangry, and it's cold out here."

Satyrna nodded, encouraging him to say yes.

He glanced around. "I'm not sure that's a good idea – hanging out in public, I mean."

"What are you outside for right now?"

"I moved inns and I needed to get food."

"Well, here's one meal handled. C'mon, let's go to our friend's restaurant – I'll ask him to let us eat in the break room," Cypha said, walking past him and gesturing with a hand.

Satyrna looked at Traphian until he sighed and turned, following them as he folded his map up.

Cypha led them to Barry's restaurant and, inside, she went right up to the bar, where Barry was wiping the counter behind the bar down.

He glanced over. "Cypha! Hey, what's up? You look like you have something up."

"Yep. Can we eat in your break room?" she asked, leaning on the bar.

He gave her a perplexed look and came closer. "What for?"

"Uh, I can give you a lowdown later, when you have a few minutes, but we've got a friend who'd rather not be seen by the public at the moment," she said, gesturing to where Traphian and Satyrna were just behind her, closing the door.

"Oh, another friend? Sheesh, what the hell have you guys been up to?"

"Long story. Can we go back there?"

Barry looked from Traphian back to Cypha. "Uh, I've got staff back there…"

She pursed her lips, looking disappointed.

"Use my office. Are you planning on ordering food?"

"Yes. I'm starving."

"Okay," he said, pulling keys out of his pocket and handing them to her. "Uh, grab a menu for your friend if he's eating too, and just go back there. I'll come and talk with you in a few minutes."

"Thanks," Cypha said, patting her hand on the bar. "You rock."

"Eh, I'm mostly just curious."

She smirked at him and turned around, pulled a menu off the hostess stand, and then gestured for them to follow her as she went around the bar, to the back left corner. "Back here," she said as she went.

Traphian looked around the restaurant as they went, but he and Satyrna followed her into the back hallway, past the restrooms, and up to one of the unmarked doors. Cypha unlocked one and held it open for them, handing Traphian the menu as he passed her.

She shut the door, leaving it unlocked, after everyone was in. "Private enough?"

Satyrna immediately went over and started moving boxes off of some of the chairs in the office, stacking them neatly along a bookcase. There were a few filing cabinets and a closed safe along the wall behind the desk with boxes and some piles of paperwork on them, but most of the desk top was visible. A couple of clipboards were piled next to a box of pens in a corner of it, and there was a lamp in the opposite corner, but otherwise, it was fairly empty.

Traphian looked around the office, nodding. "Yeah. I'm kind of impressed at how organized this is…"

Cypha snorted and sat down behind the desk, since Traphian was lingering near one of the chairs that Satyrna had cleared off, and Satyrna had already sat down in one of the others. "Do you spend a lot of time in restaurant offices?"

"I mean, not a ton, but I've worked in a few restaurants. Their offices are usually greasy and unorganized."

"Gross. I've never worked food service, but Barry's dad kept this place clean, and Barry's kept it the same. He lives upstairs."

"Oh, I see. How long have you been friends?"

"We befriended Barry our first year of high school," Satyrna said. "We all went to the same elementary because there's only one here, but he was in a different class than Dyspro and Josh for most of it. They hit it off freshman year, so he joined the group."

"He's the easiest of all of us to find," Cypha said. "But he's also the busiest, so you can pretty much just find him here. He needs another manager."

The door had opened while she was still talking, so Barry shook his head at her. "Yeah, yeah, I know. Find me someone competent enough to do it, and we'll see."

"Good luck finding that in this town," Cypha scoffed.

Barry shut the door. "Right? Anyway. Hi, I'm Barry, which you probably figured out already."

Traphian stood up and held out a hand, shaking Barry's. "Uh, Traphian. Keep that quiet though, all right?"

"Sure… why?" Barry said, glancing from Satyrna to Cypha after he'd let go of Traphian's hand. "What are you all up to? A dark guy a few days ago, and now keeping secrets?"

Satyrna just smirked halfheartedly.

"Yeah, uh, shit's gone down lately," Cypha said. "Our dark friend pissed off the knights."

Barry groaned and crossed his arms. "Seriously? Why?"

"Uh, long story. They had a tiff, and then they took all three of us into protective custody. Leah's boyfriend, Carter, went in by Dyspro while he was in custody and picked a fight, and ended up breaking his leg. He's at the hospital and getting out this afternoon."

Barry's eyebrows furrowed, looking concerned. "Fuck. How bad?"

"Uh, bad. They fractured his femur, so he had to have surgery, but thankfully they think it'll heal okay. It's just gonna take a while."

"That fucking sucks."

"Yeah."

"Does Josh know about it?"

"Yeah." Cypha rolled her eyes. "He's choosing to try to play neutral and avoid the whole situation."

"He wasn't entirely neutral," Satyrna said. "He told Teffifa where to find me and then just left. He could've ratted on her."

"And me," Traphian muttered.

"Yeah," Cypha agreed. She looked at Barry. "They had us in protective custody because our dark friend is – was? – a law enforcer that was after a criminal, and Kalyfa was afraid his target would come after us for leverage."

Barry frowned. "I guess that makes sense…"

Satyrna pointed at Traphian. "Except *this* is that criminal, and he's not a threat to us or anyone."

Barry looked at Traphian, an eyebrow raised. "Oh. So that's where you come in, huh?"

"Yeah," he said with a smirk.

"So that's why you want to hide back here?"

"Well, Malkarai's coworker is going to go back and tell their bosses that we're dead so they drop this chase for me and don't look for him. I'm not technically a criminal – I was charged with things, but never answered the charges, and was never sentenced. All I did was try and get him out, but they wanted me to shut up."

"I see."

"I mean, we came here because it's safe ground for me and Saty. It's a bonus that it's also safe for him while we try and talk about some shit," Cypha said.

Traphian looked at her, bemused. "You don't trust me?"

"Mm, not yet. Last time I met you you nearly pulled a knife on me, so yeah, you're on a probationary period."

Traphian laughed. "Okay, but that was eleven-year-old Traphian. Twenty-three-year-old Traphian saved you from a castle."

Barry snickered. "Saving the damsel in distress does not work for Cypha."

Cypha nodded in agreement.

Satyrna smiled, fondly. "Yeah, Cypha'd rather see the knife these days."

Cypha grinned and Barry laughed.

Satyrna looked up at Barry. "We met both Malkarai and Traphian when we were little. They were here when Fayta and Martra were killed."

His eyebrows raised. "Oh? Really?"

"Yeah, I figured it out after talking to Malkarai a little. He didn't tell me he was here chasing Traphian, but I actually saw him before Malkarai was in town. So, yeah…" Satyrna glanced at Traphian. "I want to be friends with Malkarai if he's still going to stay here. If he's still okay. I'd like to be friends with you too – if you're going to stay."

Traphian shrugged. "We'll see what happens. We have to survive an investigation first because I'm sure they'll come here and try to figure out what happened."

Satyrna sighed, looking troubled.

"Where's Malkarai now?" Barry asked.

"I don't know. He got hurt fighting the knights when we all got out of the castle, and then just disappeared."

"When did that happen?"

"Last night." Satyrna looked at the menu that was still in Traphian's hands and nudged it gently. "So, let's order food, because I want to get back out there, in case he comes around and needs medical help."

Traphian opened up the menu, looking down at it.

"Out where?" Barry asked.

"Saty's staying with me for a bit. Dyspro's gonna stay with his parents cuz of the leg," Cypha said, rotating the chair she was in slightly, back and forth. "Malkarai knows where the cottage is."

"Oh, well, that works if he's trying to keep hidden. You guys are pretty far out there."

"Mm-hmm."

"But, yes, let's get you food. You're fine to hang out in here as long as you need though – I don't have anything to do in here until later this afternoon."

"We'll be out of here before then," Satyrna insisted.

"So, if Teffifa is telling people you're both dead," Cypha said, pausing midsentence to swallow, "how come you're just lurking around here? Doesn't it make more sense to bolt?"

Traphian glanced up at her, hesitating with a fry halfway to his mouth. "Uh, well, Malk's still here, I assume."

"Yeah, but he was *after* you. Why are you waiting for him?"

Traphian glanced at Satyrna, who was also looking at him, and then back to Cypha. "Well… the whole reason I was fighting the system was for him. He's my little brother."

"*Actual* brother?"

"No. We've been together since he was three and I was five. We aren't related. Most likely." He tipped his head slightly. "I guess I can't say with 100% certainty that we aren't related, but we really are nothing alike. Physically, socially, mentally… Probably why we made a good team, to be honest. We have entirely different strengths."

"You don't know anything about your parents?" Satyrna asked gently.

Traphian shook his head.

"Who raised you?" Cypha asked.

"There was a caretaker where we're from. We had school there too. So, a lot of people and no one? They taught us a lot, but we were only vaguely parented."

Cypha snickered. "'Vaguely parented…' I like that."

Satyrna gave her an amused, sidelong look. "I think that describes you too."

"Probably why I like it," Cypha said with a laugh.

Satyrna looked at Traphian. "You two were kinda fighting when we met you the first time."

He chewed and swallowed thoughtfully. "Were we? I mean, it makes sense. Malk was kind of a pushover except with me. Even if we were fighting then, we weren't *mad* at each other. We were always ragging on each other. The moment someone else went at either of us though, you got both of us with claws out. We both had many chances to split up or distance ourselves from one another, but we never wanted to. We just had an understanding. The only time we ever really went in two directions was when I escaped. He was *supposed* to come with me, but he hesitated and then told me to go. I said I'd get shit in order so he could join me, but that's the last I saw him until a few weeks ago. He got reeled back in, I guess. Probably at least partially of his own choice."

"You hadn't talked to him in years?" Satyrna asked, concerned.

"Well, we'd talked. Through email. Just not in person."

"How long ago did you run away?" Cypha asked.

"I was fifteen… so seven years ago? He's the only reason I was still in *this* area though. If I was just trying to get away from home I'd have gone to a coast or left the country."

"Oh, so you guys are local?"

Traphian nodded, looking at Cypha.

"Where are you from?" Satyrna pressed.

Traphian hesitated. "South Dakota. This corner."

"Sioux Falls?"

He shook his head. "We're from a small town. Smaller than this one. That's the area though, yes."

Cypha snorted. "Sheesh, you are *really* local. I'd never have guessed that. Well, maybe I'd have guessed that looking at you. Malkarai doesn't look small town. He's like…lazy goth."

Satyrna smirked.

"Yeah, that's a good way to describe it. Malk dresses for his job. We all did. The only new part of that since I left was the coat, but it fits him. Also, we spent a lot of time traveling, and they taught us about all kinds of places, so I think it's fair to say we're pretty socially aware and worldly. He's had way more of that training than I have. I finished high school on the outside, so I got more organic world experience."

Satyrna shook her head slightly. "'Organic world experience…' Bull. That's propaganda people like you and Cypha tell yourselves to make fending for yourself way younger than you should be sound romantic."

Cypha smirked, giving Satyrna a fond, amused look.

"You both should've been taken care of and loved, not all on your own. It's impressive you've made it, but it shouldn't have been that way."

Traphian laughed and shrugged. "Yeah, but I ran away, so I don't blame anyone for it. I could've run back or asked for help, and I guess I did a few times – just not from the people I ran from. When I was in high school, I lived above this older lady who purposely didn't ask questions because she got free help around the house and a fairly steady rent check. She did a bunch of stuff for me and just didn't dig into why I asked her to. She was awesome."

"Oh, so you weren't hiding this whole time, huh?" Cypha asked.

Traphian shook his head. "I had several long-term aliases. Trebo's just the most recent one. I may have been dodging the authorities, but I wasn't trying to break laws."

"You were probably breaking a few identity and tax laws…" Satyrna muttered.

"Yeah," Traphian chuckled. "The IRS is the least of my worries at the moment though."

She sighed.

Cypha gave him a judging look as she took a long drink. When she put her cup down on the desk she said, "Wait, so, you're telling me you *chose* the name 'Trebo'?"

Traphian looked at her and nodded.

"Fuck. *Why?*"

Satyrna giggled.

"Hey, what's wrong with it?"

"It sounds so *stupid*," Cypha said with a laugh. "Where'd you get it from?"

He shrugged. "I made up a list while I was in high school, and mostly I just took from that. It wasn't one of my first choices, but I figured it was fine enough. Is my real name at least not a disgrace?"

"No, your real name is good. I like it."

"Yeah," Satyrna agreed.

"Just, maybe leave naming kids or pets to someone else," Cypha added, snickering.

He smirked and shook his head, looking down at the remains of his food and picking up another fry. "Maybe I'll get adult supervision when I pick my next one. I'm gonna need another one, I'm sure."

"Yeah, Trebo has to be retired," Satyrna agreed thoughtfully. "So, you're hinging the *where* on wherever Malkarai ends up?"

Traphian nodded. He looked up at her. "Oh, I moved, by the way. If Malkarai ends up out by you, will you let me know and tell him where I am now?"

"Sure. Will you do the same?"

"Uh… sure. How do I contact you?"

Satyrna contemplated this for a few moments. "Hmm, leave a note for me at the store."

He nodded. "That works. How often do you work?"

"Right now, I should be there most days. I have been kinda preoccupied the past few days, but I'll start working again in a day or two. I'm extra help – I'm usually in school, but it's winter break right now. Mom, Dad, and Patricia run it. Where are you now?"

"Another inn – on Eighteenth and Forest. Room 9."

"Okay, I'll remember that."

Cypha opened the desk drawer and rummaged around in it before pulling out a notepad and writing on it. "I won't."

Traphian snickered. "Where's your cottage, anyway? Sounds like it's outside of town."

"It is. It doesn't have a posted address, and it's kinda hard to find it if you aren't shown the way," Satyrna said.

"You have to follow Main until it doesn't exist anymore, and then go farther, into the woods," Cypha said, clicking the pen she had been using and tossing it back in the drawer before pulling the notepaper off the pad and shutting the drawer. "She's right, it's hard to find."

"That's enough info I could at least have a direction to try if I needed to. I should stay in though. I'm going to stock up on food again and hide until things have had a chance to settle."

"Get food from my parents' place," Satyrna insisted. "Patricia and I can talk to them and make sure that no one hears about you shopping there."

He smiled. "Thanks, I appreciate that."

"I need to get some too," Cypha said. "My last grocery trip was pretty rushed and I forgot some shit."

"Okay, we'll all go and I can introduce you to whoever is working," Satyrna said.

"If Barry's of the same mindset, I might give this place my patronage a few times too."

"He'd keep his mouth shut, yeah," Cypha said around her last mouthful of food and then swallowed. "But, I'd be wary about the other people here. Knights frequent this place."

"Maybe I won't then." He sighed. "That's a shame, I hate paying delivery fees. I'll just stock up at the store."

# 20



After parting ways with Traphian and going out to the cabin to drop off groceries and check for Malkarai, who was not there, Satyrna left a note on the table, and they went back into town to wait for Dyspro to be discharged.

Satyrna sighed, looking around the waiting room she and Cypha were sitting in.

Cypha was slouched in her chair, idly looking through things on her phone.

"Kalyfa's probably in here, isn't he?" Satyrna asked quietly after a period of silence.

Cypha looked up at her, not moving otherwise. "I guess. What happened to him?"

Satyrna was quiet for a few moments, her lips pressed together tightly. "Um, he got stabbed and then knocked out."

"Oh. Yeah, probably, but maybe not still today. Unless the stab was in an organ, I don't see why they'd keep him for that."

Satyrna inhaled deeply and exhaled silently, avoiding Cypha's gaze.

Cypha watched her for a few moments before looking at her phone. "I asked Josh what he's been doing. He said he tried to see Dyspro this morning but got turned away like we did. He's on patrol now."

"Oh. Is he going to stop avoiding us?"

Cypha snorted softly. "Probably not. I'm sure he's going to avoid us even harder now."

"Glad he's at least answering your texts."

"Oh, he's always answered them – it's just usually to turn down invites."

"He rarely talks to me."

"You don't text people."

"I guess," Satyrna said with a sigh.

Satyrna hopped to her feet when she saw Dyspro in the hospital hall, flanked by his father and youngest sister. Cypha stood too, but slower. She turned her phone off and slipped it into her coat pocket.

Dyspro gave them a grin as he reached them. He was on crutches, and his normally baggy pants were fairly snug over the cast on his broken leg. "Look!" he said, holding that leg out in front of him briefly. "You can hardly tell!"

Satyrna smiled, narrowing her eyes at him.

Cypha laughed. "Yeah, sure. Totally not obvious at all," she said sarcastically.

"Right? Regardless, I'm free!"

"No, you're not," Kirena said. "You've gotta walk around on sticks. Gimpy."

He shrugged. "Yeah, but this way I can beat anyone I want and not have my weapon taken away. C'mere, Kirena!"

She squealed and jumped out of the way as he swung one crutch at her feet.

Cypha laughed. "Feeling better, Dyspro, or is it a reaction to some drug they gave you?"

"Can't tell. If I'm depressed by tonight, you know it was a drug." Dyspro started for the door. "Come on, I want to spend as little time in this place as a free person as possible."

Outside, Dyspro walked next to Satyrna and Cypha, following Kirena and their father.

"Stay here, I'll pick you up," his father said, digging his keys out of his pocket.

"I can walk okay, Dad."

"It's snowed. I don't feel like having to check you back in for another broken leg. Wait here."

Satyrna and Cypha stayed with Dyspro as he leaned against a column outside the exit. He blinked in the light and looked around at the dark, dirty buildings, grinning. "Yay! Natural colors!"

Cypha laughed and Satyrna chuckled, shaking her head.

"Dyspro, you are really stupid sometimes."

"Hey, it's my job to be the comic relief."

"I sure hope you aren't paid a lot for that."

"Actually, I'm pretty sure I haven't been paid yet. You all owe me years of back wages."

Cypha shook her head. "You owe all of *us*."

Dyspro blew a raspberry at her and changed the subject. "I'm going to go to my parents' house for a while before I come home."

Cypha nodded. "I know. You saw my message saying that Satyrna's staying with us, right?"

"Yeah, I saw it."

"Just until I find a place of my own," Satyrna said, looking down the street. "I'll need another job though."

Cypha sighed. "You can join the search with me then."

Dyspro shrugged. "She could probably get a job easily. And when she does, she can put in a good word for you."

"I don't like taking handouts."

They both said in unison, "We know."

Dyspro laughed and Cypha couldn't help but smile.

He looked at Satyrna, who had been rather preoccupied since they came outside. She was still scanning the street. "What's up, Saty?"

She glanced at him momentarily and shook her head slowly as she looked back across the parking lot. "Nothing."

Cypha, who was on the other side of Dyspro, rolled her eyes. "You-know-who still hasn't surfaced," she said quietly.

"Oh," he replied. "He's injured, isn't he?"

"Yeah."

"How bad?"

"Bad," Satyrna muttered.

"His ass should've been in the hospital with me, then."

"Traphian said he can't," Satyrna said. "They're going to pretend they're dead, so he can't go to a hospital."

"Then what the hell is he supposed to do?"

"If he'd come out to the cottage I could *try* to fix it," Satyrna said in irritation, quietly. "But instead, he's just trying to avoid us. Or he already *died*. I *don't know*."

The others didn't respond, although Dyspro sighed heavily.

Suddenly, Satyrna tapped Dyspro on the shoulder. She pointed to a store on the other side of the street. "Look at the girl closest to the corner of the building. The one with black hair. Can you see her?"

They both nodded.

"I think she's a dark. It's kinda hard to tell from this distance, but when she turned our direction, I saw her eyes."

"Wonder what she's doing here," Cypha muttered.

"Huh," Dyspro mused. "Maybe we should tell her to get out before something awful happens to her too."

"Malkarai's problems weren't because he was dark," Satyrna said quietly.

"I guess so. I can't say I've ever seen a dark girl alone before," Dyspro said musingly.

"Me neither. Fayta always stuck to Martra like glue. Not that that helped her stay out of trouble, though…"

Satyrna frowned. "All the more reason for us to stay away from her if she is dark, right?"

Dyspro bumped Satyrna with his arm. "Hey, Saty, chin up, okay?"

"Why?"

"Because I don't know what to do with you like this."

She eyed him. "Do you really think I don't have a reason to be upset?"

"I'm just used to you being optimistic no matter what happens. I'm okay. Is that one consolation?"

"You shouldn't be hurt in the first place. And neither should Malkarai. This whole situation is my fault."

"You never pissed off Leah's boyfriend. I did."

"And I have a feeling that Kalyfa didn't like Malkarai even before you tried to help him out," Cypha added.

"But none of us should've been in that castle… He shouldn't have been hurt. He should've been able to do his work and move on…"

"Satyrna, don't blame yourself. You did your best to help the guy out. No one is gonna kill you for being nice."

"They tried to kill Malkarai for it."

"That's their dysfunction, not yours," Dyspro said. "You never did anything wrong. Besides, we backed you up. It's just as much our fault as yours. We coulda held you back and stayed away from him, but we agreed with you; he's a good guy that shouldn't be treated like crap. We offered for him to stay with us, not you."

Satyrna looked at Dyspro, a dejected look on her face. "I didn't want anyone to get hurt."

"We know, Saty. You always want the best for everyone. It's not your fault that man has enemies. He made choices too."

"His choices should've kept him alive," she murmured as Dyspro's father drove up.

"His choices are his business."

Cypha opened the front door for Dyspro and motioned to the back with a thumb. "Move it, squirt."

Kirena stuck her tongue out and hopped out of the front seat so her brother could sit up front.

Dyspro bumped Satyrna's leg with his crutch before climbing into the car. "I'm out of the hospital. Let's do something fun tonight, okay?"

"Like what?" Cypha asked, eager to change the subject.

"I dunno. Hey, Dad, what do you guys got planned tonight?"

"Your mother's working on supper. Beyond that, nothing. Why?"

"I haven't been home in ages. Let's do something together."

"Yeah, sure. You name it, and we'll see."

Dyspro smiled and looked back at Cypha and Satyrna, who had slid in after Kirena in the back seat. "You're gonna stay, right?"

"Yeah, we'll stay," Cypha said before Satyrna could opt out.

Satyrna gave her a confused look. "Really?"

"Yeah. If I'm staying, your ass is definitely staying."

Dyspro smirked and winked at Cypha, who just looked ahead, a small smile tugging at her straight mouth.

"Only for dinner, okay?" Satyrna pleaded quietly.

"Yes, yes, only for dinner. You need a distraction. This guy doesn't do anything during the daylight anyway."

Satyrna sighed but didn't protest.

Creeping along at a distance, the dark girl followed as Malkarai made his way out of town and into the woods east of town.

She had shoulder-length jet-black hair covered with a warm ski cap and had long black eyelashes. Her large, dark eyes had brown irises. She was short, maybe a few inches over five feet, and wore dark blue jeans and low-heeled brown boots under a black pea coat. There was a burgundy messenger bag over her shoulder and across her body holding a fair number of items.

He didn't go to the little cabin, like she was expecting, but stayed north of it. He'd spent most of the day in the northeast part of the woods, asleep, but then went into town and snuck around a little once it had gotten dark. He'd been moving slowly the whole time, shaky and kind of clumsy. She'd expected him to eat, but he'd just watched at a few places and was apparently retreating to the woods again.

She'd long ago figured out he was hurt somehow, but he never went to get help, so she wasn't sure how or how badly.

After watching him for twenty minutes or so and realizing that he wasn't going anywhere, she tentatively crept closer to him, trying to see how close she could get before he noticed her. She wanted to try and finally confront him, but she was scared about it too. He was curled up on the ground, lying on his right side with his arms clutched in front of him, one down by his waist and the other by his neck, both holding his coat.

She was within five feet of him before he started, turning over so his back was almost on the ground. He stared at her, eyes wide in surprise at first, but quickly narrowing.

"Who are you? What do you want?" he demanded, sounding wheezy.

She swallowed, hopping back a step. "A-are you hurt?"

"Why?"

She looked him over, seeing the saturated and torn part of his shirt on his right side, and then noticing the roll of paper towels that were half-soaked in both wet and dry blood that he had pressed against his shirt on that side. "Oh…" she said quietly in horror before looking up at his face, her expression changing to resolute. "Um! Please, stay here!"

"*What?*"

"P-please, just stay here, okay? I'll be right back! J-just me, okay? Just stay there!"

"Don't – I am trying to *hide*," he wheezed desperately, shifting like he was going to sit up.

"No, no, I know that! I won't tell anyone! Just stay right there, okay?"

She took a few more steps backward, watching to make sure he wasn't immediately moving to get up, and then turned and hurried back to town.

Malkarai's eyebrows furrowed as he watched the girl run off, his mouth open slightly in a grimace of both confusion and pain. Being startled and jumping hurt, but also, he didn't know what just happened. "What the *fuck…?*" he whispered.

He seriously contemplated moving so she couldn't find him as easily, but ultimately, he didn't move. She seemed young, naïve, sincerely worried, and reacted to the blood like a normal person would.

"Is this who's been following me?" he muttered to himself. "This spastic kitten? A fucking *dark* kid?"

He let himself back down to the ground gently, grunting and grimacing as he did so. After he shifted the paper towels so they were putting pressure on his side again, he lay there, facing upward with his coat pulled around him again.

Malkarai dozed off at some point.

He woke again with a painful jolt when he heard, "A-are you okay? You aren't dead, are you?"

"Ugh," he groaned, blinking to rewet his eyes as he stared at the dark girl, who was clutching a plastic grocery bag and staring at him worriedly. "No, I'm not dead," he retorted.

"I'm so glad," she said, sounding genuinely relieved.

"What do you want?" he demanded unkindly, shifting and pushing himself to a sitting position with one hand while he held his side with the other.

"Um, I…" she faltered before abruptly holding out the bag. "I got you things! I-I noticed you hadn't eaten, and you're hurt, so I got you some stuff to help!"

She came close enough to give him the bag, holding it steadfastly out to him until he reached up and took it, peeking inside to see what she'd gotten.

The package of jerky and the two protein bars were smart choices, the pouch of applesauce was odd, the cheese-flavored crackers were less useful but still looked mildly appetizing, and the bottle of sports drink looked way more enticing than it should've. However, the box of adhesive bandages of assorted sizes was not helpful – not for what he had wrong with him.

He looked up at her, his eyes narrowed appraisingly. "Who are you?"

She looked like she was incredibly nervous, but trying her best to be brave. She tipped her chin up slightly. "Y-you answer my questions first. I gave you things, it's only fair."

"I didn't ask for this," he responded readily.

"B-but you need them. You haven't eaten all day."

"What are your questions?"

She stammered but asked rapidly, "Is your name Malkarai? How old are you? Where were you born? How did you get to the ASA?"

As soon as she said, 'ASA' Malkarai's pallor and demeanor both changed. He stared at her, chillingly, and interrupted her before she could continue. "How do you know about the ASA?"

She faltered, her mouth open slightly as she processed the question. "Uh, um. I-" she cut herself off. "Answer one of my questions first!"

He stared at her intensely. "Twenty-one. How do you know about it? You're a civilian, aren't you?"

"C-civilian?" she asked, confused by the question.

He sighed and rolled his eyes. "Yes, you're definitely a civilian. How do you know that name?"

"I-I don't know what it means. I just know it cuz I overheard it."

"Where did you overhear it?" he insisted.

"A-answer another question!" she demanded.

"Yes."

"Wh-what question did that answer?" she asked, perplexed. "Your name?"

"There was only one yes or no question," he replied coldly. "Where did you overhear it?"

She looked like she was processing that momentarily before she replied, "I've been trying to find you for a while. I hung outside of the building in Marion for a bit, and I overheard people talking about it."

He shook his head, his expression looking more and more severe the more she said.

"I don't know what it means!" she said defensively. "I also don't know what you do, but I've seen you go to work, and I've seen you fight. This is the only job I've been able to keep up with you on though."

"If you value your life, you will never tell anyone what you've seen or mention the ASA ever again," he said seriously, staring at her.

Her lower lip quivered a bit as she stared at him, fear starting to overtake her courage.

"I'm not just lying here because it's fun, there is some really dangerous and messed up shit going on, and following me around is one of the dumbest things you could do. This name you keep throwing around could get both you and me in deep trouble, so you'd better forget it and never say it again. You need to leave me alone, and stay away from that building," he said firmly, almost hissing.

She swallowed, looking aggrieved. "When there isn't any more trouble, can we talk again?"

Malkarai scowled at her persistence. "Yeah, sure, if I'm not dead."

"Okay!" She inhaled shortly, staring at him. "Please don't die!" she cried before turning and hurrying off into the woods, toward town.

He watched her go, frowning. Eventually, he laboriously got to his feet, holding the paper towel roll against his side with his right hand and holding the bag of food and bandages in his left. He moved farther into the woods, finding a new place before he sat down and ate the food she'd gotten for him. It was hopelessly processed, but he was grateful nonetheless.

*For fucks' sake... my stupid shadow has been a civilian? I suppose it makes sense she was stealthy since she's a dark... We're the most practiced at pretending we aren't there.*

He sighed and stuffed all of the empty wrappers in the bag with the bandages before settling down on the ground how he was earlier, with pressure on his side and his coat pulled around him.

*At least she isn't one of Carlisle's assmonkeys like I was starting to fear...*

# 21

Malkarai pulled the key from his pocket as he approached the little stone cabin, scanning the area around it, and then turning and searching the woods behind him as he reached the door. He stood still for a few minutes, listening and looking.

His mysterious civilian follower hadn't returned after dropping the drug store dinner on him, at least that he was aware of. He'd spent most of the night since then asleep.

Comfortable with his solitude, he turned to the door, unlocked it, and slipped the key back into his pocket as he slowly, carefully turned the knob and opened the door.

It was surprisingly quiet. He mentally thanked Dyspro and shut the door behind him as he looked around.

The fire was burning in the fireplace still, but it was low. The main room was empty of people, and from where he was standing, he could see that Dyspro's door was shut.

He took a step to the side and noted that Cypha's door was also shut, but the extra room was open. That worked for him: he needed something from in there.

After taking two logs from the pile next to the hearth and putting them on the fire, he went over to the dishes, found a pot, and then went back to the door, moving slowly.

He scanned the area again as he went outside and got water, but returned to the cabin without incident. He turned the lock behind him after shutting the door again, and then went over to the fireplace and used the poker to pull the iron grate that was attached to the side of the interior of the fireplace out to set the pot on.

Malkarai sighed silently, putting his hands up toward the fire to warm them for a few minutes, grimacing and pressing his elbow and lower arm against his side as it twinged. He needed the hot water before he could do anything, but warming himself was too passive. His side had had such a steady ache all day while he avoided moving, the sharp jabs of pain now were both motivating and exhausting him. He looked around the room, making sure that what he needed hadn't been relocated to out here, and noticed his sword on the table, on top of a piece of paper.

After unstrapping his sheath from his belt, he picked up his sword and slid it into the sheath before setting it back down on the table. Then he picked up the note, read it, and his brow furrowed slightly as he smirked.

*Malkarai – thank you for finally doing the smart thing and coming here. I have first aid things to help you. If we're not here, please wait for us so we can help. We can tell you where Tr. moved to as well.*

*Stay put, or else.*

*-Satyrna*


He shook his head. *'Stay put, or else'... 'Or else' what, Satyrna? You'll slap me again?* He made a small noise of amusement and put the note back down. *I probably need that.*

He had no intention of waiting for or waking anyone, although the promise of actual first aid items was enticing. After holding a hand over the pot to see if the water was starting to heat up yet and accepting that it was still quite cold, he carefully took off his coat and laid it over one of the chairs at the table. Then he made his way quietly back to the open door for the extra room.

Malkarai peered inside, taking in the dim room. The moon outside was pretty bright but wasn't directly shining through the thin curtains. Regardless, he could still see the curled-up form in the bed and hear her soft breathing. He wasn't surprised that Satyrna was here, but he'd been hoping maybe she had been at home if only to make sneaking in and out easier.

Moving slowly, deliberately, and silently, he went over to the dresser and opened the drawer he remembered Cypha taking sewing supplies out of when he'd asked if she had anything he could use to mend his coat a few nights ago. He scanned the drawer, shifted a few things, and then slowly closed it, opening the drawer next to it. This one had the sewing supplies in it.

He stopped moving as he heard shifting in the bed behind him, holding his breath as he waited for her to be still again.

She didn't settle though, and he eventually turned his head, trying to see if Satyrna had woken up fully, just to be startled when he felt her arms wrap around his chest tightly, hugging him.

"Malkarai," she whispered, desperately, pressing her cheek against his upper back and the base of his neck. She apparently could feel his physical reflex to bolt, because she just squeezed more firmly, holding him in place. "Don't."

He inhaled, trying to calm his racing heart. Getting found while trying to be stealthy was an adrenaline rush – and not one he wanted right now. He felt lightheaded. After a few moments, he said softly, "I won't run."

She hesitated, but then released her hold, letting him go.

Malkarai turned around, bumping into the dresser as he looked at her.

She was frowning at him, her eyes full of worry. "Where have you been?"

"Hiding."

"Just hiding? Have you taken care of your wound?"

"That- that's why I'm here." He shifted and grabbed a spool of thread from the drawer that was still open behind his legs, and held it up.

She peered at it, having trouble seeing it in the dark, but eventually, she figured out what it was and looked back at him. "That isn't sterile."

"Yeah, well, I can't get sterile stuff…" he muttered.

"I have sterile things. Teffifa got the stuff to fix blade wounds – enough for both of you. I have the rest of it."

Malkarai sighed, glancing around the room to see if he could spot the first aid supplies. He'd just been looking for what he knew existed.

Satyrna took the thread from him, tossed it back in the drawer, and pushed the drawer shut. "Let me help you fix it properly. You've already had it over a day, you need to take care of it."

"I can take care of it. Just go back to sleep," he insisted.

"No," she said firmly. "Why do you keep trying to avoid us?"

"Because that's what started this mess!" His voice was quiet but desperate. "Why do you want to keep putting yourself in danger?"

She frowned at him, searching his face for a moment before putting her hands on his shoulders, going up on tiptoes, and kissing him firmly on the mouth.

His black eyes widened and he grabbed onto the dresser he was already leaning against. His initial reaction was shock, but he very quickly dismissed the surprise and kissed her back.

Pleased at the reciprocation, Satyrna didn't break the kiss for a minute or two, and even then, only leaned back a little, staring him in the eyes. Her eyes were wet. "Please stop running away from me."

His heart was racing again, for an entirely different reason than before. "Okay," he said, very quietly.

She smiled at him, happily. "Thank you."

Malkarai swallowed, just looking back at her, his brain still struggling to accept this declaration. He could see that more than just her eyes were wet; her cheeks were shiny in the dim light. He hadn't been aware that she was crying.

"Let me help you fix your side," she said, stepping away from him and bending over, picking up something from the floor. As she stood up, a plastic bag in her hand, she wiped her other arm over her face, drying her eyes on her sleeve.

He felt like he should ask about the tears, but since she wasn't addressing them, he was wondering if he should pretend that he hadn't seen them. "Are… are *you* okay?" he asked quietly.

She looked at him and nodded. "I'm much better now."

"Why?"

Satyrna tipped her head slightly. "'Why?' Because you ran away last night, bleeding and telling us all not to look for you. I've been afraid all day that you didn't even make it through the night and were lying dead in a ditch or alley somewhere. But you're alive, and you're here."

"You shouldn't…" he started to protest.

"Care if you're alive or not?" Satyrna interrupted. She gave him a moment to correct her, but he didn't. "In case I didn't make it abundantly clear, I'm really fond of you, Malkarai. I don't have a habit of kissing people sneaking around in my room. And you took that sword in the ribs for *me*. I'm fully invested in your well-being, so this past day was incredibly stressful and scary, and now that you've actually come here for the help you desperately need, I'm not just letting you go."

"I can't stay here," he said quietly. "This isn't over."

"Fine, I won't let you leave until I know you're out of danger, but I'm not letting you go in general, all right?"

He sighed softly, leaning more heavily against the dresser. His pulse was finally slowing, and it was making him very tired.

"*You* kissed me back. You didn't push me away. You can't deny that."

"Yeah," he muttered. "Fine."

"First thing's first, let's clean up your side and close it."

He stood up and then went into the other room, moving slowly and using the doorframe, walls, and chairs at the table to keep himself steady. He'd felt a bit dizzy even before she'd jumpstarted his heart. "I have water on to boil."

"Oh. Good," she said, putting her feet into her shoes and then following him without tying them.

"I was going to use that to sterilize the thread and needle and clean the wound."

"I have still-packaged suture thread, needles, alcohol, gauze bandages, and tape too," Satyrna said as she put the bag on the table and started taking supplies out.

"How bad was Teffifa's wound?" he asked as he held a hand over the water, which still wasn't boiling. It was pretty warm now though, so he expected a boil wasn't far off.

"She popped about eight stitches, but it wasn't terrible. Most of it looked pretty healed. I put five back in."

"She's due to get most of them out soon, but she's not great about taking it easy, especially when it comes to her arms," he said, softly.

"She's got enough scars on her, that doesn't surprise me," Satyrna said as she took a candle off the mantle, lit it in the fire, and then used it to light several other candles around the kitchen area.

"Yeah."

Satyrna glanced at him as she set the first candle back down. "You have a lot too. Is this normal for your job?"

He shrugged. "It can be. Teffifa doesn't feel pain when her emotions are extreme, so she has little reason to dodge superficial strikes in a fight. Also, I think she likes the scar tissue aesthetically."

Satyrna made an amused but disturbed face. "How does that work? Not feeling the pain, I mean."

"She has a genetically inherited chemical imbalance. Neurologically, she's a bit weird. If anything, it just makes her better at our job, so our bosses are fond of her."

"Odd… What about you?"

"I wouldn't say I like scars as a fashion statement… but when you've got as many as I do, you either grow fond of them or you hate yourself."

Her expression softened, giving him a concerned look. "Which is it?"

Malkarai ran his thumb down his jawline, tracing the scar there slowly as he looked at the fire. "Depends on the day."

Satyrna watched him, frowning. "You're a law enforcer. That was your badge I saw, right?"

He glanced at her and then nodded.

"Some secret part of the government?"

"Yes."

"And that's why you can't just quit."

"Right."

"Even though you want to."

"The risk is too high to just let people come and go like a normal job. If we can't do the job anymore, we either retire or we get another job in the system – because not everyone involved does what I do."

"But Traphian wants you to have the option to get out without that restriction?"

"Yeah."

"Is he dangerous?"

Malkarai shook his head, looking at her more steadily.

"He's a criminal that has you guys after him just because he was talking about it?"

"Right. He apparently talked a lot to you guys."

"Cypha dragged him out to lunch with us. Barry let us eat in his office. Did he hurt anyone?"

"Just a few agents, like Teffifa. His rank started too low for his skill, so he was able to evade or disable a lot of people before they sent the right caliber agent after him."

"Oh," Satyrna said quietly.

"Traphian isn't a threat. Yeah, Kalyfa's paranoia was legitimate if it was any of the other people I usually go after – but it's misplaced regarding Traphian."

"Do you think he recognized him in the castle?" Satyrna pressed worriedly.

"I don't think so. I never saw that kind of recognition from him, anyway. Traphian kept changing his hairstyle and facial hair. He even dyed it blonde and darker a few times. I have no idea what photo they gave Kalyfa, if they gave him one at all. I can see Stika not providing one. She doesn't think Traphian is actually dangerous either. Not like the people we *should* be going after."

"Who's Stika?"

"My boss."

"Did she send you after him?"

"No, her boss did. She told him it was a bad idea, but I think it was a loyalty test. He's always pulling that shit," Malkarai grumbled. "She was my handler for it though, because it was internal and local. He sure as hell got a development out of me though – just the opposite one I'm sure he was hoping for."

"He wanted you to just do the job like a good agent?" Satyrna asked tentatively.

"Yeah, I've been on auto-pilot for a few years – and it's gotten me a high rank and a good record. So, I guess he thought that I'd just been programmed, and taking down Traphian, my brother, would be a good indicator of his little project working and cement my loyalty. As soon as I figured out it was Traphian that I was after that all went out the window, though," Malkarai said quietly, sounding irritated. "Traphian knew it was me that was on him this time, that's why he came here. It was tactical."

"How so?" Satyrna pressed, leaning against the table as she looked at him.

"We have history here. I'm sure he had no idea we'd meet you guys again, but that hanging… it affected me. It affected all of us. There's a reason I blocked it out. It was mental defense. Chasing Traphian started undoing all this… this armor I built up. Meeting you again and remembering, opened the hole up further."

"That's what you wanted though, right?" she asked tentatively. "You said the other morning that you'd started getting excited about having friends again."

He sighed and looked at her, seeming jaded. "Yeah, but I can't just *have* that. Teffifa is going to tell our boss I'm dead and took Traphian with me, but while that may sever us from them… it won't make this easy. I-I still don't think it makes it safe for us to be *here*."

Satyrna frowned.

"My work isn't the only problem. I'm sure the knights are still pissed off with me – even more so after we beat them last night."

She sighed, watching him as he picked up the pot, which now had boiling water in it, and then took it over to the cold stove and set it on top of it.

"Let's give that a few minutes… it's numb, but I'm not sure that it's numb enough for actually boiling water…"

"It's numb?" Satyrna asked, perking up again in concern.

Malkarai glanced at her. "Yeah. I made it numb though – I have an anesthetic."

"Oh…" she sighed in relief.

"I've been trying to keep it clean and I put an antibiotic on it earlier. I haven't been neglecting it, I promise."

"I'm glad," she said softly. "Are these kinds of wounds… common?"

Malkarai shook his head. "Not anymore."

"All of the ones on your torso… they're old?"

He nodded absently. "These days, very little can hit me."

She pulled out the chair that held his coat and sat down in it, her arms crossed and a frown on her face. "That makes me feel worse, somehow."

Malkarai looked at her. "I chose to take that hit, Satyrna. That wasn't a mistake, or someone forcing me into it. It was a choice."

She looked up at him, her expression despondent. "But it was meant for *me*, because… because *I* hit that guy."

"The only reason there was any fighting going on was because I was there. My goal was to not let anyone else get hurt."

Satyrna sighed softly.

"Don't blame yourself for it." He dipped a finger in the water, testing the temperature. "This is tolerable now."

"Okay," she said, standing up and switching modes. She grabbed a rag from their rag box, set it on the table, and motioned for Malkarai to put the pot on it. "Take your shirt off."

After setting the pot down, he sighed and picked his cut shirt gingerly off of his side, and then pulled it off over his head. After looking at the hole in it, he just tossed it on the fire.

Satyrna gave him a perplexed look, a package of suture filament in her hands. "Um, why not just mend it?"

"That was the same one that got cut the other night – and it's just a cheap, basic T-shirt. It's not a big loss. My coat is worth mending; *that* was not."

She started gathering the supplies and set them on a chair before taking his sword and setting it against the wall near the hearth. "Lay down on the table so I can clean your wound without getting your pants wet."

He hesitated, watching her grab the note, crumple it up, and drop it in the garbage can near the stove before going to get one of the tubs from the closet by Dyspro's room. After setting the tub underneath the edge of the table, she moved the pot to the hearth and then grabbed hold of the corner of the table so he could get on it without it shifting.

He carefully laid back, his right arm behind his head and right leg dangling, so he was mostly on and over the edge.

Satyrna moved a few of the candles closer so the light was better, frowning grimly at the wound. It was about six inches long, but thankfully only deep in the center, which was slightly more toward his front on his side. She carefully tipped the water over it, focusing on washing the wound, but getting the skin around it too. She was grateful that she could only see flesh in the cut – no bone. It had overlapped his previous cut though, and that had reopened slightly where they intersected.

"I'm glad this isn't worse… I expected more scabbing though."

"I've been trying to keep it shut with pressure all day, but once I started moving the scabs that were there kinda split open."

Satyrna looked up at him, her eyebrows furrowed. "That sounds… awful."

"I'm sure it was less than ideal, but I've kept pressure on it most of the day. That shirt was saturated because I was using it as a buffer between the wound and a paper towel roll. I spent a lot of today asleep, believe it or not."

She sighed deeply, shaking her head as she focused on his side again. After several conservative rinses, Satyrna brought a candle closer to make sure there wasn't anything foreign in the wound and then set it back down. "Okay, I'm going to stitch it up."

"I can do it," he said automatically, starting to sit up.

She pushed his shoulder down and picked up the suture package she'd been holding earlier. "Stop. Teffifa taught me. Just supervise and tell me if I'm doing anything wrong. If you did it, you'd have to contort, and then it would sew up weird."

Malkarai sighed, but relaxed on the table, not protesting.

Satyrna pulled the chair with his coat on it closer and perched on the edge, carefully stitching the wounds shut. She was slow and deliberate at first but got slightly quicker as she reached the end, crouching next to the table so she could stitch the last few sutures.

Malkarai watched her as she did so, impressed at how focused and calm she was. It was a demeanor he was used to, being what he was, but the fact that she was so cool about dealing with the actual wound that had been distressing her made him smile.

"Okay, done," she said, sitting back on her heels. She looked over her work before looking up at him. "Does that look okay- What?"

He shook his head. "They look fine. Good job. They haven't taught you how to do that in nursing school?"

"Not yet. I'm not sure if it's part of the curriculum."

"Well, I'd pass you."

She laughed and stood up. "Thanks, teacher. Stay put so I can rinse it again, and I'll get you bandaged up."

"Did Teffifa get antibiotics?"

"Yeah, I have some of those too." Satyrna used the water in the pot to rinse away the errant blood from reaggravating and stitching the wound, and then set it aside. Then she picked up the alcohol, unscrewed the cap, and poured some of that over it as well.

She looked at his side while she closed the alcohol bottle. "That needs a few minutes to dry."

"Mm-hmm."

He noticed her staring at his abdomen for a few moments before turning and putting the bottle down with the other supplies and picking up a tube of antibiotic ointment.

He had very well-defined abs, but although all of his muscles were toned, none of them were arrant – he was more lean than built. Besides his face stubble and on his lower arms, he had practically no body hair. Just firm, light brown skin laced with the numerous pale scars – which covered his entire torso, but were almost non-existent on his arms and above his collarbone. If he'd cared about his physical appearance, he might've counted the lack of hair as a win, but he knew it was because of all the scar tissue that hair just didn't grow there. He was very rarely without a shirt, so what others thought of it was not something he'd ever thought about before that point in time. Right now, he was very aware of it though, and getting anxious about it because he couldn't tell what she was thinking.

He wasn't about to ask either, and just laid there silently until she crouched down again, carefully and gently applying antibiotic to the closed cuts using a cotton swab.

Then she picked up the gauze and unrolled enough to cover his side with an X-shape, covering both wounds. After she'd cut the gauze and tape and applied, she stepped back and pushed the tub of water, alcohol, and blood farther under the table so he could get up. "You're set. You're a very difficult patient."

"I thought I held very still," he protested as he gingerly sat up, trying not to bend at the waist.

Satyrna stepped closer to him and kissed him on the forehead, causing him to blush fiercely. "You did. But it was hell getting you here in the first place."

"I'm trying to think of you."

"And I think you should've come back with us after the fight." She glanced over his arms and picked one up, looking at it. "I forgot you got cuts on your arms. Can I bandage these too?"

He looked at them. "I guess. Just the big ones."

"I'm going to clean and put medicine on all of them," she stated, bringing the supplies closer.

"I don't suppose I have a choice in that, do I?" he said, bemused.

"Nope."

He shook his head slightly. "I have a box of bandages in my coat."

She gave him a curious look. "Why?"

"Uh, long story." He pointed out where they were and she dug them out from an interior pocket and opened the box.

Malkarai held his arm up for her to work on after she'd opened up one of the adhesive bandages.

After Satyrna had finished cleaning and bandaging his arm wounds, Malkarai sighed and carefully slid off the table, going unsteadily over to where his bag was still sitting on the floor on the far side of the bench. He opened the bag, pulled out a long-sleeved, dark blue T-shirt, and put it on. Once his head was clear of the fabric, he noticed Satyrna giving him a surprised look. "What?"

"It's just weird to see you in anything but black."

He blushed again, looking away evasively. "It's cold out; I want sleeves."

"Your jeans looked pretty blood-soaked…did you want to change those too?"

He glanced toward the hallway. "Not a terrible idea. I'm going to use your room, okay?"

She gestured toward it. "Go for it. Dyspro's room is empty too."

"Why? Where is he?"

"At his parents' house. His leg is broken, so he's going to stay there for a bit. The path sucks even with two properly working feet."

Malkarai frowned at her, distressed. "Yeah, Teffifa told me his leg was broken. How?"

"Relax, that isn't your fault," she insisted. "He and his ex's boyfriend got in a fight. Dyspro should've kept his mouth shut, and the boyfriend should've kept his hands off. That's their problem, not yours."

Malkarai shook his head. "He wouldn't have been in there if it hadn't been for me."

"You don't control everything, Malkarai. Stop shouldering responsibility for everyone."

He sighed. "Is Cypha okay, at least?"

"Yeah, she's fine. She has a beef with the knights, but they don't have one with her."

He picked up his bag and came over to the table. "Can I have the water and a rag so I can clean the blood off my side?"

"Oh, yeah, of course." Satyrna quickly got him a fresh rag and handed him the pot carefully.

"Thanks." He took them all into the extra room and shut the door quietly.

**226**

After cleaning up and changing his jeans, underwear, and socks, he put his boots back on, rolled the dirty clothing up, and put it in his bag. When he came back out to the main room, Satyrna had finished tidying up the first aid supplies, so she took the pot from him, emptied it in the tub, and then put it on the stove to dry. The water tub was still underneath the table.

"I can dump that outside," he said as tapped the tub with his toe before he put his bag on the table and rooted around in it.

"No need," Satyrna said as she sat at the table. "We'll dump it tomorrow when it's light outside. You shouldn't be picking heavy things up with fresh stitches."

He didn't protest that, looking at a thin, flat case about a foot long, before putting it back in the bag. "I need to take my bag with me. Don't freak out about it, okay?"

Satyrna's eyes narrowed slightly. "Why do you need it?"

"I need my computer, but I don't have a big enough pocket for it in my coat."

"Oh. That makes sense. You can leave some of your things here so it's lighter though."

"You shouldn't keep my bloody clothes here. I appreciate that you want me to be tethered here, but let me be transitory for the moment."

She looked up at him. "I'm hoping at this point you'd be tethered to *me*," she said softly.

He zipped his bag up, inhaling deeply and exhaling before sitting down across from her. "I… I can't promise anything right now. I don't know what's going to happen. Traphian and I might need to run. We might be able to just hide. I don't know. I'm sure Kalyfa is even more pissed with me."

Satyrna swallowed hard, looking at the table and shifting.

"Even if he isn't, that doesn't mean the knights would just forgive me. I would love to say that it would be great to be friends with you guys. To… to figure out whatever this is," he said, gesturing between himself and her, "but I don't know where things are going right now."

She was quiet for a few moments before asking, "Are you still suicidal?"

His eyes narrowed slightly, evaluating the depth of the knowledge behind her question.

"Teffifa told me you tried to kill yourself."

"I'm not trying to kill myself," he replied readily.

"But you're okay with someone else trying to do it?"

Malkarai shook his head. "I came here tonight to close this wound properly. I'm trying to live."

"I'm glad. She didn't just go around announcing it, by the way. I asked her if you were. She said you used to be, but she wasn't sure anymore."

"I'm not. I wasn't like that even before they sent me after Traphian."

"What's different now than when you tried to kill yourself?"

"I…wasn't stable then."

"What do you mean, not stable?"

"Emotionally injured, I guess. I've dealt with pain, hate, and stress for my whole life. That shit doesn't bother me anymore. Something happened that knocked my feet out from under me. I didn't want to try and get back up. I didn't know how to."

Satyrna didn't respond at first. After a few moments she looked up at him, her eyebrows knitted up. "Was it Arista?"

"Yeah."

"What'd she do?"

He shook his head. "I don't want to revisit it."

"But you're better now?"

"Yes. I wouldn't be bold enough to say I'm good, but I'm better."

"I'm not gonna go anywhere, okay? I'll be here. I want to help."

He stood up. "Thanks, I appreciate that. I gotta go."

"Why?"

"I shouldn't be around you, remember?"

"It's three in the morning, who the hell is going to be lurking around here right now?"

Malkarai sighed and picked his coat up from the back of her seat. He put his coat on, taking care to not dislodge anything. "I have no idea why, but there's apparently a lot of people who want to find me right now, and I can't say I appreciate it."

She smirked. "Cute."

"It's better to leave here now rather than later. I'm less likely to be noticed in the early morning hours."

Satyrna sighed. "I suppose. Just…get somewhere and rest, okay? You've lost a lot of blood. Give your side a chance to start healing."

"I'll settle somewhere as soon as I take care of something. Believe me, I know I'm off right now." He glanced at her and then at the window, a frown forming. "So… I had this suspicion that there was someone following me. They had been for the past week, at least. When I realized she was here, I thought maybe it could've been Teffifa, but she said it wasn't her. I mean, stealth isn't her thing, but I couldn't really think who else it could've been. I'm not used to being followed, so I wasn't looking for it."

"Are they friendly or not?"

"I have no idea. She confronted me earlier tonight and gave me those band-aids and some food."

Satyrna looked concerned. "Did you talk to her?"

"A little bit. I told her she needed to leave me alone because it's dangerous, and she listened after she squeezed my name and age out of me." He looked concerned and contemplative. "She seemed young."

"How young?"

"Teens. Maybe older teens. I thought maybe she could be a mercenary or a hunter… until I actually saw her. I'm almost positive she's a civilian so I really don't know what her deal is."

"Mercenary or hunter?" Satyrna asked.

He hesitated, glancing at her. "Uh, mercenaries are hired fighters. People can hire them for a variety of different tasks. Hunters… are criminal vigilantes that mostly focus on taking out government operatives."

Her eyes widened. "I'm glad she isn't either of those."

"Yeah, me too."

"What are you going to do?"

"Avoid her. It helps that I know what she looks like now."

"What does she look like?" Satyrna pressed, curious.

"She's short and has short, dark hair. She's a dark, but I could see her irises even though they were dark, so they're either brown or dark blue."

Satyrna was surprised. "She's a dark?"

Malkarai nodded slightly.

"I think I saw her – yesterday. By the hospital."

His eyes narrowed. "When?"

"Uh, around four?"

"That makes sense. I was near there then, and she's been following me. Where is Traphian now?"

"Oh, uh, he moved to the inn at Eighteenth and Forest. Room 9."

Malkarai nodded, mouthing it to himself. "Okay. Thank you."

"Are you going to go see him?"

"Not tonight. Maybe tomorrow. Depends on what happens."

"Okay." After a few moments, she said, "I have so many questions for you. Come back again soon, okay? If you ever need some heat or food or anything. Just wake me up if I'm asleep."

"I'll see what happens." Then he put his bag on over his shoulder and across his body.

Satyrna hopped to her feet and ran into her room. When she emerged, she held out his cloak. "Here. Don't freeze. If you need to, you can come here and sleep. It's going to start sticking out there soon."

"Thanks." He took the cloak, shook it out, and tossed it over his shoulders. After clasping it over his chest he looked up at her, but before he could say anything else, she stepped close to him, slipping her arms under his and hugging him tight around the chest.

Satyrna felt him go rigid, but he didn't push her away, so she didn't let go immediately. "I mean it, okay? I want you to come back."

Malkarai sighed, lifting a hand and putting it on her back.

When she let go, she looked up at him.

He shook his head and brushed some of her hair behind her shoulder. "I don't get you."

"And I don't entirely get you yet either. But I know that I like you."

"You don't understand me, I don't understand you, but you still don't want me to leave."

"I like challenges. We'll work on the getting to know each other better part."

"Later," he agreed. He picked up his sword from where it was resting against the wall, attached it to his belt, and headed for the door.

"Do you want your switchblade too?"

"I can survive without it. Hang onto it for me."

"Okay," she responded quietly as he left and shut the door.

Satyrna watched him through the window until he disappeared into the woods, and then she locked up, went back to her room, and dropped into bed.

After a few moments, she sighed heavily. *No one's made me feel like this in... ever. Wow.* She rolled over and shut her eyes. *I'm so glad he's alive.*

# 22



4:00 a.m.

In town, Malkarai spent some time searching around buildings until he found an electrical plug-in outside of a shop. After scanning the area to determine any potential interruptions or threats, he dug the laptop sleeve out of his bag and opened it. He pulled out a power cord and plugged it into the wall before taking his laptop out and setting the case aside.

Before starting the computer, he flipped a catch on the side and popped out the broadband card. After reading the specifications on the card he put it in the computer case, closed the catch, plugged the power cord in, and turned the computer on.

He interrupted the start-up process and enabled some scripts from the BIOS, disrupting the logging of his IP address and interfering with the monitoring and security programs.

After it had started, he modified and ran a few scripts, changing some variables and registry values before attempting to connect to a local wireless network.

Malkarai did a few searches on his name, trying to tunnel in on places he knew he'd normally be listed, and even trying a few wild cards. He reached dead ends in all the places.

*Wow, they worked quickly. They haven't even confirmed that I'm dead yet...*

After staring at the last screen for a few moments, he opened up another window and accessed his bank accounts. The depository account the system knew about was declared invalid, but his personal one was still active.

He sighed softly in relief and double-checked the balance before closing the window. That was still there – all $650,000 of it.

He disabled his wireless adapter and then changed his IP address one more time before turning the computer off. He shut the screen and leaned back against the wall of the building, looking around as he let the computer's battery charge.

*So far so good, but they haven't come to retrieve me or Traphian yet. I'm not sure what's holding them up... It never takes them this long to collect a body – much less an agent. I don't think they've come to town yet. I've been looking. This would usually warrant a head's involvement, and I haven't seen Stika... She relies on blending into crowds, so she wouldn't be lurking around like me or Teffifa. I haven't been blanketing the town, but still... Nothing by the hospital, nothing by the morgue...*

*I'm not sure what Traphian wants to do, but I don't feel like hiding in a hole for the next few months or the next year. If it came to that, we could leave town. Hell, we could go to Canada or something. They could follow us there, but they won't find us.*

He sighed and rested his head against the wall behind him. *Satyrna's throwing a huge wrench into this. It was so cut and clear; we'd stay here until I was sure of the situation and well enough to run, and then disappear. What the hell did you go and do that for, Satyrna? Now I have baggage.*

Malkarai shook his head slightly. *I haven't been kissed in four and a half years. It surprised the hell out of me...* **You** *surprise the hell out of me. I just did what I always do, protect civilians. But you took it personally, and now you're attached.* He sighed in exasperation. *I have to ignore it; kill it while I can. I don't have room for that too.*

He watched the street for a while, but shortly after, found that his mind had wandered back to her yet again. He scowled. *Great. She got my attention. Damn it, Satyrna... You've woken up something I'd rather had stayed dead. This could've been easy, but now I'm going to have regrets. I can't stay here. They'll find me. And there's no way in hell I'm letting you come with me. You have family, friends, and roots here. So, whatever, it'll hurt, but I can't let her get any closer. Maybe Traphian will have ideas on how to convince her.*

Malkarai sighed and put a hand over his mouth, feeling his skin heat up as he thought about that kiss again. "Goddammit."

**6:45 a.m.**

Satyrna started, pushing herself up in bed to look around. Something had jolted her out of sleep. She didn't see anyone in the pale light but felt something crinkle by her hand.

She slipped her legs underneath her and knelt back on her feet as she pulled a small slip of paper out from under the edge of her pillow. She unfolded it and held it up to the light coming from the window, but she didn't recognize the thin scrawl on the paper.

It read, *'7 tonight, 21ˢᵗ and Orchard by the trees. Just you. Bring the knife in case. Don't tell anyone I was around.'*

"Malkarai?" she murmured.

She jumped out of bed and ran into the main room, but it was dark and deserted. She went to the window, looking down the path, but there was nothing outside but dead foliage.

After looking for a few more moments she smiled faintly and looked down at the paper again. "Good boy."

232

Malkarai glanced at rooms 7 and 8 as he passed them, grateful that at least half of the rooms for this inn had exterior doors. The thought that that might've been why Traphian picked this room, if he'd had a choice, crossed his mind before he stopped in front of 9 and knocked.

He stood still, waiting and listening, but when he didn't hear a response, he knocked again.

It took another round of knocking before Malkarai heard movement. A quiet thud and then footsteps. It was quiet for a moment, and then he heard the door locks being undone.

Traphian turned the doorknob and tugged it open, but then walked away from the door, leaving it for Malkarai to open.

He pushed the door open, peering inside before stepping in and shutting it behind him. The whole room was dark, despite it being fairly light outside.

Traphian was pulling his pants on. After he'd buttoned them, he turned on a lamp on the desk in the room and turned, blinking and scratching his head as he peered at Malkarai. "Since when are you a morning person?"

Malkarai turned the deadbolt on the door. "I haven't been to bed yet."

Traphian rolled his eyes and went to his open bag on the desk chair, pulling out a T-shirt. After he put it on, he turned another light on. "Yeah, that sounds like you. I'm glad to see you aren't dead."

"Yeah, I got my priorities straight for once." Malkarai unclasped his cloak, set it on one of the chairs at the small table next to the window by the door, and then took his bag off and set it on the chair as well.

"Did you take care of that wound?"

"Yeah, Satyrna stitched me up earlier this morning."

"Awesome. Teffifa does have a functioning brain cell in her head."

Malkarai gave him a bemused look before sitting in the other chair at the table. "She's far from dumb."

"Yeah, I know – but she definitely runs on emotions, not logic."

"She's gotten better at that. The emotion is mostly just used as a weapon anymore. She's got her imbalance managed, and Shawn and Swip are her backup."

"That's good to know," Traphian said before he narrowed his eyes. "Why the hell did Stika send her after me without her keepers? Fuck, I thought she *liked* me."

Malkarai smirked. "That wasn't Stika. It was Carlisle."

"Oh," Traphian said, his mood immediately darkening. He looked at Malkarai. "Did he send you too?"

Malkarai nodded slowly.

"Glad to see that unsympathetic lizard-man hasn't changed his stripes," Traphian said acidly. "I hope this shows up as a black spot on his little personal project roster."

Malkarai smiled, considering that. "I didn't think about that. It should. Stika kept telling him that sending closer people to take you down was the dumbest of all dumb ideas. She'll never tell him, 'I told you so,' to his face, but I'm sure he can already hear it ringing in his ears all the way in Chicago."

"Good. Fucker," Traphian muttered darkly.

"Anyway… Teffifa got back yesterday. They've already started removing my existence digitally. I expected them to be in town by now, but I haven't seen anyone yet. Regardless, they'll definitely be taking the next steps sooner rather than later. What is our plan?"

Traphian moved his backpack to the floor and sat down in the desk chair, crossing his arms as he looked at Malkarai. "I haven't decided. I was waiting to see what your status was. What did you do all day yesterday?"

"Slept, mostly. I staked out the hospital, morgue, and courthouse for a bit because they need to work with the local law enforcement, and Cypha said that Kalyfa had an office in either the courthouse or town hall. They're all close to each other."

"Kalyfa was probably in the hospital. Is that why you were there?"

Malkarai shrugged. "That and they'd look for us at one."

"Right. Well, this place is seceded, so the gears are probably turning a little slower. They need to get all kinds of permission to come here for anything official. Today is more likely to have activity."

"Yeah, so we should decide our plan quickly. Do you think heading north would be too obvious?"

"Yeah, probably."

"We could try and go south then. It's farther, but it should be easier to avoid transportation and lodging than it would be in Canada in the winter."

Traphian's eyebrows knitted up. "You're willing to just run?"

Malkarai shrugged. "If we want to stay alive, that seems like the safest plan."

"Not necessarily."

Malkarai gave him a perplexed look. "Escaping isn't the safest thing to do? I mean, I know there is surveillance and stuff, but that will be everywhere. I'm pretty confident with my ability to hack most things, so that could help us buy time enough to cross a border, which would make it a lot harder for them to trap us. We had this whole thing planned out-"

"The plan when we were teenagers?" Traphian scoffed. "Yeah, that plan was shit."

Malkarai frowned. "I thought it was decent. You stayed free."

"Yeah, sure. I didn't follow our plan. Also, you are very aware, they knew where I was almost the whole time. They let me run."

Malkarai's shoulders dropped and he tipped his head slightly, giving Traphian an incredulous look. "Why do you say that?"

"Malk, you know these people have access to pretty much whatever they want. Intelligence, surveillance, investigators, you name it. I might've shaken them for a few months, but eventually, I had to resurface. I had to feed myself. If I wasn't going to break the law, I had to work. I had to go to school. I'm not sure exactly how long it took them before they found me, but they found me. They let me stay out here."

"Why?"

Traphian shrugged. "I wasn't causing problems. I didn't start causing problems until a few years ago. They even tolerated that once or twice, but then they tossed those charges on me, so I realized they weren't going to play diplomatic. I ignored them. The first time I spotted an agent who obviously knew who I was, I sold everything I could and turned transient. I wasn't *trying* to evade the ASA until they came after me first. Before that, I was just existing."

"How'd you manage to stay transient this long?" Malkarai asked, impressed.

"I had saved up quite a bit – in case you finally came and joined me and we had to do something drastic."

He frowned. "I'm sorry."

Traphian shrugged. "I made choices. You don't need to apologize for it."

"No, I do… I didn't… I didn't hold up my end."

"You had other priorities. Arista broke you, though. Well, Farad broke you first. I realized I couldn't wait for you to take off of your own accord – that's why I started pressing buttons. I was trying to drag you out." Traphian grinned and gestured at Malkarai with a hand. "Hey, look, it finally worked."

Malkarai sighed, blushing in embarrassment. "I'm sorry," he said again, quietly.

Traphian shook his head dismissively. "I'll accept that. Thanks. But right now – I don't think running is smart. Especially not *right now*."

"How come?"

"So, you have to think about what they know about this situation."

"You ran here; I followed. Teffifa's telling them that after I dug you out, we fought and I killed you, but then I killed myself. She wasn't going to be able to drag both of our bodies back, so she returned to the agency to report it so Stika could contact the authorities."

"Hm, the authorities that knew we were alive at the end of an altercation they had with us," Traphian said thoughtfully. "I know the plan. I'm wondering what that third element, the knights, have to say to her about it."

Malkarai shrugged. "That's an unknown, unfortunately. Even if Kalyfa tells Stika about what happened, Teffifa was still going to say that we killed each other off in the woods, after all the knight bullshit."

"The confusion should help," Traphian said. "But, yeah, so, the facts that they have are that we are both dead. Not running, not hiding. Just dead."

"Yeah."

"If we bolt and someone spots us, or we get new identities or forged documents, the forger could be being watched, and *that* could tip them off that something here isn't upright. If we leave, we'll be back in their jurisdiction for a lot of it. If someone is watching surveillance somewhere for something unrelated and spots one of us, then there's a breadcrumb. That breadcrumb could do a lot of damage. You get it, right?"

Malkarai nodded, looking pensive. "I stand out."

"Quite badly. My shit is old. I'm sure I've got lots of flags, but they've probably all been tripped at least once. You would trip flags of a higher urgency. We're still alive; they have no body to confirm that you died. They'll leave flags up. Now, yeah, there are no bodies to corroborate Teffifa's story, but saying that it happened in the woods is to our advantage. The woods are fantastic for claiming evidence. It snowed yesterday too. So, that might actually work out better than expected. Doing something like leaving could ruin this little perfect storm we've stumbled into. The federal authorities won't be allowed to just search here forever."

"The knights will probably tell them to buzz off and let them look first, actually," Malkarai said, hopefully.

Traphian nodded. "Most likely. So, yeah, this little oops has honestly worked out well. I think staying put and hiding for a while is the best idea. This place is seceded. And if they *don't* think we're dead, most people would not expect us to just set up camp in the very place we pulled a Houdini. They're more likely to focus elsewhere."

Malkarai made a small noise of amusement, feeling that creeping sense of excitement and optimism starting to well up again.

Traphian watched him for a few moments, seeing the change in his expression. "I take it you're okay with that plan?"

"I told Satyrna to meet up with me tonight so I could tell her what the plan was. I just… expected it to be a goodbye. Or, I guess, a note saying I was already gone."

"Yeah, there's another advantage. We have friends here."

Malkarai looked at him, his eyebrows knitting up. "Doesn't that make it more dangerous if we have connections?"

Traphian snorted. "No. Most people don't want to give shit to the authorities, Malk. They distrust them. Having friends who have even more friends is helpful to us. It'll make it a *lot* easier to hide."

Malkarai put his hands over his face, rubbing his temples and the sides of his face, back to his neck, pulling his hair out of his face briefly in the process. "Fuck," he said with a half-laugh as his hair fell back over his eyes.

"Glad you're okay with this plan. I don't know much about Dyspro, but Cypha, Satyrna, Barry, and even their friend, Josh, seem like honest, decent people. The girls think fondly of you."

"Yeah… Satyrna wants me," Malkarai muttered, staring at the dark TV evasively.

Traphian laughed. "Oh." He nodded, smirking. "Yeah, looking back with that context, I can see that now."

"I've been trying to push her away. I figured we'd have to run."

"Do you want to push her away?"

"Not really. I mean… she panicked me at first, but I like her too."

"Why'd she make you panic?"

Malkarai looked at him. "She got close and didn't cringe or flinch. She… paid attention to me. She wanted to be around me – consistently. I'm *not* used to that."

Traphian snickered. "Obviously, I've left you on your own way too long. You need someone to invade your personal space again."

Malkarai shook his head, smirking. "As happy as I am to be around you again, I'd rather have a girl in my personal space, thanks."

"Yeah, me too. Well, yes, if you think that's something, do something about it. Having friends while we burrow into hiding spots is a good thing. If the ASA ever does get wind of us, we might have to bolt… but for now, this is the safest plan."

Malkarai nodded. "We'll have to figure shit out with the knights."

"Yeah. It'll be hard to hide if they're trying to ferret us out too. Where are you planning on holing up?"

"I'm not," Malkarai replied, shaking his head slightly. "I want to keep an eye on things."

"You should figure out a place to stay eventually," Traphian said, warningly. "Also, I know you like to pretend your cuts don't exist, but that one is particularly nasty. You need to heal."

Malkarai rolled his eyes.

"You said you haven't gone to sleep yet?" Traphian stood up, not waiting for Malkarai to reply. "I'm up for the day. Sleep here."

"Where are you going to go?"

"Nowhere. One of these chairs while I watch TV with the captions on."

"I want to keep an eye on things."

"Malkarai, you can hide when it's *dark* out. That shit doesn't work as well in the broad daylight. It's not like this is a city – the shadows aren't as strong because all the buildings are short and too far apart. The plan is to hide, so stay in here and only go out when you can hide effectively."

He sighed. "Yeah, fine."

"I know, damn me and my stupid logic."

"Yep," Malkarai said shortly before unbuttoning his coat.

"When did you eat last?"

"Uh… like seven last night."

"All right, eat breakfast with me, and get some sleep."

"Stop baiting me with shit that sounds nice." Malkarai looked at Traphian, his eyebrows knitting up. "That reminds me…"

"Huh?"

"Uh, there's a girl that's been following me."

"Besides Satyrna?"

"Yeah, not her. She was following me for a bit – before Cavington even. I talked to her last night."

Traphian looked concerned. "Who is she?"

"I'm not sure. She's a young civilian. She wanted to know about my age and where I was from. She brought me food, so I told her my age and told her to get away from me. She wants to talk to me again and I agreed, but now that I know what she looks like, I intend to avoid her."

"That's weird… Is she younger than you?"

"Yeah."

"I know some chick dropped you off, but someone younger looking for you doesn't make sense. No one outside of the system should know you exist."

Malkarai shrugged. "We don't operate in a void. Satyrna and her friends knew I existed, even if they didn't know my name."

"True. You know she's a civilian?"

"No way she's a hunter or another agent, and if she's a mercenary she's the most skittish one I've ever heard of. She's a dark."

Traphian raised an eyebrow. "Think she's related to you?"

Malkarai made a displeased face. "Just because someone is dark doesn't mean they're related to me. It's a spontaneous mutation most of the time."

"Yeah, most of the time – not all of the time. Maybe she thinks you're related."

"That's nice. You're my only family," he retorted firmly.

Traphian smiled. "I definitely earned that title through years of mutual abuse, but you have to have someone out there who shares genes with you. Spontaneous mutation does not mean spontaneous generation."

"Yeah, I know, but I don't give a shit. All I know is I got abandoned twice. I don't care where I came from. You can have her if she's looking for a relative."

Traphian laughed. "That'd still make her your relative."

Malkarai rolled his eyes and stood up, taking his coat off. He picked his cloak and bag up, and put them all on the floor by the wall next to the less-used side of the bed. "I'm using your bathroom too," he said, dropping the subject. "I want a shower."

"Please," Traphian said, waving a hand dismissively as he went over to the mini fridge in the room and started digging through the grocery bags he had on top of it. "I'll figure out breakfast."

# 23



Kalyfa put a painkiller in his mouth and took a drink of water, tossing his head back gingerly. After swallowing, he looked at his desk in his office in city hall, noticing the blinking light on his phone that said he had a voicemail. He sighed and picked up the handset, holding it to his ear as he hit the button to listen to the messages, and then rapidly put his code in.

He groaned and dropped the handset on his shoulder, hitting the button to delete the message after hearing the voice of the regional agent he'd talked to just a few days ago asking him to call her at his earliest convenience.

He set the handset on the desk so he could turn his chair and unlock one of the filing cabinets behind him. After digging out a file, he looked at the phone number and then slid his chair back underneath the desk, putting his handset back up to his ear as he typed in the number.

"Karne," was the response after a single ring.

"This is Kalyfa Desfete, with the Cavington knights," he said.

"Oh, thank you for calling me back, Kalyfa."

"Yeah, no problem. Sorry that it took me a day – I was not in the office yesterday."

"That's all right. I need to talk to you about the agent that was in your jurisdiction."

"Hm?" he replied, staring across the room with annoyance on his face.

"I had sent another agent to keep an eye on him. She was not authorized to act on this mission, so she was not there in a law enforcement capacity. She returned early yesterday morning reporting that our agent and his target are both dead."

Kalyfa's eyebrows furrowed deeply as he processed that. "*Both* of them are dead?"

"Yes. She said he resisted her involvement and lost her, but she was able to find him later in the woods, bleeding out. His target was already dead. She returned without their bodies, so I was hoping that I could request your permission to come there and retrieve them."

"Where are they?"

"She just said the woods northwest of town. It was dark, and she didn't have any landmarks, so I would bring her to try to find them."

"Who do you intend to bring here?"

"Just her, myself, and probably one other agent. Her name is Teffifa Ripper, and I haven't decided on the second one yet, but probably one of her partners."

"That's it?"

"For now, yes. I don't see a need for more than that at this time."

Kalyfa moved his jaw, grinding his teeth together for a few moments, thoughtfully. "No, not yet."

"Pardon me?"

"Let me try to find them first. I have an entire squad that patrols this town regularly, let us try to find them first. If they're dead, then there is no rush. We know this area better."

"That is very true. I'm also interested in retrieving their belongings. They are… they are colleagues."

Kalyfa hesitated, glaring at the desk top. "Both of them?"

"Well… yes. Malkarai's target was an agent from our division that defected. He wasn't a convicted criminal."

Kalyfa scowled but didn't let that come through in his voice. "They send you people after those kinds of targets?"

"Only when they become dangerous problems. I'm sure he ran to your town because it was seceded, but because we have our agreement…"

"Let us look. I'll report back to you after I talk to my people and have them search first."

"Okay. Thank you, Kalyfa. I would ask, when your people do find them, please treat the area like a crime scene."

"Yeah, of course."

"I know that these things can take time, but there is a time limit on my side, so please be sure to call me back with any updates no later than Monday afternoon. If I cannot provide sufficient updates, then they may take this out of my hands, and none of us want to deal with the central authorities on this matter."

Kalyfa's lip twitched, but even with his outsider knowledge of the federal government, he agreed that he didn't want to deal with bureaucracy. "Yeah, I'll report in on Monday."

"Thank you. I'll await your next call."

"Yeah, talk to you soon."

He hung the phone up and swore out loud. He rubbed the tender spot on his head gingerly, glaring at the closed door across the room. "The fuck are you up to, Faerstathe? Did you seriously pull that shit and then just go and pull a murder-suicide in the woods afterward?"

He picked his cell phone up from where it was lying on the desk and unlocked it, opening up an app so he could contact his captains and several other knights and call a meeting.

Josh looked at the door to the knight office as it opened again, this time so Brendan could enter.

Brendan glanced around the room at the other knights that were already gathered and then went over to Josh, who was leaning against one of the big bookshelves of records, manuals, and other reference materials that were lining two of the walls in the room.

Kalyfa's desk was at the far end near the windows, but the rest of the room had a small meeting table and other chairs lined up in two rows. The chairs at the table were already mostly filled and there were a handful of people sitting in the other chairs or standing, but he couldn't see Kalyfa. In total, about a third of the squad was there.

"What's this about?" Brendan asked Josh quietly as he stood next to him.

"I know as much as you. It's about that dark that Dyspro, Cypha, and Satyrna were hanging around with."

Brendan sighed. "The one that Kalyfa said he can't give us details on? Great."

Josh just inhaled deeply and exhaled, watching the other knights with his arms crossed. He was tired and tense.

"Do you work tonight?"

"I'm at the end of a shift, so technically no. Guess we'll see what Kalyfa wants from us."

"Oh, you had the morning shift today? I thought you were on yesterday night."

"I was."

Brendan looked sidelong at Josh, his eyes narrowed. "He's gonna yell at you again."

"He wasn't around to tell me no."

Brendan just shook his head, watching as Kalyfa came in the door, a stack of paper in his hands.

Kalyfa scanned the room, taking attendance in his head before he started passing out two different photocopied papers to everyone present. He gave Brendan and Josh theirs last before giving Josh a brief, scolding look. "You're not allowed to work again until tomorrow, Garevn."

Josh's expression didn't change. "Yes, sir."

"Told you," Brendan muttered after Kalyfa had walked away.

Josh looked down at the papers. One of them was a photo of a young man with shrouding, pitch-black hair and entirely black eyes, a physical description typed out next to it with certain parts of the page that hadn't been copied, apparently covered with paper. The other sheet was a similar but differently laid out information sheet with a photo of another young adult male with short hair that looked dark but was probably lighter than the other man's. Both were printed in black and white, so the written information was their indicator of actual colors. Neither of them had a name on the page, but Josh recognized the second man.

Kalyfa sighed and then stood in front of his desk, addressing them all. "Some of you have already encountered one of these men. We followed him a few nights ago because he was lingering in town longer than he should've. His name is Malkarai Faerstathe. He's a federal agent who was sent here on assignment, but generally, they're meant to finish their work quickly and leave within hours. He'd been here three days at that point, and I was not happy about it because it also meant that the dangerous target he'd been sent to take care of was *also* lingering here, putting citizens in danger.

"They're not meant to interact with civilians, only their targets and other law enforcement. He never approached me, but he did interact with several civilians – Satyrna Hennessin, Dyspro Tanen, and Cypha Vatale. We brought them in for protective custody while I tried to deal with this uncooperative… agent." Kalyfa sighed. "Most of you know how that progressed. He showed up to argue with and distract me, and they were all removed from our custody. From what I can gather, it was by a woman and a man. I wasn't sure who they were until now."

Kalyfa picked up a photo from his desk and held it up, showing it to everyone. "Those who were in the castle the night before last, do you recognize her?"

Most of them shook their heads, peering at the photo, which was in color and clearly showed the woman's red eyes and red and black hair. Two of the others that were standing perked up though. One backhanded the one he was next to. "Yeah! Greg, that's the chick that knocked you out."

Greg made a face, putting a hand on his head. "Yeah…"

Josh recognized her too but didn't say anything.

Kalyfa sighed and set the photo face down on his desk. "Yeah, I thought so. Does anyone recognize the guy with short hair?"

"Yeah, he was fighting us at the end – when you were busy with the dark," one of the captains said. "His hair's longer than in this photo."

"He was good."

"They all were."

"The chick took down three of us."

"Who are they?"

Kalyfa sighed again, looking fed up. "Did he talk with Faerstathe?"

"Uh, I think so. While you were down and after he got injured, that guy went over and talked with him, and then he's the one that ushered everyone out. Faerstathe left on his own."

Kalyfa shook his head. "That was his target."

"What the hell…?" Brendan said, a little louder than he intended.

"Yeah, my thoughts exactly," Kalyfa said, glancing at him. "So, the woman was one of Faerstathe's colleagues. She was sent here to keep an eye on and help him out. Her name's Teffifa Ripper."

"Jesus… what a name."

"They all have names like that," Kalyfa said dismissively. "Anyway, I found out earlier this morning that Faerstathe's target was one of their colleagues who defected. Usually, like I said, they are incredibly dangerous criminals. Apparently, *something* happened, because Ripper was acting alongside this target. I don't know his real name, just several of his aliases. Based on how this guy acted in the main hall and with Faerstathe, they were probably all working together."

"Does that mean they all defected?" another captain asked.

Kalyfa made a contemplative face. "I don't think so. Ripper went back yesterday morning and told their bosses that Faerstathe killed his target and then killed himself."

"What?" several of them said, surprised.

"Seriously?" Brendan asked.

Kalyfa's eyes narrowed. "I'm not sure. That's what I was told. They asked to come and retrieve their bodies, but I told them to wait and let us find them first. They walked out of the castle alive and allied the other night, but at some point, Ripper left town and the other two are supposedly dead now. I don't know what's going on or what the timeline looks like, but I want all of you to search for these two. Find them, dead or alive. If they are dead, treat it as a crime scene so their system can investigate and then get the hell out of town. If they aren't dead… I want to talk to them."

"Like… *actually* talk to them?" Brendan asked tentatively.

Kalyfa nodded slowly, looking at him. "The danger I was worried about has passed – or didn't exist. I'm not sure at this point. But, if these two are still in town, then I want to know about it. I would toss them right back to their authorities, but they've gotten people that people in this room care about tangled up in their bullshit, so I want answers and a clearer picture of what's going on before I take action. We're *not* a haven for the greater US's criminals, and I'm not going to start now, but it's clear that we can't just force them to do anything. There are very few of us that I'd feel confident pitting against Faerstathe in a fight, and I'm not on that list anymore, thanks to Satyrna."

Brendan glanced at Josh and then back up to Kalyfa, concerned.

"What did she do?" Josh asked.

"Stabbed me in the back." When Josh made a face in response, Kalyfa added, "Literally."

"Yeah, how are you doing…?" one of the other knights who had been in the main hall asked.

"My head hurts worse than my back, but she got muscle, so I can't be in the field for a while. Thankfully, she *only* got muscle."

Josh frowned, glancing at Brendan, but he seemed surprised by this as well.

"Did you want us to pick her up too?" one of the captains asked.

"No. I'll pay her a visit in my own time. Meredith already checked; she and Vatale are out at that hunting cabin. Tanen is at his parents' house." Kalyfa looked at Josh and Brendan pointedly. "If they know where to find Faerstathe or his target, it would make everyone's lives easier if they'd just tell us. If you can spare us all the effort by asking, it would be greatly appreciated."

Josh sighed, looking away evasively. "I can ask Cypha. Saty doesn't respond and Dyspro's pissed at me."

"I can talk to Patricia and see if she knows anything or can ask her sister," Brendan offered. "I don't see Satyrna very often."

"You can do something more direct like go out and ask them point blank too, Garevn," one of the other captains said to him.

Josh made a face, eyeing him. "Have you *ever* actually talked to Satyrna Hennessin, Mason? If she's got a bug in her ass to protect something or someone, not even *I* could convince her to spill secrets about it."

Kalyfa sighed, shaking his head in resigned agreement. "He's right. She won't be cooperative. She's mother-hen-ing this guy because he's dark. We can try to pressure her, but I doubt it will go anywhere."

"Oh, hey, Kalyfa – it might not be related, but I saw this other dark in town the other day."

Kalyfa gave Isaac a surprised look. "Another one? Not *this* one?"

"Yeah, a different one. It was a girl."

"Was she alone?"

"Seemed like it."

"Odd… what does she look like?"

"Black hair, medium skin color, dark – well, obviously – dark eyes. Like the color part was dark too."

Brendan frowned, looking at Isaac. "Did she look like Malkarai?"

"Kinda, yeah?" Isaac replied, looking down at the photo. "I mean, she was way… softer. This guy just looks dangerous and kinda scary. She was more… cute. She was young and short. Hair and skin color are kinda similar though, yeah."

Kalyfa's eyes were narrowed. "Yeah, that's odd. I can't see how it would impact this search though. Just keep an eye out for her and let me know if she does anything suspicious. It's weird to see darks in general, especially when it's girls alone, but her being here isn't a problem."

"Yeah."

"Contact me if you have questions or find anything regarding Faerstathe or his target. This is a top priority until I say otherwise because their contact is waiting for me to report back with information. Organize patrols or search parties with anyone present – but try to keep it to just the people in this room for now. You've all interacted with these guys in some capacity or you're a captain. We'll only get the rest of the squad involved if we need to." He pointed at Josh without looking at him. "Except Garevn. Nobody let him help until he's had a full night's sleep."

Josh sighed and rolled his eyes. Isaac laughed.

"I'm still on for the next three hours."

"And then you're going home," Kalyfa retorted without missing a beat. "Ripper said she saw them in the northwest woods, but don't limit your search to there. We don't know that they are actually dead. If they *aren't* dead, then talk to them. Use diplomacy. Both of them are dangerous, and they obviously don't have any problem with injuring us. Don't lose those pictures, and don't copy them. You can ask people if they've seen them, but keep hold of the photos."

After they'd been dismissed, Josh pulled Brendan aside in the hall. "Hey, why'd he bring you in for this? What'd you do with these guys?"

Brendan glanced at some of the other knights as they passed them. "Uh, I was on that patrol that cornered Faerstathe the other night."

"Hm. Were you in the castle?"

"No, not when shit went down. But he caught a thief for Patrica and Satyrna outside of the store, so when he asked Patricia for help trying to figure out where we were keeping them, she asked me."

"Oh, so that's why they knew where to go?"

Brendan shrugged. "Yeah, I guess so. Were you in the castle then?"

Josh sighed and nodded, looking annoyed. "I was getting chewed out by Dyspro for not disobeying orders when Cypha and the other guy came up. I ran into Ripper a floor below and pointed out the room Satyrna was in to her, but then I left."

"Why didn't you speak up in there?"

Josh eyed him. "It didn't matter. Also, I wasn't supposed to be there."

"Oh. Are you going to help find them?"

"Not tonight, I'm tired. I'm going to go out and talk to Cypha and Satyrna before I'm off though."

"Okay. Think they'll help?"

Josh shrugged. "Not much, no. Maybe if I'm lucky Cypha will finish bitching me out before I have to clock out. I want to tell Kalyfa I tried though."

Brendan smirked.

"Also… I want to know what the fuck is going on with these two. My friends have all gotten wrapped up in this shit, so I want to know what it is."

"I mean, from what Patricia says… the dark at least sounds like a decent guy."

Josh shook his head, looking incredulous. "Decent enough that Saty would *stab* Kalyfa for him?"

Brendan shrugged, snorting softly. "I'm still trying to wrap my head around that one. What the hell happened the other night?"

Josh sighed in resignation. "Actually, saying that out loud, I'm both shocked and not shocked that she did something like that."

"Really?"

"Yeah. Saty has a temper and isn't afraid to punch or kick an asshole. If Kalyfa was harassing someone she befriended… it was just a matter of time before he pushed it too far. He's been annoying her for months."

"I know she has a temper, but… really? Assaulting the head knight? She's not that crazy."

"She's never seen Kalyfa like that. She sees him as just another guy. She doesn't care about authority. And that guy is her ex that is pissing her off, so…"

Brendan sighed, rubbing his brow. "So, she's thrown her lot in with a vigilante instead of the local law."

"Eh, she follows her heart first and the law second. She always has. We all have a soft spot for darks, and if she met this one because he helped them out with a thief… To be honest, this all makes more sense to me."

"So, are you thinking they're in the right?"

"I think this situation is fucked-up and convoluted and I want to dig into it more." Josh gestured at the knight office door half-heartedly. "Kalyfa invited me in, so you better believe I'm gonna take advantage of it."

"He invited you in cuz you're a captain," Brendan reminded him.

"Doesn't matter, I got an invite. I'm gonna try to talk to Cypha and Saty, finish this patrol, sleep, and then see what I can dig up before I go and look for them too."

"All right," Brendan said with a sigh. "I'm on in two days. If you want an extra body tomorrow, let me know."

"Sure."

**1:30 p.m.**

Satyrna shut the door behind her and started walking to town via the gently worn path, heading home for the things she'd intended to get three days earlier.

After walking for a few minutes, watching her footing since there was still some snow on the ground from yesterday, she noticed someone else when they were within twenty feet of her.

"Josh!" she exclaimed happily when she realized who it was.

He seemed surprised at her greeting. "Hey, Saty. Were you headed into town?"

"Yeah, but I can wait if you're coming out to visit." She went up to him and threw her arms around him, hugging him. "I haven't seen you in months, you jerk."

He hugged her back. "Yeah, I know. Sorry."

"Dyspro's at his parents' house."

"I know. I was coming out to see you and Cypha."

"Okay," Satyrna said, turning around and walking with him back to the house. "Thank you for helping the other night."

He sighed, color rising to his cheeks. "Yeah, no problem. Don't tell my boss."

She laughed. "Believe me, I won't tell your boss."

"What were you going to town for?"

"I have no clothes or anything out here, and I want a shower."

"Oh, I see. How long are you going to stay out here?" he asked.

"A little while. I wanna get my own place, but right now I just want to avoid town. As long as Dyspro's laid up, I figured I could keep Cypha company."

"I'm sure she'll appreciate that – more than Dyspro's company at least."

Satyrna smirked and opened the door. "Undoubtedly."

Inside, Cypha came out of her room, looking confused. She had her phone in her hand. "What'd you forget?"

"Nothing, I don't think," Satyrna said as she moved out of the way so he could come in behind her. "Look, I found a Josh!"

Cypha just raised an eyebrow, giving him a jaded look. "Wow, you *do* know where this place is?"

"Ha ha," he said flatly.

She turned on her phone screen to check the time. "Oh, it's before three. I suppose you've got to work soon?"

"Actually, I'm still working," he admitted guiltily.

"You were working the night shift yesterday," Cypha said accusatorily.

"Yeah."

"Dumbass. Does that mean this isn't a social call?"

"I mean… it's a little of both."

Satyrna frowned. "Oh… you want to talk to us as a knight?" She glanced down to his waist, realizing he had his swords on his belt. "Duh. You've been absent so long, I forgot the armed versus unarmed indicator."

Josh put a hand on the sword handle at his right hip idly, self-conscious of them now. "I want to talk to you guys cuz you're involved in some messed-up shit, and I want to know what's going on," he said, glancing at both of them. "Both as a knight and as your friend."

"But you'll tell Kalyfa what we tell you, won't you?" Cypha pressed.

"I suppose it depends on what you tell me… Look, let me tell you what *I* know, and maybe you can tell me what you know?"

"Maybe," Cypha replied bluntly. "Depends on if you have anything worthwhile."

Satyrna glanced at her, but then just looked at Josh, waiting.

He sighed and shifted. "Okay, uh, Faerstathe's boss called Kalyfa and said that Ripper, the woman that was helping Faerstathe, reported that he was dead. He killed his target and then killed himself. She asked for permission to come here and recover their bodies, but Kalyfa said no, and wants *us* to find them. Ripper said they were somewhere in the woods, northwest of town, but she wasn't sure where. Kalyfa is confused about the timeline, because the three of them left at the same time you guys did, and were apparently friendly at that time. If shit went down that night after they left, then okay, but he wants us to look for them assuming they could be dead or alive."

Satyrna frowned at him, keeping her mouth shut.

"I'm just trying to find out what you guys know. Is he dead? Do you know where he is?"

"I haven't seen the guy since the knights last did," Cypha said. "He took off."

Josh sighed and looked at Satyrna. "What about you?"

"I've been with Cypha basically the whole time," Satyrna replied.

"Hm," Josh said thoughtfully. "What about his target? The other guy that was helping him. He left with you guys."

"He and Teffifa left when we all got to the hospital," Cypha replied readily, sparing Satyrna from answering.

"Damn. Okay."

"What's Kalyfa going to do if they *are* alive?" Satyrna asked cautiously.

"I'm not sure. He's trying to figure the situation out. It sounds like he wants to talk to him. He told us not to attack, just talk."

"So he can give him back to his bosses if he's alive?"

Josh shrugged. "I don't know. He didn't say that specifically, but I know he doesn't want federal fugitives hiding here. How did you all fall in with this guy, anyway? Brendan said he caught a thief for you guys at the store, but that seems like an extreme jump to me."

"He's the dark we ran into after the hanging," Cypha said as she leaned against the wall near the fireplace.

Josh's eyes widened. "What? Seriously?"

Cypha nodded slowly.

"Yeah, and he's a really kind, smart, and interesting person," Satyrna said. "He's also incredibly dark and disillusioned and badly needs friends – because all of his were gone. I pushed him into hanging out with us to help give him a little social buffer, and it pissed Kalyfa off because he's a prick."

"He was afraid that the guy he was after would hurt you guys."

Cypha rolled her eyes. "Yeah, I heard that a few times."

"He wouldn't have," Satyrna said softly.

"Er, yeah, we're all gathering that too. His boss said that Faerstathe's target was a defector from their division, not a criminal like Kalyfa expected."

"He's Malkarai's brother," Satyrna blurted insistently. She pressed her lips together after saying that, wondering if it was too much info.

Josh's brow knitted up slightly. "Really?"

"Well, not by blood. He was there eleven years ago too. They were best friends until he ran away."

Josh frowned, contemplatively. "Do you think he'd actually kill him then?"

Cypha shrugged. "Who knows what was waiting for both of them if that wasn't how it went down?"

"I think he'd definitely kill himself if he had to kill his brother," Satyrna added.

He didn't reply immediately, thinking. "He isn't here, right?" he nodded toward Dyspro's room.

Cypha gave him a jaded look. "He's not here." She went over to his door, opened it, walked through the room, and then came back out, shutting the door behind her. "Dyspro's door is shut to keep the heat centralized where there are actually people."

"That makes sense. Can I ask you guys to let me know if he shows up?"

"I mean, you can ask," Cypha said, snarky.

"Cypha…I'm trying to help."

"I know, I just don't know *who* you're trying to help."

"Don't you trust me?"

"Of course, I trust you – I just also know how important being a knight is to you," she replied, giving him a steady look, one eyebrow raised.

Josh sighed. "That's fine. I already told Kalyfa and everyone else that you guys wouldn't tell me anything anyway. I had to say I tried. Just… stay safe, okay? I'm sure that you're fine if Malkarai and this other guy are friends since he's friends with you, but don't put yourself in the line of fire."

Satyrna nodded slightly.

"What's the other guy's name, anyway?"

"Kalyfa didn't tell you?" Cypha asked, tipping her head questioningly.

"He only had aliases, and he didn't tell us any of them."

"Traphian," Satyrna said quietly.

Josh nodded.

"Are you gonna tell Kalyfa that?"

"I don't see why it matters; I was just curious. Better than calling him, 'that other guy' in my head."

"He wasn't going by it anyway," Satyrna added.

"Probably smart, if he defected." Josh pulled his phone from his pocket and checked the time. "I should head back to town before patrol debriefs. Saty, do you want a ride to your house?"

She perked up. "Sure."

"See you for your next bi-annual appearance," Cypha said.

Josh sighed and gave her a jaded look. "I'm sorry. I've been pulling a lot of these back-to-back or day-after-day shifts."

"Yeah, I know. You're trying to," Cypha replied. "Stop being a dipshit and meet me for lunch one of these days."

"I'll try," he said sincerely.

"If you agree and then flake on me, I'm gonna come and find you at your apartment," Cypha threatened.

Josh's eyebrows just raised, the faintest look of fear on his face.

Satyrna snickered. "Play nice, Cypha."

"Not a chance." She turned and headed back to her room, waving a hand. "See you when you're back, Saty."

"Bye!"

"Bye, Cypha." Josh followed Satyrna outside and walked at her side down the path.

# 24

Malkarai woke up when the door shut. He rubbed his eyes, looking at Traphian as he walked away from the door. "Ngh, what time is it?"

"Five. Good morning, sunshine. You should get up; I ordered a pizza," Traphian replied as he set down a box on the table. He took paper plates from the bag that was on top of it and separated one for himself.

"Oh…" Malkarai pushed himself to a sitting position, blinking as he tried to get his bearings. "Fuck, I haven't had a good sleep in a week…" he muttered.

"Well, you keep doing stupid shit like avoiding buildings." Traphian sat down at the table and opened the box to get himself a slice of pizza. "I got deluxe. You can just give me your peppers."

"I eat them now," Malkarai said as he slid his legs out of the bed and stood, stumbling over to the table.

"Oh." Traphian gave him an amused smile. "Look at you, growing up and eating your spicy vegetables now."

Malkarai flipped him off halfheartedly and opened the box so he could take a piece and slide it onto one of the plates. "Thanks," he said after taking a bite, chewing, and swallowing it.

"Yeah, no problem. You owe me for half," Traphian teased.

Malkarai gave him a look but then grabbed his wallet from the table next to him, where he'd set it before going to sleep earlier, and pulled out two twenties and dropped them on the table in front of Traphian.

"I was kidding."

"I'm not," Malkarai said as he put his wallet back and picked his pizza back up.

"The pizza was like fourteen bucks, twenty with delivery and tip."

"That's nice."

Traphian sighed and moved the bills to his other side. "What's your plan for tonight?"

"I have to meet up with Satyrna at seven. After that, scope the town again."

"You should consider coming back here before it's daylight."

"I shouldn't keep coming and going from your hiding spot."

"Okay, just stay here."

Malkarai shook his head. "I appreciate the offer, but I really do need to figure out what is happening."

"At what point are you going to decide to just hole up, like you should?"

Malkarai shrugged. "Guess I'll see how things go."

"Teffifa took your phone, right?"

"Yeah."

"I have a landline phone here. You could try and call me with important updates if you can get your hands on a phone."

"Yeah, I'll get the number before I go." Malkarai ruffled his messed-up hair with his left hand, his eyes narrowing as he did so. "How scary is my hair?"

Traphian smirked. "Pretty scary. Honestly, almost back to your default."

"I knew I should've waited for it to dry…" Malkarai grumbled.

"You weren't waiting for shit. You fell asleep in like two minutes. Just wet it again – but do it right away so it dries before you go out."

"Yeah…"

"Does it stay down on its own when it's long like this?"

Malkarai nodded before taking another piece of pizza. "This is lower maintenance than it is when it's short – so it's way better for me. I fucking hated that hair gel."

"Impressive. They should've stopped making you buzz it way earlier. This is a much better choice than gravity-defying poof."

"It wasn't actually a choice. I just stopped taking care of it and figured out that long and unkempt lay better and covered my eyes. *Now* it's a choice, but it was neglect at first."

"Regardless, it's a better look for you."

"Thanks, I think. What'd you do all day?"

"Watched TV. Worked out. Washed clothes. Yours are on the bed."

"Thanks." Malkarai eyed him. "Worked out?"

"Yeah," Traphian replied with a shrug. "Abs, push-ups, squats. Shit like that."

"Huh," he said, surprised.

"You have to get creative when you're hiding in holes and can't leave or use facilities, but you need to keep your physical abilities honed. I've been on the run from trained government agents – I can't afford to get lazy."

"That's true…"

"I miss having a computer or a phone so I can actively inform myself, but the TV helps with passive information and entertainment. Books aren't a luxury I can deal with either, because they're bulky and heavy. So, yeah, I'm left with TV and exercise." Traphian leaned forward slightly, staring at Malkarai. "Do you *see* why I'm asking you to hide with me? I am so socially deprived right now, man. Doing freaking laundry was almost fun because it was something different. Also, I will make no apologies for how much blood I was or was not able to get out of your clothes. I'm pretty sure it's permanently part of the fabric now."

Malkarai laughed. "Thank you again for that. I appreciate and sympathize with your plight, but I can't hole up with you. Not yet, anyway. Let me try and figure out what's going on, and then I'll figure out where I'm going to hide."

"All right. Fine. I know, you're the best one to do this kind of stealth reconnaissance. Just, don't forget about me."

"I won't, I promise."

"And don't get your ass caught. I've put up with seven years of bullshit, I would love an actual win in this struggle."

"I will do my best to not get caught," Malkarai insisted solemnly.

**6:00 p.m.**

Satyrna shut her front door behind her and shifted her bag on her shoulder before putting her hands in the pockets of her coat to keep them warm. She'd almost reached the end of her street when she saw Brendan approaching.

She waved. "Hey, Brendan. Patricia's expecting you."

He glanced around and then walked over by her, purpose in his step. "Hey, Satyrna, I need to talk to you."

She blinked and stopped walking. "Why? What is it?"

"Why did you stab Kalyfa?"

The color flushed out of her face. She wasn't expecting a call-out like that. "H-how…?"

His brow was furrowed in concern. "You did, right?"

"Y-yes. How did you know that?" Her voice was weak.

He glanced around again and shook his head. "It isn't really a secret – well, not to the knights anyway."

She swallowed and backed up to lean against the wall. She didn't feel well.

"Are you okay?"

She shrugged, shaking her head dismissively.

"Why did you do it?"

"I don't know! I don't know why I did it!"

Brendan paused. "You care about him, don't you?"

She looked up at him, her eyes wet.

"About Faerstathe, I mean."

"Yes."

He looked at the ground for a few moments before speaking again. "Satyrna, I don't agree with Kalyfa's approach to this, but I don't necessarily think that Malkarai is innocent."

"He never meant any harm to anyone. He was here to retrieve Traphian, and that's it."

Brendan hesitated. "He wounded two knights, you know."

"They attacked him first."

"Yes, but we didn't know what we were getting into."

She narrowed her eyes. "What do you mean?"

He looked steadily at her. "He's… phenomenal, Satyrna. That man was raised to fight."

"I know he's a good fighter. I saw him in the castle… It looked effortless for him."

"You ever question why that is? Or what that ultimately means?"

She blinked contemplatively but didn't respond.

"He's taken lives before. He cut Jason and stabbed Kel in one easy swipe, without even batting an eye. He was holding back in the castle, I want you to realize. They had a plan and he was acting within it."

"I know," she said, bitterly. "I've gotten over the fighting thing. He's not a bad person. He's a just person, with a good heart. The fighting skills are part of the reason he's still *alive* – because they've made him strong."

"Was he worth potentially killing someone over? I think it was luck alone that Kalyfa didn't die, you know."

"Was it worth it for the knights to assault people, kidnap them, torture them while in forced custody, use drugs to make them more docile, force them-"

"Yeah, we did a lot of stupid shit this week. Intentions were good, but the actual actions were flawed, malicious, and in some cases, possibly illegal. Quite a few people acted against or in disregard of orders because it was supposed to be off-the-record. During our meeting this morning, Kalyfa had a very different tone overall about Malkarai and his target. He was pissed about the situation and probably in pain, but I think he was more pissed about how things happened on our side. He's still trying to weed out old elements in the knights, and this situation brought a few of those old ones to light, as well as pointed out some new ones he didn't expect."

She shook her head, glowering. "He'd better get his ass to work cleaning up his squad. If this shit happened to someone that wanted the attention, he'd have lawsuits on his hands."

"He's got a lot of office work to do while he's on medical leave, yes. Kalyfa won't let us arrest you. He wants to talk to you himself."

Satyrna eyed him. "Why?"

He shrugged. "He still cares about you. I don't know what he's planning, but I figured I'd at least give you a heads-up that he'll be looking for you."

"I-I appreciate that…"

"Josh said he would too."

"Yeah… he already did."

"Oh, okay. Good. I know you'd much rather work with him than Kalyfa. Did he tell you about what Ripper said?"

"That Malkarai and Traphian might be dead?"

"Yes."

She nodded. "I don't know where they are."

"Okay." Brendan put a hand on her shoulder. "Satyrna, please, think about this, okay? If he's still around, Malkarai Faerstathe is not a helpless little dark. He's an incredibly well-trained warrior with a very sharp mind. Now, I don't think he will hurt you. There's a lot to be said for what he did for you in the castle. I believe that the guy's upright in his moral sphere, but think about what supporting him will do for your reputation."

Satyrna didn't respond.

Brendan sighed and dropped his hand. "Are you going back out by Cypha?"

"Yes."

"All right. Be careful, okay? It's getting pretty dark. I can drive you out there if you want."

"I'll be fine. I have to stop at the store on my way."

"Okay." He started to head toward the Hennessin house, but paused and turned to add, "I'm looking out for you too, okay? Even if I didn't have a vested interest in you and your family, I wouldn't want anything to happen to you and your friends."

"Thanks, Brendan," Satyrna muttered.

"I'll see you later."

She stood there, leaning against the brick for a few minutes, examining the ground at her feet, before continuing on her way.

6:30 p.m.

The dark girl sighed in frustration, her breath visible in the air. She'd spent the greater part of the morning looking for Malkarai, but he had avoided all of his previous sleeping spots. So, she'd turned to searching for the people she'd seen him with. The frightening woman with two swords was gone; she'd seen her leave town, but the tall man with the leather coat, the brown-haired girl, and the blonde girl with short hair were all just as absent. She hadn't seen the boy who accompanied the two girls in an even longer period of time.

She considered going out to the house where the two girls were living but didn't want to run into and upset Malkarai again. She thought that maybe his friends could help guide her inquiry.

256

She leaned against a street lamp, trying to decide her next course of action. Visiting the house in the woods was a viable option, but she didn't want to be seen yet, so that was an avenue best traveled at night. It was dark now, but not dark enough to be comfortable sneaking around someone's house.

Her stomach grumbled and she put a hand over it. "Okay, maybe some food first is a good plan. Food and heat."

She looked around for a few moments before spotting a restaurant across the street. *Well, that works as well as anywhere.*

Inside, it took a few moments to get used to the murky darkness. The bar and dining area were both crowded. The only free spots were at the bar. The closest one, in the middle of the bar, was surrounded on both sides by loud, rowdy people, so she took a deep breath for courage and headed for the other empty one at the end next to a young man who seemed to be harassing one of the bartenders.

She looked at the man when she reached the seat. "Is this seat taken?"

He turned his head and stared at her blankly for a moment before he grabbed the crutches he had leaning against the bar and pulled them closer. "Oh, no, not at all. Sorry, my cripple-sticks don't need their own chair."

"It's okay, thank you."

She sat down on the stool and fixed her bag, tucking it between her back and the chair back, not noticing the smirk and head shake the bartender gave to the young man before excusing himself and turning his attention to her.

"Can I get something for you, miss?"

She looked up. "Uh, sure. Do you have cheeseburgers?"

"Of course. Fries okay?"

"Sure. And a lemonade."

"You got it. Be back in a few."

"Thanks." She idly looked around the bar, scanning the people sitting around the other sides and briefly checking to see what was on TV before she noticed that the guy next to her was looking at her.

He was trying to be subtle about it, but, being dark, subtle glances were still obvious to her. His didn't seem to be a malicious or disgusted look, so she was confused. She still pretended not to notice, just like she always did with the ill-intentioned stares.

The bartender brought her her lemonade, so she picked it up and took a sip before resting against the bar, nursing it as she avoided holding anyone's eye contact.

After a few minutes of picking at his food, the guy next to her spoke up, holding up one of the mozzarella sticks that had been mostly stripped of breading. "So, this is cheesy, and what I'm about to do is pretty cheesy too." He looked at her. "I'm Dyspro."

She stared at the cheese stick and then at him, an incredulous look on her face before she giggled nervously. "Uh, *what?*"

The bartender, who was cleaning behind the bar a short distance away, shook his head, walked over, and took Dyspro's plate, putting it on the back bar. "That was terrible. I'm taking your food away."

"No, my cheese!" Dyspro said plaintively, reaching for his plate.

She laughed, covering her mouth with a hand.

After a few moments, the bartender gave him his plate back, shaking his head at Dyspro again. He looked at the girl. "Don't let him get away with that. He needs to try harder."

Dyspro frowned at him. "You should be nice to brie, I'm injured."

"Absolutely not," he said dismissively before going over to where someone was flagging him down.

She smiled as she watched them. "I'm Rafiane," she said quietly.

Dyspro looked at her and smiled, pleased. "Rafiane?" he repeated.

She nodded.

"It's nice to meet you."

"Is he your friend?" she asked, tipping her head toward the bartender.

"Yeah. That's Barry. He owns this place."

"Oh." She looked harder at him. "He seems young for that…"

"Yeah, it used to be his dad's place, but he's been running it for the past year and a half. Is this your first time here?"

She nodded, looking back at him.

"Well, welcome." He glanced down the bar and behind her before looking back at her. "Are you here alone?"

"No," she replied automatically.

"Where are your friends then?"

She picked up her glass and took a sip evasively. "Avoiding me."

He eyed her. "Seriously, what's a girl like you doing alone in a bar?"

"Eating. And why are you so certain I'm alone?"

"I'm not getting any death glares for talking to you. Believe me; I have an eye for them."

"I doubt you'd be the one getting death glares." She looked at his crutches and changed the topic. "What happened?"

"Uh… long story. I've got a broken leg."

"Accident?"

"Well, no, it was pretty intentional."

She gave him a confused look, examining him closer. He looked fairly normal; he had short brown hair, bright, blue eyes, and a distant smirk on his lips as he stared off, somewhere down the bar. She did notice that he had pretty thick arm muscles, and the hand holding his glass had scabs like the knuckles had split recently. He was rather attractive but seemed pretty abused. "What? You intentionally broke your leg?"

"Er, well, I didn't intend for it to happen – the guy who broke it did."

"Someone broke your leg on purpose?" she said in disbelief, a trace of awe in her voice.

He shrugged. "I pissed him off. He and his buddies ganged up on me."

"Who? A gang?"

"No, some knights."

"Why would they do that? They're law enforcers, right?" She sounded wary.

"Yeah. Well, they had me incarcerated at the time, but the guy who did it was pissed at me for personal reasons."

Her eyes widened. "Incarcerated?" she whispered.

He looked at her. "Oh, no, relax. That was a bad word choice. I wasn't in prison. They were holding me because they feared for my safety. Protective custody. The boy toy of my ex saw it as a good chance to teach me a lesson."

Her discomfort was apparently obvious because he continued to reassure her.

"Seriously, I'm not a criminal, I promise. The guy who screwed my leg up is dating my ex, who's a bitch."

"That's not a good reason to beat someone up…"

"I completely agree. I mean, he picked a fight with me, and I probably should've just kept my mouth shut, but… I'm clearly terrible at doing that."

She smirked, giving him a look.

"His boss wasn't happy about it, but I don't know if he got in trouble for it or not."

"That's awful… Thanks," she said to Barry as he set a plate of fries and a cheeseburger in front of her. She took the bun off, checking what toppings were on it. After adding the lettuce and tomato from the plate to the burger, she picked it up to take a bite.

Dyspro drank some more of his drink before pursuing further conversation. "So, you're definitely not from Cavington… Are you from somewhere nearby?"

"No."

He eyed her. "This state?"

"No."

"Wow, you're really traveling. What are you doing here? I mean, it's not like Cavington is a touristy town. Honestly, we're kind of the opposite, especially for darks. Do you have friends or family here?"

She swallowed, glancing at him. She'd been unsure if he realized she was a dark or not, and now he was just dropping it casually like it didn't matter. "Kind of," she eventually replied.

"Kind of?"

"I followed someone here."

"Who?"

"I highly doubt you'd know him. He's from out of state too."

"Why then?"

"I need to find out some information from him."

"You're probably not going to be here long then, huh?"

She shrugged. "If he or his friends would stop hiding from me, no, it shouldn't be long."

"Hiding?"

She shook her head. "It's nothing you need to worry about."

He sighed. "Sorry, it's just, I know how this town is. I'm a little concerned that you're here on your own, trying to talk to someone that doesn't want to talk to you. You couldn't have had someone come along with you? No friends to help? I mean, you seem pretty friendly to me."

She looked at him out of the corner of her eye as she poked at her burger with a fry, uncomfortable. "I thought you could tell."

"Tell what?"

"That I'm a dark," she said, distressed.

He frowned, realizing that he had upset her. "Oh, no, relax," he said, soothingly. "I wasn't trying to be insensitive. I mean it, you seem really sweet." He paused and added, "I'd go along and make sure you were safe."

Rafiane blushed, shrinking in her seat slightly. "Even though I'm dark?"

"*Especially* because you're dark. I didn't mean to upset you. I don't care that you're a dark."

"Liar. Everyone around here does."

He crossed his heart and then put a hand on the one of hers that she had left lying on the bar top. "Honest, it doesn't bother me in the slightest. You wouldn't be the first dark I've befriended, okay?"

She eyed his hand. "So, we're friends now?"

"I think you need at least one here. It's not safe for girls to be wandering around alone in unfamiliar places, especially if you're dark. Darks avoid this area, so you kinda stand out. I saw you in town yesterday, actually."

She sighed and slumped back against her bag.

Dyspro looked at her appraisingly. "Is that weird?"

"Huh? No… It's just… I don't *want* to stand out. I was doing okay, keeping under the radar, but then I went and lost my lead, and… and now I don't know where to look, and…" She sighed heavily.

Dyspro motioned to Barry, who was busy down the bar. "If you ever need anything, you can go to Barry. I'm here pretty often; he's a bud of mine from high school, so I frequent the place. We'll help you out if anyone gives you any problems."

She nodded slightly. "Thanks."

"No problem." He let go of her hand. "Eat; your burger's getting cold."

She sighed but eventually returned to her meal.

After a short while, when most of her food had been eaten, Dyspro asked, "So, are you out of high school?"

"Yes."

"In college?"

"No. I'm not sure if that'll be an avenue I'll take."

"What're you gonna do instead? Do you have a job?"

"Right now, no. I've kinda been pursuing something since I graduated. I'm not sure yet what I'm going to do. It's very hard to find steady work when you're dark."

"What've you been pursuing?"

"Well, this guy I followed here."

Dyspro eyed her. "Ah, so you're that kinda girl…"

She looked at him blankly for a few moments and then her eyes widened and she put her hands up. "What?! No, no, no! It's not like that!" She pouted, staring at her lap. "I'm not just chasing some cute guy. That's so creepy and stalkerish."

"Then why are you following him?"

"I need to find out some information from him… but he won't give me it…"

"You have talked to him then?"

"Yes, but I need to find him again. I lost him…"

"You are definitely a dark, no doubt about it."

She eyed him. "What do you mean by that?"

"Getting you to give me a straight answer is damn near impossible."

She smiled apologetically, not quite done pouting. "Sorry."

He shrugged. "Eh, I'm used to it. Every dark I've known's been like that."

"Sorry."

He bumped her arm with his. "You're cuter than the rest of them though, so I'll let you get away with it."

She smiled. "You've known a lot of us?"

"Three."

"Are they still around?"

"Eh, no, not really."

"Not really?"

"Well, two of them were killed when I was nine, and the other one disappeared recently."

She frowned. "That's not a very good record."

"Well, I guess you could say it was mostly self-inflicted fates on all their parts. Doesn't make me feel any better about the fact that they're gone, though."

"This region really is awful for darks, isn't it?"

"Yeah, it's not great. So, take care of yourself, okay?"

She nodded. "I'll try…"

"Do you have a weapon?"

"A pocket knife."

"Hmm…that's not much."

"Well, I don't know how to use anything else. I'm very good at hiding."

"Hiding works. Just make sure not to get in a situation where you can't hide."

"I'll do my best. Do you have a weapon?"

"I mean, I usually have a utility knife or tools on me, but nah, I usually use my fists. But, now…" He picked up one of his crutches and hefted it lightly in one hand. "Now I have a temporary weapon set."

She giggled. "I'd like to see you use them."

He shrugged and set the crutch back down. "I'm a lot of talk. My leg aches, so I think I'll be yelling, 'mercy,' instead of egging the jerks on next time."

She smiled.

"Don't be too paranoid though, okay? If you stay out of trouble, you'll be all right. Just don't come off as suspicious, and you won't have any problems." He smiled. "That shouldn't be hard for you. I think you'd be a prize catch for anyone – especially because you're a dark."

She blushed. "Even though I'm a stalker?"

"Yeah, even though you're a little stalker."

Rafiane pressed her lips together, smirking as she looked back down at her meal. She picked her cheeseburger up and asked, "How old are you?"

"Twenty."

She eyed his drink. "So that's soda?"

Dyspro laughed. "Yeah, Barry is an ass about that. He won't serve me alcohol."

"So, you're *normally* this chatty?"

"Yeah," he said, laughing again. "I mean, not that I'd be drinking alcohol right now anyway. I'm on painkillers and have to walk home. Hobble? Whatever, you get the point. My birthday is in January, so I don't have that long before I have the option."

She looked at Barry. "Is he old enough to *serve* alcohol?"

"Yeah. He turned twenty-one in August. He still ran things before that, he just had more bartenders so he didn't get dinged for breaking the rules."

"Hm…"

"How old are you?"

"Eighteen."

His eyebrows lifted. "Really?"

Rafiane glanced at him and nodded.

"Okay, your out-of-school, no job timeline makes more sense then. Did you graduate last spring?"

"Yes."

"Hasn't this little trip been scary for you?" he pressed, looking concerned.

She shrugged. "The motivation has kept me focused. But… yes, it's been stressful."

"Seriously, please let me know if I can help you while you're here."

"Don't *you* have to work?"

"Well, right now, I'm not sure how much work I can do. But I'm a general contractor, so I'm always out and about in town, and most jobs are pretty flexible in terms of scheduling. If I need to take a break to help you get a meal without being bothered, or tell you about how to find something in town, then that's not a problem at all."

"I'll keep it in mind," she replied in a small voice.

"Do you want my number? I won't ask for yours. Just so you have an option."

Rafiane blinked, looking at the few fries left on her plate. Eventually, she put one in her mouth and nodded, reaching into her pocket and pulling her phone out.

He told her his number. She put it in her phone, checked it, and then put her phone away, feeling a little naughty and crazy. She'd just met a guy at a bar and had his number. *What the hell is happening?*

"I hope you don't need to use that cuz of something bad." He gave her a playful grin. "Just cuz you wanna see me again."

She pushed her empty plate away and took a long drink to hide her smile. Then she set the glass of ice next to her plate. "I think I'd better get going. I have people I have to find."

He was visibly disappointed. "Really? I was kinda hoping you could stay longer."

"I wish I could, but I have to go." She looked across the bar and sighed. Barry was busy filling drinks for the argumentative men in the middle of the bar. "Wow, he's busy. How much do you think this costs?"

"Nothin'."

She looked at him. "What?"

"Nothin'."

"No, seriously."

"Seriously, nothing. I got it."

She sighed. "I have enough money."

"Good, I'm glad. Save it for your next meal."

Rafiane blushed again, eyeing him. "Why… why are you flirting with me?" she asked tentatively.

He smiled at her. "Because I think you're really pretty, and after talking with you, your personality matches."

"Do you do this with a lot of girls?"

He laughed. "Well, flirt, sure, but if they end up being a bitch or are just unpleasant or boring to talk to, then I sure as hell don't offer to buy their dinner or say they can contact me or my friends later."

She sighed. "Thank you," she said sincerely.

He smiled. "My pleasure."

She held her hand out to him. "It's been nice meeting you… Dyspro, right?"

He took her hand and kissed it, instead of shaking it. "Dyspro Tanen. Rafiane?"

She blushed fiercely. "Rafiane Tavelante."

"Well, Rafiane, it's been great talking to you. I hope I get to see you around."

She smiled warmly. "Me too."

She stood up and he let go of her hand.

"Watch out for yourself."

"I will, thank you."

She put her bag over her shoulder, gave him a last smile, and then headed for the door.

Dyspro watched Rafiane until she left, and then he sighed and leaned on the bar, propping his head up with one hand, staring at his very forgotten remaining two mozzarella sticks. "Wow," he murmured.

Barry smirked as he approached to take her plate and glass. "Did you strike out, or what?"

"I mean, not really?" Dyspro replied, picking up one of the appetizers and drowning it in marinara.

"You look like someone crapped in your drink."

"Well, yeah, she left." He gave Barry a hopeful look, his eyebrows raised. "She's got my number though."

Barry laughed. "Okay, you didn't strike out. Cheer up."

He sighed. "The others were local. She isn't from anywhere near here, apparently. Why is that how it goes? I find someone that I actually like, and they aren't even from this crapheap of a town?"

"Life's not fair. Did I see that right? Was she a dark?"

"Yeah."

"Huh, I haven't seen a female one since we were kids."

"Yeah, same here."

"She's not associated with that dark guy you guys were hanging around with earlier this week, is she?"

Dyspro shrugged. "I have no idea. I don't think that guy associated with *anyone*, to be honest. It'd be kinda funny if she was, but I don't think all darks have some kind of secret network."

"Yeah, probably not. Did she leave money?"

"She tried. Add it to my tab, okay?"

"Nah, your stuff's on me tonight."

Dyspro smirked. "Thanks."

"No problem. Just don't get used to it. Consider it a get-well present."

"Now I feel cheap, getting away without actually paying."

"I aim to please."

"Oh. That girl, she's alone in town… so I told her if she had any problems to come to you or me. I figure you're easier to find than me."

"All right. I'll let you know if she comes back around."

"Thanks."

"What's her name?"

"Rafiane."

Barry nodded, his eyebrows raising briefly. "You guys are up to, what, *three* new friends this week? Should I tell Josh you're finally replacing him?"

Dyspro laughed. "Yeah, tell him that. Dickhead should've stepped up." He finished his drink and asked, "Who was the second one?"

"Oh, Saty and Cypha were in here with a tall brown-haired guy the other day. Ate in my office. His was Tray… something, I can't remember it now."

"Oh, him. That's right, Cypha mentioned they'd hung out with him a bit. Traphian."

Barry snapped his fingers. "That's it."

"We'll see if he and Malkarai stick around. Last I heard, he's still missing."

"Yeah, he hasn't been in here."

"I'd be surprised if he was. Well, I should get home. Since I'm staying with my parents, they're paying attention to when I'm out and about, and man, it's annoying."

"Did you drive here at least?"

"Yeah, Mom's letting me use her car. I should be able to work some too since I don't need to walk as much."

"That's good."

Dyspro put his coat on, dug a couple of bills out of his pocket, and threw them on the bar next to his glass. "That's to go toward my tab…"

"All right."

Dyspro gave Barry a casual salute before he tucked his crutches underneath his arms, and then he headed for the door.

# 25

Satyrna stood at the edge of downtown, searching the underbrush and trees nearby. There were quite a few residential streets here, but where she was standing was largely deserted. There was an open field here and a lighted playground across the street, but she'd been told to wait near the wood grove.

She held her hands up to her face, cupping her nose and mouth, and breathed in them, trying to warm up her nose as she scanned the street, in case he was just walking on the sidewalk.

"Do you want my cloak back? You look cold," she heard a low voice say behind her. She turned to see Malkarai emerging from the dark tree cover.

She smiled as she dropped her hands, stepping up to him as he approached. She had several bags on the ground by her feet, so she didn't stray far from them, but as soon as he was close enough, she slipped her arms around his chest underneath the cloak, hugging him. "This is fine."

He sighed, amused, and lifted his arms, hugging her back.

Satyrna smiled, resting her head comfortably on his shoulder, relishing that he was returning this hug. It was nice and warm. "Actually, I'm surprised *you* aren't colder than you are," she said.

"I haven't started wandering around yet."

"Have you been outside since this morning?"

"No, I was with Traphian."

"Oh," she said, pleasantly surprised. "I'm glad you weren't in the cold all day."

"Yeah, I showered and then slept all day. He fed me twice too."

She smiled, squeezing him gently. "Good."

"We decided on a plan."

Satyrna pulled away enough to look him in the face, not entirely letting go. "What'd you decide?" she asked eagerly, feeling anxious as she thought about what he'd previously said he'd have to do.

"I'm going to try and figure out what's going on with my employers, because I'm sure they'll show up here in person at some point, but he and I are going to hide here, in Cavington."

She inhaled, her eyebrows lifting. "Really? You're going to *stay here*? You were saying it wasn't safe."

"Traphian says running is dumb. Staying put and not interacting with anywhere or anyone new is smarter than setting off new alerts elsewhere. Teffifa told them we're dead, so we should pretend we don't exist, not test their extensive resources."

Satyrna hugged him tightly, pressing her cheek against his shoulder.

Malkarai moved one of his hands to her upper back, returning the hug. "You seem to approve of this plan."

"This is the only one where I get to keep you."

"Maybe not the only one," he said with a shrug. "It's not perfect, and it's going to rely on you and your friends wanting us around. I know *you* do, but are they willing to help us?"

"If they weren't I'd be really surprised. And I'd chew them out."

He snickered softly. "Okay."

"What do you need us to do?"

"I'm not sure yet. Right now, just pretend we are gone."

"Okay, Cypha and I are already doing that. Josh came around earlier, asking if we knew where you and Traphian went."

"He did?" Malkarai's voice sounded concerned.

"Yeah. Kalyfa's back to work and I guess your bosses called him, telling the story Teffifa told them, and they wanted to come here and find your bodies, but Kalyfa told them to hold off and has the knights looking for you."

Malkarai sighed tensely, looking around. "Thank you. That's the kind of information I wanted to find out tonight."

"Josh said he just wanted to talk to you guys and find out what's happening. He told them not to attack you if you were still alive."

"That's an improvement, I guess," he muttered.

"I don't know if Kalyfa is being upfront with the knights though. He doesn't know the whole story, and I'm sure that's bugging the crap out of him. He's been so…irrational with this whole stupid thing, I don't necessarily trust him," Satyrna grumbled.

"I wish I could find two convenient corpses to just stage in the woods. There are no bodies, so we're relying on them accepting Teffifa's word without evidence."

"Yeah, I don't think you're going to find an abundance of those around here."

"That's a good thing, it's just inconvenient for me." Malkarai was quiet for a few moments, his eyebrows knitted up. "How much do you trust Josh?"

"With my life."

He looked down at her. "Do you think he'd be willing to give you information for me?"

Satyrna sighed. "Unfortunately, I'm not sure how to answer that. He might consider it for me, but I think he'd be conflicted. Being a knight is his dream job, especially because he considers it his responsibility to do better than his grandfather did. I do think he'd be sympathetic to you, but if he had direct orders, I don't know if he'd go against them."

"I don't think asking him to be a snitch for me would make us friends. I guess, just let me know if he comes asking again, and if you're comfortable with it, let me know whatever he may tell you about what the knights are up to. We'll keep him in the dark."

"Okay. Should I keep Cypha and Dyspro in the dark?"

"Um… probably not…" Malkarai deliberated. "Well, you know them best – how well can they keep a secret?"

"Depends, for Dyspro. He means well, but he gets his foot in his mouth a lot. Cypha can keep secrets like a vault."

He snickered. "Okay, maybe just keep it to Cypha for now. Dyspro's not staying with you guys for the moment anyway."

"Yeah." Satyrna let go of him reluctantly but didn't move any farther away. He dropped his hands as well. "Will you stay with us? Or are you going to keep hiding with Traphian?"

He hesitated. "I want to keep an eye on things, so staying with Traphian is not a wise move. Me coming and going will draw attention to him. When I'm not hiding, I really stand out."

"Yeah, you are pretty unique… Does that mean you'll stay with us?"

"I'm not sure that's a good idea either."

She frowned. "Where else would be better? We're out in the middle of nowhere – there are no neighbors to see you coming and going."

"No neighbors, yeah, but remember I'm being followed. She knows about the cottage."

"She was able to follow you, and she's not what you are?" Satyrna furrowed her brow.

"Yeah. Kinda surprised me too."

"Is she just a normal person, or what?"

"Seems that way. I told her to stay away from me before she gets hurt." He shook his head, eyes on the playground across the road. "I don't think she'll just drop it that easily. She's been following me for at least two weeks."

"Do you think she'll tell them you're alive?"

"Well, whoever she may tell, I doubt it would be my employers. She could've gone through them to find out where I'm from if that was an option for her."

"Would they have told her?"

"If she was affiliated with the system, maybe. As it stands, no. I highly doubt she would've been able to talk to anyone. We're not a public group. And, even if she had gotten in contact with someone, no one would have told someone outside of the system anything about me."

"Where are you from?"

He shrugged. "I don't know."

"You don't know where they got you? Don't they keep records of what orphanages or cities the children come from?"

"Yes, they do. Everyone has access to their personal files."

"So why don't you know?"

"Because I was left there. Somebody brought me there and left me in their care when I was two."

"Your parents?"

"I doubt it. It was a rather young blonde woman. She looked nothing like me. She said that she'd found me and wanted to keep me, but couldn't make ends meet."

"So, she gave you to the government?"

"Yeah, somebody pointed her in that direction. She didn't even know that it was there before that. I doubt she had any idea what the place did besides raise orphans."

She was quiet for a few moments. "Did she say what happened to your parents?"

"No. I don't know that anything did happen to them. I just know they abandoned me."

"You think they abandoned you?"

"Yeah."

"Why do you believe that your parents abandoned you?"

"Because the woman found me on the side of the road in a carrier with my name stuck into my blankets."

Satyrna frowned, regretfully accepting this.

"If that's not abandonment, I don't know what is."

Satyrna reached forward and took his hands, squeezing them. "I'm sorry."

He shrugged. "Whatever. I can't blame them for trying to spare themselves the grief."

Satyrna frowned. "Is that really how you see dark children?" she demanded.

He looked at her. "How *I* see them? No. But I know that's how the rest of the world does."

"That girl wanted to keep you."

"But she didn't."

Satyrna sighed, aggravated by the topic. "Would you do the same?"

"As my parents did? Not on my life."

"Not everyone thinks like that…" she muttered.

"I know. I know there are more weird people like you out there, but I was abandoned, plain and simple. So, I don't know what the hell that girl's looking for, but I can't help her."

Satyrna sighed. "Well… at least she isn't with the system."

"That's the silver lining with that situation, yes. I just don't know *who* she's trying to find this information for, so I'm still going to avoid her."

Satyrna nodded. "Where are you going to stay then? Not your car, right?"

Malkarai shrugged. "The car is dead to me. It may as well not exist. Teffifa took the keys, so I'm sure they'll retrieve it. I'll probably just hide in the woods somewhere."

"You'll get so cold…"

"I sleep during the day."

She sighed and shook her head. "That doesn't matter in December, Malkarai."

"If the knights come knocking at your door, there's nowhere for me to hide there. This girl that's following me knows about it too. I just need to find something else, and if I can't find someplace indoors, then I'll find a shelter outside. There are rocks and outcroppings and things in the woods, so I can find protection from the wind and snow. Also, I do have a hat and gloves, and I'm technically wearing two coats."

"Neither of them are winter coats," Satyrna said with a defeated sigh.

"They're warm together. Once things settle down, I will too. I need to keep alert right now."

She nodded somberly. "Just don't forget you're injured."

"I won't."

"Will sneaking around and spying on things aggravate your side?"

"It might, but the way I intend to do it right now is probably safe."

"Which is how?"

"Find a good vantage point and sit there, watching."

"Oh, you're going to just watch?"

He nodded. "I'm not sneaking into anywhere. I don't know where to go, so instead I'm just going to watch a few places that I know that people dealing with this situation would go, and hope to overhear some useful information."

"You're sure they won't see you?"

"Yeah. I'm practiced at this. I stay still for long periods of time frequently. You'd be surprised how much humans rely on movement to see people. If you don't move; they don't see you. Your eyes are important." He shook his head slightly, shrouding his eyes behind his hair. "People pick out eyes, so you hide them and you look like an object. Mine are especially easy to hide."

Her eyebrows lifted as she watched him, agreeing that it was hard to see his eyes when he purposefully put his hair in front of them. "That's a little scary."

"I'm scary." He looked at her, tossing his hair out of his face, a frown on his lips. "You disapprove of all these things that have to do with me, why the hell do you want me?"

"I don't disapprove of you and I don't think that *you're* scary."

"I spend over half my time in hiding. If that bothers you, this isn't gonna work."

Satyrna sighed and squeezed his hands firmly. "It's impressive-scary, not frightening-scary. Relax."

"I don't want you getting delusions about what I am."

"Let me know more about you, and then I won't have any delusions. What I've seen so far appeals to me."

He shook his head. "Well, you'd better be prepared to take me as I am, secrets and all, because I'm not going to change for anyone anymore."

"I'm not asking you to." She reached up and cradled his jaw in her hands. "Don't get so defensive."

"I'm not a heroic figure," he muttered.

"You're a hero to me, slinking in shadows or not. I don't want you to change."

"You say that now…"

"Malkarai, stop," she said gently but resolutely. She pulled his face to hers and kissed him warmly.

He kissed her back firmly, obviously still a little aggravated. However, he put a hand on her hip as he reciprocated.

Satyrna broke the kiss with a soft sigh. "The only thing I want you to change is how negatively you think of yourself."

He shook his head slightly. "There are loads of good reasons for that."

"Fine, when this is all over and you're hiding, then you can start telling me the reasons so I can break them all down," she said, tipping her head slightly as she stared him in the eyes defiantly.

He just looked back at her, his eyes moving slightly between each of hers before he smiled faintly.

"What?" she demanded.

"I'm just getting used to someone doing this with an expression besides fear or disgust."

She sighed audibly, her eyebrows knitting up before her entire expression softened. "Better get used to it fast, because I'm not going anywhere."

"Hopefully I won't have to, either." He glanced down the street and then in the other direction. "Well, except right now. We shouldn't linger here too long."

Satyrna nodded reluctantly. "Um, before you go…"

Malkarai gave her his attention again, looking at her face, although she was looking at his chest.

"I have a small problem."

"What's that?"

"Kalyfa knows I stabbed him."

"I'd assume he does since there were a lot of witnesses."

"He… he told the knights that he'd talk to me in person."

"That's better than doing something asinine like earlier this week, and sending his people after you," Malkarai muttered.

She looked up at him, her eyes full of worry. "Malkarai… I don't know what I'm supposed to do…"

He frowned, taking in her expression. "You really are upset."

"I've never done that to anyone before… I-it was always Dyspro and Cypha who did the real rough fighting. I'd just defend myself if I needed to, and that was it. It's only been kicks and punches before this. I don't know why I did it, or what's gonna happen to me."

"You were defending me," he reminded her.

"Yeah…"

"I'm pretty sure they're angrier with me than you, Satyrna."

"Well, yes, but Kalyfa didn't just ignore it. I stabbed him." She buried her face in his cloak. "I'm scared…"

Malkarai wrapped his arms around her shoulders, holding her close. "Relax, Satyrna; he won't hurt you."

"He's gotta be angry with me."

"Well, yeah, he cares about you a lot and you stabbed him in the back – literally."

"That's why I'm so afraid. I stabbed him to save you, Malkarai. Not only did I betray him, but I physically injured him in the process."

"Do you regret it?"

"That's irrelevant, isn't it?"

"No, it's not. You could apologize and beg his forgiveness."

She shook her head firmly, turning it so her cheek was against him. "No, I won't do that. I support you, and I'm not going to go back on that just to save my own hide."

He pushed some of her hair behind her ear so he could see her face. "Well, then just steel yourself for whatever he intends to do."

She looked up at him, surprised. "That's it?"

"If you're gonna stand by it, then yeah, you're gonna have to deal with the repercussions."

She blinked, staring at the clasp on his cloak.

He touched her chin, making her look back up at him. "You're way too assertive to just take a scolding from that guy. Seriously, between the two of you, you scare me more."

Satyrna laughed shortly. "That's bull."

"Is not. You chased me down that first day and I tried to get away a half dozen times. He followed me and I got sick of it and faced him down."

Satyrna smirked. "That is not the same thing, but I appreciate the encouragement."

"He can't act like they're innocent and you're the only one who did something drastic in that fight. I didn't go there to fight; he initiated. And afterward, one of his knights retaliated against you when you were unarmed. *That* was uncalled for. Moreso than you participating in our fight."

She inhaled slowly and deeply.

"Seriously though… if he hurts you, he'll pay."

Satyrna looked him in the eyes with a shy smile. "I'm not asking you to go and beat him up for me."

"Paying for it doesn't have to mean violence – but in this case, it might. He obviously doesn't listen to reason."

She shook her head. "I don't want anyone to get hurt anymore though."

"I have a feeling this fight's not over yet."

Satyrna sighed and slipped her arms under his again, hugging him around the chest. "I hope it is. I hope the rest of it can be figured out by talking."

"I'll let you stay optimistic. Talking never works for me."

Satyrna squeezed him. "I'll do my best to help. Just tell me what I need to do."

"Go home."

She frowned. "That's not helpful…"

"Seriously, it's helpful to me. I'll be less worried about all of you if I know you're somewhere safe. I'm not far away."

She sighed. "Fine. Can I see you again soon?"

"I'll see. Go home for now. I'll be in touch."

"All right." She loosened her hold and hopped up on tiptoes, planting a kiss firmly on his lips.

He kissed her back, still holding her.

After she pulled away, he gave her a hug and a long look, and then muttered, "Stay safe," before backing up a step and then disappearing into the woods.

"You too." Satyrna sighed, watching the area where he was already lost to sight. After a few moments, she turned, gathered her things, and headed for the sidewalk.

Satyrna set the cooler she'd taken from her house next to the front door of the cottage, then shifted her bag on her shoulder and transferred a few of the grocery bags in her right hand to her left before checking to see if the door was unlocked. The knob didn't move, so she started to dig in her pocket for her keys.

Before she could get her key out, the door unlocked and opened. Cypha stood there with her hand on the door and a frown on her face. "What the hell took you so long?"

"I told you I'd be a while."

"I figured a few hours – it's been almost six," she retorted, stepping aside so Satyrna could enter.

"I'm pretty sure I told you I'd be back tonight. Whether or not you heard me is another story," Satyrna said as she put the grocery bags on the table.

Cypha sighed but shut and locked the door without further protest.

"I brought a cooler from home, so we can have meat. I got some from the store. I also got the ingredients so I can cook a few meals for us."

Cypha's eyebrows lifted as she came over to the table and peeked in the grocery bags.

Satyrna went back to the extra bedroom she'd been using and tossed the duffel bag she'd filled with clothes and other necessities on the bed.

"Okay, I forgive you," Cypha said, looking to see what one of the jars was.

"Yeah, I figured offering to cook would make you happy," Satyrna replied as she came back out, taking her coat off. She hung it up next to Cypha's near the door and then went to the table to help Cypha unload and put away the groceries.

"We need more storage space, especially if you're gonna be around here and bringing adult food options into the house," Cypha muttered as she shifted several jars to fit them better on the stacked wooden crates they were using as shelving.

"Maybe we can see what Dyspro's got stashed behind the house and build something ourselves."

"He'll probably redo it when we aren't looking."

"Whatever, that's fine. He's not out here to tell us to let him do it – and then have to wait while he finishes six other things first."

Cypha snickered. "Yeah."

"Did you eat dinner?"

"Yeah, like two hours ago."

"Okay, good. My mom fed me before I left. I'll cook for us tomorrow."

"Sure. What were you doing for six hours?" Cypha asked as she sat down at the table.

Satyrna finished putting pasta on the top of the crate shelves and then put the bag in with the other bags. "I showered, gathered up clothes and the rest of my toiletries, picked out a few books, and ate with Mom and Patricia," she said as she sat down across from Cypha. "Then I went to the store and…" she made a pensive face, re-thinking her wording, "and then I met up with Malkarai on my way back out here."

Cypha's eyebrows lifted. "Oh, you're just gonna leave that as an offhanded remark, huh?"

"Well…"

"Was this planned? Did you meet up with him specifically?"

"Yeah… he came around last night – well, really early this morning – and I helped him with his injuries. He took off again after getting bandaged up and changing clothes, but then I guess he came back before I woke up for the day and left me a note, asking me to meet him tonight. He'd asked me to not tell anyone I saw him, that's why I didn't say anything," she added defensively.

"I'm glad to hear he isn't dead and rotting in the woods like the knights were told," Cypha said, begrudgingly. "Not cool with knowing someone else was in the house last night and I slept through it entirely."

"I mean, we weren't being loud. He fought with me a little because he had intended to just stitch himself up and bolt, and I wouldn't let him, but we were still pretty quiet."

"What did he want to meet up with you for tonight?"

"He talked with Traphian and they decided what they're going to do, so he wanted to tell me the plan."

Cypha leaned forward against the table. "What's their plan?"

"They're going to stay here and hide. Traphian says that's safer than running."

"Huh," she said, surprised. "Not what I expected to hear, to be honest."

"Me neither, but I'm really happy that that's what they're gonna do," Satyrna said, a smile tugging at her mouth as she looked at the table evasively. "Malkarai is trying to see if he can find information about the situation… but otherwise he's going to keep low. Traphian already is hiding – we knew that though."

Cypha nodded thoughtfully.

Satyrna looked up at her again when she felt like she had her face under control. "Malkarai wants to keep this quiet though. He said you were okay to tell because you can keep secrets. Don't tell Dyspro for now."

"All right. Yeah, he sucks at keeping his mouth shut."

"Uh-huh. Um, I already offered, because you guys had offered earlier this week… but I said Malkarai could come here to hide."

"Yeah, that's still fine."

"He said no though, because if someone came out here like Josh did, then he couldn't really hide. I'm gonna still keep trying to convince him, but he said he's going to look for a place to hide."

"Hiding with Traphian isn't an option?"

"He's coming and going and doesn't want to draw attention to where Traphian is hiding. He spent the day with him today, but he doesn't want to keep doing that."

"I guess that makes sense. How long are they going to hide?"

"For a while. I'm not sure. It sounds like he's playing a lot of this by ear."

"Fair. How bad was he hurt?"

"Uh, well, he needed a lot of stitches. Teffifa said how many you need depends on where the injury is and how long and deep, but I think I put at least twenty, maybe thirty stitches in it."

"Damn…"

"He had a bunch of more superficial cuts on him too, but he only let me put bandages on a few of them."

"I don't think that guy stresses over wounds."

Satyrna sighed. "He should. Whether he cares about the pain or not, they can get infected."

Cypha shrugged, not protesting. "Did you get enough food to feed him if he ends up here too?"

"Yeah, at least for a day or two. Storing things doesn't work long-term out here, unfortunately. It helps that it's below freezing, but that cooler isn't huge."

"I'm already grateful for it and we haven't even eaten anything from it yet," Cypha smirked.

"Yeah, yeah, I know, you like meat. Honestly, I'm not sure how you're surviving out here without it."

"I didn't realize how spoiled I was until I moved out here. It's freaking expensive and doesn't keep worth shit if you don't have electricity."

Satyrna smiled. "Being an adult sucks more than we expected."

"There are perks, but yes. I don't feel like any of us act any differently, we just have bills and have to pay taxes. We're still doing dumb shit."

"Doing new dumb shit, even," Satyrna said with a sigh.

Cypha smirked. "Like befriending strange dark men and pissing off the knights."

"Oh, shut up," Satyrna laughed and reached across the table, swatting at her.

# 26



Rafiane stuffed her hands in her pockets and sighed as she walked down Main Street, frustrated with being unable to find *anyone* she was trying to find. She'd looked for Malkarai again this morning but came up empty-handed, so she'd started looking for his companions again. They'd proven to be just as elusive as he was.

"If he left town again, I'll be so pissed," she muttered.

She'd scouted out the house in the woods but was unwilling to knock on the door. The man with the leather jacket seemed to have disappeared. She intended to go back to the house when she felt that it was more likely to find just one person. The blonde girl kind of frightened her, and she didn't know enough about the boy to even be able to pick him out of a crowd. However, she felt all right trying to ask the brunette girl about her target. She didn't seem too disagreeable.

It was nearing noontime, and she was growing hungry, and that wasn't aiding her mood. She looked around until she saw a little food store and walked inside. There were a few people inside and only one person behind the counter. She picked up a sandwich and a bottle of soda and walked to the counter, where she put the sandwich and drink on the counter before digging some bills out of her pocket. The young woman took the money and gave her back change.

"I've seen you before."

She looked at the woman more closely but didn't recognize her. "I don't think I've seen you before."

The shopkeeper put the sandwich in a small bag. "Probably not. I just remember seeing you around. You passing through town?"

She nodded and took the bag.

"Well, I hope your visit is pleasant. Have a good day."

"Thanks." She walked out the door as a young woman with long hair came through it, running. Rafiane hopped, squeaking in surprise.

"Oh, I'm so sorry," said the runner, holding her hands up momentarily. "Are you okay?"

She looked up at the young woman and nodded. She couldn't believe her luck; she had found the brunette!

The young woman looked a little surprised to see her, as though she recognized her, but she said, "I'm sorry," again and then hurried up to the woman at the counter.

"Good job," the blonde girl said sarcastically.

The brunette ignored the jab. "Patricia, I have to talk to you."

Rafiane stepped outside, feeling awkward not finishing the action she'd started, but she lingered outside, rooting through her messenger bag to look like she was busy, hoping the brunette would come back out. She could still mostly hear the two talking.

"I'm kinda working, Satyrna – like you should be."

"Yeah, I can see that. Just let me ask you something."

"Okay, shoot. But you're going to have to be quick."

Satyrna leaned over the counter and whispered something in Patricia's ear.

Patricia sighed. "Well, maybe you should've kept your nose out of that fight."

"Absolutely not."

"You and your friends really have to stop getting involved in fights when none of you have been trained to do it."

"I don't need to listen to your pacifistic lecturing," Satyrna scoffed. "And Olivia taught Cypha and me how to throw a punch, so you can't say I have no training."

"You're not a combatant. Stop getting in fights."

"I'll be thrilled when they stop coming to me. I have to go. Don't tell them where I am, okay?"

She nodded. "All right. Watch out for yourself, Satyrna."

"I'll be fine. Bye," Satyrna said before heading out of the store, not pausing to give Rafiane a chance to stop her.

Rafiane followed Satyrna onto the street, trying to keep up with her quick pace. Her heart was beating fast, both excited and nervous. She was happy she'd finally found one of them, but was scared about approaching her.

Rafiane had just worked up enough nerve and nearly caught up to Satyrna when she tried to step around a man who prevented her from moving. She stopped short and backed up a few steps before running into someone else. She glanced back at the other person and apologized. When she turned back, the man had stepped close to her – too close for her comfort.

Her brow knitted as she sidestepped and then backpedaled, but he kept approaching.

"What's wrong, little girl?"

"Leave me alone!" she pleaded.

"Why? Do I make you nervous?"

She glanced around and realized she was in an alley, which would normally have worked to her advantage, but he pushed her up against the wall before she could dart off and disappear.

He smiled a sinister smile and put a hand on the wall next to her head. With the other hand, he drew a long switchblade, which he slid open and held up to her chin.

She pursed her lips and held onto her coat collar in fear, swallowing deeply.

"Well, tell me, little dark girl, what's a fresh score like you doing here? You trying to work these streets? Make a little money, honey?"

Her eyes were wide as she stared at the man in fright. He was much bigger than she was, and with only a slight movement, he could jab the switchblade straight into her throat. She swallowed again, but couldn't bring it upon herself to answer.

He brought his face close to hers. His breath smelled terrible and reeked of cigarette smoke too. "That's why you ran up to me, yeah. You wanted me to help sample the goods, spread the good word for ya?"

She shook her head quickly, tears starting to well up in her eyes.

"Don't be a slut in denial. I might even leave you a tip if you treat me just right."

She held her breath and pressed herself harder against the cold wall. The man kept the switchblade to her neck and wrenched her hands from her coat, opening it. She closed her eyes. *Oh God, I wish I was somewhere else. Anywhere else. Why won't someone help me?! What happened to that other person? Are they just ignoring this?!*

She started and stepped to the side when the man's hand was wrenched safely backward and his body flung against the wall and some trash cans nearby. She stepped out of the way, standing back by the opposite wall. The man stood back upright and turned around, glaring at Malkarai, who was now visible behind him.

"Oh, how sweet – a dark defending a dark. Get lost, you low-life. I found her first."

He pulled his arm back and struck Malkarai hard in the shoulder, pushing that side back for a moment, but not doing much else. It would have gotten him straight in the face had he not dodged. Malkarai sent a swift punch to the man's jaw, sending him staggering backward.

"Dirty bastard," the man hissed, coming back at Malkarai swiftly, sending several blows at his face and torso, but he didn't land a single one.

Malkarai sighed and lifted his right leg to kick the man firmly in the stomach, doubling him over.

"Shit!" the man coughed. When he stood again, he found a hard fist waiting for him. He put a hand up to his face and felt blood coming from his nose. He staggered off.

"Fine, have the dumb bitch for all I care. Shit, you probably broke my nose!"

Malkarai watched until the man was lost to sight and then he turned to her.

Rafiane was watching him in surprise. "Thank you," she said quietly.

"You need to stop following me. You're gonna get hurt."

"I wasn't following you; I didn't know where you went," she muttered. "I was following-"

"Satyrna, I know. Knock it off."

"I can't, not until I know…"

He pointed down the alley. "You know what that guy was gonna do to you?"

She glanced in that direction and responded sheepishly, "No, not really…"

"He was gonna rape you. Then he probably would've said you solicited him and gotten you in even more trouble."

She looked at him, eyes wide. "But I never-! I told him to leave me alone!"

"It doesn't matter." He stepped close to her, leaning over slightly to look into her eyes. "You and I, we don't get breaks or second chances, okay? We're dark. They don't give a shit what our opinion is. The cops won't care what you say. I'm not gonna be here all the time to save your ass. Go home before you get hurt."

"I can't!" she cried, but Malkarai turned and went around the corner.

She ran to the street, but he'd disappeared. She sighed, sniffing as she wiped the tears of fear out of her eyes.

"I can't leave yet. Why won't you just answer my questions?!"

1:00 p.m.

Dyspro, his immobilized leg out to the side as he was positioned under a sink, jumped slightly when his phone rang, shaking loudly against the plaster inside his pocket. He set down a wrench and pulled it out. "I gotta keep that on the other side…" he muttered as he opened the phone and answered it. "Hello? Barry?"

"Yeah. Hey, uh, you busy?"

"Not terribly. Replacing a U-bend. What is it?"

"That girl came back in here."

"What girl? Rafiane?"

"Yeah."

"Really?"

"Yeah… uh, she was asking for you."

"Sweet, but I can't really come there right now."

"I can have her wait, she looks spooked."

"Spooked?"

"Yeah, she said something about someone attacking her. Said you'd told her to come here if she had any problems."

"Ah, jeez… Okay, yeah, have her stay there. I'll be done with this soon, and then I'll come over."

"Okay. I'll keep an eye on her."

"Thanks."

Dyspro stuffed his phone back in his pocket and went back to work, a frown on his lips. He finished tightening the brackets and then scooted himself out from under the sink to run water and check the seals.

He cleaned up and headed for the tavern. Inside, he looked around the mostly empty dining area before going up to the bar. Barry saw him and came over.

"Where is she?"

"I took her back to the break room. This guy was hassling her."

Dyspro frowned and his brow knitted up, taking in everyone at the bar. "Who was it?"

"Relax. She's jumpy and was taking it out of proportion. I sent her back there to help her chill out."

Dyspro sighed. "All right… I'll take care of it. Thanks, Barry."

"Yeah, no problem." He went back down the bar, and Dyspro went through the door to the kitchen and, beyond that, to the break room.

Rafiane was sitting at the table, clutching a mug of something brown and hot. There was a plastic bag with something in it and an empty cellophane wrapper crumpled up next to her on the table. She looked back when she heard the slide-click of his crutches on the tile. "Dyspro!" she cried softly as she stood.

"Yeah, it's me. What's wrong?"

She dropped her eyes, cheeks flushed. She spoke quickly. "I'm sorry, I didn't want to interrupt your work, but he called you anyway, and I didn't need him to, I just needed to calm down, he scared the crap out of me-"

Dyspro stepped closer and put up his hands. "Whoa, whoa, hold on. Relax, okay?"

She swallowed, clasping her hands in front of her.

"Sit back down."

She obliged silently, grasping her mug again.

Dyspro slid into the seat across from her, resting his crutches against the table and setting his bag of tools on the floor. "Okay, what happened?"

"I was walking down the street, minding my own business, and this guy stopped me, blocked my way, and forced me into an alley… He said these really… gross things to me, and wouldn't let me get away. He pulled a knife on me and was gonna take me somewhere…"

Dyspro's eyes widened. "Did you try and fight him? Or try and escape?"

She nodded. "I tried to escape, but he had me against the wall. I locked up. I was just so scared! I called out for help, but no one on the street came and helped."

Fear flashed across his face. "Are you okay? Did he do anything?"

She shook her head. "No, no... he got beat up and ran away before anything happened. It was actually the guy I was looking for who saved me."

Dyspro blew out a heavy breath of relief. "Holy shit."

She held her hands against her cheeks. "I'm sorry. I'm still freaking out, and now you're freaked out too, and I found who I was looking for but after saving me he just said I need to go home and to stop trying to follow him. That being darks is bad enough and following him is going to put me in even more danger. Then he just sort of disappeared as soon as he left the alley and I lost sight of him."

Dyspro's brow furrowed in annoyance. "Who the fuck saves someone and then says and does that?"

"He was so... blunt about it. It felt mean. He refuses to answer my questions, but I can't go back until I know! I was really upset, and I didn't feel safe out there, so I came back here, cuz you said I could if I ever had problems... I'm really sorry; I didn't want to interrupt you while you were working-"

He shook his head. "Forget about it. I'm freelance, so once I finish one job I go to another one if I'm available. It's no problem."

She sighed, her shoulders dropping a little. "I can't go back home, not yet..."

"Who is this guy you're trying to talk to, anyway?"

"Er, I don't know if he goes by his real name here... He usually doesn't."

"Well, what's he look like?"

"Uh... he's like almost six-foot, long hair – well, down to his jaw. He's thin and strong, he's got a scar on his face. Oh," she added, "he... he looks like me."

Dyspro cocked an eyebrow. "Looks like you?"

"He's got black hair and tanned skin. Er... and he's a dark."

Dyspro sighed. "You're looking for Malkarai?" he said in disbelief.

She stared at him. "You know his name?"

"Yeah, I know him."

She stared blankly at him for a few moments before swallowing the knot in her throat. "Do you know Satyrna – I think that's her name – and the blonde girl?"

"Yeah. I live with the blonde girl. Her name's Cypha."

Rafiane put a hand over her face, blushing fiercely. "Ah, you've got to be shitting me..."

Dyspro smirked. "So, you've been following us too?"

"Well... them... I-I didn't realize that you were friends with them."

"I've kinda been in the hospital and at home lately."

"I gathered that. Malkarai won't give me the time of day, so I was hoping that his friends might be able to tell me what I need to know."

"What do you need to know?"

"Where he's from."

Dyspro shook his head. "Sorry, he never told us. He didn't tell us much."

She sighed. "He's very good at not existing. It took me so long to find him. And following? That's another story... I can't just give up now. I've never had a chance to talk to him like this, but he won't listen to me!"

"He wouldn't tell us anything either, so don't get so upset. That's just how he is."

"I know, but I'd hoped he'd talk to me – since I'm dark like him..."

"Why him? And why do you need to know where he's from?"

"It's... it's a long story. I'm sorry, I just – I don't want to talk about it."

Dyspro nodded with a sigh. "Well, Satyrna will be happy to hear that he's alive, at the very least. So, he beat that guy up?"

She nodded.

"He can't be that injured then."

"Well, I don't know, it didn't take very much to beat that guy up. I've seen him in far tougher fights. He's been really irritable lately, which doesn't make my job any easier. I'm not sure if he's tired or sick or hungry or what, but he's even less good-humored than normal."

"Is he following you now?"

She shrugged, cheeks red. "I hope not. But... I was following Satyrna at the time, maybe he was following her..."

Dyspro shook his head with a smile. "You are; you're a little stalker."

She sighed, face still burning. "I gotta find things out somehow..." she muttered.

Dyspro laughed. "You're adorable."

She just sighed loudly.

Dyspro nodded toward her mug. "What's that?"

"Hot chocolate."

"That sounds good. I'm gonna get some too. Then let's go see if we can find Malkarai, okay?"

"You're gonna help me?"

"Yeah. I wanna know where he is too, and I don't want anyone else to mess with you. I highly doubt that he'll be there every time someone tries to harass you." He stood up and tucked his crutches under his arms.

Rafiane blushed, dropping her head but looking at him through her bangs. "Thank you."

He put a hand on her head as he passed by. "Don't mention it. Stop blushing so much."

"You're being so nice though. You don't have to be."

"Why wouldn't I be? Don't be as negative as Malkarai. It's not good for your health."

She smiled as he left. "Thanks anyway," she said quietly to herself.

2:30 p.m.

"Hey, *Captain Garevn*," one of the other knights called mockingly from across the street as he and Kalyfa crossed toward him.

Josh cringed but turned and faced him. It was how the other knight said his name, not necessarily the use.

Brendan glanced at Josh. He had been standing with him at the corner, waiting to cross, but they both gave up on that when they were approached.

Kalyfa eyed the knight he was with, unamused. "Knock that shit off, Hansen."

Brendan glared at Hansen, but Josh kept his expression neutral, looking at Kalyfa for orders.

"Have you had any luck?"

Josh shook his head. "We did a sweep through the woods, but we didn't find anything. We hit the northeast side too, just in case the directions got crossed."

Kalyfa sighed and nodded slightly as he glanced around. "Honestly, I think it's more likely that they aren't dead. Either they staged something for Ripper, or they were just all in on something."

"Wouldn't it make sense for them to just be gone then?" Brendan asked.

"Yeah, probably. Faerstathe is injured. I figured he wouldn't leave town with an injury like they described, but if he's partnered up with this defector… maybe that's a feasible option for him."

Josh hesitated, but said, "Satyrna did say they were close, so that's a possibility."

Kalyfa and the other two looked at him. "Close? How close?"

"Uh, she said this guy was his brother."

"Really?" Brendan asked, perplexed. "They don't look alike."

"No, uh, not his biological brother. But, yeah, they're close. She also said that if he'd killed him, he definitely would've killed himself after."

Kalyfa shook his head. "We've had so many people search the woods, I'm almost ready to just write off the murder-suicide story as fake."

"Do you think they're no longer our problem, then?"

"I'm not sure. They haven't left town using any public transportation. I don't know if either of them had their own means of travel. Walking would be a hell of a way to travel with Faerstathe as injured as he was. Did Satyrna tell you anything else?"

"Not really. She and Cypha hadn't seen him since the knights last did."

"What about his friend?"

"I have no idea. They last saw him and Ripper at the hospital, so like fifteen to twenty minutes after Faerstathe dipped out."

Kalyfa sighed and nodded. "Okay, keep looking, and let me know if you get any leads. I'm going back to town hall until five. Report in in real-time, otherwise just let me know when you're off the street again."

"Will do," Josh replied.

Brendan nodded to Kalyfa as he and Hansen went to the left, toward downtown.

After they were out of earshot, Brendan looked at Josh. "Well, where to next?"

"Wherever any of Carter's assclown buddies aren't," Josh grumbled and went the opposite direction as Kalyfa and Hansen.

"What is Kalyfa doing about Carter? Do you know?"

"I said he should pay Dyspro's medical bills, at a minimum, but Kalyfa wasn't forthcoming with a decision on that. He suspended him for the rest of the month, pending review."

"He *should* fire him. He assaulted someone in protective custody."

"Dyspro isn't entirely innocent, but yes, you're right." Josh gestured over his shoulder. "He's ferreting out the others that were with Carter."

Brendan laughed. "Oh, so that smug-ass smirk is gonna get wiped off Hansen's face in about ten minutes, huh?"

"I fucking hope so," Josh muttered, smirking.

"Couldn't happen to a nicer guy," Brendan said with a grin. "How any of those dickheads think they would've been a better choice for a captain than you is beyond me."

"They'll ride the legacy reasoning until I die."

"Your grandfather does not run the squad anymore. It was entirely Kalyfa's decision."

"I know that. They don't care. They don't know me, so that's all they're going to latch onto."

"Well, I'm glad he picked you. No joking."

"Even though I'm four years younger than you?"

"Yeah. No one is more committed to this squad than you are besides Kalyfa. If he *hadn't* made you a captain I'd have started doubting him."

Josh sighed. "Committed… I hope that's how it looks to everyone else too."

"That's what it is, isn't it?"

"Yeah. I'm trying to prove shit."

"What, exactly?"

"That I can do this, and well. That I can do it despite what my grandfather did and what he says."

"Not for your mom?"

"Mom isn't a stain. She's respected, but she never led the squad. I'm much happier claiming to be her son than I am to claim any relation to Grandpa. Unfortunately, no one jumps to my connection to her. It's always that old asshole."

"I think of your mom," Brendan said with a shrug. "But I wasn't around when the old man was. Olivia trained me though. She trained a lot of us."

"She doesn't drop Garevn unless she has to." Josh sighed. "I should take a page out of her book and change my name."

Brendan laughed. "I mean, that's one option. I think you're beyond that helping though."

"Yeah," he muttered, looking around as they crossed a street. "If you were an injured dark hiding from the federal and local government, where would you go…?" he asked, mostly to himself.

"A hotel room."

"You need to check in to those."

"That's true. His friend could though, no one's gonna bat an eye at a young Caucasian guy."

"Hmmm… good point." Josh stopped, looking around. "Let's go ask at the hotel."

"Faerstathe kinda looks Native," Brendan added.

Josh glanced at him. "Does he?"

Brendan nodded. "I mean, it was dark when we faced off against him, but yeah, he was just… darker toned than all of us. Black hair and brown skin, but he wasn't African or Asian. So, yes, he's dark, but I thought he looked Native American too."

"Faerstathe doesn't sound Native."

"Kalyfa said all their names were weird."

"Right," Josh mused. "Honestly, that's helpful. Let's go back to my truck, we can drive over to the hotel."

"Sounds great. It's freaking cold out here." After walking for a few minutes, Brendan glanced at Josh when he pushed the walk button at a fairly busy street. "Did you ever look him up, like you said you were going to?"

"I tried," Josh said, sounding disgruntled.

"Tried?"

"Yeah, I couldn't find jack shit. I mean, he has a weird name, but every spelling I could think of, I couldn't find anything. There's nothing about this guy anywhere. I even tried his friend's name."

"Oh, you know it?"

"Yeah, Saty knew it."

"What is it?"

"Traphian," Josh replied quietly. "That's his real one. Or at least, his real one as he went by as a kid. But there's nothing about either of them."

"Did you try official databases or just the internet?"

"I tried both."

Brendan's eyebrows furrowed. "That's weird."

"Yeah. There should be *something*. Even government employees have identities. These guys don't."

"Maybe they use pseudonyms," Brendan suggested. "Ripper definitely sounds made up."

"That's possible, but would he be using it with friends?"

"I mean, why not? The US government is not known for transparency."

"It makes me nervous for my friends," Josh grumbled.

"Yeah, agreed. You think they know more than they told you?"

"Absolutely. I'm toeing a line though. I'm okay just reporting back whatever they're comfortable sharing with me, knowing that I'll report it. I'm not going to push them."

Brendan nodded in understanding. "Yeah, I respect that stance. You gonna tell them if you find out something they don't know?"

"I suppose it would depend on what I found out. Possibly. Knight affairs are important to me, but my friends are too. I'm already walking the line between the two right now. What's going a bit farther gonna hurt?"

Brendan snickered. "No argument from me."

# 27



Satyrna jolted out of sleep, confused and unsure of what had awoken her. She rolled onto her back and checked the alarm clock for the time. She sighed and set the clock back down. 4:30 was way too early to be awake, even for her.

"Satyrna," a soft voice called from a few feet away.

She sat upright, rubbing her eyes. "Malkarai?"

"Yeah." He stepped over by her bed, looking a lot like a moving shadow. It was kind of eerie. His head was hanging a little, making his face almost indiscernible under his shrouding hair.

She blinked, propping herself up with her arms. "What's up? Is something wrong? Did something happen?"

He shrugged and sat down on the edge of the bed. "Not that I'm aware of."

Satyrna curled her legs underneath her. "How are you feeling? You seem tired."

"Yeah."

"Have you been sleeping on the ground still?"

"Yeah, when I can."

"Stay here for a few hours and get some rest."

"Yeah, I intend to. I wanted to tell you I was here first."

"How's your side?"

"Irritated, but healing."

She frowned. "Irritated?"

"Yeah. It's kinda red."

"It might be infected."

"Probably is. I should've stitched it up earlier."

Satyrna reached forward and took his hand. "Malkarai, you should treat it."

"Later. I need sleep."

She rubbed the back of his hand with her thumb and then looked up at him, frowning. She put her other hand on his forehead. He shied slightly, but she persisted. "You're burning up."

"Yeah," he admitted reluctantly. "I feel feverish. Otherwise, I'd still be roughing it."

"Malkarai..." she sighed. Then she let go of his hand, scrambled out of bed, and stood. "Lay down."

"No way," he said firmly, a little energy returning to his voice.

She pushed him toward the pillow slightly. "I'm serious. Lay down."

"I'm not taking your bed, Satyrna. I'll go sleep on the bench."

"Shut up. I'll go sleep in Dyspro's bed. Lay down," she commanded.

"No, Satyrna. I'm not taking your bed."

She narrowed her eyes at him. "Malkarai, you're sick. Now shut up and take off your shoes. You're sleeping here until I'm convinced you're better."

"I can't stay here."

She crossed her arms. "Yes, you can. It's 4:30 in the morning – no one knows that you're here. Don't make me undress you."

"You know I could just leave. You can't stop me."

"Wanna see me try?"

He cast her a disgruntled look and reluctantly leaned over to untie his boots. After tossing them to the side he unclasped his cloak and then took off his coat. Satyrna picked them both up and draped them over the chest of drawers.

Malkarai gave her a tired look as she came back by him. "I have news for you; I don't usually sleep in jeans."

She sighed and spun around on her heel so her back was facing him. "Well, don't hesitate on my account."

"No, I have shorts in my bag. And boxers aren't very revealing anyway. I just didn't want you to tackle me as I went to get them."

"Oh. Well, stay here; I'll get you your bag." She headed out to the main room.

"I'm not crippled."

She came back in and handed him his bag. "No, you're running a fever and a high risk of infection. You need sleep and water and some antibiotics. You take care of resting, and I'll take care of the rest."

"How are you going to get antibiotics? They require a doctor's prescription, and I'm not going to see a doctor."

"I have an active prescription for some."

"For what?"

"My skin."

"Don't you need it?"

She felt her chin, which was pretty smooth. "Why, do you think I do?"

"Well, no, but obviously you have the prescription for a reason."

"I take them like once a week – I never remember to take them. You're far more needy right now."

Malkarai sighed and opened his bag and took out a pair of black mesh shorts. When she turned around again, he took off his jeans and knife sheaths and put on the shorts. Then he put the knives in the bag and set both the bag and the pants on the floor.

Satyrna glanced over her shoulder and then turned around. She pulled the covers back and started urging him to lie down. "Come on, down now. I don't want you to fight, okay?"

He sighed again but obliged. "If I wasn't so tired, I would be fighting, just for the record," he muttered as his head rested on the pillow.

"I wouldn't expect anything less. That's how I know you're sick." She tucked the blankets in around him and he shooed her away sluggishly.

"This isn't necessary, Satyrna."

"Shut it and go to sleep." She leaned over and kissed him on the forehead. "I'll bring you some water."

Satyrna first went to Dyspro's room, grabbed a bottle from the dresser, and then went out to the main room, where she got a clean cup and filled it with water from a jug. Then she brought both in by Malkarai.

"I got you acetaminophen so you can do something about your fever until I get you antibiotics." She handed him the cup as he sat up partially. After she'd gotten a dose out of the bottle, she handed it to him.

He swallowed the pills and some water and handed the cup back to her before settling back on the pillow.

After she set the cup down, he reached out and took hold of her hand.

She looked down at him and squeezed his hand back. "Try and relax, okay? Get some sleep."

He nodded slightly, staring at her through shrouded eyes. "Thank you."

She smiled and brushed his hair out of his eyes. "You're welcome. Anytime. Now, get some rest."

"Are you going back to bed?"

"Yep. Good, well, morning, I guess."

He smirked, squeezed her hand, and then let it go.

Satyrna tugged the curtains shut over the window and then picked up her alarm clock and phone and glanced around to see if she needed anything else before going out to the main room, shutting the door behind her. After making sure the front door was locked, she went to Dyspro's room, put the clock down on the bedside table, and threw back the blankets. She brushed out some dirt that had collected in the sheets and then climbed into bed.

Cypha opened Dyspro's door, making a great deal of noise as she did so. "There you are!"

Satyrna opened an eye, giving her a look. "What?" she groaned.

"There's a guy in your bed."

Satyrna rolled over, rubbing her eyes. "Yeah, no kidding. Why do you think I'm in here?"

"Well, actually, it'd be more fitting for you to still be in there, but whatever… pass up your chance," Cypha said with a shrug.

"Oh, bite me. He's unconscious, and I was still tired. I'll bother him later."

"I was trying to figure out why you didn't wake me up at dawn."

She shrugged. "I don't work until this afternoon. And Dyspro's got this room like a cave. It's really dark in here."

"Why is there a guy in your bed? I thought he kept saying no."

"He's sick. So, shut up so he can sleep."

Cypha glanced over at the room Malkarai was sleeping in. "Sick? What's wrong?"

Satyrna sat up, scratching her head. "He thinks his side is infected. He's running a fever and hasn't slept well in a while. So, I made him go to sleep there and relocated here. After he's slept for a while, I'm going to look at his wound. I need to get an antibiotic too." She looked up at Cypha, noting that she was dressed. "Are you going into town?"

"Yeah. Not sure where else I can apply, but I'm gonna look."

"Do me a favor and pick up some medicine for him. I have some money in my purse I can give you."

"Whatever. Just write down what you want."

She nodded and climbed out of bed.

Cypha followed Satyrna to the main room, glancing in the slightly ajar door at Malkarai. "So, how long's he been here?"

Satyrna dug through her purse on the chair for a pen. "Since 4:30 this morning."

"Well, there's his problem. No wonder he's tired. No one should be up at that time."

"I think he's nocturnal. Going to bed before daylight was probably early for him."

"Okay, animals are nocturnal, not people."

Satyrna shrugged and wrote down the name of her medication on a piece of napkin. "I guess I'd compare him to a cat, so I don't find it that weird. It's fitting."

"Turned on by that, are you?"

Satyrna gave her a look. She handed her the napkin and $20. "Here, this should be more than enough. Get the thing I wrote on there; it's under my name. You'll have to wait a few minutes for them to fill it."

Cypha took the money and note and said, "I think I'll manage it." She shook her head at Satyrna. "Seriously, Saty, stop pretending you don't like the guy. You were so down until he showed up again, and now you're back to your old self, except a little bit more hyper. And come on, sending me to go get medication? You don't wanna leave with him here."

"Whatever… I'm not gonna say you're wrong, but the reason I was so upset was because I thought he was gonna die because of me. No matter what you guys were thinking to begin with, my interest in him developed later."

"Oh, so now you are admitting to it?"

"Yeah, I guess so. I've kissed him. A few times."

Cypha raised an eyebrow. "That's awfully quick for you."

Satyrna shrugged and leaned against the wall. "He surprised the hell out of me, and I was really happy to see him."

"So, what's his take on this?"

"I'm not entirely sure. He's very anti-people, but he said he won't push me away. And he kissed and hugged me back, so… there's something there? He came back here to me when he thought he was getting sick, so I'll chalk that up to something. I'll let you know after I figure more out."

"All right. I'll bring you the meds later. How long do you think he'll be unconscious?"

"Dunno. At least 'til this afternoon. Maybe until after I have to leave for work."

Cypha nodded and pulled her coat on. "I'll come back for lunch. See ya then."

"Mm-hmm."

# 28



Malkarai woke, still tired, but feeling a lot better than before. He rubbed his eyes and then rotated an arm, trying to loosen up his stiff joints. He had a feeling that he wasn't alone though. He turned over and saw Satyrna, sitting in a chair with her feet up on the dresser, reading a book. She was looking at him.

"Good afternoon."

His brow wrinkled. "What are you doing?"

"I was reading."

"Obviously. Why in here?"

She set her book down and wrapped her arms around her thighs. "Keeping an eye on you. Besides, I was lonely. Cypha's gone. I was kinda hoping you'd wake up before I had to go to work."

He smirked and stretched before sitting up. "I see. Well, if you're hoping for social stimulation, your book might be a better choice."

She pouted. "I'd much rather talk to you."

"Unlike you, I'm not a very talkative person, Satyrna."

"It's okay. We don't have to talk."

He looked over at her slowly.

She just blinked, staring back at him. "What?"

"You're forward."

She made a face. "I have no idea what you're talking about."

He sighed and shook his head, gaze forward. "I can't tell if you're naïve or a tease."

She smirked. "Why? Am I teasing you?"

"I don't know. I'm trying to figure that one out."

She dropped her legs and stood up, stepped over to the bed, and leaned forward, putting a finger under his chin and pressing her lips against his. He responded willingly, returning the kiss and putting a hand behind her head.

Satyrna smirked and pulled away after a short while, looking him in the eyes. "You're good."

He shrugged evasively. "Can't say I'm practiced…"

Satyrna brushed his hair back, looking at his eyes closer. They were completely pitch-black except for some pale gray streaks in the irises. "Wow, your eyes are cool. I don't think you've let me see them like this in the light before."

He dropped them, embarrassed. "Meh."

She put her hand to his forehead. "Hmmm, probably shoulda checked this before that… but you still feel warm."

"I feel cold. I had the chills all morning."

"Let me look at your side, okay?"

Obligingly, he took off his shirt, avoiding eye contact.

Satyrna walked around the bed and then crouched before carefully peeling back the bandage. She glanced at it, noted the dried blood all along it, and then rolled it up. "This needs to be changed, and it could probably use a cleaning again. I'll be right back." She stood up and took the old bandage with her as she went to the main room.

Malkarai sighed, put the pillow up against the wall, and leaned back against it. He put his fingers to his neck, feeling his pulse, which was slowing down. "Gah, she makes me feel lightheaded," he muttered. "Kudos to you, Saty."

"Were you talking to me?" she asked as she walked in, a bowl in her hands.

He shook his head. "What time is it?"

"Almost one. I need to work at two, so I have enough time to get you squared away, but then you'll be on your own until Cypha's back."

He nodded and put his shirt over his shoulders. "It's cold in here."

"Yeah, but you're closest to the fireplace, so your room's the warmest one with a bed." Satyrna set the bowl down on the floor, took a cloth out of the water, and wrung it out. "This is probably gonna be cold, but try not to flinch."

"Did you just get it from the pump?"

"No, I got it before lunch and boiled it, expecting to have to do this, but I know I'm on a time limit. It's just been sitting there for a little bit."

"I see." He watched her as she dabbed at the stitched wound, carefully removing the dried blood.

After a few minutes, she glanced up at him. "So…"

"Yeah?"

"There are so many things I want to ask you, but I don't know where to start, or if you'll even answer them."

"That depends on the question, you know."

"You don't like most of my questions. I don't know what I can ask."

"Well, I'm not going to just talk, so you might as well ask and I can tell you if I'll answer it or not."

"Hmmm… All right. Those scars, where are they from?"

"Depends on the scar."

"You said they were old. Were they from when you were working when you were little?"

"Some of them, yes. The deep ones were; the shallower, more numerous ones were from my training."

Satyrna gave him a concerned, disapproving look. "Training? Did you do them to yourself?"

"No. My trainer did."

"He abused you?"

"Yeah, I guess. He called it molding, said he was shaping me."

"That's awful," she whispered.

Malkarai shrugged. "He didn't want me to get those other cuts, the deep ones. He wanted me to be able to evade everything. Eventually, it paid off. This cut is rare – very rare. I don't get hit anymore. When I do, it's usually slight. My face and this one are probably the worst ones I've ever had."

Satyrna had lines etched into her forehead as she rinsed the cloth and then went back to cleaning up the cut. "I'm sorry," she said quietly.

He put his hand on her head, brushing her hair behind an ear. "Satyrna, don't be like that, okay? I don't resent this. I'll heal. If that knight had hit you, you'd be in far worse shape than me."

"I can go to a hospital though."

"With you and me working on it, it'll be fine, hospital or not."

"If you barely get hurt, how do you know how to take care of wounds so well? Was it just from necessity from when you were younger?"

"My co-workers get banged up a lot more than me. Hell, Teffifa alone provided ample practice. She's the reason I decided to get training in it."

"Why you and not someone else?"

"I'm the one with a degree in biology – yeah, it's not medical, but it's closer to it than anything anyone else there has got. We're all in danger all the time, so knowing first aid is essential. For some of us, advanced first aid is better."

"I see." Satyrna set the cloth down on the edge of the bowl and retrieved the bag of medical supplies from the other side of the room. "She knows how to stitch herself up though."

"Yeah, she caught on after like the fifth time. Teffifa may not be as book-smart as I am, but she's definitely clever and learns quickly. So, if she's got the means, she'll do it before she gets home. She'll still come to me for the tricky ones though, like what Traphian did to her arm – or she'll just go to the hospital. We normally *can* go to the hospital. We just don't always want to bother. They ask a lot of questions and it can take a while. In Teffifa's case, she avoids the hospital if she can because she hates having to explain her imbalance and pain tolerance to new doctors at every single one."

"That makes sense…" she said as she sat down on the edge of the bed by his injured side again, digging through the bag for the antibiotic. "Um, what kind of person is Traphian?"

"Uh, speaking historically and what I can tell hasn't changed from like… six hours' worth of hanging out with him this week – he's brutally honest, chill until you pull shit, protective, stubborn, and despite his obvious willingness to break laws, very good-aligned."

Satyrna snickered as she opened up the antibiotic.

"He's always had the mindset of doing good and standing up for people, no matter what the rules are. He drove our old head agent nuts – partially on purpose. Some of the other adults too. There were others who really liked him though. Stika was one of them."

"Oh yeah?"

"Yeah. That's why she resisted sending any of us after him. She's always been fond of him. He and Arista never got along, he and Teffifa were always competing at shit, but he got along pretty well with Swip and Shawn when he wasn't stressing Shawn out by ignoring our directives. He's a polarizing person."

"Who are Swip and Shawn?"

"Our other classmates. Teffifa's partners."

"Oh. You like him though, right?" she asked as she leaned over, applying the medicine with a swab.

"Yeah. I mean, I fought with him constantly, but I love him; he's my brother. I grew up with him. I consider him the only family I've got."

"Does he feel the same?"

"Yeah," Malkarai said quietly. "He said he's been waiting all this time for me – he only started poking the bear because he saw I was stuck."

Satyrna looked up at him, taking in his serious expression. "So, whatever you two do, you're gonna do it together, huh?"

"We're going to try to, yeah."

"Well, I'm very happy that you guys decided that here is the best place to stay."

He was quiet for a few moments, solemn. "If he had thought the better idea was to run, I'd have done it. I was ready to."

"I'm not surprised by that," she said, putting the cap on the antibiotic. She tossed it in the bag and picked up the gauze, looking at him. "You were trying to bolt even before you'd talked to him."

"It just made the most sense to me…"

"Are you glad that this is the plan instead?"

"Yes," he replied immediately. "I know I'd have been happier than I was as long as I was with Traphian, but being able to stay here with you and the others… is definitely the best outcome. I'm ready to do the work to try to make it our new reality."

She held the gauze up to his side, making sure she'd estimated correctly, and then cut it. "Am I making it more desirable, or just making you panic?"

Malkarai smirked, eyeing her as she taped the bandage to his side. "A fair amount of both, I think."

Satyrna smiled. "Okay, that was a loaded question."

He leaned forward and put his shirt back on. "I came here this morning instead of to Traphian for a few reasons, yes."

"Mm, is it because I have first aid supplies?"

"He has them too. He has his own injuries he's been treating."

"Oh."

"The bandage you just threw away was actually from him. I showered when I stayed with him the other day."

"That makes sense."

He reached up and touched her cheek, brushing her hair back. "I still have no idea what it is about me you're attracted to, but I'm trying to be grateful for it instead of suspicious."

She smirked at first, and then it grew to a smile. "You know, that's very in character for you." She shook her head and stood. "You should eat something so you can take those antibiotics. Cypha picked them up for me."

"Really?" he asked, his eyebrows raising behind his hair.

"Yes. Come on, I'll get you something to eat before I have to go."

She went out in the main room, and Malkarai eased himself to the side of the bed, stretching and shivering as he left the covers. He sighed, feeling his forehead. He still felt feverish. Before following her, he extricated his cloak from his coat and wrapped it around himself.

Satyrna glanced over at him as he sat down at the table, next to the fire. "Still cold?"

"Yeah, I definitely have a fever."

"You should take some more acetaminophen with that." She stood up, abandoning the food for the moment, and went back to the room he'd slept in.

She came back to the main room, set the bottle and his cup in front of him, and then moved the prescription bottle from the other side of the table next to it.

"Thanks," he said, picking up the prescription bottle to read the label.

"Do you have any allergies or things you don't eat?"

"Uh… not that I'm aware of."

"Cool. I don't have time to cook, but I can make you a peanut butter and jelly sandwich."

"I can make that," he offered.

"Mm, I'm sure you can, but you're also sick."

Malkarai frowned at her. "If you're worried about me making you sick, maybe you should stop kissing me."

She gave him a bemused look before putting the peanut butter on the table. "I'm not worried about you getting me sick. You aren't that kind of sick. I mean, I'm your nurse right now, so I'll make it for you."

He sighed, giving her a jaded look.

"You do bring up a good point though – I don't want to give you something in addition to this infection. I'll be sad about it, but I'm going to withhold kisses on the mouth until you're feeling better."

Malkarai shook his head at her. "But kisses elsewhere are still a go?"

Satyrna smiled, focusing on the sandwich. "Yep. You should take your medicine."

He sighed, but opened both bottles, shook out the proper dosage for each, and then took the pills and washed them down with water. After setting his cup down, he closed the bottles and pushed them to the middle of the table. "Taken."

"Good boy." She pushed the plate with the freshly made sandwich across the table to him and closed up the peanut butter, jelly, and bread.

"Thanks," he said before picking it up.

After putting the food away, Satyrna sat down across from him, leaning on the table. "I feel like you barely know *me*. You've asked me almost nothing about myself. I'm the one that's willing to talk, but it's not like we've had many chances to just sit and chat casually."

"Do you *want* to talk about yourself?" he asked, eyeing her.

"Well, no, not really. I don't think I'm that interesting – I like to talk about things I'm interested in, not necessarily *myself*. I just… I just want to know about you, so I guess I figured you'd want the same – if you were interested in me, anyway."

"Just because I haven't asked directly doesn't mean I haven't observed."

"Oh?"

"I don't need to talk to people to figure them out," he said, glancing up at her before taking a drink of water.

She crossed her arms on the table in front of her. "Okay, what do you know about me?"

"You're the youngest child to married parents who own and run a store. You are going to school for nursing, but are on winter break and working at the store in the meantime. You have friends that are more than one generation deep, but you're close with your friends despite whatever your parents have to do with it. You have good relationships with all of them, even despite your avoidance of your phone. You're fairly well known in this town for several reasons. You may not want to be a public figure like Josh and Kalyfa, but because you know them and Barry and you matter to all of them, and you frequently work in a retail position, quite a few people know who you are. Because those people care about you, I imagine that also means that they think well of you. You hate injustice and bigotry, don't hesitate to stand up to defend people you respect, and are more worried about other people's feelings than your own, unless your feelings are warning you about someone else. You're also beautiful and take care of yourself – but that doesn't extend to dressing up or altering your appearance, temporarily or not. You make acquaintances quickly and easily, but friends have to pass your vibe check. If you consider them good enough to be a friend, then you're ready to take their hand and help them however you're able."

Satyrna's eyebrows had lifted very early in his speech. "Oh."

"'Oh?' Was I off?"

She shook her head slightly. "Nope, you pretty much nailed it."

He smiled and took a bite.

"Honestly, I think you might've pointed out some things I never really explicitly thought about myself," she mused, her eyebrows furrowing.

Malkarai snickered. "Sorry."

"You don't need to apologize. I was worried that you were just… I dunno, excited about the attention, but you do know me."

"If I didn't like you, I would've pushed you away, not kissed you back. I'm very romantically neglected, but I'm not a pushover. Not anymore."

"Not anymore?" she asked, smirking.

"Yep."

"When were you?"

"Most of my life."

Satyrna's smirk faded to a frown. "What changed you?"

"Traphian, Farad, Arista, three years of hard work and turning my emotions off."

"What did Traphian do?"

"Left." He ate the last bite of his sandwich and washed it down with water before continuing. "Traphian and I were partners when it came to work. We were more advanced than the rest of our peers, and we knew each other so well, it made sense. They kept saying we may not stay that way after we were contracted, but it worked then, so they kept us together. He was the more dominant of the two of us and was always the lead when we worked. He was older and I was just always shy, so it was the natural set-up. When he left, I couldn't just stand behind him and let him do the talking anymore, so I had to do his job and my own."

"I suppose that makes sense…"

"Farad was my trainer. Arista was a crutch for years – not in the field, but at home. She was my best friend after Traphian. She's been gone for almost three years now though."

Satyrna's brow furrowed. "So, you didn't work with her anymore before that?"

"We never really worked with her. She was shadowing us when we met you. Traphian and I did the work; she was an observer. Later, she did a different job than Traphian and I. It got the same results, but the methods were different."

"How different?"

"There are three general kinds of agents in our division… Combat, stealth, and social. Some agents train in more than one area, and some only focus on a single one. I'm stealth and combat. Arista was social and stealth. Traphian was combat, but he had some training in the social aspects. Not much, he had no patience for it. Teffifa is straight combat."

Satyrna looked thoughtful. "Hm, yeah, she didn't seem stealthy."

"She's very not."

"Did Arista flirt with people to get them to work with her?"

Malkarai smirked after a few moments. "Wow, you're really sharp."

Satyrna tipped her head slightly. "Well, what else was she gonna do to convince and deal with people that you and Traphian couldn't? She was a very pretty girl, even at eleven. I mean, you're attractive enough, you could probably try and do that too, but you're much better at stealth than flirting. You get embarrassed too quickly."

Malkarai frowned, his cheeks burning.

"Yes, like that. Why is that, anyway? You had to have kissed someone before. No first-timer kisses like that. You're good."

He sighed, irritated. "I never said I'd never had a girlfriend. I just said I won't talk about her."

"Hm. So, was she recent?"

He shook his head. "I'm not talking about it. This is one of the dead-end questions."

"Fine, I won't ask about her. But, she's not still around, is she? You're not claimed goods, right?"

Malkarai looked displeased. "No, I am most definitely not 'claimed,' as you put it."

Satyrna reached across the table and put her hand over his, squeezing it. "Relax, okay? I wasn't trying to upset you. I just legitimately wanted to know if I was stepping over a line."

"You are, but I'm okay with you doing so."

She looked concerned. "What do you mean?"

He chewed on his lip for a few moments before explaining. "I'm… broken. I don't trust people. I don't want to get close to people because it's hurt me in the past. I've found it's far easier to just remain alone and let nothing touch me. It's been my protection for the past few years."

She nodded, listening.

"But, because I've been like this for so long, any interaction – especially what you've been doing – is overwhelming. I mean, I don't dislike affection, not in the least, but I'm not used to it. The last time I was given affection like you're giving me… it ended with me swallowing poison."

Satyrna reached over with her other hand, squeezing his hand between hers. "I don't want to hurt you, Malkarai," she said softly.

"I know you don't, but I'm still gun-shy. So, just bear with me. I'm treading frightening waters here."

"Do you want me to stop? I can leave you alone if you'd rather be alone."

He shook his head. "No, I like you too. I don't want to be alone. I'm just... dealing with a lot right now. I'm playing dead, but I don't know what the knights or my employers are doing right now, so I know I need to hide, but I don't know where. I don't want to put you in danger, but I'm sick and not at my best, so I know I need help – at least for a little bit. I'm not asking you to go away; I'm just asking you to be patient with me."

She squeezed his hands again, giving him a reassuring smile. "I'm okay with that."

"Thanks. You probably need to get going."

Satyrna sighed, glancing around for her phone and not seeing it. "You're probably right. Are you going to go back to bed?"

"Yeah."

"Okay. I'll be back around eight-thirty tonight."

"I'll try and be up for that."

"Just focus on resting as long as you need to. Keep the curtain in that room pulled, and no one will know you're here but me and Cypha."

Malkarai turned, put a few logs on the fire, and then put the screen in front of it as Satyrna got up and went to retrieve her phone from where she'd been reading. She came back out as he was filling his water cup.

She put her coat on and then went up to him, putting a hand on his cheek and kissing him on the opposite one. "I hope the medicine helps and you feel better."

"Thanks." He gave her a small smile as she zipped her coat up. "Maybe I'll let you interrogate me some more later."

She laughed. "Only if we don't call it an interrogation."

"Mm, that'll depend on what you ask me."

She shook her head at him, amused, and went to the door. "I'll see you later."

# 29



"Crimony, he's good at hiding…" Dyspro muttered after he put the car into park on the side of the street. He and Rafiane had reached the end of town for the third time that day. She was sitting in the passenger seat with her bag at her feet.

"He's amazing at hiding. Once he found out I was following him, he became hard to track, and after I confronted him, he disappeared." Rafiane looked over at him. "Sorry, I had you out here all day with me."

"Don't worry about it. I lost nothing by it. I got a few things done for work and I got to go around with a pretty girl all day."

She blushed and clasped her hands in her lap.

"Hey, let's go out to my place. Maybe Satyrna and Cypha are out there. If Satyrna's seen him lately, maybe she can help us."

Rafiane nodded.

"Hm… she fed you peanut butter and jelly earlier, so what else do we have that's fast?" Cypha mused as she crouched next to the food, digging through the abnormally large selection.

"I'm fine with that again," Malkarai said. He was sitting on the bench. He was wearing jeans and socks, but also still had on the dark blue long-sleeve T-shirt that he had slept in.

"Variety is a good thing. My friends frequently tell me I can't live off PB&Js all the time."

He smirked. "And you listen to them with that kind of negativity?"

"Right? They're just really obnoxiously persistent, so I listen occasionally." She looked at a box of Cheerios. "How about some dry cereal?"

Malkarai made a face. "Oh, yum. Straight up sugar."

"I could make some pasta."

"You don't need to cook. I can just have another sandwich."

"Satyrna will yell at me if I have a hand in that," Cypha said, standing up and reading the box of pasta. "I don't have to make all of this, but if I open a jar of sauce, whatever you don't eat will go bad…"

"You could have some too."

"I mean, I did eat, but… I could have more. Maybe Saty'll be hungry too."

"It's pretty late, she might be."

Cypha set the box of pasta down and then crouched down to pick out a sauce. "I need to keep more rice and pasta out here. This shit's cheap and it fills you up. I could live off that and peanut butter."

Malkarai laughed. "No wonder you're so skinny."

Cypha grinned and looked up as the doorknob turned.

"Hey, Cypha," Dyspro said as he stepped inside, crutches first.

She stood up, surprised. "Dyspro, what are you doing out here?" She saw that there was someone behind him and grew nervous. "And who the hell's that?"

He glared at her. "I live here. If you're going to act like a bitch, then I'm not going to bother even coming in. We'll just leave."

"Hey, you surprised the hell out of me – and we're kinda not trusting a lot of people these days. Who's that?" she insisted.

He looked back. "You can come in. She may look nasty, but her bite's not as bad as her bark." He glared at Cypha. "Definitely not as bad."

Rafiane came inside, closed the door, and looked at Cypha. Cypha stared at her, seeing the girl's dark eyes. "What the fuck…" she muttered under her breath.

Cypha glanced over at the other side of the room, but Malkarai seemed to have disappeared into the back before the two had gotten inside.

Dyspro was giving her an annoyed look. "What's your deal?"

"Uh… I just… Look," she said more firmly, "I had no idea you were coming out, much less bringing company. Forgive me for being startled. This past week has been a little fucked-up, okay?"

Dyspro shook his head and let out a slower breath, rolling some of the tension out of his neck and shoulders. "Yeah, no, I'm a bit high-strung and defensive too, I guess. We're good. Anyway… this is Cypha," he said, gesturing to her. "Cypha, this is Rafiane."

"Uh, hi. Who are you, exactly?"

Rafiane looked incredibly sheepish and small and was standing against the door, quietly. "Um…"

"I met her at Barry's the other day," Dyspro said.

"Is she the one we spotted outside of the hospital?"

"Yeah. She's been in town a little while. I've been helping her. Is Satyrna here?"

"No. She's got the late shift at work." Cypha shifted uncomfortably. "Hey, Dyspro, I don't know if you should hang out here right now." She glanced at Rafiane briefly.

Rafiane sighed softly and stepped toward the doorknob.

Dyspro grabbed her hand and held her still. "And why not?" he demanded.

Cypha looked uncomfortable but didn't answer right away. "It's just not a good time…"

Dyspro blinked a few times before saying, "Holy crap. I'm pretty sure I saw someone else when we walked up. Cypha… do you have a guy here?"

She gave him an unamused look. "No, Satyrna does. Smartass."

His eyes widened. "Is he here?!"

"Er…"

Malkarai slipped into the main room, glaring coldly at Rafiane. "You don't listen very well, do you?"

She jumped back against the door.

Dyspro stepped between them. "Hey, hey, Malkarai, leave her alone."

Malkarai pointed past him. "Leave *her* alone?! She's the one who won't stop following *me*!"

Cypha looked between the two, her brow raised. "What the hell is going on? Who is that, Dyspro?"

Dyspro looked at Rafiane, who took a deep breath and said nervously, "My name is Rafiane Tavelante. I'm from Marion, South Dakota – like him."

Malkarai narrowed his eyes at her. "Why are you following me?"

"I'm not part of the- the *thing*, I swear." She glanced at Dyspro and Cypha.

"Yeah, no shit. I'd know you if you were. Why are you following me?"

"I-I asked you a question first," she protested, rolling her shoulders back slightly as she tried to gather her resolve. "I told you who I am. Where are you from before Marion?"

He glowered at her but didn't protest. "I don't know," he said, each word spoken distinctly and firmly. "Some girl that found me on the side of the road left me at the place I live now."

Rafiane's face brightened. "Really?"

Malkarai scowled. "Don't be so happy about that."

"No, no, no, that's what I was looking for." She stepped around Dyspro and went up to Malkarai, a bright smile on her lips. "And you're twenty-one?"

"Probably. You know, abandoned. Kinda don't have any verified details." He glared at her warily. "What are you getting at?"

She stared him in the eyes for a few moments and then hopped excitedly. "It's you! It's gotta be!"

Malkarai looked very uncomfortable. He looked from Dyspro to Cypha, but both looked just as confused. "I'm who?"

"My brother!" she exclaimed.

Malkarai blinked, mouth open slightly, aghast and at a loss for words.

Cypha looked at Dyspro, but he looked just as surprised as her.

"You have no proof of that," Malkarai said defensively, taking a step back so he was out of her bubble.

"You're the right age, you look right, you're dark, you were dropped off by a girl," she said, counting the reasons on her fingers, "and your name is right!"

"Why does the name matter? Maybe they just gave me this name because I was similar to this brother you're trying to find."

She frowned, looking contemplative but displeased by it.

Malkarai put a hand on the wall near him, shaking his head. "Just because I check some boxes doesn't mean that you can claim I'm related to you. This isn't something I care about in the slightest. I've never wanted to meet anyone I'm related to."

Rafiane pouted at him.

Dyspro looked at Cypha. "Well, they do look alike…" he mused.

"Yeah, I guess so…"

"We're both dark," Malkarai grumbled. "Of course, we look alike. That doesn't mean we're related."

Rafiane shook her head. "Not true. I have a dark friend at home – she looks nothing like me."

Malkarai scowled.

"She's got dark, dark brown hair and black and blue eyes and pale skin. We look like our parents, you and I. They both have black hair and dark eyes. But you – you've got unique eyes. They knew you had gray streaks in your eyes and nothing else but black. You're my brother."

Malkarai went over to the bench and sat down heavily. He rubbed his face in his hands, resting his palms over his eyes.

Rafiane glanced at Dyspro, confused, and then walked over. "Malkarai? Are you okay?"

"He's sick," Cypha put in.

Rafiane's expression immediately changed to worry. "Oh no. It's not bad, is it?"

"I have an infected wound. I have a fever and I'm hungry, so I'm a little light-headed," he muttered. He looked up, dropping his hands. "Not that this is helping matters any."

"Oh, you were looking bad days ago… Why didn't you get help earlier?" Rafiane pressed worriedly.

"I got help that night, but hiding in a house like this is really dangerous, so I couldn't just stay here." He shook his head, eyeing her sidelong. "I don't need to explain myself to you."

Dyspro gave Cypha a look. "Why don't you feed him?"

"I was working on it. He just woke up. Don't get on my case."

"What were you going to make?"

"Pasta, probably."

"Awesome. Get water, I'll work on it," he said, going over to the stove and pulling out two pots, one of which he handed to her.

Cypha sighed and took it, going to the door.

"You two, you obviously have shit to talk about," Dyspro said, gesturing at Malkarai and Rafiane as he put the smaller pot on the stove and then looked for spoons.

"There's nothing to talk about," Malkarai muttered.

"Sure, there is!" Rafiane insisted. She came over and sat down next to him on the bench, but he just stared at the wall across from him.

"How long have you been following me?" he asked.

"Well, I started looking last June, but I didn't find you until about two months ago. I tried following you then, lost you twice, and then did it this last time and was able to keep up."

He looked at her. "So, you haven't seen me work?"

She blinked. "Well, I've seen you follow people… and I saw you fight last week."

He looked back at the wall, a little less tense. "When the knights ganged up on me?"

"So that's what they were?"

"Yes."

"I thought maybe they were, but then I found out they were supposed to be law enforcers, and I wasn't sure anymore…"

"They were. I wasn't being dramatic – shit is fucked up here. You should go home."

She huffed. "Only after I can convince you I'm right."

Cypha came back in and set the pot on the stove, which Dyspro turned on as she closed the door. Cypha cleaned her shoes off but then went over and sat in the chair nearest the fireplace.

"I don't care if you're right or not – you're adding more danger to my plate."

"I'm not going to tell anyone you're hiding here," Rafiane insisted. "I want you to be safe!"

"You're going to draw attention to me by accident. You have to stop following me and the people I know."

"I don't need to now – I found my answer."

Malkarai shook his head, still looking disgruntled. "I still disagree."

"Just because you don't *want* us to be your family doesn't mean we *aren't*," Rafiane retorted.

"I have one person in my family, and he looks nothing like me, and I'm fine with that," he replied acidly. "He's actually looked out for me and come back for me."

"Traphian?" Cypha asked.

Malkarai glanced at her in acknowledgment but didn't reply.

"Our parents wanted to take care of you – they couldn't. They couldn't afford it and family couldn't help, so a friend took you in, but she betrayed their trust and gave you away when she couldn't take care of you anymore. They couldn't figure out how to get to where you were and try to get you back. It was *right* there, but it was completely inaccessible. No way to contact them, no way to get in without trespassing. Their friend had been your legal guardian when she gave you up, so they didn't even have that to help. Things were hard when I came around, but they held onto me extra tight because they were heartbroken about losing you."

Malkarai didn't look at her, his eyebrows getting lower over his eyes.

"You're twenty-one now – your birthday is November 13th. I'm eighteen. You were gone before I was even a thought. I didn't know about you until I was sixteen, and after I graduated Mom and Dad agreed to help me try to find you, so I tried sneaking around the building to see if you were still there, eventually saw you, and tried to follow you to talk to you a few times. This was the first I was able to do that."

"You haven't seen me work or fight except for here, right?"

Rafiane nodded, looking at him. "Right."

"Good."

"Do you believe me?"

"I believe that you believe that it's me."

"But you don't believe that I'm right?"

"I don't care if you're right," Malkarai retorted. "I've never had any desire to connect with whoever made me. I was abandoned by some woman who wasn't even my mother. No one ends up where I did if they still had family that wanted them. We don't think about getting fostered or adopted – the most important people to us are our friends and classmates who are getting trained right alongside us. Just, usually, we're there because our families are dead."

"Yours isn't, and we want to know you."

He shook his head, swallowing. "I'm not ready for that. Let me… let me get through all this bullshit I'm dealing with. Maybe I'll be able to wrap my head around this later."

Rafiane sighed. "Later is better than never. I can give you my phone number," she added eagerly, digging in her pocket and pulling her phone out.

"I don't have a phone anymore."

"Oh. Uh, can I write it down for you then?"

Malkarai shrugged.

Rafiane looked at Cypha. Dyspro was stirring dry pasta into the water on the stove.

Cypha looked around before standing up. "There used to be some notepaper out here. One sec." She went into the back of the cabin.

"Where is that woman now?" Malkarai asked.

"I don't know. They lost touch. Mom and Dad weren't pleased that she gave you up too. I mean, they hoped they'd be able to take you back – or at least be involved in your life as you grew up. But she put you where none of them could get to you."

"Too bad. I'd love to give her a piece of my mind," he grumbled.

Dyspro snorted in amusement.

Rafiane smirked. She stood up when Cypha returned and took the offered notepad and pen from her. After writing her number down, she tore the page off and went back over to Malkarai, holding it out.

He stared at it for a moment before taking it, folding it, and putting it in his pants pocket, sitting up straighter to do so.

"I'm sorry for stalking you. Thank you for finally talking to me."

He shrugged slightly.

"Can I give you a hug?"

"What for?"

Rafiane made a face at him, annoyed but starting to get used to this. "To show you I'm sorry and grateful and happy."

Malkarai sighed deeply, but grabbed onto the bench arm and used it to pull himself upright. "Yeah, fine, I guess. Avoid my waist."

Rafiane wrapped her arms around his upper torso, hugging him tight. "Thank you! I'm so happy I found you."

He hesitated, but after a few moments, he hugged her back, less tightly.

# 30



Satyrna had hurried from town, running most of the way, her purse over her shoulder and a plastic grocery bag wrapped around her hand to keep it from swinging around as she went. She still didn't feel safe being in town, knowing that Kalyfa was probably looking for her, and she was eager to get back to the cottage. The more pertinent reason for her rushing, however, was that the wind was picking up and snow was coming down hard. She wanted to get back to the house before she was caught in the storm. It wasn't far, but the woods were easy to get lost in when the path was hidden. When she caught sight of the lights in the windows of the cottage, she slowed her pace and caught her breath. She could see that someone was inside the main room, maybe three people.

When she reached the door she paused, shifting the bag, and then opened it and stepped inside. "I'm back!" she called brightly.

"Hey, Saty," Dyspro said.

She immediately saw Cypha and Dyspro, but then looked to her right, since she'd seen someone else by the bench on her way up. She had come in while Rafiane was embracing Malkarai. For a moment, she just stared at them.

Then she stepped back outside and shut the door behind her. She took a few steps away and put her red face in her hands, drawing quick breaths to calm down.

The door opened and shut behind her, but she didn't turn around. She didn't look at Malkarai when he put a hand on her arm and stepped in front of her. "What's wrong?"

"Is she from your work too?"

Malkarai's brow furrowed in confusion.

"You never let anyone near you – is she your old girlfriend or something?"

"Satyrna," he cut in, realizing why she was upset. "That's not her."

She pointed back at the house. "Then who is that? I can't compete with a dark girl, Malka-"

"I didn't lie to you, Satyrna. Arista was my girlfriend. She's gone. That's the girl that's been following me."

She blinked quickly a few times, trying to get the wetness out of her eyes, still not looking at him. "I know that. I-I remember how you described her. Why was she following you?"

"Not the reason you're apparently thinking. Come back inside, I'll explain."

He pulled gently on her arm, but she stayed still, resisting.

"Satyrna..." he sighed. "Come on, it's cold out here."

She shook her head. "I can't just walk in there and face her…I…"

Malkarai looked at her for a few moments before stepping back, taking her jaw in hand, and kissing her firmly on the lips.

Satyrna stared at him in shock for a moment before returning the kiss, her tense shoulders relaxing when she put a hand on his unoccupied forearm.

He pulled back slightly and looked her in the eyes. "Don't doubt me like that, okay? You're the only person in your position. I'm not about to let that change."

She nodded slightly, eyes wide as she stared back.

"Now come back inside. I'm freezing." He took her hand and started to lead her back to the house.

Satyrna let her eyes drop to the ground and gasped. "Malkarai, you idiot! Where are your shoes?"

"Boots take at least a minute to put on, and I wasn't sure how far you were gonna go."

She sighed loudly. "No wonder you're sick… your survival sense is very shitty."

"Better than yours, Miss Run-Away-At-The-First-Sign-Of-Awkwardness."

"At least I dress properly for it," she muttered, smiling a little anyway.

Rafiane looked at them anxiously when they got back inside. "Is everything okay? Did I do something wrong?"

Malkarai glanced at Satyrna before pulling his snow-soaked socks off and dropping them next to the fire. "Everything's fine. Satyrna, this is Rafiane – Tavelante, right?"

She nodded and held out her hand to Satyrna.

Satyrna shook it, glancing at Malkarai, hoping for an explanation. He went into the bedroom that had his clothes. "You can introduce yourself. She doesn't bite."

Satyrna cast a sulky look at him before facing Rafiane. "I'm Satyrna Hennessin. Er, who are you, exactly?"

"I'm Malkarai's sister."

Satyrna stared at her incredulously, her eyes widening. "What?"

Rafiane looked perplexed, not sure what was confusing about that. "He's my older brother."

"Allegedly!" he called from the other room.

Rafiane sighed softly and glanced back there.

Satyrna looked at Malkarai as he returned; new socks on. "What's going on? You don't know your family, I thought."

"I don't. She's been looking for me for six months."

"Oh. Well, I guess hugging him is okay then if you're his sister…"

Rafiane smiled. "That's what you were upset about?" She looked at Malkarai and giggled. "Dyspro told me that no one knew if you were still around, and I finally found you again when I saw Satyrna – but I didn't think that you two were a thing."

Satyrna blinked and glanced at Dyspro. "Dyspro…? How do you know him?"

"Um, I met him at a restaurant a few days ago, and he was really nice to me and told me to call him if I needed help, and after that guy bothered me, I went to Barry, and then Dyspro's been walking with me while I looked for you," she finished, looking at Malkarai.

"I was being a gentleman," Dyspro said proudly, stirring the pasta before turning the burner off and moving the pot off the heat.

Malkarai's eyebrows knitted up. "I was wondering why you were with him."

She smiled a little, lowering her head and playing with a button on her coat. "He's been really nice."

"Sorry about nearly running into you yesterday," Satyrna said.

She shook her head. "It's okay. I was looking for you anyway."

"Looking for me?"

"Well, looking for his friends. I followed you a short way, but I ran into trouble before I could approach you. Malkarai saved me."

Satyrna looked between the two of them. "You were there too?" she asked Malkarai, confused.

"You were following her, right?" Rafiane asked Malkarai.

He shrugged, walking over by the bench, his back turned.

"Following me?" Satyrna asked.

"Yeah, well, he certainly wasn't following me. He wanted me to go away."

"You stood up for her though, didn't you?" Satyrna said, watching Malkarai curiously.

"Well, I wasn't gonna just let her get hurt. So, I taught him a lesson and told her to go home. She doesn't listen very well."

"I couldn't go home," Rafiane protested. "I went and found Dyspro. I've been walking around with him since, looking for you. So, I did listen to you. I know it's not safe for me."

Malkarai just shook his head.

"Cypha, will you strain this so I don't need to try and maneuver that shit with crutches?" Dyspro asked, moving the pasta pot with its lid to the side of the stove closest to the door.

"Yeah," she said, standing up and taking the pot outside.

Dyspro stirred the pasta sauce in the smaller pot before knocking the spoon off and gesturing between Rafiane and Malkarai with it. "You two being related would explain a lot, you know."

Rafiane cocked her head slightly, looking at him as Cypha returned and set the pot on the stove before shutting the door and locking it. "What do you mean?"

"Neither of you can answer a straight question."

Rafiane blushed, smirking. "I dunno…sugar or alcohol helps that…"

Dyspro laughed. "Alcohol? You are eighteen, you tiny delinquent."

"So?" she protested.

Satyrna snorted. "Malkarai doesn't talk freely no matter how much he's had to drink or how delirious he is."

He held up a finger toward her. "You've never seen me affected by alcohol."

"Oh, so you will answer questions given enough booze?"

"I never said that. I just said that you've never seen me affected by it."

Cypha cast a glance at Satyrna, smirking. "You know… he's pretty hungry right now…"

She grinned.

Malkarai gave them both a look. "You are not getting me drunk."

Cypha wagged a thumb over her shoulder. "You sure? I got a bottle of rum in my room."

"Positive. My head feels funny enough as it is."

Satyrna sighed. "Sit down and stop wandering around," she commanded.

He frowned and crossed his arms. "And who made you my keeper?"

"You did when you came back here sick. Now shut up and sit down. You're tottering even when you're standing still."

Rafiane giggled as Malkarai begrudgingly sat in the chair on the other side of the room, slouching with his arms still crossed.

Dyspro smirked, pouring the sauce over the noodles in the larger pot. "Wow, she's already whipping him into shape."

Cypha laughed.

Satyrna pointed at Dyspro. "Shut up, you. I'm playing nurse right now. Don't make him get all rebellious again."

Dyspro shook his head. "Sheesh." He exchanged an amused look with Cypha.

"Oh yeah, how'd you two get here?" Cypha asked Dyspro.

"Drove."

"Good. It's snowing."

"Ugh," he said, annoyed. "We'll get going soon. It's all right that we join you guys for this pasta, right?"

"Yeah, sure, I was already worried that we'd have to make way more than we could eat."

"We'll help with it and then go."

"Sounds good."

"Malkarai," Rafiane said softly.

He looked up at her. "Huh?"

"Thank you – for saving me yesterday, I mean."

He shrugged. "It was lucky I was there. Just don't make a habit of it."

Well after Dyspro left to take Rafiane to where she was staying and head home himself, and Cypha had gone to bed, Satyrna went out to the dark main room, unable to sleep. She rubbed her upper arms before crouching down and putting two more logs on the waning fire.

"Thanks, I've been putting off doing that."

Satyrna turned and noticed Malkarai sitting on the bench for the first time. It was difficult to see him, especially with his cloak wrapped around him. "Why aren't you sleeping?"

"Why aren't you?"

"I'm not tired."

"I'm not either."

She walked over. "You need rest though."

"I know. I'll go to bed soon. A graveyard shift sleep schedule is hard to break." He shifted, dropping the leg that was resting on the seat off the edge and making room for her.

Satyrna sat down, hugging her arms close, watching the fire.

After five or ten minutes had passed, Malkarai spoke up. "You're not mad, are you?"

She shook her head, eyes on the fire. "No…"

"Then why are you so quiet?"

She looked at him, realizing he seemed anxious. "I'm just being quiet. I can do that." She paused, taking in his expression. His brow was knitted up under the long strands that covered most of his face. "Why? Was I worrying you?"

"Well, you were upset earlier."

She looked back to the fire. "I'm sorry. I'm a forgiving person, it's just… I'm really putting myself out there with you. I've never tried so hard to get someone's attention – or felt like it was so uncertain that he'd reciprocate. I was embarrassed this evening when I came in and saw that. I mean, even now, even though I know what her deal is, it doesn't mean I'm confident someone else couldn't come along and do the same thing."

"No one's gonna come up and steal me. I'm this resistant to you, and I like you."

"But you'd go back to Arista if she came back, right?"

Malkarai shifted, sitting forward from his reclined position. "She's not coming back."

Satyrna eyed him. "Rafiane found you. Why couldn't she?"

"Because of why she's gone."

Satyrna hesitated.

"I don't think I'd 'go back' to her anyway. I mean, I wouldn't shun her, but I don't think I could just take her back, no questions asked. It's different now than it was then."

"How so?"

"I nearly died because of her, several times over. I've been miserable since she disappeared, and yeah, that makes me rather resentful. Also, you're in the picture now. I don't think that being together is necessarily a good idea, but since when has that ever stopped people?"

Satyrna smiled but pursued the original subject further. "Arista disappeared?"

"Yeah."

"Out of nowhere?"

"Pretty much. She went on a mission and didn't come back."

"That's awful. Didn't they tell you what happened?"

"No. It was sealed up and classified."

"Do you think she died?"

"Well, if she didn't, she certainly didn't take any action to let me know she was alive." He sounded bitter.

"I'm sorry," she said quietly.

He shrugged evasively. "Well, that's why I tried to kill myself. I couldn't stand not knowing, waiting. She was everything, she was all I had left… and then she was gone. I was alone."

Satyrna blinked a few times, her brow knitting up. "That seems… unlike you."

"What do you mean?"

"I mean, you seem so strong, so independent. It just… doesn't make sense, that one person disappearing would make you want to kill yourself. It's not even like you were told she was dead."

Malkarai licked his lips, inhaling through his nose before speaking again. "Those scars aren't the only remnant of Farad's training…"

Satyrna turned, looking at him in concern. "What do you mean?"

"I mean, most of my private training was him fixing me."

"'Fixing you' how?"

Malkarai glanced at the window. "I think Rafiane is a good example of what I used to be like. Jumpy, nervous, kind, naïve – I hated harming people. I got overwhelming anxiety from thinking about who could be affected by us going after people, and we only got sent after criminals. They wanted me to 'work' and didn't want to send me to an orphanage – because I was dark – so they had Farad 'fix' me."

She frowned and swallowed. "How?"

"He made me feel like I was alone; like everyone wanted to hurt me, so I had to hurt them first. He told me that I couldn't and shouldn't love anyone, because no one loved me. He got rid of my weakness, but he also made me angry, sad, and a little crazy. I still had Traphian and Arista, so I knew that not everyone hated me. But Traphian and I got in a fight, and when we were supposed to leave together, I stayed behind. So, we were separated. And then, Arista disappeared without any explanation and I was weak. I thought I was strong – I put Farad in his place – but then she left the picture and I realized I couldn't survive alone."

After a few moments, Satyrna said, "You did survive though."

"Survived, sure. I certainly wasn't thriving."

"How did you keep going then? It's been a long time, hasn't it?"

"Four years. Teffifa and Stika saved my life. I guess there was enough support from my co-workers – my classmates – that I stopped thinking about killing myself. I realized that they, at least, didn't want me to die. So instead, I focused on avenging Arista. I wasn't back to normal, but I had found something to keep me going, so it was enough."

"Did things change here?"

"Yeah. Well, first of all, I didn't want to go after Traphian. I never did. And I have friends again. I have someone I felt wanted by, someone I want to stand up with and for. This is dangerous, but it's worth it."

"I don't want you to be in danger…"

"I'd rather be dead here than living alone again."

"Would it really be worth dying?"

Malkarai leaned over, put his right hand on her cheek, and turned her face to his.

Satyrna shut her eyes when she felt his mouth on hers. After a few moments, he took her hand and put it on his chest. She could feel his heart, beating rapidly.

He let her lips go enough to speak. "I haven't felt this alive in years. Yes, it's worth it."

She put her forehead against his, blushing. "Is it the attention or me?"

"Both. But the attention wouldn't make my pulse race like that if it was someone else."

Satyrna sighed and slipped her arms around him, relaxing back with him when he leaned back how he was originally.

After a short while, she spoke, softly. "This isn't going to be simple, is it?"

"No. If this is what you want, it's going to be messy."

"It's not fair."

"That's the territory you're treading in."

"Still doesn't mean it's right."

Malkarai didn't respond, rubbing her back idly, his eyes on the fire. "Satyrna, don't be mad at me if I hide this, all right?"

"Why would you hide it?"

"To spare you."

"From what?"

"Repercussions. I fear my employers."

"Oh… Do you want me to hide you too? So no one gives you problems?"

"Only from people who might know me on a professional level. I have no problem standing up for myself and you. I'm rather persuasive, and if that doesn't work, well, I'm combat-trained."

"There's no need to go picking fights."

"I never need to pick them… they always come to me."

Satyrna sighed, resting her cheek on his left pec. "What would your employers do to me?"

"Nothing physically harmful, but I could see them using you as leverage."

"Leverage?"

"They could arrest and hold you."

"They'd just hold me prisoner?"

"To bring me back, yes, it's possible. That's why I don't want anyone who knows what I am to know I have a romantic interest in you."

She frowned. "I don't know how that'll work for you, but it'll be hard for me to pretend to not be interested in you."

"You'll get better at it. I'm actually kind of practiced."

"Well, that explains quite a bit," she sighed. "You and Arista hid it too?"

"Yeah."

"Why?"

"Dating co-workers was discouraged. Pretty sure a fair number of people knew or had suspicions anyway."

"So, you didn't hide it that well, huh?"

"We did the best we could. Mostly people just figured it made sense that we were together because of how we acted."

"I have a feeling that'll happen with me too."

"I don't care if your friends and family know. It's best that they do. I just don't want it to be public knowledge. So, nothing in public. Consider it a safety precaution."

Satyrna frowned. "I'm gonna be grouchy about this arrangement. I'll do it, but not happily."

He kissed her forehead. "I'll make it up to you."

"In private?"

"Yeah, in private."

She sighed but moved on. "Malkarai, why would your employers go to such lengths to get you back? That's not legal, is it?"

"I signed an oath – a contract giving myself to them and swearing my silence. At eighteen it was legal."

"Is that why they let Traphian go – because he was underage?"

"Yeah. They didn't have a legal bond to him besides guardianship. He stayed hidden until after he was eighteen. He says they always knew where he was, but because he wasn't making any waves and he wasn't happy in the system… they let him be."

"Why did they send you after him now then?"

"To shut him up. He started trying to fight the system."

"Isn't that a violation of his rights?"

"It's a violation of a lot of things, but the system's supposed to stay secret. The government's main concern is keeping the system unknown. He knew this. He disregarded their warnings, and when they went to apprehend him, he evaded their agents."

"It's still not right, to pursue you guys like this, to not give you an option to quit."

"It's legal. Whether it's ethical or not is another story. They can't erase our memories, so they can't let us go. If we don't want to work anymore, they can find other positions for us, but we are in this for life."

"That's so wrong."

"Most people don't have a problem with it. This is what we've grown up with. What we grew up learning to do. Our trainers are usually able to tell if we're not fit for the lifestyle early on and if we fail the exams or express discomfort, they usually release us. Most people are more than happy to do the job. However, once you've signed the contract, you're in for good. I mean, there's pressure to follow through with what they've trained you for, so it's not really an even choice, but it's usually not a problem."

"So, it's too little too late for you to just leave."

"Yeah… They made sure that I wanted to do the job before I turned eighteen. They tried hard to bring me back around after I tried to kill myself, and Stika gave me a ranked position. I'm not sure how much the position had to do with Arista disappearing, but Stika said that she'd been considering me for it for a couple of years."

"How old were you when that happened?"

"Er, I thought I'd just turned seventeen, but I was still sixteen when Arista disappeared. Stika told me about the position when I was seventeen, promising me it when I was eighteen if I wanted it. I was second in command when I was still seventeen."

"What do you mean, you thought you were seventeen?"

"I picked my birthdate when I was in the system. I just made it the opposite of Traphian's."

"What's your real birthdate then?"

"*If* I'm actually Rafiane's brother, then it's November 13th, eight months later than the one I used. I always knew March 24th wasn't my real birthday, but it worked for me because I picked it."

"I understand. You would've just turned twenty-one then if the November one is right."

"Yeah, a month ago."

"What would you prefer to use?"

"I don't know. I haven't wrapped my head around this yet. I'll decide later."

"Okay. My birthday is in May. My twenty-first, I mean."

"What day?"

"The 10th."

"I'll try to remember that."

Satyrna looked at him, smiling gently. "That's six months from now."

"Mm-hmm," he replied, looking at her.

"That kinda sounds like future planning."

He smirked. "Yeah, I guess it is."

"Does that mean you're gonna keep me around that long?"

"As long as I don't fuck something up, I guess so."

"Can I officially claim you then?"

Malkarai smiled, amused. "Claim me? Yeah, I suppose you can. Quietly."

"That's still a yes," she put her head back down and snuggled in closer, watching the fire.

He chuckled lightly and sighed at her.

# 31



"Time to close up?" Satyrna asked eagerly and sat up, taking her chin off her hand as her father came out of the back, key ring in hand.

"Yup. Got somewhere to be? You've been antsy all night."

She walked around the counter to start closing up the coolers. "Kinda. Someone to see."

"Who?"

"A friend."

He looked over at her as she latched the lid down on a cooler. "A boy?"

"Yeah…"

"Boyfriend?"

"Yeah, I guess so."

He turned toward her after releasing the crash bar on the door. "How long has this been going on?"

"Just a day or two."

"What's his name?" he asked as he went back to pulling blinds and turning off the lights in the front.

"Malkarai."

"Does your sister know him?"

"Yeah, I guess so. She's met him. He caught that thief for us last week. Why?"

"Oh, really?" Dregan laughed. "The dark guy you chased down, huh?"

Satyrna smirked, her expression bright. "Yeah, that one."

"Well, he's already got a good point in my book."

"Why did you ask if Patricia knows him?"

"I overheard her and Brendan talking about some guy by that name."

Satyrna turned, staring at him. "What were they saying?"

"Damned if I know. Sounded like they wanted to know where he was."

"Oh."

"Why are you so defensive?"

She shook her head and went back to the counter to take the money out of the register. "Just on guard, I guess. I've gotten used to standing up for him."

"Is he worth standing up for?"

"Yes," she said firmly.

Her father smiled as he came behind the counter. "Well, already he sounds more favorable than the others. You never got so defensive about the others."

She sighed. "The others were well protected by their egos – hence why I didn't stick with them."

"Well, if you think he can make the cut bring him by again. I'd like to meet him properly."

"I will."

"How much do you have there?"

She put the bills and coins in a leather pouch. "$875.80."

He wrote the total of her drawer down and held out a hand. "I'll take care of the rest. Go see your boy."

She handed him the money pouch, then kissed him on the cheek and grabbed her coat and purse. "Thanks, Dad."

"Be careful walking home and tell Cypha hi."

"I will. Bye!"

She stepped outside, zipping up her coat. After moving Malkarai's switchblade from her purse to her pocket she started on her way to Cypha and Dyspro's house. She hadn't made it more than a few paces before she heard someone behind her.

Satyrna tried to see out of her peripherals but wasn't able to discern much besides the fact that there was, indeed, someone back there. Clutching the switchblade, her thumb on the trigger, she picked up her pace.

"Satyrna, slow down. I'm not going to hurt you."

She recognized that voice. She spun around, her heart racing. "Stay away from me, Kalyfa."

He stepped toward her cautiously, his hands in his pockets. He was in jeans and a brown coat. There was a long, scabbed cut on his brow and his hair seemed a little windblown. She noticed he didn't have his sword on him. "I need to talk to you. What can I do that would convince you to hear me out?"

"Hm, well, we already figured out that dragging me to your little stronghold and locking me in a room doesn't work."

He sighed but didn't reply. "I'm sorry about last week. I want you to know that my intentions were good. I cannot deny that some of the knights made terrible choices which I am dealing with. Because of the lack of information and the extremely real danger that is associated with people like Faerstathe and the people he hunts, the situation worsened. My own emotions and frustration came into play as well. If I knew everything that I knew right now, my actions would've been different."

Satyrna tipped her head to the side, still staring at him guardedly. "Wow."

Kalyfa gave her a perplexed look.

"How much did that hurt to say?"

"It didn't. How everything turned out last week hurt much worse. I wanted to protect you three, but I didn't have full information, just the most reasonable, so it put me in the wrong, and my people made very polarizing choices as well. I don't regret my actions because I feel they would've been the same if I had the same information, but that doesn't mean I don't wish that last week couldn't have gone differently."

"You're going to do something about those assholes that crossed the line, right?" she insisted.

"I have a long list of personnel-related chores to take care of, yes. You know I've never hesitated to let people go if their ideals don't align with mine. I thought I'd already handled the worst offenders, but I obviously have more work to do."

"I could file a lawsuit against that dickhead that drugged me. Don't make me feel like I have to."

"I won't."

She sighed. "Fine. I accept your apology. Is that all?"

"Thank you," he said sincerely. "Unfortunately, no."

"Then what else? It's cold out here and I want to get home."

"I need to find Faerstathe."

"For what?"

"He and I need to have a conversation. A *civil* conversation."

"Well, that would be an improvement over everything that happened last week," she said, snarky.

"Where can I find him?"

She crossed her arms. "What the hell makes you think that *I* know where he is?"

"He's disappeared."

"Uh, he's a dark. It's *what they do*."

"He hasn't left town unless he was walking, which is unlikely, since he's injured. He isn't at the hospital. He didn't try to use the clinic. He isn't in any hotel or inn. He isn't dead unless he magically buried himself. He's just gone."

"That doesn't mean I know where he is. He could've left town, you know."

"Unlikely. His target hasn't left either."

"He quit. He doesn't care where his target is."

"If his target is actually his brother, I doubt he left town without him."

Satyrna's eyes narrowed. "I see Josh is talking to you."

"Josh is worried about you guys. He's looking for them too."

"Great, if I see him again, I'll be sure to tell him to avoid Josh too."

"No, you need to tell him to stop avoiding all of us. I need to talk to him."

She scoffed. "So you can arrest him? No chance."

"His people are getting anxious. I can't keep telling them to stay out forever or it'll be suspicious or, worse, I'll cross a line. If he and his friend are trying to defect, whatever, I'll play the political role of ignorance here, but I'm not just giving unsolicited favors to someone that's fucked with me this much. I *need* to talk to him and figure out what the hell is going on."

Satyrna stared at him, not moving. "If I see him, I'll tell him."

"If I can't find him, then I'm going to tell his people this and let them come in and look for him. I don't want this, he doesn't want this, and you shouldn't want it either."

"Why? You guys know this town better – what are they going to find that you can't?"

"I don't know. They have more resources than we do, that's a simple fact. Our funding and resources rely on our citizens' taxes. There are only so many people here. They have the resources of the federal government."

"You wouldn't let them bring in a whole horde of people, would you?"

"Absolutely not. They have technology we don't though. I've got twenty-five men and women and their ambition and attention. At the moment, they would be bringing three people and who knows what skills and tools they have. The longer I delay though, the more they might try to push."

Satyrna frowned, still just staring at him. She was internalizing all of this, but no matter what he said, she would not decide for Malkarai.

"Are you going home?"

"I'm going to Cypha's."

"I'll walk you there."

"I don't think that you should."

"Because he's there."

"No, because I shouldn't be around you."

He sighed. "You know that you couldn't get any safer than walking home with me, right?"

"It's principle."

"Look, if you don't say 'yes,' I'm going to follow you anyway, so just let me walk next to you like a normal human being."

Satyrna felt like that was a jab aimed at Malkarai, but she conceded begrudgingly. "You're such a pain in the ass."

"Likewise."

She turned and started back on her way to the east end of town. Kalyfa walked at her side, hands in his pockets. They walked in silence at first.

"Do you know who this guy is?" he asked after a few blocks.

"What are you talking about?"

"I'm asking how much you know about him. If you're going to be wrapped up in his bullshit, you should at least know what the bullshit is."

"His name is Malkarai Faerstathe and, until last week, he worked for the U.S. government. I first met him and his friends eleven years ago, and the second time was last week when he grabbed a thief I was chasing down. I know his life was already difficult because of his job, and was even more so because he is dark."

Kalyfa's eyebrows were knitted up. "You met him before this?"

"Yes."

"Huh. You didn't know his last name last week."

"Well, no. I didn't run into him last week and go, 'Oh! This guy is hot! I'm gonna throw my whole life at his feet!'" she said sarcastically, rolling her eyes. "I know you think I'm that shallow, but I'm not."

"I've never thought you were like that."

"Then stop treating me like a stupid little girl that can't focus on anything. I'm fond of him because I got to know him. He's smart, kind, strong, quiet, and very clever."

"Do you know what the government made him do?"

"He wouldn't tell me details. I've put together that he went after and then worked on persuading criminals to agree to deals with the government. It was something like that."

Kalyfa shook his head. "He's picking and choosing his information."

"What makes you think I'm not?"

"You'd answer any question asked of you. Try and flat-out ask him what he does for a living. He won't answer."

Satyrna frowned but didn't respond.

"Better yet, ask him how much he makes a year. That'll clam him up real quick."

"What do you want?" she asked coldly.

"Don't you find it suspicious that he won't tell you about his job?"

"Well, first of all, he doesn't like talking about himself – at all. I've gotten him to tell me quite a bit by asking about things important to him, but details about his job are a moot point. He signed a contract that demands his silence."

"Great. But, you're telling me you're not curious? That I don't believe."

"Of course, I'm curious! But I'm not going to force him to tell me something that he can't. He's trusted me with some fairly private things. I don't feel like he's trying to trick me."

"Don't you think you should be more important than a contract signed by a man who wants to play dead?"

"Someday, maybe, but I've known him a week and a half, Kalyfa. I'm not going to ask him to drop his values and spill all of his secrets for me when we barely know each other."

Kalyfa sighed, staring ahead of them momentarily before looking back at her. "I think it'll change how you see him."

"Of course, you do. You hope it will. Otherwise, you wouldn't be belaboring this."

"I know what he is, Satyrna. It frightens me to know you're so close to him without knowing the truth."

"I think you're making huge assumptions about how close I am to him."

"Based on what you know, you're already too close."

She buried her hands in her pockets moodily. "You're playing bodyguard again."

"Look, if I knew your eyes were open, I wouldn't be so bothered. I'm fairly positive he won't intentionally hurt you, but there's too much that you don't know about him that could hurt you."

Satyrna sighed. "What the hell is it about this thing that puts me in so much danger? As long as he stays dead, they won't do anything to me. They won't know I even know him."

"He's going to have a hell of a time hiding here."

"He'd have a hell of a time hiding anywhere. At least our government isn't the one he signed the contract with."

Kalyfa was quiet for a few moments, glaring contemplatively forward. "It bothers me. He's not being honest."

"Look, just get over it already. I'm not coming back to you."

"I know you're not, and I'm not trying to push you to."

"Then why does any of this matter to you?"

"I accept that you don't want to be with me, but it doesn't mean that I don't care about you. I don't want to see you ruined."

"Kalyfa, there's seven years' difference between us. We weren't friends before we dated, and I don't think we can be now. If you just want us to be friendly, that *might* be possible – if you'd stop trying to stick your fucking nose into my business."

"Until this situation, where I was worried about your safety from a law enforcement perspective, when was I sticking my nose into your business?"

"You call me all the time. You don't take a hint that I don't want to talk to you. I never call you back."

"Satyrna, you never answered your phone even when we were together. It was even rarer for you to return phone calls. Forgive me for trying vainly to work against the system, since I couldn't see you in person."

"That doesn't change the fact that I was done with you."

A faint flash of pain crossed his features, but he responded readily. "Regardless, I wanted to talk with you. I took it at your pace though. I wasn't going to confront you if you didn't want to come to me."

"So, what are you doing now?"

"I know we're done. I'm not a moron. It's not like we parted ways because of something bad – at least that I was aware of. I'm here now because I don't want you to get put on the U.S. government's blacklist. Your friends are dismissible. I don't think the federal government would go after them except for possibly questioning. You, however, are in danger if you mean something to Faerstathe."

"He told me that," she muttered unwillingly. "I'm aware of the danger."

"Is it really worth it?"

"Yes."

"See, I think that what I know would change that answer."

"Kalyfa, come on, what he does for a living is not going to make my feelings for him completely change."

"It would if you thought about it realistically."

"Ever think that it might appeal to me?"

"Well, if it does, then you're a lot more demented than I ever thought you were."

Satyrna frowned, her brow furrowed. "I don't care if he's a spy or secret agent, Kalyfa. He was largely coerced and forced into what he did, you know."

"They're handcrafted, yes. All the more reason to avoid his kind. They're brainwashed."

"He's not brainwashed."

"Don't fall for the brainwashing too."

"I'm serious! He's aware of what the system, I think he called it, is about. He knows that they're raised to be what he was. He knows all about what you've told me. He wants out. He's wanted out for a long time, but he never saw a future outside of it before now. His brother got out, and now he wants to do the same. Why won't you just give him a chance to prove it?"

"Because he's crossed me and pissed me off."

"Wow, that's professional."

"He broke the rules and made it personal, Satyrna."

"You act like he intentionally tried to piss you off."

"I told him how it was and how he should proceed. He continued his course of action. Yes, it pisses me off. I'm pissed off on a professional and personal level. As head of the knights, I'm pissed that he broke protocol and refused to cooperate with us. On a personal level, he did it with you."

She sighed in exasperation and looked away. "That's why you want me to hate him. You're upset he's not playing your game. Way to be mature, Kalyfa."

"I want you to be aware of what he is. If you hate him because of it, well, that's your prerogative."

"You can't tell me that you have an objective stance on this."

"No, I don't. As professionals, we are at odds because he follows and enforces laws that I do not agree with. I respect his ability and prowess, but I am not on his side. As a man, I am bitter and yeah, a little jealous. I don't think you'd ever have stabbed someone for me. If he can make you happy, fine, all power to him. However, I don't want to see you hurt."

"Wow, I figured you'd love to see me hurt," she said dryly.

"Am I disappointed that we didn't work out? Yes. I've moved on though. I still think well of you and I don't want you to end up in trouble. I don't work that way. I'd rather kill people with kindness than go for an eye for an eye. I don't want people in my town to hate me, especially not someone I like. Before I had this position it had a rep for being ruthless, and I want to change that by being true to my own code. I'm not going to allow illegal shit to happen here, but I want to be a protector, not a tyrant."

Satyrna watched some paper trash blow down the sidewalk across the street silently.

"I'm not going to tell you what he is now. Try and find out for yourself. However, if he refuses to tell you, I will tell you. Then you can decide whether or not you want to be with him."

"If I do, will you leave him alone?"

"He and I have different issues to work out. What we figure out will be decided solely on a professional basis."

Satyrna nodded slowly, still staring across the street. "I doubt that," she muttered.

They were both silent for a while. When they were nearing the end of town, Satyrna spoke up again. "You do know this is part of the reason I broke up with you, right?"

"What is?"

"This isn't the best example, because, yeah, it's smart to be walked home, but you were too overprotective. It was stifling."

"You can't blame me for wanting to protect you."

"You butt in. That's what bothered me."

"Forgive me for trying to keep you out of fights. You are incredibly argumentative. I really hope that wasn't the only reason."

"No, it's not the only reason. I'm not that petty."

"Then why else?"

She made a face. "I thought you'd figured it out."

"Well, yeah, you said you just didn't like me that much. What exactly repulsed you?"

"Different ideals, mainly."

"Which ideals?"

"Marriage, family, and career."

He was quiet for a few moments. "I didn't think my ideals around those were that extreme, to be honest."

"I don't want to be completely dependent upon a man. I *never* want to just sit around, useless. I have an opposition to being nothing besides a housewife and mother."

"Okay, fine. That wasn't a hard line for me. I was mostly just letting you know I was okay with it."

Satyrna stopped, knowing that the house was just beyond the next bend in the forest. "I want to help people, Kalyfa. Yeah, sure I'll take a break when I eventually have kids, but no way would I give up nursing just because my husband could support me. I want to work, significantly contribute, and be responsible. I am not going to rely solely on a man for my livelihood."

He glanced down the path, but stayed at her side, facing her. "If that made you panic, you should've told me. I'd have talked you down then. I wasn't looking for a trophy wife."

She shook her head emphatically. "You were moving too fast. I don't want to be married for at least a couple of years. You were looking more for within a year. Kalyfa, I'm sorry, but I had, and still have, no interest in marrying you. Yeah, I had fun, but I wasn't as serious as you were. You were fine as a boyfriend, but I wasn't in love. I'm sure that sucks to hear, but you were way more invested in us than I was. I humored you for a while, but it was obvious to me that it wasn't going to get deeper, so I stopped leading you on."

He sighed. "Is Faerstathe more desirable to you?"

"To be honest, Malkarai seems more immature relationship-wise than I am. I'm not considering marrying anyone right now. What happens in the future is beyond my scope right now. Look, I know, you would like to get your life ironed out now that your position in the knights is finally stable, but don't look at me for that, all right? Yeah, I did like dating you for the most part, but when I realized that you were courting more than just dating, I had to break it off – for your sake as much as mine. Forgive me if that's a little hard to explain."

"Would it have made a difference if I took it slower?"

She shook her head. "I really don't think so. I'm sorry. I... I just didn't like you that much. Not enough for forever. It wasn't going to evolve into forever either."

He looked at the trees beyond her, his expression a little darker. "I knew it was happening, but it doesn't mean I understood." He looked her in the eye. "I was afraid I'd done something to upset you. You told me that you couldn't handle it, that you had to end it. You never told me what 'it' was. You always do that; you fly by the seat of your pants and then just let what happens happen. You can't always do that."

"I clean it up afterward."

"That's going to get harder and harder to do. Especially with Faerstathe. Make him tell you what his career was, or I will tell you. You can't be ignorant of it. It's not fair to you."

"I'll see," she replied curtly. "Good night, Kalyfa."

He sighed, looking at her for a few moments before turning and heading down the path, toward town. "Good night, Satyrna. Please, watch out for yourself."

She watched him until he was out of sight and then finished her trek to the little house just down the path. She turned the knob, found it was locked, and dug her keys out of her purse and opened it.

Cypha was just inside, looking like she had been about to open the door. "Hey."

"Hey. Why are you standing here?"

"We heard voices and weren't sure who was out there."

Satyrna came inside and shut the door behind herself, turning the lock after it had closed. "It was me. Sorry."

"You and who?" Malkarai asked, standing inside the hallway, largely shadowed.

"Kalyfa," she said distastefully.

Cypha's jaw dropped.

Malkarai strode over to the window, peeking out the corner to see if he could see him. "What did he want?"

"To talk to me. Relax; he *is* my ex-boyfriend. He was walking me home from work."

"Your ex-boyfriend that you stabbed earlier this week. What did he want?" Cypha repeated Malkarai's question.

"Well, he's apparently not going to do anything to me about that, so that's a huge relief. We mostly talked about why I left him."

"He didn't ask you about me?" Malkarai seemed confused.

"Well, yes, he did, but I just told him I had no idea where you were and that I hadn't seen you. Not sure if he accepted that or thought I was lying or what. Whatever."

"Why did you let him walk you home?"

"Because he said he was going to make sure I made it home no matter what I said, so I just let him walk next to me. I didn't let him come up to the house. I'm not a complete idiot." She pointed at Malkarai. "You should probably stay away from the window though."

He nodded and went back to the bedroom he'd been lurking near.

Cypha looked at Satyrna, trying to gauge her present state of mind. "You okay?"

"Yeah. I'm fine."

"You seem a little on edge."

"I just spent the last thirty minutes with a man that I stabbed the last time I saw him… yeah, I'm a little on edge."

"You gonna be okay?"

"I'll be fine. He's not gonna do anything to me."

"What about him?" Cypha motioned toward the room Malkarai had disappeared into.

Satyrna shook her head. "I don't know. He said what would happen between them was to be settled on a professional basis. I don't know if that means he intends to finish what he started or try and talk to Malkarai first."

"He won't be able to finish what he started, right?"

Satyrna shrugged. "I'm just hoping he tries to talk first. He's injured too, so it seems more likely than challenging him to another fight."

Cypha nodded. After a few moments, she looked over at Satyrna, her face eager. "Oh! Guess what?"

"What?" Satyrna asked, grateful for a topic change.

"I've got an interview tomorrow!"

Satyrna's brow raised, her expression much brighter. "Really? Where?"

"This shipping facility on the southwest side. It's just a seasonal position for now, but they said it could be permanent. The name's like Geiger or something."

"That's great, Cypha!" Satyrna hugged her happily.

Cypha smirked and pried her off. "Yeah, well, it's just an interview. They haven't given me the job yet."

"What'll you do?"

"Move shit around. It involves some documenting – numbers and codes and shit – and I gotta use some kind of computer system, but they said that they'd train me on everything."

"I hope you get it."

"Me too." She lowered her voice, bitter. "I'm sick and tired of mooching off people."

Satyrna smirked and messed up her hair. "Oh, chill. You're not mooching. When your friends are giving you shit it's not mooching."

"Yeah, in your warped little world, sure."

Satyrna just shrugged noncommittally.

Cypha wagged a thumb over her shoulder and mouthed, 'He misses you.' "Go talk to him," she said quietly. "You were gone all day and he was awake all day. He was like a little kid waiting for Santa, I swear."

Satyrna put a hand over her mouth to stifle a giggle. "All right."

Malkarai was sitting on the edge of the bed in the dark, elbows on his thighs. He looked over when Satyrna entered and sat up straight as she came over and sat next to him.

He took her hand, shyly. "Everything okay?"

She smiled and squeezed his hand gently. "Yeah."

"You were really scared about him confronting you. You sure I don't have to go beat him up?"

"No, not for tonight. I brought this upon myself. He said he wants to talk to you."

"What about?"

"Uh, he wants to know what the hell is going on, but… he's got a political job. I guess he's managed to keep your people out of Cavington so far, but he doesn't know how long he can do that."

Malkarai frowned. "Does he want to help me?"

"I'm not sure," she said with a sigh. "He kept going on about how he doesn't want to be as ruthless as the previous head knight, and his goal is to protect the town, but I don't know what that means for you. I didn't tell him you were here. It's up to you what you want to do."

"All right. Thanks for telling me." He paused before speaking again. "He was your last boyfriend, right?"

"Yeah."

"When?"

"Eh, like last October until late July."

"Why'd you break up?"

She laughed briefly and sighed. "That's the topic for tonight, I guess…"

Malkarai gave her a perplexed look.

"He and I were just talking about it too," she explained, shaking her head. "He kept talking about marriage and what he expected out of it, and not only did my expectations not match his, but, yeah, I liked him all right, but I did not love him."

"Did he propose to you?"

"No. Never gave him the chance. He took it harder than me. I don't think he'd ever been dumped before."

"But you'd dumped someone before," he ventured.

She held up three fingers. "He was the third. I was dumped twice, and one time was mutual."

Malkarai's brow raised. "You've had six boyfriends?"

"Before you, yes."

"That's a lot of relationships…"

She shrugged. "A few of them were pretty short."

"Why?"

"It doesn't take me very long to know if things are going to work out or not. The two where I was dumped, I liked the guy, but he couldn't handle me."

"Couldn't handle you?"

She shrugged. "I'm friendly and I guess I look nice, so I've always been frequently flirted with. If I thought the guy was kinda cute too, I'd humor him – at least until he did something that tipped my level of 'dislike' over my level of 'like.' My dating in high school was never serious. I was still kinda riding that mindset with Kalyfa, but then I realized he *was* serious… so I ended it."

"What's your mindset now?" he asked quietly.

She looked at him. "It's a lot deeper than anything I did in high school. I'm still not… courting for marriage like I know Kalyfa was. But I immediately thought you were attractive, and the more I talked to you, the more I liked being around you."

His brow knitted up. "I'm a mess…"

"You're sincere and deep. Yes, I won't try and say you have everything together – but you're kind, intelligent, and interesting."

Malkarai made a small noise in response, not an agreement, but not a rebuttal either. "Why'd the other two dump you?"

Satyrna tipped her head, trying to think of a way to summarize it. "I don't like to be sheltered and I'm very opinionated."

"Yeah, that I know."

"It gets me in trouble sometimes. They saw me in school, where I was being a good student – because school was always more important to me than boys – so if they hung out with me *outside* of class, then they got to see what my values were."

"Such as…?"

She held up her hands, counting her fingers as she listed. "If they had problems with people of color, darks, LGBTQ+ people, people with a worse situation than them, or even looked at one of my friends with distaste, I was done with them. One of them uninvited himself. The other was okay with it in theory, but couldn't handle that we actually *took action* if we saw a bigot flying their stripes. We've been dealing with shit for years – because I don't appreciate being hit on or treated like a piece of meat, or people mouthing off to my friends, or because Dyspro was too nice to the wrong girl, or someone made fun of Josh, or just because Cypha looked at someone funny. I dumped one guy because he made a rude comment about darks and wouldn't apologize for it."

Malkarai raised an eyebrow. "You have high standards."

"Two of my best friends were killed because they were dark. I have a zero-tolerance policy."

"No wonder no one's made the cut. People these days are all about protecting their own asses, especially at the expense of others. It's part of why crime is so high. You're gonna have a rough time finding someone who meets your expectations."

She eyed him, smirking. "Well, *you* do."

He squeezed her hand, ducking his head slightly.

"Honestly, the only friend that you still need to pass a vibe check with is Josh, but good luck finding him."

"Yeah, I kinda need to avoid him right now."

She sighed. "I hope someday that isn't the case."

"Yeah."

"So, yeah, I've dated a bit, but if any of those other guys had caused this much to happen in the first week… I wouldn't be holding on this tight." She leaned over and kissed his cheek. "I think it's safe to say I've matured a bit, and I see something worth holding onto."

"I'm starting to wonder if this fever is really just you overloading my circulatory system," he muttered quietly.

Satyrna laughed. "Cute."

He glanced at her. "Was it marriage in general, or specifically Kalyfa that put you off?"

"Uh, specifically marriage to Kalyfa. He's all right, but I can't see myself being married to him. There were too many things about him that drove me nuts, or that I just didn't care that much about. If I was okay being a loveless, ambitionless little housewife, he would've been a great, mostly safe choice. I'm not, though."

"Yeah, I've gathered that."

"I don't intend to rely on a guy for my survival anyway, so it's not like I *need* to be married to someone to have my life in order. I want to take care of people while I make money for myself. It's a win-win situation. I help other people, and doing so helps me. He said it wasn't a requirement, just an idea, but he had suggested that I stop working and take care of kids and the home after marriage. Unh-uh. No way."

"As opposed to…?"

"Working and just taking leave to have kids. My parents worked the whole time they were having kids and my brother and sister and I turned out just fine."

"You have a brother too?"

She looked at him. "Yeah. I haven't mentioned him?"

He shrugged. "Maybe. Is he older than your sister?"

"Yeah, by almost three years. His name's Adam."

"Where is he?"

"He lives in Madison."

"Oh… Do you still intend to have kids even if you're not married?"

"Well, no… I want a family, but not without a husband. I definitely would like to get married eventually. Just, none of the guys so far have made the cut. 'Sides, I'm only twenty. I'd like to at least be able to legally drink at my wedding."

He snickered.

"How about you? Do you want to get married?"

He shrugged.

"What about have kids?"

He just shrugged again.

"You know shrugging isn't an answer, Malkarai."

"I don't really have an opinion on the matter."

"You have to have *some* sort of opinion on it."

"Well, I can't say I have any realistic expectations of either."

"Would you be unhappy if either occurred?"

"No… I'd be ecstatic, as long as I liked the girl."

"So, you know you'd want a girl?"

"Yeah, I know that at least."

"That's something. Liked or loved her?"

"Well, loved. I doubt it'd get that far if I didn't love her."

"What would you do if you didn't love her, even if she adored you?"

He frowned, staring at the floor still. "I don't know."

"What about if you loved her and she didn't reciprocate?"

"I don't know."

"You need to take a more active stance on your wants, Malkarai."

"I don't know what I want. I'm just so happy someone wants me around."

"Don't you ever dream about the future?"

"I can honestly say no, I don't."

"Why not?"

"Because I was never optimistic enough to hope for anything like that. I was content just being alive and working day after day."

"Malkarai, I don't want you to humor me if you don't like me."

"I'm not humoring you. I honestly want to be here, Satyrna." He squeezed her hand.

She sighed and leaned against his arm. "I just don't want you to stay here because you feel like you should reciprocate. I want to know that you truly care about me. I'm not asking for love. Just a strong like, I suppose. More than just,

'Oh, this girl's paying attention to me, it's nice, I want it to continue, so I'll give her attention back.'"

"I'm not that pathetic, Satyrna. I've been wounded, but it hasn't turned me into an idiot. If, say, Cypha was doing what you are, I don't think I'd return the attention."

"Why not?"

"Because Cypha kinda scares me."

Satyrna laughed. "What?"

"I've talked to her quite a bit when you're gone. Don't get me wrong, I like her; she's a valuable ally, and I'd fight beside her any day. But her personality and mine would never mesh in a relationship."

"What about me is so different?"

"You are compassionate and gentle. And stubborn. Cypha is tough, hard, and impatient. She cares a lot, but – you know her better than me – she's proud, independent, and rough. I can't open up to rough people. I need affection."

Satyrna sighed and let go of his hand to wrap her arms around his torso and hug him. "Tough on the outside, but not inside?"

"Not at all… So, forgive me for being guarded. I bruise easily. But, it's not just her. I just used her because I've spent about as much time with her as I have you. You legitimately caught my interest. No one else has done that."

"Has she been hitting on you?"

"Uh, not that I'm aware of. Why?"

She shrugged. "Wishful thinking. I swear that girl's asexual."

"She's made a couple of comments about me if that helps any."

"A couple of comments?"

"Yeah. Apparently, my muscle tone impresses her."

"Oh, yeah, I heard one of those. It is though."

"What is?"

"Your body is pretty impressive."

Malkarai's cheeks burned.

"Why is it necessary to be so well-toned? What do you do that requires such a high level of fitness?"

He shrugged. "I don't like being scrawny."

"That's it? You seem way too trim for that."

"I'm naturally thin, the muscle tone is what I worked to get."

"Okay… Well, you can't tell me that it's necessary to be that good of a fighter just as a hobby."

"I told you, most assignments end with or involve fighting. I've been trained to not let a single hit land on me."

"Why is that so important? Why is fighting so common? I feel like most detectives and police officers don't train that much. They learn law and study cases."

"I deal directly with criminals. They tend to be violent. My life's been attempted many times. Being able to fight is an absolute necessity."

"Are you like a police officer?"

"No."

"Like what Kalyfa, Josh, and Brendan are then?"

"No."

"Then what?"

He didn't respond.

"But you are a law enforcer, right?"

"Yes."

"But you are not a lawyer…"

"No."

"So, what are you if you deal with criminals but you're not an officer or lawyer?"

"You know I can't tell you that, Satyrna."

"I don't see why a contract you signed before you faked your death should matter so much," she muttered bitterly.

"It matters because if I am discovered, or if you are discovered, my telling you would be capital treason; a violation of contract and law."

"What about a girlfriend? Can't you tell her?"

"Uh, probably not."

Satyrna sighed and let go of him, crossing her arms across her chest. "I'd hope that that wouldn't apply to a spouse."

"Well, you're not a spouse."

"They seriously tell you not to even tell your spouse though?"

"It's legally allowed."

"That's pretty low, making someone enter marriage with you before letting them find out what you do for a living."

"Did. I won't be doing it for a living anymore. It's in the past."

"How do you intend to make money now?"

"I'll figure something out."

"Stop giving us money for food then."

He seemed despondent. He'd grown unhappier since she let go of him. "I have enough money. That's not the issue. I do prefer to have some sort of income instead of leeching my savings, but I'm not worried about that right now."

"You won't be able to work for a while."

"No. But it's okay. I have enough to last me."

"How much is that?"

"Enough."

Satyrna eyed him. *Kalyfa was right... Dammit. Malkarai, why do you have to prove him right? If I didn't like you so damn much, I would be so pissed at you...*

"Forgive me for not divulging everything," he said. "How much money I have should be of no consequence to you."

"Oh Christ, I'm not a gold digger. I intend to be able to support myself. I just want to know what I'm dating."

"You're dating a dead man. I don't have a job anymore."

"Not knowing does affect my opinion of you, you know."

"I don't want it to."

"You not telling me is not affecting it very favorably, Malkarai." Her voice was aggravated.

He muttered something, but she couldn't understand it at all.

"What was that?"

"Satyrna, just… let it go, okay? I can't tell you." He sounded miserable.

She stood up and headed for the door. When he realized she was leaving he scrambled to his feet, but she went right to Dyspro's room and called to Cypha, the door open in her hand. "Good night, Cypha! I work early, so I'll walk into town with you tomorrow, so make sure I'm up!"

Cypha poked her head around the corner, confused. "Uh, 'k? Night."

Malkarai stopped and didn't pursue her any farther than the doorway, dropping his eyes as Satyrna shut Dyspro's door behind her.

He stood there for a few moments before turning back to the dark room. He kicked the dresser angrily and then fell forward onto the bed, cradling his head in his arms.

Satyrna eyed the door when she heard the loud, hollow thunk from the room Malkarai was in. She shut her eyes for a moment and then went over to the bed. She changed her clothes, climbed into the bed, and pulled the covers up to her chin, feeling awful.

*I can't let him be right. Maybe you'll be more willing to tell me if you think I'm angry with you.*

# 32



The next day, Cypha and Satyrna went into town before Malkarai was awake.

Satyrna cracked open his door and looked at him briefly. He was curled up under the blankets, facing the open side of the room and thus, away from the door. His hair was all over the place, but she couldn't see his face. She sighed and then shut the door, following Cypha, who was buttoning up her coat.

"How's my hair?" Cypha asked.

"Good. Did you wash it?"

"Yeah. Damn near got pneumonia last night."

Satyrna locked the door behind them. "Stop being an idiot and come take a shower at my house."

"Stop being an idiot and stop asking me."

"No."

"Well, then, no to you too."

Satyrna shook her head at her, adjusted her purse, and stuck her hands in her pockets as they walked down the path. It was chilly, but there was very little wind and the light snow on the ground was pretty stationary. It was the kind of weather that created ice because the snow doesn't move until it melts into sheets. The path was starting to get treacherous, so they watched their footing.

"He took off last night."

"What?"

"After you went to bed. He bundled himself up and left for a while. Said he'd be back in like an hour. He came back in shortly after I washed my hair. It was a little over an hour and a half."

"Oh…"

"Did you two get in a fight or something? He looked pissed."

"Yeah, kinda."

"Good job, Satyrna," Cypha said with a sigh. "I told you the poor guy was waiting patiently for you all day, and then you just get in a fight with him?"

"I'm trying to get him to tell me something."

"Oh, just let it go. Crimony. Is it worth upsetting him like that?"

"Yes," Satyrna said softly.

Cypha glanced over at her for a few moments before returning her attention to her footing. "What are you trying to get out of him?"

"Kalyfa said something to me that's bugging me. He said if Malkarai wouldn't tell me it, then he would."

"Why does he give a shit?"

"Because he feels it could hurt me if I don't know."

Cypha looked at her seriously as they reached the dead-end street the path connected to. "And Malkarai won't tell you?"

"No, he won't. I'm working on it."

"That's rotten."

"Yeah, and he's upset about it too. I'm not sure if it's because I keep pushing, or if it's because he wants to tell but is trying to figure out what's more important. I'm hoping it's the latter."

"What do you want to know?"

"What he is."

"What do you mean, what he is?"

"What he did for a living."

"Oh…the ever-avoided question. Well, good luck."

"Thanks. I'm gonna need it."

"Do you have an idea what it is?"

"I don't know. I just figured he would arrest people if he couldn't convince them to come back with him, but I guess that isn't what they do. Maybe they have to do it in an underhanded way? I don't understand why it's such a big deal."

"What if he never answers?"

"Then, I guess I'm going to Kalyfa."

Cypha sighed, her breath coming out in a small cloud. "I don't think Malkarai would appreciate that."

"I don't think so either. But, it's freaking Kalyfa out enough that he'd corner me and insist I need to know; perhaps I should take it to heart."

"Well, there's no doubt that Kalyfa cares about you, but don't you think he's insanely jealous of Malkarai?"

"Yeah. He told me as much. But I want to know too. I intend to at least try to get it out of him before I just find out on my own."

"Yeah, well, if you want to be with the guy, don't scare him away."

"It almost sounds like you're concerned, Cypha."

"Sounds like that, does it? Huh. Maybe I should watch what I say."

Satyrna smirked. "I don't want to scare him away."

"I was kinda afraid he wasn't gonna come back last night. I double-checked his room to make sure his bag was still there as soon as he left."

"You thought he was that upset?"

"He wasn't happy, no. I mean, the one thing he's best at is disappearing."

"True."

They walked for about ten minutes in relative silence, taking in the town. The surroundings soon changed from neat little residential houses with gradually shrinking lawns to stores, apartment buildings, and offices. Most of the businesses were open, lights on, signs on, and open signs flipped over to read as such. There were some shoppers about and others headed to work.

"How long are you gonna work today?"

"Probably just 'til this afternoon. When's the interview?"

"Ten. I wanted to get there early though."

"Good plan. Stop by when it's over, 'k? I wanna hear how it goes."

"Sure."

About five minutes later Cypha motioned across the street. "This is where I go the other direction. See ya, Saty."

"Bye. Good luck!"

"Thanks." She waved as she crossed against the walk signal, taking advantage of a gap between cars.

Satyrna watched her for a few more moments as she walked, then dropped her eyes to the sidewalk in front of her again. She felt bad and wanted to go back and apologize to Malkarai, but knew she'd never get the information she wanted if she immediately did that.

She could already feel it was going to be a long morning.

11:00 a.m.

When Malkarai woke, he didn't open his eyes at first, able to tell that it was bright before he did so. He swung an arm over his eyes and rolled over, peeking under his arm at the side of the room away from the window.

He listened and got used to the light for a while before sitting up, scratching his scalp, and then rubbing his eyes. He was pretty sure that he was alone. Satyrna might have been somewhere reading, but Cypha was almost immediately audible when she was around.

He threw back the covers and then pulled on socks and jeans before he could get too cold. After stretching and popping his back, he searched for Satyrna and came up empty-handed. Then he ate, took meds, and sat out in the main room for a while, looking at the woods, but was bored after only an hour.

It didn't take him long to decide to go into town. His side was itchy but didn't hurt, so he saw no harm in a little bit of hiding. He changed his shirt, put on his coat and boots, and locked the door behind him as he left.

Traphian turned down the volume on the TV when he heard a soft tapping at the door.

"It's me," a low, quiet voice whispered.

Traphian climbed off the bed. He unlocked and opened the door to let Malkarai in. Traphian turned the lock again before turning toward his friend. He smiled. "Glad to see you're still alive."

"Yeah, mostly."

"Where have you been hiding? I kinda expected you to call at some point."

"There's been nothing to report. Knights are looking for us, ASA still isn't here," Malkarai said with a shrug. "Kalyfa did what we expected and told them to let the knights handle it first – but there's been nothing to handle because we aren't dead bodies, you've been staying put, and I'm uncatchable when I want to be."

Traphian smirked. "Well, so far so good, I guess."

"Yeah. It's definitely not time to relax yet though."

"Oh, no, definitely not," Traphian agreed, picking up the remote and turning the volume down on the TV a few levels.

Malkarai sat on the end of the bed, watching the news Traphian had on.

There was a story on about the rising crime rate and the increase in the number of violent crimes. The reporter was pessimistic about the country's future. She even suggested the possibility of corporate involvement in a few cases.

Malkarai sighed after a few moments. "She'll be dead soon if she doesn't watch what she says."

"Someone's gotta say it. She's right."

"I know. Still, she better get a merc to guard her ass or something. This can't be a local station, is it?"

"No. It's national."

"I don't know why, but I'm surprised."

"Okay, this town is sheltered, yeah, but it's not that isolated. They do have that magical little thing called satellite TV."

Malkarai shook his head and relaxed back on the bed, leaning on his hands. "I can't imagine how much worse this country would be without the ASA."

Traphian shrugged. "You're pretty biased, you know."

Malkarai eyed him. "All right, Mr. Worldly, what would this country be like without it?"

"Worse," he agreed begrudgingly.

"So why do I feel guilty for being a part of it?"

"I don't know; cuz you're turning back into what you used to be?"

"I sincerely hope not."

"Why? What's so wrong with what you used to be?"

"I had no spine."

Traphian sighed and sat down in one of the chairs at the table. "Malkarai, you were shy, cautious, and introverted. It didn't mean you weren't a strong person. I still don't know how you put up with all the shit Farad did to you."

"I ran to you and Arista crying. That's how I put up with it," he replied in distaste. "I just ran back to the weakness he was trying to beat out of me."

Traphian stared at him for a few moments, trying to gauge Malkarai. "Don't tell me that son of a bitch actually did it…"

"Did what?"

"Broke you. He really made you believe that caring – that loving was a weakness?"

"I still loved Arista even after I snapped. He didn't beat that out of me."

"You know that guy was just trying to make your primary emotion hate instead of love, right?"

"There isn't much room for love in what we did, Traphian."

"Bullshit there isn't. None of us would've done our jobs if we didn't love something. Justice, life, peace – whatever. At the very least, I know everyone in our class was motivated by a good emotion, not just vengeance or hate."

"Mm, Swip and Teffifa might have a little of that fueling them."

"Okay, yes, maybe a little. I think Teffifa is mostly fueled by adrenaline."

"That's not wrong…"

"My point is, we all wanted to protect people. We all wanted to do good in the world, and we knew that what we were being trained to do wasn't something most people could do. There was definitely love in that."

"It's hard for me to see the love in it. My training was different from what you guys got."

"I know," Traphian scowled. "Your training wasn't training. It was abuse."

Malkarai sighed. "Yeah, I can see that now. I couldn't then."

"Because Farad was a manipulative piece of shit, and he had Carlisle's blessing. So, yeah, of course, you thought it was legit. Argh, this is getting my blood boiling again. I wanted you out of there so much earlier than this. I know, you wanted Arista out with you, but she never wanted out."

"You were angry at the time."

"Well, yeah, I wanted you with me, not in the agency still. Arista and I were at each other's throats all the time, but I respected that you wanted her to come too. I was willing to wait and help. I cared about you. It bothered me that you were still in there. I didn't think you were even trying to get out, but I didn't give up. When you told me Arista had disappeared, that's when I decided that just waiting wasn't going to cut it. I really wish you'd taken my advice and just run."

Malkarai's eyes were on the TV, but he wasn't paying attention to what was on it. "I wanted vengeance."

"You wanted to die."

"I wanted Arista back, but that apparently wasn't happening. I found what I loved that kept me going – I loved her. I deluded myself for a long time, telling myself she would just show up again one day, but it never happened. So, I just kept working my way to her."

"So, was it the work or Farad that turned you into the walking dead?"

He shrugged. "Both. You know he always had his own little bits of encouragement to throw at me. After I snapped, he didn't train me, but that didn't stop him from giving his two cents worth. The work will get to you no matter what your state of mind is."

"What do you mean by snapped? When you tried to commit suicide or-"

"No, I snapped in training. That was when I was fifteen or sixteen."

Traphian paused, waiting for Malkarai to continue. When he didn't, he urged him, "You're gonna explain right?"

Malkarai sighed. "I nearly killed Farad. He finally got to me – his words and hits finally just made me snap; and the next thing I knew, I was beating and cutting the shit out of him. When I realized what I was doing, I didn't stop right away… not until he was quiet."

Traphian raised his brow.

"I ran to Arista, covered in blood, and hid with her until that evening. I was so certain they were gonna get rid of me. We both were. We just hid in her room with the door locked until Stika came around with her keys."

"What, were you scared you killed him?"

"Honestly, I couldn't have cared less. I hated the bastard. I was afraid of the repercussions. I didn't want to be sent away from her. We talked about it. If they were going to oust me, we were both gonna run away."

"Huh…"

"That's when he decided I was done."

"So, the jackass lived?"

"Yeah. He was screwed up for a month or so, but he lived. They took me out of private training then. I got a rank raise and was allowed to go on fives solo."

"That's so wrong, you nearly kill your trainer and they reward you…"

"Yeah, no shit. Whatever. All I cared about was that they weren't gonna drug me, screw up my head, and dump me somewhere. I just wanted to stay with Arista."

"Did you ever feel right about working?"

"Well, yeah. I always thought I was doing the right thing. I never took those private ones. I always thought they were shady. I avoid gray areas. I spent too much time thinking to set myself up for shit like that."

"So, what the hell were you chasing me for?"

"At first, I didn't realize it was you. As soon as I did I tried to drop it, and they forced me. I didn't want to. I told them I didn't want to."

"How'd they force you?"

"Carlisle threatened me."

"With what?"

"Demotion. Rank loss. Revocation of privileges. I mean, I'm sure most of that would've motivated other people, but I can't say I cared. Stika always let me get whatever I wanted. Poisons, medicines, equipment, whatever. I didn't care if they said I couldn't get something anymore or made me stay out of the lab again. It'd just be one less thing to distract me. But, I was on autopilot. They never used your real name, you gotta realize. You're a mission number. They used aliases. I mean, I realized quite quickly that it was you. Especially when I found out I got the mission Teffifa failed on. That's when I called Stika and told her that I wouldn't do it. Carlisle got wind of that and threatened me. There's another reason I was leaving my phone off. I didn't feel like listening to that cranky bastard bitch at me."

"But you kept following me."

"I didn't know what to do, Traphian. You got off easy because you were underage and hadn't signed anything yet. I was fully functioning, hadn't failed a mission in four years, and hadn't seen you in longer. As Satyrna's rubbed raw, I have no aspirations for the future. I don't even know what the hell I'm going to be doing in an hour, much less next year. I didn't know if I wanted to finish the mission, fail it, or just toss everything away. I still don't. Well, that's not true. I'm fairly certain I want to stay here – hidden and dead. I just don't know what that entails yet."

"Yeah, me either. But, it's kinda been that way since I left, so I'm not stressing about it."

"How the hell can you handle that?"

Traphian shrugged. "Day by day. TV, food, booze, one-night hook-ups, long walks. Just find something that makes you happy and stick with it as long as you can."

Malkarai gave him a disgusted look. "How the hell do you look like you do if that's what you do all the time?"

Traphian smirked. "I never said that that's all I do all the time. I just said those are little perks to keep you going."

Malkarai sighed. "I guess so."

"Where are you staying? Anywhere?"

"With Cypha and Satyrna. I came down with a fever and an infected wound a few days ago, so I've been hiding in their cottage, resting under Satyrna's care."

"Wooo, nice."

Malkarai gave him a sober look.

"Oh, come on," said Traphian. "Did Arista kill your libido too?"

Malkarai replied with an exasperated glare. "I'm not a eunuch. I still have a sex drive."

"And yet you're not even the slightest bit excited to be rooming with two girls?"

"Hey, I never said I was here to ask for lodging, now did I?"

Traphian grinned. "Whatever… you've got a cute girl taking care of you, so you can't complain."

"I'm not."

"Are you doing anything about it?"

"Trying. She's mad at me at the moment."

Traphian gave him a look. "What for?"

"I won't tell her what I am."

"Why not?"

"Because, unlike you, I signed that contract. I value my well-being – and hers."

"You know she's not gonna let it go, right? I mean, she may at first, but you know it'll still be bugging her. She'll ask again."

"Yeah, I know."

"Don't you think it's safer for her to know what she's dealing with?"

Malkarai paused. "You mean dealing with me or with them?"

"Both. I mean, if she wants to be involved with you, shouldn't she know what you are?"

"What if she decides I'm not worth sticking with? Then I've got a random girl who knows about the system. Good job me."

"How's she gonna know if you're worth sticking with when you're not completely truthful?"

"I don't know, Traphian. Maybe it's better if she would just give up on me."

Traphian shook his head. "I don't think it's a good idea for anyone to give up on you."

"I don't need to be babysat."

"Maybe you do. Look, that girl; she's a very rare catch, Malk. She's cute, she's tough, she's smart. Hell, she's going to be a nurse! A nice, respectable profession. She'll always have work to do. Believe me, that's a plus with people. The ones that don't work are obnoxious as hell. They expect to be carried. This one, for whatever reason, you have completely snagged her interest. Don't just chuck it away on some formality."

Malkarai didn't respond, staring at the television as he let Traphian's words soak in.

"Do you even like her?"

"Yes."

"How much? Cuz you can't compare her to Arista, you know. That's not healthy."

"I haven't been comparing her to Arista. They're entirely different people."

"How much do you like her then?"

"I like her a lot. It's just… I'm stuck between not wanting her to be in more danger because she knows, and putting her in a different kind of danger because she doesn't know what I'm up against."

"Well, I can't help you decide that. Obviously, she feels that she's safer knowing your enemies."

"Yeah. But she doesn't know who they are, so I don't entirely trust her opinion."

"Which makes sense." Traphian shook his head. "Well, I guess you need to decide if she's worth investing in. If you think she's worth it, I think you should consider telling her. If you don't think she'll stick around in the long run…well, there's your answer."

Malkarai shook his head slowly. "See, I'm torn between what I want to be true and reality. I don't know her well enough to know how permanent this is. She's dated a lot of guys, Traphian. I don't know how serious she is about me."

"You want her to be serious?"

"Yes."

"As serious as Arista?"

"Not immediately; Arista and I were in love. I'm not unrealistic – I certainly don't feel that way and I don't expect her to. I just want to know that she's going to try and stick with me. I don't want her to run at the first sign of problems. I mean…I might…but I don't want her to be hurt."

"Man, if she hasn't run yet, she's got to have a fair bit of backbone. She helped you in that brawl. She caught you when you took a sword in the abdomen and then tried to follow when you ran off. I mean, even now, she's taking care of you, right?"

"I took the hit for her."

"Does that make a difference?"

"Yes. She feels grateful and kinda guilty. I don't want to have this based purely on that. I've been trying to tell her there's more to me than what she sees now."

"Like hiding in plain sight, sneaking around in vents, scaring the crap out of people, hacker skills, and making homemade incendiaries?"

Malkarai laughed. "I forgot about those. I haven't made one in years."

"That's a shame; they were fun. They ever let you get another cat?"

"No. Teffifa has one. She said we could share him, but he doesn't really like anyone but her. It wasn't the same. I got other pets without their permission."

"Like what?"

"Mice, gerbils. I have a scorpion right now. Well, did. She'll die if no one feeds her."

"Oh, that's nice and cuddly."

"I was experimenting with her venom."

"Not on yourself, I hope."

"Not too often."

"Dumbass, that shit can kill you."

"Yeah, I know," he replied soberly.

Traphian sat up suddenly. "That's what you did! You tried to poison yourself!"

"No, I *did* poison myself. Stika had my stomach pumped and they gave me three anti-venoms. I was numb for almost a week. It was blissful. I was sad I had to go back."

"To work?"

"To feeling." He continued before Traphian could comment. "Stika wouldn't let me even touch the key to the lab until early this year, and that was mostly necessity – so I could teach."

"I wouldn't let you go back at all."

Malkarai shrugged. "If I was going to do it, I would've found another way. Why try and go the route they're expecting you to take?"

Traphian stared at him for a few moments. "You know, she could tell you were suicidal."

"Satyrna? Yeah, I know. She slapped me when she realized it."

"Good."

Malkarai eyed him.

"How serious are you two?"

"I'm not sure."

"Well…what have you done?"

"Hugged, kissed. Yelled at each other."

"So farther than a second or third date."

"Yeah, sure. I don't have a hierarchical array for judging what position a relationship's in, Traphian."

"Watch more TV. Okay, my suggestion: wait a little longer. Give it a week or so. Give her a chance to not be pissed at you. She's gotta get used to you not talking about some shit. Make your decision next week. We've got a lot of shit to get through. If you're still on the fence, telling her *before* we try to dodge the ASA hurdle is unwise."

Malkarai nodded slowly, looking out the window behind Traphian now. The thin shades were pulled, so there was natural light shining in, but it was hard to see out or in. The thick, light-blocking curtains were completely open. "Hey, will you do me a favor?"

"Yeah, sure."

"Will you walk her home?"

"Huh?"

"She's at work. Last night Kalyfa approached her and then followed her home. He was just making sure she was safe, but I'd rather he stayed away from her."

"Why don't you?"

"Cuz, first of all, I'm supposed to be at the house, not in town. Secondly, the knights are looking for me."

"They're looking for me too."

"You blend in better. Besides, you should talk to her outside of when she's worrying or bitching about me being missing."

Traphian sighed. "Yeah, all right. When's she off work?"

"Two, I think. She and her sister usually switch in the middle of the afternoon."

"I'll go at 1:30. I gotta get some more food anyway."

"Thanks."

"Yeah, whatever. Just don't screw it up, okay?"

"Why does that make a difference to you?"

"Cuz I'm not gonna try and make you look good if you're just gonna screw it up later. Looks bad on my credibility."

Malkarai laughed. "Oh, shut up. You're the federal criminal here. What credibility are you talking about?"

"Oh, bite me."

# 33



Satyrna leaned against the counter, resting on her elbows and staring out the window. The store was empty, and she'd already set up the displays her mother had asked her to, so now she was just waiting for her sister to show up so she could leave.

She stood up straight when she saw someone walk by the window and open the door. When he stepped inside, she realized it was Traphian.

"Hello," she said, a bit of confusion in her voice.

He glanced up at her. "Oh, good, you are still here. Hey."

"What do you mean, 'I'm still here?'"

He walked to one side of the store and started picking out food items. "Malk seemed sure but not positive that you worked 'til two."

"You've seen him? Have you been to our house?"

He smirked at her wording. "No. He visited me."

Her brow knitted up. "When? Last night?"

"No, an hour ago. Did he escape last night too?"

"I guess he's getting restless," she sighed, propping her chin up with a hand. "He was never very patient with healing."

"Why'd he send you to me?"

He picked up a loaf of bread and moved to pick out some single-serving, microwaveable entrees and soup. "To provide knight-repellent. Apparently, you have a problem with them following you."

Satyrna raised an eyebrow. "Did he tell you this?"

"Well, yeah. I've been hiding in my room like a hermit for three days. I don't know what's going on."

She hesitated. "You sure he's not just jealous cuz my ex-boyfriend walked me home yesterday?"

He shrugged. "He seemed legitimately concerned. Plus, I think he wants you to not think I'm a creeper."

Satyrna stared at the floor for a few minutes, trying to decide what this meant. Did Malkarai want her to ask Traphian since he couldn't tell her himself? Maybe he just wanted to distract her. She wasn't sure.

He brought the armful of food he had up to the counter and let it tumble to the surface.

"Out of food again?"

"Yeah. I'm going to stock up for the long run this time. The knights are dragging their feet, so the other threat is still looming. Seems like we're gonna hafta hide for a little bit longer."

"Where do you get your money from?" Satyrna asked as she started ringing his items in the register.

He gave her a look. "That's kind of a personal question."

"Well, I mean… you're not working; you're running from people like him. He's not working either anymore. I just don't understand where you guys are getting your money from." She shrugged. "You don't have to answer. I'm just curious."

"Well, he's made money working for the people I ran from. I made money on my own, working different jobs since I left. I sold a lot of things before I uprooted myself, and I had savings. I don't have a ton, but so far, I've had enough to last me for this escapade I've been on. I didn't have to start running until a few months ago."

"Oh, so you have different incomes."

"Yeah. Our work when we were under eighteen or below a certain skill level was never paid. What we made automatically went to pay for our schooling, room, and board. So, I was never paid for my work there."

"But he was?"

"Yeah; he was an active agent for four or five years."

"How much did he make from it?"

Traphian shrugged. "Got me, Satyrna. I don't know what the pay's like. I was too young to give a shit when I left."

She sighed. "$28.60."

He took out his wallet and gave her two twenties. "Why are you trying to find out his income anyway?"

"I was told I should be aware of it."

"By who?"

She gave him his change. "By Kalyfa."

He put the bills in his wallet and dropped the change in his jeans pocket. "Yeah, Malkarai's number one fan. What the hell do you trust him for?"

"I used to date him. He insists I should know what Malkarai is and how much he makes. He said it was unfair for me to not know basic information like that – said it would change my view of him."

Traphian sighed and leaned against the counter. "Did you tell Malkarai this?"

"No. I wanted to see if he would tell me just on his own."

"He won't, Satyrna."

She frowned, displeased by the certainty with which he said this. "Why not?"

"Because he doesn't want to put a target on your head if things don't work out between you two."

"What makes him think I'd tell anyone?"

"That's irrelevant. He wants to play it safe. He cares about you, you know. He doesn't want to make you any more desirable to the ASA than you already are."

"If I'm already a target, what the hell is knowing what they are going to do to harm me?"

"It's not a crime to know Malkarai. It's a crime to know about the system without legal documentation. Yeah, if you never spoke of it, you'd probably be safe. They can't read minds. But he doesn't want to risk it."

"For his own sake or mine?"

"Well, both. He doesn't want them to have a reason to suspect you of knowing, nor does he want them to punish him for squealing."

Satyrna sighed. "So, I should just give up? That's what you're telling me?"

"Nah. Keep trying if you want to. I'm just telling you, that's how he feels about it. Don't expect him to talk easily."

"Is he always this hard to get info out of?"

Traphian smirked. "Yeah."

"Crimony... what a pain in the ass."

"Yeah, that's Malkarai. A royal pain in the ass."

"What's the big deal? Why doesn't he ever talk about himself?"

Traphian's expression was more serious as he considered this question. "Well, mainly it has to do with what he's been through. He's lived through a lot of shit he doesn't like to talk about – or he's lost things he cared about, and no one likes to think or talk about things like that."

"Does he really not think about the future?"

"He used to think about everything – overthink, really. Now I think he does everything he can to avoid thinking. About the past, the future, most of the present... I think he tries to stick with what he's doing at the moment and not look past it."

Satyrna frowned. "That's sad."

Traphian shrugged. "I can't say I blame him. I try not to think about things like that too much either. Makes life easier."

"I want to know about him, though. I want to know why he is the way he is. I want to know him better. I don't think I'll get him to talk about his personality or feelings like that, so I settle for learning about what he's been through or what he thinks about other people and topics. That helps me understand why he is the way he is now."

"Oh, I understand. And you'll probably get him to talk if you haven't already. It's just hard to get him to spill. It isn't impossible; just hard."

"Got any freebies for me?"

"Er…he's a cat person."

Satyrna smiled. "You know, I probably could've guessed that."

"Why do you say that?"

"I don't know; he just seems to act like one. A cat, I mean."

Traphian nodded reflectively. "Yeah, that he does. He used to have one. It slept with him in his bed before it would take off for the night. It didn't come back one day and they wouldn't let him get another one."

"Why didn't it come back? Did it run away?"

He shrugged. "Dunno. Maybe. Might've got run over, or someone else took it in, or one of any number of things. I thought the thing liked him though, so I'd guess it was probably something bad that kept it from returning. He started sleeping with stuffed animals after that. He missed its company."

Satyrna smiled. "That's cute."

Traphian smirked. "I should stop lowering his masculinity."

"No, please, continue."

He shook his head and shifted, looking out the window at the front of the store.

"Did you have your own rooms where you lived?"

"When I was there, we shared one. We had bunk beds. Malk was on top cuz he was always smaller. Most kids shared rooms. Arista and Teffifa shared one for like a month before they got split up, but they were a rarity. Teffifa stressed Arista out, and they just didn't mesh. After I left, Malkarai stayed single though, I think. No one else his age to pair up with besides Arista or Teffifa, but they don't do co-ed rooming. Shawn and Swip were already paired up and did well together, so they wouldn't split them. I'm sure that being alone didn't help his self-inflicted isolation any. After he reached active status he got another room – a bigger room – for himself, I'm sure. They don't make adults have roommates."

"You all lived in the same building though?"

"Lived, ate, trained, taught, learned; yeah. We only left to work or take tests. At fourteen they let you go into town with groups for a short amount of time, and at eighteen you have free range."

"Doesn't that get…boring?"

"Incredibly, but we got to work fairly often, so it wasn't too awful. It's also in the middle of the woods, so we were allowed to go outside and play." Traphian snickered. "They didn't have their eye on us 24-7, otherwise we would've gotten tons of shit for these," he moved his right arm. "Probably would've had it removed."

Satyrna stared at his arm for a moment. "Oh, the dragon scars?"

"Yeah."

"You're not allowed to do anything like that?"

"We are, but he was twelve and I was thirteen when we did it. Arista scolded us – well, me, really, for making Malk do it. Shawn and Teffifa thought it was cool as hell. She wanted to do it too, but we wouldn't let her use ours."

"Was it your idea?"

"It was both of ours. I said it'd be cool to get a tattoo or something, he suggested branding."

"Crimony… didn't he realize how much that would hurt?"

"Yeah. He didn't care. I don't think he liked needles. Burning his flesh? No problem." Traphian laughed. "I'd be oblivious if I didn't know by now that Malk's odd."

"Not to mention no one would give pre-teens tattoos."

"Yeah, that too." Traphian nodded toward the street. "Here comes your sister."

"Yay!" Satyrna ducked down and got her purse and coat out from under the counter as Patricia came inside and up to the counter. "This morning was awful. It felt like it took days."

Patricia looked at Traphian, pausing for a few moments before nodding. "Hey…"

He waved casually and glanced back at Satyrna. "Why's that?"

"It was slow, and I wanted to get home."

Patricia sighed and set her purse on the counter. "Where you're harboring a boy, you naughty little hussy."

"Ssshhh!" Satyrna hissed, whispering, a finger to her lips. "Mom's in back!"

Patricia just eyed her. "You'd better hope Dad doesn't find out that you and Cypha are keeping him there."

"How's that so different from Dyspro being there?"

"You aren't infatuated with Dyspro." She took off her coat. "Besides, they know him. If Dyspro were to do anything to you, he'd have the sense to know that there'd be repercussions. They don't know Malkarai, thus, they don't trust him."

Satyrna sighed and looked at Traphian in exasperation. "This is the kinda shit I've had to deal with every time I dated. I could never let him meet my family until he'd been properly prepared."

Traphian shrugged, a smirk on his lips. "I'm not so sure that Malkarai would ever be properly prepared. He doesn't have his own family to relate to, you know."

She sighed and slipped her coat on. "I know. He has no idea how to treat Rafiane."

"Who?"

Satyrna looked at him. "Oh! That's right! You've been a hermit! So, there's a girl that's been following Malkarai – he thought it was Teffifa at first, but it wasn't. It was this girl named Rafiane who's been trying to find him for months."

"Why?"

"Because she's pretty sure he's her older brother."

Traphian scoffed. "No shit. Man, I fucking called that."

Patricia leaned on the counter, giving Satyrna a perplexed look. "He didn't know he had a sister?"

"He was abandoned as a baby. Apparently, his family lives where he did-"

"Really?" Traphian asked, surprised.

"Yeah, I think so. They knew where he was but couldn't take him back. When she found out about him, Rafiane didn't accept that like her parents. She wanted to meet him and let him know he had family. Well, she didn't catch up to him until he stopped moving – here."

"Huh… Wow. Does he agree that the facts line up?"

"I mean, sorta. He told her he doesn't want to think about this right now and he definitely wasn't happy or excited to hear *why* she was following him. He's glad it's a personal and not a professional reason though."

"Yeah, that makes sense." Traphian scoffed. "Never thought he'd find family first."

"You thought you'd find yours?"

Traphian shrugged. "Nah, he just never cared to find it, that's all. Sounds like he's still of that mindset." He dug out his wallet, opened it, and showed Satyrna and Patricia a picture of a woman with brown hair that went to her shoulder blades. The picture was well-worn, so she couldn't tell her eye color or much about her clothes, but she had a cheerful, friendly smile on her face.

Satyrna glanced up at him. "She kinda looks like you."

"She's my mom."

"Oh…"

He closed his wallet and put it away before leaning against the counter. "Well, I'm pretty sure she is, anyway. Stika, one of the other agents – the one Malk worked under, actually – gave me that when I was little. She said that it was with me when I came there."

"What do you mean?"

"I was abandoned by kidnappers that got scared – at least, that's the story. They didn't know where I was from, just that I'd been dropped. I don't like the vague details associated with the whole thing, so I'd always kinda hoped I'd find out the truth someday – find out who she is. Malkarai respected that, but never really understood. He never expressed any interest in finding his family. He was aware of where he came from, that he'd been abandoned. He's always been bitter about that."

Satyrna nodded.

"Is this strange…in your work?" Patricia asked tentatively, not sure she was asking the question right.

"Being abandoned or dropped at the agency? Yeah, kinda. Most of our co-workers were orphans found in orphanages or homes. We all grew up together, being trained to be what Malkarai is and what I was supposed to be."

"I didn't realize you were all estranged."

"Yup. That's how they justify handcrafting us. They figure they're giving us a greater opportunity than we'd ever have coming out of an orphanage or children's home."

Satyrna hesitated before responding. "Did they?"

Traphian shrugged. "Depends on the person. I obviously didn't appreciate it. Teffifa loves it. Most of the people there really like the job."

"What about Malkarai?"

"That's something you'll have to ask him yourself."

"He quit," Patricia put in.

Satyrna glanced at her. "Yeah, but he quit because he was lonely and unhappy."

"Ask him." Traphian stood up. "You're gonna make him nervous. I should get you out there."

"He's that worried about me?"

"Yeah. He thinks that Kalyfa unnerved you."

Patricia shook her head with a sigh.

Satyrna cast her a look. "What?"

"A little overprotective, isn't he?"

"Hey, you know, I don't make crap out of Brendan and how much he coddles you. Don't make crap out of my guys."

"Whatever, you need someone to watch your butt, but isn't not trusting you to walk home alone in the middle of the day a bit much?"

"He wanted to keep Kalyfa away from me."

Traphian nodded in agreement but didn't say anything.

Patricia sighed. "Still, it's not like Kalyfa's gonna hurt you, Satyrna."

Satyrna put her purse strap over her shoulder and walked around the counter. "That doesn't mean that I feel safe around him."

Patricia shook her head.

"I'm not asking you to adore him, Patricia. Just respect that I do, okay?"

She just gave her sister a patronizing look. "Don't get in trouble."

Satyrna shook her head as she turned toward the door. "Don't worry about me."

Outside, Traphian gave her a look. "So, your family doesn't approve of him?"

"My parents just know I've got a new boyfriend. I've given them a few details, but I'm trying to keep it G and not mention too much of what happened last week. Patricia at least seems to agree with me on that, but she's never approved of anything without a good reputation. Malkarai doesn't have one according to her, so he's the unknown, a risk. Last week the knights that she respects were at odds with him but then she watched him save me from being cut down by one, so she's trying to see where he shakes out."

"He is a risk though."

She shrugged. "I like risk. See, I have things pretty good. My brother appeased my parents' desire for a college-educated child, and my sister has always been the good little girl, always there to help and support. She'll be the first married too. Me? They got all those wishes fulfilled, so I'm pretty much free to do whatever the hell I want. They're protective of me, yeah, but they scold me far less than either of them. There're a lot of things that I value that my parents aren't comfortable with though."

"Like?"

"Like equality, peace, love, and some adventure."

"They don't like equality and peace?"

"They like them, but getting either of those involves fighting."

Traphian shook his head. "Oh, well, yeah, I knew that…"

"I've gotten more black eyes than my brother and sister combined." Satyrna grinned. "Proud of every one of them too."

"Is that why you're interested in Malkarai? Because he's an adventure?"

"I'm interested in Malkarai because I'm attracted to him."

"That didn't really answer my question," he muttered.

She looked at him. "Oh, you want to know *why* I'm attracted to him?"

"Yeah."

"Uh… well, physically, I think he's gorgeous. Tall, thin, muscular, tan skin, and black hair. I kinda like how his eyes are always hiding, but his eyes are really cool, so it's like it's special – like I'm special – when I can see them… Anyway…" she cleared her throat, feeling uncomfortable discussing this with a guy.

Traphian sighed softly. "Yeah, girls always thought he was cute. Lucky bastard ended up growing into a babe magnet instead of being incredibly awkward. He easily could've gone the other way."

Satyrna smirked, blushing.

"You know, as long as they don't care about his eyes. So, his eyes don't freak you out, huh?"

She shook her head. "I mean, I've had friends before with dark eyes, so they're not new to me. I've always been fascinated with them because of Fayta and Martra. However, I'm aware that they don't like it when people pay a lot of attention to their eyes, so I haven't asked him any of the many questions I have about them. But I am, I'm interested, not scared of them. It is a little weird to not be able to tell where he's looking right away though – his irises are hard to see."

Traphian nodded. "Most darks have colored irises. Malk's are almost completely black. What are his supposed sister's eyes like?"

"Um, dark. Black too, I think. Maybe a dark brown. I can tell where she's looking easier than Malkarai, but I didn't notice a color. His hair's covering his eyes too though; she's got bangs, but they don't cover her eyes."

He nodded. "So, not the same as his?"

"No, not exactly. Anyway, I noticed most of that stuff right away, but just because I thought he was good-looking and I was interested in his eyes weren't good reasons to pursue him like this. The more I talked to him, the more I was drawn to him. See, I want a guy that's tough – I mean, truly tough, not just a beefed-up, steroid-drunk, ego-machine. Malkarai's tough. He's so obviously dark, but he hasn't been trodden on because of it. He isn't a pushover. He can back up everything he does – be it with words or fighting. He's smart, he's clever, but he's soft-spoken. I like that he doesn't talk just for the sake of talking. Yeah, he's got a lot of downsides – like being terminally depressed and a pessimist – but I don't see problems as a deterrent. Flaws and issues make things more interesting, in my opinion. I don't want a perfect guy. I'm not perfect, so why the hell would I expect that out of anyone else?"

Traphian nodded, encouraging her to continue.

"And I… I can just tell when people are good. I've always been able to see past tough or undesirable exteriors and see what a person really is like. I mean, I'm not clairvoyant… I just have very good gut feelings. I can usually feel how they feel about things."

"Empathetic."

"Yeah. Cypha was one example of that. She tried her damnedest to be the toughest kid ever, but even though she picked on and beat up everyone who looked at her funny, I tried to be her friend. She's nothing like that now – cuz Josh and Dyspro and I were her friends. She was lonely and abused, and had grown very defensive because of it. I'd trust Cypha with my life. Malkarai was similar. He tried to make us leave him alone, and I was willing to respect that. I wanted to make life for him easier here, but I wasn't going to force anything on him. I could tell, though, that he wanted the social interaction. He wanted to be around people. He acted anti-social, but he was hurt and gun-shy. I wanted to know why, and that got me closer to him. The more I learned, the more I saw what he was like, the more I cared."

Traphian nodded slowly, watching the street in front of them. They were in the residential district now.

"Er… that's all, I suppose… Why did you want to know, Traphian?"

He hesitated. "I wanted to know you weren't playing around with him. I think he could handle the disappointment, but to tell you the truth, I'd tell him if you didn't seem sincere. He's got a lot of danger riding on his shoulders, and having a significant other tossed into the mix does not reduce the danger."

"So, does he want to be with me?" she asked quietly.

Traphian looked at her. "Haven't you asked him yourself?"

"He never answers straight questions like that. He always dances around the answer. I mean, he's kissed me and held me and told me what danger there was being with him, but I'm not sure what all of that means. I asked if I could claim him and he said yes, but he hasn't said any kind of declaration to me, you know?"

"Seems to me like he wants to be with you. He just doesn't want you to be hurt."

Satyrna shook her head vehemently. "That's just it though! I feel like I'm something he's enjoying only as long as it's safe. I don't want that. I want to mean something..."

Traphian didn't respond, thinking.

"Traphian?"

"You need to have this discussion with him," he responded quietly. "He can't read minds either. Let him know how you feel about this."

She nodded slightly. "I will. You think that's a better approach than letting him think I'm angry that he won't trust me?"

"With Malkarai? Definitely. Yeah, he'll try and make you not mad at him, but it doesn't mean he'll give in to your wants. If you want to get information, it's better to take the gentle approach. He's kinda like a porcupine or one of those pill bugs. The greater the fuss, the more he armors himself. If you want to get to him, take it slow."

She smiled at him. "Thanks, Traphian."

He shrugged. "Don't mention it."

"You're still pretty protective of him, huh?"

"Old habits die hard."

"He doesn't need it anymore, you know."

"Physically, no. I'm pretty sure his mental and emotional state's in worse shape than it ever was when I was around."

Satyrna frowned. "You think so?"

He nodded and dropped his eyes to the ground a yard or two in front of his feet. "The more I talk to him the more I can tell." He glanced at her. "That's why, so long as you're after him for the right reasons, I encourage you two to be together."

She pursed her lips for a few moments, chewing that over. "Well, thanks for your blessing, I guess. I want to try and help him. I mean, maybe I can't fix everything that Arista and his trainer did to him, but I can help. At the very least, so long as I have a say in it, he'll never consider taking his life again."

"That's a good start. Also, if he's told you about his trainer and Arista... he trusts you more than you realize."

She looked at him, her eyebrows lifted. "Really?"

Traphian nodded. "They aren't people he talks about freely."

She smiled, looking pleased as she looked forward again.

# 34



Satyrna looked around inside while dislodging her key from the door. "Malkarai?" she whispered.

Traphian pointed to the corner by the table and Malkarai moved, finally catching Satyrna's eye.

She gave him an exasperated look as she stepped inside.

"What?"

"Am I going to have to play hide-and-seek every time I enter a room you're in?"

"Not every time – but most," Traphian responded, shutting the door behind him.

Satyrna sighed as Malkarai stepped around the table by her. He kissed her on the temple. "Forgive me," he said softly. "I trust you – I don't trust him."

She shook her head. "It's fine. I don't care to run into him again either. 'Sides," she glanced at Traphian, "I was able to dig up some more dirt on you."

Malkarai's brow knitted up and he gave Traphian a look, but Traphian was avoiding his gaze by looking around the room and down the hallway.

"Primitive, but kinda cool. Wow, this is a perfect hiding spot. There's no electricity or anything, is there?"

"No wired power. Cypha has a solar charger for small appliances like her phone."

"Nice," Traphian said, impressed.

"Yeah, no electronic trail is a plus. What did you tell her?"

"About your cat and your needle aversion. She thinks you're a psycho."

Malkarai looked at Satyrna, who gave Traphian an unamused look before turning back to Malkarai. "I don't think you're a psycho. However, branding was a pretty screwed-up choice."

"I'd rather deal with a minute of scorching pain than a few hours of someone stabbing my skin with a needle, over and over. Both would throb for hours to days afterward, so I wanted to get the worst part over quicker. What's so screwed up about that?"

"You were twelve!"

"We were not naïve twelve-year-olds, Satyrna. Even at that age, we had seen so much weird shit, branding was not that screwed up, okay?"

"What kind of weird shit?"

"Piercings in places they shouldn't be; people cutting their tongue so it looked like they had two; people half-skinning their fingers and then sewing them together so they grew together." He held up a hand, his forefinger and middle finger together and the ring finger and pinkie finger together to illustrate. "Some people you couldn't even see what their real skin color was because they were so covered in tattoos, or prosthetics, or implants. Traphian and I immortalizing our friendship with a little dragon brand wasn't that screwed up, okay?"

She cocked an eyebrow at him. "You saw this regularly?"

"Well, not regularly, but often," Traphian put in.

She looked between the two. "Who the hell were you hanging out with?"

"Criminals," they both responded.

"But it isn't necessarily criminals that do crap like that," Malkarai added. "A lot of regular people modify their bodies. Life outside of Cavington is an entirely different experience, Satyrna. This town is very sheltered. Your policing system here is very effective. Well, effective at keeping out people who don't fit your demographic."

"Well, keeping out criminals is okay, right?"

Malkarai crossed his arms as he leaned against the table. "They didn't want me here either, remember?"

She stared at him, her expression going from receptive to despondent. "I'm sorry…"

He shook his head and stood up, walking over to the fireplace to put some more wood on the fire. He tossed the last two pieces on the low flames. "Don't be sorry. I don't blame you for whatever thinking this place has put in your head. You at least have your eyes open enough to be able to tell true criminals from people who are just different."

Satyrna didn't respond, staring at the fireplace. After a few moments, she turned and took the hatchet from where it rested against the wall next to the stove. "I'm going to get some more wood."

Malkarai turned and started toward her. "No, I should go and-"

She seemed ready for rebuttal. "Why? Because you're a guy? I don't think so. You're injured. Stay here and talk with your friend." She swung the hatchet up, letting the wooden handle rest on her shoulder.

Malkarai stopped, watching her go a little helplessly.

After the door had shut, Traphian laughed. "She's spunky. I like her."

Malkarai looked at him. "Did I upset her?"

"Nah. Relax."

"I'm not sure what the hell's going through her head."

"She's a girl; of course, you don't. Chill out."

Malkarai sighed and leaned against the table again, looking at his feet. "Does she seem mad at me?"

"She seems frustrated, but not mad. You know she was just trying to get you to talk, right? She's trying to figure out how you work."

"I was hoping she wasn't mad. I mean… I don't know what I'm supposed to apologize for. I just refused to tell her something."

"You could apologize anyway. It can't hurt your chances. She wants you to trust her."

"I… can't. Not yet."

"Yeah, well, you both need to talk more. It'll help things work out."

Malkarai nodded slowly.

"She's sacrificing things too, you know."

Malkarai looked up at him.

"You're in danger because you chose to defect, but she's contesting some of the most important things in her life because she wants to be with you."

"What do you mean?"

"The important things in your life are the system and your friends. Well, you lost your friends until you came here and met more, but you decided they were more important than work, choosing them over your safety, right?"

Malkarai nodded, urging him to continue.

"Well, to her, the most important things are her friends and her family and both the values they've instilled in her and their approval of the things she does. Yeah, there's a certain amount of rebelliousness in her, but inherently, if her family or friends don't approve of something, it will affect her actions."

"So, you're saying her friends and family don't approve of me?"

Traphian shrugged. "Her sister's distrustful because she doesn't know you. She doesn't seem to fear you, per se, but her perception of you has changed since Satyrna told her you two are together. You don't know her parents either. My point is, you said it yourself; you're the unknown here – the unwanted. She knows this. But, what should matter to you is that she doesn't care. She knows what people think of you – both as a dark and as an agent, even if she doesn't know details about the agent part – but she doesn't care."

Malkarai seemed very sober. "I know. I've told her that people aren't going to approve of this. She's too pigheaded to sit down and consider it."

"I'm not so sure that's true. I think she has considered it."

Malkarai looked at him, waiting for him to continue.

Traphian shook his head. "Unh-uh. I'm not elaborating. Talk to her about it. That's not my place."

"So, what the hell are you telling me all this for?"

"Giving things a nudge. You guys don't have much time to make up your minds, you know."

Malkarai looked away, eyes on the floor. "I still haven't seen any sign that they've come for me or you."

"You've been laid up here for a few days."

"Yes, that's true, but I looked around while I was in town, and I was keeping track of everything before I got sick."

"They're bound to come. They lost an agent – there's no way they'd let this fall solely to the local police's responsibility. Kalyfa can hold them off for a while, but not forever."

Malkarai turned his head, hearing the hollow, distant thwacking of the axe.

Traphian smirked. "She's doing her best to keep you in line."

"Shut up."

"Whatever. Deny it if you want, but you'd tell me to kiss your ass if I'd talked to you like she does."

Malkarai gave him a look. "If you talked to me like she does I'd tell you to keep your distance; I don't swing that way."

Traphian sighed in exasperation and slugged him in the back of his shoulder. "You're a pain in the ass."

4:00 p.m.

A short while after Traphian left, when Malkarai was looking through the food to figure out what they could make for supper, Satyrna bundled up in her coat and gloves again. Malkarai looked up and watched her anxiously.

"Where are you going?" he asked quietly.

She smiled and put a hand on his shoulder momentarily as she passed. "Relax – I'm just going to cut some more wood. That won't last us through tonight."

"Oh…"

She picked up the axe and opened the door. "Be back soon."

Satyrna headed around the side of the house and started following her path from earlier to the tree she'd downed. The sun would set soon – in about forty-five minutes. She needed to get a few more pieces cut quickly.

It was very cold and windy. It wasn't snowing, but there was still snow on the ground in several layers. It was mildly treacherous because the first layer was frozen to the dead leaves and brush on the ground, and there was a softer layer of about half an inch of powder on top.

She weaved through the trees before reaching an incline. The tree was just beyond the bottom of the hill.

Satyrna reached up and grabbed onto a branch to help her descent. On her second step, she slipped on the leaves and fell, sliding and landing on her butt at the bottom of the incline.

She hissed out a cuss word. She'd hit her tailbone on something.

After a few moments, she bent her legs to stand up and stopped moving, feeling a searing pain in her right knee. She tilted her leg and gritted her teeth.

Her jeans were cut and quickly soaking up dark blood. The axe was a few feet away, its blade mostly clean, but there were already a few drops of blood in the snow.

"Shit…"

She reached out to her knee, not sure if she should pull the cloth back or hold it to staunch the bleeding. She glanced at it quickly, decided that the skin was still attached, and pressed her palm against the joint. It stung. The cold air did not agree with the raw, open flesh.

Satyrna sat for a few minutes applying pressure, trying to determine what was best to do. Eventually, she decided that, even if it meant moving it, she needed to get inside. She reached over, grabbed the axe, and used it to heft herself to her feet.

She winced, a scowl on her face, but let go of her leg and immediately set about getting up the incline, using the axe as a climbing tool.

It hurt a lot. Each step sent a jab of pain through her knee, and it was bleeding pretty heavily.

About halfway back, she stopped, her breathing ragged, letting her knee rest. She examined it, poking the cloth aside gingerly.

The skin went with the cloth.

She drew her breath quickly, steeled her jaw, and stood up again. Her stomach felt suddenly unsettled and she felt sweat on her forehead. She inhaled deeply and continued steadfastly, trying to keep the lame leg immobile.

By the time she reached the house, her sock had grown warm and then cold as the air had cooled the blood.

She'd stopped using the hatchet before she dropped it outside of the door and staggered inside.

Malkarai looked up from the book of hers he'd started reading. When he saw she was limping and bloodstained he jumped to his feet.

"What happened? Were you attacked?"

"No, I'm a klutz," she said through clenched teeth as she sat heavily on one of the chairs at the table.

He shut the door and went over by her, pulling the other chair around in front of her. He leaned over and examined it, touching her leg carefully. "Jeez… What happened?"

"I slipped down a hill and hit my tailbone. I must've caught my leg with the axe when I fell."

His brow tightened slightly, but otherwise, his calm, appraising expression didn't change. "Can you bend it?"

"I wasn't – it hurt like hell when I moved it-"

"Pain's irrelevant. Can you move it?"

She nodded slightly and flexed her knee a little to prove it.

He tipped his head, examining it from the side. "Good. It doesn't seem to have hit any tendons. Okay, we're going to have to get your pants off to look at it."

She glanced at him, an eyebrow cocked.

He sighed. "Look, if you think you can roll your pants up without dying in pain, go for it."

"Actually, I was thinking that I'm pretty sure the skin would come off with my pants."

He leaned over, looking at it closer. She could barely tell that he was touching it. "You'll be fine. There's enough holding it. We should get it off the cloth though. I'll let you do that, okay?"

She nodded slightly and bent over her leg to gingerly get to work, pulling the blood-stained material off her knee.

Malkarai stood up and went into the room he'd been using. He came back with the bag of medical supplies and something made of black, shiny, soft mesh cloth. She held the jeans back and looked up at him, confused when he handed her the clothing. "What's tha- Oh, your shorts?"

"Yeah. Put them on if you're so modest. You need to get your jeans off though."

"Er… hold my jeans back, okay?"

"Sure. Just a moment."

He went to the stove, got a small pot, filled it with water, put it on the stove, and turned on the burner. Then he grabbed the basin they'd been using for wound washing.

He came back and set the tub down. Then he took over keeping her knee and jeans apart as she stood up and started unbuttoning and unzipping her pants. After pulling them down as far as her thigh she put her hand down her pant leg and took over holding her flesh to her knee. He untied her snow boots and took them and her bloody sock off, setting them aside, before pulling her pants off the rest of the way.

After she pulled his shorts on and sat down, she looked at him, her hands between her thighs, palms flat on the seat.

He caught her eye and laughed at her flushed cheeks, which was contrasting drastically with her otherwise uncharacteristically pale complexion. "What?"

"Congratulations."

"On what?"

"On being the first guy to see me minus pants."

He laughed again and shook his head as he grabbed the basin and put it under her leg. "No wonder you're so skittish. Well, thank you. I feel honored." He stood up and went back over to the stove. "Just a few more minutes and this will be boiling."

"That's going to hurt."

"Yes, probably. I'll leave it cool down though. I think you'll probably need stitches. Is it all right if I give them to you, or do you want to go to the hospital?"

"Um, I don't want to walk all the way to the hospital. It's a long way."

"I can carry you."

Satyrna shook her head emphatically. "You're not healed yet either. It's fine, you can do it."

"I have a local anesthetic."

She blinked. "Really?"

He nodded. "That's why my wound was numb when you tried to take care of it."

Satyrna turned her head and leaned over to look at her knee, her teeth clenched. "I'm already grateful for the offer."

Malkarai turned to the stove to check on the water. When it had started boiling, he picked up the pot and a hot pad and then moved around the table to where Satyrna was sitting. He put the pot down on the pad on the table and sat in the chair across from her, moving so the chair was in front of hers.

"Put your leg up on the rung of my chair."

She obliged, pulled the leg of the shorts up her thigh to keep her knee bare, and leaned forward a little, assisting as he looked closely under the piece of skin that had been sliced.

"Hmmm…I think it's just flesh. I'll stitch it, and you should be fine."

"You sure it's not more serious?"

"Yeah. It just looks like dermis."

"Hurts like hell."

"I'd imagine it does." He got the anesthetic out of his coat and set out all the supplies on the table, and then he unscrewed the cap of the alcohol and tested the water. "It's still hot, but not scalding, so I'm going to wash it out."

Satyrna nodded, holding onto the edges of her chair.

He proceeded to wash the wound with the water, and then the alcohol. Afterward, he sprinkled some of the powdered medicine on her wound before finally stitching it up.

"Does this sort of thing happen often?" He asked as he worked.

She looked up at him, not sure if he was joking or not. "Um, no…Why?"

He shrugged. "You're very calm, considering you almost cut a chunk out of your knee with an axe. You're pale, but that's normal."

She shrugged. "I'm going to be a nurse. Losing my head over blood or cuts would result in a very short career."

"Even when it's your own?"

"Yes."

He leaned forward and kissed her forehead.

Satyrna watched him, a smirk on her lips. "What's that for?"

"A token of my admiration."

She cocked her head slightly. "Not used to girls being able to handle blood, or what?"

"Or pain. Not gentle ones. Teffifa practically bathes in it, but she's a lunatic. You've got a lot of guts. You can handle a lot. I find that admirable. And attractive."

Satyrna smiled.

# 35



After getting stitched and cleaned up, Satyrna returned to working on dinner while Malkarai gathered the wood she'd never retrieved.

She sighed, half-crouching by the stove, her bad leg out to the side, staring at the selection of food items in the box. "We need meat again," she murmured. She stood up, went to her purse, and dug her phone out. She turned it on and dialed Cypha.

Cypha answered after two rings. "Yeah?"

"Hey, when are you coming home?"

"Uhh…in an hour maybe. Why?"

"Could you pick up ground beef, salsa, and lettuce?"

"Yeah. What for?"

"Tacos?"

"Wow, you're spoiling me," she replied, genuinely impressed.

"Stop eating nothing but peanut butter and jelly, and meat won't be such a treat for you."

"Then I won't feel so blessed when I get it."

Satyrna sighed. "I'll see you when you get here."

"'K. Bye."

With nothing to do before the food arrived, she picked up the book Malkarai had been reading and sat down to pick up where she left off.

There was a knock on the door. Satyrna looked up, curious. Dyspro, Cypha, or Malkarai wouldn't knock. They knocked again and Satyrna set the book down and looked out the window. She couldn't see who it was, but there was definitely someone out there. It didn't look like Dyspro and certainly wasn't Malkarai or Cypha.

"Traphian?" she murmured. *He was just here though.* She went to the door and hesitated before opening it. At home, she wouldn't be so cautious, but very few people knew about this house, much less visited it. She opened the door a crack and looked out. Kalyfa was standing outside, his hands in his pockets. She narrowed her eyes. "Go away."

Kalyfa sighed. "Satyrna, please, stop with the animosity."

"No. Go away. I don't want to talk to you."

"Well, that's fine, because I'm not here to talk to you."

Satyrna stared at him through the narrow opening. "Who are you looking for?"

"Faerstathe."

"I told you, he's not here."

"What do you think I am?"

"You don't want me to answer that question," she said.

"Let me in, okay? Whether he's here or not, I know you're in contact with him, and I need to tell him something."

"You can tell me through the door."

"It's not quick, and it's cold out here. Look, I walked all the way here, please, just let me in for a few minutes." He held his hands out and turned from side to side slightly. "I'm unarmed."

"Are you off the clock?"

"I'm never really off the clock, but no, I'm not counting this as an official action."

Satyrna stared unwelcomingly at him for a few moments, but then eventually opened the door. At least, if he was inside, Malkarai would have a chance to see that things were amiss and then not enter.

Kalyfa stepped inside and shut the door behind him, looking around the room.

Satyrna crossed her arms and leaned against the table, not letting him get near one of the chairs. "Well, spill. What do you need to tell him?"

"Do you know what he is?"

"No! I'm working on it, okay?! What the hell do you need to tell him? Say it and get out."

"I would rather tell him myself. I need a decision from him."

"Tell me and I'll let you know his decision."

"Time's of the essence, Satyrna. If you know where he is, I need to know too."

"I'm not letting you see him, Kalyfa."

Kalyfa sighed and walked back toward the bedrooms, glancing in Malkarai's first, then in Dyspro's. Cypha's door was mostly shut, so he reached out to push it open.

She followed, grabbing his sleeve. "What the hell are you doing?"

"Looking to see if he's hiding back here."

"I told you, he's not here! Now get the hell out of there!"

He looked at her calmly, staring her in the eyes for a few moments. "Why are you so defensive, Satyrna?"

She scowled. "Because you are unwanted here, and this is Cypha and Dyspro's home, not mine. Now get out of here. Now."

He sighed. "Satyrna, I don't want to take legal measures with this, okay? If I feel that he is here, I can get a warrant to search the place. Not that there's much left to search."

"Don't be an asshole."

"I *need* to find him."

"So you guys can stick a needle in his arm? Screw you. I'd warn him to leave town before I let you know where he was."

"I have a proposition for him, but I need a decision now. I came here myself because my men have failed to locate him, and this is the most likely place for him to be hiding."

They heard a gentle thunk against the door and Satyrna's gut dropped when she heard the doorknob turn. She spun, mostly just to spare herself letting Kalyfa see the look of dread on her face. She hoped that it was Cypha, home early, but her hopes were in vain.

Malkarai came inside, kicked the door shut behind him, set the hatchet down, and dropped the wood by the fireplace. When he glanced up at Satyrna he noticed Kalyfa behind her in the dim light and, in an instant, had the axe in his hands again, brandished and at a ready stance.

Kalyfa glanced at Satyrna and shook his head.

"Let her go, Desfete."

Kalyfa lifted his arm that Satyrna was still clutching. "Uh, she's holding me, Faerstathe."

Satyrna let go of him and walked over to Malkarai moodily. "He needs to tell you something."

He noticed she was flushed, so he put a hand on her bicep and looked her in the eyes. "You okay?"

"Yeah. I'm fine. Pissed, but fine."

Malkarai let his hand drop to take hers and faced Kalyfa, still holding the axe in his other hand. Satyrna appreciated the gesture, but Kalyfa didn't. He stared coldly at Malkarai.

"What do you want?" Malkarai asked quietly.

"Your friends are going to be here tomorrow. I need to know what the hell we're telling them."

Malkarai's eyes narrowed. "Why aren't you telling them the truth?"

"The truth? The truth that you and your buddy are poorly faking your deaths by just digging yourselves into holes and hiding, making my entire squad look incompetent because we can't find evidence to get these assholes to stop breathing down our necks without wrapping up people we care about in the process? That truth?"

Malkarai frowned, just glaring at him.

"I certainly don't want you here, but I want her and her friends under investigation by your black ops division even less. So, fucking talk to me, so I can try to handle this situation with the least amount of fallout for everyone involved," Kalyfa finished, firmly.

"Fine. What do you want to know?" Malkarai asked, his voice still quiet, but acidic.

"What exactly are you two trying to pull? Why didn't you do your job and go back with Ripper? Why are you *still here*?" Kalyfa gestured to Satyrna. "She's made it pretty clear that you two hitting it off happened as a later thing, so why Cavington? Also, I'm not armed and have no intention to pick another fight with you at this moment, so how about you extend the courtesy and drop that axe?"

Malkarai set the axe down by the fireplace and then looked back at Kalyfa, who moved into the sitting part of the main room before facing him and Satyrna again. "Teffifa lied so Traphian and I can get away from the system. He left seven years ago and I was supposed to go with him, but… shit happened. I was on auto-pilot, so he came here because he knew it would be more difficult for me, but also because we had history here."

"What history?" Kalyfa demanded, his eyes narrowing.

"We were here when the two dark kids were executed."

Kalyfa looked at Satyrna.

"He wanted me to confront him, but more than that, he wanted to wake me up. I was already having enough issues with being sent after my best friend, but then I ran into Satyrna, who dredged up what was a dark enough memory that I'd blocked it out, and then you and the knights confronted me, so I had multiple points of conflict going on – which all could've been solved by finishing my job and leaving, but that was the number one thing I didn't want to do. I was ready to just let you do what you'd threatened, and kill me in the castle, but when I went to tell Traphian to leave, he told me that Teffifa was here and offered his help."

"I did *not* approve that note threatening to neutralize you. What the fuck was your goal with the shit in the castle?"

Malkarai shrugged. "To prove to you that you didn't know what you were messing with, with the added perk of getting those three free again."

"It was protective custody, you asshole. I was trying to keep them safe from your fucking target."

"My target wasn't a threat to anyone."

"They usually are."

"I won't argue that, but maybe if you wanted to have an actual conversation with me, don't bring your squad as backup. I don't really consider all of you a threat, but that doesn't mean I can't see a threat when it's made. I had a fucking phone."

"I was never given a phone number for you. I was just informed you were here and given your target's rap sheet. I expected you to stop being a concern after four hours, but you were still here three days later. I can't tell the rest of my squad *why* I was concerned about you being here, so I've also been dealing with that bullshit, because half of them think I'm just being overprotective of my ex-girlfriend, and *that's* a fucking terrible color to be painted as a controversial leader that's still trying to break the underlying loyalty to the previous ideals for the squad."

Satyrna glanced at Malkarai, but he just kept his eyes on Kalyfa. "I can't help your political issues."

"No, you can't, but good news, I've already thought about how I would like this to play out."

"How?"

"You finish first. Why didn't you two leave?"

"Traphian says staying put is safer than running away and setting off alerts elsewhere when we're supposed to cease existing – especially because Cavington isn't under federal jurisdiction."

Kalyfa's eyebrows knitted up. "Yeah… that's actually smart."

"He's pretty intelligent, and he's also been doing this for seven years."

"Is he here too?"

"No, he's hiding somewhere else. I'm here because Satyrna was taking care of my injuries. Otherwise, I probably would've found somewhere more neutral or at least less obvious to hide. The last thing I wanted to do was put her and her friends in more danger, but I needed medical help."

"At least we have the same goal. Okay," Kalyfa said as he crossed his arms, "this is what I propose. If you two are determined to stay and sever all contact with your division, then I will help."

Satyrna's eyebrows raised in surprise. Malkarai's eyes narrowed slightly, obviously more distrustful than excited.

"This is not because I like you or give a shit about your freedom. I can see the advantages of doing this, so I want payment. I'm going to go along with this lie that you and Ripper concocted. I'd like to fake a compromised crime scene and gather evidence to help support it."

"Okay… It would have to be good. We're trained in crime scene protocols, even if we don't normally care about them in the field."

"So are we. I'm not concerned about my people's abilities. I'm not doing this for free though. I'm ready to just hand you two over if you don't agree to payment."

"What do you want from me?"

"I want you to work for me. Unofficially and off the record."

Malkarai made a bewildered face at first. "I thought you hated me."

"Oh, I am not fond of you, no. However, you apparently have skills. I want the knights to get stronger and be more effective more than I care about stroking my ego. We would work out the details of what this entails later, but I'd want you to train us and also keep an eye out for federal threats, and possibly help us with them if they arose. Not directly, because I wouldn't want them to get wind of you still being alive, but there's plenty you can do without being visible."

Malkarai shrugged slightly. "That sounds like something I could do."

"I'll put this all into place immediately, but I want it to hinge on something."

"What?"

"I want you to fight me."

Malkarai's eyebrows knitted up. "That ended poorly for you last time."

"Both times other people were involved. I want a fair, one-on-one fight so I can more properly judge your abilities and make sure this is worth it to me. No tricks, no games, no outside involvement. Show me you can actually fight like you claim because right now your supposed skills seem like a tall tale."

Malkarai sighed. "What's the point?"

"Professionally, I want your skills to work for this town in return for our discretion, and this is proof you have them. Personally, prove to me this is worth the headache, paperwork, and cover-ups."

"How much of this has jealousy motivating it?" Satyrna grumbled.

Kalyfa eyed her briefly. "I won't lie and say jealousy is uninvolved."

"We were done before Malkarai was in the picture."

"I know that. It doesn't mean that I'm not bitter."

"Just me, or Traphian too?" Malkarai asked.

Kalyfa looked back at him. "For the fight, just you. I'm not pleased he infiltrated our base as easily as he did, but you're the main cause of my irritation right now. I'd prefer that he was also involved in this deal, but we can figure out how later. He hasn't been a part of this system for seven years."

"I'm not his keeper. He'll have to decide if he wants to be part of this too."

"Do you know where he is?"

"Yes."

"Do you think he'll agree to it?"

"Probably, but I'm still not going to decide for him."

"We need to take action tonight before your people are in town."

"Let me call him." Malkarai looked at Satyrna. "Can I use your phone? Is it charged?"

She glanced between Malkarai and Kalyfa before looking back to Malkarai and nodding. "I thought he didn't have a phone."

"His room does."

"Oh, right. I'll get it." She pulled her hand free of his and went back to Dyspro's room, limping after taking a step, having forgotten her knee was injured until it painfully reminded her.

Kalyfa's eyebrows knitted up as he watched her go, looking down to see the large bandage around her mostly exposed knee. "What's wrong with your leg, Satyrna?"

She rummaged around in the dark in Dyspro's room for a few moments before coming back out. "I fell earlier and cut my leg with the axe."

He looked alarmed. "How bad was it? Do you need to go to the hospital?"

"The hospital was too far away. Malkarai cleaned it and stitched it shut," she replied as she handed Malkarai her phone after typing in a passcode.

Kalyfa looked at Malkarai critically. "The hospital would've been safer."

"I can't show my face in public," he replied as he went over to the extra bedroom, where he had the number stashed in his coat.

"He knows how to take care of a wound and give stitches," Satyrna said defensively, looking at Kalyfa. "Also, I'm almost a nurse, I know something about what to do."

Kalyfa continued giving her a disgruntled look before nodding to her knee. "Keep an eye on it and see a doctor if it doesn't look right."

"Yes, yes, I will," she said with a sigh.

Malkarai came back out to the main room, looking at Kalyfa, the phone still up to his ear. "He agreed. When do you want to do this?"

"Now. We're running out of time to fix up and edit things."

"Okay." Malkarai looked at the floor. "Not sure if you heard him, but now," he said to Traphian. "Meet us on Main Street. Just get on it and walk east until you meet up with us."

Kalyfa nodded slowly in agreement. "Make sure he has whatever he'd have on his person if he was fighting you."

Malkarai pulled the phone from his ear, searched the screen, and then switched the phone to speaker mode. "Bring your sword, backpack, and coat." He looked up at Kalyfa. "Are you going to take our things from us?"

"Depends on the items. I plan to pretend that someone found you, called you in, the cops responded and then the morgue collected you, but you were cremated after a thorough examination and recording, because we get random criminals showing up frequently, and we don't store their bodies because we want the space for actual citizens."

"That's convenient."

"We have little pity for when the US's garbage wanders in here just to die."

Malkarai snorted.

"Well, this sounds exciting and underhanded. I'm definitely in," Traphian said over the phone.

Satyrna smirked, covering up her mouth to stifle a laugh.

"Great. Get moving. Come on, Faerstathe. I have a shitload of work to do tonight."

"See you soon," Malkarai said to Traphian and then hit the 'end call' button before handing Satyrna her phone. "When do you want to do this fight, anyway?"

"The end of the month. You're injured, and I have a hole of my own to deal with."

"All right. Let me get dressed," Malkarai said before going into the extra room to get his coat and weapons.

Kalyfa eyed him as he went.

"What?" Satyrna demanded.

"Where are you staying? That's a twin in there, isn't it?"

"Dyspro's room," she replied flatly, still staring at him.

He looked back at her but didn't say anything else.

Malkarai came back out after a few minutes, belt and cloak on and his sword in hand. He brushed Satyrna's cheek with the thumb of his free hand and kissed her. "I'll be back soon."

She nodded slightly. "You're upsetting him," she whispered very quietly.

He smiled wickedly. "I know; isn't it satisfying?"

She giggled quietly and pecked his lips before he sheathed his sword and turned to Kalyfa, who looked rather displeased.

Malkarai motioned to the door. "After you."

Kalyfa moved to the door and exited, not giving Satyrna another glance.

On their way into town, Kalyfa said only one thing, when they were still in the woods. "You hurt her, and I'll cut your balls off."

Malkarai paused, considering how to answer this and not get decked. "I'm sure I'll be too busy taking care of her and whatever problems she gets herself into to ever hurt her."

Kalyfa didn't reply, only grunted, apparently accepting that as a suitable response.

# 36

Malkarai glanced at Traphian as he looked all the way around them while they followed Kalyfa into a building near the police station. The place was empty and most of the lights were off, but Kalyfa had keys for everywhere he was taking them.

"Anxious?" Kalyfa asked offhandedly.

"Yeah," Traphian said. "Going into official buildings with a law enforcer is kind of antithetic to everything I've been living for the past how many years."

Malkarai smirked and Kalyfa shook his head but didn't reply. "I called in a few knights to help us, for speed, mostly."

"Are they read-in?"

"No, but they're ones I trust to keep this quiet, even without knowing all the details. I called in Garevn and Kariden." When Malkarai didn't respond, Kalyfa glanced back at him. "Josh and Brendan."

"Oh," he replied, approvingly.

"The rest are too polarized for me to deal with at this exact moment, or I've kept them uninvolved."

"That works for me."

"Who are they?" Traphian asked Malkarai.

"Josh is Satyrna, Cypha, Dyspro, and Barry's friend. Brendan is Patricia's boyfriend."

"Oh, right."

They followed Kalyfa downstairs and down a dimly lit tile hallway, past a sign that said, 'Morgue' and into a room that was labeled, 'Autopsy Theater.'

Josh, Brendan, and a shorter woman with brown hair pulled back in a half-pony, jeans, and a T-shirt underneath a stained lab coat were standing near one of the two metal autopsy tables in the room. They all looked over as Kalyfa, Malkarai, and Traphian entered.

Josh made a small noise, impressed. Brendan smirked. "And that's why you're the boss."

Kalyfa gave him a perplexed look. "What do you mean?"

"Twelve of us couldn't find a trace of either of them, but you found them both."

"Oh. Satyrna and Cypha were hiding Faerstathe, and Faerstathe called his friend," Kalyfa said offhandedly as he walked over to the woman. "I paid them an unofficial visit. Since none of this is following the rules, it seemed pointless to keep dancing."

"Yeah, fair."

"I wouldn't have asked any of you to do that. It was fine that all of you followed the rules. We're out of time though." Kalyfa turned to address everyone instead of just the knights. "Anyway, this is Traphian and Malkarai. Josh, Brendan, and Lisa, our city coroner."

Lisa waved halfheartedly. "Well, on Monday and Tuesday, anyway."

"Yeah, which is another reason I think this will work. This office is not fully staffed because we don't need it to be. We're going to fake some photos and document your belongings, and then after we're done here, we'll go out to the woods and take a few crime scene photos. I borrowed a police camera so they can enter it properly into their evidence."

"Are there date and timestamps on the camera?" Malkarai asked.

"Nope, it's pretty primitive, and not digital. We're also using two different cameras. Lisa will use her own."

"Are you going to confiscate some of our stuff?" Traphian asked, shifting as he crossed his arms.

"We do confiscate found weapons, but I intend for those to be lost to bureaucracy because I'd rather you remained armed. Do either of you have wallets on you?"

"I mean, yeah, but it doesn't have my real name in it," Traphian said with a shrug.

Malkarai shook his head. "At this stage, I'd have left it in my bag."

"Where would your bag be?"

"On a normal mission, in my car or at a police station or with my handler. In this case, somewhere I stashed it."

"Okay, that will just be missing. Did either of you have a phone?"

"No," Traphian replied immediately.

"Teffifa took mine – and my badge with my credentials."

"Okay, that helps us muddy the waters," Kalyfa said before looking at Lisa. "We'll want you to take samples so they can DNA test them if they want."

"You bet."

"All right, we have a lot of work to do, so let's get started. Lisa, give us orders," Kalyfa said, turning to her.

Satyrna woke and opened her eyes when she felt a hand on her shoulder. Malkarai was crouched in front of her at the side of the bed that he'd been using for the past few days. She sat up, rubbing her eye with the back of her hand. "Jeez, I fell asleep…"

"Don't get up on my account."

"No, no, I was waiting for you. I wanted to make sure nothing happened."

"Nothing happened. It went fine. Traphian and I are now legally dead. Kalyfa has promised to get our accounts and identities straightened out in a few days. Traphian's also gonna move again. He really does respect Traphian more than me. He was confused as hell that Kalyfa was being so nice."

"Yeah, well, Traphian isn't after me." She shrugged. "He's a douchebag."

"A douchebag who is so not over you."

"Yeah. Whatever. That's his dysfunction, not mine."

Malkarai played with the end of a strand of her hair, smiling at her. "I can't blame him. You're pretty enchanting."

She sighed, blushing. "You realize what this means, right?"

"Hmm?"

"You're safe."

"Not quite. I have to stay invisible for a few days."

"But you will be."

"Mm-hmm."

"We get to spend more time together without being paranoid about who's looking around the corner."

"So we hope, yes."

"You can meet my parents."

Malkarai raised his brow. "Maybe I could go back into hiding again."

She poked him. "I'm serious, Malkarai. I want you to meet them."

"Why?"

"Because I'm taking this seriously. I want them to know who you are so they can be at ease."

"They'll probably be more at ease without knowing me, Satyrna."

She frowned. "Knock it off, okay? Being dark does not make you a bad person. Stop thinking like that. It's bad enough other people think it, darks shouldn't think it too."

He sighed and said, after a few moments, "You're that serious, huh?"

She grabbed his hand with both of hers. "Yes. I don't know how things will go down the line, but I want to try and make this work. So, I wanna do it right, even though all this strange shit is going on. I want to at least do this normally."

He shrugged. "Well, I guess we're following your lead then, cuz I'm not an expert on normal."

"Okay, well, truth; being honest is important here. You're putting a lot on the line for this, but I am too. No, I won't die if things don't work out how we want them to, but I'm going to put in as much as I ask from you, okay?"

He nodded. "Sounds fair."

"Yes, I am a virgin. Surprise. My panties have never seen the light of day before today. Well…you know what I mean."

He smirked. "I probably could've guessed. That doesn't matter to me either way. I'm not."

She raised her brow. "Okay, surprise on my end."

He laughed, a little uncomfortable. "Really?"

"Yeah, you strike me as very naïve."

He shrugged. "I'm not naïve. I'm… very shy and private. I lived with the same people my whole life. There were five other people my age, and I was the youngest. Yeah, we talked about sex, but that was it. Maybe the others did it regularly, I don't know, but I spent most of my time with Arista. It was her work, so she wasn't curious. Girls were told all about it – and I do mean all about it, and guys were just told, 'Don't do it. We'll beat the shit out of you.' So, I just kinda stayed away from it."

"You did it."

He shrugged. "She knew what she was doing. I didn't. I was confused, and then after she was gone, I was too hurt to get close to anyone. I'm done talking about that. It makes me embarrassed."

Satyrna smiled and kissed his forehead, which was, indeed, a little warm. "I may be naïve in terms of the world, but there are a lot of things that make you uncomfortable, and I think they're cute."

"Thanks," he replied sarcastically.

"Did you eat supper?"

"Yeah. Traphian and I ate in his room after we were all done."

"There're leftovers from tacos."

"I'll have some tomorrow. I'm fine tonight. I'm tired."

She started to get off the bed. "I'll let you go to–"

He grabbed her arm and gently held her. "Nah, stay there."

She stared at him. "Huh?"

He let go and started untying his boots. "Stay with me for a little while."

She blushed fiercely. "I'm wearing your pajamas. What are you gonna wear?"

He glanced at her and snickered. "Relax. I'll leave my jeans on. I just wanna cuddle a little. I'm finally letting myself get excited that I get to be with you."

"Letting yourself?"

He pulled up his pant legs and started unstrapping his knives. She hadn't even realized he'd put them on. "I was setting myself up for the worst, so I was hesitant to get too close. But, thanks to Kalyfa and how much he wants you to be safe and happy, I'll get to stay."

"I was so afraid he'd try and turn you over."

He stood up and shook his pants back down. "He's apparently smart enough to see something he can use to his advantage if he keeps his personal grudge partially out of the equation. Besides, I had my sword and my knives, so he wouldn't have been able to pull that shit, even if he'd called in a lot of other knights to help without us realizing it."

Satyrna sighed and lay down on the pillow again as he lay down next to her and wrapped his arms around her.

"Malkarai…"

"Hmmm?"

"Since it's gonna be safe… will you tell me?"

"Tell you…?"

"What you were?"

He brushed her hair out of her face and kissed her. "Satyrna, I can't do that."

"Even with them so close?"

"Especially with them so close. We'll revisit that later, okay?"

"I have other ways of finding out, you know."

He stopped moving, not taking that lightly.

"I don't want to have to resort to it, but I will if I need to."

"Satyrna… I can't tell you, okay? I guess, I'd rather you waited for me to tell you, but if you really can't wait, I can't stop you from searching." He sounded hurt.

She frowned and buried her head under his chin, trying to ignore the sentimental part of her conscience telling her she was a jerk.

Malkarai put a hand on the back of her head, feeling unsettled. Despite his tiredness, she fell asleep before he did. He didn't bother to rouse her when he realized she'd fallen asleep, just gave her a kiss and made sure his arm was secure around her so she wouldn't roll backward and fall off the side of the twin bed.

He rested his cheek on her head gently, holding her close.

# 37



Kalyfa bent his elbows so his hands were near his shoulders and stretched his arms backward, carefully, grimacing as he flexed his shoulders. His back was stiff and he was tired, but he was expecting the ASA rep and her subordinates, so clocking in late to catch up on sleep wasn't an option today.

He was able to take a long drink of his water before there was a knock on the door. He set the bottle down and sighed as he went over to open it.

"Good morning," he said, motioning for them to enter. "Stika Karne, right?" he asked the first woman who came in.

She nodded and held out a hand. "Nice to meet you in person, Kalyfa." Stika had a kind but tense face, her brown hair pulled up in a ponytail. She was middle-aged, tall, and seemed strong. She was dressed in a black suit with a blue blouse underneath. "This is Swip Reed and Teffifa Ripper," she said, gesturing to her companions as they entered, in that order.

Swip was a handsome, fit young man with short, light brown hair and a clean-shaven face. He was wearing a dark blue winter coat and jeans. Teffifa was wearing a long, leather trench coat that was open to show a red T-shirt and torn jeans. Her black and red hair and red eyes contrasted starkly with her average, approachable-looking fellows. She was much shorter than both of them as well.

Although Kalyfa had seen photos of all three of them, this was the first time he'd seen any in person. He'd looked up their records recently enough, that he knew that Stika was only ten years older than him and Reed and Ripper were the same age as the two thorns in his side, so barely in their twenties, but all of them put him on edge, partially but not entirely because he knew what they were capable of.

He nodded to Swip and Teffifa and then shut the door behind them and motioned for them to come over to his desk. As they sat down, he said, "Thank you for being patient. I've had a selection of my people looking for them all weekend."

"Have you had any developments since we talked yesterday?"

He leaned forward against his desk. "So, one of my men checked with the police and found out that someone had found two people in the woods Saturday, but because there was no present danger, the police had handled the whole incident without notifying us. They took photos and found no identification, so they classified them as John Does and sent them to the city morgue. We get random non-citizens entering town frequently. They only need to check in or register if they intend to move here. However, when it comes to criminals, if they do anything illegal, they're subject to our laws once they step on our soil. With that said, finding random people dead is unfortunately not a new situation here. People like to come here, on what they feel is neutral ground, and deal with their disagreements. Sometimes that results in bodies that don't belong to us. Our morgue is not meant to hold bodies for a lengthy period, so if we have no ID to notify next of kin and they are not citizens, the coroner will perform an autopsy, record all findings and belongings, and then send them for cremation. The coroner is only in the office on Monday and Tuesday, and cremations will usually be performed Wednesdays or Thursdays, depending on the availability of the technician."

Stika was frowning, looking concerned. "So, they were found and subjected to this process?"

"Yes, it appears so. One of my men contacted the police on Sunday, but the officers involved were not back in the office until Tuesday, and by then they'd already been autopsied and sent for cremation, which was done on Wednesday, which was when I was finally looped in."

She sighed softly, looking at his desk.

Teffifa was and had been watching Kalyfa closely, but Swip looked from Kalyfa to Stika after a few moments.

"They did take photographs of the scene and the coroner has records, as well as her findings from the autopsies. I can get those records for you."

"Yes, please," Stika said, looking back up at him. "What about their belongings?"

"Well, the weapons are confiscated and kept by the police force. I can see about trying to get them, but it might take a little bit. If their belongings are not identifiable, they are donated. Their clothes looked pretty messy, so I think they were disposed of."

"What about money?"

"Money is usually held in case of someone claiming them after the fact, but I don't remember seeing any money identified in their belongings."

"You have a list of those effects?"

Kalyfa nodded and leaned back, picking up a folder from the side of his desk. "I need to make copies for you still. I just got these when I got in this morning – which was only a few minutes ago."

"Okay. We have several things we need to try to retrieve."

"All right? Like what?"

"Malkarai drove here, so we need to locate his car. He also had a computer on him. While it's unlikely anyone could access protected information on it, it's still an asset of significant value."

Kalyfa nodded and opened up the folder, flipping over a few pages and scanning the list of effects for Malkarai. "I don't see keys or a computer on him…"

"We have the keys. Teffifa grabbed them before she left."

"Oh, okay," he replied, glancing at Teffifa. "Not his computer?"

"It wasn't on him," she said flatly.

"It was probably in his bag," Stika added. "It might be in his car, but we won't know until we locate it."

Kalyfa nodded thoughtfully. "I can check if we have any cars impounded."

"I'd appreciate that."

"I can track it," Swip piped up, holding up his phone.

Kalyfa gave him an appraising look. "Can you track any vehicle?"

Swip smirked. "Nah. We put chips in our cars. As long as it hasn't malfunctioned or fallen off, I'll be able to initiate and track it. Checking if it's impounded is still helpful though, because I won't be able to retrieve it if it's locked up."

"Okay. Give me the information, and I'll see what I can find." Kalyfa stood up. "Let me go and copy this for you first, and then you can go and look around."

After Kalyfa had left, Swip looked at Stika. "I've never been involved in something like this – is that normal?"

Stika looked at him, her expression still tense. "Which part?" she asked patiently.

"The whole cremation after less than a week thing."

"Unfortunately, yes. These seceded towns *are* frequent targets for our criminals for exactly the reasons he listed. Not every town has that short of a timeframe, but most have something similar. It's, unfortunately, very appealing to people who want to get rid of bodies."

Swip swore under his breath. "Wow, you learn something new every day…"

"Perhaps we should have a special class on seceded towns. We usually don't have to chase people, and this is out of our jurisdiction, but obviously, they are still something we can deal with."

"Yeah."

"I should've tried to drag them to my car," Teffifa muttered, staring at the back window, above the filing cabinets.

Swip turned, looking at her. "What purpose would that have served?"

"We'd have actual bodies to deal with. I figured they wouldn't be found that easy in the woods, but obviously, these people spend more time outside than I do."

"You made the right call, Teffifa," Stika said. "I'm sure Traphian came here on purpose. He knew it would logistically be more difficult for Malkarai and us. I just wish it hadn't ended up like this."

"Yeah," Teffifa muttered.

Stika sighed and pulled her phone out of her pocket when it started vibrating and then ringing. She looked at the caller ID and hesitated with her thumb over the 'decline' button.

Swip glanced at it, seeing 'Carlisle' on the screen. "Are you gonna talk to him?"

"I don't want to, but I probably should. Apologize to Desfete for me if I'm still talking when he returns," she said before standing up and swiping to answer the call.

She walked to the corner of the room, her head down as she greeted him tersely.

Swip watched Stika for a few moments before looking at Teffifa and taking in her bothered expression. Her eyebrows were knitted up and eyes darting like she was thinking, mouth pulled in a frown. "You okay, Teff?"

"Mm," she replied shortly.

"Are you stuck?"

"Just thinking."

He smirked. "Ah, that's why you look like you're in pain."

Teffifa's eyes snapped to him and then narrowed before she backhanded him, smirking. "Shut up, ass."

He laughed and put his hands up too late to block her.

Her smirk faded quickly, but he looked pleased anyway.

"I hope this car chip tracking thing works. I've never had to use it outside of testing it in our own parking lot."

"Oh no, I'm sure you're so sad about playing easter egg hunt with a car," she said sarcastically.

"Gotta find the fun where you can. This whole situation is shitty." He was quiet for a moment before saying, "A shit-uation if you will…"

"I'm gonna report you for unprofessionalism and Stika'll leave you in the car all day," Teffifa threatened, entirely kidding, although her tone didn't sound like it.

"She can't do that," he replied nonchalantly. "You can't talk to people, and she's too stressed out. You both need me today."

"You tell yourself whatever you need to get through the day."

Stika sighed audibly as she came back over by them. "That's just wonderful," she grumbled.

"What's wrong?" Swip asked.

The door opened, so Stika waved a hand dismissively. "Later."

Kalyfa came over, flipping through the papers before he handed a new folder to Stika. "There you go, that's a copy of everything I've got. I expect to get some more information in today, and then I'll make copies of that for you too."

"Thank you," she replied, taking the folder.

"Did you want me to assign a knight so you had someone local to help?"

"Er, just a phone number is plenty."

"All right. Just call me, then. I'll let you know before I leave the office, but I expect to be here most of the day."

Stika nodded. "Thank you. I wasn't sure how long we were going to stay in town, but we'll for sure be gone before the end of the day."

"Oh," Kalyfa said flatly. "There's no rush."

"I appreciate that, but unfortunately, I'll have to get back to the agency sooner rather than later. Something came up."

"I see."

"We'll check back in person at least once before we leave. Let me know when you get more paperwork to collect. You have my cell number."

"I will."

"Thanks." Stika nodded toward the door. "Teffifa, Swip. Let's go find the car."

"Oh, right, the specs," Swip said as he stood up.

Kalyfa went around the desk and pulled over a notepad, sliding it to Swip, who picked up a pen and wrote down the make, model, color, year, and the license plate number and state of the car.

"You had that memorized…?" Kalyfa said, impressed.

Swip grinned. "Cars are my thing. Let Stika know if you guys have it in impound."

Kalyfa nodded and slid the notepad in front of him as Swip followed Teffifa and Stike to the door.

Outside of the office, Stika said, quietly, "Carlisle is coming to Marion." She sounded deeply annoyed, bordering angry.

"What the hell for?" Swip asked.

"He has nothing better he can do, so he's showing up in person to pretend he has a dick to wave around." She cleared her throat, composing herself better. "He had a special interest in both Malkarai and Traphian, and this did not go the way he wanted it to."

"Great," Teffifa grumbled sourly.

"Yeah," Stika agreed, glancing down the hallway before opening the door to the stairs. "This shit is his fault. I get to do the politics dance of making that abundantly clear without being a bitch."

"Good luck," Swip said sincerely.

"Thanks. At least we're going back with evidence. Let's make it even better by finding the car and a computer."

Swip pulled his phone from his pocket again. "On it."

Satyrna woke with the side of her face against Malkarai's shoulder. He'd shifted so he was on his back, holding her at his uninjured side, her arm across his chest. She didn't move, listening to him breathe.

She shut her eyes, breathing in his warmth.

She was happy – happy that something seemed to be going right, happy that she felt comfortable where she was, albeit a little nervous having spent the night in bed with a guy, even though she knew it had just been sleeping. She felt like this was something she could get used to though. However, that's why she wanted more than anything to know exactly what it was that she was holding.

She could hear Cypha was up and moving around, so she wasn't surprised when she heard the door creak open slightly. She opened an eye a tiny amount to see Cypha raise her brow and shake her head before going back to the main room.

Satyrna settled back, deciding to deal with that later, enjoying her position far too much to bother explaining now.

The door creaking must have roused Malkarai though, because she felt his arm squeeze her back slightly and then all the muscles in his torso tensed as he stretched. He relaxed with a sigh and looked down at her when she opened her eyes.

"Morning," he said softly, a smile on his lips.

She smiled back and burrowed in under his chin again. "Morning. We've been caught."

"Oh? By who?"

"Cypha."

He shrugged. "I'm only concerned if you are."

"I'm not. So, what happened to just cuddling?"

"I dunno. You're the one who decided to fall asleep. Who am I to deny you?"

She shook her head slightly, playing with his sleeve idly.

"Are you supposed to work today?"

"Yup."

"When?"

"I'd say, judging by the light outside, I probably should've been there already."

"Oops."

"Yeah. Whatever, I'll get there when I get there." She shifted so she could look him in the face. "So, you've gotta hide for a few days, right?"

"Mm-hmm."

"What about after that?"

"Kalyfa said that we'd get things worked out so we can stay under their radar but could live normally."

"Are you gonna have to get another name?"

He paused, thinking that over. "Yeah, probably."

"What are you gonna use?"

"Well… I'm considering using Rafiane's last name – Tavelante. Whether I'm her brother or not, they wouldn't expect me to use that name, and there's a decent chance they don't know about it."

"Only a decent?"

Malkarai shrugged. "I mean, it's the government. I don't know what kind of searches they did when I showed up on their doorstep. That person has a birth certificate somewhere, but he's apparently missing."

"Your first name is pretty unique… I suppose it wouldn't be too hard to find that if they were looking."

He nodded slightly, looking up, thinking. "Well, I could just change it slightly, use that Biblical name. My signature is kinda illegible anyway."

"Malachi?"

"Yeah."

She was quiet for a few moments. "I like yours better."

He snickered and squeezed her momentarily. "Thanks. We'll work that out later. You need to get to work."

"I'd rather stay here."

"Me too. But, responsibility beckons. We'll do this again soon."

He kissed her forehead and she sighed and climbed out of bed. It was very cold outside of the blankets. She immediately felt goosebumps on her legs. "Eeek…"

He laughed at her as he sat up and put his feet on the floor. "Go put normal pants on."

She touched the gauze on her knee, wincing slightly. "I'm going to rebandage my knee first…"

"All right."

Malkarai followed Satyrna into the main room, where she greeted Cypha and then dug through the bag of first aid supplies before sitting by the fire.

Cypha eyed both of them suspiciously. "Good morning, guys."

Malkarai couldn't help but smirk as he sat down on the hearth. "Morning."

Satyrna looked at her after pulling her old bandage off. "So, what's new with you?"

Cypha crossed her arms. "Not as much as with you."

"Oh, now that's not fair; I asked you first," she replied pleasantly as she started cleaning away dried blood from the uncut skin.

"I got a call back from that place earlier."

Satyrna stopped and looked up. "Really?"

"They want me to start training on Monday."

Satyrna squealed. "That's great!"

"Congratulations," Malkarai said, a lot more calmly.

"Thanks. Okay, now what the hell were you two doing?" She paused. "If you think I don't wanna know the answer, don't say a damn thing."

Satyrna laughed. "Relax, Cypha."

She pointed at Malkarai. "If she gets pregnant Dyspro and I are gonna screw you up."

Malkarai raised his brow.

Satyrna chucked the roll of medical tape at her. It hit her in the shoulder. "Cypha! Come on!"

Cypha looked at Satyrna, still serious, not at all abashed. "Better us than your father."

Satyrna glared at her.

"We never did anything, Cypha," Malkarai said. "She fell asleep and I didn't care to move her."

"You could've used Dyspro's bed," she insisted.

"But I didn't want to," he replied simply.

Satyrna was still glowering. "Cypha, whether you guys like it or not, he and I are together now. Thanks to Kalyfa, we can stay together. Now stop policing us, and don't threaten him."

"Oh. Congratulations. I actually don't mind; I was just standing up for your sensibilities because I know how *you* are." Cypha looked back and forth between them. "So everything went okay with the knights last night?"

"Yes. Traphian and I have to keep hiding for a little bit, but we get to stay."

"Good job on Kalyfa for sucking his pride up enough to do that."

Malkarai smirked.

Satyrna held out her hand to Cypha. "Can I have the tape back?"

She reached over, picked it up from the ground, and tossed it to her. "Do you have to work today?"

"Yeah, I should've been there fifteen minutes ago. I'll use this thing on my knee as an excuse." She looked warningly at Cypha. "Not a word to my parents about us sleeping together."

Cypha made a face. "Of course not."

Malkarai smirked but didn't say anything.

Satyrna placed the last piece of tape on her leg, smoothing it with her fingers. Then she stood up and headed back to Dyspro's bedroom to change.

Cypha leaned against the table, her chin propped up with a hand. "I like you better than the others she's landed," she said, unsolicited.

"Um, thanks?"

"It's about time she actually was serious about a guy she dated. Kalyfa's the only one she even had a second thought about, but it really wasn't the second thought she should've had."

"You weren't a fan?"

"No way. He's fine, whatever. Him and her? No, that was a terrible match-up, and I'm glad she eventually ended it."

"Why was it terrible?"

"If you can't hang with a person's friends, I don't think that's a good match. He did not mesh with us. We're too feral for him. Besides, him being around was one of the reasons Josh ducked out. No one wants to hang out with their boss."

Malkarai snorted, amused. "Noted. Uh, if it makes you feel better, I wore my jeans to bed. I have no desire to push her to do anything she doesn't want to."

Cypha waved a hand at him. "Whatever, you're her boyfriend. If I had been aware of you being that serious before this conversation, it would've gone differently. I knew she was crushing on you bad, but I didn't know you liked her back."

He nodded slowly. "I'm willing to give this a try."

Satyrna came out with new clothes on. "Your shorts are on your bed. I hope we have donuts or something today. I'm starving."

"Maybe I'll come and meet you for lunch," Cypha offered.

"Sounds like fun. Malkarai, you want me to bring some more books out here for you or something?"

"That'd be great," he replied, mutedly enthusiastic.

She smirked. "I'll see what I can dig up." She threw her coat on and grabbed her purse. "See you guys tonight."

"See ya at lunch."

"Oh, yeah. At lunch." She waved as she went out the door. On her way down the path, Satyrna took out her phone and opened it, deliberating as she stared at the screen until it went black. Then she hit a button, opened her contacts, and called Josh.

He answered, sounding very lethargic and muffled. "Mmello?"

"Morning, Josh. Sorry, did I wake you?"

"Oh, no. I was awake."

She smirked. She had totally woken him up. "I have a request."

"What's that?"

"I'd like you to find something out for me. Could you?"

She heard him groan like he was stretching. "Depends on what it is, Saty."

"I figure you'd have access to this – it sounds like the knights have some information on it."

"On what?"

"I need to know what Malkarai is."

"Er… what do you mean, exactly?"

"What he does – or, did, I guess."

He sighed. He sounded more awake now. "I've been trying to find that out myself. I figured you'd know by now."

"No. He hasn't told me."

"Hasn't or won't?"

"Well, both. Do you know what Kalyfa offered to him?"

"Yeah. He had me help last night. The ASA, whatever that stands for, is supposed to be here by now."

"Mm-hmm. Damn."

"Hey, Satyrna?"

"Yeah?"

"Is it true? You and Faerstathe are together?"

"Yes."

"Was he there when I was earlier this week?"

"No. He didn't show up until a day or so later."

"Okay, you guys didn't lie to me."

"No, we just omitted some things."

"Now that this is being handled, we can all go back to being open with each other, right?"

"As long as you're going to, sure," she replied, glancing around before crossing a street, limping slightly.

"I was being open with you guys."

She sighed. "Do you think any of the other knights know what he is?"

"Just Kalyfa, I think. Brendan tried helping me. He couldn't find anything either. According to the data we have access to, your boy doesn't exist."

"Huh… That's weird. Rafiane was able to find him. I wonder if she used a paper trail or not."

"Who?"

"Uh, she claims to be his sister. Dyspro's been running around with her. He's been estranged from his family since he was little, but she was able to find him this summer and catch up to him here because he stopped moving for a long enough period of time, and she claims he's her older brother."

"And Dyspro's running around with her?"

"Yeah. He thinks she's cute."

He sighed. "Why the hell won't he talk to me?"

"He's being a whiny little bitch. Just walk up to him and make him talk to you."

Josh laughed. "Wow, Saty. You're in a feisty mood this morning."

"I'm aggravated. I want to know. I need to know. And I don't want to go to Kalyfa to find out. I don't want to give him that satisfaction."

"Why won't Faerstathe tell you himself?"

"I don't know. He keeps feeding me this line of bull that I'm safer not knowing, and he keeps saying the contracts say he can't say anything. I think he just doesn't want to be guilty of squealing if I decide to dump him. I know he's insecure."

"He does seem more akin to shadows than people."

"Yes, but I wish he'd change his tune. I need to know what I'm up against!"

"You said Kalyfa's willing to tell you?"

"He told me he would if Malkarai wouldn't, yes. But I don't want to let him feel good about himself. He's only being this generous to Malkarai because being around Malkarai makes me happy and he found a way to benefit from it himself."

Josh sighed. "Even your enemies love you, Satyrna. I'd love to be in your shoes."

"No, you wouldn't. You'd be walking with a limp and have a boyfriend who doesn't exist and an ex-boyfriend who is still bothering the hell out of you, as well as an overprotective sister breathing down your neck, an unknown government agency to be afraid of, and you'd be late for work."

He laughed. "Okay, point taken. Well, I don't know what to tell you. I can't help. Sorry."

She sighed in resignation. "Will you meet me at work at two?"

"What for?"

"Will you go with me to see Kalyfa?"

"You're gonna ask him?"

"Yeah. I gotta know. Especially if the ASA's in town. Damn it, I wish I even knew what that meant!"

"Yeah, I'll meet you. Will you answer your phone if I call?"

"Probably not. I'll call you back if I see it though."

He snickered. "All right. I'll see you at two."

"Bye, Josh."

"Bye."

After Josh hung up, Satyrna looked at the phone to call the store and explain to whichever parent had opened why she wasn't there yet.

Swip frowned, staring at his phone and using his fingertips to move the digital map around a few times, trying to figure out why the blinking dot on it was saying there should be a car right here.

Stika was talking on the phone, sitting in the car they'd driven from South Dakota that day, on the shoulder of a county road. Teffifa was standing a few feet behind him, her hands in her pockets.

"What's wrong with it?" she asked.

Swip huffed, looking around again before crouching and looking in the scrubby gravel-strewn grass of an ill-used road or ATV path. "Nothing, I don't think. I was kidding when I was talking about the chip falling off. They're well secured; it would have to be purposefully tampered with to fall off…"

"What color is it?"

"Dark blue four-door sedan, Iowa plates."

Teffifa walked forward and crouched down next to Swip, reaching a hand in his coat pocket and digging around.

He gave her a surprised look, lifting an arm out of the way. "What the hell?"

She found the keys in it, looked at the icon on the remote, and then glanced at the silver car behind them. Then she stood, went around to his other side, and dug around for the other set of keys. Once she found them, she stuffed the first set in his second pocket and stood up, holding it above her head while she hit the 'lock' button repeatedly.

Swip stood up as they both heard a horn honk in the trees in front of them.

Teffifa smirked smugly, looked at the keys so she could find the 'unlock' button, hit it twice, and then tossed him the keys before walking the path to the woods.

Swip caught the keys and sighed as he followed her.

About twenty yards from the road, parked amongst trees and brush, was the car. It was dusted in snow, but the tail lights were illuminated from Teffifa using the remote.

"Hold up," he said, switching to the camera app on his phone.

Teffifa stood back while he took a few photos, and then she went up to the car with him, helping to brush the snow off the windows.

They both peered in after clearing them. Swip snapped a few pictures through the windows.

"I don't see anything," she said.

"Yeah… me neither. This is definitely the car though. Let me check the trunk." Swip looked at the keys again and pushed the button to pop the trunk. It took two pushes before it popped audibly. "I think the battery is low."

"It has been freezing for the past week."

He went over to the trunk and opened it, taking a photo before scanning the contents of the trunk and inventorying the bags in it. "I don't think any of these are his…" he muttered. "Looks like just the standard kits."

"That blows."

"Yeah. I'm gonna try and start it and let it run a little. If we can start it, I'll have you drive it."

"Yeah, sure."

Swip closed the trunk and went up to the driver's door. He climbed in and put the keys in the ignition, turning the car over. It took two tries, but eventually it rolled over and the engine started. "Awesome." He called out the open door to Teffifa, "Help me get out of these trees, we'll let it idle by the road until Stika's off the phone."

Teffifa gave him a thumbs up and then walked away to help direct him down the path.

**11:00 a.m.**

When there was a knock on the door, Malkarai jumped, having not heard anything in at least an hour. He set Satyrna's book down on his bed and eased off of it, listening intently. The person knocked again, and then he heard a soft voice call out, "Is anyone in there? It's Rafiane!"

He sighed and went to the door to let her in. After peeking out the window, he opened the door enough for her to hop inside, and then shut and locked it again.

She rubbed her ears with her gloved hands. "It is disgustingly cold out there."

"It's December and we're in Minnesota. Marion's no better."

"I know." She dropped her hands, a bright smile fixing itself to her face. "How're you?"

He crossed his arms and leaned against the wall. "Getting better."

"Healing-wise or in general?"

"Well, both. Where's your bodyguard?"

"He's busy at a business on this end of town, so I came out to visit. Cypha says you two are legit now."

"Yeah. What about you? Did you fall for his charm yet?"

She blushed dark red. "Shush. Dyspro's a really nice guy, but I was here to find you. Is it true that you get to stay here?"

"At least until New Year's. After that, it'll depend on how well I fight. Kalyfa can't just offer things without strings attached."

"You'll win. I know it."

He smiled. "Thanks for the vote of confidence. Just, keep all of this quiet, okay?"

"I will. Cypha said not to tell anyone else too."

"Good. Hey, Rafiane, I think you should stay inside as much as you can the next few days, okay?"

"Why?"

"Because the ASA might recognize you. I don't need anything to stick out to them. What I'm trying to do is very risky."

"Why would they recognize me?"

"They caught you on the cameras a few times."

"Oh…I didn't realize that."

"Yeah. Stika thought it might've been me, but obviously it was not. She wrote it off officially as a mountain lion or wolf or something, but she really thought it was a person."

She nodded. "Yeah, I'll keep in for a little bit, Malkarai."

"Thanks. I don't want anyone to get hurt or caught."

"After this is all over, would you come home with me for a little bit?"

"Marion's probably the most dangerous place for me."

"I…I know, but I'd like you to meet our parents."

His eyes narrowed and looked out the window evasively. "I can't say I want to meet them."

She frowned. "They only did it for your well-being, Malkarai. They didn't mean anything malicious by it. It hurt them to have to give up their first child like that."

"I still haven't entirely accepted this story you've told me. Yeah, some of the shit lines up, but what I know about then is colored with government lenses. I was two when I was given to the government – I can't rely on my own memories."

"I…I can get photos. Your age and appearance and name all match up, and the story about the woman abandoning you. Those all are the same."

"I also really don't want to connect with my family. It hurt me a lot too. I don't care to stir up more hurt."

"They'll be happy to see you've grown up so well, especially if you're free to live wherever and do whatever you want now."

"And I'll just be upset and angry that I couldn't have grown up there instead of a few miles away."

"I know. I wish you could've too, but that's not what happened. Why can't you just be happy that you have us now? We are."

"You've talked with them?"

"Yeah. I told them I found you."

He sighed. "So, I can't tell you to just forget about the whole thing then."

"Of course not!" She huffed, stepping back. "Malkarai, knock it off. You want to keep your friends and Satyrna, right?"

He nodded once.

"So why is family so much different?"

"These friends haven't abandoned me yet."

She shook her head. "Please… please give them a chance. Mom and Dad really want to see you."

"What are their names?"

"Huh?"

"Your parents. What are their names?"

"Oh, Micale and Dorena."

"Tavelante."

"Yes."

He nodded once in recognition. "I may use that name to hide."

She raised her brow. "Really?"

"Yeah. I won't be able to go as Malkarai Faerstathe. The government's already hidden or deleted all records of anyone by that name existing. So, Malkarai Tavelante will suddenly no longer be missing, I guess."

Rafiane smiled brightly. "Okay."

"I might have to change my first name too. I'm not sure yet. Ideally, I'd like to keep it, but it might be too suspicious. It's a very unique name."

"Yeah, Mom and Dad picked unique names for both of us."

He hesitated. "I wish I knew if the government changed mine or not."

"Do you think they did? Why would they pick the same name?"

"I think it would've been convenient for them to grab the name of an already recorded dark kid and assign it to me with a new last name. They always change the names of kids who join the system, the kids just usually have a say in it because they're normally about ten. I was a toddler, so it was assigned."

"Hm. I see. Well, I'm still confident you are *actually* Malkarai Tavelante," she said. Rafiane looked around. "Are you alone here?"

"Yeah. You apparently ran into Cypha and Satyrna's been at work since ten."

"I'll keep you company for a little bit then. What were you up to?"

"Reading. Not much else to do out here."

She dug into her bag and pulled out a half-sized notebook and two pens. "Let's play a game."

"What?"

She turned around and sat down at the table. "Let's play a game. Come on. It'll pass the time until Dyspro comes and gets me."

He hesitated, but then uncrossed his arms, walked over to the other seat, and sat down. "All right. What are we playing?"

She smirked. "Something we played all the time in study hall when we were pretending to study."

"We?"

"Me and Abby, my best friend from back home. She's the other dark I told you about."

"Oh. Well, explain, please. I never really had a study hall to pass time in."

She sighed and handed him a piece of paper and a pen. "All right, big brother, I'll teach you how to play games I learned in grade school."

He stuck his tongue out at her and she grinned.

# 38



Josh glanced at Satyrna as he held the door to the courthouse open for her. "You're much quieter than you were this morning."

She looked around the lobby before looking back at him. "I don't know where his office is. I never visited him here."

"We're going to see Kalyfa," he waved at the receptionist, who gave him a permitting nod. "Down here," he motioned and led her down a hallway to the right.

"I'm nervous. I still feel like I'm betraying him."

"He should've told you a detail like this."

"He said he would, in time. I don't think we have time."

Josh nodded and then pushed open a door to a stairwell and went up.

"Does he know we're coming?"

"I told him we'd be by this afternoon, yes. He said to be careful. They're probably around. So, we should zip it."

Satyrna nodded slightly, feeling tense as she realized that any of the people they were passing could be agents like Malkarai was. She doubted that, on second thought. She'd recognized a few of them, and none of them had felt anything like being around Malkarai or Teffifa at first had made her feel – like she was in the presence of a soldier or a hunting dog – that nervous, guarded, but not safe, feeling. Like the person she was standing next to could save her life before she realized it'd happened, but also that they could take it even quicker.

On the second floor, Josh led her to the right, toward the back corner of the building.

"Here, but his door's shut," Josh said, stopping outside of a closed door. It had a frosted glass pane set in weathered wood like the rest of the office doors in this hallway.

"Knock?"

He knocked on the wood and hesitated.

"I'll be with you in a moment," Kalyfa called from within.

Satyrna looked at Josh as he turned and went to lean against the wall across from the door. "Are they in there?" she whispered.

"Probably."

"Should we wait? Should we come back later?"

"They won't hurt you, Satyrna. Don't act suspicious and they will barely notice you."

She took a deep breath, reminding herself that they had no idea she even knew Malkarai and Traphian. "Right."

A few minutes later the door opened and three people stepped outside with Kalyfa.

Josh stood up straight, putting forward a more professional posture. Satyrna didn't move, just watching them.

Swip flashed Satyrna and Josh a charming smile and said, "At ease," to Josh in a vaguely inappropriate voice before turning back toward Kalyfa.

Josh flushed red, looking uncomfortable. Satyrna eyed Josh, but didn't say anything.

Teffifa was next, followed by Stika.

Stika shook Kalyfa's hand last. "Thanks for your cooperation. We're going to continue our sweep to see if we can find any of their belongings, and I'll call before we leave," she said tersely.

"Take your time. I'll be here until five, but after that, you'll have to get my cell number."

"Thanks. We'll probably be gone by four, I need to get back to the agency. I appreciate the assistance." She nodded to him and then started down the hallway, the others following.

As she passed, Teffifa winked at Satyrna but otherwise didn't acknowledge her presence.

Kalyfa sighed and crossed his arms before looking at Josh, who had returned to normal color, and Satyrna. "Come in."

They followed him inside and Josh closed the office door.

"So that was them," Satyrna said quietly.

"Yeah, those were the dark's friends."

"They didn't seem all that bad to me," Josh put in.

Kalyfa sat down heavily in his chair. "No. They're fairly normal-looking people. Faerstathe and Ripper are probably the weirdest ones in the bunch."

Satyrna raised an eyebrow. "I don't see what's so weird about him."

Kalyfa looked up at her momentarily. "He's a dark. That's what his novelty is. Usually, agents are social, friendly people. He's not. She isn't either – Ripper, I mean. It pissed me off that he brought her into the castle. She's imbalanced. I'm surprised that none of my people were cut down."

"Because she's a woman…?" Josh asked both tentatively and doubtfully.

"No, because she's literally, medically diagnosed as such."

"She's not that bad of a person, Kalyfa," Satyrna protested.

"No, when you get her calm, she's not. She's been the most agreeable of all of them, probably because we've been trying to match stories. When she's angry or excited, get the hell away."

"How do you know?" Satyrna asked, a slight sneer in her voice.

Kalyfa turned in his chair and dug through a folder that was sitting on top of a filing cabinet behind him. He tossed a stapled packet of papers across the desk at her. "It's in her personnel record."

Satyrna picked it up and looked at the first page. Below a bold warning about how the information was not for unauthorized eyes, there was a black and white picture of Teffifa. She had kind of a sinister, smirking smile on her face, but otherwise looked pretty normal. The grayscale didn't show the red eyes or hair. Satyrna read the list next to her picture.

Designation: Teffifa Ripper

Age: 22

Height: 5'3"

Weight: 125 lbs.

Hair: Brown

Eyes: Gray

Rank: 15

Level Approved: 5

District: Northwestern

Agency: 6

Style: Twin Swords, Knives, Daggers

Notes: Dyes hair black and red, wears red contacts. Has a medically diagnosed chemical imbalance that blocks pain and narrows focus. Most often occurs when in combat. Do not approach when in this state.

Satyrna looked up at Kalyfa, and he reached over and took the packet from her. "I can't let you look at the rest."

"You have one on Malkarai, don't you?"

He nodded once. "And that man you just saw, Swip, and their leader, Stika. Because Cavington is outside of federal jurisdiction, we require updated information on all the agents in this district before we'll allow them into town, otherwise, they will be charged as criminals for performing their job within city limits. If one from somewhere else comes here, I'm sent information on them as well. I'm sent new data every year, and then I destroy the old. The stipulation is that I'm not supposed to let people see it though – they're for my knowledge only."

"You let me see it."

"You knew everything on that page besides her rank."

"I didn't know that wasn't her real hair or eye color."

Kalyfa scoffed. "She's a freak, but she's not *that* weird."

"I guess I could've guessed the eyes though. What's the rest of it?"

"Mission details of note. Classified shit. Anyway, you're here because Faerstathe won't tell you, right?"

"Yes."

He opened his desk drawer and slid a smaller packet across the desk to her. "That's for you to keep."

Satyrna picked it up hesitantly and read the first page. It looked just like Teffifa's, but Malkarai wasn't even trying to manage a smile in his picture.

Designation: Malkarai Faerstathe

Age: 21

Height: 5'10"

Weight: 170 lbs

Hair: Black

Eyes: Black

Rank: 16

Level Approved: 5

District: Northwestern

Agency: 6

Style: Swords, knives, daggers, darts, poisons

Notes: Dark. High stealth capability. Works at night in secluded areas. Will always call to report success or target may not be found. Always get location details. Probably will not be seen until finished, if at all. Works alone.

She sighed. "That doesn't tell me much that I don't know." *I know far more about him than that...*

"The other pages will," said Kalyfa.

She hesitantly flipped the front page back. There was a lot of data on the page. A rap sheet on some other person, his picture, and later down the page, a picture of him again, looking quite dead. She hid her surprise. "What is this?" she asked quietly.

"There are a few records of his completed missions in there. I think that'll give you a good enough idea of what it is that he does."

She read the page with greater care and then stared blankly at the last picture, trying to look like she was reading and not trying to wrap her head around what was on the page. Eventually, she flipped to the next page. This was similar to the previous, only it was a woman. Neither of the 'after' pictures looked particularly gruesome – the people were just dead. "Does he locate bodies?"

Kalyfa snickered quietly. He was reclined in his chair. "No. He makes bodies."

She looked up at him, fighting hard not to react. "He kills people."

He nodded once, slowly.

She blinked. "W-what's legal about that? I don't understand."

Kalyfa shrugged and sat forward. "It's the federal government's shady alternative to needles or prisons. They handcraft killers and send them after the people they approve. His whole division is secret. Division 53 of Homeland Security – otherwise known as the ASA or American Security Association. You'll never find it doing an internet search, but you might find yourself on a watch list you didn't want to be a member of."

Satyrna felt her brow beginning to betray her response. She held the papers out to him. "Thank you," she said stiffly.

He put a hand up. "Keep it."

She looked at Josh. "I'm ready to go."

Josh nodded.

"Satyrna," Kalyfa said softly.

She turned and looked at him.

"Please, don't dismiss this. I didn't make that information up. And, I'm willing to allow his decision to change."

She frowned. "You hope that it will."

He shrugged. "I'm not an assassin like him. I don't care to kill anyone."

Her control was at its breaking point. She turned back to Josh. "Let's go."

He opened the door and glanced at Kalyfa as she went outside, but then followed without saying anything.

Outside the courthouse, Josh looked over at Satyrna and saw that tears were coming down her cheeks. He stopped and put an arm around her shoulders, dipping his head so he could see her face. "Saty, are you okay?"

Her voice was taut, the packet gripped tightly in her hands. "Why couldn't he have been anything else? Th-there's nothing right about that…"

Josh was quiet for a few moments. "It depends on who it was he was killing, you know."

"Why does that matter?!"

"If he's killing criminals, then it's a whole lot more right than killing whoever someone wanted knocked off."

He felt her shudder and then reached for the sheet.

"Let me see it."

She let him take and open it to one of the mission pages. He read the details through quickly and then put a finger on something on the page. "Here, this guy was a murderer and a rapist, Satyrna." She looked, blinking to clear away the tears. He flipped the page. "And this woman was an extortionist, child abuser, and rapist. Wow, that's kind of a weird combo." He flipped to the next one. "And this one was a repeated murderer." He flipped to the last page but was quiet.

"What's that one?" she asked quietly.

"Traphian – well, Trebo. Treason and evasion of custody. He doesn't count, right?"

She shook her head slowly. "Malkarai said he never approved of this mission. No wonder he had such a hard time…they wanted him to kill his best friend…"

Josh put a hand on her shoulder, handing her the papers back. "See, Saty… Kalyfa wants you to hate him. He's not going to put it in that context for you. He gave you all the info you need though. Read them through."

She shook her head. "I don't wanna know details. Whether they were criminals or not, he killed them."

"Kalyfa's no saint either. None of us are. We've all had to do things we regret to protect people."

"Have you ever killed anyone?"

"I haven't, no. I know Kalyfa has."

"There's so much more that you guys do though. If this is all he did, then what does that make him?"

He didn't respond. "You know, the people we bring in, if they did things bad enough to warrant the death penalty, someone's gotta do them in. Does that make us any better than the guy who puts the needle in the person's arm? We're the reason they're there in the first place."

She was quiet for a few moments. "This involves planning, it's an act of conscious will. He chases these people down before he kills them. He doesn't just walk into a room, inject someone, and then leave. He runs them down and… and-"

Josh hugged her and watched her, but she didn't say anything else. After a few minutes, he asked, "Would you like me to walk you home?"

She nodded.

"Cypha and Dyspro's place or yours?"

"Mine."

"All right."

He walked her to her house and parted ways at her door.

"Thanks, Josh," she murmured.

He stared at her, wanting to do something, but he had no idea what he could do. "You gonna be okay?"

She shrugged and turned to the door. "We'll see. Bye."

"Bye."

Inside, she waved at her mother, who was sitting in the living room, reading, and continued up the stairs.

"Satyrna? I thought you were going back to Cypha's."

Satyrna paused and then unwillingly turned and descended the few steps she'd made it up. "I'm going to stay here tonight."

"Oh. All right. Dinner'll be ready at seven. I'm going to take it to your father and sister at the store. Want to go with?"

"No. I want to lie down."

Her mother frowned and set her book down on her lap. "Oh, honey, you look ill. Are you all right?"

She shrugged. "I've felt better."

"Is it your knee? Do you think it's infected?"

She'd honestly forgotten about her knee. "Oh… maybe. I don't know. It feels fine."

"It might be a cold or the flu. Go rest. I'll bring you up something to eat."

Satyrna nodded listlessly and turned to go upstairs. "Thanks, Mom."

In her room, she pushed the door shut behind her without turning the light on, took off her coat and let it drop to the floor, tossed the papers on her bed, and followed, landing heavily, her head just shy of the pillows. She curled her arms up under her chin, staring out the window.

She shut her eyes tight as she felt tears run down her cheeks again. *Damn it, Malkarai… What the hell is wrong with you? You're an* **assassin***? I could've dealt with a spy or some kind of secret agent, but someone who kills people for a living? I mean… what the hell is that?!*

She punched the mattress, an angry sob escaping her. "Damn it!"

Swip leaned against the silver car as they reached it, resting his arms on the roof as he looked at Stika. She stopped a few feet from the car, reading some of the paperwork she was holding again. He glanced at Teffifa, who was scanning the area, her hands in the pockets of her coat, the front still open.

"So, what's the plan? Where should I drive?"

Teffifa glanced at him and then looked at Stika.

After a few moments, Stika closed the folder. "What would you two do?"

Teffifa didn't reply.

"Well, I'd check the mission or other donation places."

Teffifa shook her head slightly. "Good luck being able to tell Malkarai's clothing from anyone else's."

"All he ever wore was black," Swip countered.

"Yeah, black T-shirts out of multi-packs. It's not like they ever had logos, decals, or sayings on them."

"Whatever. His coat was incredibly distinctive. He had it made for him, didn't he?"

"He had it made and then modified it, yes," Stika said. "There weren't enough pockets for his liking. His coat won't be at a thrift store though, he was wearing it." She sighed and rubbed her face. "Malk… what the hell did we do to you?" she muttered and then opened up her car door.

Swip and Teffifa glanced at each other, but Teffifa looked away quickly and opened up the back door behind Stika.

He sighed and then stood up and opened the driver's door before climbing into the car. "So, closest secondhand store?" he said as he started the car and then pulled his phone out of his pocket.

"Yes. We'll think of other options on our way. Scan alleys for his bag, Teffifa."

"Yes, ma'am."

Stika raised an eyebrow at the title and then looked at Swip, who was looking up an address on his phone.

"Five places. Closest is about five blocks from here," he said as he set his phone down in the mount on the dashboard and put the car into gear.

3:30 p.m.

Teffifa yawned as she walked down the men's aisle in a thrift store, idly moving hangers of musty-smelling clothing as she passed them. She wasn't really looking, not expecting to find either Malkarai or Traphian's clothes here. It was possible they dumped them, but unlikely. She figured it was more likely for both of them to hide the old things than donate.

She glanced toward the register where Stika was asking the cashier if either a black duffel bag or a blue backpack full of items had been turned in by anyone.

Swip stretched as he came up to Teffifa. "Nothing?"

"Nothing."

"I wonder what happened to their stuff."

"Probably stolen."

"Hope Malk didn't have anything confidential on him."

"Yeah."

"We still haven't found his computer either."

"Oh. Right. No way a normal techie could get into that though. It's more likely to be wiped than hacked."

"I guess so," Swip agreed. "Maybe we should've looked at pawn shops."

"Do they have them here?"

Swip took out his phone and looked it up as Teffifa dug through a bin of empty purses and bags. "Two."

"Well, tell Stika. We're running out of time."

They went over to Stika, waiting for her to finish with the cashier. When she was done, she turned and asked, "Anything?"

Teffifa shook her head and Swip said, "Nope. There are two pawn shops in town though. His computer could've been pawned."

"Hmm, yeah, you're probably right."

"What else could he have had on him? We're not supposed to carry valuables."

Stika motioned to the door and then led them outside before replying. "No, we're not; you're right. I'm trying to find his things because his bank account was empty."

"It was?" Teffifa asked in surprise.

Stika nodded.

"Where the hell did his money go?" Swip asked, perplexed.

"They don't know. He withdrew it all. I don't know if he was keeping it in cash somewhere or what. Malkarai was too smart to leave a trail."

Teffifa frowned.

"So, you just don't want the money to fall in someone else's hands, or what?"

"Yeah. It's his money. There are things I know he'd rather it was used for if he wasn't able to use it – instead of some punk using it to buy drugs or something."

"Like what?" Teffifa asked.

"Well, since Traphian's gone too, probably school supplies or lab equipment. A donation to his college. I don't know. There are a lot of options besides just letting it go."

Swip sighed. "Should we report that, or something?"

Stika shook her head. "The upper levels are already looking into it. I just wanted to see if it was in cash on his person. It's their problem."

"Oh, all right."

"We'll look at the pawn shops for his computer though. They will want me to try and recover that."

"This would've been easier if we'd come right away," Swip shook his head as he unlocked the car.

"Yes, but these seceded towns make everything harder. The reps agreed that it was better to let the local authorities try and clean up first."

"They obviously fucked that up," Swip muttered as they all climbed into the vehicle.

"That's why Traphian ran here in the first place," Stika agreed. "He knew everything would be more complicated if he was in a separated area."

Teffifa buckled in and put her feet on the bottom of Stika's seat, chewing on her forefinger as she looked out the window. She was starting to wonder just how many layers to this cover-up there were. Her role wasn't going to change, but the more they investigated this, the more she realized she was only playing a part, not orchestrating it. She'd had to lie a whole lot less than she expected.

"You're right though; it's been too long. If we find nothing at the pawn shops, we'll head back to Marion. By this point, the trail's too cold, and I've got a Carlisle shitstorm showing up at home."

"All right," Swip said as he started the car.

Patricia walked out where her parents were sitting together on the couch, watching TV, holding the kitchen phone to her shoulder. "Hey, do you guys know where Satyrna is?"

Her mother looked up at her. "Yeah, she's upstairs."

Patricia sighed. "Seriously? Why isn't she answering her phone?"

"She didn't feel well. She's probably asleep. Why? Who's asking?"

"Cypha. She said she was expecting her and she never showed, and she's been trying to call her for hours."

"Well, she's here. Let her know."

Patricia turned on her heel and went back to the kitchen, where Brendan was sitting at the table, trying to spin a pen in his hand. She put the phone back up to her ear. "Hey, Cypha?"

"Yeah?"

"She's in her room, apparently. Mom says she wasn't feeling well."

"Oh, well, she could've told us. Her phone ringing as much as I was calling her had to've annoyed her."

"It's probably off."

"Probably. I wish she'd just get rid of the damn thing. Then we'd stop trying to rely on her using it." Cypha sighed. "All right. Tell her I called, and in the future, I want her to let me know if I should expect her or not. I was worried."

Patricia hushed her voice, well into the kitchen. "You mean he was worried."

"We both were. Thanks, Patricia."

"Yeah. No problem. Bye."

She hit the 'end' button on the phone and set it in the charger. "Why does my sister stress me out so much?"

"Because you worry about her too much."

"Someone's got to."

Brendan snickered. "Hon, everyone worries about that girl. You're not alone."

She slid into the chair across from him and leaned across the table. "He's staying out there with them. I mean, if Mom and Dad knew that!"

He shrugged. "Your parents don't know a thing about him."

"Yeah, well that's not much more encouraging."

"Are you ever gonna approve of one of her boyfriends?"

"Probably not," she replied truthfully. "Kalyfa was the best one, and I still didn't think he was that great."

Brendan snickered and patted her hand. "That's why you're mine."

"Seriously, what the hell attracts her to these crazies?"

"She likes challenges."

"Kalyfa wasn't challenging enough for her?"

"Not that kind of challenge. They were a compatibility challenge. She wants people with problems. She's a fixer. Kinda like you, but more ambitious."

"What's that supposed to mean?"

"Patricia, you're trying to fix her as we speak."

She sighed, propping her chin up on her hand. "I don't know what she sees in that guy."

Brendan shrugged. "He's a dark. I'm sure very few have seen what he truly has to offer. He's tough though, I'll give him that. And not just anyone will take a sword to the ribcage for another person."

"So, I suppose you encourage this pairing, huh?"

He shrugged again. "I encourage whatever makes her happy. That's the least we can hope for, right?"

"I guess so. Still wish she'd try and act a little more normal though."

He smirked. "Half of Satyrna's personality is her over-living. Just let it go. At least he isn't a criminal."

Patricia's brow knitted slightly, but she let the topic slide.

11:30 p.m.

Satyrna jolted out of sleep, her eyes to her window. She was still lying on her stomach, head in her arms. She sat up, rubbing her eyes, trying to get the nightmare she'd been having out of her head.

She'd been reliving that night in the castle when Malkarai had been injured. It'd started off with her clutching him close to her when she realized he'd been hit;

when she saw the blood and the pain in his face – the fear that had paralyzed her when she saw what had happened.

It had changed though, and she remembered seeing him charging her – but he didn't charge her to protect her – he charged her and stabbed *her* in the side. She felt the pain and shock. His face was like it was in the photo: careless, emotionless, cold. The only warmth she'd felt was her blood. That's when she'd woken, shaking, feeling cold and sweaty.

She rubbed her arms and spotted his face on the packet, which was still lying askew on the bed. She reached out and struck it with her hand, sending it to the floor between her bed and the window.

She put her palms over her eyes for a few moments before running her fingers back through her hair. *I can't believe that I feel like this, still, over a killer. I should just want to break this off, no questions asked, but I'm trying to tell myself it's not true, that it's a big hoax, that it can't be true, but I know it is. What else would keep Traphian running for so long?*

*That's why he was so cold... That's why he felt like a predator. He's a manhunter. What if I'm the one he's hunting now?*

She bent over, putting her forehead against the comforter again, squeezing her eyelids shut tight.

*No. I really feel like he cares about me. You don't fake things like what happened last night. The problem here isn't whether or not he's been truthful; he has. Unlike what Kalyfa's saying, Malkarai hasn't lied to me, I just never grasped exactly what he was talking about. The problem is what it means to me now that I'm not ignorant.*

She reached for the end of her bed and grabbed a stuffed dolphin from the small pile of plush animals lying there before climbing under the covers and burying her face in it, head on her pillow.

*It could've been normal... it could've been – not perfect – but great. But you're a murderer. An assassin! What the hell am I supposed to think about that?*

# 39



Cypha's eyebrows raised in surprise when Satyrna answered her call.

"Hello?" she asked, less than enthused.

"Satyrna! Jeez, where the hell have you been? We haven't heard from you in two days. Are you sick?"

"No."

"Why haven't you come back out here then?"

"I just haven't."

Cypha turned and leaned against the wall, catching Malkarai's gaze. He was sitting on the bench, elbows on his knees. He looked pretty downcast. "Communication's a good thing, you know. At first, we thought something happened to you, and then we thought you were sick. I mean, throw us a bone here."

"Sorry." She didn't sound very sincere.

Cypha hesitated. "What's wrong?"

"I don't wanna talk about it."

"Did something happen?"

"No."

Cypha chewed on the inside of her lip for a few moments before speaking again. "Hey, Malkarai would like to speak to you."

"I'm at work. I can't talk."

"Even for a moment?"

"No. Bye."

Cypha pulled her phone away from her ear to check what she suspected, that Satyrna had hung up. She shut her phone and looked at Malkarai. "Did you do something to upset her?"

He shook his head slowly. "Did she say I did?"

"No, but she apparently doesn't want to talk to you. She got off the phone pretty quick there."

He frowned, staring at the floor. "Is she working?"

"She said she was."

He groaned and put his hands over his face. "Shit!"

"What?" Cypha asked, startled.

"I know what she did…"

"What? What did she do?"

He turned around and looked outside. "She told me she could find out what I am without me telling her. Damn it! When it's dark, I'm going to town."

Cypha shook her head. "No way, they've gotta still be around. You can't go into town."

"I'll be fine. Even if they're here, they won't be able to see me."

"What if they're with her? What if they figured out you know her? Maybe she's trying to keep you safe."

"Well, if that's the case then it's already over. I won't let them keep her if that is what's going on."

"Don't make the past two weeks be for nothing, Malkarai. Yeah, she's a psycho twit sometimes, but don't screw that all up because something's bothering her."

He shook his head. "No, she needs to have this explained. Otherwise, it might compromise everything."

Cypha sighed and crossed her arms. "Am I wasting my breath?"

"Yes. I'm going once it's dark."

She threw her hands up and went back to her room. "Fine! Just don't come crying to me if your ass gets caught."

4:30 p.m.

Dregan glanced around the store to make sure that there was no one inside to help and then ducked down to open a box and start stacking the items on the counter. About halfway through the box, he heard the bell on the door ring as it opened and grabbed a few more items before standing up straight to watch the store again.

Malkarai entered and glanced around the store quickly before going to the counter where Dregan was standing.

Dregan asked, curiously, "Can I help you?" He felt like he recognized him, but couldn't place it.

"I'm looking for Satyrna. Is she still working?" He was soft-spoken, but not unfriendly.

"She's on her break. What do you need?"

He paused and then held out a hand. "Sorry, are you her father?"

"Yeah…" he said, taking his hand.

"I'm Malkarai," he explained, as he shook his hand.

"Oh! Uh, sorry, I'm Dregan Hennessin. I was thinking that I recognized you, but it wasn't clicking. Thank you."

Malkarai dropped his hand when Dregan let go of it, looking perplexed. "Um, for what?"

"For catching that thief for us. You ducked out without really getting the credit you deserved for it."

"Oh, there's no need for thanks."

"Most people won't try and do anything like that. They're scared to get involved."

Malkarai shrugged. "I'm a law enforcer. It was practically reflex."

"You're a law enforcer? Are you a cop?"

He shook his head. "I was more investigation-oriented. I've left that position since I moved here though."

"Any idea what you'll be doing here?"

"I might end up helping the knights some. I'm looking for a more permanent job though."

"Law enforcement again?"

He shook his head slowly. "Nah. I might try my hand at some teaching. I have a general sciences teaching degree."

"Really?"

He nodded. "I was a teacher for my subordinates, so I taught science and different weapon skills."

"How old are you?"

"Twenty-one. We had accelerated programs, but even so, I was only able to teach for a year or so."

"Hmmm." Dregan nodded, impressed.

Malkarai looked to his left when he saw movement, spotting Satyrna coming up from the back.

"Hey, Dad, I'm ba- What are you doing here?" She almost hissed the last part.

Her father raised his brow, surprised at her greeting.

Malkarai sighed. "I was talking to your father. We need to talk."

She sighed, looking aggravated. She looked at her father. "Is it okay?"

He motioned toward him. "Feel free."

Satyrna finished coming down the aisle, grabbed Malkarai by the sleeve, and led him out of the store.

Malkarai looked at Dregan in surprise as she did this. "Er, nice meeting you again."

He nodded, crossing his arms as he watched his daughter, a bemused expression on his face.

Outside, Satyrna pulled him into the alley and spun to face him. "Are you crazy?" she demanded, her voice an emphatic whisper. "You're going to get caught!"

He crossed his arms. "I'll be fine. Now what the hell is wrong?"

"What do you mean, what the hell is wrong? You just walked through town to see me when Teffifa and two other people are here, trying to find out where your shit is!"

"How do you know that?"

"I ran into them the other day. Teffifa, a man, and a woman."

He stared at her, shocked. "You ran into them?"

"Yeah. At the courthouse. Relax, they didn't even say anything to me. Teffifa winked, and that was the extent of the attention they paid me."

"You're positive?"

"Yes."

He paused, tense. "What did the others look like?"

"She was tall and had straight brown hair; he had short brown hair and was wearing a dark blue coat."

"Stika – that makes sense, and…" he looked like he was trying to figure out the second one. "Who the hell has a coat like that?"

"Swip."

He looked up at her. "How'd you know his name?"

"Kalyfa. What kind of name is that?"

"It was his nickname. His real name used to be like Stewart or something."

"The point is, they're here, and they're looking for you."

"They think I'm dead. They're looking for my bag. They would not be looking at a grocery store for something like that. They'd check lost and founds, thrift stores, and donation boxes. That or dark alleys like this."

Satyrna sighed, turned around, went back to the back door, put her key in the lock, and opened it up. "Get in here."

He followed her into the store room, where there were a lot of boxes stacked along the walls, a garage door at one end, and a corner full of cleaning equipment.

He watched her closely as she turned and faced him again. "So, how'd you find out?" he asked softly.

"How'd I find out what?"

"I know you know. How'd you find out? Who told you?"

She put up a finger, then went to the next room. After a few moments, she returned and shoved a bunch of papers at him.

He took them and looked at them, flipping through to see all the documents. He recognized them though, so he didn't need to look at them very long. "Who gave these to you?"

"Does it matter?"

"Yeah, because they chose missions they deemed important."

"It doesn't matter, Malkarai! You're an assassin! That's what matters!" she kept her senses enough to keep her voice low.

He looked her in the eyes. "So, do you find me repulsive now? Is that why you're avoiding me?"

She crossed her arms and looked away. "I don't know what to think. You told me. You never told me what you do when you catch people, but you told me… You told me it was something people would see as bad. I just assumed I was more open-minded than most, so I ignored your warnings."

"Are you open-minded enough to listen to my side of it?"

She looked at him but paused before nodding.

"I want you to understand two things. First of all, I chose my missions carefully. I only went after people who'd already been dealt the death penalty, or who would've been had they ever been present at a trial. I stand by the fact that I am a law enforcer – a protector. Secondly, you should understand that not everyone functions the same way I do. Yes, it's true; there are private missions that pop up. Even the federal government will overlook things when paid enough money. I never took those targets. I've always been in constant conflict with my morals and conscience with this. I never took a life until I was twelve. I assisted, yes, but it was always Traphian who would finish our missions. We consider it a kill if it's our mission, regardless of details. Seeing someone die in front of you changes you. Doing it yourself changes you more."

She frowned, a look of distaste on her face.

"Yes, I've taken lives. But I'm not a murderer. I'm an executioner."

"I can't believe the government actually funds an organization like that."

"There's a reason you've never heard of it, Satyrna. We've been around for over 250 years."

She stared at him in disbelief, her jaw dropping open slightly. "250 years?"

He nodded once. "The ASA's old, but you'll never find any record of any of its members or any of its facilities. Our victims' fates are covered up. Some are said to have died in prison, others are said to have been shot or cut down on the streets. The minor ones just disappear. It varies. We don't deal with that part. There's an entire other sector of the system that deals with hiding our identities and our targets' fates."

She shook her head. "It's so wrong, sending people to kill people…"

"And hanging's more civilized?"

She blinked. "No. But the noose or the needle doesn't have to go home to a wife and kids at the end of the day and try to make people understand why they do what they do."

"A needle can't chase a fugitive across state lines and into hiding. What I do protects people. That's why I stayed. I wanted to protect people. I wanted to keep people from having to mourn like I did. I wanted evil to go away. One of those bastards took Arista away. It killed me. That's why I've been blindly working for the past few years – because it hurt – but I could make a difference because I was still alive."

"Why wouldn't you tell me?" she asked quietly.

"Because I was afraid of something like this, where you wouldn't understand. Satyrna, look, we've only known each other like two weeks. This isn't something I can tell people right after I meet them. I needed to know that I can trust you. Whoever told you was irresponsible and would probably get in deep shit if anyone ever discovered they'd made copies of these documents."

"What's the bigger issue? You not wanting me to know, or you being afraid of what the government will do to you?"

"I don't know what the bigger issue is. Yeah, it's really bad to let you know about this organization, but I didn't want to lose you. I didn't know how you'd take it. I'm subjective when it comes to what I do. I feel that it's okay. But I know that there are reasons the government keeps the ASA secret, and thus, I'm not sure what an outsider's view of it would be. That unknown was making me hesitant. That's why I wanted to wait until the end of the month. I wanted to be able to figure you out better. I wanted to wait and see if you'd even be able to handle it."

She sighed.

He stepped closer to her, reaching a hand up to brush her hair away from her cheek. "Satyrna…"

She looked at him, still not speaking.

"What are you thinking?" he asked.

"I'm thinking that I still don't know what to say…"

"I understand if you can't handle it…" His expression said he would understand, but he wouldn't be happy about it.

"Will you let me digest it some?"

He nodded. After a short pause, he asked, "Will you come back out tonight?"

"Yeah. I'll come out there. I'll give you an answer then."

His hand hovered near her cheek for a moment and then he dropped it to his side. "All right."

Satyrna found herself wishing he'd kissed her, and so she felt unsatisfied when he went to the door.

"I'll see you tonight. Tell your father I said goodbye, but I'm going to take the back way."

She nodded and he opened the door and was gone.

Satyrna stood there for a few minutes, thinking, and trying not to at the same time.

"Why do I feel like crying?" she murmured.

Once she felt she had her face under control, she went up to the front by her father.

"I'm back. You can go eat."

He looked over at her. He was sitting on one of the stools, leaning on the counter. "That was your boyfriend, right?"

She nodded.

"He seemed all right. Wears a lot of black."

She shrugged. "He likes black." *More like he likes not being seen...*

"He seems pretty accomplished for only being your age."

She paused. "Er, like what?"

"Has a degree, had a job in law enforcement, used to teach people. He can barely drink."

"Oh, yeah. He's really smart."

"Is he going to visit his family?"

"For Christmas? Probably not."

"Bring him then. Your brother's gonna be here for the holidays."

Satyrna's face brightened a little. "Really? Adam's coming home?"

"Yup. For a week and a half. The more the merrier."

She nodded. "I'll see."

"He knows a lot of stuff, huh?"

She sighed. "Yeah, well, he never had much of a social life before he came here. He took lessons and learned instead."

Her father snickered and stood up. "Well, I'm sure you'll break him of that. I'm gonna go eat supper. Holler if you need help."

"'K."

Satyrna leaned heavily on the counter as her father went into the back. "Christ, even Dad approves of him. Except for that glaring little black blemish, you're damn near perfect, aren't you?" she muttered darkly.

# 40



Satyrna walked to Cypha's house slowly, eager, but dreading what she'd have to face when she reached the person she was so eager to see.

All the conflicting emotions made her want to crawl into her bed again and die. She'd started out disgusted and appalled, convinced she'd never want to see him again, but as soon as she'd thought about never seeing him again, she'd had an overwhelming desire to run back and throw her arms around him and not let go.

That's when she'd started trying to justify it to herself. She tried to tell herself he had no choice; that he had been brainwashed, that it was the government's fault. But she knew she was lying to herself. She'd told Kalyfa herself; he wasn't brainwashed. He was perfectly aware of everything he was doing.

What was bothering her was that she was trying to protect him.

She knew what he'd done. It made it less abominable that it was criminals he'd killed, and it made her feel a little better knowing that the criminals apparently hadn't been mutilated in any way. She didn't want to think that he enjoyed the act of killing. But it still bothered her that he'd been killing people for a living. She still didn't know how much he made, or if that was at all a factor in who he chose or how much he worked.

Part of her wished she'd stayed ignorant. She wanted to stay blissfully dumb. She wanted to let things progress with him like they had been before this. She had been happy. But now, instead of worrying about someone or something else taking him away, she wasn't sure if she should even keep him herself. Instead of seeing him how she did the morning before she found out – sleepy and smiling at her, happy, protective, and exposed – the cold, emotionless photo from his work information kept popping into her mind. When she concentrated hard to bring that happy memory back she felt both better and worse at the same time – but at least, there was less fear and more confusion when she thought of him like that.

Logic said she should cut her losses and leave him. Logic said she shouldn't be with someone who conflicted with her moral structure. Logic said that he was dangerous, that the things surrounding him were dangerous, that attaching herself to him was dangerous. Her heart didn't care what logic said.

It wasn't that he cared about her. She'd been looked at with adoring eyes before, gotten in trouble for making decisions based on them, and learned from her mistakes. It made things more complicated – made forgiveness and acceptance more desirable. But what mattered was that she kept thinking of him like that; she couldn't stop thinking about him. Everyone was right. She'd fallen for him. And she wasn't sure how deeply, but this was certainly testing it. Her unwillingness to let him go was making her realize that it must be deeper than she thought.

She stopped when she realized that the trees around her had dissipated. She could see the light from the fire burning inside the little stone house, smoke curling into the starry black sky from the chimney. There didn't seem to be any candles lit inside, but that wasn't surprising. Cypha had taken to going to bed early to save on candles and wood used.

That didn't mean Malkarai was asleep though. She was sure he was sitting there in the firelight, being a shadow like normal.

She sighed and then went to the door, digging her keys out of her pocket. She hesitated before slipping it into the lock, fighting a flight reflex. The fight won out and she put her key in the lock and turned it and the knob. Once inside, she looked over to the shadowed area by the bench first but didn't see anyone. Then she looked at the table and realized Malkarai was sitting in a chair near the hearth, in plain view, watching her.

"Found you."

He smiled faintly. "Good job."

She shut the door and set her purse on the table. "Is Cypha in bed?"

"Yeah."

"Okay."

He watched her as she took off her coat and sat in the other chair, resting her arms on the table.

"Did you eat?" she asked.

"Yeah. You?"

"I ate before you showed up at the store."

He watched her in silence, patiently. She knew it was her place to say something, but she didn't want to. She wanted to pretend none of this had ever happened.

Eventually, his eyes looked down, possibly at her hands. She felt like he was trying to decide if it was okay to take one. For some reason, the loss of eye contact gave her more strength.

"I don't want you to go away."

He looked up again.

"But... I'm not okay with what I found out. I'm less upset than I was when I first found out, but I'm not okay with it. I do appreciate why you've done what you've done, but I don't condone it. I have never felt that the death penalty was humane. I do agree that some people are inhumane and thus deserve to reap what they sow, but I would never agree to someone killing someone else, whether it be for justice or their own personal advancement. When that becomes okay, it's only a small jump before cops are killing protestors and subversive groups just because they go against the status quo."

Malkarai said, "ASA targets are never those people. We only deal with capital criminals who escape prison or evade capture by either monetary or physical means. I agree – cops should not have this power. Most people should never have this power. When they have it, then little kids get hanged in public for petty larceny. That's why we're trained like we are. We're raised in a closed environment, watched carefully. There's a specific sort of demographic they need for us to be useful. Not everyone makes it through training."

"What makes the ASA so different from the mob then?"

He shrugged. "We're here to protect the civilians, not anyone's financial investments or political power. We take care of politicians sometimes too."

"It's the ASA that picks who lives and dies then, huh?"

"On one level. The heads pick missions too, and then offer them to us. If none of us agree to it, it probably won't be finished. We don't just report for duty, get handed a piece of paper, and then follow the instructions. As people are chosen, we are allowed to check out the new targets and work as we wish or feel the need to. We pick who we go after."

"So, aren't the worst people ignored then?"

He shook his head. "Those people are the ones we group together for. The worse the person, the more committed we are to removing them from society."

Satyrna's brow knitted and she looked over at the stove. "I'm not trying to justify whether or not the ASA is okay... that's an entirely different issue. I'm trying to resolve in my mind the fact that you killed for a career."

"If you can't handle it, Satyrna, don't try to tell yourself that you will later. It won't get easier."

"I can forgive the past. I've come to that conclusion. I can't forgive things that may happen when we're both aware of everything."

"What do you mean?"

She turned her head toward him, looking him in the face at first and then letting her eyes drop until they rested on his arms, which he had crossed loosely across his chest. "When I see your hands, feel them touching my face or holding my hand, I don't think of what they've done before. Even now, I don't think of them as things that have been stained with blood and taken people's lives. When you hold me, I don't think of you as hard or brutal or... a predator. That's what I felt like you were at first. Not a sexual predator, of course, but like a hunter.

"Now... now that you've let me see you – the you that was under whatever you had built up since Arista left – when you hold me, I feel safe and happy and warm. When I see you, I feel happier. No matter what I told myself, nothing that I discovered was that much of a surprise. You'd told me what you were, if not directly. The way you acted, the way you treated people, the way you moved, spoke... I'm surprised I never suspected something like this earlier, Malkarai. The shock was that it was the truth."

He snorted softly. "I really acted like a predator?"

She nodded slightly. "You were not easy to approach. I kept telling myself that there was a reason you were that way and that you couldn't be like that on all levels, and I was right. I just never stopped to think about what the reason was you were like that in the first place. I just wanted to see more beneath the surface, because the more I discovered, the more I liked, the more I fell…"

"Fell?"

She looked away, at her hands, her cheeks flushed. "I fell for you."

He didn't respond at first, and she continued, not giving him a chance to.

"But as much as I want to be with you, I can't if you can't agree to a few things."

"What do you want me to do?"

"I don't want you to kill anyone anymore. I don't care if they're a criminal or not. No one else."

He nodded. "Easily done."

"Also, I know why you were the way you were before, and I don't want you to be like that. I won't ask you to forget Arista. You should never forget her. But I want you to let her go. As long as I'm here, I don't want her to be."

He reached forward and took her hands in his, scooting his chair a little closer to the table. "Already done," he whispered. "The only thing that's been bringing her to mind is when you push me to share information. I stopped thinking about her when you came into the picture. On my own, I was pushing the knife deeper. You took it out."

She snickered a little at his use of metaphor and squeezed his hands. "You're morbid but cute. Last thing."

"Yes?"

"Whatever you did or said to my father, I want you to start making that your normal interaction with people."

"What?" Malkarai was a little surprised at the change in terms.

"He liked you. I don't know what you said to him exactly, but he approved of you. He didn't think you were quiet, or creepy, or anything he usually thinks about darks. He didn't say, 'Well, that guy's a few eggs short of a dozen' or something stupid like that. Yes, he's said that about at least two of my boyfriends before. He thought you were okay. Hell, he invited you to our house for Christmas."

Malkarai blinked and laughed a little, unsurely. "Uh, Satyrna, I was using my business mode there."

"Business mode?"

"I was being social – approachable. I talked about myself. I went out on a limb to try and impress him."

"Huh. So that's why he never commented about that."

"I figured I already looked goth, I didn't need him to realize I was anti-social right away."

"Why don't you do that all the time?"

"Because it's hard as hell. When I need to make a really good impression, I'll do that. Normally, I don't like making eye contact while talking, I don't like speaking up, and I don't like talking about myself – at all. And doing it coolly and without faltering? It's rough. But I don't want your parents to think I'm a freak. I can't hide my eyes, so I know I have to beat all the dark stereotypes and make them trust me – even though the majority of them are true about me. I also figured talking myself up a little couldn't hurt since avoiding the question didn't seem to help me make any friends."

Satyrna nodded in agreement. "He did comment on the black clothing, but he was more impressed with how well-learned you are. So, yeah, whatever you told him your profession and schooling were, he liked it. We're going to stick with that story for everyone. What did you tell him?"

"That I was in investigative law enforcement. I dropped the private investment shit since everyone here seems to know I was a law enforcer, thanks to Kalyfa's way too loose tongue. I did tell him that I had a degree in general sciences – which I do – and that I taught my subordinates. So, all truth. Just, you know, no mention of the ASA."

"Where are we gonna say you're from?"

"Rapid City. It's far enough away from Marion to not immediately ring bells. I'll be using Tavelante for everything."

"You'll still be going by Malkarai?"

He nodded. "I have no attachment to that last name, but because it already exists it makes things immensely easier."

"What about Traphian?"

"They're still working on his things. He can't use his birth name or any of his aliases, so he's gotta make up another one."

"Poor Traphian."

"Yeah. Whatever, he'll be fine. And we have input on the name, so he isn't going to go by something as lame as Trebo," Malkarai made a face of distaste.

Satyrna laughed. It felt like the tension had mostly lifted. She felt much better. Laughing was possible now.

"He was never very imaginative," Malkarai sighed.

She smiled, staring at him.

He smirked a little, feeling her gaze. "What?"

"That's such a small part of you, why is it so glaringly important?"

"My job?"

She nodded once. "Well, what you do when you finish a job."

He shrugged. "Because it's the one unknown. I'm pretty normal otherwise. You know, for a dark."

She shook her head and shifted. "Nah, you're normal for anyone. You're just quieter than most people." Her voice changed to a mildly irritated tone. "And can hide in broad daylight."

He leaned forward and reached up to her chin, pulling it close to him so he could kiss her. Satyrna responded willingly. She could feel the rest of the tension melt away.

When he pulled away, she stood up and moved around the table to sit down on his lap, her arms wrapped around him.

"Oof," Malkarai said softly, half-laughing. He slipped his arms around her waist and held her close, hugging her for a minute or so before Satyrna kissed him fervently. He smirked slightly and responded agreeably, deepening the kiss. Satyrna smiled but reciprocated.

After a few minutes, Satyrna pulled away, putting her hands on his shoulders. "Okay, we're done, before I do something I regret."

He smirked and put his forehead against hers. "Would you really regret it?"

She didn't answer. "I have a few more questions."

"Well, I'm in an agreeable mood, so you'll probably get answers."

"Good. Your income. How much were you paid, and how much do you have?"

"Well, right now my income has flatlined, of course. They've deleted all records of my existence and closed my pay accounts."

She frowned. "So, you have nothing?"

"No, I have plenty of money. I didn't keep my savings in their account. I always took my money out of my pay account and put it in a private one. I figured that it was safer, in case I did decide to join Traphian someday."

"Oh… smart thinking."

"Mm-hmm. It's paid off now. I'll be set for a while, whether I work or not."

"How much were you paid for working for them?"

"Before I turned eighteen, most of my money went back to the agency to pay for schooling and housing. After that, a certain amount was still automatically taken out of my paychecks for housing, and I had to pay for whatever college-level courses I took."

"All right."

"Well, I suppose I should explain that we weren't paid by the hour. We were paid by the mission. Also, we were only paid if we were successful. If we failed, someone else would have the chance to finish the objective. The harder the mission, the more the pay." He reached over to the end of the table and picked up the packet. She realized he must've taken it with him earlier. "Okay, yeah, that's on here." He showed her the stats sheet on the front and pointed to the 'rank' and 'level approved' lines. His were '16' and '5' respectively. "See this?"

"Yes."

"My rank was how far I'd made it in training. There isn't much of a max, because people can get new ranks based on how much they train. I was pretty far up there though. Most of the veterans hover around rank 20. Up until rank 15, you are approved for a new mission level every three ranks. Level one is the easiest, and level five is the hardest. Sometimes we'll get a rank six, but those usually require groups for safety's sake."

"So, you could go after fives?"

"Yeah, I was skilled enough to go after the hardest – the worst – people solo. I probably could've had a higher rank than 16, but after I was made Stika's second hand and achieved rank 15, I focused more on my secondary profession, teaching, and dealing with all the administrative crap she needed me to take care of."

"Oh, I forgot you were given a position. What did it mean? What did you do?"

"She's the head of our agency, Stika, the woman you apparently saw with Teffifa and Swip. She's in charge of all the finances of the agency, making sure that we have enough food and supplies, or making sure that the people in charge of that are doing their job. She also has authority over all the agents in the agency. She enacts punishments for digressions, awards levels and other achievements, and makes sure that everything's running smoothly. She's also our emissary to the higher levels of the government. When administrative problems arise, she takes care of them. She deals with the internal agents far more than the rest of us, much to our gratitude. The agents are usually a bunch of pricks."

Satyrna snickered softly.

"Anyway, what I did was assist her. I usually dealt with finances and budgeting more than the other tasks, but when she went on missions, I took care of her job. Thankfully, though, Stika knew that I preferred to not have a leadership position, so she rarely went on missions. She's paid a salary, so she doesn't need to work in the field anymore. I was paid a smaller salary for being her second hand, as well as for all the missions I did. So, because of my dual income, I'm sitting on quite a bit of money now, even despite getting my degree and various training programs. I hated having downtime. It's why I have so many skills."

"How much?"

"Well, level fives, which is what I did most of the time, pay about $9,000 to $11,000 a mission. I could usually do two, maybe three missions a month. This one I was on was abnormally long. My salary was about $100,000 a year before they took all the fees and housing costs out."

Satyrna raised her brow. "Wow…" she said mutedly.

"I've got $650,000-something in my account right now."

She rested her head against his, staring at the sheet, but not really looking at it, not sure how to respond to that.

"So, you understand why I don't like to discuss the amount I was paid, right?"

"That's a lot of money…" she replied softly.

"Yeah. But it's not all blood money. I worked hard when I was there. I have no moral hang-ups about using that money now."

"I guess so, but it's still a lot. I doubt my parents have anywhere near that much in their savings…"

He rubbed her back with his hand and set the papers down on the table. "Your parents have three children of post-college age. Also, the reason we are paid so much is they intend for the money to last us until we die. So, after we retire, which is usually in our forties or fifties, we don't have to do any other work. The way I figure, they've made it all that much easier for me to stay hidden."

"I wouldn't go spending it all to begin with."

He shook his head. "No, I wasn't going to. I intend to use a little to get things going but then rely on whatever income I can dig up here. I'll save it for whatever might come later."

She nodded slightly, her head still resting against his.

"You okay, Saty?"

"Yeah, I'm just trying to fathom that much money, I guess."

"It's not that much, in the grand scheme of things."

"Today it is. Especially for someone our age. Yeah, inflation's still gross, but work's hard to come by."

He shrugged and slipped his other arm back around her, hugging her close. "Look at it this way, with all the shit we've already got to worry about, at least money isn't one of them."

She laughed slightly and nodded, leaning back a little. "Yeah, that's true."

He kissed her lips briefly and then said, "Hey, I have a question."

"Yeah?"

"Stika… how'd she look?"

She shrugged. "In charge. I dunno."

"I meant emotion-wise."

"Oh. Serious. Swip smiled at us and flirted with Josh and Teffifa winked, but Stika didn't even glance at us. She looked nice enough, but she was obviously preoccupied. Why?"

Malkarai made a face at first. "Fucking Swip… At least *he* seemed normal." He sighed and shook his head, looking contemplative. "If there's one thing I regret, it's leaving Stika without giving a warning. She relied on me a lot."

"Because you were her second hand?"

"Yeah."

"It's not like you could've given her a warning, Malkarai. They think you died. They think that you and Traphian killed each other."

He nodded slightly.

"Isn't that something she could've expected?"

"I don't know. Maybe. She knew I wasn't happy about this mission, but her hands were tied. The upper levels ordered me to take it. That's not something that happens often, and I never like it when they do. I'm sure she's probably sad if anything."

"That you're gone?"

"Yeah. And that I had such a shit mission for my last one. She liked Traphian. She kept denying their requests to let us track him down. It kept getting sent to the Southwestern and Midwestern divisions even though he was in our district. Eventually though, they got fed up with transporting agents up here and demanded she put it in the system. Teffifa took it, but she didn't realize it was him until she found him. I think she faltered too."

"Really?"

"Yeah. That's what she made it sound like. She was bitching about how he shouldn't have gotten her off guard, he shouldn't have been able to catch her. I think it threw her, even when she was in bloodlust. She was never one of our best buddies, but we were all close to the people in our age group."

"Was Swip part of that?"

He nodded. "Swip, Shawn, Teffifa, Traphian, Arista, and myself. I took it the hardest, but they were all down when Arista disappeared, and everyone was confused when Traphian left. I was the only one who knew where he went. I'm sure they were just expecting me to go sooner or later, be it of my own doing or something else."

"They took pictures of you two, right?"

He nodded.

"Pretending to be dead?"

"Yeah."

"What did you guys decide to pretend you did?"

"I killed him and then killed myself. We faked an entry wound on him down here," he pointed to the soft spot right below the middle of his ribcage, "and we faked like I split my arm from elbow to wrist."

She blinked, staring at him in surprise. "You'd slit your arm? That's not instantaneous, Malkarai…"

He shrugged. "How I was before, it wouldn't have mattered. All that would've mattered was that it would've been fatal. And the wound we faked, it would've been fatal within a minute or so, at least. It wasn't a weak, second-guessing slash."

"But, would you have really killed Traphian too? I mean, even if you'd given up, why would you kill him too?"

"Because, if I didn't, they'd still blame him for my death anyway, and then his difficulty would be raised, and thus he'd become more of a priority target. Unless he completely disappeared, they would track him down and kill him. There wouldn't even be a chance of capture at that point. It'd be more humane for me to just finish it there."

"Will they believe that?"

"I hope so. Until you threw me off course, it was hovering around my first choice for a plan of action."

Satyrna blinked. "Really?" she asked quietly.

"Yeah. Traphian owes you just as much as me."

She let go of his torso and reached up to cradle his head in her hands. "Do you still feel like that?" she asked softly.

"Suicidal?"

She nodded once.

"No. The complete opposite. I want to fight to live now."

"Honest?"

"Satyrna, look at where I am." She glanced down and around, not sure at first what he was talking about. He laughed and pulled her against his chest. "Oh, you're cute. If I still wanted to kill myself after this, well, then I'd better hurry up and spare everyone else the wasted oxygen, because I must be a complete idiot."

She pressed her nose against his neck. "I'm serious."

"So am I. I don't want to die. I want to stay here with you and with your friends. I get to see my brother again, and, well, I found out I have a little sister. You undoubtedly saved me."

Satyrna smiled and squeezed him. "Will you come with me to Christmas at my house?"

"Yes."

"Good. My brother's gonna be there, and you can work on making my sister respect you."

"I thought she was okay with me."

"She was okay with you until you were of significant interest to me, then her required standards were raised."

He sighed. "Figures."

"She's easier to please than my dad though. When you're trying, anyway. I usually don't bother to try."

"I'm sure she doesn't give a shit what schooling I have though."

"No, probably not."

"So how do I win her favor? Or your mother's, for that matter."

"Patricia, it's about accomplishments, actions, and how you treat people. My mother? Be nice to me and make her smile. You already have one thing going for you in my mother's eyes."

"What's that?"

She pointed to her knee.

"I can sew, so I'm okay?" he ventured.

"Well, that's a plus, but no. You can take care of me. I'm pretty self-sufficient, but when things got too bad for me to deal with alone, you were able to fix me up yourself."

He smirked. "So, being able to clean up after you, that's a good ability then?"

She nodded.

He snickered and kissed her, slowly and deliberately. "All right, I think I can manage that."

# 41



Cypha sat at a table for two in the nearly deserted tavern, the other chair empty. The only other people there were one waitress, one bartender, presumedly a cook, most of the usual drunks, and a couple near the back of the room, but they were hanging all over each other, too engaged to notice anything else happening in the building. Barry was even out, visiting his mother's family in Owatonna. Her father was there, but he was stone drunk, too washed up to notice her – if he even knew what she looked like.

She looked up briefly as another couple came in, and sighed, swirling the ice in her drink. Then she toasted to the empty chair across from her. "Well, here's to another merry Christmas."

As she drank deeply from the glass, the waitress, Roxy, came over to her. She had very curly, dark brown hair that was pulled back in a pony, brown skin, and freckles. When Cypha had first shown up a different waitress was working, but it seemed Roxy was running the dining area solo now.

"Hey, Cypha, spending Christmas alone?"

"Yep. Why does he have you working on Christmas Eve? I thought he liked you."

Roxy shrugged. "My family's doing everything this weekend, so I volunteered. I make good money when I work odd hours, especially holidays."

Cypha nodded slowly, staring straight ahead of her. She didn't see how she got good tips on nights like this, but whatever floated her boat. "I haven't seen Leah in a while."

"Oh, you didn't know? Barry fired her."

Cypha looked up at Roxy in surprise. "What? Really? Why?"

Roxy smirked, glancing at the bar. "Well, it was her boyfriend that broke Dyspro's leg. Technically Dyspro works for Barry too, and even if he didn't, they're best friends. It was a 'conflict of interests.'"

Cypha laughed. "Wow. Well, that makes my fucking night." She eyed Roxy. "You aren't friends with her, are you?"

"Dyspro's nicer than she is, so nah. She was kind of a backstabber."

"Good."

Roxy smiled. "You want a refill?"

"Yeah, sure, why not?"

"All right."

Roxy took Cypha's nearly empty glass and went to the bar. She returned soon after and set the glass down on the table.

"Dyspro and Satyrna with their families?"

Cypha nodded.

"Why aren't you?"

"Don't have one."

"Oh, I didn't know that. Why don't you celebrate the holiday with your friends then?"

She gave Roxy a look, even though the waitress' question was innocent enough. "Cuz I hate Christmas, that's why. I think those two over there might want to order."

Roxy glanced at the newly arrived couple but turned back to Cypha briefly before departing.

Cypha sighed and laid her head down on an arm on the table. She flicked her glass with a fingernail, watching the liquid inside tremor slightly. She heard the door open again, and then felt the icy wind blow in, but didn't lift her head. The bartender said something to the arrival or arrivals, and then they responded. It was a man who spoke. She turned her head so that she could see, still resting it upon her arm, and then watched him for a few moments. He was alone. He ordered something and looked around the tavern, still standing.

She turned her head back and continued staring at her glass. A few minutes later she jumped slightly when she heard someone behind her say, "Cypha, right?"

She lifted her head and pushed her hair out of her eyes. "Oh, hey, Traphian."

"What are you doing in here alone?"

She leaned back in her chair and sighed. "Celebrating the holiday."

He chuckled and looked about the tavern. It was dark as usual, but it had strands of Christmas lights hung up around the room and a wreath in each window. The festive decorations didn't seem to lift the heavy mood inside though. "Sure picked a depressing spot to do so."

"Yeah, well, Christmas is depressing, and I'm depressed. Why're you here?"

"Thought I'd get a drink and then grab something to eat. I saw a little cafe that was open 'til 9:30. Do you care if I sit with you, or do you want to be alone?"

She shook her head. "No, go ahead. It'll be nice to have someone to talk to."

He sat down and shed his coat on the chair back. "Didn't you get invited over by any of your friends?"

"Yeah, I got two invites. I turned them down."

"And then came here alone?" he asked, incredulous.

She sighed. "I never accept. Honestly, the only reason I'm not at home avoiding everything is I've gotten too used to people being around, and Malkarai and Satyrna have both been gone almost all day."

"Oh. Yeah, he was at my place most of the day. Satyrna was at her parents', right? That's where he went this afternoon."

"Yeah."

"You just prefer to lone it?"

"Yeah."

"I guess I don't blame you. I never got the point of all this celebrating myself. I mean, I understand why the Church celebrates it, but I didn't ever get the parties."

She shrugged. "It's a reason to get your family together. I mean, it's a good thing to gather up your family once in a while, but it's not a whole lotta fun if you're lacking one."

"Yeah, there's nothing wrong with it, but I find it a lonely time of the year."

"No family, no point."

"Exactly."

"I'm avoiding particular people and avoiding feeling like an unwanted invader." Cypha took a drink and motioned to the bar with her glass. "This is about as close as I get to having my family together for the holidays. I'm fine with it; I don't want to spend any time with him anyway."

Traphian looked back to where she had gestured and noticed the loud, gangly man in the middle of three others, laughing uproariously at something. His dirty blonde hair was similar in color to Cypha's. The other three had brown hair. "Is that your father?"

"Yeah. Pretty sure he has no idea I'm still alive, much less what I look like though."

He turned back.

She smiled devilishly. "I'm definitely better off than that son of a bitch though, so I can't complain too much."

He was quiet for a moment. "How come he doesn't know you're alive?"

"He dumped me in a trash can when I was four or five. Figured I'd die. Well, I didn't. I spent like a year and a half in a home and then ran away. Came back here and have been here since."

"He's guilty of child endangerment and abandonment then."

"Yeah, he spent time in prison. Obviously a totally satisfactory amount," she said sarcastically.

"Where's your mother?"

"No clue. I'm sure she's no better than him though, if she's still alive."

"You ever ask him where she is?"

"I've never talked to him, and I don't want to. I'd end up socking him in the face before I got an answer out of him. That's why I'm sitting at this sad couple's table instead of at the bar where I can talk to Marvin at least."

"Anger's pretty deep here, I see."

"Yep."

He glanced back over his shoulder. "Pretty sure you'd win."

She shrugged. "I don't know, he's bigger than me and he's kinda lanky, and he looks strong enough. I'm not that great of a fist-thrower either. I guess I could make do with kicking though. If I pulled another blade in here, they'd kick me out for good. That's what Roxy told me, anyway."

"Who's Roxy?"

"The waitress. Barry probably wouldn't kick me out for good. If he did, Dyspro would sweet-talk him for me. He might make me eat in the back from then on though."

He snickered and then looked up as Roxy set a glass in front of him. He thanked her and she smiled and went back to the bar.

"God, I'd hate to have her job," said Cypha.

"Why?"

"Gotta serve insolent people all day, get paid little, and tipped even less. Plus, you gotta act happy all the time and be friendly."

Traphian chuckled. "Can't do that?"

"I'm not the service sort."

"What do you do then?"

"I'm working at a shipping facility right now."

"Oh, well, that works then."

"Yeah. So, you get to play dead, right?"

He nodded.

"You're gonna stay here, right?"

"Most likely. The local government is willing to offer me immunity – at least from the federal government. I'm not gonna pass that up recklessly."

"Valid. Where are you staying now?"

"The knights put me up in a temp apartment, but it sucks, so I started looking for a place for Malk and me to rent."

"Oh, that's cool. He's getting antsy about not having electricity or running water. So he went to your place this morning?"

Traphian nodded absently, watching Roxy as she passed by. "Used my shower. It's a big get-together at Satyrna's place, right?"

"Yeah, he's meeting the whole fam and Dyspro's family is there."

"So Rafiane is too?"

"Yeah, pretty sure. Dyspro invited her back for it."

"Malk's gonna need therapy after that." Traphian laughed. "Good luck, sucker."

Cypha smirked. "You should work on getting a job."

"Yeah, I've been looking. Most of the apartments won't even call me back if I can't say I have a job. I'll look harder when I'm sure that Malk and I are staying here. He still has to do this stupid fight against Kalyfa. I'm optimistic because I know how Malk fights, but I still feel like maybe I should wait and see if we need to bolt."

Cypha made a face. "I hope you don't. Satyrna will be absolutely awful if he up and left."

He smirked. "I'm sure she's great motivation for him not to lose, yeah. That's why I *am* looking."

"What can you do for work?"

Traphian shrugged. "A lot of stuff. I'll probably end up somewhere in food service though. I enjoy cooking."

She laughed shortly. "Really?"

He nodded, looking at her.

"I never would've guessed that."

"Me neither, to be honest. It was one thing they didn't teach me in the system, so I kinda learned to enjoy figuring out what I could make out of what I could manage to scrape together. It was a challenge. I've had to cook for myself since I ran away."

"That's awesome. Malk can't cook, can he?"

"Not that I'm aware of. Honestly, he's terrible at even remembering to eat at times."

She snickered and stared at him for a few moments. "He was trying to arrest you, right?"

"Somethin' like that."

"You don't resent that?"

"No, he didn't want to do it. That's why it took him two weeks to even talk to me. Malkarai's always been like my little brother. I looked out for him all the time, but he was my best friend and he looked out for me too. I've been waiting for years for him to do this, so I'm just happy he finally joined me."

"That's cool that you two are still friends after all that." Cypha took a sip from her glass and then wiped a bit of wetness off her lower lip with her finger, staring at the almost empty glass. "Oops."

"What?"

She sighed. "I'm getting drunk again. Cut me off, okay?"

He raised an eyebrow, smirking. "Why?"

"Cuz I'm… angry when I'm drunk."

Traphian laughed. "All right. Noted."

"I really don't need to get in another fight." She sighed, folding her arms and resting them on the table. "I want to keep this job."

After a few moments, he asked, "What are you planning on doing tonight?"

"I don't know. Maybe get something to eat, then go home and try not to think. Go to sleep."

He chuckled. "Sounds like a plan. Sounds a lot like mine."

She laughed.

"You wanna go to that cafe with me?" Traphian asked. "It looked a hell of a lot less dreary than this place."

She sighed and looked at the drink she held in her hands. "I would, but I don't have any money yet. I get paid on Friday. Dyspro's got a tab here; he always pays for us. Plus, he works here sometimes, stocking things and fixing what needs to be fixed, so Barry gives him big discounts."

"Don't worry about it, I'll pay for you."

She shook her head. "Nope."

"Why not?"

"Cuz it's not like you're working. Save your money."

"I've got enough, don't worry. Malkarai keeps reverse pick-pocketing me whenever he's over, and I decided to pretend I didn't notice because I think it's relieving some of his guilt."

She snickered and sighed, looking down at the table and flicking her finger against her glass uncomfortably.

He leaned forward and took hold of her hand so that she looked up at him, affronted. Traphian ignored this since it was only a look and she didn't pull away. "Look, it's not charity or anything. I don't know, think of it as a date or something. I'll take a pretty, neglected woman out for something to eat on Christmas Eve, simple as that. Hopefully, it'll be something good to think back on. Can you live with that?"

Cypha blushed fiercely. "I have booze in me, you'd better watch how you step, buddy."

He just raised an eyebrow, not intimidated. "Chill, okay? I'm kinda lonely. Being stuck in a single room for three weeks with no outside interaction besides Malkarai and television makes one pretty desperate for human contact. Please come with me?"

She turned her drink in her free hand, trying to ignore the one he still had a hold of, then glanced up. "Fuck it; why not?"

He smiled, let go of her hand, and slipped his coat on. Cypha downed what was left of her drink and stood, putting her coat on. She dug some money out of a pocket, tossed it on the table next to her empty glass, and started for the door, where she waited. Traphian stopped at the bar to pay and then she followed him outside.

"It was over here," he gestured to the west and she walked with him.

After a few minutes, she asked, "Did you mean that 'pretty' bullshit or were you trying to butter me up out of desperation?"

Traphian grinned. "Are you going to punch me if I meant it?"

"I'm considering punching you regardless, to be honest."

He laughed.

She smiled, eyeing him in amusement – because his laugh was not condescending, just entertained.

"Wait an hour to decide if you wanna punch me or not, and I'll let you."

"Deal."

10:00 p.m.

Malkarai took Satyrna's hand as they turned the corner away from her house.

"That went well," she said.

He rolled his eyes. "Oh yeah, real smooth."

"What?"

"Your brother thinks I'm a creeper and everyone knows that I got into some rough shit earlier this month and had to change my identity. Yeah, things are working out great."

Satyrna sighed, staring at the ground in front of her. "Yeah, whatever… so you're a fighter. We know plenty of them. Brendan is one too. They don't know all of the details or how messed up it was. Despite it being such a hot topic, everyone miraculously kept their mouths shut about me stabbing Kalyfa. Adam's just being a shithead because he was one of the ones that thought me hooking up with Kalyfa was a great idea. They went to school together and he's impressed he was picked to be head of the knights, so of course he's pissed I didn't like him that much. Now that Brendan finally actually proposed to Patricia, hopefully he'll stop bothering me, and by proxy, you."

"Satyrna, most people don't get involved in sword fights, okay? Not even the knights. Yeah, your mother was grateful I could take care of you when you got hurt, but you know neither of your parents want you involved with someone who regularly deals with shit like that."

"Kalyfa did."

"There's nothing unknown about Kalyfa's profession. You said yourself, that people think his position is something great."

"That's not true, that there's nothing unknown about his job. You know, they're not aware that there are other parts to your job. They probably just figure you're like him – that you're a typical law enforcer. You're all sensitive about it because you know there are differences. Let it go, okay? When I was Kalyfa's girlfriend I was in danger too. Probably more, if you think about it. He was and is more…public. More well-known. You were secretive, and now you're retired."

"I doubt that his enemies are more dangerous than mine."

"The public was aware of him, they're not aware of you. There's a reason he was so overprotective, Malkarai. He should've dropped it after it all ended, but that's his thing, not mine."

Malkarai sighed, not answering. He was searching the street in front of them idly, keeping an eye out for threats.

"I'm all right with keeping our relationship quiet – especially if you think it'll keep both of us safer," Satyrna said. "But I want you to realize that I'm not okay with hiding it like it's something to be ashamed of. I'm perfectly aware of what being with you means."

"Thank you, I'm glad… but there's a lot that you don't know, and the ignorance helps with being brave about it, I guess. I feel like I know just enough to realize that there's a lot of danger out there that I don't know about."

She squeezed his hand firmly. "That's not something we need to worry about right now, is it?"

He shook his head.

"What you did before, what you worried about before – you should try to leave it in the past. Once this stupid thing with Kalyfa is over, then we can just worry about the future. A future *together*."

He was thoughtfully silent. After a minute or so, he looked across the street and then pulled her across by the hand. "Let's take a detour."

"What?" she replied, a little surprised, but following regardless.

"We're gonna take a different way home."

"All right."

He led her north for a few blocks and then east, toward a brighter, cleaner, newer part of town. There were houses here with varying-sized lawns, all cozily nestled along friendly, well-lit streets. Satyrna's family lived in town, where the older, dark brick buildings were prominent. Here the houses were older than turn-of-the-century suburbia but were still strictly residential. They were built in a period where homes were still unique, built differently each time with different floorplans, colors, and materials, instead of the industrial cookie-cutter houses that had become popular around the turn of the millennium. The homes that had been built with this method were on the western edge of town.

Satyrna looked around her as he turned onto a street she was pretty sure ended in a dead end. "Where are we going, Malkarai? This doesn't go anywhere."

"Yeah, it does," he replied simply. "You've probably seen it before, but I found it earlier and wanted to come back."

Satyrna just shrugged.

Malkarai turned into a small block park and headed along one of the lightly snow-covered, winding, diagonal sidewalks to the center of the park. Amid some bushes and leafless trees was a gazebo with a brightly lit and decorated Christmas tree inside.

It was very different from the one at the Hennessins' house. Theirs was a fairly realistic fake tree with dozens of mismatched heirloom ornaments, reflective garland, and an angel at the top. This was a real evergreen, had a paper chain garland, and bore only glass balls amongst the multi-colored lights. The top was adorned with a silver star.

There were streetlamps along the sidewalks, but inside the gazebo was dark except for the glow from the tree.

Malkarai shrugged, nodding toward the tree. "Well, this is it."

She squeezed his hand gently, watching him. She knew what he was motioning to, but she wasn't sure what 'it' was. "I've never been here before," she said after a few moments.

He glanced at her. "Really?"

"Yeah. Dyspro's family lives on this end of town, but they're a few blocks south. We never came this far north to play."

"This is the kind of place I'd like to live someday," he said, his attention on the tree.

"Er…a park?"

"No, this kind of neighborhood. I don't like cities, and towns are okay for work and shopping, but I want to live someplace where there are other people, but enough space to still feel separated and private. I want greenery. And, most of all, I want peace. A neighborhood where they put up a tree in the middle of a park for no reason aside from making people happy is the kind of place I want to live."

Satyrna leaned against his shoulder, wrapping her arms around his. "What brought this on?"

"You said I should look at the future and think about what I want."

She smiled and shut her eyes.

After a few moments, he looked at her, dislodged his arm, and wrapped both of them around her. Satyrna hugged him back, gazing at the tree with her cheek against his shoulder.

"Here?" she asked.

He shrugged slightly. "Wherever life may take me. But this is what I want."

"What's it like where you lived before?"

"Similar, but we didn't have any neighbors. We were way back in the woods behind a locked gate. We lived and played behind a fence."

"Gross."

He shrugged. "We were kinda lucky. The other agencies didn't even have woods, just lawns – or sand, like the one in Arizona. The base in Chicago is in the city."

She was quiet for a few minutes before asking, "Have you ever celebrated Christmas before?"

"We kinda did. We put up a tree, lit candles, and had a big dinner on Christmas, but it was never religious. Very few of us were, and since we ran it, that's just how it worked."

"Are you religious?"

"No. We were free to explore them if we wanted, but most of them said not to do what my entire job consisted of."

"Huh," she said softly. "Did you enjoy tonight?"

"Yeah. It was… stressful, but I did enjoy myself."

Satyrna smirked. "Stressful, yeah, that's my family."

"It was a lot of firsts for me. I was afraid I was going to make an ass out of myself."

"What firsts?"

"Meeting my girlfriend's parents, being at a family Christmas, meeting family period… Yeah, it was mildly nerve-wracking," he finished dryly.

"Says the man who hunted felons."

"Yes, says the man who hunted top-class felons. Your family made me nervous."

She squeezed him for a few moments. "Well, you did fine. No ass-making was done."

"I'll take your word for it. I felt like an eyesore all night."

"Aside from Adam, who just doesn't like you because you aren't Kalyfa, no matter what excuses he's trying to make for his assholery, I think it's safe to say you had a positive impression on everyone. I'm happy with how tonight went."

Malkarai sighed. "If you're happy with it, then I'll try to be too."

"That sounds like a wise plan." Satyrna shifted, rubbing the ankle of one boot against the panty-hosed knee of her other leg. "I'm cold."

"All right." His arms loosened their hold and then he kissed the top of her head, moving down to her forehead, down her nose, and then stopping at her lips, kissing her passionately.

Satyrna felt a chill go down her spine, gripping the back of his coat in both hands and standing on tiptoes to be closer to him.

Malkarai slipped a hand behind her head, running his fingers into her hair, holding her close to him for a few more moments before releasing, pecking her softly on the lips, and pulling back. He ran his hand down her back, stroking her hair, before letting it rest on her waist and turning to go. "Okay, let's go home."

She clutched onto his coat on his far side, her arm around his back. When they were back on the street she asked, "What do you want for Christmas?"

"To wake up holding you again."

She blushed, taken off-guard by his response. "Er, well, that can be done."

"What would you like?"

She was quiet for a few moments before answering softly, "The same thing… even after that."

He squeezed her waist. "I'll see what I can do about that."

Satyrna looked around when they'd opened the door and stepped inside Cypha and Dyspro's house. It was dark, and the fire was low behind the screen. "Cypha?"

Malkarai shut and locked the door behind them before unbuttoning and taking off his coat.

After searching the other rooms Satyrna came back out, taking her coat off as she re-entered the main room. She put her coat down over his, on the back of a chair, before fluffing the red satin knee-length dress she was still wearing from the party. "She's not here. Wonder what she's up to."

"Are you concerned?"

"Not really. She turns down everyone's invites to holiday parties, but it doesn't mean she just stays home. If she's not back in the morning, then I'll get concerned." She gave him a smile. "Our lives usually aren't that interesting, I promise."

"Good." Malkarai snickered as he put a few pieces of wood on the fire and, when he stood up, stopped Satyrna from lighting a candle.

She gave him a curious look as he took her hands, setting the candle and the matches down. Satyrna cocked an eyebrow, smirking. "Did you want to turn in already?"

Malkarai dropped his hands, still holding onto hers. He leaned forward, kissing her softly. "Not explicitly."

Satyrna blushed, squeezing his hands. When he'd leaned back she inhaled quietly, looking from his mouth to his eyes. "What instead then?"

Malkarai smirked slightly. "I figured we could enjoy having the place to ourselves for a little while. I'm pretty amateur when it comes to romance, but I'd like to give it a shot anyway."

Satyrna giggled, loosing her hands from his and running them up his chest and over his shoulders, hugging him around the neck.

Malkarai kissed her neck gently as he slid his arms around her waist, holding her close to him.

"Amateur, huh?" she said breathily.

"Painfully."

"Guess I've only been with Neanderthals before now then."

Malkarai laughed and slid his hand up and down her lower back. "I meant what I said earlier though… you look really nice in this."

Satyrna blushed.

He kissed her ear gently. "Feel really nice too."

"I guess you've only been around me in sweater season." She felt her skin burn and heard Malkarai chuckle softly in her ear.

"You know, for how confident and just effortlessly sexy you are, you get so flustered from intimate contact."

"I'm not used to you being intimate," she replied quietly.

"Is this a problem? I can back off if you want me to."

"No, no," she said quickly. "You just strike me as so reserved, and, well… I'm so…"

"Not?"

Satyrna tweaked his ear through his hair, smirking. "Incredibly attracted to you. I guess I'm just used to having to fight tooth and nail to get close to you. I'm not easy. Although now you have me worrying that I'm coming off that way."

He shook his head slightly. "Not easy – just more comfortable expressing yourself. So, I'm surprised I can make you this bothered."

Satyrna smirked, still blushing. "You have no idea how attractive you are, do you?"

"Guess not. I think I'm creepy."

She shook her head slightly and kissed him gently. "I guess your confidence doesn't come from your looks then."

"Nope. My confidence comes from knowing that close to no one out there can touch me."

Satyrna made a small noise. "Wow. I really did accomplish the impossible."

Malkarai snickered, dropping an arm and sliding it under her thighs, picking her up and moving over by the bench. "I meant combat-wise, but yes, I suppose you did accomplish the impossible."

Satyrna ran her fingers through his hair as he sat down on the bench, letting them both get comfortable before he met her lips warmly with his own.

"Mmmm…" she murmured, holding onto his head, her fingers in his soft, fine hair – something she hadn't noticed before. After they'd parted to breathe, she said softly, "I guess it's because you've been in hiding for the past three weeks so I've avoided touching it, but I don't think I've ever noticed how soft your hair is."

He laughed. "Thanks? I don't know how Cypha washes her hair with just water from that pump. My hair's looked like shit, but I've been keeping the rest of me clean." He shook his head in disbelief. "I never would've dreamed that at some point in my life, I'd be taking the equivalent of a sponge bath."

Satyrna laughed. "Wasn't a goal of yours, huh?"

"Well, I may not have had many goals before this month, but no, bathing outside of a shower or bathtub was never one of them. I'm not complaining though; this has been the ultimate hiding place. Zero digital trail, seclusion, no address. Hell, the people who live here don't even own it."

She smiled. "Never really thought about it that way. I thought that they were silly when Dyspro said they were going to live here and be caretakers, but the longer they're here the more I like it. Plus, it's kept Cypha off the streets, which is great."

"And now it's hiding a fugitive quite effectively."

Satyrna snickered. "Which I'm happy about."

Malkarai shut his eyes, kissing her warmly and deeply.

Satyrna slid her fingers back around the base of his head again.

After a few minutes, they broke off the kiss, and she rested her forehead against his. "Let's get ready for bed," she said quietly. "Before Cypha gets home."

He smirked and let go of her so she could slide her legs off of his lap. "Okay. Let me grab my shorts and you can get ready in there."

She kissed him on the nose and then headed back for the bedrooms.

# 42

December 30, 2036
4:00 p.m.

Satyrna looked around the little stone house as she set her purse down on the table, but it seemed to be empty. "I'm home," she called, checking anyway.

She didn't receive a response, as she expected, so she peeked into the extra room Malkarai had been using for the past three weeks. "Malkarai?"

There was no reply, so she turned and went back outside.

She went through the woods a short distance before she heard heavy breath, peaking in small grunts occasionally. He came into view after only a short distance. He was practicing in an open area mostly cleared of snow, scuffed and worn bare by his use from the past week, wearing just a T-shirt, jeans, and boots. She stopped and leaned forward against a tree, watching him around it. The T-shirt was sticking to him, so she assumed he'd been out here a while.

Malkarai swiped and jabbed at the air with his sword, pausing before swinging wide. "Hey, Satyrna," he said without looking in her direction.

"Hey," she responded quietly, watching him as he pulled a quick circuit, spinning somewhere in the middle, and ending in a hard strike that would've landed at about abdomen height on a person. He moved too quickly – too strategically – for her to catch everything he was doing. However, it boggled her mind that he could do it all while talking to her. He seemed more out of breath today than before, though, so he was quiet for now.

Rotating his shoulders and passing the sword in between his hands to avoid stretching with the weapon in hand, he walked over to where his coat was draped over a rock.

"Done for today?" she asked.

He sat down and picked up a cup of water he had nestled in the snow next to the rock. "Not quite. I'm still a little stiff. Feels loads better than it did last week though."

"Don't get pneumonia," she scolded weakly.

"I'll be fine." He took a sip and looked at her. "How was apartment-hunting?"

She shrugged. "Mildly fruitful. I'm not really in love with any of the places, but they'll do. I gotta see what I can get for a second job in the meantime."

He looked at her for a few moments, elbows on his knees, holding the glass between them. "You seem bothered. What's up?"

She shook her head slightly. "It's tomorrow…"

"Yep," he replied, still watching her.

"It didn't bother me until… well, now. I'm worried you two are gonna seriously hurt each other."

He shrugged. "Blame Kalyfa for that one. I have no urge to fight this guy."

Her brow was knitted up. "So why don't you just tell him no? Why do you have to fight him?"

"He's the one who gave me the ultimatum. If he thought I would turn tail and run, he was wrong. Perhaps, when I was younger, I would've done that, but not now. I have pride now, and since I know he's also trying to prove to you that you made the wrong choice, I *need* to correct that."

Satyrna looked at her feet. "I don't need a fight to know my choice was right."

He set the glass down and stood up, leaving the sword to rest as he stepped over by her. He brushed some of her hair behind her ear and kissed her forehead. "I'm glad to hear you say that, but this unfortunately isn't about proving it to you – although you better believe I won't embarrass you by losing."

She sighed. "I'd rather this whole stupid thing didn't happen," she said quietly.

"Do you want me to stay?"

"Of course, I do…"

"Then it's going to happen," he said firmly as he stepped away and picked his sword up again. "He hinged this cover-up on me proving my skills."

Satyrna swallowed the knot in her throat, staring at the ground.

Malkarai wiped his forehead on his shirt sleeve and started a circuit, practicing weapon and foot placement.

"If I felt like it'd do any good, I'd go and give him a piece of my mind, but he didn't listen to me even when I was his girlfriend. He'd just pat me on the head, tell me it'd be okay, and then do whatever the hell he wanted to anyway. I was hoping you'd be different."

"I am different," he muttered. "Believe me, I hear you, Satyrna. My only other option is to give up and leave Cavington, which neither of us wants. I'm going to play by his rules and beat him at his own game."

"If you beat him too badly, that could ruin the arrangement anyway."

Malkarai shrugged and turned, jabbing under his arm and behind him with his blade. "I have control."

"Do you have enough control to not badly injure him, and still win?"

He glanced over at her, not pausing. "Yes."

"Aren't you afraid that he'll resent you after this…?"

"Honestly, I kind of expect that he will. You picked me of your own free will, and I'm still here. We could've just existed peacefully, but he needs to pull this shit and attempt to prove that he's the better fighter, when he isn't. If he'd had me do a debate, he probably would've kicked my ass soundly, but he picked combat."

Satyrna snorted and sighed, begrudgingly amused by that.

"I want to stay here, and he wants me to train his people. If he needs proof I can do it, fine."

"Do you think that's that important to them?"

"Yeah. They were humiliated by us. Teffifa, Traphian, and I opened their eyes."

"You guys kinda snuck up on them."

"Exactly. Two agents and a former one were able to infiltrate their stronghold and defeat a group of them before they hardly even realized it. They figured out quickly that not even a group of seven of them could take me down, and their leader and a captain couldn't do it either. I am not confused at all that Kalyfa wants to know what we know."

Satyrna watched as he walked over to the rock and picked up his sheath. After wiping the blade on a dry part of his shirt to get the wet residue from the snow off of it, he slipped it carefully into the leather apparatus. Then he set the sword down on the rock and proceeded to stretch.

"Now you're done?" she asked.

He bent over, grasping the toes of his boots – although he was nearly able to touch his shins with his head, so the toe-touching was only to keep his hands off the ground. "Yeah. It's getting dark and a stuffed-up head won't help me tomorrow."

Satyrna raised her brow. "Wow, you're flexible."

He smirked and winked at her, causing her to blush.

"So, wanna go get something to eat in town?" she asked, changing the subject quickly.

He laughed and stood up, stretching his shoulders. "Yeah, sounds good."

"Good. I asked Dyspro, Rafiane, Cypha, and Traphian to come."

He slung his sword belt over his shoulder. "What for?"

She shrugged. "We haven't had everyone together since the last fight. I want to try and not think about what's gonna happen tomorrow, so let's go have a little fun."

"All right." He picked up his coat and the glass of water. "Let me change my shirt and we'll go."

"'Kay." She followed him out of the clearing and back to the house, watching the sword bounce against his back. She had a sudden urge to grab the thing and just chuck it into the woods but only looked away with a sigh. *Why the hell am I attracted to the guys that play with blades?*

Outside of Barry's tavern, Malkarai squeezed Satyrna's hand and let go. She glanced at him but accepted it with a sigh and pulled the door open. It only took a few moments to spot the others at a round table in the far corner. Satyrna pointed and Malkarai nodded, pushing her back slightly to motion for her to go first. She waved at Barry and then headed back by the others.

Rafiane waved when she saw them and Cypha looked over her shoulder. Traphian was sitting in the corner of the room, reclined, looking elsewhere in the restaurant. Dyspro wasn't at the table, but his coat was on the chair next to Rafiane's.

"Hey," Cypha greeted. "Took you long enough."

Satyrna nodded at Malkarai. "He was still practicing and had to change. Where's Dyspro?"

"Bathroom."

"It's nice to see you again, Rafiane. You were home for a bit again, right?"

She nodded, smiling at Satyrna. "I'd been away from home for a while, so being back was nice, but Dyspro invited me back for New Year's stuff."

"Did he officially ask you out yet?" Cypha asked before taking a sip of her drink.

Rafiane blushed, but smiled. "Yeah… a week or so ago…"

"Oh, he never said anything. What an ass."

"Congrats!" Satyrna said brightly. "I mean, assuming you said yes."

She giggled. "Yes, I said yes."

Satyrna jumped when something poked her in the back of the knee. She turned and gave Dyspro an amused look. "Watch it or someone's gonna take those things away."

He pouted. "You'd really steal the crutches from a poor cripple?"

Cypha snorted. "Cripple, my ass."

He sat down between Rafiane and Cypha, propping his crutches against the wall. "Sit. I'm hungry. Some people have been working all day."

"Uh, yeah, both of us too," Satyrna replied, sitting next to Cypha.

Traphian gave Malkarai a look. "What have you been doing? Cuz you certainly haven't been working."

"Training," he answered, sitting between Traphian and Satyrna.

"It's tomorrow, right?" Rafiane asked quietly.

He nodded.

"How healed are you?" she asked.

"Uh, we took the stitches out last week, and the infection was gone long before that. It's seemed fine."

"He'll be healing for a while, but it's probably good enough as long as he doesn't pull anything stupid," Satyrna added.

Traphian laughed. "Malk would never do that."

"Of course not," Malkarai said flatly.

Satyrna gave them both a scolding look and Cypha laughed.

"Are you worried?" Dyspro asked.

Malkarai just shrugged. "I'm better than him. He could get lucky though."

"She helped you last time, right?" Dyspro motioned at Satyrna.

"Yeah. I was also pretty distracted too. Your siblings were making me nervous."

"Why?"

"Because I didn't want them to get hurt." Malkarai shook his head. "I don't like talking about these things before they happen. I think better during them if I haven't planned or analyzed anything."

"Really?" Traphian asked, an eyebrow cocked.

He nodded. "I got better at a lot of shit after I stopped thinking. Anyway, when's the cast coming off, Dyspro?"

"On the third. I'll have to wear a brace for a while. Then I'll be wanting my bedroom back, thank you very much." He motioned back and forth between Malkarai and Satyrna. "Deal with that how you will."

"I'm getting my own apartment, stop fretting," said Satyrna.

"And I'm still looking for one for us," Traphian said, motioning to Malkarai.

"You two are going to live together?" Dyspro asked incredulously.

Malkarai nodded absently, looking at the bar. "Yeah. We lived together for twelve years already – unless he turned into a total slob, I'm actually looking forward to being able to live with him again."

"Well, I'm not a total slob," Traphian said musingly.

Malkarai smirked.

"I'm surprised you two aren't getting a place," Dyspro said, gesturing between Malkarai and Satyrna.

Satyrna blushed, surprised. Malkarai looked amused. "As nice as that would be, I'm pretty sure Satyrna's family would have a few words to say in opposition."

She sighed, an exasperated look on her face. "And then some. It took enough convincing for them to support me getting my own place, even if it's financially better to have a roommate, I'm not ready to have that kind of fight." She looked at Cypha. "Unless you want to move back to town…"

Cypha made a face. "Thanks for the offer, but I like paying nothing for rent."

Satyrna snorted. "Cheap ass."

"Yep."

At this point, they were interrupted by the waitress, who took Satyrna and Malkarai's drink orders and asked everyone if they wanted food.

After ordering, Cypha asked Satyrna, "Did you invite Josh?"

Dyspro looked at Satyrna but didn't say anything.

Satyrna nodded. "He's working."

Cypha sighed. "He's always fucking working."

"Pretty much," Satyrna said with a smirk. "At least he's back to talking to us."

Rafiane asked, "So, you're going to be staying too, Traphian?"

"If Malkarai is, yes."

"Aww, isn't that cute," Dyspro said with a grin. "You two usually follow each other around?"

Traphian sighed and Malkarai's face flushed.

"He used to," Traphian replied. "Then he pulled the ultimate 180 and didn't follow the one time I really wanted him to."

"So now you're following him?"

Traphian shrugged. "We both agreed to stay. It's safest here, and if he's okay staring at my mug, I'd prefer to be with my friends for a change."

"What was the time you really wanted him to follow?" Rafiane asked Traphian innocently.

"When I ran away from the agency and he didn't."

She looked at Malkarai, taken aback. "You could've escaped?"

He shrugged.

Cypha eyed Malkarai. "How come you never followed him?"

Malkarai pushed his hair behind his left ear, making the long scar from his ear to his chin plainer to see. It was pretty obvious since he never pushed his hair back. "Arista was looking a lot more desirable than him at that moment in time."

Traphian rolled his eyes. "Malk, Arista was always more desirable than me."

Malkarai shrugged in agreement. "Yeah, well, you knew exactly why you didn't wanna be there. I had nothing against the place yet. I hadn't decided my opinion yet."

"Oh, you had an opinion all right. Your opinion was that Farad's head should explode. Daily."

Malkarai nodded. "Okay, I had an opinion on that. I meant I didn't have anything against the system."

Traphian shook his head with a sigh.

Cypha pointed at Malkarai's face. "So, what's the story on the scar then?"

He pointed at Traphian. "He did it."

She gave Traphian a look. "Yeah, well, I wouldn't go with you either if you went around cutting up my face."

He gave Malkarai an annoyed look and then explained, "We had a fight and it escalated to fist-throwing, and, eventually, knives. It's not like I meant to,"

Traphian grumbled. "He was swiping at me too; I just had the shitty luck to land a hit."

Dyspro narrowed his eyes at Traphian, a smirk on his face. "So, you celebrated your victory and ran away?"

"No," Malkarai said quietly. "He dropped it immediately and took care of me all night. It was me who held a grudge. When he ran away, I didn't. I stayed with Arista."

Satyrna found his hand under the table and squeezed it gently.

"I don't even remember what we were fighting about," Traphian said, staring past Dyspro and Rafiane to the center of the restaurant.

"I do."

He looked sidelong at Malkarai. "Let me guess–"

"Arista," they both said.

Traphian laughed and looked away. "Yup."

Malkarai smirked.

"She was the only thing you got worked up about."

"She was the only thing you wouldn't let go."

"Yeah, well, whatever. What's done is done. You turned out okay."

Malkarai laughed aloud. "Yeah, I'm the definition of 'okay,' just like Teffifa's the definition of 'sane.'"

Traphian sighed. "Oh, shut up." He let his rebuttal rest there though because the waitress showed up with Satyrna and Malkarai's drinks and asked if anyone wanted refills.

"This thing tomorrow is just a pissing contest, right?" Dyspro asked after the waitress had left.

"I hope so," Traphian said.

"I mean… mostly? Kalyfa really does want to kick my ass, so I can't just go into it cocky and sloppy," Malkarai said.

"What if he does win?"

"He made it sound like he'd stop protecting me because he wouldn't consider me good enough to train the knights and work with him."

"That's a stupid move on his part," Cypha said.

Malkarai shrugged. "It is, but he's fighting personal and professional motivations here. I understand not wanting to work with someone you dislike, even if it is a good idea in theory."

Satyrna sighed in annoyance. "I shouldn't have humored him and dated him."

"I told you you shouldn't have," Cypha said, smirking.

"Yeah, but you were like the *only* one," Satyrna protested. "Everyone else was telling me to at least give him a try. Especially my family."

"I'm obviously the only sane, logical one. You all should really take my word for it more often."

Dyspro laughed. "Cypha, I'm supposed to be the funny one. You can't take my job. Stay in your lane."

Cypha smirked as Satyrna and Rafiane snickered. "Sure, let me know when you're ready to be funny, and I'll let you give it a try."

Malkarai looked over as the flickering light from the fire was blocked for a few moments. He was lying on the bed in the extra room at the cabin, arms behind his head, fully clothed on top of the covers but not wearing shoes.

Satyrna paused and then stepped over by the bed when her eyes had adjusted enough to see him.

"Cypha asleep?"

"Mm-hmm," she responded, sitting on the edge of the bed.

He moved one arm from behind his head and wrapped it around her waist. "Will you stay with me tonight?"

Satyrna hesitated before looking down at him. She squeezed his hand against her side. "Yeah. Are you sure you won't sleep poorly like that? You don't want to be stiff tomorrow."

He sat up and shifted, hugging her from behind. "Honestly, I sleep better when you're with me."

She put a hand on his arm, applying pressure. "I never would've guessed you were this cuddly three weeks ago."

"Is that a problem? If you're uncomfortable with it, you don't have to, Satyrna."

She shook her head. "No, I don't feel pressured or threatened by you. I'm okay with it. I like cuddling with you. You just… used to flinch so hard when I touched you."

He squeezed her gently for a few moments. "I love this. I… need this. Yeah, physical contact used to startle me. After Ash disappeared, I didn't have anyone to cuddle or hug besides Traphian and Arista – and as much as I loved both of them, hugging wasn't a common thing. Even when Arista and I were together, we didn't touch a lot of the time."

"Who is Ash?" Satyrna asked, perplexed.

"She was my cat."

"Oh," she sounded relieved. "I thought there was yet another person who was taken from you. A cat is bad enough…"

"I'm still trying to figure out what role parents and family are supposed to play in a normal person's life because I lacked it. I'm mad at my own, whether they are also Rafiane's or not, for not letting me grow up where I felt loved and wanted. Traphian and I filled that void with each other. That's why we're as loyal as we are – we decided we were family, and to hell with anyone who wants to take that from us. Because people certainly tried."

"Like your trainer."

"He wasn't the only one, but yeah. He's also a big reason why I… flinch."

"Does it hurt?"

"No, it… I actually don't usually feel things on my torso. It doesn't hurt. But being touched when I'm not expecting it startles me because my reflexes have become so honed. I didn't have anyone left in my life that *wanted* to touch me. Most people actively avoided it. I can't promise that I won't flinch anymore, but touching and holding you makes me really happy, so I'm glad that you're okay with me doing it."

She put a hand on the side of his head, resting her head against his. "I am. I obviously prefer it when my affection is returned, so of course I like it."

He kissed her temple. "Thanks for being patient with me."

"Likewise."

# 43



It was dark as Malkarai made his way into town, following the path from the cottage to Main Street. He was trying hard to not think about the fight in front of him, but that unfortunately meant that he kept thinking about it. Trying to fight off the tactical part of his brain that was exploring moves and attacks he could use against a taller man with a broadsword, he tried to focus on what he intended to do after the fight.

That wasn't working well either, however. All he wanted to do was kick Desfete's ass as quickly as possible so he could go back to Satyrna, knowing that nothing was going to stop him from doing so.

He sighed heavily, watching his breath against the clear, dark sky. *From killing machine to mush in three weeks. Christ, Malkarai. No wonder Farad was so hard on you. When there's a cute girl who wants to be with you, the last thing you want to focus on is sticking a knife in some guy.*

*Just get in there, fight like hell, and leave. Decide later what you'll do. And stop thinking about her, you moron. Goddamnit...*

Malkarai slowed to a stop and shut his eyes for a few moments, taking a deep breath. Counting slowly in his head, he stood for several minutes, meditating and calming. They'd all learned meditation early on, and most trainers used it at the end of sessions, but he had never used it in the field except for when he was young. When he was young it had always been because he was afraid. He was far from afraid now, but the fights he'd fought in the past five years had never mattered quite like this one, nor did they have such personal consequences.

He needed to find whatever state it was he'd been hunting in for the past few years or Kalyfa might actually beat him.

After a few minutes, he heard a familiar, "Hey," and opened his eyes, looking up to see Traphian standing a few feet from him. He had his sword strapped to his back, the hilt sticking up from the back of his coat collar.

"Hey."

"You ready, or do you need a few minutes?" Traphian asked, looking serious.

"I'm as ready as I'll ever be. Thanks for coming," Malkarai said as he started walking again.

Traphian joined him, walking at his side. "I know you said I didn't need to be armed, but..."

"No, it's fine. I mostly just wanted someone there for *me* if I got more messed up than I intended to."

"Yeah. I'll be ready to defend you if anyone tries and pulls the shit they did last time."

"I appreciate it."

"I know you said you don't like to plan, but I know you have one. Care to share it?"

Malkarai inhaled silently and exhaled audibly through his nose. "I intend to be professional, but I'm planning on clearly illustrating the difference in our skills."

"Okay, good."

"These guys, especially Kalyfa, are practiced and trained, but they're very one-dimensional, and that's why we'll always beat them one-on-one."

"Agreed. Are you going to play by their rules or ours?"

"A combination of both. I won't cross his lines, but I'm not going to just act like we're in a competition with judges. He wants to see my skills – okay."

"Are you going to use your combat knives?"

"I don't think I'll need to."

Traphian smirked.

Josh glanced at the balcony, where some off-duty knights were gathered, milling about and talking quietly. He and Brendan were the only two that Kalyfa had allowed to be in the hall, and he'd already told them they had to stay at the top landing of the left-hand stairs. The right-hand stairs were blocked off. The way down from the balcony to the first floor was a lot more inconvenient.

All of the training equipment had been tidied up and put away or pushed to the sides of the room so that the main area was clear. The only piece of furniture remaining was a small foldable table by the front door.

"You're clear on your orders?" Kalyfa said, looking at Josh until he looked back at him.

"Yeah. No one on the main floor until you say it's over," Josh replied.

"Including us," Brendan added. "Why don't you want us on the balcony too?"

"I expect Faerstathe to bring his shadow, at minimum."

"That *would* be smart," Josh muttered.

"Yeah, so just keep him with you. If he doesn't bring anyone and needs medical attention, he'd probably be civil if one of you helped him."

"Sure," Brendan agreed.

Kalyfa turned to the door when he heard the large brass knocker on the door hit thrice. He motioned for Josh and Brendan to go up, and then went to the door. Malkarai stood outside, looking windblown but solemn. Traphian was standing just behind him, his hands in his pockets and his eyebrows furrowed.

"Great, I don't need to have any of my people haul your ass out of here for medical care."

"I hope you brought your own babysitter," Traphian replied flatly.

Kalyfa eyed him.

"Can I watch from the door?"

Kalyfa shook his head, opened the door farther so they could come in, and pointed up to where Josh and Brendan were standing on the landing. "There are off-duty knights watching from the balcony. Stand with Josh and Brendan on the stairs. They're under explicit orders to not intervene or seek revenge in any way, and Josh and Brendan will enforce this should it occur."

"Sure, sure," Traphian said dismissively as he went over to the stairs. "Sounds great."

Kalyfa closed the door behind Malkarai, who unbuttoned his coat and unstrapped his sword sheath from his belt, still next to the door.

Malkarai took his coat off and set it on the floor as he looked at the table. Then he unsheathed his sword and put the sheath next to the wall by the table.

"Are you ready?" Kalyfa asked as he walked further into the room, perturbed at Malkarai's lack of engagement.

Malkarai looked at him. "I'm here, aren't I?"

"Are you even taking this seriously?" Kalyfa asked as he faced Malkarai again from a short distance away, close to the center of the room.

"Yes, I am taking this seriously. You want an example of my experience and skillset, so I intend to demonstrate it." He held his hands out, his sword in one of them. "I mean, that's why you want this fight, right? We're not just doing a dick-measuring contest about who can fight better, yeah?"

"Cut the shit. Yes, this is so you can prove you're even a third as capable as your mission briefs imply you are."

Malkarai rolled his eyes. "Lucky you, I have two lessons planned for you today." He hefted his sword, moving with intent toward Kalyfa, who held his sword at ready, on guard. "Let's get started. First lesson: don't bring a sword to a knife fight."

Kalyfa narrowed his eyes and rushed Malkarai – the logical way to start a fight.

Malkarai, however, took a few quick steps backward, grabbed one of the table legs, and chucked it at Kalyfa.

Unprepared for this, Kalyfa put his arms up to block but was hit directly by the table.

While his opponent was dealing with the projectile, Malkarai dropped his sword and pulled his switchblade from his pocket, but didn't open it. He charged and pushed right into Kalyfa's chest, grabbing Kalyfa's right wrist to keep the sword clear as he stabbed the butt end of the closed knife into his exposed ribcage twice. When Kalyfa's left arm moved to block that spot, Malkarai jabbed him in the jaw below his ear, and then once more in the kidney when he raised his arm to protect his head.

Malkarai then shoved Kalyfa away, causing him to trip over the table and fall to the stone floor heavily.

His black eyes narrowed and cold, Malkarai looked up at the knights. "Fights aren't duels. Duels have rules. If you are in a location or situation where you can't bring a sword to bear, you will be overwhelmed by a shorter, faster weapon that will not suffer in a constricted space."

He looked at Kalyfa, who was getting to his feet, his expression betraying the pain he was feeling from those last two hits in particular. His breathing was hard but controlled. The knights could probably just see his mask, but Malkarai could see him struggling.

Malkarai put his switchblade away as he walked back to his sword, still keeping an eye on Kalyfa as he rearmed himself. "Okay, time for lesson two." He pointed his sword at Kalyfa, indicating his readiness. "Don't push my fucking buttons."

Kalyfa growled, grimacing as he charged again.

Malkarai went to meet him this time, running toward him and preparing to stop what he assumed would be a full, over-the-shoulder downward swing.

However, Kalyfa stopped short, not taking the final step and shortening his swing to bring his sword over his shoulder and forward into a two-handed thrust instead, aiming right for Malkarai's chest.

Malkarai was in a poor position to defend against this attack and let go of his sword with his left hand so he could throw his body back and to the left to twist out of the way, still taking a cut to his left shoulder as he did so. He swung his sword around, deflecting Kalyfa's as he spun back to face him again.

Kalyfa adjusted his footing and pulled back his sword to stab again, but Malkarai was already back around and deflected the stab even quicker this time. Malkarai stepped into Kalyfa's space, bringing his sword up to strike Kalyfa between the eyes with his pommel. Kalyfa had been trying to bring his sword around again and Malkarai had suffered a slight cut on the arm from the blade, but he didn't acknowledge it.

Watching Kalyfa stumble backward, dazed and bleeding from the nose, Malkarai said, "We're done here."

"No!" Kalyfa shouted over him. "I'm not done yet!"

Malkarai's eyes narrowed but he did not raise his weapon.

Kalyfa balanced himself with his sword before inhaling through his nose and spitting the blood that he'd inhaled on the floor.

Malkarai scowled. "When will you be done, Kalyfa? When you can't respond? When you're dead? What fucking use is that?" He stepped toward Kalyfa, swiftly lifting his sword and then letting it go, throwing it hard over and beyond Kalyfa.

Kalyfa watched the sword's path for just a moment, but then looked back to Malkarai – more specifically, Malkarai's fist as his nose was crushed. The sword clanged loudly behind them.

"There's your remedial lesson! Are we finished?" Malkarai yelled as Kalyfa was knocked backward, stumbling a step before falling on his rear and rolling onto his side.

He brought a shaky hand up to his face, stuttering, "We-we're done."

"I'm not doing this pointless shit again. I still agree to this deal, and I'll work for you and train your men. You don't control or own Traphian or me. You have no bearing on whether or not Satyrna and I are together, and you'd better start acting like you understand that."

Malkarai walked over to where his sword had landed and plucked it up before looking up at the balcony and gesturing to his left, where Traphian was still standing with Josh and Brendan. Malkarai called loudly to the knights, "I win. We demand a certain amount of respect. You give us shit, and you're not learning a damn thing. We've agreed to work with you because there's a mutually beneficial plan in place. Get down here and help him."

As Malkarai went back to the door, the knights moved, leaving the balconies to head down the stairs. Traphian, Brendan, and Josh were the first ones down but were followed shortly after by a handful of other knights.

Traphian went directly over to Malkarai and Josh followed unsurely behind him, glancing over at Kalyfa. Kalyfa was quickly surrounded and helped to a sitting position by other knights though, so Josh turned his attention to Malkarai and Traphian.

"Are you going to get your injuries looked at?" Josh asked.

Traphian glanced at Malkarai as he sheathed his sword and then reattached his sword sheath.

"Yeah, by Satyrna," Malkarai grumbled. "I'm not going where he's going."

Traphian snickered. "Want to come to our victory party, Josh?"

Josh looked uncomfortable, glancing over at Kalyfa again. There were so many people around him though, he shook his head slightly and looked at them. "Yeah."

Malkarai smirked at him, picked his coat up, put it on, and then went to the door. "Let's go."

He opened the door, and the three of them left the castle.

**9:00 p.m.**

Satyrna sighed, pacing the floor between the door and the hallway. Cypha, who was sitting at the table trying but failing to read a book, eyed her, looking over at Dyspro and Rafiane. They were sitting on the bench, his arm around her, intermittently chatting. Dyspro caught Cypha's eye and shook his head slightly.

"Yo, Saty, you're cooling all the warm air down before any of it can get to us," he said.

She stopped, exhaling grumpily. "I want to go. I should've gone."

"He wouldn't have let you," Cypha said, looking at her over her book.

"The stupid boys are fighting over me," she groaned.

"Partially. Honestly, it's better you aren't there because of that," Cypha said matter-of-factly.

"Yeah, don't endorse their stupidity. Pretend you don't care!" Dyspro encouraged.

Satyrna gave him an amused look.

They all jumped when the knob clicked and then there was a knock on the door.

Satyrna practically pounced on it, unlocking and opening it quickly before throwing the door open.

Josh was startled and jumped back a step, running into Malkarai as he did so. Traphian laughed in surprise.

Satyrna looked around at all three of them, confused. "What the- where- I was just expecting Malkarai."

"Welp, you got extras," Traphian chuckled.

"Uh, hi," Josh said sheepishly. "Can we come in?"

Satyrna stepped out of the way immediately. "Yeah, of course."

They all came in, cleaning their shoes off on the rug before Satyrna could shut the door. As soon as she did so, she went up to Malkarai, putting her hands on his face. "What happened? Are you hurt? Did you beat him?"

Malkarai snickered breathlessly, a little startled but not pulling away. "Not really. Yeah, I beat him."

Satyrna wrapped her arms around his neck, hugging him. "Oh, thank God."

"Yeah, you've picked the superior fighter this time," Josh said as he leaned against the stove.

Satyrna didn't let go of Malkarai, who hugged her back, but she gave Josh a look over his shoulder, smirking. "Thanks for the modifier, Josh."

He just smiled at her.

Cypha put her book down, finally abandoning it. "Where'd you guys come from? Were you watching?"

"Yeah," Traphian replied as he sat down in the chair by the fireplace. "Malk asked me to come with him to make sure he made it out of there intact."

"There were a bunch of knights watching," Josh said.

"We stole Josh afterward," Traphian added.

"Kalyfa had plenty of help," Josh said dismissively, obviously still feeling a little guilty about leaving.

Satyrna let go of Malkarai, unbuttoning his coat and patting his torso down, checking her hands for blood. "Where are you hurt? Do I need to stitch anything up?"

"Probably not," Malkarai said reassuringly before shrugging his coat off and hanging it on the hook on the wall over Dyspro's coat. "I've got a few shallow cuts, but Kalyfa's definitely worse off." He showed her his arm and shoulder – looking at the injuries for the first time himself. "Okay, maybe stitches on my shoulder?"

Satyrna gave him a bemused look.

"Hey, it's better than last time," Malkarai protested.

"What'd you do to him?" Cypha asked.

"Broke his nose, hit him in the forehead. Jabbed him in the ribs, kidney, and jaw with the back of a knife."

"Threw a fucking *table* at him," Traphian laughed. "And that was the damn *opener.*"

Cypha laughed and Rae's eyes widened as she covered her mouth.

"You did *what?*" Satyrna asked, flabbergasted.

"Threw a table at him," Malkarai said meekly. "So I could ambush him with the jabs."

Dyspro scoffed. "I thought it was a sword fight."

Malkarai glanced at him. "We fight with our whole bodies – the weapon is just an added tool."

Traphian nodded in agreement.

Josh made a small noise. "That's not how we are taught. Is that the difference?"

"Part of it, I'm sure," Malkarai said.

Satyrna frowned, picking up Malkarai's right hand and looking at his split knuckles. "What happened to your hand?"

"Oh. I punched him in the face. That was the final blow."

She sighed. "So… this is from his teeth…?"

"Yeah, probably."

Satyrna sighed even louder and went to gather the restocked first aid supplies from the extra bedroom. She returned quickly. "Josh, Traphian, could we use the seats at the table?"

"Sure," Josh said, going over to the bench and sitting down next to Rafiane.

Traphian also stood up and brought his chair around for them, moving over to the chair across from the bench and sitting down.

Satyrna pulled a chair out for Malkarai and then went to work on cleaning and disinfecting his injuries, sitting in the seat Traphian had vacated.

"Is Kalyfa gonna be okay, or is he fucked up?" Cypha asked, watching Satyrna clean Malkarai's shoulder.

"I mean, he's gonna have a hell of a day tomorrow, but he'll probably be back to normal within a week, tops," Malkarai said. "Maybe have black eyes for a while."

"Nothing permanently debilitating though?"

"No."

"He's not gonna pull something stupid like hide in the woods for two days," Traphian said, smirking at Malkarai.

Malkarai flipped him off with his left hand and Satyrna smacked his hand and pushed his arm back down so she could keep working with his shoulder.

Josh looked over to Rafiane and Dyspro. "You must be Rafiane. Did I say that right?"

She smiled and nodded. "Hi."

"I'm Josh."

"The traitor," Dyspro added coldly.

Rafiane glanced between Josh and Dyspro, confused.

Josh sighed and Cypha rolled her eyes visibly.

"I convinced Kalyfa to pay for your medical bills out of Carter's paycheck," Josh said to Dyspro. "Also, he's suspended for like six months."

Cypha snickered. "So he has to recertify before he comes back?"

Josh glanced at her, smiling. "Exactly."

"Nice."

"The four guys that were with him got a month's suspension too. The guy that drugged Satyrna and the one that tried to hit Satyrna but *did* hit Malkarai have been fired."

"Good," Satyrna said heatedly.

Dyspro sighed. "Okay, fine. I forgive you."

"Gee, thanks," Josh said, still smiling, although his eyebrows were knitted up.

"Is this gonna be a regular occurrence again, or just a holiday-only occasion?" Cypha asked, looking at Josh.

"Er, I'm gonna assume you mean me visiting and *not* fucking with the knights," Josh said unsurely.

"Yeah, let's not make me breaking my leg an annual occurrence," Dyspro put in.

Cypha shrugged and held her hands up, looking thoughtful. "I mean…"

Josh continued, eyeing Cypha. "Yes, I'm going to try and make it more regular. It seems like we're getting a little more wrapped up together, and also Satyrna's finally free of Kalyfa."

"I've been free of that tumor since July," she said shortly, unwrapping an adhesive bandage for Malkarai's lower arm.

"You've been *trying* to get rid of him since then," Josh corrected.

"He'd better fucking figure it out quick," she said succinctly as she applied the bandage. "I've been with Malkarai for three weeks and already like him more and am more comfortable with him than I was at the peak of my time with Kalyfa."

"Oh, I told him to knock it off too," Malkarai reassured her. "In less nice words."

"Good. I have far better things to worry about than that asshole."

"Like how much practice for your job your new boyfriend is giving you?" Cypha said with a grin.

Traphian snickered.

"Hopefully he stops giving me homework once my practicals start up," Satyrna responded coolly.

"Mm, depends on how bad the knights I have to train are," Malkarai mused.

## To be continued in The Haven...

# About the Author

E.M. Johnson is a technical writer by day and a fiction writer by night with four books (The Dark, The Haven, The Hunt, and The Shield) in the Division 53 Series. There are more Division 53 books planned, and two other series just waiting for their time to shine.

E.M. has a BFA in English Writing and a BSBA in Information Systems with Management from Drake University. She was born and raised in Iowa, but loves to travel. She is married and has two young daughters. In addition to writing, she is an avid gamer, artist, and sewist that loves fantasy, adventure, action, and realistic, deep characters.

## Connect with E.M. Johnson:

Website: Division53.com

Bluesky: @division53.bsky.social

Facebook: @Division53 @EMJohnsonAuthor

Instagram: @asbiecat @division53_dolls